CAPTURED IN TIME

CAPTURED IN TIME

Five centuries of South African writing

Written, compiled and edited by John Clare

JONATHAN BALL PUBLISHERS
Johannesburg & Cape Town

Published in trade paperback in 2010 by
JONATHAN BALL PUBLISHERS (PTY) LTD
PO Box 33977
Jeppestown
2043

ISBN 978-1-86842-378-1

Cover design by Michiel Botha, Cape Town
Maps by Jan Booysen, Pretoria
Picture research by Harold Thompson
Typesetting and reproduction by Triple M Design, Johannesburg
Set in 10.75/14 pt Dante MT and 10/14 pt Myriad Pro Light Semi Condensed
Printed and bound by CTP Books, Cape

CONTENTS

INTRODUCTION

For all its beauty, South Africa is not an easy country to embrace. Its history is violent and stained with racism. Its present, also disturbingly violent, is marked by disparities of wealth and poverty as extreme as anywhere in the world. Yet it is also a place of hope. Three-hundred-and-fifty years of European colonialism and authoritarian white rule have given way to a vigorous, non-racial democracy.

To set that in a living context – to explore South Africa's present through the prism of its past and to do so in the words of those who have lived and created that past and this present – is the aim of this book. Drawing on eye-witness accounts and personal responses, it offers readers, be they visitors or residents, a kaleidoscopic introduction to South Africa's history, politics and literature. Here, with a few exceptions, are the words not of historians, biographers or journalists but of natives, settlers, explorers, hunters, travellers, missionaries, soldiers and politicians as well as of novelists, playwrights and poets. From the works of 108 of them, I have chosen some 200 extracts and a score of poems that I think best illuminate this glorious but sometimes tortured land. The silence of those who occupied it first but left no written record can only be noted and lamented.

Among my sources[1] is the journal of Jan van Riebeeck, the first Dutch governor of the Cape, who sowed so many of the seeds of what was to come. His absorbing daily record of the settlement's first 10 years is the most detailed account in history of a colony's founding. Then there are the intimate letters of Lady Anne Barnard, who witnessed the transfer of power from the Dutch to the British at the end of the 18th century; the reminiscences of intrepid travellers such as John Barrow and William Burchell, who found themselves roaming over an apparently trackless land that was being ruthlessly depopulated of its original inhabitants; the tales of hunters such as William Cornwallis

Harris and Roualeyn Gordon Cumming, who found – and bloodily despoiled – a country teeming with game; and the vivid memoirs of Thomas Pringle, the Scottish poet who was one of the 1820 Settlers, and Thomas Baines, one of South Africa's finest painters, whose subjects included the 19th-century frontier wars against the Xhosa.

Here, too, are the diaries of Nathaniel Isaacs, who could only look on while Shaka, the brilliant but psychopathic Zulu king, slaughtered his people, and of Francis Owen, who was forced to watch Dingane, half-brother and slayer of Shaka, massacring a party of Voortrekkers, an event that was to leave an indelible mark on South African history. Then there are the works of David Livingstone, the formidable missionary-explorer, outraged by the way the Boers treated the blacks; of Sir Harry Smith, one of the great English satraps, who waged war on the Xhosa frontier and liked the 'kaffirs' to kiss his boots; of Mahatma Gandhi, who, having had the temerity to buy a first-class train ticket to Pretoria, wondered if he would ever reach his destination alive; and of Winston Churchill, taken prisoner by a Boer War general who was later to become the Union of South Africa's first Prime Minister.

In the vanguard of a platoon of visiting English novelists came Anthony Trollope, who travelled at the rate of 30 miles a day by horse-drawn cart to Kimberley and described the 'largest and most complete hole ever made by human agency'. Others included Rider Haggard, who worked as a colonial administrator in Natal while gathering material for *King Solomon's Mines*; Rudyard Kipling, friend and admirer of Cecil Rhodes, the arch-Imperialist who *was* King Solomon; Arthur Conan Doyle, a Boer War volunteer who became one of its most vivid chroniclers; and John Buchan, whose heroes instinctively knew where the white man's duty lay. They and others like them, shaped South Africa in outsiders' eyes.

The home-grown novelists I have drawn on include Olive Schreiner, author of *The Story of an African Farm*, one of the weirdest of literary classics; Sir Percy FitzPatrick, whose delightfully sentimental *Jock of the Bushveld* has had to be bowdlerised for contemporary South African consumption; Alan Paton, author of *Cry, the Beloved Country*, now unfairly accused of Uncle Tom-ism; and South Africa's two Nobel Literature prizewinners, Nadine Gordimer and John (JM) Coetzee, both masterly dissectors of the excrescences of apartheid.

Racial exploitation is the dark thread that runs through South Africa's history from Van Riebeeck onwards, dominating its politics and animating its literature. Emphasising that continuity are the thoughts of three of apartheid's earliest architects: Cecil Rhodes, who was determined to keep 'illiterate barbarians' in their place; Alfred (Lord) Milner, Britain's all-powerful man in South Africa at the turn of the 20th century, who fully subscribed to Rhodes's white supremacist vision; and Jan Smuts, one of the founders of the League of Nations, whose internationally-celebrated idealism did not extend to the country of which he was Prime Minister for 14 years.

And then, miraculously drawing a line under 350 years of history, comes Nelson Mandela, apartheid's most famous victim, who became its nemesis.

Finally, in perceptive studies of the Truth and Reconciliation Commission, urban and rural crime and AIDS, three deeply engaged writers describe post-apartheid South Africa's efforts to heal the wounds of the past and grapple with the pandemics that afflict the present.

Here, then, is South Africa in the raw through the eyes of those best equipped to see.

As this is a personal selection, I should say something of my own background. My family moved to South Africa in 1953, when I was 12. In Cape Town, I went to a (whites only) Church school, where hardly anyone – apart from my close friend Richard Turner, who was later assassinated – seemed shocked by apartheid, and then to university in the year the government closed it to non-white students. My second year coincided with the Sharpeville massacre, when police shot dead 69 Africans demonstrating against the pass laws; in my third year, the banned African National Congress (ANC) committed itself to 'armed struggle'; and in my final year Mandela was jailed for what turned out to be 27 years. As a student, I ran a night school in one of the African townships. After leaving university, I joined the South African Liberal Party, which stood for 'one man, one vote', and first worked as a journalist on a black newspaper. Forced to leave the country in 1965, I was not allowed back for 25 years, since when I have been a regular visitor, fascinated as much by what has changed as by what has not. Inevitably, such experiences have influenced what follows.

Readers unfamiliar with South Africa's colonial history may find a brief outline helpful.

The Dutch occupied the Cape in 1652 with the intention of setting up a refreshment station for their ships on the way to the East Indies. Over the next 150 years, the settlement expanded steadily, driven by land-hungry Boers (farmers) careless of the existence of those who were there first. By the end of the 18th century, whites and blacks had begun to clash on the eastern frontier, 600 miles from Cape Town. Britain then seized the colony from the Dutch, briefly in 1795 and finally in 1806. Soon afterwards, to escape British rule, the Boers headed north on their Great Trek, establishing what became the independent republics of the Orange Free State and the Transvaal[2]. On the eastern frontier, the British continued the war against the Xhosa, which was to last intermittently for 100 years. They also laid claim to Natal,[3] which brought them into conflict with the Zulus, whom they finally defeated in 1879. By then, diamonds had been found at Kimberley, gold was soon to be struck in the Transvaal and the independent republics' days were inevitably numbered. Britain, having provoked and won the Boer War (1899-1902), promptly handed the Afrikaners, as they were now called, control of a unified but segregated South Africa.

They denied the vote to the black majority of the population, claimed title to 93 per cent of the land and spent most of the 20th century enforcing 'grand apartheid' – total separateness. Once the rest of Africa had shaken off colonialism, the Afrikaners' position became untenable and they capitulated. In 1994, after South Africa's first democratic election was won by the ANC, Nelson Mandela became president.

The book is arranged largely chronologically – although following a theme some-times takes precedence – because South Africa, perhaps more acutely than anywhere else, can really be understood only in terms of its past. As I hope will become clear to the patient reader, every step along the way pre-figured the next.

Writing about a country that has been so tortured by racial distinctions makes a note on terminology essential.

The Dutch settlers called the first two groups of indigenous peoples they encoun-tered Bushmen and Hottentots. 'Bushmen' came from Bossiesman (variously spelled), Dutch for outlaw or bandit, and 'Hottentot' from the clicking sounds in their speech, which the Dutch heard as tot-tot-tot-ing. Both terms came to be seen as offensive and have been replaced by, respectively, San and Khoi-khoi. The latter is what the Hottentots called themselves and means something like 'men of men'. San, though, is the derisory name they gave their diminutive countrymen. To avoid embarrassment, the two words are now usually elided and Khoisan is used for both. For the sake of historical clarity – and without intending any offence – I have continued to use Bushmen and Hottentots. Yellowish brown in colour, they are distinct from the third, blacker, group that the set-tlers encountered, who are now called Africans and were principally Xhosa and Zulu. The Dutch, and later the English, referred to them all as kaffirs (also variously spelled), derived from the Arabic for infidel. It eventually came to be seen as a term of abuse – much like 'nigger' – and was replaced, successively, by Native and Bantu, both now rejected. Finally, there are the people who resulted from the mingling of white (or pinkish grey), yellowish brown and black, the most numerous of whom are known as Cape Coloureds.

South Africa's present population of 47 million is approximately 75 per cent black, 11 per cent white, mostly of European descent, 9 per cent Coloured, and 2.5 per cent Asian, mostly of Indian descent. They speak a total of 11 official languages, among which those most widely used at home are Zulu (24 per cent), Xhosa (18 per cent), Afrikaans (13 per cent) and English (8 per cent). Not for nothing did Archbishop Desmond Tutu, the Nobel Peace prize-winner, dub this the 'rainbow nation'.

NOTES
1 For a full list, see pages 507–511
2 Now divided into the four provinces of Gauteng, Mpumalanga, Limpopo and North West.
3 Now KwaZulu-Natal.

TIMELINE

1488 Bartholomew Diaz rounds the Cape

1497–98 Vasco da Gama rounds the Cape and reaches India

1602 Dutch East India Company founded

1652 Van Riebeeck establishes a refreshment station at the Cape

1658 First slaves imported

1685 Louis XIV revokes the Edict of Nantes

1688 Huguenot settlers arrive

1760 First Europeans cross the Orange River

1778 Great Fish River declared the Cape Colony's eastern boundary

1779 First 'Kaffir War'

1792 Second 'Kaffir War'

1795–1803 First British occupation

1799 Third 'Kaffir War'; Dutch East India Company dissolved

1806 Second British occupation

1807 Slave importation prohibited

1811–12 Fourth 'Kaffir War'

1816 Shaka becomes King of the Zulus

1819 Fifth 'Kaffir War'

1820   British settlers arrive in Algoa Bay

1828   Shaka murdered, succeeded by Dingane; Hottentots made equal before the law with whites

1833   Slavery abolished: slaves to be liberated after five years

1834–35   Sixth 'Kaffir War'

1835   Voortrekkers begin Great Trek north

1838   Piet Retief and followers murdered by Dingane; massacre avenged at Battle of Blood River (16 December); Boers declare independent republic of Natalia

1843   Britain annexes Natalia

1846–47   Seventh 'Kaffir War'

1848   Britain annexes Orange River Sovereignty

1850–53   Eighth 'Kaffir War'

1852   Boers granted independence in the South African Republic

1854   Boers granted independence in the Orange Free State

1856–57   Great Cattle Killing

1860   First Indian indentured workers arrive in Natal

1867   Alluvial diamonds discovered in Kimberley

1871   Diamond mining begins; Britain annexes diamond fields

1872   Cape Colony granted self-government

1877   Britain annexes South African Republic, renames it Transvaal

1878   Ninth (and last) 'Kaffir War'

1879   Anglo-Zulu war: British defeated at Isandlwana (January); Zulus defeated at Ulundi (July)

1881   Boers defeat British at Majuba Hill

1883   Kruger becomes president of the South African Republic

1886   Gold discovered on the Witwatersrand

1890   Rhodes becomes Prime Minister of the Cape Colony

1893   Mahatma Gandhi arrives in Natal

1894   Glen Grey Act introduces segregated land tenure

1895–96   Jameson Raid; Rhodes resigns

1897 Milner appointed Governor of the Cape and High Commissioner of South Africa

1899 Boer War begins (11 October)

1900 Britain annexes Orange Free State and Transvaal; scorched earth policy begins

1902 Boer War ended by Peace of Vereeniging (31 May)

1906 Transvaal and Orange River Colony granted self-government; Bambata rebellion in Natal

1909 Britain grants South Africa Dominion status

1910 Act of Union; Botha becomes Prime Minister

1912 Forerunner of ANC founded

1913 Natives Land Act declares 93% of South Africa 'white'

1919 Botha dies, Smuts becomes Prime Minister

1924 Hertzog defeats Smuts, forms Pact government with Labour

1925 Afrikaans replaces Dutch as an official language

1927 Immorality Act bans extra-marital inter-racial sex

1933 Hertzog-Smuts Fusion government

1936 Cape African limited franchise abolished

1939 Hertzog quits, Smuts takes over; Vorster and other Nazi sympathisers interned

1946 UN condemns South Africa's racial policies

1948 Malan's National Party introduces Grand Apartheid

1952 Defiance (of Unjust Laws) Campaign

1954 Strijdom succeeds Malan

1955 Congress of the People adopts Freedom Charter; Sophiatown bulldozed

1956 Cape Coloureds removed from common voters' roll

1958 Verwoerd succeeds Strijdom

1960 Sharpeville massacre

1961 ANC and PAC banned

1962 Mandela jailed

1966 Verwoerd assassinated, succeeded by Vorster; UN brands apartheid 'a crime against humanity'

1970 Steve Biko founds Black Consciousness Movement

1976–77 Soweto riots

1977 Biko dies in custody

1978 Vorster quits, succeeded by Botha

1983 United Democratic Front founded

1985 State of Emergency declared

1986 US bans new investment in South Africa

1987 Government begins secret talks with Mandela

1989 Botha ousted, succeeded by De Klerk

1990 Mandela released (11 February)

1994 First democratic elections (27 April); ANC wins 62.5% of the vote; Mandela becomes president

1999 Second democratic elections; Mbeki succeeds Mandela

2003 AIDS claims its millionth victim

2004 Third democratic election

2009 Fourth democratic election; Mbeki ousted, succeeded by Zuma

NOTE TO READER

The figures in brackets (1 through 125) that appear throughout the text refer to the list of Acknowledgements on pages 503–508, which is numbered accordingly. The page reference(s) for each extract is given after the source.

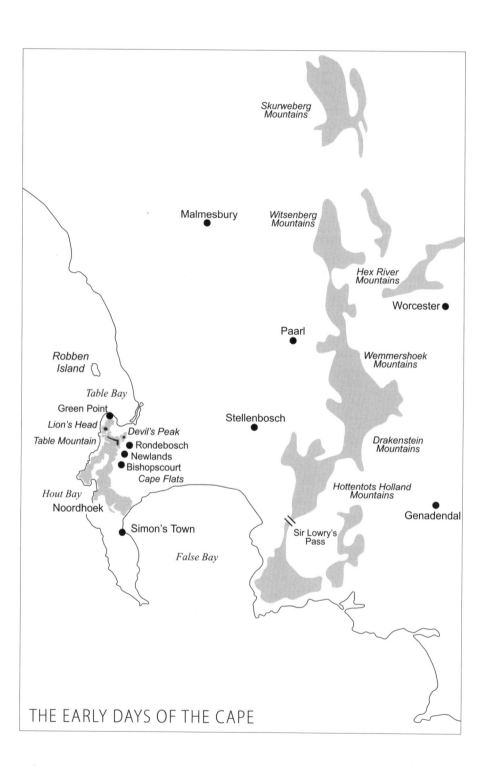

Skurweberg
Mountains

Malmesbury

Witsenberg
Mountains

Hex River
Mountains

Worcester

Paarl

Robben
Island

Wemmershoek
Mountains

Table Bay

Green Point
Lion's Head
Table Mountain

Devil's Peak
Rondebosch
Newlands
Bishopscourt
Cape Flats

Stellenbosch

Drakenstein
Mountains

Hout Bay
Noordhoek

Hottentots Holland
Mountains

Simon's Town

Genadendal

Sir Lowry's
Pass

False Bay

THE EARLY DAYS OF THE CAPE

FIRST CONTACTS:
A HEDGE OF BITTER ALMONDS

The Lusiads (1), a delightfully readable epic poem by Luis de Camoes, is the first eye-witness account of southern Africa by a European writer. Born in Lisbon, De Camoes sailed for India in 1553, 65 years after Bartholomew Diaz, his countryman, first rounded what he named the Cape of Storms but which his King, seeing it as the gateway to the East, preferred to call the Cape of Good Hope. After roaming about the East for 17 years, De Camoes returned home and, in 1572, published his great work. Its subject is the second Portuguese voyage round the Cape, and the first to reach India, told in the words of Vasco da Gama, the expedition's leader, who set sail from Lisbon in July 1497 with four ships and 170 men. Sticking to the known facts, De Camoes has Da Gama and his crew landing five months later – where the extract begins – on a 'sandy beach' at present-day St Helena Bay, about 100 miles north of Cape Town, a 'land where no one seemed to have ventured'. The sequence of what happened next – tentative contact, gifts of trinkets, questions about the riches of the interior, growing suspicion, violent resistance and bloody reprisal – was to set the pattern for the next 300 years.

24 By now the moon at her shifting post
     In the first sphere had five times shown
     Her crescent face, five times her full,
     Since the fleet began our long voyage,
     When from the topmost lookout
     A keen-eyed sailor holloed: 'Land! Land!'
     Impatiently, our people rushed on deck
     All peering eastwards at the tiny speck.

25   Looking at first like clouds, the range
     Of mountains we had glimpsed grew clearer;
     The heavy anchors were prepared;
     As we approached we struck sails;
     Then in order to discover in parts
     So remote, precisely where we were,
     Using the astrolabe, that instrument
     It took skill and ingenuity to invent,

26   We went ashore at an open stretch,
     Where our men quickly scattered
     To reconnoitre this welcome land
     Where no one seemed to have ventured;
     But I, eager to know where I was,
     Stayed on the sandy beach with the pilots
     To measure the sun's height, and use our art
     To fix our bearing on the cosmic chart.

27   We found we had long ago left behind
     The southern Tropic of Capricorn,
     Being between it and the Antarctic,
     That least-known region of the world.
     At this, my companions returning,
     I saw a stranger with a black skin
     They had captured, making his sweet harvest
     Of honey from the wild bees in the forest.

28   He looked thunderstruck, like a man
     Never placed in such an extreme;
     He could not understand us, nor we him
     Who seemed wilder than Polyphemus.
     I began by showing him pure gold
     The supreme metal of civilization,
     Then fine silverware and hot condiment:
     Nothing stirred in the brute the least excitement.

29 I arranged to show him simpler things:
   Tiny beads of transparent crystal,
   Some little jingling bells and rattles,
   A red bonnet of a pleasing colour;
   I saw at once from nods and gestures
   That these had made him very happy.
   I freed him and let him take his pillage,
   Small as it was, to his nearby village.

30 The next day his fellows, all of them
   Naked, and blacker than seemed possible[1],
   Trooped down the rugged hillsides paths
   Hoping for what their friend had obtained.
   They were so gentle and well disposed
   It caused our friend Fernao Veloso[2]
   To try his hand as anthropologist
   And discover how such people could exist.

31 Trusting to his strong arm, Veloso
   Was too confident he would be safe;
   But after much time had elapsed
   While I watched for some signal,
   I was scanning the horizon anxiously
   For the adventurer, when he appeared
   On the rough track scurrying to the shore
   A great deal faster than he went before.

32 Coelho's[3] boat was quick to take him
   Off, but before it could make a landing,
   A bold Ethiopian[4] grappled with him
   To prevent him making an escape;
   More and more came after Veloso,
   By now surrounded and helpless;
   We sprang to the oars but, as we bent our backs,
   There sprang from ambush a battalion of blacks.

33 Countless arrows and stones rained
   On the rest of us in a thick cloud,
   And not tossed to the wind aimlessly
   For it was there I got this leg wound;
   But we, as the aggrieved people,
   Returned so superadded a reply
   It was not just those bonnets that they wear
   Were crimson at the end of this affair!

34 As soon as Veloso was safe and sound
   We rowed quickly back to the ships,
   For, given this people's bad faith
   And brutish lack of courtesies,
   We were not likely to obtain from them
   Any news of the India we desired
   Except that it was many moons away,
   So I ordered full sail without delay.

35 Soon, one of the men said to Veloso
   (As everyone was relaxing, laughing):
   – 'Veloso my friend, that hill's obviously
   Better to come down than go up ...'
   – 'Absolutely,' said the bold adventurer
   'But up there, when I saw so many
   Of those dogs approaching, I looked about me,
   Knowing you'd be scared to death without me.'

36 He said that as soon as they mounted
   The crest, the black men of whom I speak
   Refused to let him proceed, threatening
   To kill him if he persisted;
   When he turned back, they laid an ambush
   So when we sought to rescue him,
   They could dispatch us to eternity
   And rob our corpses with complete security.

As Da Gama and his crew sail on south, they have a terrifying vision of the giant,

Adamastor. A 'fearful creature' who personifies the Cape of Storms, he upbraids them for 'trespassing' on his territory and accurately foretells their and their successors' fate.

37 Five more suns had risen and set
    Since we embarked from that beach,
    Cutting seas no other nation had braved,
    With the winds gusting favourably,
    When that night as we kept watch
    At the sharp prow and at our ease,
    A cloud above the mast loomed huge and high
    Blackening out completely the night sky.

38 So fearful it looked, so overpowering,
    It put great terror in our hearts;
    The dark, invisible waters roared
    As if frustrated, pounding on some reef.
    'Oh Omnipotent and Sublime,' I cried,
    'What demon does this region hold,
    Rising before us in this dreadful form
    For it seems something mightier than a storm?'

39 Even as I spoke, an immense shape
    Materialized in the night air,
    Grotesque and of enormous stature,
    With heavy jowls, and an unkempt beard,
    Scowling from shrunken, hollow eyes,
    Its complexion earthy and pale,
    Its hair grizzled and matted with clay,
    Its mouth coal black, teeth yellow with decay.

40 So towered its thick limbs, I swear
    You could believe it a second
    Colossus of Rhodes, that giant
    Of the ancient world's seven wonders.
    It spoke with a coarse, gravelly voice
    Booming from the ocean's depths;
    Our hair was on end, our flesh shuddering,
    Mine and everyone's, to hear and behold the thing.

41 It addressed us: 'O reckless people,
   Bolder than any the world has known,
   As stubborn in your countless,
   Cruel wars as in vainglorious quests;
   Because you have breached what is forbidden,
   Daring to cross such remote seas,
   Where I alone for so long have prevailed
   And no ship, large or small, has ever sailed,

42 Because you have desecrated nature's secrets
   And the mysteries of the deep,
   Where no human, however noble
   Or immortal his worth, should trespass,
   Hear from me now what retribution
   Fate prescribes for your insolence,
   Whether ocean-borne, or along the shores
   You will subjugate with your dreadful wars;

43 No matter how many vessels attempt
   The audacious passage you are plotting,
   My cape will be implacably hostile
   With gales beyond any you have encountered;
   On the next fleet which broaches
   These turbulent waters, I shall impose
   Such retribution and exact such debts
   The destruction will be far worse than my threats.

44 'Here, in my reckoning, I'll take sweet revenge
   On Dias[5] who betrayed me to the world,
   Nor is he the only Portuguese
   Who will pay for your foolish persistence;
   If what I imagine comes to pass,
   Year by year your fleets will meet
   Shipwreck, with calamities so combined
   That death alone will bring you peace of mind.

45   As for your first viceroy,[6] whose fame
     Fortune will beacon to the heavens,
     Here will be his far-flung tomb
     By God's inscrutable judgement,
     Here he will surrender the opulent
     Trophies wrung from the Turkish fleet,
     And atone for his bloody crimes, the massacre
     Of Kilwa, the levelling of Mombasa.

46   Another will come,[7] a man of honour,
     Noble, generous, and a lover
     Bringing with him a beautiful lady,
     Love's due reward for his virtues;
     Vindictive fate will deliver them,
     To these harsh, implacable shores;
     They will have time to contemplate my curse,
     Weathering shipwreck to endure far worse.

47   'They will watch their dear children,
     Fruits of such love, perish of hunger;
     They will see harsh, grasping people
     Tear her clothes from the lovely lady,
     And her body of such crystal beauty
     Exposed to frost and the scorching winds,
     After marching so far in the terrible heat,
     Tramping the rough sand with her delicate feet.

48   'Those who avoid their dreadful fate
     Must witness further sufferings,
     Two hapless lovers falling victim
     To the parched, relentless bush;
     After softening the very rocks
     With tears distilled from grief and pain,
     They lie embraced, their souls already flown
     Their wretched gaol of exquisite flesh and bone.'

49 The fearsome creature was in full spate
Chanting our destiny when, rising
I demanded: 'Who are you, whose
Outlandish shape utterly dumbfounds me?'
His mouth and black eyes grimaced
Giving vent to an awesome roar,
Then answered bitterly, with the heavy voice
Of one who speaks compelled and not by choice:

50 –'I am that vast, secret promontory
You Portuguese call the Cape of Storms,
Which neither Ptolemy, Pompey, Strabo,
Pliny, nor any authors knew of.
Here Africa ends. Here its coast
Concludes in this, my vast inviolate
Plateau, extending southwards to the Pole
And, by your daring, struck to my very soul …'

Adamastor spends the next 10 verses describing his antecedents after which Da Gama
resumes the story.

61 By now Apollo's team of four
Were bringing back the sun's chariot
And Table Mountain was revealed to us
To which the giant was transformed.
At long last, hugging this coast,
Our prows were pointing eastwards;
I followed it some miles, and once again
Turned for the shore and landed with my men.[8]

62 The people who owned the country here,
Though they were likewise Ethiopians,
Were cordial and humane, unlike
Those others who proved so treacherous;
They came towards us on the sandy beach
With dancing and an air of festival,
Their wives along with them, and they were driving
Humped cattle which looked sleek and thriving.

63 Their wives, black as polished ebony,
    Were perched on gently lumbering oxen,
    Beasts which, of all their cattle
    Are the ones they prize the most.
    They sang pastoral songs in their own
    Tongue, sweetly and in harmony,
    Whether rhymed, or in prose, we could not gauge
    But like the pipes of Virgil's golden age.

64 These, as their smiling faces promised,
    Dealt with us as fellow humans,
    Bringing sheep and poultry to barter
    For the goods we had on board;
    But as for news of what we sought,
    For all our desire to converse with them,
    Neither with words nor signs could we prevail,
    So we once again raised anchor and set sail.

65 By now we had made a complete circuit
    Of black Africa's coast, pointing
    Our prows towards the equator,
    Leaving the Antarctic in our wake.
    We passed Santa Cruz[9] where Dias,
    Having rounded the Cape of Storms,
    And planted a memorial column,
    Not knowing of his triumph, turned for home.

66 From here we sailed on many days
    Into both fair and wretched weather,
    Charting a new course on the ocean,
    Swept along only by our hopes,
    At times fighting the sea itself
    As, changing its moods wilfully,
    It conjured up a current of such force
    Our ships could make no headway in their course.

But make headway they did, finally reaching India in May 1498. In July the following year,

Da Gama returned to Portugal with a cargo of pepper and cinnamon and was rewarded with the title of Admiral of the Indian Seas. For the next 100 years neither Portugal nor any other European power took much interest in Southern Africa. The Portuguese, finding few natural harbours and no evidence of gold or slavery, preferred to develop their trade with the East Indies (present-day Indonesia).

In June 1580, eight years after *The Lusiads* was published, Francis Drake sailed past the Cape in the 'Golden Hind' on his voyage of circumnavigation. Dismissing the Portuguese assertion that it was 'the most dangerous cape in the world, never without intolerable storms', he famously recorded: 'This cape is a most stately thing, and the fairest cape we saw in the whole circumference of the earth.'

By the 1590s the Dutch were ready to take up the challenge. Following in Da Gama's wake, they began a lucrative trade in spices and cloth based on Batavia – present-day Jakarta – on the north-west coast of Java. The trade soon became the monopoly of the Dutch East India Company, which was founded in 1602 as the world's first venture in corporate capitalism and rapidly grew into a powerful state-within-a-state. One of its employees was Jan van Riebeeck, who had trained as a surgeon and been sent to Batavia in 1639, when he was 20. An ambitious young man, he switched to administration and rose in the ranks. By 1651, the Company had decided to establish a refreshment station at the Cape, growing fruit and vegetables to help combat the scurvy that blighted its crews on their eight-month voyage to the East. Van Riebeeck, who had called in at the Cape some years earlier, was appointed its first Commander. On 6 April 1652, after a relatively speedy three-and-a-half month passage from Amsterdam, his ship, *Dromedary*, anchored in Table Bay and so set South Africa's colonial history in motion.

Three days later, Van Riebeeck, who was to prove a shrewd and energetic leader, had chosen where the Company's first fort was to be built – on the site of present-day Cape Town's Grand Parade – and personally paced out its dimensions. A fortnight later he moved his family and baggage ashore and set up home 'for the time being in a make-shift wooden hut, rather roughly constructed'.

Happily for posterity, Van Riebeeck's instructions from the Company included: 'You are without fail to keep a true record and journal of everything that happens about you.' From this (2) we know that for the 100 men, including a troop of soldiers, and 25 women and children in his party, the first few months – it was winter at the Cape – were grim. Living in leaky tents made from old sail cloth, they suffered severely from the cold and discomfort. Most were struck down by dysentery; many died. Almost everything they planted – the main exceptions were cabbages and carrots – was destroyed by heavy rain and the Cape's notoriously strong winds. Moreover, the natives, whose fires they could see burning on the mountains across the bay, unaccountably kept away, making it impossible to barter for cattle and sheep.

Soon, the settlers were reduced to a diet of groats and peas. By September, they were beginning to grumble. One, found to be 'the instigator of the discontent over food', was sentenced to 100 lashes 'as a deterrent to others'. Not until October, six months after the landing, did a party of natives offer the first animals for bartering: three cattle and four sheep, exchanged for copper plate and tobacco. It was nowhere near enough and, to make matters worse, the Company's ships, which had been expected to call in on their way to Batavia, failed to materialise. On 11 November 1652, Van Riebeeck sorrowfully recorded: 'If it does not please the Lord to send us relief soon through cattle being brought by these natives or the arrival of ships from the Fatherland (of which in view of the time elapsed there is little hope), it will certainly come to this, that we shall soon have to stop the work for a time on account of the weakness of the men. The supplies of peas, groats, meat and bacon are running out. These have been made to last considerably longer by our good hauls of fish, without which we should have exhausted our provisions by now … May the Lord grant that the natives will soon come to us with plenty of cattle.'

Enter at this point, Harry the Hottentot, who was to become a critical factor in the early development of the Cape as well as the principal character of Jan van Riebeeck's Journal. Properly called Chief Autshumato, he was the leader of the Kaapmans, also known as the Watermen. Twenty years earlier, he had been taken to Java on an English ship and learned a little of the language, on which scanty basis he became Van Riebeeck's interpreter and, for many years, main point of contact with the natives. We hear of him at length for the first time in an entry dated 13 November 1652, a revealing account of each side's efforts to get the measure of the other.

Sitting at table in the afternoon, and conversing with the Hottentot Harry – who speaks a little broken English, and whom we daily feed from our table in order to make him all the more favourably disposed towards us – we questioned him closely, as we have often done before, about the circumstances of the different inhabitants of this place. He gave us to understand by means of signs and broken, hybrid English that this Table Valley was annually visited by three tribes of people, similar in dress and customs. One is called the Strandlopers, or as they call themselves in the broken English they have learned, Watermen, because they live on mussels which they find on the rocks and some roots from the earth. As far as we have observed they are not above 40 or 50 in number and, in any case, have no cattle. The second kind are those from Saldanha, called by them Saldanhamen, who arrive here every year with countless cattle and sheep. The third kind were called by him

13

Fishermen, who after the departure of the Saldanhamen arrive here with cattle only and no sheep, and who subsist by fishing, without boats, from the rocks with little fishing lines. On this they are very keen. The Watermen and Saldanhamen, according to Harry, are continually at war with these Fishermen (about 400 to 500 strong), one side always seeking to harm the other as much as possible. He further gave us to understand that we should do the Watermen and the Saldanhamen a great favour if we would by specious behaviour entice the Fishermen to come to us, on the pretence of wanting to barter copper for their cattle, as is usually done every year. Then, having them in our power, we should kill them with their women and children and take their cattle – to which end, he believed, all the Watermen and Saldanhamen would be inclined to contribute their power and strength. In regard to this we gave him no indication as yet of our intention, but replied that when those people arrived we would see what they were like; meanwhile, however, we are leading him by the nose as plausibly as is expedient and flattering him so that in due course we may gain more knowledge and more confidences from him with regard to one or two matters.

He further gave us to understand that these Fishermen were always travelling in secret and hiding from the Saldanhamen, not daring to make fires like the Saldanhamen, for when the Saldanhamen (whose numbers are countless) saw their fires, they always sought to catch them; and of this the Fishermen were greatly afraid. They lived beyond the mountains east of the Cape towards the bay De Sambras[10] and in that direction; the Saldanhamen lived towards the west and north from here near the bays of Saldanha and St Helena, where the yacht has now gone to look for trade etc. The Watermen live permanently in this Table Valley and behind the Lion and the Table Mountain. The oft-mentioned Harry alone remains with us with wives and children to serve the Company as interpreter as far as he is able. His people, the Watermen, have retired behind the Lion and the Table Mountain, where they exist on mussels from the rocks, and roots which, with great difficulty, they dig from the earth with long, sharp, round iron rods.

A month later, his frustration growing at the Hottentots' reluctance to trade, Van Riebeeck suggested a ruthless solution to the Company.

The Saldanhars with thousands of cattle and sheep came so close to our fort that their cattle nearly mingled with ours. Could not, however, get the bartering properly under way. Every now and then they would offer a lean, inferior beast and a sheep or two for sale, with the result that no more than 20 sheep, 3 cows and 5 calves were obtained, they being very unwilling to part with any more cattle. It is very sad to behold such fine herds of cattle and to be unable to purchase anything worth while; and although, to allure them and to make them eager, we offered them ⅓ more copper than previously for each beast, and in addition treated them with all the friendliness in the world, they could not be swayed. Whether they have already been glutted with copper (there being perhaps no consumption of it among them), or whether they are holding back out of envy or mischievous incitement, we cannot really tell. If only we could know! – for it would be a pity to see these herds leave without being able to do further trading. To-day we had ample opportunity of depriving them of 10 000 head of cattle had we been allowed to do so. If we are ordered to do this, it can always be done at some future date; this would suit us even better, for the Saldaniers trust us more and more as the days go by. Once we had possession of so many cattle, we could maintain an adequate supply by breeding; moreover we should have no fear of the English touching here and spoiling the cattle trade with the natives. These people daily give us sufficient cause by stealing and carrying away our possessions; we are so often subjected to this that we have enough reason for taking revenge by capturing them or their cattle. If one cannot get the cattle from them by friendly trading, why should one then suffer their thieving without making any reprisal? This would only be necessary once: with 150 men ten or twelve thousand cattle could be secured without the danger of losing a single person. On the other hand many savages could be captured without a blow as they always come to us unarmed; they could then be sent to India as slaves. This, however, requires more consideration and wiser judgment than ours alone; it is only in passing that we refer to it on this occasion. It could be considered and deliberated more fully later on, after more experience, in the event of our receiving higher orders to that effect.

Although Van Riebeeck continued to urge his solution, the 'higher orders' – from those he termed 'our Lords and Masters in the Fatherland' – never came and the infant settlement's plight deepened. Only the arrival of some of the Company's ships in April 1653, the first anniversary of the landing, kept starvation at bay. Sixth months later, to Van Riebeeck's dismay, Harry's Hottentots murdered a Dutch herd-boy and made off with the 42 cattle the settlers had managed to accumulate – the first serious such theft in

South Africa's colonial history and by no means the last.

In April 1654, on the second anniversary, Van Riebeeck recorded: 'The men are already beginning to starve because they cannot subsist on the ration of bread and meat. In order to fill their bellies we are constantly compelled to give them to eat whatever we can obtain, namely penguins or other birds, which they would otherwise hardly touch.' Later that month, adding insult to injury, the Hottentots grazed what Van Riebeeck estimated to be 20 000 cattle and sheep within sight of the fort 'but would not part with a single beast'. By 10 February 1655, the Commander was at last beginning to understand that the natives were seriously aggrieved and had, in fact, imposed a trade embargo. At issue was the most fundamental question of all: whose land was it?

Our men from the forest came to report that the place was full of natives, who had very few cattle and who molested them a great deal both on the road and in the forest. The men accordingly asked for more soldiers to protect them and their carpenter's tools, etc., as they could hardly keep these safe from the Hottentots any longer. They also stated that the natives had given them to understand that they intended to come to our fortress in large numbers and look for a good opportunity of attacking us and robbing us of the copper, of which we have a large quantity in the fort. In reply to this the natives were told that we were willing to give them copper for their cattle and thus trade with them in friendship. They had answered, however, that we were living upon their land and they perceived that we were rapidly building more and more as if we intended never to leave, and for that reason they would not trade with us for any more cattle, as we took the best pasture for our cattle, etc. This, the Strandlopers here at the fort, have also told us time and again in broken English. Will consequently have to keep a closer watch than before, in order not to be caught unawares, through overconfidence, by a surprise attack, as happened with the theft of our cattle. Indeed, the natives are becoming so bold that we are almost forced to do our work with a tool in one hand and a weapon in the other all the time, or at least to post soldiers with each worker and almost everywhere, or else they cause our men the greatest annoyance in the world.

Only last night it happened that about 50 of these natives wanted to put up their huts close to the banks of the moat of our fortress, and when told in a friendly manner by our men to go a little further away, they declared boldly that this was not our land but theirs and that they would place their huts wherever they chose. If we were not disposed to permit them to do so they would attack us with the aid of a large number of people from the interior and kill us, pointing out that the ramparts were only constructed of earth and could easily be surmounted by them; *item* that they also knew how to break down the palisades, etc. It is therefore becoming more and more evident to us that these rogues are emboldened by kind treatment; and whatever Harry may be conspiring with the people in the interior to the Company's prejudice is difficult to tell – at any rate, one can surmise that he is doing little good. We should therefore take good care and every precaution, as said before, that we are not unexpectedly attacked. It is indeed true that the fort would not easily be taken by them, but since all our men have their hands full and are steadily occupied with their work, with hardly anyone so far being spared for separate guard duty, they would be able to massacre us almost to a man.

We have therefore divided the men into 3 watches, one of which is to mount guard fully armed every third night, and nevertheless carry on with its appointed work during the day. Some are also to keep guard separately, some in the gateway and others in searching the bushes all round the fort for Hottentots that might be gathering in secret somewhere. We shall thus prevent them from surprising our men at work, of which we are becoming more apprehensive every day, more particularly because we can see from the large number of fires burning everywhere that the land hereabouts is full of Hottentots, and our men, without giving any provocation, suffer much annoyance from them even close to the fortress. We dare not, however, resist them too much, as we still enjoy to a fair extent the convenience of their assistance in fetching firewood, although we almost have to beg and beseech them to do so, and whenever the whim seizes them they simply refuse altogether. In that case almost all our men have to work and tire themselves almost to death carrying wood in order to keep the cook's pot boiling, as the wood nowadays, right up against the Table Mountain, has to be fetched fully a mile and even so is quite scarce.

Later in 1655, Harry relented. He told Van Riebeeck he now understood that, unlike previous, shipwrecked Dutchmen, they intended to stay and he had decided to make the best of it. So he lifted the embargo but, as quickly became apparent, it was a short-sighted move. For as the Company's herds increased, so the Kaapmans – the middlemen in the trade with the other Hottentots – profited hugely and could afford to buy more cattle of their own. Soon the competition for pasturage around Cape Town became severe, the situation aggravated by Van Riebeeck's decision to plough up part of present-day Rondebosch, round the side of Table Mountain, where, he calculated, the prevailing winds were barely a tenth as strong. As an experiment, he decided to plant wheat, oats, barley and rice there.

In February 1657, the pressure on land increased again, when, after a two-year campaign, Van Riebeeck finally persuaded the Company to release some of its servants and allow them to become 'free burghers', each granted 26 acres on which to grow grain and tobacco and breed cattle. 'Individual tenants with a personal interest and the prospect of profits', Van Riebeeck had argued, 'would be more industrious than the Company's servants, who are quite content to do as little work as possible.' The Company's agreement marked the point at which its refreshment station – 'a cabbage patch on the way to India' – truly became a settlement. Harry did not miss the significance. By July 1657, he was demanding to know where he and his people were to live and graze their cattle now that the Dutch were building houses and cultivating the land. Van Riebeeck suggested they head inland towards present-day Stellenbosch, Paarl and Malmesbury. But that, Harry explained, was the Saldanhars' land. Come the summer, the Saldanhars would arrive there in great numbers and kill them. Would the Commander, he wondered, join forces with him in attacking the Saldanhars and seizing their cattle? 'He was told,' Van Riebeeck recorded stiffly and apparently unconscious of the irony, 'that the Hollanders were not a nation to rob another of its property.'

As tension grew, it was Van Riebeeck who made the first move. In July 1658, he lured Harry into the fort and had his 110 cattle rounded up. One of the Kaapmans was shot dead and another wounded. Establishing another long South African tradition, Van Riebeeck then sent Harry to Robben Island, from where, 18 months later, by night in a small rowing boat, he became the first prisoner to escape alive. The Kaapmans retaliated by stealing cattle and burning the free burghers' farmsteads. Although the two sides were now effectively at war, it was not until 19 May 1659 that the council Van Riebeeck headed met at the fort and issued a formal, fateful declaration.

Finally, by a unanimous vote, after full and very lengthy discussion, the following resolution was agreed upon.

'Since we see no other means of securing peace or tranquillity with these Cape people, we shall take the first opportunity practicable to attack them with a large force and, if possible, take them by surprise. We shall capture as many cattle and men as we can, but shall avoid, as far as is possible, all murderous bloodshed. The prisoners we shall keep as hostages, so that we may restrain and bring to submission those who may evade us. By this means

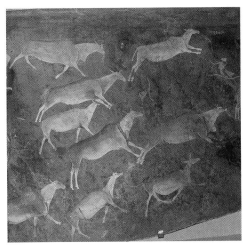

Left: The Bushmen – South Africa's first inhabitants some 30 000 years ago – left thousands of rock paintings like this one found in a cave in the Drakensberg Mountains. The eland it portrays were central to their spiritual beliefs.
[Iziko Museums of Cape Town]

Below: The Landing of Jan van Riebeeck at the Cape of Good Hope – a highly stylised Victorian image by Charles Bell, a British colonial official, of the first contact between the Dutch commander of the Cape and the Hottentots who grazed their stock there. The reality was rather more brutal: the Hottentots were rapidly dispossessed.
[National Library of South Africa, Cape Town]

Bottom: Table Bay crowded with ships of the Dutch East India Company, which established the colony in 1652 as a maritime refreshment station on the way to and from the East Indies and ruled it for 150 years. The painting, by the Dutch artist, Aernout Smit, is dated 1683.
[Aernout Smit. Cape Town, 1683. Iziko Museums of Cape Town]

Above: Despite being warned that it was 'a very absurd and dangerous undertaking', Anders Sparrman, an eminent Swedish naturalist and explorer who sailed with Capt Cook, spent eight months travelling around the Cape by ox wagon in 1775–76. [National Library of South Africa, Cape Town]

Below: Hottentot Ornaments &c – Anders Sparrman's intricate drawings of a milk basket, shell necklace, pipe, shoe, woman's head band and man's belt illustrated his *Voyage to the Cape of Good Hope*, first published in English in 1785. He was an unusually sympathetic observer of Hottentot life. [Smithsonian Institute Libraries]

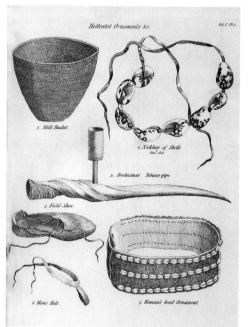

Top: Francois Le Vaillant, a French ornithologist and adventurer, was the most widely read of the early writers about the Cape, where he lived and travelled extensively from 1781-85. He collected more than 2 000 species of birds as well as insects, mammals and plants. [Princeton University Library]

Above: A portrait of a Hottentot woman by Le Vaillant, who delighted in the 'rural simplicity' of the Hottentots' lives and lamented that they, 'once masters of this whole portion of Africa', had been deprived by the Dutch of 'their rights, their authority, their peace and their happiness'. [MuseumAfrica]

Left: William Burchell's drawings of the ox wagon in which he travelled thousands of miles around South Africa between 1810 and 1815. An explorer, naturalist, artist and author, he amassed an enormous collection of plants, insects, skins and skeletons.
[HAROLD STRANGE LIBRARY]

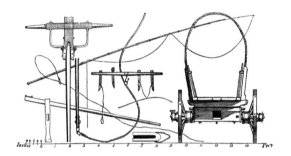

Below: William Burchell's painting is of himself drawing his ox wagon as it was ferried across the Berg River, north east of Cape Town, at the beginning of one of his many journeys into the 'unknown regions of Southern Africa'.
[WILLIAM BURCHELL. *CROSSING THE BERG RIVER.* NEW YORK PUBLIC LIBRARY]

Bottom: A Bushman kraal (settlement) painted by William Burchell, who was inspired in his travels by his determination to 'investigate man in an uncivilised state of society' and 'propose the means of his betterment'.
[MUSEUMAFRICA]

Above left: John Barrow, an able and ambitious civil servant, was sent to the Cape in 1797, after the British had taken it from the Dutch, to report to his government on the state of the new colony. He did so in notably caustic terms. [MUSEUMAFRICA]

Above right: Clever, glamorous and highly engaging, Lady Anne Barnard arrived at the Cape in 1797, when her husband was appointed Secretary of the Colony. Over the next five years, she recorded her vivid impressions in watercolours, diaries and a stream of letters. [NATIONAL LIBRARY OF SOUTH AFRICA, CAPE TOWN]

Below: Genadendal – Valley of Grace – was South Africa's first missionary settlement, established in idyllic surroundings by the Moravians in 1737 to encourage Hottentot converts to be 'industrious, religious and happy'. The Dutch, though, saw it as a refuge for the workshy and shut it down for 50 years. [MUSEUMAFRICA]

we hope to restore peace, the more so because we feel sure that the true Saldanhars, enemies of the Kaapmans, will care as little about their fate as they did in Harry's case, but will more freely come to deal with us in greater security than before, since these Kaapmans have always been found to be the chief hindrance to this.

'For carrying out the above, orders have been given to have everything in preparation, and the Council prays that it may please the Lord God to attend us with His blessing and His help. Amen.

'Thus done, resolved and determined in the fort of Good Hope on the above date.

(Signed) 'Jan van Riebeeck,

'Roeloff de Man,

'The mark of Hendrick Boom,

'Abraham Gabbema,

'The mark of Jan Reijnierssen,

'Pieter Everaerts.'

This resolution was not even an hour old when news came of the theft of all Brinckman's cattle, at least 30 in number, as well as all his sheep (above 70); also the rest of Vasagie's and Van Roon's cattle. Brinckman's comrade, Sijmon in't Velt, after he had fired upon the Hottentots, had been attacked and cruelly murdered with assegais; he had received 7 wounds. In addition a slave had received a wound. The interpreter Doman, who had been one of the attackers, had picked up Sijmon's gun and made off with it. He had been pursued by 7 free burghers but is, we fear, unlikely to be overtaken, and there is a danger that our men will also be lost.

Orders were therefore immediately given to despatch the soldiers mentioned to the free burghers' houses to help protect them as much as possible from further misfortune, and to make all preparations for the prevention of further disasters, since 4 farms are already in complete ruin, brought to a standstill in the midst of the ploughing and sowing season. This is most detrimental to our agriculture.

No sooner had this report reached the fort than all the Hottentots in this vicinity took to flight with women, children and everything else.

20th Dark, grey skies. All the Company's livestock were brought to the fort from the grain-field, except most of the sheep, because the sheep-shed here cannot take any more, and the Company's oxen used for drawing the plough and the wagons, as these are needed to keep the farming operations going.

Furthermore, as we see that the Kaapmans cannot be brought round by friendly means, but that, in fact, they threaten to rob us of all our cattle before they will desist, and to kill anyone who even attempts to prevent them, full permission has been granted to all our people to seize them or shoot them down wherever they can do so, that is, those they can catch anywhere near their houses or happen to encounter elsewhere. Each man must remain at his home to protect his own property until such time as further orders are given for taking the field for this specific purpose. This will be after our scouts, who have been sent out, return and bring full information where would be the best place to get at the Kaapmans, so as to do them the most harm and once and for all properly to put fear into them.

Only the interpreter Eva remained in the Commander's household, and she appeared to be most dismayed when she saw all the preparations and heard about the plans, for, as she can speak and understand Dutch well, it was difficult to keep anything from her. She said that the Kaapmans who were still at the fort yesterday had tried to entice her away with them, but that she had preferred to remain here. Her only fear was that if any of Oedasoa's people[11] should come here they would also be killed, but she was assured that precautions would be taken against any such happening. It was explained to her that we had endured the Kaapmans' insolence quite long enough; and that, although as recently as last Sunday we had tried through her agency to get them to make peace with us, they had spurned our approach and had indeed that very afternoon murdered a free burgher most miserably and had stolen 70 sheep and 40 head of cattle, apart from previous robberies. This was a matter which made the Lord God sorely displeased with these people (who knew nothing about Him). We shall therefore offer all possible resistance, and also cause them as much harm as lies in our power. Because they have not heeded the voice of friendship, we shall by forceful means make them more reasonable and co-operative. In this just cause the Lord God would moreover help and support us.

That end was achieved after just two skirmishes. In the first, in July 1659, five Kaapmans armed with assegais ambushed a soldier who was driving some oxen from Groote Schuur, the Company's newly-built granary in Newlands. The assailants were intercepted by four mounted guards who shot three of them dead and wounded a fourth. A month later, soldiers scouting down the west side of the Cape Peninsula, near present-day Noordhoek, found a settlement of Kaapmans, killed three of them, destroyed their huts and 'hurled their assegais and bows and arrows into the sea'. The Hottentots had had enough. They fled 50 miles north to Saldanha Bay and sued for peace. Van Riebeeck recorded: 'They explained that they had begun the war against us because we had put all the best ground under the plough and they had thought they would be able to prevent this by stealing the oxen we used for ploughing. On being asked why they wished to come back to the Cape now and make peace, they had replied that the Cape was their birthplace and their own country with an abundance of fresh water and that their hearts continually hankered after it.' On 6 April 1660, the eighth anniversary of the landing – an occasion that was now observed as 'an annual day of prayer and thanksgiving for the safe arrival here and the success of the settlement' – Van Riebeeck recorded, with admirable frankness, the terms of the conquerors' peace that set the seal on South Africa's future. It was based on subjugating the natives, dispossessing them of their land and segregating them from the Europeans, so establishing a pattern that was to be elaborated with increasing intensity for the next 330 years.

At the fort to-day, peace was renewed with the chief and overlord of the Kaapmans, with Harry and with all the principal men and elders. Mutual promises were given that the one would no longer molest the other, but there were none of the stolen cattle left for the Kaapmans to return. Instead, they said that they would do their best to see that as many as possible were from time to time brought by other tribes in the interior. They strongly insisted that we had been appropriating more and more of their land, which had been theirs all these centuries, and on which they had been accustomed to let their cattle graze, etc.

They asked if they would be allowed to do such a thing supposing they went to Holland, and they added: 'It would be of little consequence if your people stayed here at the fort, but you come right into the interior and select the best land for yourselves, without even asking whether we mind or whether it will cause us any inconvenience.' They therefore strongly urged that they should again be given free access to this land for that purpose. At first we argued against this, saying that there was not enough grass for their cattle as well as ours, to which they replied: 'Have we then no reason to prevent you from getting cattle, since, if you have a large number, you will take up all our grazing grounds with them? As for your claim that the land is not big enough for us both, who should rather in justice give way, the rightful owner or the foreign intruder?'

They thus remained adamant in their claim of old-established natural ownership. They said that they should at least be allowed to go and gather bitter almonds, which grow wild in abundance there, and to dig for roots as winter food. This likewise could not be granted them for they would then have too many opportunities of doing harm to the colonists and furthermore we shall need the almonds ourselves this year to plant the proposed protective hedge or defensive barrier. These reasons were, of course, not mentioned to them, but when they persisted in their request, eventually they had to be told that they had now lost the land as the result of the war and had no alternative but to admit that it was no longer theirs, the more so because they could not be induced to restore the stolen cattle which they had unlawfully taken from us without any reason. Their land had thus justly fallen to us in a defensive war, won by the sword, as it were, and we intended to keep it.

Against this they complained bitterly, saying that the colonists and others who lived in the country had done them much mischief, by sneaking off with either a sheep or a calf on occasion, by snatching off their beads and armlets from their ears and arms and giving them to their slaves, or by beating and striking them, without the Commander's knowledge – and there is some truth in this. Unable to bear this any longer, they had determined to take their revenge by stealing the cattle, and they roundly declared that they had had cause enough for this. In answer to this, they were reminded of the many exemplary punishments meted out by us to those against whom they had brought in charges of such molestation. If they were not satisfied with that, but preferred every time to take their revenge by means of robberies and thefts such as those mentioned, peace could never be maintained between us, and then by right of conquest we should take still more of their land from them, unless they were able to drive us off. In such a case they would, by virtue of the same right, become the owners of the fort and everything and would remain the owners for as long as they could retain it. If this alternative suited them, we would see what our course of action was to be.

Whereupon they replied that this was a story of bygones and that they were satisfied never to contemplate doing our people any more harm, but to bring us their grievances against any who molested them, so that such men might receive their just punishment at our hands in accordance with the evidence obtained. They would do the same on their side and they expected the Commander to come out one day to show them the routes they will be allowed to use and the limits beyond which they are to remain. This was postponed until the ships have departed from the roadstead. So peace was concluded and the chief Gogosoa, Harry, and all the principal men, numbering about 40 persons in all, were presented with gifts of copper, beads, and tobacco and then treated so well to food and drink that they were all merrily tipsy. If we had wanted to, we could have kept them there as prisoners, but for many weighty reasons this was considered inadvisable, for we could always manage that and in the meantime we could sound them further to discover their real attitude.

The 'proposed protective hedge or defensive barrier' had absorbed Van Riebeeck almost from the start. Initially, the Company had wanted him to build a canal 10 feet wide and 6 feet deep right across the Cape Flats isthmus from False Bay to Table Bay, an undertaking he regarded as laborious, expensive and 'quite impractical'. Instead, 'to prevent the Hottentots from driving our cattle away', he favoured a hedge of bitter almonds and thorn trees. This time, he got his way. Parts of the hedge can still be seen in Cape Town's Kirstenbosch Gardens. The entry is dated 25 February 1660.

To-day the boundary of the Cape settlement was measured and found to be a distance of 3,673 roods. The route taken was as follows: from the seashore at the first watch-house, Kijck Uijt, out behind the farmlands of the free burghers and the Company, then over the top of the Bosheuvel as far as the foot of the Bosbergen and up to and including the forest of the free sawyer Leendert Cornelissen. Of this total, 1,320 roods is the distance between the shore and the principal watch-house projected for mounted guards. The remaining distance is 2,353 roods. It is proposed to plough up the land in a strip one rood wide and sow and plant it with bitter almond trees and all sorts of fast-growing brambles and thornbushes. This belt will then be so densely overgrown that it will be impossible for cattle or sheep to be driven through and it will take the form of a protective fence, like those with which some lords and squires mark off the boundaries of their territories in certain parts of Germany and in the district of Cologne. They also have circular watch- or guard-towers here and there, with heavily barred entrances to protect the farmers against attacks from outside. Our already completed watch-houses and their adjacent barriers will serve a similar purpose in our case. This ploughing and planting is considered to be the cheapest and quickest system, since the ploughing is not more than 2 or 3 weeks' work. The bitter almonds are ripe towards the end of March or the beginning of April and can then be gathered in large quantities for sowing along this strip in the next rainy season. The thornbushes can be planted at the same time. In 4 or 5 years' time all this should have grown into a fine, dense hedge, good enough to serve for the purpose mentioned, for we have found that these bitter almond trees grow as luxuriantly as any willow in the Fatherland and produce thick trunks and branches. Indeed when these trees are mixed with brambles and thorn-bushes, even human beings would have great difficulty in penetrating the hedge, so that there would be much less chance for cattle getting through, except when they are permitted to pass in and out through the barred entrances at the watch-houses at the discretion of the mounted guards. Within the compass of this hedge, the whole settlement and all the grain farms, forests, etc. will be beautifully enclosed as in a half-moon, and everything will be well protected against raids by the Hottentots.

Eight months later, he noted: 'Our whole settlement has been fenced in, giving us a feeling of great security.' The Hottentots, of course, would have felt the opposite. In December 1660 Van Riebeeck observed: 'The Hon. Company has recently acquired such large numbers of livestock through the flourishing trade – which has been so much desired – that we have had to employ mounted and other guards to graze the animals at quite a distance beyond the set perimeter. As we become better stocked with cattle, we shall have to deprive the Kaapmans of all the Cape pasturage as the Hon. Company will soon need it for all its own livestock.' And so it transpired. Indeed, in 1672, 10 years after Van Riebeeck had left, the Company sought to legitimise his conquest by 'buying' the whole of the Cape from Saldanha Bay to the Hottentots Holland Mountains. In return for 'full, perpetual and hereditary' ownership, it paid two Hottentot chiefs a quantity of 'tobacco, beads, brandy and other trifles'. (Even 166 years later, when the Voortrekkers thought the Zulus had given them half of Natal, Europeans still did not seem to understand that the indigenous people of South Africa never believed that ownership of land, which belonged to the community, could be transferred.)

Meanwhile, foremost among the other issues claiming Van Riebeeck's attention was agriculture. In addition to fresh meat, the Company's ships urgently needed a reliable supply of fruit and vegetables to counter the lethal effects of scurvy. The voyage from Holland to the Cape – two-thirds of the way to Batavia – commonly took four months but often much longer. The ships were frequently becalmed around the equator for four weeks or more. Most carried between 250 and 350 men but some as many as 500. The death rate averaged 5 per cent but sometimes exceeded 10 per cent. Van Riebeeck kept a meticulous record. The *West Vrieslandt*, for example, left Holland in May 1658 with 351 men. By the time she arrived at the Cape five months later, scurvy had killed 72 and left 150 'very ill'. The *Maersveen*, which sailed from Holland in November 1660 with 348 men, took four-and-a-half months having being 'delayed by calms for 54 days and nights near the equator, which she had crossed three times'. She arrived in the anchorage in a 'pretty desolate state'; 73 of her crew had died, including the skipper, 80 were ill and the rest 'so weak they could not moor her'. The *Wassende Maen* sailed from Texel in April 1661 and was becalmed for five weeks. Of her 258 crew, 23 had died and 'most of the others were badly smitten'.

Poignantly, some seafarers already knew how scurvy could be prevented. As early as 1601, Sir James Lancaster, an English East India Company captain, had sailed into Table Bay with his crew intact after insisting that they drink three spoonfuls of lemon juice every morning of the voyage. It was to be nearly another 200 years before officialdom took notice.

For those who did not die, recovery was generally rapid, given the right diet. Hence the importance of cultivating the Company's gardens – still preserved at the top of what is now Adderley Street. Almost anything that grew close to the ground and thus out of the violent winds did well there as long as it was not 'scorched by extreme drought and prolonged heat', as from time to time it was. In Rondebosch, sheltered from the wind, peas, beans and orange and lemon trees flourished and so did grain. And it was not long before Van Riebeeck discovered that viticulture had a future, too. In August 1658, on his own, recently-acquired 200-acre private estate at Bosheuvel – present-day Bishopscourt – he laid out, 'during the waning moon, which is the correct time', a 'splendid' vineyard.

All this, however, required a great deal of labour, for which the Hottentots showed no appetite. The answer, Van Riebeeck decided, as early as 1654, was to import slaves. Initially, the Company demurred and it was not until four years later that the first batch arrived. The *Amersfoort*, one of the Company's ships, had intercepted a Portuguese slaver off the coast of Brazil en route from Angola with a cargo of 500 male and female slaves. The *Amersfoort* took half of them – 'leaving the old and unserviceable' – of whom 170, predominantly children, survived the voyage to the Cape. It was for their benefit that Van Riebeeck built South Africa's first school. A couple of months later, the *Hasselt* sailed in from Dahomey with 228 slaves – 'an exceptionally fine, strong and lively lot' – obtained there on the Company's instructions. Although 100 were sent on to Batavia, slaves now outnumbered the settlers. That was to remain so – with far-reaching consequences for white South Africans' attitude to manual labour – until slavery was abolished nearly 180 years later. By then, an estimated total of 63 000 had been imported.

Another subject to claim Van Riebeeck's attention was the exploration – distinctly tentative, as it turned out – of the interior. He sent the first party of volunteers inland three years after landing 'to see whether any other native peoples are to be found, and whether better minerals are to be obtained than those we have here'. Having travelled northwards, they returned three weeks later to report that 'they had come across a certain people of very small stature, subsisting very meagerly, quite wild, without huts, cattle or anything in the world, clad in small skins like these Hottentots and speaking almost as they do'. It was the first time Van Riebeeck's men had encountered Bushmen.

A second expedition was mounted two years later with instructions to find a new source of cattle – Harry's trade embargo was then in force – and 'at the same time to make inquiries to find out whether a fair quantity of ostrich feathers, elephant and hippopotamus tusks, rhinoceros horns, civet, amber, gold, honey and the like are to be obtained from them'. Having journeyed to the area around present-day Paarl and Worcester, this party, too, returned three weeks later with just 10 cattle and 41 sheep. Irritated, Van Riebeeck immediately despatched a third group 'to visit said natives with a supply of copper, tobacco and pipes to see whether a goodly number of cattle can be bought from them on friendly terms'. But the natives had moved on and the group returned in a month empty-handed. A year later, in February 1659, Van Riebeeck decided to raise his sights. He sent an expedition north to find the fabled kingdom of Monomotapa – present-day Zimbabwe – which the Portuguese had known to be rich in gold, as well as 'new tribes, towns or villages and anything else that might be discovered'. The seven volunteers left with an ox-wagon loaded with cloth, beads, bracelets, sewing needles, copper, brass, lead, tobacco and spices 'to find out if any of these commodities are in demand'. They also took with them a copy of Van Riebeeck's dauntingly detailed instructions for explorers, effectively a conqueror's handbook.

I.

As soon as you have crossed the first river you should begin thenceforth to note by the compass the direction of your course and to record how many hours you have travelled, noting to within a half-hour how much longer or shorter the stage has been, just as the helmsman does at sea, so that this information may be presented on a chart to our Lords and Masters in the Fatherland. This must first and foremost be observed and on no account be neglected.

2.

In addition you must record where you find clayey soil or arable land, sandy or stony soil or mountainous country; where there is water or where there are running rivers and what course they take. Observe too if there are any minerals anywhere in the mountains or in the rivers, where silver or gold may be extracted. Also note whether the whole route could be negotiated by wagons and give names to some of the noteworthy places and inquire the names of the people and their chiefs and towns, so that in future we shall know them.

3.

Whenever you meet any tribes you should also notice what they subsist on, what chiefs they have, what clothes they wear, what they live on, what religion, what dwellings and what fortified places they have. Find out what they desire most to acquire, and whether they possess honey, wax, ostrich feathers, elephant tusks, silver, gold, pearls, tortoise-shell, musk, civet, amber, any fine pelts or anything else.

4.

Note what edible fruit or root crops are to be found and if ever you come to the coast, mark all bays and river mouths, noting the direction of the rivers, what supplies of water there are and what wood or refreshment, etc. is to be found there. Also whether oysters or mussels with pearls, or tortoises whose shells could be made into combs and other articles are obtainable anywhere.

5.

Ascertain the strength of the tribes, also with whom they live in peace and with whom in enmity and the reasons for this. Find out the commonly accepted names of the tribes and in particular the names of their important chiefs or kings. Discover too what settlements, towns and villages they have, as well as their equipment for waging war.

6.

Sound such people on their attitude towards our nation and find out if they are barbarous, or kindly-disposed and are in some degree civilized and have a system of government. In order that you may know precisely how to record all these things, we have appended for your further attention and guidance a copy of the memorandum prepared by the Hon. Directors to be consulted in the writing of reports. With the aid of this and of our verbal instructions we trust that you will now be well aware of what your duties are in every respect, in order to gain honour for yourselves and earn the reward promised you in proportion to the merit of whatever you discover. God grant that this may be considerable. In conclusion, we herewith wish you a prosperous journey there and back under the protection of the Great Guardian of the faithful. We shall daily pray for you that He in His grace may abide with you. Amen.

In the fort of Good Hope,
4 February 1659.

(Signed) Jan van Riebeecq.

Alas, the hapless explorers were back in a month saying all they had found was a 'country everywhere so barren, parched and ill-supplied with pasturage and water' that they had been forced to give up. 'Their journey,' Van Riebeeck noted, 'has thus been of very little value.' He, though, was not one to give up. In November 1660 he offered a bounty to anyone willing to undertake another expedition to Monomotapa 'and promise not to return within 3 or 4 months'. In the event, the 13 volunteers were back within two months, saying they had been 'unable to cross the steep Mountains of Africa, fully twice the height of Table Mountain' – assumed to be today's Hex River Mountains, a formidable 6 000ft-high barrier. 'The expedition,' Van Riebeeck noted, 'was practically fruitless.' He initiated three more attempts in 1661, each ending in failure and variously reporting 'a country so barren and salty it was impossible to traverse', 'as solid and dry as a plank', 'nothing but sand dotted with molehills'.

Those failures apart, Van Riebeeck, faithful Company servant that he was, had reason to be satisfied with what he had achieved. Thanks to him, a fragile toe-hold on the southern tip of Africa had become not only a productive settlement but a secure base from which to explore and settle the interior. Replaced as Commander at his own request in May 1662, Van Riebeeck was assigned to a post in Batavia, where he died 15 years later at the age of 58.

NOTES

1 Poetic licence: the people Da Gama encountered here would have been yellowish-brown rather than black; he himself described them as 'swarthy' or 'tawny'.
2 One of Da Gama's shipmates.
3 Nicolau Coelho, commander of one of Da Gama's ships.
4 Then the term for all Africans south of the Sahara.
5 Bartholomew Diaz, who first rounded the Cape in 1488, was drowned in 1500, three years after Da Gama's voyage.
6 Francisco d'Almeida, killed at the Cape in 1510.
7 Manuel de Sepulveda, shipwrecked off Natal with his wife and two small sons in 1552. They walked 200 miles to Mozambique, where they were killed.
8 Near present-day Mossel Bay, 200 miles east of Cape Town.
9 An island at the mouth of the Great Fish River, half way between present-day Port Elizabeth and East London.
10 Near Mossel Bay, where Da Gama had landed in 1497.
11 Oedasoa was the overlord of the Kaapmans.

CHAPTER 2

INTO THE INTERIOR:
BUSHMEN AND HOTTENTOTS

Among the novelists who have best evoked South Africa's interior are John Buchan and Olive Schreiner. Buchan arrived in 1901 as a member of Lord Milner's 'kindergarten', a group of bright young men, all Oxford bachelors, charged with reconstructing the country after it had been devastated by the Boer War. Although he stayed only two years, John Buchan fell in love with the place and set *Prester John*, one of his best-known novels, in the far north of the Transvaal. Here, in an extract from his autobiography (3), published in 1940, he offers a bird's-eye view.

The country is like an inverted pie-dish, a high tableland sloping steeply to the ocean on south and east, less steeply to the Zambesi in the north. Its selvedge of coast land is temperate in the south, and as it sweeps north becomes sandy desert or tropical flats. The pie-dish contains every variety of landscape. In the Cape peninsula you have the classic graces of Italy, stony, sun-baked hills rising from orchards and vineyards and water-meadows. On the high veld you have grey-green plains, which carry the eye to an immense distance. The mountain rim from the Drakensberg to the Rhodesian scarp breaks down in wild kloofs and pinnacles to the bushveld; and the streams, which begin as strings of pools on the veld, are transformed first into torrents and then into sluggish tropical rivers. That is the general configuration, but there are a thousand hidden nooks which recall to every traveller his own home, for it is the most versatile of lands. Yet there is a certain subtle unity in the landscape, something indefinable which we know to be South African. This has much to do with the climate, which I take to be the best in the world, not because there are no discomforts – for there are many – but because no climate that I know produces so keen a sense of well-being. One could go supperless to bed in the rain on the bare veld, and awake whistling from pure light-heartedness. Whoever has once drunk Vaal water, says the proverb, will always return, and for certain the old enchantress lays a spell which is ill to loose. The scent of a dung fire or wood smoke or mimosa, the creak of a wagon axle, a mule coughing in the dust, and a dozen other little things are still to me as evocative of memories as the 'smell of the wattles in Lichtenburg' was to Mr. Kipling's Australian.

There was little of the country which I did not see, from the Cape peninsula, where from shining seas the staircase of the hills climbs to the many-coloured Karroo, to the dull green forests of the Zambesi. But it was the northern plateau which I explored intensively: the castled summits of Mont aux Sources and Basutoland, where the streams descend in sheer veils of lawn to Natal; the scarp whence one looks into the Swaziland and Zululand glens, and, further north, across a hundred miles of bush to the dim outline of the Lebombo; the ridges which huddle behind Lydenburg into the sunset; the lake country of Ermelo; the endless spaces of the high veld; the Zoutpansberg and other ranges of the north, honeycombed with caves and secret waters; the Limpopo running its fantastic course from its springs on the edge of the Rand through high veld and bushveld to the lush flats of Mozambique. I used every kind of transport – Cape cart, mule wagon, horses of all kinds from half-broken Argentines and Texans to handy little Boer ponies – anything Remounts provided, for in those days we could not be particular. Often I had company, but often I had lonely rides and solitary bivouacs. There is something to be said for leaving youth a good deal alone that it may discover itself.

Two pictures I have always carried to cheer me in dismal places. One is of a baking noon on the high veld, the sky a merciless blue, the brown earth shimmering in a heat haze. I am looking into a wide hollow where a red road like a scar descends and disappears over the next ridge. In the bottom there is a white farm with a clump of gum trees, a blue dam, and blue water-furrows threading a patch of bright green alfalfa. An outspan fire is sending up spirals of milky blue smoke. A hawk is hovering far above, but there are no sounds except the drone of insects, and very far off the jar of an ungreased axle. The air is hot but not heavy, pungent and aromatic. I have never had such a sense of brooding primeval peace, as from that sun-drenched bowl brimming with essential light.

The other picture is the Wood Bush in the North Transvaal which lies between Pietersburg and the eastern flats. You climb to it through bare foothills where the only vegetation is the wait-a-bit thorn, and then suddenly you cross a ridge and enter a garden. The woods of big timber trees are as shapely as the copses in a park laid out by a landscape-gardener. The land between them is rich meadow, with, instead of buttercups and daisies, the white arum lily and the tall blue agapanthus. In each cup is a stream of clear grey-blue water, swirling in pools and rapids like a Highland salmon river. These unite to form the Bruderstroom which, after hurling itself over the plateau's edge, becomes a feeder of the Olifants. Here is a true lodge in the wilderness, with on the one side the stony Pietersburg uplands, and on the other the malarial bushveld. The contrast makes a profound impression, since the Wood Bush itself is the extreme of richness and beauty. The winds blow as clean as in mid-ocean, soil and vegetation are as wholesome as an English down. I have entered the place from different sides – by the precipitous road up the Bruderstroom, by the Pietersburg highway, from the north along the scarp, and once from the bushveld by a tributary glen where my Afrikander pony had to do some rock-climbing; and on each occasion I seemed to be crossing the borders of a *temenos,* a place enchanted and consecrate. I resolved to go back in my old age, build a dwelling, and leave my bones there.

Olive Schreiner was born in the Karoo and worked as a governess for Karoo farmers, which was the genesis of her first novel, *The Story of an African Farm*. This description is from a collection of essays (4) published posthumously. (She died in 1920.)

If we return to the Western districts of the Cape Colony, and leaving the coast belt, climb one of the high mountain ranges that here, as everywhere else, bound the coast belt separating it from the centre of the country, we shall find to our surprise that on reaching its summit, we make hardly any descent on the other side; and that what appeared from the south to be a high mountain range was merely the edge of a vast plateau. We shall find ourselves on an undulating plain, bounded on every side by small fantastic hills. The air is dry and clear; so light that we draw a long breath to make sure we are breathing it aright. The sky above is a more transparent blue than nearer the coast, and seems higher. There is not a blade of grass to be seen growing anywhere; the red sand is covered with bushes a few inches high, clothed with small, hard leaves of dull, olive-green; here and there is an ice-plant, or a stapelia with fleshy, cactus-like leaves, or a rod-like milk bush. As far as the eye can reach, there is often not a tree or a shrub more than two feet high; and far, in the distance, rising abruptly out of the plain, are perhaps two solitary flat-topped mountains; nearer at hand are small conical hillocks, made of round iron-stones piled so regularly on one another that they seem the work of man rather than nature. In the still, clear air you can see the rocks on a hill ten miles off as if they were beside you; the stillness is so intense that you can hear the heaving of your own breast. This is the Karoo. To the stranger, oppressive, weird, fantastic, it is to the man who has lived with it a scene for the loss of which no other on earth compensates.

As you travel through it after fifteen, twenty, or fifty miles, you may come upon a farm. The house, a small brown or white speck in the vast landscape, lies at the foot of a range of hills or a small 'kopje', with its sheep kraals on the slope behind it, of large brown squares, enclosed by low stone walls. Sometimes there is a garden before the house also enclosed by stone walls, and containing fruit trees, and there is a dam with willow trees planted beside; sometimes there is no dam and no garden, and the little brown mud house stands there baking in the sun with its kraals behind it; the only water for men or beasts coming from some small unseen spring. Throughout the Karoo there are few running streams; the waters of any fountains which may exist are quickly drunk up by the dry soil, and men and animals are largely dependent on artificial dams filled by rain-water. The farmer makes his livelihood from flocks of sheep which wander over the Karoo, and which in good years flourish on its short dry bushes.

In the spring, in those years when rain has fallen, for two months the Karoo is a flower garden. As far as the eye can reach, stretch blots of white and yellow and purple fig flowers; every foot of Karoo sand is broken open by small flowering lilies and waxflowers; in a space a few feet square you may sometimes gather fifty kinds of flowers. In the crevices of the rocks little flowering plants are growing. At the end of two months it is over; the bulbs have died back into the ground by millions, the fig blossoms are withered, the Karoo assumes the red and brown tints which it wears for all the rest of the year.

Sometimes there is no spring. At intervals of a few years great droughts occur, when for thirteen months the sky is cloudless. The Karoo bushes drop their leaves and are dry withered stalks, the fountains fail, and the dams are floored with dry baked mud, which splits up into little squares; the sheep and goats die by hundreds, and the Karoo is a desert.

For the first 100-or-so years after the settlement's founding, Bushmen and Hottentots were what chiefly attracted the attention of those who ventured into the interior. At first, however, they travelled little further than Van Riebeeck's men had, and met with as little success. For example, Olof Bergh (5), a Company ensign, was sent north by Commander (later Governor) Simon van der Stel in October 1682 – 30 years after Van Riebeeck landed – with instructions to barter beads and tobacco for cattle with the Namaqua (or, as his scribe has it, Amacqua) Hottentots. By 24 November, the party had reached the Groen River near present-day Garies in the Kamiesberg Mountains, about 250 miles north of Cape Town. Bergh's journal vividly records the difficulties of the journey and the frustrations of trying to do business with the Hottentots in an atmosphere of mutual suspicion and hostility.

Tuesday, Nov. 24th. Early this morn we fared forth over and amongst dry and barren mountains of moderate height. We marched on various courses in the sultry and hot weather, finding like yesterday neither water nor pasture [...] We climbed upon an enormous rock and have mapped the high peaks ahead of us beyond which lay the Amacquas with their kraals. About three o'clock this afternoon we marched on till set of sun along the aforesaid river which was clothed with thorn trees, reeds and grass [...]

Wednesday, Nov. 25th. Early this morning the Ensign sent the Amacqua Hottentots to their kraals to say they must come to us with their cattle if they were willing to barter. About 6 o'clock we broke camp and proceeded towards the high peaks passing over ridges and mountains of fair size until we came again to the aforesaid river, where it was overgrown with many thorn trees. There came 3 or 4 other Amacquas, one of them a Captain with the Company's 'chiap'[1] upon his staff and above thereon was the name Heijbe. We marched farther along the river till about 10 o'clock, when we came to a great plain clothed in long grass. There was good water in the river here and there and round about were many thorn trees. The Amacquas said that there would be little pasture farther on. We have unyoked the oxen and allowed them to graze [...] This afternoon the Ensign has sent some Amacquas to their kraals to say they should come and trade with us. The two afore-mentioned Captains and a third Amacqua remained here; they were regaled by us as usual. We have pitched our tent and have placed all the goods from the wagons therein and then constructed a 'kraal' for the cattle. We named the place at which we camped the Grass-plain, the river the Green-thorntree River.

Thursday, the 26th November. At midday the Ensign caused the Amacquas to be asked why they tarried so long and where their people's kraals were. They have sent back, on the Ensign insisting, three of their Hottentots and said they would be with us by the morning. We kept the Captains with us.

Friday, the 27th November. This morning the Ensign again caused the Captains to be asked if the people of their kraals were soon to be with us, for it appeared they were making a mock of us and were out to deceive us, and we were well on our guard. The Captains sought to leave us, saying, 'You Dutchmen at the Cape are masters, but the Amacquas are masters here.' To this impertinence the Ensign could hardly listen. He caused them to be told that wherever the Dutchmen came, there they sought friendship, but if they cheated them and made them angry they counted all the Amacquas as naught and would quickly be their master, but if they shewed goodwill the Dutchmen would also. Because we have consumed all of our sheep except three, we have kept the three aforesaid Captains with us against their will the better to obtain such cattle as we require on the way if they did not wish to barter with us. There arrived meanwhile some of their Hottentots with 6 oxen, 5 calves and 6 sheep, whereof the Ensign obtained 2 oxen, 2 calves and 6 sheep by barter. We could not agree about the rest, for they wished to have much more for them than they were worth. At midday there came again a party of Hottentots and quite 50 or 60 women, but they brought no cattle with them. They came for naught else but to prate with our Hottentots and to gaze at us. They at last left us and again came others both men and women. This went on throughout the entire day, without bringing us more cattle than an ox and two sheep which the Ensign traded. They said they would return with many cattle in the morning. They all left this evening except one Captain, whom we kept with us on pretext that if their nation despoil us of cattle they would have to try to get him back.

Saturday, 28th November. This morn there came to us a great number of Hottentots, both men and women, well over 200. They brought no cattle save only an old and meagre cow, a calf and 2 sheep. The Ensign obtained the calf and 2 sheep by barter. They remained near us sitting round about and prating of naught save tobacco. They giggled and laughed with our Hottentots, poking fun at us, so it seemed, and had they the chance would have treated us as enemies, so that it was hardly to be endured. They said outright they would not trade with us, pretending that their cattle had been taken from them; from others we learned that this was untrue and they merely sought to cheat us. At midday we again packed our goods on the wagons and left about one o'clock. We returned the way we had come. We could have done another day's journey, but turned back for there was nothing more to be achieved for the service of the Company; moreover, our wagons were beginning to fail us and we might find less water on the return journey and be put to the greatest embarrassment.

Six years later, Van der Stel sent Ensign Isaq Schrijver on a more elaborate and, as it turned out, fruitful expedition to the Eastern Cape. Taking two wagons and accompanied by 20 Dutchmen and a number of Hottentots, he was to find, and trade for cattle with, a group then known as the Inquahase or Inqua Hottentots. Led by a 'captain' called Heikon (variously spelled), they were believed to be based near present-day Graaff-Reinet, some 500 miles by modern road from Cape Town. Once the party passed Oudtshoorn, 250 miles to the east, they were in country unknown to Europeans. Besides its tantalising references to shipwrecks, castaways and cannibals, Schrijver's diary provides a glimpse of Hottentot society before the settlers engulfed it. We join the explorers in February 1689 on the 47th day of their journey as they approached the Camdeboo Mountains.

Saturday 12 dto. We set our course N.E. by E. with the approach of day until about 9 o'clock in the forenoon we came to a high mountain range. We camped here at the entrance to the kloof at the said river Kalniga.[2] The sergeant with 2 of our men and 5 of the Hottentots who are with us, were sent from here to the neighbouring mountains to see if any kraals lay on the other side. Our guides, however, said unanimously that this was Heikon's land and that he with his kraals sometimes lay at this river. We sent the master-miner with 2 assistants to the other side of the neighbouring mountains to see if they could find any minerals. The wind blew from the W. by N., bringing hot and clear weather. The sergeant with his company returned at sunset. He reported to us that he had found the mountains covered everywhere with good grass land, but he had been unable to see any kraals. By evening the master-miner and his men also returned. He said he had failed to find minerals anywhere.

Sunday 13 dto. We continued to rest here and stayed in camp all day. At day-break, however, we sent out 3 Hottentots to search for Heijkon's kraal. Meanwhile our men were cheerfully occupied making a kraal for the cattle.

Monday 14 dto. found us still at the aforesaid resting place. We remained in camp awaiting with great longing the Hottentots sent out by us; they have not returned to-day.

Tuesday 15 dto. Six Hottentots of Heikon's kraal came to us early this morn-ing. They said that they had not met the Hottentots sent by us, but that one of the Sonquas had arrived at their kraal and told them of our coming. They reported that Heijkon was very pleased at our arrival and was already on the march to meet us and he requested that we await him here at this place. We therefore instantly sent 2 of the said Hottentots back to him with some small gifts in order that Heijkon might haste the more to come to us.

But it was to be another four days before Heijkon showed up.

Saturday 19 dto. About 1 o'clock in the afternoon 9 of Heikon's deputies ar-rived: they besought us in his name not to go hence before their Captain came. When they had delivered their message each received a piece of to-bacco and also a portion for their Captain, and they immediately hastened at their best pace back to him. When an hour had passed he at last arrived with fully 150 followers under guidance of our Hottentots sent out on the 13th.

This Captain is of great stature and more robust than any of our men, and on the average bigger of body and limbs than the Cape Hottentots. He is well proportioned, courageous and strong; his face and his beard, however, are like that of the Cape Hottentots. This Captain has great authority over his people, all his behests are carried out and brought to a finish at the dou-ble. His people are more humble than our Hottentots. In the beginning they were very afraid and shy of us, even the Captain himself shook and shivered when he saw us, but this quickly passed when he perceived the crown of copper which was set upon his head. He was most pleased by this and was in high feather. In the drinking of arrack he bore himself frugally, but had

little or no knowledge of smoking tobacco. After he had given us information and replied well to our questions, he betook himself with his company
of followers to his kraal before sundown.

His neighbours told us the following: The Kubuquas lay 5 days' journey
hence on the sea coast; they inhabit small houses made of clay. They own
much cattle and trade with them, living at times in great enmity and causing
each other great damage and destruction.

The district where the Kubuquas lay was pointed out to us E.S.E. In these
territories the Damaquas also inhabit small houses of clay and are a numerous people rich in cattle, living on the sea coast. This tribe is provided
with beads, copper and iron which they know how to obtain from stranded
ships. They have also (according to the assertion of Heijkon) people of our
fashion with them. Further away lie three nations on the sea coast who are
richly provided with cattle. They are called the Ganumqua, Namkunqua
and the Ganaqua, from whom the Inquahase Hottentots barter dagha,[3]
which is used by them as the Indians use opium or amphion. Towards the
North lie yet other three nations called the Glij, Brij and Blij, from whom the
Inquahase barter flat thin copper plates which they resell to the Kubuquas
and Namaquas. Finally there is a nation of people known by them named
Briqua, who are eaters of men.

Sunday 20 dto. Early this morning came the Captain Heijkon, chief of the
Inquahase Hottentots, accompanied by more of his people than yesterday.
We began to barter, favoured by a lovely day.

Monday 21 dto. Captn. Heijkon with his followers came again amongst us and
stayed until the afternoon. They bargained mostly for strong drink, of which
they had imbibed all too freely yesterday.

Tuesday 22 dto. Captn. Heijkon had arranged a feast in his kraal with the
result that not one of them came to us all day; we passed it, however, in
bartering. Towards evening we learned the reason why Heijkon had not visited us during the day. This was the reason thereof. One of our people shot
a bird yesterday after he had left us. He appeared to be in high dudgeon at
this, for it is their custom that if any of his people kill game, be it tiger, lion,
hartebeest or such like, he may not eat of it or enjoy the same ere Captn.
Heijkon has received a fat sheep as an offering; the which seemed strange

to us or that he appeared to wish to hold us to this custom. On this account we again sent him an offering of a few beads with which he was well pleased and appeased.

Wednesday 23 dto. The Hottentots of Heijkon's kraal came to us to barter very early. About 9 o'clock in the forenoon their Captain visited us too and left us in the afternoon.

Thursday 24 dto. Captn. Heykon and his followers again visited us and spent the day in barter.

Friday 25 dto. After Captn. Heijkon and his people had stayed with us until noon and the trading had proceeded readily, the said Captn. Heijkon took leave of us about 1 o'clock in the afternoon. He said that he must of necessity go for fear that his kraal might be raided by the surrounding Sonquase Hottentots and that he durst not therefore abide longer with us. He commended himself, however, to the favour of the Honourable Company and the Great Captn. He hoped that we might soon return bringing with us assegais for him. He appeared to be well satisfied and contented with the trade-goods we had bartered with each other. This morning the wind was very changeable, but in the afternoon we had a N.N. Easter accompanied by heavy rain.

Saturday 26 dto. About 7 o'clock in the mirk of morning as we stood upon our departure, Captn. Heykon came once again and for the last time; he accompanied us a little way. He repeated his requests of yesterday and at last took leave of us. We have obtained by barter more than 500 cattle and a flock of sheep here.

Having seen long service at the Cape, both Bergh and Schrijver were too used to Hottentots to remark much on their customs. Even Van Riebeeck in his 2 500-page journal had little to say about them, although he, like everyone else, did note the Hottentots' partiality to tobacco and liquor and – when, for example, they were alarmed by looking in a mirror – 'the peculiar antics and entertaining eccentricities of these strange people'. He observed, too, that 'they are averse to living in our houses; they are like the birds that prefer ranging the open air to living in the finest halls of kings … It is also a grievous punishment for them if they are not allowed to mess and wallow like swine in all kinds of dirt and filth.'This last was what was apt to catch the eye of explorers such as Anders Sparrman (6), though he was less judgmental about the 'dirt and filth' than most. An eminent Swedish naturalist, Sparrman had studied under Linnaeus, the botanist and father of modern taxonomy, sailed round the world with Capt Cook, visiting the Antarctic, New Zealand and the South Pacific islands, and returned to the Cape in 1775. After describing the Hottentots' physical features, he went on:

In order to finish the picture I have here given of the Hottentots, the next thing I have to describe is their dress, and method of painting themselves. This latter (if painting it may be called) consists in besmearing their bodies all over most copiously with fat, in which there is mixed up a little soot. This is never washed off; on the contrary, I never saw them use any thing to clean their skins, excepting that when, in greasing the wheels of their waggons, their hands were besmeared with tar and pitch, they used to get it off very easily with cow-dung, at the same time rubbing their arms into the bargain up to the elbows with this cosmetic: so that as the dust and other filth, together with their sooty ointment and the sweat of their bodies, must necessarily, notwithstanding it is continually wearing off, in some measure adhere to the skin, it contributes not a little to conceal the natural hue of the latter, varying from a shiny soot-brown to a dark brown-yellow mixed with dirt.

What has enabled me to determine the natural complexion of the Hottentots to be of a jaundice-like colour, was merely the scrupulous nicety of some few farmers' wives, who made one or two of their Hottentot girls scower their skins, that they might not be too filthy to look after their children, or to do any other business that required cleanliness.

It is asserted by many of the colonists, that by this washing the Hottentots looks are not at all improved. They seem to think, that their natural yellow-brown hue was to the full as disagreeable as that which is produced by their besmearing themselves; and that a besmeared Hottentot looks less naked, as it were, and more complete, than one in his natural state; and that the skin of a Hottentot ungreased seems to exhibit some defect in dress, like shoes that want blacking, &c. Whether this fancy is most founded in custom or in the nature of things, I shall leave to others to determine.

Besides the pleasure the Hottentots enjoy in besmearing their bodies from head to foot, they likewise perfume them with a powder of herbs, with which they powder both their heads and bodies, rubbing it in all over them when they besmear themselves. The odour of it is at the same time rank and aromatic and seems to come nearest to that of the poppy mixed with spices. The plants used for this purpose are various species of the diosma, called by the Hottentots bucku[4] and considered by them as possessing great virtues in curing disorders. Some of these species are very common round about the Cape; but one particular sort, which I am told grows about Goud's rivier[5], is said to be so valuable, that no more than a thimble full of it is given in exchange for a lamb.

The Hottentots, with their skins dressed up with grease and soot, and bucku-powder, are by this means in a great measure defended from the influence of the air, and may in a manner reckon themselves full dressed. In other respects, both men and women are wont to appear quite undressed; indeed, I may say naked, except a trifling covering, with which they always conceal certain parts of their bodies.

Also much remarked on was the Hottentot language, which includes a range of clicking sounds – or, as the Dutch heard it, 'tot-tot-tot-ing'. Similar clicks are present in the languages of South Africa's two largest groups, the Zulu and the Xhosa, collectively referred to at the time as Kaffirs or Caffres. Carl Peter Thunberg (7), a contemporary and countryman of Sparrman's, who arrived at the Cape in 1772, was one of the first to try to describe the phenomenon.

The Hottentot language is not everywhere the same but has very different dialects; all of them, however, are commonly pronounced with a kind of smack, or clacking of the organs of speech. This clacking I observed to be made in three different ways, which renders it almost impossible for the Europeans to speak it properly, although their children, who have been brought up among those of the Hottentots, learn to speak it fluently. The first of these modes of clacking is the dental, in which the tip of the tongue is struck against the teeth. The second is the palatial,[6] when the noise is made by the tongue striking against the palate. The third, or guttural, is the most difficult of all, and performed quite low down in the throat, with the very root of the tongue. These clackings are the more difficult to perform, as they must be made at the very instant of uttering the word, and not before nor after. They occur not only in the beginning, but likewise in the middle, of a word; and sometimes two clackings occur in a word of two or three syllables. When several Hottentots sit conversing together, the sound is very like the clacking of so many geese. That the pronunciation of the language is troublesome to them, was very evident to me, from the gesticulations they made, and from the circumstance that they wearied their lips. They could talk, however, with a tobacco pipe in their mouths, but in very short sentences only. The language of the Caffres I observed was much easier, and was spoken with much less clacking, which was heard in some few words only.

Thus the inhabitants of this southernmost promontory of Africa have a proper language; but, in other respects, are so rude and uncultivated as to have no letters, nor any method of writing or delineating them, either on paper, in wood, or on stone. It is in vain, therefore, to seek for any kind of learning, or any antique records, among them; and few nations in the world, perhaps, are less enlightened than they.

What Thunberg calls the Hottentots' 'lack of enlightenment' was another frequent theme of the early explorers' reminiscences, as was the Hottentots' 'idleness'. Anders Sparrman, who journeyed for nine months deep into the Eastern Cape, was unusually perceptive about this. We join him on 1 September 1775 at a Hottentot kraal near present-day Stormsvlei in the Western Cape.

As I wished to try if I could not hire a Hottentot or two into our service, the oldest man in the craal presented his son to me, a youth of nineteen or twenty years of age, saying, that he could be very well spared in the craal, in case I could persuade him to follow me. Upon this I crept into the young man's hut, and found him lying under his cloak, in the way I have described above when speaking of his countrymen in general, with his knees drawn up to his nose, almost like a *foetus in utero*. I spent a great deal of time to no purpose, in representing to him the great advantages he would gain by going with us; such as a cow with calf, knives, brass tinder-boxes, glass beads, and other tempting articles; in short, presents to an uncommon value, all which I offered him as a premium for half a year's service; but as I considered it equally base to deceive a poor Hottentot as any other person, I did not dissemble to him, that our expedition would be of some duration: though, on the other hand, as the Hottentot nation is not absolutely insensible to the pleasures of the chace any more than to the calls of ambition, I at the same time represented to him, that an expedition of this sort would of itself afford him no small degree of pleasure, and on his return would give him some consequence in the eyes of his companions; but all was in vain. With as little success did I endeavour to set before him the pleasure he would have in smoking a better sort of tobacco, a quantity of which I had taken with me, and intended to bestow it very plentifully on any one that should accompany me in my journey. I likewise put him in mind, that he would not find so costly an article as tobacco, nor even victuals abound greatly, if he staid at home.

Notwithstanding all this, I found him absolutely immoveable in soul as well as in body; excepting, indeed, that with regard to the latter, he now and then threw out a whiff of tobacco from the left side of his chops; and that two or three times, on my repeatedly requesting him to let me know his mind on the subject, he at length, though not without some difficulty, prevailed on himself to open his mouth, and answer me with a short but decisive, *No!* The extreme indolence of the lad, his very cavalier reception of me, the clouds of smoke that filled his cabin and made my eyes smart most horribly, together with the swarms of fleas I observed in it, excited in me just at that time the greatest indignation, as well as the utmost contempt for the Hottentot nation: though, when I afterwards came to consider the matter more impartially, as the lad, from his habits as well as nature, could very easily make shift with a moderate quantity of food, and with this could and actually did enjoy what to him was a real substantial pleasure, viz. his ease and tobacco, I could not well suppose that my offer would have any weight with him.

At last, however, I made him another proposal of a different nature, which was, that he, for a very moderate premium, should, for a few days only, help us to lead our oxen to Zwellendam, where I was in hopes of getting somebody in his room. To this he answered as quick as thought, *Ja, Baas,* (Yes, Master,) got up in an instant, and had nothing more to do than to hang his tobacco-pouch on his arm, in order to be quite ready for his journey. After this, he went straight to my waggon, and with all the ease and alacrity imaginable, did every thing that was requisite to it; so that he no longer appeared to be the same lazy fellow, with whom I had just before been bargaining.

The principal reason of this disposition that prevails with most Hottentots is, perhaps, that their wants are extremely few; and consequently, being without care or employment of any kind, they are inactive and idle. From this cause again, a famine or general want of the necessaries of life arising, will naturally stimulate their usually half-starved bodies into activity and vigorous motion, at least, till their more pressing wants are relieved. On the other hand, such children of Hottentots as from their tender years have been in the service of the colonists, and have been used to work, do not yield the palm of briskness and agility to any other nation whatever. It appears to me, therefore, that one cannot accuse any natural disposition of theirs, as being a hindrance to their rising from their present very barbarous and unpolished state to a much higher degree of civilization.

Though the father of the Hottentot I had just hired did not take the least part in his son's resolve, yet at their parting he showed, that he possessed the affections of a father. In fact, they seemed to take a tender farewell of each other; on which occasion, the old man repeatedly importuned us in the most friendly manner to use his son kindly.

The Bushmen, however, were another matter. Here, with a harshly anthropological description of these tragic people, is John Barrow (8), who arrived at the Cape in 1797 after the British first took it over from the Dutch and spent seven months surveying the new colony on his government's behalf.

Whether they are considered as to their persons, their turn of mind, or way of life, the Bosjesmans are certainly a most extraordinary race of people. In their persons they are extremely diminutive. The tallest of the men measured only four feet nine inches, and the tallest woman four feet four inches. About four feet six inches is said to be the middle size of the men, and four feet that of the women. One of these that had several children measured only three feet nine inches. Their colour, their hair, and the general turn of their features, evidently denote a common origin with the Hottentots, though the latter, in point of personal appearance, have the advantage by many degrees. The Bosjesmans, indeed, are amongst the ugliest of all human beings. The flat nose, high cheek-bones, prominent chin, and concave visage, partake much of the apeish character, which their keen eye, always in motion, tends not to diminish. The upper lid of this organ, as in that of the Chinese, is rounded into the lower on the side next the nose, and forms not an angle, as is the case in the eye of an European, but a circular sweep, so that the point of union between the upper and lower eyelid is not ascertainable. It is perhaps from this circumstance that they are known in the colony under the name of *Cineeze,* or Chinese Hottentots. Their bellies are uncommonly protuberant, and their backs hollow; but their limbs seem to be in general well turned and proportioned. Their activity is incredibly great. The klip-springing antelope can scarcely excel them in leaping from rock to rock; and they are said to be so swift, that, on rough ground, or up the sides of mountains, horsemen have no chance in keeping pace with them. And, as the means of increasing their speed in the chace, or when pursued by an enemy, the men had adopted a custom, which was sufficiently remarkable, of pushing the testicles to the upper part of the root of the penis, where they seemed to remain as firmly fixed and as conveniently placed as if nature had stationed them there. It is highly probable that such an operation, in order to be effectual, must be performed at an early period of life. Some were said to have one up and one down, which may have given rise to the Hottentots being characterized in the *Systema Naturae* as *Monorchides*.

The tone of such observations made it all the easier for the settlers to treat the Bushmen as sub-human. In a concerted drive along the Cape's northern border in 1774, they killed more than 500. Again, it is Anders Sparrman, the Swedish explorer, now, in January 1776, in the Eastern Cape some 100 miles north of Port Elizabeth, who gives an uncharacteristically balanced account of the conflict between the Dutch and those who had taken possession of the land at least 25 000 years earlier.

The lower *Sneeuwbergen*, or Snow-mountains, are inhabited the year throughout; but on the higher range of hills the winters are severe enough: this circumstance is said to make the colonists remove into the plains below in Camdebo. The inhabitants, indeed, of the more distant *Sneeuwbergen* are sometimes obliged, according to report, entirely to relinquish their dwellings and habitations, on account of the savage plundering race of Boshiesmen, who from their hiding-places, shooting forth their poisoned arrows at the shepherd, kill him, and afterwards drive away the whole of his flock, which perhaps consists of several hundred sheep, and forms the chief, if not the whole, of the farmer's property. What they cannot drive away with them they kill and wound, as much as the time will allow them, while they are making their retreat. It is in vain to pursue them, they being very swift of foot, and taking refuge up in the steep mountains, which they are able to run up almost as nimbly as baboons or monkeys. From thence they roll down large stones, on any one that is imprudent enough to follow them. The approach of night gives them time to withdraw themselves entirely from those parts, by ways and places with which none but themselves are acquainted. These banditti collect together again in bodies to the amount

45

of some hundreds, from their hiding-places and the clefts in the mountains, in order to commit fresh depredations and robberies. One of the colonists, who had been obliged to fly from these mountains, was at this time passing to *Agter Bruntjes-hoogte* with his family, servants, and herds, in order to look out for a new habitation. He informed us, that the Boshies-men grew bolder every day, and seemed to increase in numbers, since people had with greater earnestness set about extirpating them. It was this, doubtless, which has occasioned them to collect together into large bodies, in order to withstand the encroachments of the colonists, who had already taken from them their best dwelling and hunting-places. An instance was related of the Boshies-men having besieged a peasant with his wife and children in their cottage, till at length he drove them off by repeatedly firing among them. They had lately carried off from a farmer the greater part of his sheep. Not long before this, however, they had suffered a considerable defeat in the following manner. Several farmers, who perceived that they were not able to get at the Boshies-men by the usual methods, shot a sea-cow[7], and took only the prime part of it for themselves, leaving the rest by way of bait; they themselves, in the mean while, lying in ambush. The Boshies-men with their wives and children now came down from their hiding-places, with an intention to feast sumptuously on the sea-cow that had been shot; but the farmers, who came back again very unexpectedly, turned the feast into a scene of blood and slaughter. Pregnant women, and children in their tenderest years, were not at this time, neither indeed are they ever, exempt from the effects of the hatred and spirit of vengeance constantly harboured by the colonists with respect to the Boshies-man nation; excepting such, indeed, as are marked out to be carried away into bondage. Does a colonist at any time get sight of a Boshies-man, he takes fire immediately, and spirits up his horse and dogs, in order to hunt him with more ardour and fury than he would a wolf or any other wild beast. On an open plain, a few colonists on horseback are always sure to get the better of the greatest number of Boshies-men that can be brought together, as the former always keep at the distance of about a hundred or a hundred and fifty paces, (just as they find it convenient) and charging their heavy fire-arms with a very large kind of shot, jump off their horses, and rest their pieces in their usual manner on their ram-rods, in order that they may shoot with the greater certainty; so that the balls discharged by them will sometimes, as I have been assured, go through the bodies of four, five, seven, or eight of the enemy at a time, especially as these latter know no better than to keep close together in a body. It is true, that, on the other hand, the Boshies-men can shoot their arrows to the distance of two hundred paces, but with a very uncertain aim, as the arrow must necessarily first make a curve in the air; and should it even at that distance chance to hit any of the farmers, it is not able to go through his hat, or his ordinary linen or coarse woollen coat.

In the district of *Sneeuwberg* the *land-drost*[8] has appointed one of the farmers, with the title of *veld-corporal,* to command in these wars, and as occasion may require, to order out the country people alternately in separate parties, for the purpose of defending the country against its original inhabitants. Government, indeed, has no other part in the cruelties exercised by its subjects, than that of taking no cognizance of them; but in this point it has been certainly too remiss, in leaving a whole nation to the mercy of every individual peasant, or in fact, of every one that chuses to invade their land; as of such people one might naturally expect, that interested views, and an unbridled spirit of revenge, should prevail over the dictates of prudence and humanity. I am far from accusing all the colonists of having a hand in these and other cruelties, which are too frequently committed in this quarter of the globe. While some of them plumed themselves upon them, there were many who, on the contrary, held them in abomination, and feared lest the vengeance of heaven should, for all these crimes, fall upon their land and their posterity.

Among those who evidently did not fear the vengeance of heaven were the settlers who trapped and killed scores of Bushmen in a ravine near Calvinia, about 180 miles north of Cape Town. Called 'Oorlogskloof', it is now part of a nature reserve renowned, ironically, for its Bushman rock paintings. The following poem by Jonty Driver (9) was published in 1994.

Oorlogskloof

The others go too near the edge.
This is Oorlogskloof
Where the San were slaughtered:
The old men, the old women,
The young men, the young women,
The children, their mothers, their fathers,
The pubescent girls

The adolescent boys
The priests
The artists, the song-makers and the trackers
Carvers of arrowhead and knobkerrie
And those who knew how to talk to the Dutch farmers.

Since no one owns the land or the cattle
The San steal. They also fall down dancing
When the sounding stones are pounded with stones,
And the stones make the brain's music inside.
They talk to eland
As eland talk to elephants
They read the wind
They see a lizard hiding ten yards away
They are not to be trusted
They hide among rocks
And they know as much about poison as cobras.

So the Dutch farmers drove them like monkeys
Into this canyon without an outlet
And then killed them one by one, as they stepped
Toward the waterfall which not even
The San could climb. No one counted the dead.
And when the last old woman had been dragged
From behind the rocks
And her throat cut
And the last baby thrown against a rock face
The Dutchmen went away
To their homesteads, churches, wives and children.
The guns were primed to deal with the next species.

Our guide tells us he hears their ghosts sometimes
When he hunts what little is left down there:
Dassies, duikers, baboons. Leopards? we ask.
No leopards, he's certain. No, no leopards –
Only the ghosts of the San still retreating
When the hot wind blows along Oorlogskloof.

Almost as poignant is a story told by Col Robert Gordon, a Dutch soldier of Scottish extraction, who, before he committed suicide in 1795 – the year the British first took the Cape from the Dutch – was head of the garrison at Cape Town Castle. On 13 November 1777 he was near the Sneeuberg Mountains north of Graaff-Reinet when he recorded in his journal: 'These so-called Bushmen or Chinese have a famous chief called Koerikei, or "Bullet-Escaper". Veld Wagtmeester [a local official] Van der Merwe told me that, after an action which he had commanded, this Koerikei, standing on a cliff out of range, shouted out to him: "What are you doing on my land? You have taken all the places where the eland and other game live. Why did you not stay where the sun goes down, where you first came from?" Van der Merwe asked him whether he did not have enough country as it was. He replied that he did not want to lose the country of his birth and that he would kill their herdsmen, and that he would chase them all away. As he went off he further said that it would be seen who would win.' As, of course, it was.

The following extract, written nearly 50 years later, is an epitaph for a dying people. It comes from *Travels and Adventures in Southern Africa* by George Thompson (10), an English businessman who spent 40 years in the country, travelled widely and paid Thomas Pringle, the 1820 Settler, poet and pamphleteer, to ghost-write his memoirs. In July 1824, Thompson was in the Roggeveld Mountains in the Northern Cape staying with Veld-Commandant Jan Nel, the local magistrate.

The Bushmen on this frontier, whatever may have been the original condition of their progenitors, are now entirely destitute of cattle or property of any description; and now that the larger game have been generally destroyed, or driven out of the country by the guns of the Boors and Griquas, they are reduced to the most wretched shifts to obtain a precarious subsistence, living chiefly on wild roots, locusts, and the larvae of insects. The wandering hordes of this people are scattered over a territory of very wide extent, but of so barren and arid a character, that by far the greater portion of it is not permanently habitable by any class of human beings. Even as it is, the colonists are perpetually pressing in upon their limits, wherever a fountain, or even a temporary vley or pool of water is to be found: but had this territory been of a character less desolate and inhospitable, there can be little question that it would have been long ago entirely occupied by the Christians. They are continually soliciting from the Government fresh grants beyond the nominal boundary; and at present are very urgent to obtain possession of a tract lying between the Zak and Hartebeest Rivers. In defence of these aggressions they maintained to me that the Bushmen are a nation of robbers – who, as they neither cultivate the soil, nor pasture cattle, are incapable of occupying their country advantageously; that they would live much more comfortably by becoming the herdsmen and household servants of the Christians, than they do at present on their own precarious resources; and finally, that they are incapable of being civilized by any other means, as the failure of the Missionary establishment among them at the Zak River had evinced. At this institution, I was told, the most strenuous exertions had been employed by the missionary Kicherer, for many years, to engraft upon them habits of industry and foresight, but totally without avail; for he had been ultimately forced to abandon the enterprise, and the station was now in ruins [...] Whatever may have been the causes of the failure of Missionary attempts to civilize the Bushmen, I fear that the usual conduct of the farmers towards them has been rather of a description to render them more barbarous and desperate, than to conciliate or civilize them [...]

Nel informed me that within the last thirty years he had been upon thirty-two commandoes against the Bushmen, in which great numbers had been shot, and their children carried into the Colony. On one of these expeditions, not less than two hundred Bushmen were massacred! In justification of this barbarous system, he narrated many shocking stories of atrocities committed by the Bushmen upon the colonists – which, together with the continual depredations upon their property, had often called down upon them the full weight of vengeance. Such has been, and still, to a great extent, is the horrible warfare existing between the Christians and the natives of the northern frontier, and by which the process of extermination is still proceeding against the latter, in the same style as in the days of Barrow.

It struck me as a strange and melancholy trait of human nature, that this Veld-Commandant, in many other points a meritorious, benevolent, and clear-sighted man, seemed to be perfectly unconscious that any part of his own proceedings, or those of his countrymen, in their wars with the Bushmen, could awaken my abhorrence. The massacre of many hundreds of these miserable creatures, and the carrying away of their children into servitude, seemed to be considered by him and his companions as things perfectly lawful, just, and necessary, and as meritorious service done to the public, of which they had no more cause to be ashamed, than a brave soldier of having distinguished himself against the enemies of his country: while, on the other hand, he spoke with detestation of the callousness of the Bushmen in the commission of robbery and murder upon the Christians; not seeming to be aware that the treatment these persecuted tribes had for ages received from the Christians, might, in their apprehension, justify every excess of malice and revenge that they were able to perpetrate.

Writing in 1806, John Barrow, the British government official, came to much the same conclusions about the fate of the Hottentots – expressed, though, in rather more robust terms. Allowance should almost certainly be made for his prejudice against the Dutch.

Twenty years ago, if we may credit the travellers of that day, the country beyond Camtoos[9] river, which was then the eastern limit of the colony, abounded with kraals or villages of Hottentots, out of which the inhabitants came to meet them by hundreds in a groupe. Some of these villages might still have been expected to remain in this remote and not very populous part of the colony. Not one, however, was to be found. There is not in fact in the whole extensive district of Graaff Reynet a single horde of independent Hottentots; and perhaps not a score of individuals who are not actually in the service of the Dutch. These weak people, the most helpless, and in their present condition perhaps the most wretched, of the human race, duped out of their possessions, their country, and their liberty, have entailed upon their miserable offspring a state of existence to which that of slavery might bear the comparison of happiness. It is a condition, however, not likely to continue to a very remote posterity. The name of Hottentot will be forgotten or remembered only as that of a deceased person of little note. Their numbers of late years have been rapidly on the decline. It has generally been observed that wherever Europeans have colonized, the less civilized natives have always dwindled away, and at length totally disappeared. Various causes have contributed to the depopulation of the Hottentots. The impolitic custom of hording together in families, and of not marrying out of their own kraals, has no doubt tended to enervate this race of men, and to reduce them to their present degenerated condition, which is that of a languid, listless, phlegmatic people, in whom the prolific powers of nature seem to be nearly exhausted. To this may be added their extreme poverty, scantiness of food, and continual dejection of mind, arising from the cruel treatment they receive from an inhuman and unfeeling peasantry, who having discovered themselves to be removed to too great a distance from the seat of government to be awed by its authority, have hitherto exercised, in the most wanton and barbarous manner, an absolute power over these poor wretches, whom they had reduced to the necessity of depending upon them for a morsel of bread. There is scarcely an instance of cruelty, said to have been committed against the slaves in the West-India islands, that could not find a parallel from the Dutch farmers of the remote districts of the colony towards the Hottentots in their service. Beating and cutting with thongs of the hide of the sea-cow or rhinosceros, are only gentle punishments, though these sort of whips, which they call shambocs,[10] are most horrid instruments, being tough, pliant, and heavy almost as lead. Firing small shot into the legs and thighs of a Hottentot is a punishment not unknown to some of the monsters who inhabit the neighbourhood of Camtoos river. And though death is not unfrequently the consequence of punishing these poor wretches in a moment of rage, yet this gives little concern to the farmer; for though they are to all intents and purposes his slaves, yet they are not transferable property. It is this circumstance which, in his mind, makes their lives less valuable, and their treatment more inhuman.

In offences of too small moment to stir up the phlegm of a Dutch peasant, the coolness and tranquillity displayed at the punishment of his slave or Hottentot is highly ridiculous, yet at the same time indicative of a savage disposition to unfeeling cruelty lurking in his heart. He flogs them, not by any given number of lashes, but by time; and as they have no clocks nor substitutes for them capable of marking the smaller divisions of time, he has invented an excuse for the indulgence of one of his most favorite sensualities, by flogging them till he has smoked as many pipes of tobacco as he may judge the magnitude of the crime to deserve.[11]

Francois Le Vaillant (11), a French naturalist and explorer, who spent four years at the Cape from 1781, offered a mordant summary of what had befallen the natives since Van Riebeeck (whom he calls 'Riebek') had arrived 130 years earlier. Like John Barrow, he was no friend of the Dutch, but it is hard to fault his analysis of their behaviour.

When, in 1652, the surgeon Riebek, returning from India to Amsterdam, opened the eyes of the directors of the company to the importance of an establishment at the Cape of Good Hope, they wisely thought that such an undertaking could not be better carried out than by the very genius who had had the idea of it. So, duly mandated, well supplied, armed with all that could contribute to the success of his undertaking, Riebek soon arrived in Table Bay. His shrewd policy was to appear as an able peacemaker and he used all the devious means necessary to attract the goodwill of the Hottentots, and covered the lip of the poisoned cup with honey. These masters of this whole portion of Africa by imprescriptible right, these savages, were won over by these cruel lures, and did not see at all how this culpable debasement was taking away their rights, their authority, their peace, and their happiness. Why should these men, indolent by nature, unattached to any particular piece of land, like true cosmopolitans, not in the least inclined to agriculture, be concerned that some strangers had come to take a little piece of useless and often uninhabited land? They thought that a little further, or a little nearer, was immaterial. It did not matter where their flocks, the only wealth worthy of their note, found their food, as long as they found some. The Dutch held out great hopes for their greedy policy after such a peaceful beginning, and as they are especially skilful and tougher than others in seizing the advantages given by chance, they did not fail to finish off the work, by offering to the Hottentots two highly seductive lures: tobacco, and brandy. From this moment on, no more liberty, no more pride, no more nature, no more Hottentots, no more men. These unfortunate savages, enticed by these two baits, stayed as close as they could to the source providing them. On the other side, the Dutch who could get an ox for a pipe of tobacco or a glass of brandy, tried to keep, as much as possible, such valuable neighbours. Imperceptibly the colony spread and got stronger. Soon one saw rising on foundations that it was too late to destroy, this redoubtable power which dictated laws to this whole part of Africa, and rejected violently all that might resist its ambitions and greedy advancement. News of the company's riches spread and attracted new colonists every day. It was decided, as is always the practice, that might was sufficient right to spread as much as one wanted to. This logic nullified the sacred and respectable rights of property. On several occasions, they grabbed indiscriminately more than was needed, taking all the land that the government or individuals it favoured thought good and suited them.

The Hottentots, thus betrayed, harried, squeezed out everywhere, divided and took two totally different paths. Those still interested, in keeping their flocks went far into the mountains towards the north and the north-east. But this was the smaller group. The others, ruined by some glasses of brandy and a few plugs of tobacco, poor, stripped of everything, never thought of quitting this country. But, renouncing absolutely their habits as well as their ancient and gentle origins, which they no longer even remember today, they basely came to sell their services to the whites. The whites, who are no longer submissive foreigners, but have suddenly become enterprising and proud masters and farmers, do not even have enough workers to cultivate their large farms, and so completely pass on the difficult work and drudgery to these unfortunate Hottentots, who became increasingly degraded and bastardised.

It was all, of course, inevitable or – as a character in *Dusklands*, an early (1974) novel by JM Coetzee, the Nobel Literature prize-winner, cynically explains – 'a necessary loss of innocence …The herder who, waking from drunken stupor to the wailing of hungry children, beheld his pastures forever vacant, had learned the lesson of the Fall: one cannot live forever in Eden. The Company's men were only playing the role of the angel with the flaming sword in this drama of God's creation. The herder had evolved one sad step further towards citizenship of the world. We may take comfort in this thought …'

Not all the early travellers based their observations on anything they had actually seen. Probably the most ludicrous – though he is still solemnly cited by some modern anthropologists – was the German, Peter Kolben. He arrived in Cape Town in 1705, stayed eight years and published *The Present State of the Cape of Good Hope* in 1731. Having condemned other writers for their reliance on 'invention and hearsay', he went on: 'I take this opportunity to tell the reader (a matter I have seen and affirm) that Negroes are born white. But in ten or fourteen days after the birth, the colour changes into a deep black all over them, excepting the palms of their hands and the soles of their feet, which remain whitish as long as they live.'

Of course, 'anthropology' of this kind cuts both ways, as Mazisi Kunene, the celebrated Zulu poet, demonstrated in *Emperor Shaka the Great* (12), his epic verse biography of the Zulu king, published in 1979. Here he records the impact of Europeans arriving in Natal in the early 19th century. (The translation is Kunene's.)

> For many years there were rumours of the arrival of the Pumpkin Race.
> In truth, the teller of tales informs us
> It was the great King Sobhuza[12] who, in a dream, foresaw these events.
> He solemnly told his councillors, at the Assembly:
> 'Through a vision I saw nations emerging from the ocean.
> They resemble us but in appearance are the colour of pumpkin-
> porridge.
> They speak a language no different from that of nestling birds,
> Quick and given to staccato sounds like wild animals.

They are rude of manner and are without any graces or refinement.
They carry a long stick of fire.
With this they kill and loot from many nations.
Sometimes they seize even children for their sea-bound furnaces –
A veritable race of robbers and cannibals!'
Those at the Assembly were deeply disturbed by this horrific dream.
Some denounced the prevalence of dreams,
Certain no such dream would ever come true.
But there were others who affirmed its truth,
Claiming their own story-tellers had told them as much.
It was clear the great king was not alone in these dreams.
The narrators of ancient tales tells us:
Once as the sea lay calm, throwing off only trembling waves,
A strange race emerged from the ocean.
Their hair hung down like husks of maize.
Against them many a mother warned her curious child,
Telling her how once a young boy stared at them,
Eager to see the truth of their form.
But as they neared they began to chase after him.
Only by remembering the advice of Mkhulu[13] was he saved.
To him he had said: 'There are creatures out to kill and rob.
These Nanabahules[14] are a threat to every man.
By asking for water and food they prepare to seize whole villages.
For, indeed, they possess insatiable appetites.
Should you see them, flee, my grandson, flee for your life.
For they run as if they possess the wings of the wind.
To escape them only this stratagem will save you:
Throw chunks of bread (these they never leave),
Which they shall devour like hungry vultures,
To them food is more precious than the human race.
They would annihilate whole nations on earth
To feed endlessly their great appetites.'
It was this story that saved his life;
As he fled he could hear fierce growlings as they fought for bread.
Such stories were prevalent throughout Zululand.
They were known as people-whose-ears-are-shot-through-by-the-rays-
of-the sun.

NOTES

1 The Company called chiefs 'captains'; those with whom it came into contact were given a cane topped with a copper knob engraved with the Company's logo, known as a 'chiap'.
2 Now Kariega River.
3 Dagga, better known as marijuana.
4 More commonly, 'buchu'.
5 Gourits River.
6 i.e. palatal.
7 Hippopotamus.
8 Magistrate and local administrator.
9 i.e. Gamtoos; the river is about 50 miles west of Port Elizabeth.
10 i.e. sjamboks.
11 In 1823 the number of lashes a slave could be given was limited to 25.
12 King of what is now Swaziland.
13 Grandfather.
14 Whites – literally, big-bellied monsters.

CHAPTER 3

INTO THE INTERIOR:
THE TRAVAILS OF TRAVEL

South Africa's fine, modern highways make it difficult to imagine what a hardship travel was in the 18th and early 19th centuries. As you soar up the passes that slice through the mountains around Cape Town, it takes an effort to appreciate what mighty and daunting barriers these were to the Europeans who first penetrated them. Their wagons were drawn by 'spans' of at least a dozen oxen, straining to haul their loads over steep, stony ground under the vicious crack of the sjambok, a whip made of rhino or hippo hide. The way was unmarked, the destination unknown and the hazards presented by man and beast could only be guessed at. The further north they went, the drier and more inhospitable the land became; the further east, the more precipitous the ravines and impenetrable the bush. Travelling often by moonlight to avoid the excoriating heat of the day, they rarely covered more than three miles an hour or 15 miles a day.

But first, of course, the travellers had to arrive in Table Bay and that could be anything but plain sailing. Indeed, their experiences readily explain the origin of the myth of the Flying Dutchman, condemned to sail the seas round the Cape until Judgement Day. In 1812, for example, just getting into the Bay took the ship carrying the Rev John Campbell (13), director of the London Missionary Society, nearly two weeks.

On the 11th of October, when in full expectation of reaching Cape Town on the succeeding day, the wind changed to the south east, and blew directly against us with much violence, and soon raised the sea mountain-high. The day following it blew with redoubled fury, which obliged us to lay-to under a reefed topsail and gib, driving away from our port. On the 14th, the storm continued tremendously awful; about three o'clock in the morning, we were almost upset by a dreadful sea breaking over us: the tumbling of chairs, and the rattling of plates and glasses, prevented all sleep. Perhaps of all scenes which the human eye has an opportunity of beholding, such a storm, in such a latitude, is the most grand, majestic, and awful. In the evening the storm began to abate.

On the following day, at noon, we found the storm had driven us more than a hundred miles beyond the latitude of the Cape, and two hundred miles further to the westward in longitude. At noon we were able again to direct our course towards the Cape; but on the 17th, when within about a hundred miles of it, violent squalls from the south east drove us again out to sea; and in the evening the sea rose and raged as high and furious as ever. About nine o'clock the elements seemed conspiring to effect our destruction, which produced a very serious meeting for prayer, in the cabin, for our preservation from the fury of the raging storm. During prayer, the violent heaving of the ship rendered it almost impossible to remain in one posture.

At one, next morning, a powerful sea broke over the stern, and came rushing down into our cabin: when at breakfast the same thing was repeated. On the 20th, our allowance of water was a second time reduced. On the 21st, at five P.M. a seaman from the mast-head descried land, which on the following day, we found to be the south side of the entrance to Saldanha Bay. Having seen no land for ten weeks, the sight was peculiarly gratifying. At eleven A.M. Table Mountain, which stands immediately behind Cape Town, was seen from the deck. On the 23rd, at two o'clock in the morning, a squall, which lasted three hours, drove us again out to sea; but at noon, the wind becoming favourable, we were brought by the evening within eighteen miles of our port, and next morning at ten A.M. by the good providence of God, we cast anchor in Table Bay, opposite to Cape Town; exactly four months after sailing from Gravesend.

Two years earlier, the explorer, William Burchell (14), had a similarly frustrating experience. He, however, having come to the Cape to 'investigate man in an uncivilised state of society', was content to while away the time – stormy as it was – in philosophical reflection.

Baffling winds frequently impeded our progress, and put the sailors' patience to trial; but the novelty of the scene, and the interesting objects before me, absorbed the whole of my attention. Eager to become acquainted with the details of what I saw, I long occupied myself in scrutinizing, with a telescope, every rock and ravine; though as yet we were too far off to allow my impatient curiosity to be gratified.

We continued till evening frequently tacking and working our way slowly towards Table Bay, where we hoped to cast anchor in the course of the night. The moon had just risen, glittering on the tops of the waves, and, casting its light on the projecting crags of the mountains, spread a beauty and solemnity over the scene, that heightened the effect of every occurrence. At this time we were abreast of Green Point at the entrance of the bay.

The moment we had passed beyond the shelter of the Lion Mountain, a furious wind suddenly and unexpectedly assailed the vessel; pouring out of the clouds, as it seemed, its boisterous fury upon us. A poetic imagination would certainly have fancied that the skins given by Aeolus to Ulysses had been carried to the top of Table Mountain, and there all cut open at once.

The vessel was rapidly driving out to sea again; in the utmost hurry the sailors flew up the rigging, and took in all sail possible. We strove to beat into the bay, but a whole hour's struggling against the storm proved all in vain; and the fore top-sail being split, we were compelled to wear the ship, and retreat to the shelter of the Lion Mountain to bend another sail.

Towards morning we made a second attempt, but were repulsed by a wind more furious than before; so that we considered ourselves fortunate in being able to regain our former shelter. Here we continued the whole of this and the following day, standing off and on within the lee of the Lion Mountain, experiencing alternate calms and gales; at one moment the ship rolling in a dead calm, and at the next, if we happened to exceed the limit of our shelter, running with the gunnel under water, through waves whose tops were blown away in spray by the fury of the south-easter: yet the weather appeared fine and the sky cloudless.

We often approached to within half a mile of the shore, where with a glass we could discern people at work, and dust driven up in clouds. Some spots appeared of a beautiful purple and others of a yellow colour, occasioned most probably by the abundance of flowers. So tantalizing a view, after a protracted and tedious voyage, would have induced me to attempt a landing almost at any rate; but the surf, which lined the whole coast with a fringe of white, plainly showed the danger and even impracticability of the attempt at such a time; I therefore contented myself with making a drawing of the view; which in this bearing, more than in any other, presents a resemblance to a lion quite sufficient to justify the name the mountain has received; and is probably that in which the likeness was first observed. To a ship keeping the Lion's Head and the middle of the northern side of Table Mountain in a line, and being at the distance of about two miles, the mountain exhibits the form of a *lion couchant*, whose fore-paws are extended forward, and form the southern point of Camp's Bay, while the tail is very well represented by the flat land of Green Point.

The first discoverers of a land presenting such grand features of bold and mountainous outline, must have felt that the occurrence itself was full of interest; but when at the same time they knew that they had thus passed the barrier which had stopped all former navigators, at least of the later ages, and had now opened a way to the Eastern world, the doubling of this celebrated promontory must have been an event which might justify the highest exultation. As I looked upon the mountains and the shore, my imagination carried me back to that period when its peaceable inhabitants, the simple Hottentots, roamed freely over the country, enjoying the liberty of nature, nor dreaming that a day could ever arrive when they must resign all to some unknown race of men, coming upon them from the ocean, an element which no tradition had ever told them could be travelled on by man [...]

The idea, that the land was now before me where I was to become acquainted with my fellow-creatures living in primeval simplicity, caused a pleasing glow in my mind, and I imagined myself already in the midst of their tribes, delighted at the novelty of the scene, and acquiring new views of human nature. Not aware that the ardor of a youthful imagination concealed every difficulty, I could see none which could disappoint my hope of traversing in any direction the unknown regions of Southern Africa; and believed that once safely landed, every obstacle to my progress would vanish. My impatience, therefore, at remaining on the sea so long after coming in sight of the harbour, began to render my confinement to the ship exceedingly irksome.

In fact, it was another 10 days before Burchell's ship could drop anchor. Once ashore, travellers had to prepare themselves for the kind of journey that Anders Sparrman, the Swedish naturalist, had been warned would be a 'very absurd and dangerous undertaking'.

I was chiefly dissuaded from the journey, as being a very absurd and dangerous undertaking, especially as, being a stranger, as yet unacquainted with
Africa, and far from rich, I must necessarily subject myself to every kind of
inconvenience; but since I saw nothing impossible in the affair, at least not
in making the experiment, I pursued my design. With this view I formed an
acquaintance and even friendship with Mr. Daniel Ferdinand Immelman, a
young African,[1] who before this had, merely for the sake of pleasure, made a
little trip into the country, to which he was induced by the following spirited
reflection: that it was very little either to his honour or to that of the other
African colonists, that they had neglected investigating their own country, so
that they would soon be obliged to apply to me and other strangers, for intelligence concerning themselves and the very place of their residence [...]

Mr. Immelman provided himself with a good stallion for which he gave
fifty rix-dollars; I had already bought an ordinary nag for thirty-four, and
a new baggage-waggon, about the size of the ammunition-waggons in
Sweden, but covered over with a tilt made of sail-cloth, and finished in the
same manner as those in which the peasants usually travel in this colony. The
price of it was likewise what was usually given for these carriages, that is,
about two hundred rix-dollars, reckoning seventy-four for the wood-work,
and eighty for the iron-work; the yokes, the hind chains, and those for the
traces, the sail-cloth covering, and a box for the coom,[2] made up the rest of
the sum. To draw a waggon of this kind there are usually required five pair
of oxen, which I therefore bargained for at eight rix-dollars a head. I further
took with me medicines of several sorts, as well for our own use, as for that
of the peasants, to whom they might be of great service, and procure us
a better reception. I likewise provided myself with a small stock of glass
beads, brass tinder-boxes, steels for striking fire with, and knives, together
with some tobacco; all these were commodities peculiarly acceptable to the
Hottentots. We likewise took with us an oaken cask, made for the purpose
of keeping serpents and other animals in brandy; also several reams of paper
for drying plants, with boxes and pins for insects, and at the same time some
necessary changes of apparel. Neither did we forget to take with us plenty
of tea, coffee, chocolate, and sugar, partly for our own use, and partly to
insinuate ourselves into the good graces of the yeomen, who, by reason of
the great distance they are at from the Cape, are often without these necessaries. I was told indeed, that liquors would infallibly answer this purpose
much better; but the room they took up, their weight, and the expence of

them, prevented me from taking any with me. We were well provided with sewing needles of several sorts, as by means of these, and a few good words, we should be enabled to gain the good graces of the farmer's daughters, as well as their assistance in collecting insects. I bought too thirty odd pounds of gunpowder, with a small quantity of which we filled several horns, which we kept near at hand; the remainder we emptied into a leathern bag, and locked it up in my chest, by way of keeping it out of the way of the lighted pipes of the Hottentots. We took with us shot of different sizes, about seventy pound in weight, with a tolerable stock of balls, lead, and moulds for casting. It is certain, that the expence and quantity of this ammunition, was much more than we were advised to take with us, or than I myself thought necessary. On our return to the Cape, however, after an eight month's journey, it was almost all used. I would therefore advise every body, who may hereafter undertake an expedition of this kind, to stock themselves well with powder and shot. Every shot does not hit its mark, and not a little is expended in the shooting of small birds; some too must be spent in shooting at marks. Besides, it may happen, as it did to me and my party, that for several weeks together, one may have little else to live upon than what falls before one's gun; not to mention, that prudence requires one to be prepared with ammunition against the hostile attacks of the Boshies-men and Caffres.

As the colonists here are enjoined by the laws to seize and bring to the Cape all such as travel about the country without being able to shew a permission in writing for that purpose, I therefore solicited and obtained the Governor's pass, requiring that I should pass every where free and unmolested; and at the same time that the inhabitants should assist me as far as lay in their power, on receiving a reasonable compensation. In another letter, the people belonging to the Warm Baths in Hottentots Holland were enjoined to find me in lodging; for this remedy I was resolved to try against the chills that I had contracted in the Antarctic circle.[3]

Roualeyn Gordon Cumming (15), a fanatical hunter reputed to have killed more game than any man before or since, travelled and lived in an ox-wagon almost continuously from 1843 to 1848. He describes one with a connoisseur's passion.

The Cape waggon is a large and powerful, yet loosely-constructed vehicle, running on four wheels. Its extreme length is about eighteen feet, its breadth varying from three and a half to four feet; the depth of the sides is about two feet six inches in front, but higher towards the back of the waggon. All along the sides two rows of iron staples are riveted, in which are fastened the boughs forming the tent, over the waggon usually five feet high, with an awning of Kaffir mat, and a strong canvas sail over all, with 'fore-clap' and 'after-clap', the colonial names for two broad canvas curtains, that form part and parcel of the sail, and hang in the front and rear of the waggon, reaching to within a few inches of the ground. In the front is placed a large chest occupying the extreme breadth of the waggon, on which the driver and two passengers of ordinary dimensions can sit abreast. This is called the fore-chest, and is secured from sliding forwards by two buffalo rheims, or strips of dressed hide, placed across the front of it, and secured to the sides. A similar chest is fastened in like manner to the rear of the waggon, called the after-chest. Along the sides of the waggon, and outside it, are two longer and narrower chests called side-chests; these are supported by two horizontal bars of hard wood riveted to the bottom of the waggon, and are very convenient for holding tools and all manner of odds and ends too numerous to mention. The fore and after chests are likewise extremely useful for containing clothing, ammunition, and a thousand small articles in daily use. Along the sides of the tent are suspended rows of square canvas bags, called side-pockets, in which the traveller keeps his hair-brushes and combs, razors, knives, tooth-brushes, soap, towels, or anything else he may wish to have at hand. In one of these bags I usually placed my luncheon – often a slice of elephant's trunk.

The traveller sleeps upon a sort of cot, termed a 'cardell'. This cardell is a light, strong, oblong-frame, about eight feet in length, and occupies the breadth of the waggon. It is bored all round with small holes, through which strips of hide are interlaced, forming a sort of network on which the mattress rests. This cot is slung across the waggon, and is attached with thongs to the bows of the tent, its elevation being regulated by the cargo, which is carefully stowed away beneath it in the body of the waggon. Suspended underneath the hind part of the vehicle is a strong wooden framework called the trap, on which the pots and gridirons are lashed during a march. The waggon is steered by a pole, called the dissel-boom, to the end of which is fastened the trektow, a stout rope formed of raw buffalo-hide. It is pulled by a span, or team, consisting of twelve oxen, which draw the waggon by yokes fastened along the trektow at regular intervals by means of strips of raw hide. Passing through each end of the yoke, at distances of eighteen inches from one another, are two parallel bars of tough wood about a foot and a half in length; these are called yoke-skeys. In inspanning, the yoke is placed on the back of the neck of the ox, with one of these skeys on either side, and towards the ends are notches in which is fixed the strap, made of twisted hide; this, passing under the neck of the animal, secures him in the yoke.

Besides these straps, each pair of oxen is strongly coupled by the buffalo rheims, which are used in catching and placing them in their proper order, preparatory to inspanning. A rheim is a long strip of prepared hide with a noose at the end; it is made either of ox or buffalo hide, and is about eight feet long. A waggon likewise is provided with a tar-bucket, two powerful iron chains which are called the rheim-chains, and a large iron drag called the rheim-schoen; also the invariable whip and jambok, the former consisting of a bamboo pole upwards of twenty feet in length, with a thong of about twenty-five feet, to the end of which is sewn with 'rheimpys', or strips of dressed steinbok-skin, the 'after-slock', and to this again is fastened the 'fore-slock', corresponding with the little whipcord lash of the English coachman. The 'fore-slock', about which the waggon-drivers are very particular, is about a yard in length, and is formed of a strip of the supple skin of a particular variety of antelope prepared in a peculiar manner. The skins of only a few species of antelopes are possessed of sufficient toughness for this purpose. Those most highly prized amongst the colonists are the skins of the hartebeest, koodoo, blesbok, and bushbuck; when none of these are to be obtained they use the skin of a he-goat, which is very inferior. The colonial waggon-driver wields this immense whip with great dexterity and grace; as he cracks it he produces a report nearly equal to that of a gun, and by this means signals his leader, who is, perhaps, herding the oxen at the distance of a mile, to bring them up when it is time to inspan.

The 'jambok' is another instrument of persuasion, indispensable in the outfit of every Cape waggon. It is made of the thick, tough hide, either of the white rhinoceros or hippopotamus. Its length is from six to seven feet; its thickness at the handle is about an inch and a half, and it tapers gradually to the point. These jamboks are exceedingly tough and pliant, and are capable of inflicting most tremendous chastisement upon the thick hides of sulky and refractory oxen. Those manufactured from the skin of the hippopotamus are very much superior to those of the rhinoceros, being naturally of a much tougher quality, and, if properly prepared, one of them will last for many years.

Henry Lichtenstein (16), another naturalist, took a particular interest in how the wagons were driven. He had ample time to observe it for he set off from the Cape in October 1803 with Jan Janssens, the last of the Dutch governors, on a 4 500-mile journey that took six months. (His reference to 'Bastards' was not meant to be offensive. It – or the more polite 'Baasters' – was the term then officially applied to the offspring of whites and Hottentots. The missionaries re-named them Griquas but not all Baasters were convinced. They reckoned their original name bespoke white blood, so raising them – in South African eyes – above the Hottentots.)

The waggons, according to the weight of their lading, and to the length and difficulty of the way they have to go, are drawn by eight, twelve, and even sometimes by sixteen oxen. These are yoked together two and two by a beam over the back of the neck, which is fastened by a thong of leather under the neck, and two others running on each side of the hams [...]

As drivers to these waggons, Hottentots or Bastards are generally preferred since they know best how to keep pace with the oxen, as well as how to dress and tend upon them. No reins are used; the drivers manage the animals with merely calling to them; every ox has his particular name, and by pronouncing the word *hot* or *haar*, they turn to the right or left according to the signification of the word used. The well-known whips with bamboo handles from fourteen to sixteen feet in length, and lashes of at least an equal length, with which a dexterous driver can readily strike any of his cattle from the first to the last, are very seldom used among a well-ordered team; never unless any of the poor creatures happen to be extremely weary, or the difficulties to be encountered in the way render a more than usual exertion of strength necessary.

This perpetual calling to the animals, which is done in a high rough-toned voice not easily to be imitated, and which is more intelligible to the oxen themselves from the tone in which it is done than from the expression used, is indescribably wearisome to the traveller, who is compelled to ride in the waggon. In very narrow and bad roads, however, the driver does not depend wholly upon his vocal powers for managing his *atelage*; a boy is then added, who leads the fore-most oxen by a thong fastened to the horns. It is, indeed, extraordinary to see how a boy can with so much dexterity lead so long a team through heights and depths, over hills and crags, without risk either to himself or to the vehicle he has under his care. This is principally done when the team consists of more than sixteen oxen, for the driver alone can hardly manage above that number, partly because the most spirited being selected for the leading oxen, while the strongest are reserved for the hinder ones, they are more difficult to be kept in order, and partly because the little stones slipping about under their feet are apt to throw the middle yokes out of their ranks, and one pair will perhaps be inclining to one side while the next draws towards the other. Is a river to be passed, the poor boy must often wade through the water up to his chin, still holding the thong fast, to prevent the fore oxen stumbling or reeling in the middle of the stream, and oversetting the whole equipage.

The strength of the draught oxen here is easily exhausted. On a level road, with only a moderate load, and if the air be tolerably cool, they will get on as far in an hour as a man who walks pretty quick; but if the way be sandy, the load be heavy, or the sun be very hot, they cannot at all keep pace with him. The distance from place to place is reckoned by hours; but in different parts they compute differently as to the quantity of ground that may be gone over in an hour. It is calculated that a distance of eight hours with a team of twelve oxen, and the customary load of twenty hundred weight, may without difficulty be performed in a day, rising early in the morning, or in the very hot season of the year rather travelling all night, and resting in the middle of the day. Such a distance is here called a *schoft*, and all greater distances are calculated by so many *schofts*, or days journeys.

The Rev John Campbell, who suffered such a stormy and protracted arrival in Table Bay, was anxious that the London Missionary Society, which had given him the task of inspecting its outposts, should appreciate the difficulties of travelling round the colony. As an example of what he was up against, he described his struggle through the Outeniqua Mountains in March 1813, when he was on his way to the mission station at Bethelsdorp, near Port Elizabeth.

We all rose on the morning of the 9th by break of day, in the hope of re-commencing our journey. Mr. Standard yoked thirty-two excellent oxen to our two wagons, and happily we were once more in motion. After travelling about four miles we reached the cliffs, which had engrossed a great part of our conversation for several days past. I confessed they exceeded, in difficulty of passing, what I had previously conceived. The steep descent continued for about half a mile; there was a step in the rock, about two feet perpendicular in height, which went direct across the path, and which the wagons must descend; also a quick dangerous turn in the descent, where the rock was smooth, like glass. There one of our wagons took a swing, and was nearly over the edge of the path; had it gone over, it must have fallen down several hundred feet. On reaching the bottom we crossed the river, about two hundred yards above its entrance into the sea. The cliff that was then to be climbed, deserved to be called the 'hill of difficulty'; however, up the oxen went, and after many a lash, and many a fall, and the loss of some blood, they dragged all safe to the summit, and we went forward on our journey with cheerfulness, until a little after sun-set, when we halted in front of a wood, which our Hottentots said was infested by elephants, none of whom, however, were seen or heard by any of us.

Our road next morning lay across the wood, which had a most venerable appearance, from the extraordinary loftiness and great thickness of the trees. In the middle of it our attention was completely drawn from the trees of other ages, to a long, rocky, and steep ascent in the road. The first wagon, though twenty-six oxen were yoked to it, was two hours before it reached the summit; and the second, with the same oxen, was three hours. The bustle and the anxiety of our minds during these five hours were considerable. The last wagon, at one part of the road, was about two hours in moving forty yards; sometimes from the oxen falling, or ineffectually drawing, because not drawing at the same time, or getting into disorder, or resting. Another person and myself were busy filling up holes in the road. This minuteness of description in the early part of the journey will assist friends to form a correct conception of African travelling.

On arriving at the head of the steep rise, the rain descended, and drenched most of us to the skin. Though we were some hundred feet above the level of the sea, we were only at the base of a high mountain, whose top was hid in a cloud, over which our wagons must pass; we therefore halted, to refresh and prepare our oxen for the tiresome task.

At three P.M. we began ascending the mountain; on reaching its summit, a very extensive view of the surrounding country opened to us. At five we descended a long and steep declivity, at the bottom of which is a place called Little Hell, for what reason I could not learn, as there is nothing terrific about it. We had now a much higher mountain to get over, whose top we had not yet seen, being enveloped in clouds. Though near sun-set, in order to lessen the labour of next day, we determined to ascend part of it; accordingly we scrambled up about a quarter of a mile, and there halted for the night. The Hottentots found a spring of water.

March 11. Began to climb the mountain about half past five, A.M. and reached the top about nine. One part was a sharp turn round the corner of a spur some hundred feet high, at the bottom of which we saw the remains of two wagons lying, that had fallen over it. At one time the fore wheel of my wagon got upon the top of the mud parapet, on the edge of the spur, when all hands went to work to lift it off, which we happily effected. We were an hour and a half in getting round this turn. The summit is called the Devil's Head. Though our prospect from the top was very extensive, neither house, nor man, nor beast, nor any cultivated spot, was included in it; all was dull wilderness.

One of the most engaging records of early travel is to be found among the letters of the clever and glamorous Lady Anne Barnard (17). They were written to Lord Melville, her 'dear friend' and confidant, whom she had once hoped to marry. A member of William Pitt the Younger's first Administration, Melville was chiefly responsible for the annexation of the Cape in 1795. In 1797, he appointed her husband, Andrew Barnard, Secretary of the Colony, and enjoined Lady Anne – her title derived from her position as the eldest child of an Earl – to write to him 'freely about everything that occurred'. A year after landing at the Cape, she set off on her first journey into the interior by way of what is now Sir Lowry's Pass over the Hottentots Holland Mountains. She told Lord Melville all about it.

Sunday, May 6th, 1798. After making a tolerable breakfast from our own tea, just with the addition of some fresh eggs, which we bought, we started. We hired a team of oxen to carry us to the foot of the Hottentot Kloof, which we reached in about an hour, having passed but one farmhouse by the way, and not a single tree or bush. At the bottom of the ascent we found a Boer ready with twelve splendid oxen ready to be put to the waggon. They seemed to dislike the business they were going on, and lowed piteously when they found themselves in the yoke. The ascent is about two miles; for the first mile, wherever the eye turned there was heath, sand, sea, mountain, scarce a house to be seen, no cultivation, and, of course, no population. As we looked back over the wide prospect we were leaving, bay succeeded bay, and hill hill, carrying on the eye over a scene of infinite beauty. The path was very perpendicular, and the jutting rocks over which the waggon was to be pulled were so large that we were astonished how they were accomplished at all, particularly at one part called 'The Porch.' At length we reached the summit, and the new Canaan opened to my eye; hillock upon hillock, mountain behind mountain, as far as the eye could reach, a slight thread of rivulet here and there winding through the valleys like a silver eel. Our descent was much easier accomplished. We went down on foot, and when we got to the bottom we found the waggon safe, and the horses put to it again. I was horrified to see how much the poor oxen had suffered in our service; their sides were streaming down with blood which the knives of the savage drivers had brought forth. They are very cruel here to their cattle – the whip is an implement of torture, and is sometimes supplemented by knives; the drivers are sufficiently good anatomists to know exactly the vital parts to be avoided. We travelled on over a tract of country still innocent of the plough, passing by three rivers, or *rivieres,* as they are called here, of which the Palmite was the greatest. Then along a dangerous pass, which with a high loaded waggon and eight horses in hand was not very pleasant, but our driver was extraordinarily skilful. We at last reached the farmhouse where we were to stop for the night. The name of the farmer was Jacob Joubert, a mere Boer; his wife received us – a plain, stupid, but civil woman, strange to say without any children. We made a good dinner with them of some boiled fowls, with plenty of potatoes and butter – a repast fit for an emperor.

Monday, May 7th, 1798. We started at seven o'clock in the morning, the weather glorious, and all our animals well. We had to engage a further team of twelve oxen to carry us over Howe-hook, another tremendous hill. These cattle were so strong that they pulled us with ease up perpendicular ascents, which made me think that they would pull us like Elijah up to heaven. The vegetation, of tender green and olive and brown, was fresher than the day before. The rocks appeared to be of a bastard white marble, but they said they were limestone; and a lot of the most brilliant everlasting flowers, pinked with black hearts, grew among the heath. The descent was two miles, and before us opened a wide desert, pathless, untenanted; one little bit of smoke only ascended to heaven – it looked like the fire-offering of Cain. Probably it was the fire of some poor Hottentot cooking his humble mess. We now got on to what is called 'The Great Road,' tolerably well beaten by waggons. We were going on to a Mynheer Brandt's, where we intended to pass the night; but we stopped halfway at a farmhouse to rest the horses and have something to eat. I was very tired, and I thought the *stoep* in front of the house the pleasantest of all seats. We made the best meal we could, having as a table the top of an old barrel.

I wanted to stay here all night, but the coachman said that he could go on and reach our destination before sunset. He was mistaken, for after we had gone some time the sun set with a vengeance. There is hardly any twilight here, and in this case there happened to be no moon, so within a quarter of an hour we were plunged from light into total darkness. The road was very rough, and though I made Hector walk at the head of the horses to be doubly sure, suddenly the waggon began to rock. 'Sit tight! ' shouted Mr. Barnard. I felt the wheel sinking on the side I was, and, in a moment, down we came like a mountain. The waggon was overturned, my head lower than my heels, and everything in the world, it seemed, was above me. Cousin Jane, Johnny, and I were laid low; Mr. Barnard escaped, and rushed to see how we were. I felt half suffocated with the luggage, and my arm seemed broken, but presently, when they had unpacked me, I crawled out safe on the heath. Presently Jane also emerged, and there we were, bruised, but with no bones broken; it was really a miraculous escape. While they were trying to get the waggon straight again, though they had great fear of doing it, I walked about to discover in the darkness where we were, while Jane sat on a stone, a statue of patience, condoling with herself for the bruises on a white marble arm, the rest of her being preserved, in a most literal sense of the word, for a cask of ginger had had its topknot knocked off in the fall, and had poured its contents in at Jane's neck and out at her toe, by which means she was a complete confection. I could not help laughing, and sat down to count my bruises with her, when we were startled by hearing a voice in the darkness behind us saying, 'Well, to be sure, this is the devil's own circumstance.' I found it proceeded from Cousin Johnny, who had embarked the whole of his fortune, amounting to thirty dollars, in Jane's netting case, which happened to be the only thing lost in our tumble. We all crept after it on our hands and knees in the darkness, but nowhere was it to be found, nor had we a tinder-box to strike a light. 'Well,' said he, with a cornet's philosophy, 'here's for a light heart and a thin pair of breeches,' and he kicked out his foot to emphasise his words, and lo and behold! it struck against something which jingled. I leave you to imagine his transports. Everything was replaced in about an hour, and off we started. But fresh perils awaited us, for we had to cross the river; fortunately the ford was marked out by a stick or two, and we got over it safely. Never was anything so welcome as Mynheer Brandt's house. We entered through a kitchen filled with slaves, many of them with very little covering on. Under the guidance of Gaspar, who turned out to be a man of many talents, we made a most excellent supper, with a little hot wine and water to crown it. Decent beds rendered no trouble in unpacking necessary.

Travellers faced other hazards too. Col Robert Gordon (18), the Dutch soldier and explorer whom we heard earlier on the plight of the Bushmen, reached the Garie or Great River on Christmas Eve 1777. He renamed it the Orange River after the Dutch Ruling House and called the high gorge through which it flows at this point the Oranje Poort.

The Oranje Poort, which is half an hour long and a good quarter of an hour wide, is a natural opening between two mountains. I dismounted among the trees and gave a Hottentot the horse to lead as I wanted to climb the mountain. I saw my Hottentot disappear in front of me, with a great cry. The horse jumped back and the poor fellow screamed for help. Going to him I saw that he was in a deep pit which the wild people[4] make in hippopotamus paths to trap these animals and made so that one cannot see them. With the aid of a long stick I helped the terrified Hottentot from his prison. He was so full of dust that he could not see. They dig the pits 14 to 18 foot deep with an oval diameter of about six foot. They take the soil away in skins and then lay sticks across it, pushing the same into the soil on both sides so that the path remains level. Then they cover everything and make what looks like a hippopotamus foot-print across it with the result that one cannot see anything […]

I wanted to see if I could cross this river on horseback and spent some time looking at it. Eventually found this impossible to do on horseback. I then decided to ride away from the river and following a hippopotamus path through some reed on a hillock, fell unexpectedly into a pit which the wild people had made for hippopotamus, my horse going with me. While falling, I pulled at the horse's bridle violently so that most of the underside of its body fell below. Dust and stones fell on me from all sides so that in order not to smother I struck up with both hands and made an opening. I gripped the horse and began to beat it, working at both ears, closing them tightly, because I had heard that this was a good thing. The poor animal stood still, sweating in its death-agony and the suffocation of the pit. Being unhurt and completely in control of myself, I saw that the pit was eight foot high above me and that I had to make an attempt quickly because breathing had become very difficult. I therefore jumped as high as I could and fortunately remained hanging with my shoulders and feet in the hole above the horse that had started to thrash violently. I now gathered all my strength and worked myself upwards with three or four thrusts, like a chimney sweep. With one hand I snatched at one of the remaining sticks which was at the edge of the hole and where it was still firm enough to hold me and thus with every good fortune got free of the danger. I talked to my poor horse and the creature was calm once again. I then ran as fast as I could to the wagon and fetched people with a spade in order to save the creature but when we arrived at the hole we found that the animal had died of suffocation; the sweat stood like water on its body. It would also have taken us nearly half a day to dig it out. Since the pit was about 16 foot deep, it appeared incomprehensible to my travelling companions and to me how I had got out of the hole without help.

Another hazard for travellers was locusts, described here with admirable detachment by Henry Lichtenstein, the naturalist.

We had scarcely passed the northern entrance to the kloof, when we perceived by our side one of those enormous swarms of travelling locusts which I had hitherto wished in vain to see. It had exactly the appearance of a vast snow-cloud, hanging on the slope of the mountain, from which the snow was falling in very large flakes. I spurred my horse up the hill, to the place where I thought the swarm seemed the thickest. When I was within a hundred paces of them, I heard the rushing noise occasioned by the flight of so many millions of insects: this constantly increased the nearer I approached; and when I got into the midst of them, it was, without any exaggeration, as loud as the dashing of the waters occasioned by the mill-wheel. Above, below, and all around me, the air was filled with, and almost darkened by these insects. They settled about the bodies of myself and my horse, till the latter was so much teased and fretted, that he became extremely restless, turning his back constantly towards the side on which their flight was directed. Every stroke of the riding-cane swept twenty or thirty to the ground, and they lay there so thick that it was impossible to take a step without trampling a number to death. I gathered up some for my collection, but found them all injured; even those who flew before me were obliged almost immediately to settle themselves. Those that settled were indeed only the wounded of the party, such as had a leg or wing broken in their flight by coming in contact with their neighbours: these formed a very small part of the whole enormous mass. Those that flew the highest rose to fifty or sixty feet above the ground; those which did not rise to more than twenty feet, rested at every hundred paces, and then flew on again. They all took exactly the same course, not going with the wind, but in an oblique direction against it, directly toward the fields of the Hottentots. I was very much alarmed for the young corn; but on my return I learnt that the swarm had done no mischief; it had gone over at the distance of a thousand paces from the fields. They never deviate from the straight line, so long as the same wind blows. The bushes around were already eaten quite bare, though the animals could not have been long on the spot, since an hour earlier our oxen had been grazing, without the persons who attended upon them having seen a single locust. Finally, that I might complete my survey, I rode against the swarm so as to pass them, and found that the train extended in length to between two and three thousand paces; in breadth it could scarcely exceed a hundred.

A striking account of one of nature's most effective antidotes to swarming locusts was given later by Arthur Cowell Stark (19), the great South African ornithologist, who was killed by a Boer shell during the siege of Ladysmith.

The well-known 'Locust Bird' is of gipsy-like habits, migrating here and there without much regard to season, and frequently appearing suddenly in a district for several days or weeks in flocks numbering tens of thousands, to disappear as suddenly, often for many years. These Starlings are in fact so largely dependent for food upon the migrating swarms of locusts that they are compelled to remain in touch with these insects for the greater portion of the year [...] When pursuing a flight of mature locusts these Starlings perform various extraordinary and beautiful aerial evolutions with the object of intercepting and surrounding a portion of the swarm. Starting in a dense 'ball-like' mass, they suddenly open out into a fan-shaped formation, then assume a semi-circular arrangement, and finally end by forming a hollow cylinder in which a portion of the locusts are enclosed; as the imprisoned insects are destroyed, the Starlings gradually fill up the hollow of the cylinder until they again assume their 'ball' formation and proceed to follow the remaining locusts. The ground below the flock is covered with the droppings of the birds and the snipped-off legs and wings of locusts.

But what most struck 18th-century naturalists such as Sparrman, Thunberg, Le Vaillant and Lichtenstein was the Cape's astonishing profusion of indigenous flora. The Cape Peninsula alone boasts more than 2 000 unique species, later painstakingly catalogued in the seven-volume *Flora Capensis* by a team of botanists who spent 30 years on the task. Only slightly less ambitiously, Mary Maytham Kidd painted 800 of them for her book, *Wild Flowers of the Cape Peninsula* (20), which was published in 1950. The foreword was written by Jan Smuts, the former Prime Minister, an enthusiastic and knowledge-able amateur who was intrigued by the theory that the flora owe their uniqueness to a lost continent.

Our Cape plants belong to a flora which is unique and to which a great deal of mystery attaches. A large number of plant families belonging to our flora are found nowhere else in the world, and have only distant relatives in a few Southern countries like West Australia and South America. And the question of the origin of this unique flora has intrigued students of the geographical distribution of plants. Great authorities, like Sir Joseph Hooker, who made a special study of the question, and Charles Darwin, inclined to the view that they derive from a lost continent now under the Indian or Southern ocean, of which Antarctica is now the main survival, and that the Northern limits of the lost continent may have reached as far north as the tip of South Africa, and may thus have passed on its unique southern flora as far north. It is noteworthy that the Cape flora is confined to this southern tip of Africa, as I have already stated, and that the rest, even of South Africa, is covered by a northern flora which has reached so far south.

Such at least is the speculation, and for the rest the frozen Antarctic holds its secrets, which may, however, eventually be revealed by the discovery of plant fossils under its ancient ice cover. Only then, if at all, will this mystery be solved.

True it is that when the European botanists came to the Cape in the seventeenth and eighteenth centuries they found here an unrecognizable plant life, quite unlike that of Europe. New names had to be invented for whole families, not to mention numerous genera and species. Everything looked new and strange. A new botanical world had been discovered, of unique and strange characters. Such is our Cape flora. Some exotics have indeed since come from oversea. Still more plants are intruders, which have come by land from the North, in the ways common in plant migration. But the bulk of this flora was indigenous and new to science. We can imagine the surprise of these early European botanists at this strange sight, this faery land of flowers from nowhere. They must have been, like stout Cortes and his gallant band when they stared upon the vast Pacific, 'silent upon a peak in Darien'. Northern botanists, determined to prove a Northern origin for our botany, have done their best to assimilate our flora to that of the north. But in vain: the strange, fascinating lady keeps her secret and her charm. The mystery probably points to some ancient tragedy in the life-history of this great globe itself. Who knows?

The best summary of many of the early travellers' experiences came from the poetically-mind William Cornwallis Harris (21), an ex-Indian Army officer who arrived at the Cape in 1836 with the intention of killing – and sketching – as many wild animals as he could. Here, he is approaching the Orange River on his way to Kuruman, the missionary outpost established seven years earlier by Robert Moffat.

We had now fairly quitted civilization, and were entering upon a sterile inhospitable region sparingly inhabited by Bushmen – the remnant of Hottentot hordes, and the wild aborigines of the country – who, gradually receding before the encroachments of the European Colonists, have long since sought refuge in the pathless desert.

From this point until we reached Kuruman, a distance of three hundred miles, the number of our oxen became daily diminished by the effects of a drought which had prevailed, and which had so completely removed every vestige of vegetation, that they were frequently compelled to pass two days without tasting food or water. Extensive – to the eye bound-less, plains of arid land with neither eminence nor hollow, were on all sides expanded to the view: of these the prevailing colour was brownish yellow, variegated with a few black and sickly shrubs. Scarcely an object met the straining eye but an ostrich sometimes striding in the distance, or a solitary vulture soaring in the sky. Over the wide desolation of the stony waste not a tree could be discerned, and the only impression on the mind was – that of utter and hopeless sterility. Occasionally however as we advanced, the sameness of the scene was varied by a wide stretching undulation. Our caravan was then the only object in the landscape upon which the eye could repose. Waggon after waggon slowly rising to view, the van was to be seen advancing over the swell, whilst the cattle and sheep were yet hidden from the sight. The world before us was still nought but earth and sky – not a green herb enticed the vision, not a bird winged through the air: the loud cracking of a whip rolling in suppressed echo along, the sun-baked ground alone disturbed the silence of the sultry atmosphere, which gave to the azure vault of heaven the semblance of an unnatural elevation from the globe.

Whilst the days were oppressively hot, and the sky unveiled by a cloud, the nights were piercingly cold – our feelings during the latter indicating as well as the thermometer, that the temperature was near the freezing point: and to add to our discomfort, fuel was rarely procurable. In the morning, the ground was sometimes covered with hoar frost: but the absence either of vapour or cloud to diminish the heat of the sun, soon dispelled the appearance, and rendered visible the nakedness of the land. Mirage in these regions, flickering in the distance, presents to the thirsty traveller an illusion as tempting as tantalizing. Blue and delusive lakes of which the surface seems agitated by a ripple, recede as he advances – and ultimately disappearing, 'leave not a wreck behind.'

But the monotony of this wearisome journey was not always unbroken by events. We halted the first day on the borders of what appeared to be a body of water many miles in circumference – an oasis in the desert, towards which after a sultry march of twenty miles, lured by the appearance of several waggons on its brink – both man and beast rushed with impetuosity. We soon perceived to our disappointment that we had been deceived by a saline deposit of immense extent at which a party of Boors were engaged in obtaining salt for the use of the Colonists: but it was long ere the broken hearted oxen discovered that what they had understood to be water, was a mere mineral efflorescence in the desert.

The fourth day brought us to the magnificent Orange river – the only stream within many hundred miles that is entitled to the appellation. Emerging from desolation and sterility the first glimpse that we obtained of it realized those ideas of elegant and classic scenery which exist in the minds of poets. The alluring fancies of a fairy fiction, or the fascinating imagery of a romance, were here brought into actual existence. The waters of this majestic river, three hundred yards in breadth, flowing in one unbroken expanse, resembled a smooth translucent lake; and as its gentle waves glided past on their way to join the restless ocean, bearing on their limpid bosom as in a polished mirror, the image of their wood clothed borders, they seemed to kiss the shore before bidding it farewell. Drooping willows clad in their vest of vernal freshness, leaned over the bank – and dipping their slender branches into the tide which glistened with the last rays of the setting sun – seemed fain to follow: whilst at intervals, the wrecks of stately trees that had been torn from their roots by the violence of the torrent during some vast inundation, of which the traces on the shore gave evidence – reared their dilapidated heads in token of the then resistless fury of that flood, which now appeared so smooth and tranquil. To those who may conceive this description overcharged I will only remark, that the sight of water after days in the desert, is probably one of the most delightful sensations that a human being can experience.

NOTES
1 i.e. a European born in Africa.
2 Axle grease.
3 On his voyage with Captain Cook.
4 i.e. Bushmen.

CHAPTER 4

THE CAPE 150 YEARS ON:
BOERS, SLAVES AND LANDSCAPES

The end of the 18th century was a watershed. After governing the Cape for nearly 150 years, the Dutch East India Company was bankrupt; in 1799 it was dissolved. Revolutionary fervour had driven the Prince of Orange out of Holland, now renamed the Batavian Republic. Anxious to prevent the Cape from falling into Napoleon's hands, Britain stepped into the vacuum. Apart from its strategic importance, however, the new colony was not then much of a prize. Since the welcome influx in 1688 of nearly 200 Huguenots – French Protestants fleeing Catholic persecution after Louis XIV revoked the Edict of Nantes – immigration had not been encouraged, although there had been a steady trickle of German settlers. In the 1790s, Cape Town had a population, not counting Hottentots, of just 15 000, 10 000 of whom were slaves, and nowhere else was bigger than a village. Yet the Company's territory had expanded in a great arc, beyond the Orange River 600 miles to the north and beyond the Great Fish River 600 miles to the east. Van Riebeeck's handful of Dutch free burghers with their 26-acre grants of land and a fine disregard for the rights of the natives had turned into a wandering tribe of farmers – 'Trekboers' – with an insatiable hunger for land and an utter contempt for the natives. The mechanism of their haphazard expansion was described by Cornelius (CW) de Kiewiet (22), one of South Africa's most elegant and perceptive historians. His *History of South Africa Social & Economic* was published in 1941.

It became a deeply ingrained habit of frontier society for each man to have such a farm of 6,000 and even 10,000 acres. When the youth left his father's farm, it was to take up his birthright, which was a farm of his own. The method of measuring their farms exceeded even the unprecision of medieval land measurement. To measure his 'hide' the Boer walked his horse from a central point for half an hour to each of the four cardinal points. A Boer 'hide' was thus about the size of a medieval 'hundred'. In this wise a relatively small population could push outwards the frontiers of the Colony with astonishing speed.

In theory the frontiersmen could not move on to fresh land without the sanction of the administration. In theory also the administration acquired sovereign title to all land upon which its colonists settled. But since allegiance and the authority of government came to rest ever more lightly upon the men of the frontier, there developed amongst them an attitude towards land not unlike that of the natives themselves. Though in strict legality the land tenure was not in freehold and was revocable at the will of the administration, actually the Trekboers availed themselves of the land with the utmost freedom. On the farthest frontier men did not always register their farms or pay their dues. The eighteenth century in South Africa did not develop the precise doctrine of Crown Lands which was of such importance in the history of land settlement in Australia, New Zealand, and Canada. At an early moment there was born the attitude that the right of public domain was qualified by the right of the individual to acquire land either at no cost or at a nominal rental. The claim of each man to a farm of not less than 6,000 acres became ultimately an inborn right. In subsequent South African history few factors are of greater importance than the uncontrolled and haphazard method of Boer land settlement and the habits which were bred by the Company's loss of control over Boer expansion.

A factor of similar importance to subsequent South African history was the Boers' determination to escape regulation of any kind. Like the free burghers before them, they resented the Company's – or, indeed, any authority's – interference in their affairs and, especially, the imposition of taxes. That, as much as their hunger for limitless and virtually free land, was what drove them on into the interior, with the consequences De Kiewiet describes.

In the long quietude of the eighteenth century the Boer race was formed. In the vast, unmysterious, thirsty landscape of the interior lay the true centre of South African settlement. When the Trekboers entered it with their flocks and tented wagons, they left the current of European life and lost the economic habits of the nations from which they had sprung. Though they never became true nomads, the mark of nomadism was upon them, and their dominant traits were those of a restless and narrow existence. They had the nomad's appetite for space and possessed the hardness and courage of men of the saddle who watch their flocks and hunt their meat. Their wealth was in their cattle and in their sons and grandsons, who were born numerously and who thrived amazingly. Their life gave them a tenacity of purpose, a power of silent endurance, and the keenest self-respect. But this isolation sank into their character causing their imagination to lie fallow and their intellects to become inert. Their virtues had their obverse qualities as well. Their tenacity could degenerate into obstinacy, their power of endurance into resistance to innovation, and their self-respect into suspicion of the foreigner and contempt for their inferiors. For want of formal education and sufficient pastors, they read their Bibles intensively, drawing from the Old Testament, which spoke the authentic language of their lives, a justification of themselves, of their beliefs and their habits. Continued immigration, even of such small groups as the French Huguenots, would have done much to keep them abreast of some of the thought of the new Europe of the Enlightenment. Instead the remotest corner of Europe was better informed.

Approaching the Great Karoo in 1797, John Barrow, the British government official, had put it even more sharply.

At the head of this little valley we were to take leave of every human habitation for at least sixteen days, which is the ordinary time required to cross over the Great Karroo, or arid desert, that lay between us and the distant district of Graaf Reynet. It therefore became necessary to supply ourselves here with a stock of provisions, as nothing whatsoever is to be had on the desert except ostrich eggs and antelopes. To those travellers who are furnished with a good waggon and a tent, the want of habitations is no great loss; for few of them, behind the first range of mountains, have any sort of convenience, comfort, or decency. Among the planters of Africa it is true there are some who live in a decent manner, particularly the cultivators of the grape. Many of these are descendants of the French families who, a little more than a century ago, found an asylum at the Cape of Good Hope from the religious persecutions that drove them from their own country. But a true Dutch peasant, or boor as he styles himself, has not the smallest idea of what an English farmer means by the word comfort. Placed in a country where not only the necessaries, but almost every luxury of life might by industry be procured, he has the enjoyment of none of them. Though he has cattle in abundance he makes very little use of milk or of butter. In the midst of a soil and climate most favourable for the cultivation of the vine, he drinks no wine. He makes use of few or no vegetables nor roots. Three times a-day his table is loaded with masses of mutton, swimming in the grease of the sheep's tail. His house is either open to the roof, or covered only with rough poles and turf, affording a favourable shelter for scorpions and spiders; and the earthy floors are covered with dust and dirt, and swarm with insects, particularly with a species of the *termes*, which, though not so destructive as some others of this genus, is nevertheless a very troublesome and disagreeable animal. His apartments, if he happens to have more than one, which is not always the case among the grazing farmers, are nearly destitute of furniture. A great chest that contains all his moveables, and two smaller ones that are fitted to his waggon, are the most striking articles. The bottoms of his chairs consist of thongs cut from a bullock's hide. The windows are without glass; or if there should happen to be any remains of this article, it is so patched and daubed as nearly to exclude the light it was intended to admit. The boor notwithstanding has his enjoyments: he is abso-lute master of a domain of several miles in extent; and he lords it over a few miserable slaves or Hottentots without control. His pipe scarcely ever quits his mouth, from the moment he rises till he retires to rest, except to give him time to swallow his *sopie,* or a glass of strong ardent spirit, to eat his meals, and to take his nap after dinner. Unwilling to work, and unable to think; with a mind disengaged from every sort of care and reflexion, indulging to excess in the gratification of every sensual appetite, the African peasant grows to an unweildy size, and is carried off the stage by the first inflammatory disease that attacks him.

How different is the lot of the laboring poor of England, who for six days in the week are doomed to toil for twelve hours in every day, in order to gain a morsel of bread for their family, and the luxury of a little animal food for the seventh day!

The consequences of the Boers' territorial hunger were precisely the boundary disputes, cattle thefts and house burnings foreshadowed in Van Riebeeck's time. Again, the los-ers were the native inhabitants: the Bushmen, whom the Boers hunted to death; the

Hottentots – now decimated by smallpox – whom they virtually enslaved; and, increasingly, the Xhosa – universally referred to at the time as 'kaffirs' – whom they steadily deprived of their land. War between the settlers and the Xhosa first broke out on the eastern frontier in 1781 and was to continue intermittently for the next 100 years. Henry Lichtenstein, the naturalist who accompanied Governor Janssens during the brief reassertion of Dutch control of the Cape between 1803 and 1806, took the frontier turmoil as the starting point for his relatively sympathetic meditation on the Boers in their isolation.

When the perpetual dangers in which the solitary Inhabitants of this district live are duly considered; when we reflect that they are continually in apprehension of the inroads of these most uncouth of all savages, of the Caffres, who swarm in the neighbourhood, and of bands of christian deserters and fugitive Hottentots who are roving about, it is scarcely to be comprehended how they can have any pleasure in existence. In making an estimate besides of the portion of happiness dispensed to them, many other things are to be taken into the account. The frightful drought of the country, in which often not a drop of rain falls for three months together, where only here and there a little muddy spring, or a stagnated pool in the otherwise dried up bed of a river offers drink either for mankind or for the cattle; where, except the thinly scattered mimosas, whose delicate leaves scarcely afford any shade, not a bush is to be seen; where a continued contest is to be maintained with wild beasts as well as wild men; – these must all be taken into the estimate, and in order to have their due weight allowed them must have been seen. An eye witness alone can properly judge of the joyless state of existence to which these people seem doomed. He cannot, without a great degree of astonishment, contemplate the force of habit, and witness what privations men are capable of, to whom, from their earliest youth, every thing beyond what will satisfy the mere wants of life has been totally unknown.

Yet it is much easier to comprehend how the present generation can be satisfied here, than how the first settlers could ever think of establishing themselves in so inhospitable a waste. That character must have been peculiarly framed, which could abandon all those enjoyments the mind receives from social intercourse, all the delights and advantages of friendship for a situation where really nothing was to be found but what is requisite to satisfy our first physical necessities. One should be almost tempted to consider complete indolence as the prevailing feature of such a character, and to pronounce that all other considerations must have been sacrificed to the indulgence of it; for this country would be wholly uninhabitable, were it not for the nourishment it affords in such abundance to the sheep; but these yield such extraordinary produce, that with a tolerable flock a whole family may be entirely supported without the owner being obliged to contribute the least exertion of his own. From two thousand sheep a thousand lambs may be calculated upon annually, after allowing deductions for what may die or be stolen. Six hundred wethers are requisite for feeding a family the year through, including the slaves and Hottentots, and in many a colonist's family no other food but mutton is ever tasted: four hundred will then remain for sale to the travelling butchers, which are worth about six hundred dollars, and that money supplies the remaining wants of the family. All the trouble that the colonist has is to see that his Hottentots go out with the flocks in the morning, and that the sheep are brought home safe at night. Some, indeed most of them, visit their flocks in the course of the day, and in the time of lambing they sometimes stay with them the whole day. The remainder of the time passes in trivial household employments, or in frequently repeated devotional exercises, only a little variety is sometimes sought in the chase.

In parts favourable to the feeding of cattle the lot of the inhabitant is somewhat happier, for such countries are also favourable to agriculture, and sufficient corn may be raised to supply the family abundantly with bread. Milk besides affords a very pleasant and wholesome article of food, and from the butter which is annually carried to the Cape Town a handsome capital is in time amassed. In most places the litter is left useless to dry away in the kraal, but an active farmer will collect it, and by the liberal use of it procure excellent garden products, and perhaps so large a quantity of corn, that besides what is necessary for his own use he will have some left for sale. Yet again it must be observed that these fair appearances may be at any moment destroyed by the robberies of the Bosjes-mans, the inroads of the Caffres, a sudden storm, or the murrain among the cattle; and the latter seems produced equally from want of water during the great heats in some places, and from the cold and damp of winter in others. It is only the extreme facility of produce that can in any degree counterbalance these contrarieties.

Is it surprising that men, who not only have no excitement to activity, but who would, if disposed to exertion, often find that it had been exercised wholly in vain with regard to themselves, by degrees learn to think of nothing but indulging the natural propensity of their nature to indolence; that they grow constantly more and more indifferent to the higher enjoyments of the mind and heart, and sink gradually into a sort of demi-savages, seeming to live only to satisfy the wants which they have in common with the whole animal creation, of sleep and food? One medium for supplying the latter want is here offered so bountifully by nature, that her other gifts are so much the more inexorably withheld. Man holds out his hand to receive her bounty without admiring it; he suffers the other privations to which he is doomed without feeling them as privations; therein consists his principal source of happiness, that he does not know the value of these things of which he is deprived. In an almost unconscious inactivity of mind, without any attractions towards the great circle of mankind, knowing nothing beyond the little circle which his own family forms around him, the colonist of these parts passes his solitary days, and by his mode of life is made such as we see him. We may not be compassionate, but we ought not to be angry with him, for the character of a man is not formed by himself; it arises from the circumstances under which he is placed; it is derived in great measure from the nature of the country which he inhabits. It is with these things always in mind, that I wish my readers to form their judgments of the character of the African colonists.

A dominant feature of life in the Cape Colony at the end of the 18th century was slavery, yet another of Van Riebeeck's legacies. Numbering then nearly 30 000, the slaves had been imported in more or less equal proportions from Mozambique, Madagascar, India and Ceylon, and Indonesia. The settlers, it was noted, had become so completely dependent on them that they could scarcely trouble to lift a finger for themselves. As the Company itself observed in 1755: 'Wherever Europeans dwell among inferior races who perform most of the manual labour, they are tempted to look upon work as degradation. They cultivate luxurious habits and acquire expensive tastes.' True to its Calvinist roots, the Company then imposed sumptuary laws on the Cape specifying, for example, that only the governor could ride in a gilded coach, only senior merchants and their wives were permitted to use umbrellas and women were forbidden to wear dresses with trains.

Both Francois Le Vaillant, the French naturalist, who travelled widely through the Cape in the 1780s, and John Barrow, writing in 1806 on the eve of Britain's prohibition of the slave trade, were impressed by the way the slaves were treated – by comparison, in Le Vaillant's case, with conditions on the plantations in the West Indies and the American South.

For twelve leagues around the Cape the colonists no longer employ Hottentots. They prefer to buy Negroes, who are not so lazy and because they can rely on their services. The Hottentots, carefree and fickle by nature, often disappear at the approach of hard labour, leaving their masters in a plight. It is true that the Negroes also run away but their hopes of freedom are vain as they are soon recaptured. They are brought to the bailiff of the district where their owner can claim them. After the owner pays a small fee and the slaves get a very light beating, they are returned to him. Indeed, in no other country in the world are slaves treated in a more humane manner than in the Cape.

The Negroes from Mozambique and Madagascar are considered the strongest labourers and the most loyal to their masters. When they are landed at the Cape they usually go for one-hundred-and-twenty to one-hundred-and-fifty piastres each. Indians are more particularly sought after for domestic work or as town employees. Malays are also found in this type of employ. They make both the most intelligent and the most dangerous slaves. Assassination of their master or mistress is only a minor crime in their eyes and, in the five years I spent in Africa, I saw this heinous crime committed time and again. They walk to the scaffold calm and composed. I even heard one of these wretched criminals tell Mr Boers that he was delighted he had committed his crime. Although he had been quite aware of the kind of death he would be made to suffer, he nonetheless was eager to see his end approach because he would then immediately find himself back in his native land. It is a wonder that such a violent misconception does not cause even greater tragedies.

The Cape Creole slaves are the most highly valued. They fetch twice the price of the others and, if they are highly skilled, their price becomes exorbitant. A cook, for instance, sells for eight to twelve hundred rix-dollars, and others according to their talents. They are always decently clothed, but they walk barefoot as a sign of their slavery.

A stranger arriving in the Cape is surprised to see so many slaves who are as white as the Europeans. But astonishment stops when one knows that the young Negresses, provided they are attractive, each has a soldier with whom they spend Sundays as they like. Out of self interest the master turns a blind eye on the disorderly conduct of his slaves as he looks forward to the product of these licentious relationships.

John Barrow, however, drew a comparison closer to home.

In full possession of all the vices that must infallibly result from the condition of slavery, there is yet no part of the world where the domestic slaves of every description are so well treated, and so much trusted, as at the Cape of Good Hope. They are better clothed, better fed, and infinitely more comfortable, than any of the peasantry of Europe. Yet such are the bad effects which the condition of slavery produces on the mind, that they are incapable of feeling the least spark of gratitude for good and gentle usage, whilst, under the severe hand of a rigid and cruel master, they become the best of slaves. It may be considered as an axiom or self-evident truth, that such are and always will be the consequences of degrading man to the lowest of all conditions, that of being made the property of man.

The Dutch use little prudence or precaution with regard to their domestic slaves: in the same room where these are assembled to wait behind their masters' chairs, they discuss their crude opinions of liberty and equality without any reserve; yet they pretend to say that, just before the English got possession of the Cape, and when it was generally thought the French would be before-hand with us, the slaves who carried the sedan chairs, of which no lady is without one, used very familiarly to tell their mistresses, 'We carry you now, but by-and-by it will be your turn to carry us.' The proportion of slaves to whites, of both sexes and all ages, in the town, is not more than two to one: but that of slave men to white men is near five to one.

The field slaves belonging to the farmers are not, however, nearly so well treated as those of the town; yet infinitely better than the Hottentots who are in their employ. The farmer, indeed, having a life-interest in the one, and only five-and-twenty years in the other, is a circumstance that may explain the difference of treatment. The one, also, is convertible property, an advantage to which they have not yet succeeded in their attempts to turn the other. The country slaves, notwithstanding, are ill fed, ill clothed, work extremely hard, and are frequently punished with the greatest severity; sometimes with death, when rage gets the better of prudence and compassion.

The bad effects that a state of slavery invariably produces on the minds and habits of a people, who have the misfortune to be born and educated in the midst of it, are not less felt at the Cape than in the warmer climates. Among the upper ranks it is the custom for every child to have its slave, whose sole employment is to humour its caprices, and to drag it about from place to place lest it should too soon discover for what purposes nature had bestowed on it legs and arms. Even the lower class of people think it would be degrading to their children to go out as servants, or be bound as apprentices to learn the useful trades, which, in their contracted ideas, would be to condemn them to perform the work of slaves.

A probably fictionalised account of a slave auction in Cape Town was given by Robert Semple, the Scottish traveller, in *Walks and Sketches at the Cape of Good Hope* (23), published in 1803.

In one of our morning walks about the town, observing a considerable crowd before the door of a house, my friend and I went up and inquired what was going forward, and were informed that it was a public sale of all the effects of a colonist deceased. Scarcely had we joined the crowd, when the auctioneer mounted upon a chair and struck for some time upon a round plate of brass, as a signal that the auction was going to begin. Immediately all was attention. Numbers of articles were put up and disposed of till, growing tired of the scene, we were going away; a short pause, however, and then a murmur in the assembly, announced that something else than trifles was going to be produced. We accordingly waited a moment, and soon saw a black man coming forward through the crowd. 'Ah!' said Charles, 'they are going to dispose of the family slaves; let us stop a little longer.'

The first that was put up was a stout native of the Mozambique coast. His look was sad and melancholy, his hands hanging down clasped together as if they were bound, and his eyes fixed upon the earth. When he heard that his lot was determined, and that he was sold for six hundred rix-dollars, he raised his eyes up heavily to look for his new master, and followed him out of the crowd without speaking a word; but we thought that his cheek was wet with tears, and perhaps we were right; for the purchaser told us, with some expressions of compassion, that he had been a great favourite of his deceased friend. Many more were put up, the household of the deceased having been very numerous, but on the countenances of all of them sorrow and the humiliation of slavery were the predominating features. At length an object was presented which almost made us weep; a mother was brought forward with a little girl of three years old clinging to her, which they wished to tear from her, whilst she, dreading the threats of her owners, feebly told her child to leave her at the same time that she folded her arms round it. 'Put them up together, put them up together,' said every voice; it was consented to, and the woman kissing her child and leading it by the hand, advanced to the spot appointed. Whilst they were bidding for her, she looked anxiously round in every countenance, as if imploring compassion. Her price was bade up to seven hundred dollars, which the auctioneer repeated a long time without anybody seeming willing to say more. 'The man who has bought her and the child,' said one who stood next to us, 'has the reputation of being very cruel to his slaves.' 'Has he?' said Charles, whilst the blood rushed into his face, 'but he has not got them yet.' 'Seven hundred and ten,' cried he with a voice trembling with eagerness. Everybody turned their eyes upon us, and the mother and the little child looked full in Charles's face. 'Seven hundred and twenty,' said the man, starting up; ' fifty,' said the other; 'eight hundred,' bade Charles; the man bit his lips, a long pause ensued; 'eight hundred and one,' said a mild-looking old man whose humanity I was well acquainted with. Charles drew back, and the poor slave was allotted to a mild master.

Francois Le Vaillant, who was the most widely read of the early writers about the Cape – his book was a best-seller across Europe – gave his readers a brief sketch of Cape Town towards the end of the 18th century.

Cape Town is situated on the slopes of Table Mountain and the Lion and forms an amphitheatre which extends to the sea-shore. The streets, though wide, are not at all practical because they are poorly paved. The houses, almost all of the same design, are attractive and spacious. They are covered with reeds to prevent accidents that might arise from heavier roofs when strong winds blow. The interiors display no frivolous luxury and the furniture is in simple and noble taste. There are no wall-hangings; some paintings and mirrors are the main decorations.

The entry to the city by the square in front of the castle presents a superb vista, with some of the most beautiful buildings grouped there. Along one side you note the Company garden, on the other the fountains whose water comes down Table Mountain by a ravine that one sees from the city and anywhere in the bay. The water is excellent and provides abundantly for the consumption of the inhabitants as well as for the provisioning of ships calling in the harbour.

In general, I found the men well made, and the women charming. I was surprised to see that the women dress and adorn themselves with the same fastidious elegance as our French ladies, but they have neither their style nor their graces. As it is always the slave women who breast-feed the master's children, the great familiarity between them has a strong influence on manners and education. The education of the men is even more neglected, if we except the children of the rich who are sent to Europe to be educated, for the only teachers one finds at the Cape are teachers of writing.

Almost all the women play the harpsichord; it is their only talent. They like to sing and are mad about dancing; thus rarely a week passes without several balls taking place. The officers of ships calling in the bay often give them the occasion for offering a ball. When I arrived, the Governor used to give a public ball once a month, and the people of importance followed his example.

Carl Peter Thunberg, who arrived in Cape Town in 1772 and was later to be called the father of Cape botany, preferred striding about the mountains. Indeed, he was said to have climbed Table Mountain 15 times. Another favourite destination was Lion's Head, which, as he discovered, played a vital role in the settlement's precarious security.

During my stay in town, I visited several times the Lion's Head (*Leeuwe-kop*) a mountain that stands to the westward of Table Mountain, and rises to an almost inaccessible peak; from this peak it runs out in a long sloping ridge, and terminates in a curved eminence, called the Lion's Tail (*Leeuwe-staart*). Below its peak, the Lion's Head is so steep in one place, that if one wishes to ascend to it, a rope has had to be fastened to the rock, by the help of which, one must clamber up by a side that is almost perpendicular. On the very top of the peak, where a perpetual guard is placed for the purpose of discovering the approach of ships, there is a small hut, with a fireplace in it for dressing provisions; three guns, one of which is fired for every ship that is seen; and a flag-staff to hoist a flag on. By the number of guns fired, government is immediately informed whether it is a single ship or a fleet that approaches. In the evening, the sentinel goes down to his house, which is situated in the cleft between Table Mountain and the Lion's Head. When the ships that are descried, approach, a flag is hoisted on the Lion's Back (*Leeuwe-rug*), and when they enter the harbour, the colours are hoisted on the citadel, till they have saluted it. If any ship should come within sight of the Cape, and afterwards pass by it, the flag on the Lion's Back is struck, as soon as it disappears. The flag that is hoisted varies every month, and is like a watchword on the field of battle; for the colour of the flag is appointed by the directors in Europe, and made known only to the respective regencies at Batavia and the Cape, and in sealed letters to the captains of the outward and homeward bound ships. Thus the captains of the ships may discover, if on a sudden eruption of war, the Cape is fallen into the hands of the enemy, and in such case, keep away from the harbour. In time of war, when any great fleet is descried making its approach, the whole colony through the interior parts may be summoned with the greatest expedition, by the firing of guns, the hoisting of flags, and the kindling of fires, which are disposed at certain places, and distributed at such distances, that these signals may always be seen or heard from one place to the next.

Robben Island is situated at the entrance of the harbour, about six miles from the town. The ships that run into the harbour must always pass by this island, which then hoists the Dutch flag. Sometimes, when a strong south-east wind prevents the ships from entering, they anchor beside it. This island was formerly the resort of a great number of seals, whence it also derives its name; but now these animals having been driven away from it, it is become the retreat of chameleons, quails and prisoners for life (called here bandits), who are obliged to collect every day on the seashore a certain quantity of shells, which are burned to make lime for the buildings erected by the Company. These prisoners for life are not only black slaves who have been guilty of misdemeanours, but also Europeans, who have committed heinous crimes.

No one climbed Table Mountain more enthusiastically – or more loyally – than Lady Anne Barnard. Her route in 1797 was up what is now called Platteklip Gorge, the most unforgiving of ascents. The 'fine spring of water', of which she saved a bottle for her 'cher ami', Lord Melville, is still there. Her companion was the energetic and ambitious John Barrow, who, thanks to Melville's patronage, was later to be knighted, become the chief civil servant at the Admiralty and the father of Arctic exploration.

I must now tell you a little about a Cape expedition of mine. Having been told that no woman had ever been on the top of the Table Mountain (this was not literally true, one or two having been there), and being unable to get any account of it from the inhabitants of this town, all of whom wished it to be considered as next to an impossible matter to get to the top of it, as an excuse for their own want of curiosity, and having found the officers all willing to believe the Dutch for ditto reason, laziness to wit, there was some ambition as a motive for climbing, as well as curiosity. And as Mr. Barrow is just one of the pleasantest, best-informed, and most eager-minded young men in the world about everything curious or worth attention, I paid him my addresses and persuaded him to mount the mountain along with me. We were joined in the plan by two of my ship-mates, officers, and my maid chose to be of the party. I had a couple of servants, and a couple of boxes with cold meat and wine. Mr. Barrow and I slung round our shoulders tin cases for plants, of which we were told we should get great variety on the top of the mountain. It is 3,500 feet in height, and reckoned about three miles to the top of it from the beginning of the great ascent, the road being (or rather the conjectured path, for there is no road) necessarily squinted in the zigzag way which much increases the measurement of the walk. At eight o'clock in the morning Mr. Barrow and I, with our followers, set off. We reached the foot of the mountain on horseback, and dismounted when we could ride no more – indeed, nothing but a human creature or an antelope could ascend such a path.

We first had to scramble up the side of a pretty perpendicular cascade of a hundred feet or two, the falls of which must be very fine after rains, and the sides of which were shaded with myrtles, sugar trees, and geraniums. We continued our progress through a low foliage of all sorts of pretty heaths and evergreens, the sun at last beginning to beat with much force down on our heads, but the heat was not, though great, oppressive. Wherever we saw questionable stone or ore, Mr. Barrow attacked it with a hammer, which I had luckily brought for the purpose, but he found the mountain through all its strata, of which there are innumerable, composed of iron stone, and that at least to the quantity of fifty per cent. It made me smile to see the signs of human footsteps, in the quantity of old soles and heels of shoes which I came across every here and there. I suppose these relics have lain time immemorial, as leather, I believe, never decays, at least not for a great while. They proved that the Dutchmen told fibs when they said that few people had tried to get up this mountain. The sun and fatigue obliged me frequently to sit down; and as I had an umbrella with me, a few minutes always recruited me. At last, about twelve o'clock, the sun began to be so very hot that I rejoiced at the turn of the mountain, which I saw would soon bring us into the shadow, before we reached the great gully by which we were to get out on the top. Redoubling my activity, at last we made the turn, but it was wonderful the sudden chill which instantaneously came over us; we looked at our thermometers, and in a second they had fallen under the shadow fifteen degrees, being now 55, and before, on the brow of the hill, they were 70. We had now come to a fine spring of water, which fell from the top of the rock, or near it, over our heads; we drank some of it with port-wine, but it was too cold to have been safe, if we had not more way to climb. I saved a bottle of it for you, cher ami. Opposite there was a cave cut in the rock, which is occasionally inhabited by run-away negroes, of which there were traces.

Once more we set off, and in three hours from the bottom of the mountain reached the very tip-top of this great rock, looking down on the town (almost out of sight below) with much conscious superiority, and smiling at the formal meanness of its appearance, which would have led us to suppose it built by children out of half a dozen packs of cards. I was glad on this pinnacle to have a bird's-eye view of the country, the bays, and the distant and near mountains. The *coup d'oeil* brought to my awed remembrance the Saviour of the World presented from the top of 'an exceeding high mountain' with all the kingdoms of the earth by the devil. Nothing short of such a view was this. But it was not the garden of the world that appeared all around; on the contrary, there was no denying the circle bounded only by the heavens and sea to be a wide desert, bare, uncultivated, uninhabited, but noble in its bareness, and (as we had reason to know) possessing a soil capable of cultivation, a soil, which submits easily to the spade, and gratefully repays attention. On the top of the mountain there was nothing of that luxuriancy of verdure and foliage, flower or herbage, described by travellers; there were roots and some flowers, and a beautiful heath on the edge of the rocks, but the soil was cold, swampy, and mossy, covered in general with half an inch of water, rushes growing in it, and sprinkled all over with little white pebbles, some dozens of which I gathered to make Table Mountain earrings for my fair European friends. We now produced our cold meat, our port, Madeira, and Cape wine, and we made a splendid and happy dinner after our fatigues. When it was over I proposed a song to be sung in full chorus, not doubting that all the hills around would join us – 'God save the King.' 'God save great George our King,' roared I and my troop. 'God save – God save – God save – God save – God save – God save – God save – God save – great George our King – great George our King – great George – great George – great George,' repeated the loyal mountains. 'The impression is very fine,' said Mr. Barrow, with his eyes glistening. I could not say 'Yes,' because I felt more than I chose to trust my voice with, just then, but I wished 'great George our King' to have stood beside me at the moment, and to have thrown his eye over his new colony, which we were thus (his humble viceroys) taking possession of in his name.

My servants shot a few pretty birds, which you shall see by-and-by, and we found it time to return home, which we could not reach, we saw, before six o'clock at night. Nothing was more singular than to look down far, far below, on the flag raised on the top of the Lion's head, a rock perpendicular, of some hundred feet, on the top of a great North Berwick law. It is round this rock that there is a constant necklace of clouds playing; but on this day all was clear. The person who keeps guard on this rock is drawn up by ropes fixed in a particular manner.

If it was difficult to ascend the hill, it was much more so to descend. The ladies were dressed for the occasion, else – I need not say more after the word 'else.' The only way to get down was to sit down and slip from rock to rock the best way one could. My shoes I had tied on with some yards of tape, which had been a good scheme. At last we reached home, not more tired than I expected we should have been, and more than ever convinced that there are few things impossible where there is, in man or woman, a decided and spirited wish of attainment.

Writing 80 years later, RM Ballantyne (24), inveterate traveller and author of *The Coral Island*, the children's classic, was as enchanted as Lady Anne by the clouds that decorate Cape Town's semi-circle of mountains and as struck as all visitors are by the phenomenon known as the South-Easter.

It is pretty generally known that there is a 'tablecloth' at Capetown. Its proper resting-place is Table Mountain. When the flat top of that celebrated hill is clear, (I write of the summer season), the thirty thousand inhabitants of Capetown may go forth in comfort if they can stand the blazing sunshine, but as surely as that pure white cloud – the tablecloth – rests on the summit of Table Mountain, so surely does the gale known as the 'south-easter' come down like a wolf on the fold.

The south-easter is a sneezer, and a frequent visitor at the Cape in summer. Where it comes from no one can tell: where it goes to is best known to itself: what it does in passing is painfully obvious to all. Fresh from the

Antarctic seas it swoops down on the southern shores of Africa, and sweeps over the land as if in search of a worthy foe. It apparently finds one in Table Mountain, which, being 3582 feet high, craggy and precipitous, meets the enemy with frowning front, and hurls him back discomfited – but not defeated.

Rallying on the instant, the south-easter rushes up over its cloud-capped head and round its rugged sides, and down its dizzy slopes, and falls with a shriek of fiendish fury on the doomed city. Oceans of sand and dust are caught up by it, whirled round as if in mad ecstasy, and dashed against the faces of the inhabitants – who tightly shut their mouths and eyes as they stoop to resist the onset. Then the south-easter yells while it sweeps dust, small stones, twigs, leaves, and stray miscellanies, right over Signal Hill into the South Atlantic.

This is bad enough, but it is a mere skirmish – only the advance guard of the enemy. Supposing this attack to have been commenced in the morning, the remainder of the day is marked by a series of violent assaults with brief intervals of repose. In rapid succession the south-easter brings up its battalions and hurls them on the mountain. It leaps over the moat and ramparts of the 'castle' with fury, roars down the cannons' throats, shrieks out at the touch-holes, and lashes about the town right and left, assaulting and violating, for the south-easter respects neither person nor place. It rattles roofs and windows, and all but overturns steeples and chimneys; it well-nigh blows the shops inside out, and fills them with dust; it storms the barracks and maltreats the soldiers; it compels the shutting up of sun-umbrellas, or reverses and blows them to ribbons; it removes hats and bonnets by the score, and sweeps up small pebbles in its mad career, so that one feels as if being painfully pelted with buck-shot; it causes the shipping to strain fearfully at its cables, and churns the waters of Table Bay into a seething mass of snow and indigo.

All this time the sun shines intensely in a cloudless sky, and beautifies the 'cloth' which floats on Table Mountain, undulating on its surface, or pouring over its edge like a Niagara of wool, to be warmed into invisibility before tumbling half-way down the mighty precipice that backs the town.

The last word on the Cape at the end of the 18th century belongs to Lady Anne Barnard, here describing to Lord Melville the symbolic transfer of power from the Dutch to the British.

The Castle, Cape of Good Hope: August 10th, 1797. I must begin my letter, my dear Friend, by telling you of the steps which have been taken to bring the people of the Cape into harmony with our English Government. There was a Proclamation to the effect that during a certain time, which was an ample one, they might come from all quarters and take the oath of allegiance to His Majesty. The gates of the Castle were thrown open every morning, and I was surprised to see so many come after what I had heard. Firstly came a number of well-fed, rosy-cheeked men, with powdered hair, and dressed in black. They walked in pairs with their hats off, a regulation on entering the Castle on public occasions which, in former days, Dutch pride imposed. They were followed by the Boers from the country – farmers and settlers who had come some very great distance. I think that many of them seemed very sulky and ill-affected; their manner seemed to say: 'There is no help for it. We must swear, for they are the strongest.' They are very fine men, their height is enormous; most of them are six feet high and upwards, and I do not know how many feet across; I hear that five or six hundred miles distant they even reach seven feet. They all came to the Cape in waggons, bringing a load of something to market at the same time. They were dressed in blue cloth jackets and trousers and very high flat hats. In fact, they struck me as overdressed, but the Hottentot servant who crept behind each, carrying his master's umbrella, on the other hand, was underdressed. He seemed to have little else to carry except a piece of leather round his waist and a sheep-skin round his shoulders; one or two had a scarlet handkerchief tied round the head, sometimes an old hat ornamented with ostrich feathers, but very often they were bareheaded. I was told the Hottentots were uncommonly ugly and disgusting, but I do not think them so bad. Their features are small and their cheek-bones immense, but they have a kind expression of coun-tenance; they are not so ugly as the slaves of Mozambique. I must try to sketch a face of every caste or nation here; the collection cannot be short of twenty.

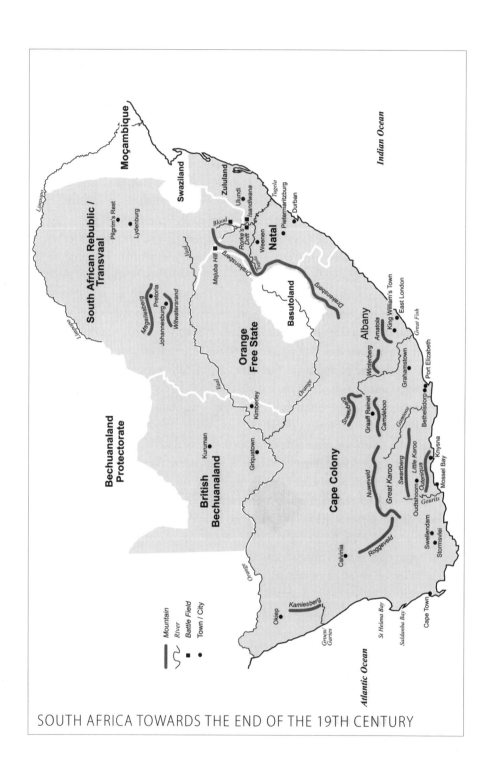

SOUTH AFRICA TOWARDS THE END OF THE 19TH CENTURY

CHAPTER 5

ANIMALS AND HUNTERS

Out of the Ark's grim hold
A torrent of splendour rolled –
From the hollow resounding sides,
Flashing and glittering, came
Panthers with sparkled hides,
And tigers scribbled with flame,
And lions in grisly trains
Cascading their golden manes.
They ramped in the morning light,
And over their stripes and stars
The sun-shot lightnings, quivering bright,
Rippled in zigzag bars.
The wildebeest frisked with the gale
On the crags of a hunchback mountain,
With his heels in the clouds, he flirted his tail
Like the jet of a silvery fountain.
Frail oribi sailed with their golden-skinned
And feathery limbs laid light on the wind.
And the springbok bounced, and fluttered, and flew,
Hooping their spines on the gaunt karroo.
Gay zebras pranced and snorted aloud –
With the crackle of hail their hard hoofs pelt,
And thunder breaks from the rolling cloud

That they raise on the dusty veld.
O, hark how the rapids of the Congo
Are chanting their rolling strains,
And the sun-dappled herds a-skipping to the song, go
Kicking up the dust on the great, grey plains –
Tsessebe, Kudu, Buffalo, Bongo,
With the fierce wind foaming in their manes.

From: 'The Flaming Terrapin'

Thus Roy Campbell (25), one of South Africa's most distinguished poets, in his re-creation of the Flood, published in 1924.

That wild animals were abundant was known from the start. Before Van Riebeeck even stepped ashore at Cape Town in April 1652, his men had killed a large hippo, 'the weight of two fat oxen'. Two weeks later, they caught a young one and discovered 'the meat tastes like that of a calf'. The first few months of his Journal contain repeated references to 'countless whales in the bay', 'whales in the bay, lying in the sun and disporting themselves', 'the bay again full of whales … close to the shore they made a great hub-bub, blowing and behaving noisily' – accompanied by regret that 'we have neither the equipment nor the people to catch them'. There were leopards and rhinos in the neigh-bourhood, too, but the lions were the real menace. 'Last night,' Van Riebeeck recorded on 23 January 1653, 'the lions seemed almost to storm the fort to get at the sheep, which are kept inside at night. A large number of them had followed the scent, roaring horribly and loudly as if they wanted to tear everything to pieces.' By June 1656 the situation had become serious.

16th During the forenoon the Commander, walking in the gardens, saw tracks of wild beasts everywhere, and shortly afterwards a bold lion jumped up just outside the gardens not more than 40 or 50 paces from him and leisurely made off towards the Table Mountain. The sergeant and the huntsman, with 4 or 5 soldiers, were sent after it with firelocks, and fully 200 Hottentots followed immediately, driving all their sheep and cattle. They cornered the lion in a deep kloof on the slopes of the Table Mountain, so that its only way of escape was by breaking through the sheep, which the Hottentots had placed in front of them as a breastwork for their defence. The lion lay hid-den under a bush and the Hottentots stood outside the flock of sheep, and between them and the cattle. Whenever the lion showed itself and, roaring, tried to break out and seize a sheep, they hurled their assegais at it over the sheep, with great noise and shouting, on which the lion retreated. It was a very singular spectacle. As the Hottentots could not hit it, the sergeant who was with our huntsman and the others, who were about 8 or 10 paces away from the lion, fired first but missed, whereupon the huntsman sent three bullets through its head – an excellent shot – causing it to drop dead at once. Then the Hottentots showed themselves brave men and would have stabbed the animal a hundred times after it was dead, but they were prevented from doing so – after 3 or 4 assegais had already been plunged into the body – in order not to ruin the skin, which could now be nicely repaired and hung up in the large hall used for a church. The carcase was therefore brought home in a cart and was found to weigh 426 Dutch pounds and to be 5½ feet long without the tail (which was 3½ Rhineland feet in length), and on its feet 3½ feet high. It was therefore quite as sturdy as an average English or Java pony. When it was cut open, a good deal of the flesh of the horse it had devoured last night was found in its stomach, as well as some porcupine quills and legs, etc.

17th Fine weather and wind as above. In view of the heavy losses inflicted on the Company's livestock by wild beasts, it was resolved to-day to offer the following rewards: for catching or shooting a lion, 6 reals of eight, a tiger or wolf, 4, and a leopard, 3. The huntsman had in the meantime been rewarded with 2 tankards of Spanish wine, 3lbs. of tobacco and 2 reals of eight.

However, the offer did not seem to make much difference. Soon, Van Riebeeck was recording that three sheep had been devoured by a lion near the Company's granary at Rondebosch; another had mauled two of his private plough-oxen at Bishopscourt; a soldier had been devoured while fishing near present-day Green Point; and in Newlands three lions were 'daily causing loss' among the free burghers' livestock.

Wild animals could also be an embarrassment to travellers, as Carl Peter Thunberg, the Swedish naturalist, discovered. In November 1772 he was riding towards Knysna, about 250 miles east of Cape Town, with his friend, John Auge, the distinguished super-intendent of the Company's gardens, and one of the Company's soldiers.

In the afternoon we arrived at Koukuma' Rivier. We forded over one of its branches, and intended to pass through a thicket to a farm which we dis-covered on an eminence on the other side of this thicket, belonging to one

Helgert Muller; but we had not advanced far into the wood before we had the misfortune of meeting with a large old male buffalo, which was lying down quite alone, in a spot that was free from bushes, for the space of a few square yards. He no sooner discovered Auge, 'who rode first, than roaring horribly he rushed upon him. The gardener turning his horse short round, behind a large tree, by that means got in some measure out of the buffalo's sight, which now rushed straight forwards towards the serjeant, who followed next, and gored his horse in the belly in such a terrible manner, that it fell on its back that instant, with its feet turned up in the air, and all its entrails hanging out, in which state it lived almost half an hour. The gardener and the serjeant in the mean time had climbed up into trees, where they thought themselves secure. The buffalo after this first achievement, now appeared to take his course towards the side where we were approaching, and therefore could not have failed in his way to pay his compliments to me, who all the while was walking towards him, and in the narrow pass formed by the boughs and branches of the trees, and on account of the rustling noise these made against my saddle and baggage, had neither seen nor heard any thing of what had passed. As in my way I frequently stopped to take up plants, and put them into my handkerchief, I generally kept behind my companions, that I might not hinder their progress; so that I was now at a small distance behind them.

The serjeant had brought two horses with him for his journey. One of them had already been dispatched, and the other now stood just in the way of the buffalo, who was going out of the wood. As soon as the buffalo saw this second horse, he became more outrageous than before, and attacked it with such fury, that he not only drove his horns into the horse's breast and out again through the very saddle, but also threw it to the ground with such violence, that it died that very instant, and all the bones in its body were broken. Just at the moment that he was thus occupied with this latter horse, I came up to the opening, where the wood was so thick, that I had neither room to turn my horse round, nor to get on one side. I was therefore obliged to abandon him to his fate, and take refuge in a tolerably high tree, up which I climbed. The buffalo having finished this his second exploit, suddenly turned round, and shaped his course the same way which we had intended to take.

From the place I was in, and the eminence I had gained, I could plainly perceive one of the horses quite dead, the other kicking with its feet and endeavouring to rise, which it had not strength to do, and the other two horses shivering with fear, and unable to make their escape, but I could neither see nor hear any thing of my fellow-travellers and companions, which induced me to fear that they had fallen victims to the first transports of the buffalo's fury. I therefore made all possible haste to search for them, to see if I could in any way assist them; but not discovering any traces of them in the whole field of battle, I began to call out after them, when I discovered these magnanimous[2] heroes sitting fast, like two cats, on the trunk of a tree, with their guns on their backs, loaded with fine shot, and unable to utter a single word. I encouraged them as well as I could, and advised them to come down, and get away as fast as possible from such a dangerous place, where we ran the risk of being once more attacked. The serjeant at length burst out into tears, deploring the loss of his two spirited steeds; but the gardener was so strongly affected, that he could scarcely speak for some days after.

Many others, though – made of sterner stuff – were drawn to South Africa by the prospect of encountering large numbers of wild animals and killing them. Foremost among them were the two former Army officers, William Cornwallis Harris and Roualeyn Gordon Cumming. Here, to give a flavour of what excited these 'Nimrods' – they gloried in the Biblical reference   are their accounts of hunting giraffe, which they also knew as 'cameleopards' or 'camelopards'. First, Cornwallis Harris, astride his 'trusty steed', north of the Vaal River in 1837.

To the sportsman, the most thrilling passage in my adventures, is now to be recounted. In my own breast, it awakens a renewal of past impressions, more lively than any written description can render intelligible; and far abler pens than mine, dipped in more glowing tints, would still fall short of the reality, and leave much to be supplied by the imagination. Three hundred gigantic Elephants, browsing in majestic tranquillity amidst the wild magnificence of an African landscape, and a wide stretching plain, darkened far as the eye can reach, with a moving phalanx of Gnoos and Quaggas, whose numbers literally baffle computation, are sights but rarely to be witnessed; but who amongst our brother Nimrods shall hear of riding familiarly by the side of a troop of colossal Giraffes, and not feel his spirit stirred within him? He that would behold so marvellous a sight must leave the haunts of man, and dive, as we did, into pathless wilds, traversed only by the brute creation – into wide wastes, where the grim Lion prowls, monarch of all he surveys, and where the gaunt Hyaena and Wild Dog fearlessly pursue their prey.

Many days had now elapsed since we had even seen the Cameleopard – and then only in small numbers, and under the most unfavorable circumstances. The blood coursed through my veins like quicksilver, therefore, as on the morning of the 19th, from the back of *Breslar*, my most trusty steed, with a firm wooded plain before me, I counted thirty two of these animals, industriously stretching their peacock necks to crop the tiny leaves which fluttered above their heads, in a mimosa grove that beautified the scenery. They were within a hundred yards of me, but having previously determined to try the *boarding* system, I reserved my fire. Although I had taken the field expressly to look for Giraffes, and had put four of the Hottentots on horseback, all excepting Piet had as usual slipped off unperceived in pursuit of a troop of Koodoos. Our stealthy approach was soon opposed by an ill tempered Rhinoceros, which with her ugly calf, stood directly in the path; and the twinkling of her bright little eyes, accompanied by a restless rolling of the body, giving earnest of her intention to charge, I directed Piet to salute her with a broadside, at the same moment putting spurs to my horse. At the report of the gun, and the sudden clattering of hoofs, away bounded the Giraffes in grostesque confusion – clearing the ground by a succession of frog-like hops, and soon leaving me far in the rear. Twice were their towering forms concealed from view by a park of trees, which we entered almost at the same instant; and twice on emerging from the labyrinth, did I perceive them tilting over an eminence immeasurably in advance. A white turban, that I wore round my hunting cap, being dragged off by a projecting bough, was instantly charged by three Rhinoceroses; and looking over my shoulder, I could see them long afterwards, fagging themselves to overtake me. In the course of five minutes, the fugitives arrived at a small river, the treacherous sands of which receiving their long legs, their flight was greatly retarded; and after floundering to the opposite side, and scrambling to the top of the bank, I perceived that their race was run. Patting the steaming neck of my good steed, I urged him again to his utmost, and instantly found myself by the side of the herd. The stately bull, being readily distinguishable from the rest by his dark chesnut robe, and superior stature, I applied the muzzle of my rifle behind his dappled shoulder, with the right hand, and drew both triggers; but he still continued to shuttle along, and being afraid of losing him, should I dismount, among the extensive mimosa groves, with which the landscape was now obscured, I sat in my saddle, loading and firing behind the elbow, and then placing myself across his path, until, the tears trickling from his full brilliant eye, his lofty frame began to totter, and at the seventeenth discharge from the deadly grooved bore, bowing his graceful head from the skies his proud form was prostrate in the dust. Never shall I forget the tingling excitement of that moment! Alone, in the wild wood, I hurried with bursting exultation, and unsaddling my steed, sank exhausted beside the noble prize I had won.

When I leisurely contemplated the massive frame before me, seeming as though it had been cast in a mould of brass, and protected by a hide of an inch and a half in thickness, it was no longer matter of astonishment that a bullet discharged from a distance of eighty or ninety yards should have been attended with little effect upon such amazing strength. The extreme height from the crown of the elegantly moulded head to the hoof of this magnificent animal, was eighteen feet; the whole being equally divided into neck, body, and leg. Two hours were passed in completing a drawing; and Piet still not making his appearance, I cut off the tail, which exceeded five feet in length, and was measurelessly the most estimable trophy I had gained.

Nine years later, in June 1846, Gordon Cumming was near Kuruman, in the Northern Cape. 'This day was to me rather a memorable one,' he records, 'as the first on which I saw and slew the lofty, graceful-looking giraffe or camelopard, with which, during many years of my life, I had longed to form an acquaintance.'

Although we had now been travelling many days through the country of the giraffe, and had marched through forests in which their spoor was abundant, our eyes had not yet been gifted with a sight of Tootla[3] himself; it was therefore with indescribable pleasure that, on the evening of the 11th, I beheld a troop of these interesting animals.

Our breakfast being finished, I resumed my journey through an endless gray forest of cameel-dorn and other trees, the country slightly undulating and grass abundant. A little before the sun went down my driver remarked to me, 'I was just going to say, sir, that that old tree was a camelopard.' On looking where he pointed, I saw that the old tree was indeed a camelopard, and, on casting my eyes a little to the right, I beheld a troop of them standing looking at us, their heads actually towering above the trees of the forest. It was imprudent to commence a chase at such a late hour, especially in a country of so level a character, where the chances were against my being able to regain my wagons that night. I, however, resolved to chance every thing; and directing my men to catch and saddle Colesberg, I proceeded in haste to buckle on my shooting-belt and spurs, and in two minutes I was in the saddle. The giraffes stood looking at the wagons until I was within sixty yards of them, when, galloping round a thick bushy tree, under cover of which I had ridden, I suddenly beheld a sight the most astounding that a sportsman's eye can encounter. Before me stood a troop of ten colossal giraffes, the majority of which were from seventeen to eighteen feet high. On beholding me they at once made off, twisting their long tails over their backs, making a loud switching noise with them, and cantered along at an easy pace, which, however, obliged Colesberg to put his best foot foremost to keep up with them.

The sensations which I felt on this occasion were different from any thing that I had before experienced during a long sporting career. My senses were so absorbed by the wondrous and beautiful sight before me that I rode along like one entranced, and felt inclined to disbelieve that I was hunting living things of this world. The ground was firm and favourable for riding. At every stride I gained upon the giraffes, and after a short burst at a swinging gallop I was in the middle of them, and turned the finest cow out of the herd. On finding herself driven from her comrades and hotly pursued, she increased her pace, and cantered along with tremendous strides, clearing an amazing extent of ground at every bound; while her neck and breast, coming in contact with the dead old branches of the trees, were continually strewing them in my path. In a few minutes I was riding within five yards of her stern, and, firing at the gallop, I sent a bullet into her back. Increasing my pace, I next rode alongside, and, placing the muzzle of my rifle within a few feet of her, I fired my second shot behind the shoulder; the ball, however, seemed to have little effect. I then placed myself directly in front, when she came to a walk. Dismounting, I hastily loaded both barrels, putting in double charges of powder. Before this was accomplished she was off at a canter. In a short time I brought her to a stand in the dry bed of a water-course, where I fired at fifteen yards, aiming where I thought the heart lay, upon which she again made off. Having loaded, I followed, and had very nearly lost her; she had turned abruptly to the left, and was far out of sight among the trees. Once more I brought her to a stand, and dismounted from my horse. There we stood together alone in the wild wood. I gazed in wonder at her extreme beauty, while her soft dark eye, with its silky fringe, looked down imploringly at me, and I really felt a pang of sorrow in this moment of triumph for the blood I was shedding. Pointing my rifle toward the skies, I sent a bullet through her neck. On receiving it, she reared high on her hind legs, and fell backward with a heavy crash, making the earth shake around her. A thick stream of dark blood spouted out from the wound, her colossal limbs quivered for a moment, and she expired.

I had little time to contemplate the prize I had won. Night was fast setting in, and it was very questionable if I should succeed in regaining my wagons; so, having cut off the tail of the giraffe, which was adorned with a bushy tuft of flowing black hair, I took 'one last fond look,' and rode hard for the spoor of the wagons, which I succeeded in reaching just as it was dark.

No pen nor words can convey to a sportsman what it is to ride in the midst of a troop of gigantic giraffes: it must be experienced to be understood. They emitted a powerful perfume, which in the chase came hot in my face, reminding me of the smell of a hive of heather honey in September.

Another astonishing sight much remarked on by the hunters was the migration of the springbok, 'pouring down like locusts from the endless plains of the interior', as Cornwallis Harris put it. Here the phenomenon is described by Gordon Cumming.

The springbok is so termed by the colonists on account of its peculiar habit of springing or taking extraordinary bounds, rising to an incredible height in the air, when pursued; the extraordinary manner in which they are capable of springing is best seen when they are chased by a dog. On these occasions away start the herd, with a succession of strange perpendicular bounds, rising with curved loins high into the air, and at the same time elevating the snowy folds of long white hair on their haunches and along their back, which imparts to them a peculiar fairy-like appearance, different from any other animal. They bound to the height of ten or twelve feet, with the elasticity of an india-rubber ball, clearing at each spring from twelve to fifteen feet of ground, without apparently the slightest exertion. In performing this spring they appear for an instant as if suspended in the air, when down come all four feet again together, and, striking the plain, away they soar again, as if about to take flight. The herd only adopt this motion for a few hundred yards, when they subside into a light elastic trot, arching their graceful necks and lowering their noses to the ground, as if in sportive mood; presently rolling up, they face about, and reconnoitre the object of their alarm. In crossing any path or waggon-road on which men have lately trod, the springbok invariably clears it by a single bound and when a herd of, perhaps, many thousands have to cross a track of the sort, it is extremely beautiful to see how each antelope performs the surprising feat, so suspicious are they of the ground on which their enemy, man, has trodden. They bound in a similar manner when passing to leeward of a lion, or any other animal of which they entertain an instinctive dread.

The accumulated masses of living creatures which the springboks exhibit on the greater migrations is utterly astounding, and any traveller witnessing it as I have, and giving a true description of what he had seen, can hardly expect to be believed, so marvellous is the scene. They have been well and truly compared to the wasting swarms of locusts, so familiar to the traveller in this land of wonders. Like them they consume everything green in their course, laying waste vast districts in a few hours, and ruining in a single night the fruits of a farmer's toil. The course adopted by the antelopes is generally such as to bring them back to their own country by a route different from that by which they set out. Thus their line of march frequently forms something like a vast oval, or an extensive square, of which the diameter may be some hundred miles, and the time occupied in this migration may vary from six months to a year.

Fifty years later, WC Scully (26) witnessed one of the animals' last migrations. In 1892, he was the resident magistrate at Okiep – by his account, a god-forsaken town – in Namaqualand. When he could, he headed for 'the cleansing fires' of Bushmanland in the Northern Cape.

It was my fortune then to witness about the last great 'trek', as the annual migration of springbuck from east to west across the desert is termed. The number of buck involved in such a phenomenon varied according to circumstances. The amount of rain that may have fallen in the central plains is one of the determining factors in this respect. There can never again be a trek on such a large scale. Fencing, the increase of population and the general distribution of arms of precision among people have almost exterminated that hapless, at one time innumerable, host for whose use, if there be any such thing as design in creation, the Great Bushmanland Desert must have been made.

The idea underlying the trek seems to have puzzled hunters and naturalists from time immemorial. To me the explanation is simple and obvious. In summer a certain amount of rain falls in Bushmanland, but in winter that tract is absolutely rainless. It is bounded on the west by a range of granite mountains which spring from sandy plains. Here no summer rains fall, but in early winter the south-west wind brings soaking showers and the sandy plains lying among the mountains become clothed for a few weeks with rich, succulent vegetation. This occurs at the season when the springbuck fawns are born and when, consequently, the does require green food. Hence the westward trek, which is, I believe, of hoar ancient origin.

A view of the trek when at its height was an experience not to be forgotten. It would be fruitless to attempt an adequate description of it. In dealing with myriads, numbers cease to have any significance. One might as well endeavour to describe the mass of a mile-long sand-dune by expressing the sum of its grains in ciphers, as to attempt to give the numbers of antelopes forming the living wave that surged across the desert in 1892 and broke like foam against the western granite range. I have stood on an eminence some twenty feet high, far out on the plains, and seen the absolutely level surface, as wide as the eye could reach, covered with resting springbuck, whilst from over the eastern horizon the rising columns of dust told of fresh hosts advancing.

I had to issue a hundred rifles and many thousands of cartridges from the Government store to the farmers to enable them to protect their crops. The farmers used to bring back carcasses by the waggonload to their wives, by whom the meat would be made into biltong. Over and over again the waggon would go out from the same farmhouse, always, while the trek lasted, returning with a full load.

After the wave had receded, the western margin of Bushmanland was like a ploughed field; all the grass roots, all the shrubs, were lying loose on the surface, beaten out by the hoofs. At many points the invading host broke through the line of defence and overran the cultivated fields. One hapless springbuck was shot in the graveyard at O'okiep, of all places in the world.

The trek ended more suddenly than it began. In a single night the springbuck totally disappeared.

Elephants, given the value of their tusks, were inevitably a prime target for the early white hunters. Gordon Cumming boasted of killing 100. Cornwallis Harris had his first sight of them in 1837 in the Magaliesberg Mountains, west of present-day Pretoria.

Leaving the waggons to proceed to a spot agreed upon, we again took the field about ten o'clock, and pursued the track indefatigably for eight miles, over a country presenting every variety of feature. At one time we crossed bare stony ridges, at another threaded the intricacies of shady but dilapidated forests; now struggled through high fields of waving grass, and again emerged into open downs. At length we arrived amongst extensive groups of grassy hillocks, covered with loose stones, interspersed with streams, and occasional patches of forest in which the recent ravages of Elephants were surprising. Here to our inexpressible gratification we descried a large herd of those long sought animals, lazily browsing at the head of a distant valley, our attention having been first directed to it, by the strong and not to be mistaken effluvia with which the wind was impregnated. Never having before seen the noble Elephant in his native jungles, we gazed on the sight before us with intense and indescribable interest. Our feelings on the occasion even extended to our followers. As for Andries he became so agitated that he could scarcely articulate. With open eyes and quivering lips he at length stuttered forth *'Dar stand de Oliphant.'* Mohanycom and 'Lingap were immediately despatched to drive the herd back into the valley, up which we rode slowly and without noise, against the wind; and arriving within one hundred and fifty yards unperceived, we made our horses fast, and took up a commanding position in an old stone kraal. The shouting of the savages, who now appeared on the height rattling their shields, caused the huge animals to move unsuspiciously towards us, and even within ten yards of our ambush. The group consisted of nine, all females with large tusks. We selected the finest, and with perfect deliberation fired a volley of five balls into her. She stumbled, but recovering herself, uttered a shrill note of lamentation, when the whole party threw their trunks above their heads, and instantly clambered up the adjacent hill with incredible celerity, their huge fan-like ears, flapping in the ratio of their speed. We instantly mounted our horses, and the sharp loose stones not suiting the feet of the wounded lady, soon closed with her. Streaming with blood, and infuriated with rage, she turned upon us with uplifted trunk, and it was not until after repeated discharges, that a ball took effect in her brain, and threw her lifeless on the earth, which resounded with the fall.

Turning our attention from the exciting scene I have described, we found that a second valley had opened upon us, surrounded by bare stony hills, and traversed by a thinly wooded ravine. Here a grand and magnificent panorama was before us, which beggars all description. The whole face of the landscape was actually covered with wild Elephants. There could not have been fewer than three hundred within the scope of our vision. Every height and green knoll was dotted over with groups of them, whilst the bottom of the glen exhibited a dense and sable living mass – their colossal forms being at one moment partially concealed by the trees which they were disfiguring with giant strength; and at others seen majestically emerging into the open glades, bearing in their trunks the branches of trees with which they indolently protected themselves from the flies. The back ground was filled by a limited peep of the blue mountainous range, which here assumed a remarkably precipitous character, and completed a picture at once soul-stirring and sublime!

Those averse to killing animals for pleasure will be struck by the moral and aesthetic confusion in all this. Cornwallis Harris – despite noting the tears trickling from a 'magnificent' giraffe's eye – seemed, at best, only dimly aware of it. Consider, for example, the contrast he draws in this account of a typical day's hunting between his own actions and those of the 'savages' who accompanied him.

We soon perceived large herds of Quaggas and Brindled Gnoos, which continued to join each other until the whole plain seemed alive. The clatter of their hoofs was perfectly astounding, and I could compare it to nothing, but to the din of a tremendous charge of cavalry, or the rushing of a mighty tempest. I could not estimate the accumulated numbers, at less than fifteen thousand; a great extent of country being actually chequered black and white with their congregated masses. As the panic caused by the report of our rifles, extended, clouds of dust hovered over them; and the long necks of troops of ostriches were also to be seen, towering above the heads of their less gigantic neighbours, and sailing past with astonishing rapidity. Groups of purple Sassaybys, and brilliant red and yellow Hartebeests, likewise lent their aid to complete the picture, which must have been seen to be properly understood, and which beggars all attempt at description. The savages kept in our wake, dexterously despatching the wounded Gnoos by a touch on the spine with the point of an assagai, and instantly covering up the carcases with bushes, to secure them from the voracity of the vultures, which hung about us like specks in the firmament, and descended with the velocity of lightning, as each discharge of our artillery gave token of prey. As we proceeded, two strange figures were perceived standing under the shade of a tree; these we instantly knew to be Elands, the savages at the same moment exclaiming with evident delight, *Impoofo, Impoofo,* and pressing our horses to the utmost speed, we found ourselves for the first time, at the heels of the largest and most beautiful species of the antelope tribe. Notwithstanding the unweildy shape of these animals, they had at first greatly the speed of our jaded horses, but being pushed, they soon separated; their sleek coats turned first blue and then white with froth; the foam fell from their mouths and nostrils, and the perspiration from their sides. Their pace gradually slackened, and with their full brilliant eyes turned imploringly towards us, at the end of a mile, each was laid low by a single ball. They were young bulls, measuring upwards of seventeen hands at the shoulder.

I was engaged in making a sketch of the one I had shot, when the savages came up, and in spite of all my remonstrances, proceeded with cold blooded ferocity to stab the unfortunate animal, stirring up the blood and shouting with barbarous exultation, as it issued from each newly inflicted wound, regardless of the eloquent and piteous appeal, expressed in the beautiful clear black eye of the mild and inoffensive Eland.

In 1850, only 13 years later, Thomas Baines, the artist and explorer, stood on the banks of the Vaal River, 'the classic ground of the late adventurous traveller, Captain Harris', and wondered: 'Where now, alas, are the unbounded herds portrayed by his equally spirited pen and pencil? All, or nearly all, are now destroyed by the unsparing Boers; the stately eland no longer browses beneath the shady thorn, nor the tall giraffe crops its topmost foliage; the mighty rhinoceros is slain; the giant elephant destroyed; and the broad river, though strong, yet clear, reflects the brightest stars and the moon, now rising in all her loveliness, on its placid surface, unruffled by the shapeless bulk of the sea cow rising for breath.'

In fact, Baines rather exaggerated the dearth. Ten years later, he was present at the most grotesque hunt South Africa had ever seen. The occasion was the state visit of Queen Victoria's second son, 16-year-old Prince Alfred. For his entertainment, an estimated 30 000 animals – predominantly buck – were rounded up by 1 000 Africans on horseback and driven across the plains into a valley near Bloemfontein. There the Prince and his party effortlessly slaughtered hundreds.

Other hunters in search of abundant game kept pressing north, among them Roualeyn Gordon Cumming, who had vowed to 'penetrate into the interior farther than the foot of civilised man has yet trodden'. On the banks of the Limpopo in a single afternoon in June 1847, he shot three crocodiles, discovered a 'troop of five or six beautiful leopards', 'came suddenly upon a lion and lioness lying in the grass, and took a couple of shots at the lion, missing him with my first but wounding him with the second barrel', and shot a hippopotamus, 'putting three balls into his head, when he sank, but night setting in, we lost him'. At dawn the next day, he watched a herd of buffalo crossing the Limpopo and then stalked 'an antelope of the most exquisite beauty, utterly unknown to sportsmen or naturalists'. Having shot this 'princely old buck' – 'the ball had cut the skin open along his ribs, and, entering his body, passed along his neck and lodged in his brains' – he modestly christened it *Antelopus Roualeynei*'. As *The Quarterly Review* remarked when the first edition of his *Five Years' Adventures* appeared in 1850: 'The endless and too often useless slaughter of God's creatures will be revolting to most minds'. The book did, though, enjoy enormous popularity, not least for passages such as this on the 'mighty and terrible king of beasts'. It is March 1846.

The night of the 19th was to me rather a memorable one, as being the first on which I had the satisfaction of hearing the deep-toned thunder of the lion's roar. Although there was no one near to inform me by what beast the haughty and impressive sounds which echoed through the wilderness were produced, I had little difficulty in divining. There was no mistake about it; and on hearing it I at once knew, as well as if accustomed to the sound from my infancy, that the appalling roar which was uttered within half a mile of me was no other than that of the mighty and terrible king of beasts. Although the dignified and truly monarchical appearance of the lion has long rendered him famous among his fellow quadrupeds, and his appearance and habits have often been described by abler pens than mine, nevertheless I consider that a few remarks, resulting from my personal experience, formed by a tolerably long acquaintance with him both by day and by night, may not prove uninteresting to the reader. There is something so noble and imposing in the presence of the lion, when seen walking with dignified self-possession, free and undaunted, on his native soil, that no description can convey an adequate idea of his striking appearance. The lion is exquisitely formed by nature for the predatory habits which he is destined to pursue. Combining in comparatively small compass the qualities of power and agility, he is enabled, by means of the tremendous machinery with which nature has gifted him, easily to overcome and destroy almost every beast of the forest, however superior to him in weight and stature.

Though considerably under four feet in height, he has little difficulty in dashing to the ground and overcoming the lofty and apparently powerful giraffe, whose head towers above the trees of the forest, and whose skin is nearly an inch in thickness. The lion is the constant attendant of the vast herds of buffaloes which frequent the interminable forests of the interior; and a full-grown one, so long as his teeth are unbroken, generally proves a match for an old bull buffalo, which in size and strength greatly surpasses the most powerful breed of English cattle: the lion also preys on all the larger varieties of the antelopes, and on both varieties of the gnoo [...]

One of the most striking things connected with the lion is his voice, which is extremely grand and peculiarly striking. It consists at times of a low, deep moaning, repeated five or six times, ending in faintly audible sighs; at other times he startles the forest with loud, deep-toned, solemn roars, repeated five or six times in quick succession, each increasing in loudness to the third or fourth, when his voice dies away in five or six low, muffled sounds, very much resembling distant thunder. At times, and not unfrequently, a troop may be heard roaring in concert, one assuming the lead, and two, three, or four more regularly taking up their parts, like persons singing a catch. Like our Scottish stags at the rutting season, they roar loudest in cold, frosty nights; but on no occasions are their voices to be heard in such perfection, or so intensely powerful, as when two or three strange troops of lions approach a fountain to drink at the same time. When this occurs, every member of each troop sounds a bold roar of defiance at the opposite parties; and when one roars, all roar together, and each seems to vie with his comrades in the intensity and power of his voice. The power and grandeur of these nocturnal forest concerts is inconceivably striking and pleasing to the hunter's ear. The effect, I may remark, is greatly enhanced when the hearer happens to be situated in the depths of the forest, at the dead hour of midnight, unaccompanied by any attendant, and ensconced within twenty yards of the fountain which the surrounding troops of lions are approaching. Such has been my situation many scores of times; and though I am allowed to have a tolerably good taste for music, I consider the catches with which I was then regaled as the sweetest and most natural I ever heard [...]

At no time is the lion so much to be dreaded as when his partner has got small young ones. At that season he knows no fear, and, in the coolest and most intrepid manner, he will face a thousand men. A remarkable instance of this kind came under my own observation, which confirmed the reports I had before heard from the natives. One day, when out elephant-hunting in the territory of the 'Baseleka,' accompanied by two hundred and fifty men, I was astonished suddenly to behold a majestic lion slowly and steadily advancing toward us with a dignified step and undaunted bearing, the most noble and imposing that can be conceived. Lashing his tail from side to side, and growling haughtily, his terribly expressive eye resolutely fixed upon us, and displaying a show of ivory well calculated to inspire terror among the timid 'Bechuanas,' he approached. A headlong flight of the two hundred and fifty men was the immediate result; and, in the confusion of the moment, four couples of my dogs, which had been leading, were allowed to escape in their couples. These instantly faced the lion, who, finding that by his bold bearing he had succeeded in putting his enemies to flight, now became solicitous for the safety of his little family, with which the lioness was retreating in the back-ground. Facing about, he followed after them with a haughty and independent step, growling fiercely at the dogs which trotted along on either side of him. Three troops of elephants having been discovered a few minutes previous to this, upon which I was marching for the attack, I, with the most heartfelt reluctance, reserved my fire. On running down the hill side to endeavour to recall my dogs, I observed, for the first time, the retreating lioness with four cubs. About twenty minutes afterward two noble elephants repaid my forbearance [...]

In winding up these few observations on the lion, which I trust will not have been tiresome to the reader, I may remark that lion-hunting, under any circumstances, is decidedly a dangerous pursuit. It may nevertheless be followed, to a certain extent, with comparative safety by those who have naturally a turn for that sort of thing. A recklessness of death, perfect coolness and self-possession, an acquaintance with the disposition and manners of lions, and a tolerable knowledge of the use of the rifle, are indispensable to him who would shine in the overpoweringly exciting pastime of hunting this justly celebrated king of beasts.

Agog though Victorian readers may have been, David Livingstone, who for five successive years played host to Gordon Cumming at his mission station near the present-day border with Botswana, was less impressed. 'To talk of the majestic roar of the lion is mere majestic twaddle,' he observed sniffily. 'The silly ostrich makes a noise as loud, yet he never was feared by man.' Indeed, one was 'in much more danger of being run over when walking in the streets of London than of being devoured by lions in Africa'. In fact, though, Livingstone himself was very nearly devoured by a lion near the mission station in 1844. 'I have great cause for thankfulness that I escaped with my life,' he wrote at the time. 'He shook me as a cat does a mouse, and had the mercy of the Lord not prevented could easily have torn me to pieces.'

Perhaps Thomas Pringle's poem 'Afar in the Desert' (27) best, or at least most charitably, captures the hunters' roaming spirit – not, though, that he approved of hunting. Coleridge thought it 'among the two or three most perfect lyrics in our language'. It was first published in 1824.

Afar in the Desert

Afar in the Desert I love to ride,
With the silent Bush-boy alone by my side:
When the sorrows of life the soul o'ercast,
And, sick of the Present, I cling to the Past;
When the eye is suffused with regretful tears,
From the fond recollections of former years;
And shadows of things that have long since fled
Flit over the brain, like the ghosts of the dead:
Bright visions of glory – that vanish too soon;
Day-dreams – that departed ere manhood's noon;
Attachments – by fate or by falsehood reft;
Companions of early days – lost or left;
And my Native Land – whose magical name
Thrills to the heart like electric flame;
The home of my childhood; the haunts of my prime;
All the passions and scenes of that rapturous time
When the feelings were young and the world was new,
Like the fresh bowers of Eden unfolding to view;
All – all now forsaken – forgotten – foregone!
And I – a lone exile remembered of none –
My high aims abandoned – my good acts undone –
– Aweary of all that is under the sun –
With that sadness of heart which no stranger may scan,
I fly to the Desert afar from man!

Afar in the Desert I love to ride,
With the silent Bush-boy alone by my side:
When the wild turmoil of this wearisome life,

With its scenes of oppression, corruption, and strife –
The proud man's frown, and the base man's fear,
The scorner's laugh, and the sufferer's tear –
And malice, and meanness, and falsehood, and folly,
Dispose me to musing and dark melancholy;
When my bosom is full, and my thoughts are high,
And my soul is sick with the bondman's sigh –
Oh! then there is freedom, and joy, and pride,
Afar in the Desert alone to ride!
There is rapture to vault on the champing steed,
And to bound away with the eagle's speed,
With the death-fraught firelock in my hand –
The only law of the Desert Land!

Afar in the Desert I love to ride,
With the silent Bush-boy alone by my side:
Away – away from the dwellings of men,
By the wild deer's haunt, by the buffalo's glen;
By valleys remote where the oribi plays,
Where the gnu, the gazelle, and the hartèbeest graze,
And the kùdù and eland unhunted recline
By the skirts of grey forests o'erhung with wild-vine;
Where the elephant browses at peace in his wood,
And the river-horse gambols unscared in the flood,
And the mighty rhinoceros wallows at will
In the fen where the wild-ass is drinking his fill.

Afar in the Desert I love to ride,
With the silent Bush-boy alone by my side:
O'er the brown Karroo, where the bleating cry
Of the springbok's fawn sounds plaintively;
And the timorous quagga's shrill whistling neigh
Is heard by the fountain at twilight grey;
Where the zebra wantonly tosses his mane,
With wild hoof scouring the desolate plain;
And the fleet-footed ostrich over the waste
Speeds like a horseman who travels in haste,

Hying away to the home of her rest,
Where she and her mate have scooped their nest,
Far hid from the pitiless plunderer's view
In the pathless depths of the parched Karroo.

Afar in the Desert I love to ride,
With the silent Bush-boy alone by my side:
Away – away in the Wilderness vast,
Where the White Man's foot hath never passed,
And the quivered Coránna or Bechuán
Hath rarely crossed with his roving clan:
A region of emptiness, howling and drear,
Which Man hath abandoned from famine and fear;
Which the snake and the lizard inhabit alone,
With the twilight bat from the yawning stone;
Where grass, nor herb, nor shrub takes root,
Save poisonous thorns that pierce the foot;
And the bitter-melon, for food and drink,
Is the pilgrim's fare by the salt lake's brink:
A region of drought, where no river glides,
Nor rippling brook with osiered sides;
Where sedgy pool, nor bubbling fount,
Nor tree, nor cloud, nor misty mount,
Appears, to refresh the aching eye:
But the barren earth, and the burning sky,
And the black horizon, round and round,
Spread – void of living sight or sound.

And here, while the night-winds round me sigh,
And the stars burn bright in the midnight sky,
As I sit apart by the desert stone,
Like Elijah at Horeb's cave alone,
'A still small voice' comes through the wild
(Like a Father consoling his fretful Child),
Which banishes bitterness, wrath, and fear,
Saying – MAN IS DISTANT, BUT GOD IS NEAR!

Pringle's reference to ostriches hiding their nest 'from the pitiless plunderer's view' recalls another of Gordon Cumming's observations.

In the evening two of the Hottentots walked in to camp, bending under a burden of ostrich-eggs, having discovered a nest containing five-and-thirty. Their manner of carrying them amused me. Having divested themselves of their leather 'crackers,' which in colonial phrase means trousers, they had secured the ankles with rheimpys,[4] and, having thus converted them into bags, had crammed them with as many ostrich-eggs as they would contain; the remainder they left concealed in the sand, for which they returned on the following morning. While encamped at this vley[5] we fell in with several nests of ostriches, and here I first ascertained a singular propensity peculiar to these birds. If a person discovers a nest, and does not at once remove the eggs, on returning he will probably find them all smashed; the old birds almost invariably destroy them, even when the intruder has not handled the eggs or so much as ridden within five yards of them. The nest of the os-trich is merely a hollow scooped in the sandy soil, generally amongst heath or other low bushes, and in diameter about seven feet; it is believed that two hens often lay in one nest – the hatching of the eggs is not left, as is generally believed, to the heat of the sun, but, on the contrary, the cock relieves the hen in the incubation. These eggs form a considerable item in the Bushman's cuisine, and the shells are converted into water-flasks, cups, and dishes. I have often seen Bush-girls and Bakalahari women, who belong to the wandering Bechuana tribes of the Kalahari desert, come down to the fountain from their remote habitations, each carrying on her back a kaross or network containing from twelve to fifteen ostrich-egg shells, which had been emptied by a small aperture at one end: these they fill with water and cork up the hole with grass.

A favourite method adopted by the wild Bushman for approaching the ostrich and other varieties of game is to clothe himself in the skin of one of these birds, in which, taking advantage of the wind, he stalks about the plain, cunningly imitating the gait and motions of the ostrich until within range, when, with a well-directed poisoned arrow from his tiny bow, he can generally seal the fate of any of the ordinary varieties of game. These insig-nificant-looking weapons are about two feet six inches in length; they consist of a slender reed, with a sharp bone head, thoroughly poisoned with a com-position of which the principal ingredients are obtained sometimes from a succulent herb, having thick leaves, which yield a poisonous milky juice, and sometimes from the jaws of snakes. The bow barely exceeds three feet in length; its string is of twisted sinews. When a Bushman finds an ostrich's nest he ensconces himself in it, and there awaits the return of the old birds, by which means he generally secures the pair. It is by means of these little arrows that the majority of the fine plumes are obtained which on state occasions grace the heads of the fair throughout the civilised world.

Europe's demand for the ostrich's fine plumes was soon to stimulate a farming industry that by the early 1880s was producing South Africa's third most valuable export after wool and diamonds. The market crashed during the First World War. Travellers such as William Burchell were far more interested in the eggs, each weighing about 3lbs. Here he describes how best to cook one.

We made our dinner from the ostrich-eggs; each of the Hottentots eating whole one, although containing as much food as twenty-four eggs of the domestic hen. It is therefore not surprising that I found myself unable to accomplish my share of the meal; even with the aid of all the hunger which a long morning's ride had given me. The mode in which they were cooked, was one of great antiquity; for all the Hottentot race, their fathers, and their grandfathers' fathers, as they express themselves, have practised it before them. A small hole the size of a finger was very dextrously made at one end, and having cut a forked stick from the bushes, they introduced it into the egg by pressing the two prongs close together; then by twirling the end of the stick between the palms of their hands for a short time, they completely mixed the white and the yolk together. Setting it upon the fire, they continued frequently to turn the stick, until the inside had acquired the proper consistence of a boiled egg. This method recommends itself to a traveller, by its expedition, cleanliness, and simplicity; and by requiring neither pot, nor water, the shell answering perfectly the purpose of the first, and the liquid nature of its contents, that of the other.

For the most literate celebration of hunting – as well as for an introduction to the 'warlike Zulus', of whom we shall hear more later – we turn to *Jock of the Bushveld* (28), Percy FitzPatrick's 1907 classic tale of a man and his dog, set for the most part in what is now the Kruger National Park. They are in search of impala.

We had gone out after breakfast, striking well away from the main road until we got among the thicker thorns where there was any amount of fresh spoor and we were quite certain to find a troop sooner or later. The day was so still, the ground so dry, and the bush so thick that the chances were the game would hear us before we could get near enough to see them. Several times I heard sounds of rustling bush or feet cantering away: something had heard us and made off unseen; so I dropped down into the sandy bed of a dry donga and used it as a stalking trench. From this it was easy enough to have a good look around every hundred yards or so without risk of being heard or seen. We had been going along cautiously in this way for some time when, peering over the bank, I spied a single impala half hidden by a scraggy bush. It seemed queer that there should be only one, as their habit is to move in troops; but there was nothing else to be seen; indeed it was only the flicker of an ear on this one that had caught my eye. Nothing else in the land moved.

Jock climbed the bank also, following so closely that he bumped against my heels, and when I lay flat actually crawled over my legs to get up beside me and see what was on. Little by little he got into the way of imitating all I did, so that after a while it was hardly necessary to say a word or make a sign to him. He lay down beside me and raised his head to look just as he saw me do. He was all excitement, trembling like a wet spaniel on a cold day, and instead of looking steadily at the impala as I was doing and as he usually did, he was looking here there and everywhere; it seemed almost as if he was looking at things not for them. It was my comfortable belief at the moment that he had not yet spotted the buck, but was looking about anxiously to find out what was interesting me. It turned out, as usual, that he had seen a great deal more than his master had.

The stalking looked very easy, as a few yards further up the donga there was excellent cover in some dense thorns, behind which we could walk bold-ly across open ground to within easy range of the buck and get a clear shot. We reached the cover all right, but I had not taken three steps into the open space beyond before there was a rushing and scrambling on every side of me. The place was a whirlpool of racing and plunging impala; they came from every side and went in every direction as though caught suddenly in an enclosure and, mad with fear and bewilderment, were trying to find a way out. How many there were it was quite impossible to say: the bush was alive with them; and the dust they kicked up, the noise of their feet, their curious sneezy snorts, and their wild confusion completely bewildered me. Not one stood still. Never for a moment could I see any single animal clearly enough or long enough to fire at it; another would cross it; a bush would cover it as I aimed; or it would leap into the air, clearing bushes, bucks and everything in its way, and disappear again in the moving mass. They seemed to me to whirl like leaves in a wind eddy: my eyes could not follow them and my brain swam as I looked.

It was a hot day; there was no breeze at all; and probably the herd had been resting after their morning feed and drink when we came upon them. By creeping up along the donga we had managed to get unobserved right into the middle of the dozing herd, so they were literally on every side of us. At times it looked as if they were bound to stampede over us and simply trample us down in their numbers; for in their panic they saw nothing, and not one appeared to know what or where the danger was. Time and again, as for part of a second I singled one out and tried to aim, others would come racing straight for us, compelling me to switch round to face them, only to find them swerve with a dart or a mighty bound when within a few paces of me.

What Jock was doing during that time I do not know. It was all such a whirl of excitement and confusion that there are only a few clear impressions left on my mind. One is of a buck coming through the air right at me, jumping over the backs of two others racing across my front. I can see now the sudden wriggle of its body and the look of terror in its eyes when it saw me and realised that it was going to land almost at my feet. I tried to jump aside, but it was not necessary: with one touch on the ground it shot slantingly past me like a ricochet bullet. Another picture that always comes back is that of a splendid ram clearing the first of the dense thorn bushes that were to have been my cover in stalking. He flew over it outlined against the sky in the easiest, most graceful and most perfect curve imaginable. It came back to me afterwards that he was eight or ten yards from me, and yet I had to look up into the sky to see his white chest and gracefully gathered feet as he cleared the thorn bush like a soaring bird.

One shot, out of three or four fired in desperation as they were melting away, hit something; the un-mistakable thud of the bullet told me so. That time it was the real thing, and when you hear the real thing you cannot mistake it. The wounded animal went off with the rest and I followed, with Jock ahead of me hot on the trail. A hundred yards further on where Jock with his nose to the ground had raced along between some low stones and a marula tree I came to a stop – bush all round me, not a living thing in sight, and all as silent as the grave. On one of the smooth hot stones there was a big drop of blood, and a few yards on I found a couple more. Here and there along the spoor there were smears on the long yellow grass, and it was clear enough, judging by the height of the blood-marks from the ground, that the impala was wounded in the body – probably far back, as there were no frothy bubbles to show a lung shot. I knew that it would be a long chase unless Jock could head the buck off and bay it; but unless he could do this at once, he was so silent in his work that there was little chance of finding him. The trail became more and more difficult to follow; the blood was less frequent, and the hot sun dried it so quickly that it was more than I could do to pick it out from the red streaks on the grass and many coloured leaves. So I gave it up and sat down to smoke and wait.

Half an hour passed, and still no Jock. Then I wandered about whistling and calling for him – calling until the sound of my own voice became quite uncanny, the only sound in an immense silence. Two hours passed in useless calling and listening, searching and waiting, and then I gave it up altogether and made back for the waggons, trying to hope against my real conviction that Jock had struck the road somewhere and had followed it to the outspan, instead of coming back on his own trail through the bush to me.

But there was no Jock at the waggons; and my heart sank, although I was not surprised. It was nearly four hours since he had disappeared, and it was as sure as anything could be that something extra-ordinary must have happened or he would have come back to me long before this. No one at the waggons had seen him since we started out together; and there was nothing to be done but to wait and see what would happen. It was perfectly useless to look for him: if alive and well, he was better able to find his way than the best tracker that ever lived; if dead or injured and unable to move, there was not one chance in a million of finding him.

There was only one kaffir whom Jock would take any notice of or would allow to touch him – a great big Zulu named Jim Makokel'. Jim was one of the real fighting Zulu breed; and the pride he took in Jock, and the sort of partnership that he claimed in tastes, disposition and exploits, began the day Jock fought the table-leg and grew stronger and stronger to the end. Jim became Jock's devoted champion, and more than once, as will be seen, showed that he would face man or beast to stand by him when he needed help.

This day when I returned to the waggons Jim was sitting with the other drivers in the group round the big pot of porridge. I saw him give one quick look my way and heard him say sharply to the others, 'Where is the dog? Where is Jock?' He stood there looking at me with a big wooden spoon full of porridge stopped on the way to his mouth. In a few minutes they all knew what had happened; the other boys took it calmly, saying composedly that the dog would find his way back. But Jim was not calm: it was not his nature. At one moment he would agree with them, swamping them with a flood of reasons why Jock, the best dog in the world, would be sure to come back; and the next – hot with restless excitement – would picture all that the dog might have been doing and all that he might still have to face, and then break off to proclaim loudly that every one ought to go out and hunt for him. Jim was not practical or reasonable – he was too excitable for that; but he was very loyal, and it was his way to show his feelings by doing something generally and preferably by fighting some one. Knowing only too well how useless it would be to search for Jock, I lay down under the waggon to rest and wait.

After half an hour of this Jim could restrain himself no longer. He came over to where I lay and with a look of severe disapproval and barely control-led indignation, asked me for a gun, saying that he himself meant to go out and look for Jock. It would be nearer the mark to say that he demanded a gun. He was so genuinely anxious and so indignant at what he considered my indifference that it was impossible to be angry; and I let him talk away to me and at me in his exciting bullying way. He would take no answer and listen to no reason; so finally to keep him quiet I gave him the shot-gun, and off he went, muttering his opinions of every one else – a great springy strid-ing picture of fierce resolution.

He came back nearly three hours later, silent, morose, hot and dusty. He put the gun down beside me without a word – just a click of disgust; and as he strode across to his waggon, called roughly to one of the drivers for the drinking water. Lifting the bucket to his mouth he drank like an ox and slammed it down again without a word of thanks; then sat down in the shade of the waggon, filled his pipe, and smoked in silence.

The trekking hour came and passed; but we did not move. The sun went down, and in the quiet of the evening we heard the first jackal's yapping –

the first warning of the night. There were still lions and tigers in those parts, and any number of hyenas and wild dogs, and the darker it grew and the more I thought of it, the more hopeless seemed Jock's chance of getting through a night in the bush trying to work his way back to the waggons.

It was almost dark when I was startled by a yell from Jim Makokel', and looking round, saw him bound out into the road shouting, 'He has come, he has come! What did I tell you?' He ran out to Jock, stooping to pat and talk to him, and then in a lower voice and with growing excitement went on rapidly, 'See the blood! See it! He has fought: he has killed! Dog of all dogs! Jock, Jock!' and his savage song of triumph broke off in a burst of rough tenderness, and he called the dog's name five or six times with every note of affection and welcome in his deep voice. Jock took no notice of Jim's dancing out to meet him, nor of his shouts, endearments and antics; slowing his tired trot down to a walk, he came straight on to me, flickered his ears a bit, wagged his tail cordially, and gave my hand a splashy lick as I patted him. Then he turned round in the direction he had just come from, looked steadily out, cocked his ears well up, and moved his tail slowly from side to side. For the next half-hour or so he kept repeating this action every few minutes; but even without that I knew that it had been no wild-goose chase, and that miles away in the bush there was something lying dead which he could show me if I would but follow him back again to see.

What had happened in the eight hours since he dashed off in pursuit can only be guessed. That he had pulled down the impala and killed it seemed certain – and what a chase and what a fight it must have been to take all that time! The buck could not have been so badly wounded in the body as to be disabled or it would have died in far less time than that: then, what a fight it must have been to kill an animal six or eight times his own weight and armed with such horns and hoofs! But was it only the impala? or had the hyenas and wild dogs followed up the trail, as they so often do, and did Jock have to fight his way through them too?

He was hollow-flanked and empty, parched with thirst, and so blown that his breath still caught in suffocating chokes. He was covered with blood and sand; his beautiful golden coat was dark and stained; his white front had disappeared; and there on his chest and throat, on his jaws and ears, down his front legs even to the toes, the blood was caked on him mostly black and dried but some still red and sticky. He was a little lame in one fore-leg, but there was no cut or swelling to show the cause. There was only one mark to be seen: over his right eye there was a bluish line where the hair had been shaved off clean, leaving the skin smooth and unbroken. What did it? Was it horn, hoof, tooth, or – what? Only Jock knew.

Hovering round and over me, pacing backwards and forwards between the waggons like a caged animal, Jim, growing more and more excited, filled the air with his talk his shouts and savage song. Wanting to help, but always in the way, ordering and thrusting the other boys here and there, he worked himself up into a wild frenzy: it was the Zulu fighting blood on fire and he 'saw red' everywhere.

I called for water. 'Water!' roared Jim, 'bring water'; and glaring round he made a spring – stick in hand – at the nearest kaffir. The boy fled in terror, with Jim after him for a few paces, and brought a bucket of water. Jim snatched it from him and with a resounding thump on the ribs sent the unlucky kaffir sprawling on the ground. Jock took the water in great gulpy bites broken by pauses to get his breath again; and Jim paced up and down – talking, talking, talking! Talking to me, to the others, to the kaffirs, to Jock, to the world at large, to the heavens, and to the dead. His eyes glared like a wild beast's and gradually little seams of froth gathered in the corners of his mouth as he poured out his cataract of words, telling of all Jock had done and might have done and would yet do; comparing him with the fighting heroes of his own race, and wandering off into vivid recitals of single episodes and great battles; seizing his sticks, shouting his war cries, and going through all the mimicry of fight with the wild frenzy of one possessed. Time after time I called him and tried to quiet him; but he was beyond control.

Once before he had broken out like this. I had asked him something about the Zulu war; and that had started a flood of memories and excitement. In the midst of some description I asked why they killed the children[6]; and he turned his glaring eyes on me and said, 'Inkos, you are my Inkos; but you are white. If we fight tomorrow, I will kill you. You are good to me, you have saved me; but if our own king says "Kill!" we kill! We see red; we kill all that lives. I must kill you, your wife, your mother, your children, your horses, your oxen, your dog, the fowls that run with the wagons – all that lives I kill. The blood must run.' And I believed him; for that was the Zulu fighting spirit. So this time I knew it was useless to order or to talk: he was beyond control, and the fit must run its course.

The night closed in and there was quiet once more. The flames of the camp fires had died down; the big thorn logs had burnt into glowing coals like the pink crisp hearts of giant water-melons; Jock lay sleeping, tired out, but even in his sleep came little spells of panting now and then, like the after-sobs of a child that has cried itself to sleep; we lay rolled in our blankets, and no sound came from where the kaffirs slept. But Jim – only Jim – sat on his rough three-legged stool, elbows on knees and hands clasped together, staring intently into the coals. The fit worked slowly off, and his excitement died gradually away; now and then there was a fresh burst, but always milder and at longer intervals, as you may see it in a dying fire or at the end of a great storm; slowly but surely he subsided until at last there were only occasional mutterings of 'Ow, Jock!' followed by the Zulu click, the expressive shake of the head, and that appreciative half grunt, half chuckle, by which they pay tribute to what seems truly wonderful. He wanted no sleep that night: he sat on, waiting for the morning trek, staring into the red coals, and thinking of the bygone glories of his race in the days of the mighty Chaka.

That was Jim, when the fit was on him – transported by some trifling and unforeseen incident from the hum-drum of the road to the life he once had lived with splendid recklessness.

It was not until the 1920s that people began to take pleasure in looking at animals in the bushveld without wanting to kill them. That they were able to do so was almost entirely due to the energy and persistence of James Stevenson-Hamilton, a British Army officer who fought in the Boer War. In 1902, when the war ended, the British administration appointed him warden of the Sabi game reserve in the eastern Transvaal. It had been established just before the war by Paul Kruger, the Boer President. Over the next 20 years, Stevenson-Hamilton, brushing aside hostility and disbelief, devoted himself to converting a relatively small reserve into a vast national park. In his memoir, *South African Eden* (29), first published in 1937, he described how the breakthrough came.

In 1923 the South African railway authorities conceived the idea of running, during the cold weather, a service of fortnightly tourist trains to points of interest in the Transvaal. This service, which became known as the Round-in-Nine, because it took nine days to complete the tour, was a model of efficiency, cheapness and comfort for the passengers. All the most interesting places, and those containing the finest scenery, were embraced. Citrus orchards at Nelspruit and mountain passes at Pilgrim's Rest were inspected, finishing up with sea bathing and a dance at Lourenco Marques. When the programme of the service was shown to me I was a little disappointed, though perhaps hardly surprised, to discover that these tourist trains were scheduled to pass through the reserve by night on every occasion, and of course without stopping.

I called on the system manager, whom I knew, and mooted the idea of allowing each train to make a halt while passing through, or at least to make the journey in daylight. 'But why?' he asked me, with a surprised air.

'Well,' I said, 'perhaps some of the people might like to look at the game.'

He looked at me steadily for a moment or two, as one does at a person of whose complete sanity one is not quite sure, then he leaned back in his chair and burst into a hearty laugh. When he had recovered a little, he gasped out, 'What! Look at your old wildebeests! What on earth do you suppose anyone wants to see *them* for? But look here' – suddenly struck by an idea – 'I'll make a bargain with you. If you will allow us to stop and have a little shooting – I promise we won't bring more than a single rifle on the train – I am sure that would amuse the passengers. We could put an expert shot on board, and some of them might like to have a go themselves. Anyhow, if you will agree to that I think I could arrange for an hour's halt.'

Well, well! Twenty years' work of building, and no more helpful suggestion at the end than one to allow neophytes to practise with lethal weapons on semi-tame animals. But that was still the public attitude towards game even so recently as 1923.

However, I did not allow myself to be unduly discouraged, and ultimately it was settled that the train, without rifle and expert hunter, should stay the night at the siding opposite Sabi Bridge. There we would arrange a campfire for the passengers, and next morning, very early, proceed to Newington (at that time within the sanctuary) to remain there for an hour in daylight.

I don't think anyone was more surprised than the railway authorities when they discovered at the conclusion of the first tour that the short halt in the game reserve was, to the majority of the passengers – mainly townspeople from Johannesburg – by far the most interesting and exciting part of the whole trip. Later, it was agreed that more time in the reserve should be spent by the tourist train, and it was further arranged that a ranger should travel on it, and at each halt take the passengers for a little walk in the bush. The campfires, too, became a great attraction; the people sat round the huge blaze, alternately singing choruses and shivering with delight at the idea of being watched, from the dark bush close at hand, by the hungry eyes of beasts of prey, though I am sure every wild beast within earshot had long fled headlong from the clamour.

One of the stewards on the train, having possessed himself of a lion-skin, would sometimes envelop himself in it and would come crawling stealthily into the ring of firelight, to be greeted with shrieks from the more timid of the ladies, while the bolder of the men would assume protective attitudes. To add to the realism, our South African Police sergeant at Sabi Bridge could give a very passable imitation of a lion's roar through a long glass tube. While his confederate was advancing, he would, from a place of concealment, provide the necessary vocal accompaniment. The tourists loved thrills, and De Laporte[7], our humorist, always did his best to gratify them; asked if there was any danger from snakes, he assured them that in his experience mambas had boarded the train on only two occasions! A couple of lion, he added, might always be noticed waiting for the train at a certain mile-post, ready to race it to the next one.

The interest betrayed by the public in the animals, and the remarks I overheard when mixing with the passengers, made me at last confident that, could only our national park scheme mature, it would become popular, and therefore an asset to the country. It was beyond measure encouraging to feel that the South African public, despite tradition, might be content to look at animals without wanting to kill them.

Directly the South African railway administration realised that the Sabi reserve held potential publicity value, it at once became, in the person of Sir William Hoy, the general manager, a wholehearted supporter of its development into a national park.

The Kruger National Park was finally designated in 1926.

NOTES

1 Now Goukamma.
2 At the time, it meant great in courage – ironical in the context.
3 Derived from the Xhosa word for giraffe.
4 Strips of hide.
5 A shallow lake.
6 i.e. the children of the Boers.
7 One of the rangers.

CHAPTER 6

'KAFFIR WARS', SETTLERS AND MISSIONARIES

On the eastern frontier, the colonists pressing up the coast ever northwards clashed bloodily and repeatedly with the Xhosa expanding southwards. Over the course of 100 years, they fought nine, increasingly ferocious 'kaffir wars'. The first two, in 1781 and 1793, took place under Dutch rule and amounted to little more than skirmishes. The third, which started in 1799, has been called Britain's first war against black men in Africa. It was ended by the Dutch in 1803 when they briefly resumed control of the Cape. The fourth, which started in 1811, was a determined campaign by the British to drive the Xhosa back across the Great Fish River, half-way between Port Elizabeth and East London. About 20 000 blacks were dispossessed of their land, had their homes burnt, their cattle seized and their crops destroyed. It was the first large-scale removal in South Africa's history, and there were many more to come.

By now, the Xhosa were themselves under mounting pressure on their eastern frontier as thousands fled south from Natal to escape the murderous upheavals precipitated by the empire building of Shaka, the Zulu king. So in 1818, in the fifth 'kaffir war', the Xhosa attempted to repossess their land in an area centred on present-day Grahamstown that Britain had renamed Albany. They failed. The British drove them back across the Great Fish, seized more than 20 000 of their cattle and decided that Albany would be the ideal place to settle 5 000 British immigrants. They would act as a first line of defence against 'kaffir incursions', help Anglicise a Dutch-populated colony and relieve the Mother Country of some of the social pressures – unemployment was widespread – that had built up in the wake of the Napoleonic wars. As *The Times* reported on 14 July 1819: 'A sum of £50,000 has been voted by the House of Commons, upon the motion of the Chancellor of the Exchequer, for the assistance of such unemployed workmen as wish to emigrate to one of our colonies. The colony selected by Government is that of the Cape of Good Hope. It is on the south-east side of Africa, remarkable for the mildness of the climate and the general fertility of the soil […] Such an arrangement may be productive of much good to this country, and to those adventurers who adopt it. Parishes will thus possess the means of recommending employment, and the great probability of ultimate comfort, to those able bodied individuals chargeable upon them, who have no work and cannot starve; and the redundancy of population, so much complained of in these days, may be materially diminished.'

And so aspirant 1820 Settlers, as they came to be known, were offered free passages to South Africa and 100-acre grants of land that was unoccupied only because the Xhosa had been driven off it. About 80 000 applied, 4 000 were chosen, and another 1 000 elected to pay their own way. Among the chosen was a party of 25 Scots assembled by Thomas Pringle (30), impoverished poet and friend of Sir Walter Scott. After calling in at Simon's Town, the British naval base near Cape Town, their ship sailed on up the east coast to Algoa Bay and a town soon to be named Port Elizabeth. Pringle beautifully captures the settlers' anticipation.

We sailed out of Simon's Bay on the 10th of May, with a brisk gale from the N.W., which carried us round Cape L'Aguillas, at the rate of nearly ten knots an hour. On the 12th, at daybreak, however, we found ourselves almost becalmed, opposite the entrance to the Knysna, a fine lagoon, or salt-water lake, which forms a beautiful and spacious haven, though unfortunately rather of difficult access, winding up, as we were informed by our captain, who had twice entered it with the Brilliant, into the very bosom of the magnificent forests which cover this part of the coast. During this and the two following days, having scarcely any wind, and the little we had being adverse, we kept tacking off and on within a few miles of the shore. This gave us an excellent opportunity of surveying the coast scenery of Auteniqualand and Zitzikamma, which is of a very striking character. The land rises abruptly from the shore in massive mountain ridges, clothed with forests of large timber, and swelling in the back-ground into lofty serrated peaks of naked rock. As we passed headland after headland, the sylvan recesses of the bays and mountains opened successively to our gaze, like a magnificent panorama, continually unfolding new features, or exhibiting new combinations of scenery, in which the soft and the stupendous, the monotonous and the picturesque, were strangely blended. The aspect of the whole was impressive, but sombre; beautiful, but somewhat savage. There was the grandeur and the grace of nature, majestic and untamed; and there was likewise that air of *lone-someness* and dreary *wildness*, which a country unmarked by the traces of human industry or of human residence seldom fails to exhibit to the view of civilized man. Seated on the poop of the vessel, I gazed alternately on that solitary shore, and on the bands of emigrants who now crowded the deck or leaned along the gangway; some silently musing, like myself, on the scene before us; others conversing in scattered groups, and pointing with eager gestures to the country they had come so far to inhabit. Sick of the wearisome monotony of a long sea voyage (for only a few had been permitted by the Cape authorities to land at Simon's Bay), all were highly exhilarated by the prospect of speedily disembarking; but the sublimely stern aspect of the country, so different from the rich tameness of ordinary English scenery, seemed to strike many of the *Southron* with a degree of awe approaching to consternation. The Scotch, on the contrary, as the stirring recollections of their native land were vividly called up by the rugged peaks and shaggy declivities of this wild coast, were strongly affected, like all true mountaineers on such occasions. Some were excited to extravagant spirits; others silently shed tears.

Coasting on in this manner, we at length doubled Cape Recife on the 15th, and late in the afternoon came to an anchor in Algoa Bay, in the midst of a little fleet of vessels, which had just landed, or were engaged in landing, their respective bands of settlers. The Menai sloop of war and the Weymouth store-ship were moored beside the transports; and their crews, together with a party of military on shore, were employed in assisting the debarkation.

It was an animated and interesting scene. Around us in the west corner of the spacious bay, were anchored ten or twelve large vessels, which had recently arrived with emigrants, of whom a great proportion were still on board. Directly in front, on a rising ground a few hundred yards from the beach, stood the little fortified barrack, or blockhouse, called Fort Frederick, occupied by a division of the 72nd regiment, with the tents and marquees of the officers pitched on the heights around it. At the foot of those heights, nearer the beach, stood three thatched cottages and one or two wooden houses brought out from England, which now formed the offices of the commissaries and other civil functionaries appointed to transact the business of the emigration, and to provide the settlers with provisions and other stores, and with carriages for their conveyance up the country. Interspersed among these offices, and among the pavilions of the functionaries and naval officers employed on shore, were scattered large depots of agricultural implements, carpenters' and blacksmiths' tools, and iron ware of all descriptions, sent out by the home government to be furnished to the settlers at prime cost. About two furlongs to the eastward, on a level spot between the sand-hills on the beach and the stony heights beyond, lay the camp of the emigrants. Nearly a thousand souls, on an average, were at present lodged there in military tents; but parties were daily moving off in long trains of bullock wagons, to proceed to their appointed places of location in the interior, while their place was immediately occupied by fresh bands, hourly disembarking from the vessels in the bay. A suitable background to this animated picture, as viewed by us from the anchorage, was supplied by the heights over the river Zwartkops, covered with a dense jungle, and by the picturesque peaks of the Winterhoek and the dark masses of the Zureberg ridge far to the northward, distinctly outlined in the clear blue sky.

The whole scene was such as could not fail to impress deeply the most un-concerned spectator. To us, who had embarked all our worldly property and earthly prospects – our own future fortunes and the fate of our posterity, in this enterprise, it was interesting and exciting to an intense degree.

It being too late to go ashore that evening, we continued gazing on this scene till long after sunset – till twilight had darkened into night, and the constellations of the southern hemisphere, revolving in cloudless brilliancy above, reminded us that nearly half the globe's expanse intervened between us and our native land – the homes of our youth and the friends we had parted from for ever; and that here, in this farthest nook of Southern Africa, we were now about to receive the portion of our inheritance, and to draw an irrevocable lot for ourselves and for our children's children. Solemn re-flections will press themselves at such a time on the most thoughtless; and this night, as we swung at anchor in Algoa Bay, so long the bourne of all our wishes, many a wakeful brain among us was doubtless expatiating, each according to the prevailing current of thought, in serious meditation on the future or the past.

Although he was writing 50 years later, RM Ballantyne, whom we left admiring Cape Town's 'tablecloth', had the 1820 Settlers firmly in mind when he described the business of getting ashore with one's luggage at Port Elizabeth.

Standing on the shores of Algoa Bay, with the 'Liverpool of South Africa' –

Port Elizabeth – at my back, I attempted to realise what must have been the scene, in the memorable '1820,' when the flourishing city was yet unborn, when the whole land was a veritable wilderness, and the sands on which the port now stands were covered with the tents of the 'settlers.'

Some of the surroundings, thought I, are pretty much as they were in those days. The shipping at anchor in the offing must resemble the shipping that conveyed the emigrants across the sea – except, of course, these two giant steamers of the 'Donald Currie' and the 'Union' lines. The bright blue sky, too, and the fiery sun are the same, and so are those magnificent 'rollers,' which, rising, one scarce can tell when or where, out of a dead-calm sea, stand up for a few seconds like liquid walls, and then rush up the beach with a magnificent roar.

As I gazed, the scene was rendered still more real by the approach from seaward of a great surf-boat, similar to the surf-boats that brought the settlers from their respective ships to the shore. Such boats are still used at the port to land goods – and also passengers, when the breakers are too high to admit of their being landed in small boats at the wooden pier. The surf-boats are bulky, broad, and flat, strongly built to stand severe hammering on the sand, and comparatively shallow at the stern, to admit of their being backed towards the beach, or hauled off to sea through the surf by means of a rope over the bow.

As the surf-boat neared the shore, I heard voices behind me, and, turning round, beheld a sight which sent me completely back into the 1820 days. It was a band of gentlemen in black – black from the crowns of their heads to the soles of their feet, with the exception of their lips and teeth and eyes. Here was the Simon Pure in very truth. They were so-called Red Kafirs, because of their habit of painting their bodies and blankets with red ochre. At this time the paint had been washed off, and the blankets laid aside. They were quite naked, fresh from the lands of their nativity, and apparently fit for anything.

Shade of Othello! – to say nothing of Apollo – what magnificent forms the fellows had, and what indescribably hideous faces! They were tall, muscular, broad-shouldered, small waisted and ankled, round-muscled, black-polished – in a word, elegantly powerful. Many of them might have stood as models for Hercules. Like superfine cloth, they were of various shades; some were brown-black, some almost blue-black, and many coal-black.

They were coming down to unload the surf-boat, and seemed full of fun, and sly childlike humour, as they walked, tripped, skipped and sidled into the water. At first I was greatly puzzled to account for the fact that all their heads and throats were wrapped up, or swathed, in dirty cloth. It seemed as if every man of them was under treatment for a bad cold. This I soon found was meant to serve as a protection to their naked skins from the sharp and rugged edges and corners of the casks and cases they had to carry.

The labour is rather severe, but is well paid, so that hundreds of Kafirs annually come down from their homes in the wilderness to work for a short time. They do not, I believe, make a profession of it. Fresh relays come every year. Each young fellow's object is to make enough money to purchase a gun and cattle, and a wife – or wives. As these articles cost little in Africa, a comparatively short attention to business, during one season, enables a man who left home a beggar to return with his fortune made! He marries, sets his wives to hoe the mealies and milk the cows, and thereafter takes life easy, except when he takes a fancy to hunt elephants, or to go to war for pastime. Ever after he is a drone in the world's beehive. Having no necessity he need not work, and possessing no principle he will not.

As the boat came surging in on the foam, these manly children waded out to meet her, throwing water at each other, and skylarking as they went. They treated the whole business in fact as a rather good jest, and although they toiled like heroes, they accompanied their work with such jovial looks, and hummed such lilting, free-and-easy airs the while, that it was difficult to associate their doings with anything like *labour*.

Soon the boat grounded, and the Kafirs crowded round her, up to their waists sometimes in the water, and sometimes up to the arm-pits, when a bigger wave than usual came roaring in. The boat itself was so large that, as they stood beside it, their heads barely rose to a level with the gunwale. The boatmen at once began to heave and roll the goods over the side. The Kafirs received them on their heads or shoulders, according to the shape or size of each package – and they refused nothing. If a bale or a box chanced to be too heavy for one man, a comrade lent assistance; if it proved still too heavy, a third added his head or shoulder, and the box or bale was borne off.

One fellow, like a black Hercules, put his wrapper on his head, and his head under a bale, which I thought would crush him down into the surf, but he walked ashore with an easy springing motion, that showed he possessed more than sufficient power. Another man, hitting Hercules a sounding smack as he went by, received a mighty cask on his head that should have cracked it – but it didn't. Then I observed the boatmen place on the gunwale an enormous flat box, which seemed to me about ten feet square. It was corrugated iron, they told me, of, I forget, how many hundredweight. A crowd of Kafirs got under it, and carried it ashore as easily as if it had been a butterfly. But this was nothing to a box which next made its appearance from the bowels of that capacious boat. It was in the form of a cube, and must have measured nine or ten feet in all directions. Its contents I never ascertained, but the difficulty with which the boatmen got it rested on the side of the boat proved its weight to be worthy of its size. To get it on the shoulders of the Kafirs was the next difficulty. It was done by degrees. As the huge case was pushed over the edge, Kafir after Kafir put his head or shoulder to it, until there were, I think, from fifteen to twenty men beneath the weight; – then, slowly, it left the boat, and began to move towards the shore.

Assuredly, if four or five of these men had stumbled at the same moment, the others would have been crushed to death, but not a man stumbled. They came ashore with a slow, regular, almost dancing gait, humming a low monotonous chant, as if to enable them to step in time, and making serio-comic motions with arms and hands, until they deposited safely in a cart a weight that might have tested Atlas himself!

It seemed obvious that these wild men, (for such they truly were), had been gifted with all the powers that most white men lay claim to, – vigour, muscle, energy, pluck, fun, humour, resolution. Only principle is wanted to make them a respectable and useful portion of the human family. Like all the rest of us they are keenly alive to the influence of kindness and affection. Of course if your kindness, forbearance, or affection, take the form of action which leads them to think that you are afraid of them, they will merely esteem you cunning, and treat you accordingly; but if you convince a Kafir, or any other savage, that you have a disinterested regard for him, you are sure to find him grateful, more or less.

A few weeks after coming ashore, Thomas Pringle's party – it included his father and two brothers – headed inland. Their assigned destination was nearly 200 miles to the north, in the foothills of the Winterberg Mountains. Pringle describes the last stage of the journey.

It were tedious to relate the difficulties, perils, and adventures, which we encountered in our toilsome march of *five days* up this African glen; – to tell of our pioneering labours with the hatchet, the pick-axe, the crow-bar, and the sledge-hammer, – and the lashing of the poor oxen, to force them on (sometimes twenty or thirty in one team) through such a track as no English reader can form any adequate conception of. In the upper part of the valley we were occupied two entire days in thus hewing our way through a rugged defile, now called Eildon-Cleugh, scarcely three miles in extent. At length, after extraordinary exertions and hair-breadth escapes – the breaking down of two wagons, and the partial damage of others – we got through the last *poort* of the glen, and found ourselves on the summit of an elevated ridge, commanding a view of the extremity of the valley. 'And now, *mynheer*,' said the Dutch-African field-cornet who commanded our escort, '*daar leg uwe veld*' –'there lies your country.' Looking in the direction where he pointed, we beheld extending to the northward a beautiful vale, about six or seven miles in length, and varying from one to two in breadth. It appeared like a verdant basin, or *cul de sac*, surrounded on all sides by an amphitheatre of steep and sterile mountains, rising in the back-ground into sharp, cuneiform ridges of very considerable elevation; their summits being at this season covered with snow, and estimated to be about 5000 feet above the level of the sea. The lower declivities were sprinkled over, though somewhat scantily, with grass and bushes. But the bottom of the valley, through which the infant river meandered, presented a warm, pleasant, and secluded aspect; spreading itself into verdant meadows, sheltered and embellished, without being encumbered, with groves of mimosa trees, among which we observed in the distance herds of wild animals – antelopes and quaggas – pasturing in undisturbed quietude.

'Sae that's the lot o' our inheritance, then?' quoth one of the party, a Scottish agriculturist. 'A weel, now that we've really got till't, I maun say that the place looks no sae mickle amiss, and may suit our purpose no that ill, provided thae haughs turn out to be gude deep land for the pleugh, and we can but contrive to find a decent road out o' this queer hieland glen into the lowlands – like ony other Christian country.'

Descending into the middle of the valley, we unyoked the wagons, and pitched our tents in a grove of mimosa-trees on the margin of the river; and the next day our armed escort, with the train of shattered vehicles, set out on their return homeward, leaving us in our wild domain to our own courage and resources.

Our wearisome travels by sea and land were at length terminated; and it

was remarked that exactly six months, to a day, had elapsed, from the departure of the party from Scotland to their arrival at their destined home. With
the exception of myself and two or three other individuals, all the party
had embarked at Leith for London on the 29th of December, 1819; and we
reached our African location on the 29th of June 1820. For six long months
we had been pilgrims and sojourners – without any other home since we
left London than the crowded cabin at sea, and the narrow tent on shore.
Now we had reached the 'Promised Land,' which was to be the place of our
rest; and it may be conceived with what feelings of lively interest most of us
assembled the following morning to sally forth on an exploratory excursion
to the upper extremity and lateral recesses of the valley.

Some months later, Pringle, who had been living with one of his brothers, decided to set
up home for himself. The bee-hive hut he built was of the kind that still dominates many
of South Africa's rural areas.

The site which I fixed upon for my residence was about three miles distant
from my neighbours on either side; Mrs. Rennie and her family being on
the stream above me, and Captain Cameron below, with rocky heights and
clumps of shrubbery intervening. I selected an open grassy meadow, with
a steep mountain behind, and the small river in front, bordered by willow-
trees and groves of the thorny acacia. It was a beautiful and secluded spot;
the encircling hills sprinkled over with trees and bushes, and the fertile
meadow-ground clothed with pasture, and bounded by cliffs crowned with
aloes and euphorbias.

As the hut I was about to erect was still only intended for a temporary
residence, I adopted, with some variations, the mode practised by the coloured natives in constructing their slight habitations. Drawing a circle on
the ground of about eighteen feet in diameter, I planted upright round this
circle about twenty tall willow-poles; digging, with an old bayonet, holes in
the ground, just large enough to receive their thicker ends. I then planted
a stouter pole exactly in the centre, and, drawing together the tops of the
others, I bound them firmly to this central tree with thongs of quagga's
hide. With the same ligature pliant spars or saplings were bound round the
circle of poles, at suitable intervals, from bottom to top; and thus the wicker
frame or skeleton of a cabin was completed, in the shape of a bee-hive or
sugar-loaf. It was then thatched with reeds, the ends of the first layer being

let about a couple of inches into the earth. Spaces were left for a door and a small window; but neither fire-place nor chimney formed any part of our plan. A convenient door, to open in two halves, was soon constructed of the boards of some packing-cases; and a yard of thin cotton cloth stretched upon a wooden frame formed a suitable window.

With the assistance of my Hottentot servants I then proceeded to plaster the interior to the height of about six feet, with the composition mentioned elsewhere.[1] When the plaster was dry, the whole was washed over with a sort of size-paint, composed of pipe-clay and wood-ashes diluted with milk, forming a handsome and durable greyish stone colour. Thus secured externally, the next point was to lay a dry and firm floor below foot. Following the custom of the country, I directed a dozen or two of large ant-hillocks, of which there were hundreds within view, to be broken up and brought into the hut, selecting those that had been previously pierced and sacked by the ant-eater. This material, from having been apparently cemented by the insect architects with some glutinous substance, forms, when pounded and sprinkled with water, a strong adhesive mortar, which only requires to be well kneaded with trampling feet for a few days, in order to become a dry and compact pavement, almost as solid and impenetrable as stone or brick.

Less impregnable, though, were the settlers. Knowing nothing of Africa and, for the most part, little about farming (contrary to what they had been told, the soil was far from 'generally fertile'), they soon found themselves the target of marauding bands of Bushmen and angry groups of dispossessed blacks. As Noel Mostert, the historian of the eastern frontier, put it: 'The operation was probably the most callous act of mass settlement in the entire history of empire. It is at any rate hard to think of any other occasion when some 4 000 people were at one go dumped in such an alien environment, wholly ignorant in most cases of how to plant a potato, largely innocent of any real knowledge of the historic background of the region they occupied, and certainly ignorant of how to cope with the natural dangers of their surroundings.' In fact, most gave up and migrated to the towns, among them Pringle, who found the tough measures required to defend his 'inheritance' hard to square with his liberal sentiments. After a thwarted attempt to publish a newspaper in Cape Town critical of the colonial administration, he returned to London and became secretary of the Anti-Slavery Society.

The principal – often, indeed, the only – voice of Enlightenment liberalism in the colony was that of the missionaries, and the Boers quickly came to loathe them for it. They also disliked the missionaries' settlements, which they saw as refuges for work-shy

Hottentots. The first of these, Genadendal – Valley of Grace – had been set up by the Moravians in 1737 about 75 miles east of Cape Town. Forced to close after only a few years, it re-opened in 1792 and was later visited by Lady Anne Barnard on her journey into the interior.

Thursday, May 10th, 1798. We set off again in our waggon, favoured with another charming day. Our object this morning was to see those humble missionaries who, sent by the Moravian Church about seven years ago, have made so great a progress in converting the Hottentots to Christianity. I had heard much of them, and I desired with my own eyes to see what sort of people Hottentots are when collected together in such an extensive *kraal* as that which surrounds the settlements of the fathers. Hitherto I had only seen the servants of the farmers kept to hard work and humiliating subjection. We travelled on over rough ground, and after about four hours arrived at the base of the Baviaan and Boscheman's Kloofs, where the settlement was. Each step we now took we found a bit of grass or a few cattle, a *kraal* or a hut, a cornfield, a little garden, and a general look of peace and prosperity, which seemed to me the tacit manna of the Almighty showered down upon His children. The fathers, of whom there were three, came out to meet us in their working jackets, each man being employed in following the business of his original profession – miller, smith, carpenter, and tailor in one. They welcomed us simply and frankly, and led us into their house, which was built with their own hands five years ago. They told us that they were sent by the Moravian Church in Germany; that their object was to convert the Hottentots and render them industrious, religious, and happy; that they had spent some time in looking out for a proper situation, sheltered, of a good soil, and near water; that they had found it here, and had procured some Hottentots to assist them in the beginning of the work, and by their treatment of them had gradually encouraged more to creep around them. 'This gate,' said one of the fathers, 'and all the ironwork is my *broeder's* making.' The other two had raised the walls, which were of clay mixed with stone. The tailor had taught the Hottentot women to make rush mats of a sort of reed, with which the floor of the church was covered. They asked us to step in to see the church; we found it about forty feet long and twenty broad; the pulpit was a platform raised only a few steps above the ground, and matted with some rushes, on which were three chairs and a small table, on which was a Bible. I regretted very much that it was not Sunday – then I should have found the whole community, about three hundred Hottentots, assembled to Divine worship. The fathers said I should still see them, as at sunset every day, when business was over, there were prayers. Presently the church bell was a-ringing, and we begged leave to make part of the congregation. I doubt much whether I should have entered St. Peter's at Rome, with the triple crown, with a more devout impression of the Deity and His presence than I felt in this little church of a few feet square, where the simple disciples of Christianity, dressed in the skins of animals, knew no purple or fine linen, no pride or hypocrisy. I felt as if I was creeping back seventeen hundred years, and heard from the rude and inspired lips of Evangelists the simple sacred words of wisdom and purity. The service began with a Presbyterian form of psalm; about one hundred and fifty Hottentots joined in the twenty-third psalm in a tone so sweet and loud, so chaste and true, that it was impossible to hear it without being surprised. The fathers, who were the sole music-masters, sang in their deep-toned bass along with them, and the harmony was excellent. This over, the miller took a portion of the Scripture and expounded it as he went along. The father's discourse was short, and the tone of his voice was even and natural, and when he used the words, as he often did, *myne lieve vriende,* 'my beloved friends,' I felt that he thought they were all his children.

We made a most excellent supper, and the fathers ate with us. I must say they had excellent appetites – they urged one another on. 'Broeder, eat this,' and 'Broeder, take another slice,' and 'Ledi, ask him, he likes it.' This was *à propos* of one of our cold hams, for they had not tasted one since they left Germany, they said. So, of course, we left what remained of it for them. Our cask of madeira and our gin were next produced, and they gladly partook of it, as it was a day of *fête.* They had accustomed themselves to do quite without wine, and even without meat, living on the simplest fare. Their position, they told us, was one of great danger, for the Boers disliked them for having taken the Hottentots away from the necessity of laborious servitude, and 'over and over again,' they told us, 'the farmers had made plots to murder us. The last plot, which was to shoot us with poisoned arrows, we discovered and were able to prevent.' Mr. Barnard was very much interested in this, and promised to speak to the Governor to see what was best to be done for their security. We spent the night in a small sitting-room on a couple of cane sofas very comfortably.

The most politically influential of the 19th-century missionary bodies was the London Missionary Society. Its most powerful spokesman was Dr John Philip (31), a radical Evangelical whose concern for the rights of the dispossessed threatened the 'total ruin of our country', according to one of the leaders of the Boers' Great Trek out of the colony. Even 150 years later, Philip's name could still raise Afrikaners' hackles. His account of his first visit to the Cape in 1819 began with a stern defence of missionary endeavour.

While our missionaries, beyond the borders of the colony of the Cape of Good Hope, are everywhere scattering the seeds of civilization, social order, and happiness, they are, by the most unexceptionable means, extending British interests, British influence, and the British empire.

Wherever the missionary places his standard among a savage tribe, their prejudices against the colonial government give way; their dependence upon the colony is increased by the creation of artificial wants; confidence is restored; intercourse with the colony is established; industry, trade, and agriculture spring up; and every genuine convert from among them made to the Christian religion becomes the ally and friend of the colonial government. The materials of our conquests, made in this way, will bear examination. Triumphs gained by such weapons occasion no tears, and present no disgusting details: they are the triumphs of reason over ignorance, of civilization over barbarism, and of benevolence over cruelty and oppression.

It may be an easy thing for a theoretical European, looking at one of our missionary institutions, to imagine and assert that the work might have been accomplished by other means. Philosophers and projectors had a hundred and fifty years to try their skill upon the Hottentots before our missions commenced, and what was done? – nothing! When the missions began in South Africa, we found the poor natives as far from a state of civilization, as they were at the first introduction of Europeans among them. They were deprived of their country; from a state of independence they were reduced to the miseries of slavery; their herds of cattle followed their lands and passed over into the hands of their intrusive neighbours; and all they had gained in return for these sacrifices, were a few beads, tobacco, and spirits, and a number of vices unknown to them in their former ignorance.

The 'theoretical European' Dr Philip almost certainly had in mind was the traveller and explorer, William Burchell, who lived for a time at the mission station in Klaarwater, now Griquatown, in the far Northern Cape. In October 1811, having attended a Sunday service in their meeting house, he reflected on what the missionaries were trying – and failing – to achieve and concluded with a modest proposal: would they not do better to teach the natives a useful trade?

The ceremony of marriage, according to Christian rites, had not been introduced at Klaarwater longer than three years; nor, indeed, could the greater part of these people be persuaded to adopt it. The restrictions which it had been endeavoured to lay upon their former customs, had rendered the missionaries rather unpopular; and the law for reducing the number of wives from two, often three, and sometimes four, to one, in a nation consisting of more females than males, did not meet with many advocates in either sex. However, since its first introduction, about a hundred, as I was informed, had submitted to it.

This meeting-house serves also for a school-room, where some of the children attend, principally in the evenings, although in a desultory manner, to be instructed in reading, and a few in writing. Once or twice in the week, a greater number are assembled to repeat a catechism, and to have it explained suitably to their capacities. This business, which generally occupies about an hour, concludes with an extempore prayer, and a verse of some psalm or hymn sung by the whole party.

This is the ordinary routine of the business of the mission, as I observed it during the four months which, at different times, I spent at Klaarwater. And, with respect to its effects in forwarding the object of it, I cannot say that they appeared to me very evident: certainly, I saw nothing that would sanction me in making such favorable reports as have been laid before the public.

The enthusiasm which, perhaps, is inseparable from missionary affairs, may create some optical delusion in the mind's eye, that may cause it to see those things which are not visible to a more temperate and unbiassed observer; but still, it is much to be lamented that the community at home are misled by accounts (I speak generally) catching at the most trifling occurrence for their support, and showing none but the favorable circumstances; and even those, unfairly exaggerated. Deception never yet supported any cause for long. Every sensible and reasonable person must be too well aware of the difficulties attending the civilization of wild nations, to expect more than slow and gradual advancement, or to be disappointed or deterred by the untowardness of savages, or by their resistance to novel doctrines. Whatever aversion the African tribes, taken generally, may have to new opinions in religion and morality, they will not, I am sure, reject any proffered instruction in such arts as have for them an evident utility. Why not, therefore, begin with this? As the trial has, I believe, never been made, the objection that such a plan will not succeed, cannot yet be fairly urged against it; while those who have an opportunity of getting at the truth, know that the evangelizing scheme has too often ended in nothing. If there really do exist so much goodwill and such disinterested philanthropy, towards all the untutored savages of the globe; and this has, it cannot be denied, shown itself in a variety of shapes, combined always with religious enthusiasm; why, therefore, has it not shown itself in some endeavour directed exclusively to the object of instructing them in those arts and practices, from which we derive those superior comforts which, in a worldly point of view, distinguish us from them? Why have no missionaries been sent to them with this as their first great object? Because, perhaps, our philanthropy is not strong enough to stand purely by itself, without the enthusiasm of a religious devotee. But I hope not to be misunderstood; for though I well know that nothing can stand without the support of genuine religion, I mean, that as mere men, and having to deal with mere men, there is no absurdity in trying how far worldly means are likely to produce those good effects on our fellow-creatures, which we are so desirous of witnessing.

In time, the missionaries did focus their efforts on education and training. Indeed, in the first half of the 20th century many of South Africa's black élite owed at least part of their education to them. For most of the 19th century, though, the missionaries concentrated on 'civilising the barbarians' by converting them to Christianity, stamping out polygamy and enforcing a European dress code. The effect was to hasten the destruction of traditional African society, so exposing Africans to the very exploitation the missionaries deplored.

Dr Philip's main concern, however, was with the rights of the Hottentots, who were effectively bonded labourers kept in a state of semi-slavery. He concluded his work on *The Condition of the Native Tribes* with a bitter summary of how they were treated – and a rousing peroration.

The Hottentots, despairing of help from every other quarter, now look to the justice and humanity of England for deliverance; and they now justly and humbly ask, why they may not, like the colonists, be allowed to bring their labours to the best market? Why they should be compelled to labour for two or for four rix-dollars (equivalent to three or six shillings sterling money) per month, when they might be receiving twenty or twenty-five rix-dollars per month, if permitted to dispose of themselves as a free people? Why they may not be exempted from the cruelties exercised upon them without any form of law? Why they should be arbitrarily flogged in the public prison, upon the mere *ipse dixit* of their masters? Why, on complaining of bad usage to a magistrate, they should be put in prison till their master appear to answer the accusation brought against him; – and why they should be flogged if their complaints are held to be frivolous? Why they should be liable to punishment at the mere caprice of a magistrate, and without any trial? Why they should be made responsible for the loss of their master's property, and thereby kept in perpetual bondage, without ever receiving any wages? Why they should be treated as vagabonds, and be liable to be disposed of at the pleasure of any local functionary in whose district they may reside, if they do not hire themselves to a master? Why they should be given to any master, by such an authority, without ever having been consulted on the subject? Why they should be liable to have their homes violated, their children torn from them, and from the arms of their distracted mothers, without having the smallest chance of redress? Why they should be denied, by the justice and humanity of Britain, the boon prepared for them by the Batavian government,[2] when the Cape of Good Hope fell into the hands of the English? And why these intolerable oppressions should continue to be imposed upon them, in direct violation of the proclamation of the colonial government, declaring, that the original natives of the country, the Hottentots, must be considered and treated as a free people, who have a lawful abode in the colony; and whose persons, property, and possessions ought, for that reason, to be protected, the same as other free people?

The interest of the colony cannot require that such a system of cruel oppression should be continued; and it is impossible that the justice, the humanity, and the magnanimity of the British government can suffer longer that evils so enormous should exist in any of its foreign dependencies. Let justice be done to the Hottentots; let them be exempted from the oppression of the local authorities of the country; let them be at liberty to bring the produce of their labour to the best market; let them have all the genial stimulus arising from the elevated cares of a family; let them feel all those powerful energies which arise from seeing the support, – the lives of their children dependent upon their labour; let the churches of the colonists be thrown open for their devotional exercises; let the ministers of the colony be enjoined to recognise them as a part of their charge; and let not this interfere with the self-denied labours of those who are willing to impart to them the first elements of instruction; – and, when those invidious distinctions which mar all fellowship but that which arises from a partnership in guilt are done away, the loathsome appearances which now deform the face of our African Society, and which indicate a rottenness deeply seated at the core, may be expected, under the impartial administration of equal laws, the fostering wing of the British constitution, and the purifying influence of Christian instruction and evangelical ministrations, gradually to pass away along with them.

To use the eloquent language of Mr. Wilberforce, –

'Africa will then become the seat of civilization, because the seat of liberty – the seat of commerce, because the seat of liberty – the seat of science, because the seat of liberty – the seat of religion, because the seat of liberty – the seat of morals, because the seat of liberty – the seat of happiness, because the seat of liberty!'

Dr Philip's rhetoric did not fall on deaf ears. In 1828, the year his book was published, the British government made the Hottentots, to the outrage of the Boers, equal before the law with whites and free to move about as they wished.

However, to Robert Moffat (32), running the London Missionary Society's station at Kuruman, 1 000 miles to the north, the 'eloquent language of Wilberforce' must have seemed a world away. As this unusual insight into the frustrations of missionary life makes clear, he was disillusioned and close to despair.

We shall now return to our labours among the Bechuanas, which had already been carried on for about five years.

The natives had by this time become perfectly callous and indifferent to all instruction, except it were followed by some temporal benefit in assisting them with the labour of our hands, which was not always in our power. The following extract from a letter written at this time, depicts our real situation: – 'I often feel at a loss what to say relative to the kingdom of Christ, at this station. A sameness marks the events of each returning day. No conversions, no inquiry after God, no objections raised to exercise our powers in defence. Indifference and stupidity form the wreath on every brow – ignorance, the grossest ignorance of Divine things, forms the basis of every action; it is only things earthly, sensual, and devilish, which stimulate to activity and mirth, while the great subject of the soul's redemption appears to them like an old and ragged garment, possessing neither loveliness nor worth. O, when shall the day-star arise on their hearts! We preach, we converse, we catechise, we pray, but without the least apparent success. Only satiate their mendicant spirits by perpetually giving, and we are all that is good, but refuse to meet their demands, their praises are turned to ridicule and abuse.'

Our time was incessantly occupied in building, and labouring frequently for the meat that perisheth; but our exertions were often in vain, for while we sowed, the natives reaped. The site of the station was a light sandy soil, where no kind of vegetables would grow without constant irrigation. Our water ditch, which was some miles in length, had been led out of the Kuruman River, and passed in its course through the gardens of the natives. As irrigation was to them entirely unknown, fountains and streams had been suffered to run to waste, where crops even of native grain (sorghum), which supports amazing drought, are seldom very abundant from the general scarcity of rain. The native women, seeing the fertilizing effect of the water in our gardens, thought very naturally that they had an equal right to their own, and took the liberty of cutting open our water ditch, and allowing it on some occasions to flood theirs. This mode of proceeding left us at times without a drop of water, even for culinary purposes. It was in vain that we pleaded, and remonstrated with the chiefs, the women were the masters in this matter. Mr. Hamilton and I were daily compelled to go alternately three miles with a spade, about three o'clock P.M., the hottest time of the day, and turn in the many outlets into native gardens, that we might have a little moisture to refresh our burnt-up vegetables during the night, which we were obliged to irrigate when we ought to have rested from the labours of the day. Many night watches were spent in this way; and after we had raised with great labour vegetables, so necessary to our constitutions, the natives would steal them by day as well as by night, and after a year's toil and care we scarcely reaped anything to reward us for our labour. The women would watch our return from turning the streams into the watercourse, and would immediately go and open the outlets again, thus leaving us on a thirsty plain many days without a drop of water, excepting that which was carried from a distant fountain, under a cloudless sky, when the thermometer at noon would frequently rise to 120 in the shade. When we complained of this, the women, who one would have thought would have been the first to appreciate the principles by which we were actuated, became exasperated, and going to the higher dam, where the water was led out of the river, with their picks completely destroyed it, allowing the stream to flow in its ancient bed. By this means the supply of water we formerly had was reduced to one-half, and that entirely at the mercy of those who loved us only when we could supply them with tobacco, repair their tools, or administer medicine to the afflicted. But all this, and much more, failed to soften their feelings towards us. Mrs. Moffat, from these circumstances, and the want of female assist-ance, has been compelled to send the heavier part of our linen a hundred miles to be washed […]

Our attendance at public worship would vary from one to forty; and these very often manifesting the greatest indecorum. Some would be snor-ing; others laughing; some working; and others, who might even be styled the noblesse, would be employed in removing from their ornaments cer-tain nameless insects, letting them run about the forms, while sitting by the missionary's wife. Never having been accustomed to chairs or stools, some, by way of imitation, would sit with their feet on the benches, having their knees, according to their usual mode of sitting, drawn up to their chins. In this position one would fall asleep and tumble over, to the great merriment of his fellows. On some occasions an opportunity would be watched to rob, when the missionary was engaged in public service. The thief would just put his head within the door, discover who was in the pulpit, and, knowing he could not leave his rostrum before a certain time had elapsed, would go to his house and take what he could lay his hands upon. When Mr. Hamilton and I met in the evening, we almost always had some tale to tell about our losses, but never about our gains, except those of resignation and peace, the results of patience, and faith in the unchangeable purposes of Jehovah. 'I will be exalted among the heathen,' cheered our often baffled and drooping spirits.

Nonetheless, Moffat soldiered valiantly on. He translated the Bible into Sechuana, printed it on his own press and finally returned to London in 1870 after a mission lasting 53 years.

One of Moffat's visitors at Kuruman had been David Livingstone (33), who married his elder daughter before pressing on north to evangelise among the Bechuana. There, in the early 1850s, Livingstone encountered some of the Boers who had trekked from the Cape Colony to settle in what became the Transvaal. Like Dr Philip, he did not like what he saw.

An evocative painting by Thomas Baines commemorating the landing at Algoa Bay in 1820 of 5 000 ill-equipped and ill-prepared British settlers. The scheme was later described by one historian as 'probably the most callous act of mass settlement in the entire history of empire'. [THOMAS BAINES. LANDING OF THE BRITISH SETTLERS. ALBANY MUSEUM]

'All among the Hottentots capering ashore' – a contemporary cartoon by George Cruikshank predicting the fate awaiting the 1820 Settlers at the mercy of cannibals and predators. However, their real problems were that they had been assigned frontier land belonging to others and knew little about farming. [MUSEUMAFRICA]

Left: Thomas Pringle, impoverished Scottish poet and friend of Sir Walter Scott, led a party of 25 Settlers seeking a new life 200 miles into the rugged and war-torn interior. He returned to Britain six years later to become Secretary of the Anti-Slavery Society. [MuseumAfrica]

Below: Wagon crossing a River by Thomas Baines, an English artist and explorer who arrived at the Cape in 1842 and spent the next 30 years painting events and scenery across southern Africa. This picture is set on the eastern frontier, where whites and blacks fought each other throughout the 19th century. [MuseumAfrica]

Bottom: An African village by Samuel Daniell, who was appointed official artist to a British expedition to the Northern Cape in 1801. He turned his field sketches into a fine collection of aquatints published in 1805 as *African Scenery and Animals.* [MuseumAfrica]

The Giraffe by Sir William Cornwallis Harris, an ex-Indian Army Officer who arrived at the Cape in 1836 with the intention of killing – and sketching – as many wild animals as he could. He regarded hunting 'stately' giraffes as particularly 'thrilling'. [MuseumAfrica]

Hunting the Wild Elephant by Cornwallis Harris. As he recorded in his *Narrative of an Expedition in Southern Africa*, 'Streaming with blood, and infuriated with rage, she turned upon us with uplifted trunk.' [MuseumAfrica]

The Quahkah – i.e. quagga – by Samuel Daniell, who sketched animals from life in their natural habitat and was praised for his accuracy and attention to detail. The quagga, a subspecies of zebra, was hunted to extinction in the 19th century. [MuseumAfrica]

The Gnu, another fine aquatint by Samuel Daniell. A kind of antelope, also known as wildebeest, gnus were a favourite target of 19th-century wildlife hunters. [MuseumAfrica]

Above: Ivory and Skins for Sale in the Grahamstown Market by Thomas Baines, a sketch first published in 1866 by the *Illustrated London News*. Killing elephants and selling their tusks was how hunters like Cornwallis Harris funded their expeditions. [THOMAS BAINES. MR. HUME'S WAGGONS. ALBANY MUSEUM (HISTORY)]

Left: A portrait of Shaka, King of the Zulus, based on the only known drawing of him from life. It was made by Lt James King, an ex-Royal Navy officer, who met and befriended Shaka in 1825 and was given command of one of his regiments. [MUSEUMAFRICA]

Below: Zulu kraal by George French Angas, an English artist who arrived in South Africa in 1846. He spent two years in Natal and the Cape, travelled widely and published a collection of hand-coloured lithographs called *Kafirs Illustrated* in 1849. [MUSEUMAFRICA]

Another adverse influence with which the mission had to contend was the vicinity of the Boers of the Cashan Mountains, otherwise named 'Magaliesberg'. These are not to be confounded with the Cape colonists, who sometimes pass by the name. The word Boer simply means 'farmer', and is not synonymous with our word boor. Indeed, to the Boers generally the latter term would be quite inappropriate, for they are a sober, industrious, and most hospitable body of peasantry. Those, however, who have fled from English law on various pretexts, and have been joined by English deserters and every other variety of bad character in their distant localities, are unfortunately of a very different stamp. The great objection many of the Boers had, and still have, to English law, is that it makes no distinction between black men and white. They felt aggrieved by their supposed losses in the emancipation of their Hottentot slaves, and determined to erect themselves into a republic, in which they might pursue, without molestation, the 'proper treatment of the blacks'. It is almost needless to add that the 'proper treatment' has always contained in it the essential element of slavery, namely, compulsory unpaid labour [...]

The tribes who still retain the semblance of independence are forced to perform all the labour of the fields, such as manuring the land, weeding, reaping, building, making dams and canals, and at the same time to support themselves. I have myself been an eye-witness of Boers coming to a village, and, according to their usual custom, demanding twenty or thirty women to weed their gardens, and have seen these women proceed to the scene of unrequited toil, carrying their own food on their heads, their children on their backs, and instruments of labour on their shoulders. Nor have the Boers any wish to conceal the meanness of thus employing unpaid labour; on the contrary, every one of them, from Mr. Hendrick Potgeiter and Mr. Gert Krieger, the commandants,[3] downward, lauded his own humanity and justice in making such an equitable regulation. 'We make the people work for us, in consideration of allowing them to live in our country.'

I can appeal to the Commandant Krieger if the foregoing is not a fair and impartial statement of the views of himself and his people. I am sensible of no mental bias toward or against these Boers; and during the several journeys I made to the poor enslaved tribes, I never avoided the whites, but tried to cure and did administer remedies to their sick, without money and without price. It is due to them to state that I was invariably treated with respect; but it is most unfortunate that they should have been left by their own Church for so many years to deteriorate and become as degraded as the blacks, whom the stupid prejudice against colour leads them to detest [...]

It is difficult for a person in a civilized country to conceive that any body of men possessing the common attributes of humanity (and these Boers are by no means destitute of the better feelings of our nature) should with one accord set out, after loading their own wives and children with caresses, and proceed to shoot down in cold blood men and women, of a different colour, it is true, but possessed of domestic feelings and affections equal to their own. I saw and conversed with children in the houses of Boers who had, by their own and their masters' account, been captured, and in several instances I traced the parents of these unfortunates, though the plan approved by the long-headed among the burghers is to take children so young that they soon forget their parents and their native language also. It was long before I could give credit to the tales of bloodshed told by native witnesses, and had I received no other testimony but theirs I should probably have continued skeptical to this day as to the truth of the accounts; but when I found the Boers themselves, some bewailing and denouncing, others glorying in the bloody scenes in which they had been themselves the actors, I was compelled to admit the validity of the testimony, and try to account for the cruel anomaly. They are all traditionally religious, tracing their descent from some of the best men (Huguenots and Dutch) the world ever saw. Hence they claim to themselves the title of 'Christians', and all the coloured race are 'black property' or 'creatures'. They being the chosen people of God, the heathen are given to them for an inheritance, and they are the rod of divine vengeance on the heathen, as were the Jews of old. Living in the midst of a native population much larger than themselves, and at fountains removed many miles from each other, they feel somewhat in the same insecure position as do the Americans in the Southern States. The first question put by them to strangers is respecting peace; and when they receive reports from disaffected or envious natives against any tribe, the case assumes all the appearance and proportions of a regular insurrection. Severe measures then appear to the most mildly disposed among them as imperatively called for, and, however bloody the massacre that follows, no qualms of conscience ensue: it is a dire necessity for the sake of peace. Indeed, the late Mr. Hendrick Potgeiter most devoutly believed himself to be the great peacemaker of the country.

CW de Kiewiet, the historian, took a longer and more understanding view of the up-heavals that engulfed South Africa for much of the 19th century.

The native wars, from major campaigns to unheralded skirmishes, were spectacular phases in a lengthy process of encroachment, invasion, extrusion, and dispossession. For the most part the wars were not caused by the inborn quarrelsomeness of savage and warlike tribes, but by the keen competition of two groups, with very similar agricultural and pastoral habits, for the possession of the most fertile and best-watered stretches of land. In the arid regions the struggle was for the 'eyes' of good land, near the invaluable springs or fountains. It is a bootless effort to ascertain the responsibility for each war. Ama-Xosa tribesmen were skilled and daring cattle thieves; Zulu impis thundered their knees against their war shields; the black nodding plumes of Swazi warriors were feared in the Transvaal; Natal lived for a generation in terror of a great native uprising; upon every frontier the story of burning houses was familiar. Yet the general causes of these wars were seen most clearly in their effects. They can be seen in the loss of native land, in the growing inability of the natives to maintain themselves in more restricted and less fertile areas, and in the diminishing means of independent livelihood of the tribes. Fielding's comment that 'the sufferings of the poor are less observed than their misdeeds' has much meaning in frontier history. It was no chance that the great majority of wars came in seasons of drought. The relationship between the tortured barrenness of a South African drought and native uprisings is too obvious to be missed. Burned under a cruel sky, as empty of moisture as the soil was of nourishment, the cracked and cropless land was often the trigger of revolt. Yet not all the frontier lands passed into European hands by violent means. There were cessions made by chiefs who put their marks on pieces of paper which they did not always understand, or afterwards always respect. Land was bought with harness, guns, and cases of brandy. It was acquired by the process of turning a permission to graze into the right to occupy. In the background of frontier land settlement was many a sordid story of land speculation. Many a missionary, not always innocently, was the tool of land-sharks. These locked up great blocks of land and almost literally compelled the Boers in the Republics to wrest the land they wanted from the natives.

The complex process of dispossession was made more difficult to regulate by the differing attitudes of whites and blacks towards the ownership of land. In the European mind ownership was more important than use; in the Bantu[4] mind use was more important than ownership. Native borders were open, vague, and imprecise. They encouraged trespass. The notion that a signature or the gift of a spavined horse gave a white man the right to hold land to the exclusion of all others was foreign to the native mind. Even more foreign was the notion that land where all men's beasts had grazed without let could be reserved for the herds of a single individual.

Between the native policies of the British colonies and the Dutch Republics no very significant distinction can be drawn. In all of them the process which allotted the privilege of land to the Europeans and the duty of labour to the natives was similar. In the new society which was being created the possession of land was a badge, and dispossession was a stigma. The endowment of the whites and the disendowment of blacks obeyed the social and moral rules to which the ruling group was attached. Similarly, the abstention of one group from hard physical labour, and the subjection of the other were more than economic differences. They were social differences as well.

In December 1834, in the biggest incursion of its kind, 15 000 Xhosa crossed the Great Fish River and advanced into the Cape Colony along a front that stretched 90 miles to the sea. They destroyed or severely damaged 800 farmhouses and captured more than 100 000 cattle, a cataclysmic event for the colonists that brought to the fore one of the most bizarre characters in South Africa's colonial history. Harry Smith (34), a veteran of the Napoleonic wars, was energetic, vain, prone to histrionics and driven by an insatiable lust for glory. He had arrived at the Cape to take command of the garrison in 1828, when he was 41. For the next six years, he mostly rode, hunted and chafed at his inactivity. So when news of the Xhosa invasion reached Cape Town, he was, as he recounts, more than ready to leap into the saddle. And what a ride it was!

The Kafir tribes, which for many months had been greatly agitated and excited, at length burst into the Colony in what was for the moment an irresistible rush, carrying with them fire, sword, devastation, and cold-blooded murder, and spoiling the fertile estates and farms like a mountain avalanche. Such were the reports received from the Civil Commissioners and the Commandant of the troops. His Excellency Sir B. D'Urban[5] determined to dispatch me immediately, with full powers civil and military to adopt whatever measures I found requisite, while he would himself follow as soon as possible. His Excellency told me a sloop of war was ready to take me to

Algoa Bay. I, however, preferred riding post, and the horses were laid for me for a seven days' ride, 600 miles. It was needless to start until the horses were on the road, so I had two days to make arrangements, and to ship military stores of every description, ordnance, etc. One half of the 72nd Regiment was to proceed in waggons, the other by sea.

On the night of the 31st December, I dined with Sir B. D'Urban at Cape Town (my own dear little cottage at Rondebosch being four miles off), and after dinner His Excellency and I had a long conversation. I fully ascertained his views and desires, and then made a resolution in my own mind never to swerve from his principles where circumstances admitted of their application. He on his part was most frank, honest, and decided, saying, 'You now understand me thoroughly. Rely on my support in every way, and my perfect readiness to bear all the responsibility.'

I parted with this noble soldier and able statesman at half-past twelve, drove out to my cottage, and lay down for three hours. I then started with a single Hottentot for a ride of 90 miles the first day [1st January, 1835], the heat raging like a furnace. My orders, warrants, etc., were sewn in my jacket by my own dear wife. From the anxiety and exertion of the previous day's running about Cape Town from store to store, and the little sleep I had had, as I rode the first 25 miles to the first change of horses I was half tired, but I got a cup of tea at the post-house, and never felt fagged again.

I arrived at Caledon at one o'clock, when it was threatening a heavy thunderstorm. I had then 25 miles to ride. The storm came on violently, the rain poured behind me, but I reached my stage, Field Cornet Leroze, by three, perfectly dry. The next day I started before daylight, and got to Swellendam to breakfast. I had two heavy, lazy brutes of horses. In Swellendam I wrote letters of instructions to that able fellow the Civil Commissioner, Harry Rivers, and I then started for an additional ride of 70 miles. I found the Buffeljagts river out. My first horse from Swellendam had a 20-miles stage, but through having to go up the river to ford, this noble little four-year-old had 30 miles, which he did, crossing the river too, in two hours and twenty minutes. I was so pleased with him, I wrote to Rivers to buy him and bring him up with the burghers. He bought him for £18 5s. I afterwards rode him very hard for two years, and sold him to Sir George Napier for £50. This day was excessively hot. I reached my stage at three o'clock.

I started the next day for George, with a long ride of 100 miles before me. At the second stage I found no horses and was kept waiting one hour. I got to a Field Cornet's where there was a great assembly of burghers enrolling their names for service, and a great dinner prepared at twelve o'clock, at which I was fool enough to eat, the remainder of my ride to George being rendered thereby a great exertion. Unfortunately, after a ride of 100 miles, I found all the civil authorities and inhabitants prepared to receive me, a ceremony I could readily have dispensed with. I soon got rid of these well-meant attentions, had a hot bath, lay down, and dictated letters to the Civil Commissioner, Mynheer de Bergh, until eleven at night.

I was off before daylight with a tremendous ride before me, over mountains, etc., etc. About halfway I met the mail from Grahamstown, and such a task as I had to open it! Not till I had opened the last bag did I find the packet of letters I wanted from the Commandant and the Civil Commissioner, Grahamstown. Their descriptions of disaster, murders, and devastations were awful; the Commandant talked of the troops being obliged to evacuate Grahamstown. I made comments on all these letters, and resolved to reach Grahamstown in two days. The heat to-day and the exertion of opening the letter-bags were fatiguing. On my arrival at my stage, I got hold of the Field Commandant Rademeyer, and sent on expresses all night to have the horses ready a day before they were ordered, being determined to reach Uitenhage the next night (the fifth from Cape Town),–500 miles.

Off two hours before daylight. One river, so tortuous is its bed, I had to cross seven times. I galloped through, and was as wet for hours as if I had been swimming, with a sun on me like a furnace. About halfway to Uitenhage, the heat was so excessive my horse knocked up, and no belabouring would make him move. About half a mile off I saw a sort of camp, went up, and found a Dutch farmer with his family, herds, flocks, etc., fleeing from the scene of devastation. I told him who I was, where and what I was going for, and asked him to horse me to the next stage, about seven miles. To my astonishment (for nothing can exceed the kindness and hospitality of the Dutch Boers on ordinary occasions), he first started a difficulty, and then positively refused, which soon set my blood boiling. He was holding a nice-looking horse all ready saddled, so I knocked him down, though half as big again as myself, jumped on his horse, and rode off. I then had a large river to cross by ferry, and horses were waiting for me. The Boer came up, and was very civil, making all sorts of apologies, saying until he spoke to the guide who followed me, he did not believe that in that lone condition I could be the officer I represented myself. The passion, the knocking him down, the heat, etc., was very fatiguing, and I reached Uitenhage at five o'clock, having been beating grass-fed post-horses from three in the morning until that hour, and ridden over some very bad and mountainous roads, 140 miles. To my horror, the Civil Commissioner (though a very worthy, good man) had all the town turned out to receive me, and a large dinner-party to refresh me, while I wanted repose. To add to this, a Colonel Cuyler, an officer retired on half-pay, of great experience and abilities on this frontier, waited on me. He was very communicative, of great use to me, but, being as deaf as a beetle, the exertion of calling loud enough for him to hear (although naturally I have a very powerful voice) I cannot describe. I had a wash, went to the great dinner – I dare not eat, quite to the astonishment of my host – soon retired, got hold of his secretary, and lay on my back dictating letters until twelve o'clock, when, fairly exhausted, I fell asleep.

Off again next morning for Grahamstown. If the previous day's work had been excessive, it was short of what I this day encountered from the wretched brutes of knocked-up horses laid for me. About half way I found the country in the wildest state of alarm, herds, flocks, families, etc., fleeing like the Israelites. Everything that moved near a bush was a Kafir. I was forced to have an escort of burghers on tired horses, and oh, such a day's work, until I got within ten miles of Grahamstown! There I found awaiting me a neat clipping little hack of Colonel Somerset's (such as he is celebrated for) and an escort of six Cape Mounted Rifles. I shall never forget the luxury of getting on this little horse, a positive redemption from an abject state of misery and labour. In ten minutes I was perfectly revived, and in forty minutes was close to the barrier of Grahamstown, fresh enough to have fought a general action, after a ride of 600 miles in six days over mountains and execrable roads, on Dutch horses living in the fields without a grain of corn. I performed each day's work at the rate of fourteen miles an hour, and I had not the slightest scratch even on my skin.

If it be taken into consideration that there was no previous training, that I started without sleep almost and after two days' excessive fatigue of mind and body in Cape Town, embarking stores, troops, etc., the little sleep I had on the journey from being obliged to dictate letters and give orders, the excessive heat, the roads, the horses, then it must be admitted a performance of no ordinary exertion for a man who, when it was over, was ready and required to use every energy of mind and body.

As Smith set to work, he explained in a letter to his wife: 'I look upon the wily Kafir as a wild beast and try to hunt him as such.' Sir Benjamin D'Urban, the governor, agreed: 'The Kafir is the worst specimen of the human race I have ever had to deal with … They are treacherous and irreclaimable savages.' For a near-contemporary – and rather more rounded – account of the Xhosa, we cannot do better than turn to George McCall Theal (35), South Africa's most prolific historian. He worked in the area as a teacher and journalist in the 1860s.

In South Africa the word Kaffir is often used in a general way to signify any black native who is not the descendant of an imported slave, but on the eastern frontier of the Cape Colony the term is usually restricted to a member of the Amaxosa tribe [...]

The Kaffir of the coast region is a model of a well-formed man. In general he is large, without being corpulent, strong, muscular, erect in bearing, and with all his limbs in perfect symmetry. His skull is shaped like that of a European; but here the resemblance ends, for his colour is a deep brown, and his hair is short and woolly. His intellectual abilities are of no mean order, and his reasoning powers are quite equal to those of a white man. He is haughty in demeanour, and possesses a large amount of vanity. For anything approaching frivolity he has a supreme contempt. The men are handsomer than the women, which is owing to the difference in their mode of living [...]

Until European clothing was introduced, the dress of the Kaffirs was composed of skins of animals formed into a square mantle the size of a large blanket, which they wrapped about their persons. The skin of the leopard was reserved for chiefs and their principal councillors alone, but any other could be used by common people. Married women wore a short leather petticoat at all times; in warm weather men and children went quite naked. No covering was ordinarily worn on the head, though a fillet, intended for show, was commonly bound round it, and a fantastic headdress was used by the women on certain festive occasions.

They are fond of decorating their persons with ornaments, such as shells, teeth of animals, and beads, used as necklaces, copper and ivory rings on their arms, etc. They protect their bodies from the effects of the sun by rubbing themselves all over with fat and red clay, which makes them look like polished bronze. Their clothing is greased and coloured in the same manner.

They live in villages, large or small according to circumstances. Their habitations consist of hemispherical huts formed of strong wickerwork frames thatched with reeds or grass; they are proof against rain or wind. The largest are about twenty-five feet in diameter, and seven or eight feet in height in the centre. They are entered by a low, narrow aperture, which is the only opening in the structure; their interior is smoky and dirty, and not seldom swarms with vermin. The villages are usually in situations which command a good view of the surrounding country.

The Kaffirs are warlike in disposition and brave in the field, though when fighting with Europeans they seldom venture upon a pitched battle, owing to their dread of firearms. Their weapons of offence are wooden clubs with heavy heads, and assagais or javelins. The assagai (a corruption of a Portuguese word derived from the Latin *hasta*) consists of a long, thin iron head, with both edges sharp, and terminating in a point, and is attached by thongs to a slender shaft or rod. Poising this first in his uplifted hand and imparting to it a quivering motion, the Kaffir hurls it forth with great force and accuracy of aim. The club is used at close quarters, and can also be thrown to a considerable distance. Boys are trained to the use of both these weapons from an early age. Before the introduction of firearms the Kaffir used a shield to defend his person. It was made of ox-hide stretched over a wooden frame, and varied in size and pattern among the clans [...]

A battle between Kaffirs consists of a series of individual encounters, in which the bravest combatants on each side challenge each other by name, and when one falls, another is called upon by the victor to take his place. The height of ambition is to be mentioned in one of the rude chants which the bards, whose principal employment is to sing the praises of the chief, compose on the occasions of festivals, and to hear one's name received with applause. The brave wear on their heads the feathers of the blue crane, which are given to them by the chief as tokens of distinction, and which no one else is permitted to wear [...]

Horned cattle constitute their principal wealth, and form a medium of exchange throughout the country. Great care is taken of them, and particular skill is exhibited in their training. They are taught to obey signals, as, for instance, to run home upon a certain call or whistle being given. In former days every man of note had his racing oxen, and prided himself upon their good qualities as much as an English squire does upon his blood horses. Ox racing was then one of the institutions of Kaffirland, and was connected with all kinds of festivities.

The care of cattle is considered the most honourable employment, and falls entirely to the men. They milk the cows, take charge of the dairy, and will not permit a woman even to touch a milksack. When Europeans first visited them they had, in addition to the ox, domestic dogs and an inferior breed of goats, the last not considered of much value. Barnyard fowls were also found in their possession, but adults made no use of either their flesh or their eggs.

The Kaffirs are an agricultural as well as a pastoral people. They cultivate the ground to a large extent, and draw the greater portion of their food from it. A species of millet, called by the colonists Kaffir corn, was the grain exclusively cultivated by them prior to the advent of Europeans. Of this they raise large quantities, which they use either boiled, or bruised into a paste from which bread is made. They were acquainted with the art of fermenting it and making a kind of beer, which they were fond of drinking, and which soon caused intoxication [...]

They have a system of religion which they carefully observe. It is based upon the supposition of the existence of spirits who can interfere with the affairs of this world, and who must therefore be propitiated with sacrifices. These spirits are those of their deceased chiefs, the greatest of whom has power over lightning. When the spirits become hungry, they send a plague or disaster, until sacrifices are offered and their hunger is appeased. When a person is killed by lightning no lamentation is made, as it would be considered rebellion to mourn for one whom the great chief has sent for. They have no idea of reward or punishment in a world to come for acts committed in this life, and each of the commonalty denies the immortality of his own soul.

In olden times, when common people died, their corpses were dragged away to a short distance from the kraal, and there left to be devoured by beasts of prey; but chiefs and great men were interred with much ceremony. A grave was dug, in which the body was placed in a sitting posture, and by it were deposited his weapons of war and ornaments. When it was closed, such expressions as these were used: 'Remember us from where you are. You have gone to high places. Cause us to prosper!'

They believe in the existence of a Supreme Being, whom they term Qamata, and to whom they sometimes pray, though they never offer sacrifices to him. In a time of great danger a Kaffir will exclaim, 'O Qamata, help me!' and when the danger is over he will attribute his deliverance to the same Supreme Being. The Kaffirs cannot define their belief concerning Qamata very minutely, and they do not trouble themselves with thinking much about the matter […]

A corollary to the belief in malevolent spirits is the belief in witchcraft. Certain persons obtain from the demons power to bewitch others, and thus sickness and death are caused. The same individual who acts as a priest acts also as a witch-finder. In olden times the person whom the witch-finder pronounced guilty was liable to confiscation of property, torture, and even death. The priest and witch-finder professes also to have the power of making rain, and of causing the warriors of his clan to be invulnerable in battle. When following any of these occupations, he attires himself most fantastically, being painted with various colours, and having the tails of wild animals suspended around him.

Before the supremacy of the Europeans it was seldom that the individual who filled this office died a natural death. Sooner or later he would fail to cause rain to fall when it was needed, or warriors whom he had made invulnerable would be struck down, or something else would happen which would cause him to be regarded as an impostor. He was then generally tied hand and foot and cast into the first stream at hand. Nevertheless, implicit confidence was placed in his successor, until he, too, met the same fate […]

The snake is treated with great respect by the Kaffirs. If one is found in a hut, the people will move out and wait patiently until it leaves. The owner will say that it is perhaps the spirit of one of his ancestors who has come to visit him in this form. It may be only an ordinary snake, he will add, but it is not advisable to run any risk, lest harm should befall his house.

In the division of labour the cultivation of the ground falls to the woman's share, as does also the collection of firewood, and the thatching of the huts. A man who meddles with work of this kind is regarded as an intruder into a domain not his own. The females look upon it as pertaining to them, just as in England they look upon housework […]

Ingenious as they are, the men are far from being industrious. A great portion of their time is spent in visiting and gossip, of which they are exceedingly fond. They are perfect masters of that kind of argument which consists in parrying a question by means of putting another. They are not strict observers of truth, and, though not pilferers, they are addicted to cattle lifting. According to their ideas, stealing cattle is not a crime; it is a civil offence, and a thief when detected is compelled to make ample restitution; but no disgrace attaches to it, and they have no religious scruples concerning it.

Such, in brief, are the Kaffirs.

Within nine months of Harry Smith's arrival on the frontier, the sixth 'kaffir war' was over. The Xhosa were defeated, their cattle seized and their homes and crops destroyed. Supposedly at their request, a great chunk of their territory, extending 100 miles to the east of the Great Fish River and containing a population of 100 000, was annexed to the Crown as the province of Queen Adelaide with its capital at King William's Town. Smith was appointed great panjandrum. In a victory address to an assembly of 'Kaffir chiefs', he set about instructing his subjects – he called them 'my children' – on how to become good Englishmen.

Whoever it was among you who first suggested the idea of your becoming British subjects, deserves to be marked by you as a man who has rendered you the most eminent service. Did not your great father, Gaika,[6] on his death-bed, assemble his sons around him and with his dying breath tell them to hold fast the word of peace with the English? This you did not do: what ensued? You were almost utterly destroyed, soon would have been annihilated, and driven from your native country; your women and children were starving, almost the prey of wild beasts, and the widows of 4000 of your warriors lament their husbands slain during the war; the greater part of your cattle starved or taken; your plunder, so treacherously seized from the Colony, lost to you from the robberies of others; you were in a lamentable, nay, a deplorable plight; you sought and asked for mercy – it was granted you. You also begged to be received as British subjects; this has been granted you, and you are now the subjects of the most powerful nation, whose laws, manners, customs, and institutions are the wonder of the world.

This was your state when I took you 'out of the bush,' since which three moons have barely passed over your heads; land has been given you, your gardens are flourishing; your clergymen are returned to you, hoping to forget your sins in observing your penitence; a trade is established for you; your persons and property are protected by the equity of the British law – no man can now be 'eat up,'[7] unless found guilty of crime, and condemned by your judges; and in place of being the beaten, the degraded, humbled, mortified people you were in the bush, you are taken by the hand, and called 'brother' by the greatest nation under the protection of Almighty God.

You tell me that you are naked and ignorant, that I must teach you to clothe yourselves, to know good from evil, that you are willing to learn, and that you wish to be real Englishmen. Mark me, then. Years ago the English were as naked as you, and ignorant as you, as cruel as you were in the late war; but the bright day which has opened upon you, dawned upon them; they first learnt to believe in the omnipotent power of Almighty God, who judges every man according to his actions; worshipped, honoured, and obeyed Him; they loved their neighbours as themselves, and respecting their property, ceased to be thieves; they believed all that the ministers of God told them; they sent their children to be taught to read and write; they learnt the use of money, and carried on an honest trade with each other, selling their skins, etc., and buying clothes as you see us all now dressed. Some were labourers in the field, some tended the herds and flocks, some made implements of husbandry, built houses, made arms, and every other thing you see your brother Englishmen possess; while others made laws to govern the whole, under the King, whom we all love. Thus civilization gradually advanced, while we became acquainted with the works of art; knowledge increased, we threw off the yoke of despotism and barbarism, cast away our vicious habits, and put to death or banished by the Law every one who by sin, crime, and wickedness was a pest and an enemy to society at large.

Do you suppose that we have all these things by lying sleeping all day long under a bush? No; but by habits of daily industry, working as you see me do, and all the people around me, each day becoming wiser than the other: and by avoiding the evils of yesterday, striving to improve ourselves to-day. Such now may be your case, provided you cease to do the following things:–
I. First, to 'eat up' one another. This is theft.
II. To murder or kill any one.
III. To believe in witchcraft. This is all folly and ignorance of the worst description. Did not Eno's[8] 'rain-maker' desire you to go to war, and encourage you by telling you that you would beat the English, the greatest nation in the world, whose power exceeds yours as much as the waters of the Keiskamma do the pools of the Penla rivulet? How dare the villain tell you such lies? Was he not the first man shot when the troops moved on Eno's kraal, after I came amongst you, and was then as much your bitter enemy as I am now your true friend?
IV. Perjury, or giving false witness against any one.
V. Setting houses on fire, and destroying property.
VI. Rape. And above all (having this day taken the oath of allegiance) –

VII. Treason, or lifting up your hand against the King, the Governor, his officers, magistrates, soldiers, and subjects.

The British Law punishes these crimes with death; by avoiding them we have become the great, powerful, and enlightened and happy nation you see, going about the world teaching others to imitate us, and we are now instructing you. Do you wish to be real Englishmen, or to be naked, and almost wild men? Speak, I say, that I may know your hearts.

★　★　★

You have spoken well; your brothers will assist you. This day has his Excellency the Governor clothed your Chief Magistrates and Field Cornets according to their rank, to show you how England expects her subjects to appear. From this time henceforth no more presents of clothes will be given you; by trade (as we do) you must clothe yourselves, and look no more to me for presents but for some important and good service rendered to the State. Such I will reward, because his Excellency the Governor loves to reward merit.

Since you have been under my protection the oldest men tell me there has been less crime than they ever knew: but this, though it pleases me, does not satisfy me. There shall be no stealing, one from the other; above all, from the King – or, as you would term it, the Great Kraal – the Governor or his people. Beware, I say, of theft, and as I protect you, so will I punish you, until the Law, by the rigour with which I will wield it, shall root out this evil from amongst you. Our clergymen will teach you what God expects from you, what you must do to expect God's mercy and love in the next world: thus you will all learn to love God.

You may send your children to school, or you are wicked and base parents; and by your good example and speaking the truth, teach them what they may become with the advantages of an education, which you have not, and could not receive. Above all, do not despair or despond, or say, 'We are poor people; we know nothing.' Rouse yourselves: remember what I have told you, that the English were once as you now are, and that you may become what they are at present.

In the great change of laws by which you are now governed, one of the most important is that of not tolerating your being 'eaten up.' Now, this protects the weak; the strong from time immemorial possessed amongst you this power, which custom made a right of the Chief, though it was a curse to you: do not therefore suppose that the English Law while it protects one part injures the other. No, such is not the case; your Chiefs who from custom possessed this power by which their kraals were filled with cattle, and by which they were enabled to reward those who performed good service, must, your merciful and provident governor says, receive an equivalent; besides, being now your magistrates, much of their time and attention will be taken up for your advantage. You must therefore contribute to their support and dignity.

A regulation is now framing that each kraal pay so many cattle or calves in the hundred annually to each other on the day the ox is paid to the King of England for the land which you possess, and which he had conquered from you. No time will be lost in carrying this arrangement into effect. Thus you see, Macomo, Tyalie, Umhala, and the others of your kindred who from birth possess rights and privileges, you will be hereafter amply provided for.

To the heads of kraals and villages do I now address myself. You are responsible for the good conduct of the people of your village; if you exert yourselves and do your duty, crime will be checked and ultimately stopped. No man ought to be absent without your knowledge. No man can return with cattle or horses without your knowing it, and whenever a crime shall have been committed by a kraal, I will make the whole responsible to me, if they do not produce the offenders and the stolen property. You shall leave off this wicked practice of stealing from one another in the way you do; the English Law will make honest men of you – you shall not steal.

You must see that your people are active and industrious, that they work in the garden; it is the duty of men to work in the fields, not of women; they ought to make and mend your clothes and their own, and to keep the children clean, wash your clothes, cook your food, and take care of the milk. You well know from observation what work the English do, and what their women; this you must imitate, and not sleep half your time and pass the rest in drowsy inactivity; these things you must do, and you will soon reap the fruits of your labour.

Magistrates and all assembled! As you wish to be real Englishmen, you must observe their manners and customs in everything; and as you are rapidly ceasing to believe in witchcraft, and at the death of any of your friends and relatives (an affliction to which we are all liable) beginning to omit the witch dance and the burning your huts and clothes, so do I now call upon you to bury your dead, as you see we do, and not drag out the corpse ere the vital spark is extinct, and cast it forth for food for wild beasts and birds of prey – the thought, even, makes a Christian and a civilized man shudder. To the first man who has the misfortune to lose one of his relatives, if he decently inter him, will I give an ox. How can you bear to see those whom in life you loved and cherished – your aged father, who taught you your manly exercises and provided you with food; your mother, who nursed you as a child, who attended you in your sickness, who for years watched over you, contributing to your wants or wishes; your brother, sister, nearest relation and dearest friends, dragged from amongst you ere dead, and thrown out to the dog? We English not only make coffins to bury our dead, but raise upon the spot where our dearest friends' earthly remains are deposited, monuments to perpetuate their virtues; and when wicked men whose lives have been forfeited to the offended laws of our country for any of the crimes which I have enumerated to you are buried (for we even bury them also), such spot is marked with the ignominy it deserves; and our youth, as they pass the tomb of the good man, have an example of the respect due to virtue set before them; or are taught to abhor the crime which merited an ignominious death by the wretched mound which marks the sinner's grave. Thus as you loved your relatives in life, so you are bound to cherish their memory, and deposit their mortal remains in their parent earth. Englishmen not only do this, but the clergyman prays over the grave, and these matters of moment connected with the immortality of your souls the missionaries will teach you when you attend Divine worship. But your dead you must bury, as I point out, if you wish to be real Christians and Englishmen.

At this great meeting let me impress upon you, that all previous animosities among yourselves be forgotten, and while the great English nation now regard you as British subjects and brothers, love your neighbours as yourself, fear God, honour your King, and the Governor, his representative.

Alas for Harry Smith, his bracing brand of imperialism made the British government blanch. It repudiated the annexation of Queen Adelaide province and recalled the governor, Sir Benjamin D'Urban. Smith was relieved of his command and despatched to India. Within seven years, however, he was back covered in glory having wrested the Punjab from the Sikhs. In his absence, the seventh 'kaffir war' had broken out and Sir

Harry Smith, as he had now become, was appointed governor of the Cape Colony. He arrived in Cape Town on 1 December 1847. Noel Mostert (36), the historian, takes up the story.

The Cape Colony was ecstatic. Cape Town was illuminated and the windows of the solitary house that remained unlit were smashed by a mob. Finally, it was generally agreed, Britain had done the right thing by sending to the Cape the one man sympathetic to the cause of the colonists and who more than anyone else could be relied upon 'to put the Kaffir in his place'. That in all likelihood it was the worst appointment that she yet had made during her entire tenure of the Cape Colony was, for the more sober-minded, plainly evident the moment that Harry Smith stepped ashore at Algoa Bay on 14 December.

Walking up from the beach, Smith went to a local hotel to show himself to the excited crowd from a window, from where he spotted his old adversary Maqoma astride his horse in the throng. Their sudden consciousness one of the other was quickly picked up by the crowd, which became attentive audience for what followed. There are various accounts of the incident, the principal details of which are, however, in agreement. Smith, holding Maqoma's attention, drew his sword half-way from the scabbard, held it for a minute, and then drove it back 'with an expressive gesture of anger and scorn'. The phrase was Harriet Ward's, who was disposed to romanticize. In another, more reliable account Maqoma after this gesture came forward, arm extended, to shake Smith's hand. He may have regarded the sword play as an acceptable small joke. But there was nothing funny about what followed. Maqoma was forced to prostrate himself before the Governor who, placing his foot upon his neck, declared: 'This is to teach you that I have come to teach Kaffirland that I am chief and master here, and this is the way I shall treat the enemies of the Queen of England.'

Once again, Sir Harry annexed the former province of Queen Adelaide, renamed it British Kaffraria and proclaimed himself paramount chief of the Xhosa. He called another assembly of chiefs and, having addressed them at length from horseback, instructed them to kiss his foot 'in token of submission'. Later, he had a throne built before which the chiefs were required to prostrate themselves.

The Boers, however, were less easy to subdue, as we shall see in the next chapter.

NOTES

1 A mixture of mud and cow dung.
2 The Dutch, during their reassertion of control between 1803 and 1806, had been planning to remedy some of the injustices.
3 Both were Voortrekker leaders.
4 Like so many South African terms, now regarded as derogatory; it meant black African.
5 Sir Benjamin D'Urban, the governor of the Cape Colony.
6 A paramount chief, whose son, Maqoma, led the 1834 invasion.
7 To be 'eaten up' was to be arbitrarily accused of witchcraft and have one's property confiscated.
8 Another Xhosa chief.

CHAPTER 7

'VACILLATION VARIED WITH TYRANNY'

The Scorpion

Limpopo and Tugela churned
In flood for brown and angry miles
Melons, maize, domestic thatch,
The trunks of trees and crocodiles;

The swollen estuaries were thick
With flotsam, in the sun one saw
The corpse of a young negress bruised
By rocks, and rolling on the shore,

Pushed by the waves of morning, rolled
Impersonally among shells,
With lolling breasts and bleeding eyes,
And round her neck were beads and bells.

That was the Africa we knew,
Where, wandering alone,
We saw, heraldic in the heat,
A scorpion on a stone.

William Plomer (37)

By 1834, the Boers had had enough. Resentful at being conquered by the British and made subject to their laws, they insisted on the right to live as they chose in the land of their birth. The Bushmen, Hottentots and Xhosa had, of course, felt much the same about the advent of the Dutch – and with rather more reason – but the parallel would not have recommended itself to the Boers. What they chiefly resented were the British government's insistence on Hottentots' rights, its inability to suppress the turmoil on the eastern frontier and its decision to emancipate the slaves. That Act had been passed in 1833, emancipation in the Cape Colony, where there were more than 35 000 slaves, to be completed five years later. So over the next four years, 6 000 Voortrekkers (pioneers), as they became known – a quarter of the Europeans in the Eastern Cape – accompanied, naturally, by their 5 000 'coloured' servants, quit the colony and headed north. An iconic event in Afrikaner mythology, it was likened to the exodus of the Israelites from Egypt and came to be known as the Great Trek. The reasons behind it were spelled out in the *Grahamstown Journal* on 2 February 1837 (38).

Manifesto of the Emigrant Farmers

A document has been handed to us, with a request to give it publicity, purporting to be the causes of the emigration of the colonial farmers, of which the following is a literal translation:

Numerous reports having been circulated throughout the colony, evidently with the intention of exciting in the minds of our countrymen of prejudice against those who have resolved to emigrate from a colony where they have experienced, for so many years past, a series of the most vexatious and severe losses; and, as we desire to stand high in the estimation of our brethren, and are anxious that they and the world at large should believe us incapable of severing that sacred tie which binds a Christian to his native soil, without the most sufficient reasons, we are induced to record the following summary of our motives for taking so important a step, and also our intentions respecting our proceedings towards the native tribes which we may meet with beyond the boundary:

1. We despair of saving the colony from those evils which threaten it by the turbulent and dishonest conduct of vagrants, who are allowed to infest the country in every part; nor do we see any prospect of peace or happiness for our children in any country thus distracted by internal commotions.

2. We complain of the severe losses which we have been forced to sustain by the emancipation of our slaves, and the vexatious laws which have been enacted respecting them.

3. We complain of the continual system of plunder which we have ever endured from the Caffres and other coloured classes, and particularly by the last invasion of the colony, which has desolated the frontier districts and ruined most of the inhabitants.

4. We complain of the unjustifiable odium which has been cast upon us by interested and dishonest persons, under the cloak of religion, whose testimony is believed in England, to the exclusion of all evidence in our favour; and we can foresee, as the result of this prejudice, nothing but the total ruin of the country.

5. We are resolved, wherever we go, that we will uphold the just principles of liberty; but, whilst we will take care that no one shall be held in a state of slavery, it is our determination to maintain such regulations as may suppress crime, and preserve proper relations between master and servant.

6. We solemnly declare that we quit this colony with a desire to lead a more quiet life than we have heretofore done. We will not molest any people, nor deprive them of the smallest property; but, if attacked, we shall consider ourselves fully justified in defending our persons and effects, to the utmost of our ability, against every enemy.

7. We make known, that when we shall have framed a code of laws for our future guidance, copies shall be forwarded to the colony for general information; but we take this opportunity of stating, that it is our firm resolve to make provision for the summary punishment of any traitors who may be found amongst us.

8. We propose, in the course of our journey, and on arriving at the country in which we shall permanently reside, to make known to the native tribes our intentions, and our desire to live in peace and friendly intercourse with them.

9. We quit this colony under the full assurance that the English Government has nothing more to require of us, and will allow us to govern ourselves without its interference in future.

10. We are now quitting the fruitful land of our birth, in which we have suffered enormous losses and continual vexation, and are entering a wild and dangerous territory; but we go with a firm reliance on an all-seeing, just, and merciful Being, whom it will be our endeavour to fear and humbly to obey. By authority of the farmers who have quitted the Colony,

(Signed) P. RETIEF

'P Retief' was Piet Retief, who went on to lead a party of Voortrekkers north across the Orange River and then east over the Drakensberg Mountains. From there they espied the promised land of Natal, which, however, had quite enough problems of its own. Much of it had been laid waste between 1816 and 1828 by Shaka, the 'Zulu Napoleon'. He, too, had forged an army, created an empire, instigated a reign of terror and killed lots of people – in his case, an estimated one million. Believed by some modern historians to have been impotent, Shaka – also known as the 'Zulu Nero' – took a perverse pleasure in mass murder, as Nathaniel Isaacs (39), then an 18-year-old trader, witnessed. The entry in his diary is dated 11 November 1826.

His majesty rose early this morning and collected his warriors [...] He told his people that he was going to select a spot on which to build a kraal, but he had no such design; he sought only to carry into effect one of his usual inhuman executions, or horrible butcheries. I suspected his design, and sought to learn his purpose, because, having before been witness to similar proceedings, I could distinctly perceive by his manoeuvres, and judge from the arrangements, that he no more contemplated seeking a site for a building, than he did of being merciful to an unfortunately offending native. The poor wretches who were to be sacrificed that day being selected, were sent under pretext of viewing the parts adjacent, and to report a congenial spot for building. Chaka then sat down, and desiring his people with great earnestness and precaution to be secret, stated that he had had a dream which greatly concerned him. He dreamt that a number of his boys had had criminal intercourse with his girls in the palace, and that while he was teaching them songs last night, many of them were debauching his women, and had thus polluted his imperial establishment. This offence he declared himself determined to punish with rigour; his people applauded his resolution, and said, 'Father kill them for they are not fit to live.' The revengeful and unappeasable Chaka, seeing his subjects partake of his feelings, and hearing them demand that he should execute summary punishment upon the supposed violators of the purity of the imperial seraglio, said, 'that the spirit of an old and favourite chief, Umbeah, had visited him several times and warned him against the designs of his people, who, when he called them out on public purposes, took advantage of his temporary absence, entered into his palace, and polluted his females;' that this had been done last night he protested he had every proof, confirmed by the communications of the spirit of his forefathers. That it was so now he had no doubt, for many of his people yet remained in the kraal who ought to be present at the conference, but were indulging in amours with the girls of the palace. 'Look,' said he, 'at the Maloonga (meaning me), you see he is a man, he knows that it is improper to stop at home in my absence.' The people reluctantly acquiesced in all he said, fearing the awful consequences that might befall the girls, not that they esteemed them, but because they were property. Meanwhile, two or three of the men got up and went towards the kraal, not, it was thought, with any criminal design, but for the purposes of nature, when they were immediately killed.

The king now arose, and the people followed him, keeping about twenty yards in his rear; and every time he stopped they kept bending to the ground, agreeably to their custom. 'Now let me see,' said he, 'if there be a man among you: how are we to secure the people in the kraal?' Some said by surrounding it. 'Well,' said he, 'how will you manage it, will they not see you, and many of the guilty escape?' Here the people appeared at a loss, or were most probably willing that those in the kraal should escape. Chaka, therefore, conceived that the best plan would be, when his followers approached the kraal, for a few of them to run on each side and the remainder shortly to follow them, and then, while those within stood unsuspectingly looking on, for all to unite again suddenly, and surround the whole kraal. A party was directed to remain with the king, lest something should be apprehended, who also might be employed in taking the people out of the huts and putting them in the cattle kraal. The people about Chaka were unanimous in applauding so ingenious a stratagem, and, declaring themselves ready to execute orders: this diabolical tyrant immediately marched his party into the kraal.

I went to secure my boys as I feared the approaching massacre, – the inhuman tragedy about to be performed, and was extremely anxious that they should not take a part in it. The king at first beat his aged and infirm mother with inconceivable cruelty, and to the astonishment of all, as he had ever manifested towards his parent a strong filial affection. He then became in such a violent and savage rage, that, knowing his want of temper to discriminate objects, and apprehending something for my own personal safety, I withdrew to my hut.

When all the poor unoffending creatures were collected in the cattle kraal, many of them being sick, their number amounted to one hundred and seventy girls and boys, a great many of whom were his servants and girls from his seraglios. Nothing could equal the horror and consternation which pervaded these poor miserable and devoted wretches, who, surrounded and without hope of escape, knew they were collected to sate some revengeful feeling of their tyrant, but were nevertheless ignorant of the cause, for they felt that they were innocent. Chaka, in an instant, on missing me, sent to call me, and rebuked me for leaving him, when I mentioned that I had been to drive the strangers out of my hut, and secure my boys; he shook his finger a good deal at this, as a mark of his approbation. Everything being ready for the bloody scene, to complete this unexampled sanguinary massacre of un-offending beings, he called his warriors, that had surrounded the kraal, and told them that his heart was sore, and that he 'had been beating his mother Umnante, because she had not taken proper care of his girls.'

He then ordered the victims intended for destruction to be brought to him, and those whom he selected his executioners immediately despatched. He began by taking out several fine lads, and ordering their own brothers to twist their necks, their bodies were afterwards dragged away and beaten with sticks until life was extinct. After this refined act of monstrous cruelty, the remainder of the victims in the kraal were indiscriminately butchered. Few of the poor innocent children cried or evinced any sorrow, but walked out as if inwardly conscious they were about to be removed from a state of terror to 'another and a better world.'

There being so many of the victims, it took the warriors a considerable time to perform their inhuman duty, and thus fulfil the bloody order of their savage master.

The tyrant was left alone, with the exception of the interpreter and my-self, who were forced to witness the tragic scene, when, with a smile, he asked me 'why I did not assist in killing the Umtaggarties,' or people not fit to live, and otherwise appeared to exult at the success of his stratagem, and at the destruction of the innocent.

The warriors, after having done their infernal work of extermination, returned to the monster, and saluted him in their accustomed manner, by squatting on their hams. His majesty then addressed them, saying: 'You see we have conquered all our enemies and killed a number of Umtaggarties, I shall now consult Umbea and find out the rest.' Meanwhile he told the chiefs to kill some bullocks, and to thank the spirit, and then observed, 'To-morrow I shall kill all those who have offended since I have reigned, there will then be nothing wanted to make you and me happy.' After this, he arose and went into his palace, and the people after paying the usual respect retired to their huts, to take certain roots, for having killed their relatives; – these, they say, prevent their grieving, which is punished with death.

On the other hand, not being moved to tears could also have lethal consequences, as Thomas Mofolo (40), the Basuto author, explained in his pioneering novel, *Chaka*. Written in Sesotho and published in 1925, it was the first attempt at a psychological study of the Zulu tyrant, a man who 'craved to witness death'.

In those days, that is to say when King Chaka was in the very middle of the years of a man's life, the time when life is most enjoyable, when he who has been working begins to taste the fruit of his labours, when he sees the cattle and the goats he has earned beginning to multiply, and the people enjoying their milk; the time when he watches with satisfaction as the children of his loins are running around and playing; at that very time in his life King Chaka began to suffer untold pain in his soul. He suffered even though he was a king, instead of enjoying his large kingdom and enormous wealth which were the longings of his heart. Chaka was a king of kings, and the renowned of the earth paid tribute to him, and came to him crawling on their knees or on their stomachs, their heads bowed low. Where he sat, there was always a young warrior shading him with his shield, and his courtiers were continually declaiming his praises, acclaiming him and greeting him with salutations which were greatly flattering, which were spoken with much respect. Yet, in the midst of all that adulation, he began to suffer extreme pain in his soul.

The number of his warriors was equal to the stars in the sky, and no king before him had ever had so many; but even more important, they were invincible, and they fought against the winds and the storms till they conquered them, to say nothing about other human beings. He ought therefore to have been happy in the knowledge that all these things had come into being, and were of the nature they were, because of him. And yet, in the midst of all that wealth and all that glory he began to suffer pain and a gnawing sense of discontent in his soul.

What, we may ask, was his heart yearning for now? What was the object of its whimpering? What was it hankering after? What was it that he could wish for and be denied? But, in the midst of all these things, his heart lacked peace and contentment, nothing pleased him any more, his thoughts were in turmoil and were not able to calm down and to make firm decisions.

Chaka was a warrior who saw much blood in his growing up, blood that was spilt by him personally; now that he no longer went to war with his armies, therefore, he longed to see people dying by his own hand. He craved to witness death. Whenever he did not see that spectacle he became truly sick, and he desired that as his armies were shedding blood in battle, his right arm should remain steeped in gore here at home.

To still the throbbing in his heart, he called for a big feast, and as the people were enjoying themselves, he kept his eyes open for those he might find an excuse to remove from this world, by means of whom he might quench the thirst that was burning inside him. Some were killed right there during the festivities for, it was said, they sang out of tune or danced out of step, and thus spoiled the king's feast. Now since people do not have the same strength in their chests, those who feared to be killed for singing out of tune kept quiet so that their voices should not be heard; but that very silence of theirs became the misdeed for which they were killed, for it was said that they despised the king's feast. In these modern days, when a sermon is moving, people often cry; even in those days of darkness also, good dancing and singing did often make people cry, especially the elderly who were no longer able to participate in the games. On that day also many people's hearts were moved when they saw those uniformly adorned warriors, each division having its own dress, and when they remembered what they themselves used to be like in their days. They wept then. Some induced their weeping artificially, and said they were crying because they were moved by the king's feast.

Chaka asked what was the cause of their weeping, and they explained, and then he said: 'It amazes me that you are moved to tears by watching my warriors at their games, and not by me who am a wonder, by me who created all these things; you are not moved by my person, you are moved by the beauty of a garment not by him who is wearing it, and who made it, and by that act you are despising me.' When he spoke those words, he raised his little spear and pointed it upwards, and those poor people were killed, and yet they had acted under the mistaken belief that the king would be pleased that they were moved to tears by the magnificence of his feast. The people who were adept at the games, and the ones with beautiful voices who sang most tunefully, were also killed, for it was said that they made the people cry and usurped the glory of his majesty. And now the people were at a loss to know what it was that might please the king since the good singer, the bad singer, and the one who kept quiet were all killed alike. These ones we have just told about were the ones who were killed during the day, in the middle of the festivities.

When the night was advancing, when the people turned in for the night, Chaka took his regiments and killed the majority of the people who had come to the festivities at his own invitation, saying that they had been plotting against him; and the menials of the king to whom that task was entrusted, carried out this order quietly, and hundreds of people simply disappeared in the middle of the night, and were no more. And now his heart began to feel happy, and things began to look normal again, and he was able to derive some joy from them, now that he had done this deed; he could taste his food again, and that painful thirst which had seized him was diminished, and he felt like a human being again. He repeated such acts many times to douse this heat that seared his insides. The reason for arranging the feast was that he should be able to kill the people easily when they were all gathered together in one place.

Two years after the massacre that Nathaniel Isaacs had witnessed, Shaka was murdered by his half-brother, Dingane, who then assumed the Zulu throne. The Rev Francis Owen, who had been sent to Zululand by the Church Missionary Society 'to diffuse the light of the Gospel among the Heathen tribes', first encountered him in July 1837. But Dingane, as Owen soon discovered, was more interested in acquiring gunpowder and bullets. Owen's reluctance to provide them was to make preaching the Gospel to a frankly sceptical audience an exceptionally uphill task. His diary (41) entry for 26 November 1837 – a Sunday – begins: 'The most memorable, at the same time, most painful day since the commencement of the Mission…'

Dingarn called me to him, and told me he was *very sore*. The white people, he said, were not *one with him*. They granted him some things, but other things they withheld (alluding to the gun-powder): yet he was ready to do all the white people asked him: first one teacher' asked to instruct his people, then another, and he granted all! Yet he could not have his wants supplied in return! He said, moreover, that I was like the rest: that I was one with the white people; for when he asked me only to *lend* him a bullet mould, I refused, this shewed that I was like them. I told him that I was ready to do him every service in my power, consistently with my duty to my God, my king, and my country. He said it was no use for me to 'twist myself out' of the charge that he brought against the white people, for it was evident that I opposed his having fire arms as much as they did. I told him I did not mean to twist myself out of this charge, that I desired his good, chiefly the good of his Soul, which I had come in the first place to promote, and that I was ready to teach him anything else besides God's word consistently with my duty to my country. He said it was in vain for me to shelter myself under the pretence that I desired his good, because I did not lend him the bullet mould. He repeated over and over again the substance of what he had said, addressing himself to his servants, all of whom acknowledged, and then he said he would tell me plainly that *he was offended*. When I asked if he was offended at me, he told me *not to ask that question*. I must infer it from what he had said. At length I told him it was Sunday, whereupon he bid me to address his people and teach them the word of God. At the same time he sent Masipulu, his head servant to tell the Indoonas[2] that they were all to be quiet and listen attentively to me. A dead pause immediately ensued. I went forward, feeling in my heart, that I was called to testify Christ publickly in this place for the last, and the only time! Having advanced within a convenient distance from the men, the king sitting a good way behind, I commenced by telling them that they all knew that there was a great chief above the sky. Dingarn now sent a message to us to tell us to speak up, as we did at Nabamba. Raising our voices I proceeded to say that this king was greater than all kings, greater than my king, greater than their king: that they ought to fear their parents, they ought to fear their king, but much more ought they to fear the great God; they ought to do what their parents bid them, what their king bid them, and also what God bid them! We have none of us, however, done what God has told us to do. We are all sinners before him; He is displeased at us: each of us has a soul that must live for ever when the body is dead, but that our Souls, by reason of sin, are filthy and that they must be *washed*. Until this moment the greatest stillness and attention prevailed, but now the contradiction began, and such a cavilling and stormy audience never did I before address. It is impossible to give an adequate idea of the dispute which lasted for nearly 2 hours; one cavil succeeded another or was repeated 10 times, whilst no reply was made to my answers. The indoonas and the king were the chief objectors, the latter sitting at some distance behind and speaking low, his servant Masipulu shouted out to my Interpreter all his remarks. First I had to turn to the Indoonas then to the king as they successively opposed me. When I had begun to speak of the need of spiritual washing in order to introduce the Gospel the subject was treated with scorn. One asked if we were to be washed in the river. I said not with water, but with blood! Whose blood was the natural reply. The blood, I answered, of the Son of God, who was Jesus Christ. Where is he? they asked. In heaven, I said, but once he came down to earth, and ... Whom did he leave behind to wash us? He washes us himself with his own blood. It is not our bodies that he washes, but our Souls. He washes all who come to him by faith. Away, it's all a lie. I persisted in crying that Jesus Christ shed his blood, and that if they believed in him, that he came down from heaven, that he died for them, their souls would be saved. They asked me how this person was killed and who killed him. I said, wicked men nailed him to a tree. Dingarn then asked if it was God that died. I said, the Son of God. Did not God die, he asked? I said God cannot die. If God does not die, he replied, why has he said that people must die? I told him it was because all people were sinners, and death was the punishment of sin, but He would raise us all again from the grave. This gave rise to innumerable cavils. They wanted me to tell them the day and the hour when we should rise again, who would be witnesses of the resurrection, who would be alive at that day. They said if any generation had been seen to rise from their graves they would believe. I told them that Jesus Christ rose again the third day, and that he was seen by his 12 servants, and afterwards by 500 persons at once, and that his servants raised a great many other people. Dingarn asked me how many days Jesus Christ had been dead. If only 3 days (said he), it is very likely that he was not dead in reality but only *supposed* to be so! I said, that when he was on the tree a soldier pierced his side from which came forth blood, and that blood, I said, if believed in washes away sin. After a great deal more combat they told me I need not speak anything more about the resurrection, for they would not believe it. They had no objection to God's word, but they did not believe in the resurrection. Previous to this, however, I asked them why should it be thought an incredible thing with you, that God should raise the dead? Could not he who formed us at first, bring us into being again! They said they were formed by their Parents, but would not tell me how the first man was formed. At length they told me to say no more about the dead – leave them where they are, *go to the sick* and keep them from dying, for this is easier than to raise the dead. It is impossible to relate all that I said and all that they said. Whether all this contradiction was designed or not I cannot tell. Dingarn at length told me that the sun was hot and that I must tell him when I had done. I said I had only one question to ask. Did they not believe that the spirits of their ancestors survived their bodies. He said, all they believed about them was this, that when a person was sick the doctor was consulted who sometimes said that the spirit of the sick man's father had caused the sickness, hereupon he advised the sick man to appease his father's spirit with a bullock, and after this he sometimes got better. I said it would be much wiser for a sick man to pray to God that his sins might be forgiven. Notwithstanding the contradiction, I felt encouraged to think that God had enabled me to bring the truth before them, and tho' they did not understand it and would not believe yet, they could not avoid remembering (perhaps for ever), that it was by blood sin was to be cleansed and that he who shed this blood was now in heaven and ready to wash all who believed in him! This doctrine indeed now appeared to be 'foolishness' to them and as such utterly rejected: but I was encouraged to hope that the Spirit himself would hereafter unfold it to them, shewing them its true import and necessity. It might I hoped be a foundation on which to build at a future time, and doubtless they would remember more, than if my discourse had proceeded in a natural strain. I many times broke away from their cavillings and exhorted them to believe instead of objecting. The king once asked if all men would go to heaven? I told them plainly, if you believe the words which I now speak you will go to heaven, but if you believe them not you will all go to hell. They wanted me to give a proof that Christ was now in heaven; as who had seen him there. What the persons who took him up into heaven said when they came back again. Umthela remarked that if he saw a bird fly ever so high in the air and he looked at it steadfastly it always came down again. I told them he went up by his own power, in the sight of his disciples and that he would surely come again, when every eye should see him.

But there was an infinitely more memorable and painful day to come. Piet Retief, having espied his promised land, now had to obtain it from Dingane, who knew that even then hundreds of ox-wagons were pouring over the Drakensberg. Could the Boers, Retief asked, please have Natal, from the Drakensberg east to the sea and from the Tugela River to the Umzimvubu, more than 200 miles to the south? 'But of course,' he understood Dingane to say, and Francis Owen was on hand to draw up the deed of cession. On 4 February 1838, Retief and about 70 followers arrived to celebrate the agreement, leaving their guns, as was customary, at the gates of Dingane's kraal. Two days later, Owen was on hand to witness the bloody consequences.

Feb. 6th. – A dreadful day in the annals of the mission! My pen shudders to give an account of it. This morning as I was sitting in the shade of my waggon reading the Testament, the usual messenger came with hurry and anxiety depicted in his looks. I was sure he was about to pronounce something serious, and what was his commission! Whilst it shewed consideration and kindness in the Zoolu monarch towards me, it disclosed a horrid instance of perfidy – too horrid to be described – towards the unhappy men who have for these three days been his guests, but are now no more. He sent to tell me not to be frightened as he was going to kill the Boers. This news came like a thunder stroke to myself and to every successive member of my family as they heard it. The reason assigned for this treacherous conduct was that they were going to kill him, that they had come here and he had *now* learned all their plans. The messenger was anxious for my reply, but what could I say? Fearful on the one hand of seeming to justify the treachery and on the other of exposing myself and family to probable danger if I appeared to take their part. Moreover I could not but feel that it was my duty to apprize the Boers of the intended massacre whilst certain death would have ensued (I apprehended) if I had been detected in giving them this information. However, I was released from this dilemma by beholding an awful spectacle! My attention was directed to the blood stained hill nearly opposite my hut and on the other side of my waggon, which hides it from my view, where all the executions at this fearful spot take place and which was now destined to add 60 more bleeding carcases to the number of those which have already cried to Heaven for vengeance. There (said some one), they are killing the Boers *now.* I turned my eyes and behold! an immense multitude on the hill. About 9 or 10 Zoolus to each Boer were dragging their helpless unarmed victim to the fatal spot, where those eyes which awaked this morning to see the cheerful light of day for the last time, are now closed in death. I lay myself down on the ground. Mrs. and Miss Owen were not more thunderstruck than myself. We each comforted the other. Presently the deed of blood being accomplished the whole multitude returned to the town to meet their sovereign, and as they drew near to him set up a shout which reached the station and continued for some time. Meanwhile, I myself, had been kept from all fear for my personal safety, for I considered the message of Dingarn to me as an indication that he had no ill designs against his Missionary, especially as the messenger informed (me) that the Boer's Interpreter, an Englishman from Port Natal was to be preserved. Nevertheless, fears afterwards obtruded themselves on me, when I saw half a dozen men with shields sitting near our hut, and I began to tremble lest we were to fall the next victims! At this crisis I called all my family in and read the 91st Ps., so singularly and literally applicable to our present condition, that I could with difficulty proceed in it! I endeavoured to realize all its statement and tho' I did not receive it as an absolute provision against sudden and violent death, I was led to Him who is our refuge from the guilt and fear of sin, which alone make Death terrible. We then knelt down and I prayed, really not knowing but that in this position we might be called into another world. Such was the effect of the first gust of fear on my mind. I remembered the words, 'Call upon me in the day of trouble and I will hear thee.' But of the Boers, Dingarn, the Mission, the Providence of God, I had other thoughts. Dingarn's conduct was worthy of a savage as he is. It was base and treacherous, to say the least of it – the offspring of cowardice and fear. Suspicious of his warlike neighbours, jealous of their power, dreading the neighbourhood of their arms, he felt as every savage would have done in like circumstances that these men were his enemies and being unable to attack them openly, he massacred them clandestinely! Two of the Boers paid me a visit this morning and breakfasted only an hour or two before they were called into Eternity. When I asked them what they thought of Dingarn, they said he was good: so unsuspicious were they of his intentions. He had promised to assign over to them the whole country between the Tugala and the Umzimvubu rivers, and this day the paper of transfer was to be signed. My mind has always been filled with the notion that however friendly the two powers have heretofore seemed to be, war in the nature of things was inevitable between them, but I dreamed of the ultimate conquest of the Boers who would not indeed be the first to provoke, but who would be the sure defenders of their own property, and the dreadful antagonists of the Zoolu nation, who could hardly be kept from affronting them, not to mention that real or imaginary causes of quarrel could not fail to exist between two such powerful bodies. The hand of God is in this affair, but how it will turn out favourably to the Mission, it is impossible to shew. The Lord direct our course. I have seen by my glass that Dingarn has been sitting most of the morning since this dreadful affair in the centre of his town, an army in several divisions collected before him. About noon the whole body *run* in the direction from which the Boers came. They are (I cannot allow myself to doubt) sent to fall or to join others who have been ordered to fall unawares on the main body of the Boers who are en-

camped at the head of the Tugala, for to suppose that Dingarn should murder this handful and not make himself sure of the whole number with their
guns, horses and cattle would be to conceive him capable of egregious folly,
as he must know that the other Boers will avenge the death of their countrymen. Certain it is as far as human foresight can judge; we shall speedily hear
either of the massacre of the whole company of Boers, or what is scarcely
less terrible of wars and bloodshed, of which there will be no end till either
the Boers or the Zoolu nation cease to be.

Owen was right about the fate of the other Boers encamped at the head of the Tugela.
At a place now called Weenen, which means weeping, nearly 300 were slaughtered
together with their 250 servants. Psalm 91, which Owen read to his family, contains the
words: 'Thou shalt not be afraid for the terror by night; nor for the arrow that flieth by
day; nor for the pestilence that walketh in darkness; nor for the destruction that wasteth
at noonday.' Oddly, on hearing of the massacre, John Philip of the London Missionary
Society, observed: 'The retributive hand of God is visible in all of this.'

The Boers, of course, had their revenge. Led by Andries Pretorious, their chief commandant, they invaded Dingane's territory in November 1838. On 16 December, 468 of them,
drawn up in a laager (circle) of 64 wagons, were attacked by about 10 000 Zulus. In what
came to be known as the Battle of Blood River, three Boers were wounded and 3 000 Zulus
killed. The eye-witness was Jan Bantjes (42), who was acting as Pretorious's secretary.

Sunday, the 16th, was a day as if ordained for us. The sky was open, the
weather clear and bright. Scarcely was the dawn of day perceivable, when
the guards, who were still on their posts, and could scarcely see, perceived
that the Zoolas were approaching. Now, the patrols were all together in the
camp, having been called in the day previous by alarm signals of the cannon. The enemy then approached at full speed, and in a moment they had
surrounded the camp on all sides. In the meantime the day began to dawn,
so that they might be seen approaching, while their advanced lines had already been repulsed by the firing from the camp. Their approach, although
frightful on account of the great number, yet presented a beautiful appearance. They approached in regiments, each captain with his men following
him. In the same way the patrols had seen them come up the day previous,
until they had all surrounded us. I could not count them, but it is said that
a Caffer prisoner had given the number of 36 regiments, which regiments
may be calculated at from 9 to 10,000 men. The battle now commenced, and

the cannons were discharged from every gate of the camp; the battle then became violent, even the firing from the muskets from our side as well as from theirs. After this had been kept up for full two hours by the watch, the chief Commandant (as the enemy was continually bestorming the camp, and he was afraid that we would get short of ammunition), ordered *that all the gates of the camp should be opened, and the fighting with the Caffers take place on horseback.* This was done, and to our regret, they took to flight so hastily, that we were obliged to hunt after them [...]

Thus the Zoola commando was pursued for more than three hours, and we returned, as we were all short of ammunition. The chief Commandant ordered the cleaning of the guns, and that every man should provide himself with ammunition. This was complied with, and balls were also cast. Prayers and thanksgivings were offered to God, and after Divine Service had been performed, the chief Commandant again sent a strong party to pursue the Zoolas as far on as they could; but they returned in the evening, not having been able to come up with them. The next day we counted the number of the slain; those who had been killed about and near the camp, of which some have not been counted, with those who had been over-taken and killed, we found amounted to, the lowest certain number, more than 3000, besides the wounded.

The day – known afterwards as the Day of the Covenant in honour of a pre-battle deal the Boers had apparently done with their God – is commemorated by a laager of 64 bronze wagons at the site and in a series of marble tableaux at the huge Voortrekker Monument on a hill over-looking Pretoria. Its foundation stone was laid on the 100th anniversary of the Battle of Blood River. At noon on 16 December a shaft of sunlight shines through a hole in the dome on to a marble cenotaph 40 metres below, so 'symbolising God's blessing on the lives and endeavours of the Voortrekkers'.

What followed is one of the more bizarre periods in British colonial history. The Boers, emboldened by their victory at Blood River, had declared an independent republic, which they called Natalia. Five years later, however, Britain annexed it and so the Boers trekked back over the Drakensberg, some to the area between the Orange River and the Vaal, and some to join other Voortrekkers further north between the Vaal and the Limpopo. In 1848, Britain – in the person of Sir Harry Smith – annexed the former, calling it the Orange River Sovereignty, and then in 1854, by when Smith had been sacked, handed it back, allowing the Boers to form the independent republic of the Orange Free State. In 1852, those who had crossed the Vaal were allowed to establish what they called the South African Republic, only to see it annexed in 1877 and renamed Transvaal, Britain's policy now being to turn South Africa into a self-governing confederation. In 1881, the infuriated Boers finally drove the British out at the battle of Majuba Hill in what was later to be called the First Boer War. As JA Froude, the eminent English historian, who visited South Africa at the time, observed: 'The story of our rule at the Cape is a story of vacillation varied with tyranny.'

Delicate tribute to 'those resolute trekkers' was later paid by Francis Carey Slater (43) in his 1924 poem, 'The Karroo'.

Once, as I wandered by night on the fringe of the moonlit desert,
Lapped in a vision I saw pictures of days that are dead:
Groups of horsemen rode by me – with rifles slung at the shoulder –
Bronzed and bearded and stern, silent and watchful they rode.
Hard after these there followed, drawn by the slow-footed oxen,
Waggon on resolute wagon – white-sailed ships of the veld!
Maidens with mirthful faces, framed in the sun-bonnet homely,
Peeped from the rocking waggons that rumbled steadfastly on.
Almost I heard the rattle of chains and the creaking of yoke-skeis,
As onward the waggons lumbered over the limitless plain.
On, unfaltering on, invincibly journeyed the trekkers,
Onward over the desert, melting away like a cloud.

* * *

Gone are those resolute trekkers – pilgrims who passed through the
  desert;
Vanished the pioneers who strove with its obstinate soil:–
Gone, and they gallop no more the plains in the diamond morning;
Clamber no more the kopjes, watching the set of the sun;
Vanished, they plough no more, they sow not nor gather the harvest;
Linger no more on the stoep while star-buds open their eyes;
Never list they to the bleat of flocks that nibble and wander;
Saunter no more in the kraal while milk croons soft in the pail;
Never with prayerful eyes will they search through the passionless
  heavens,
Seeking for birds that tarry – grey-winged shadows of rain!
Blind to the dawn's red deluge and the purple surge of the sunset –

Suns no longer shall smite them, nor ever the moon enchant.
Stern was the conflict and long, but the desert has broken and crushed
    them,
Drained to the lees their life-blood, wasted them body and bone:
Drops in the sea of its silence, grains on the shores of its vastness,
Merged are they in its fabric – one with the infinite veld!

William Plomer (44) struck a similar note in *Turbott Wolfe*, his 1926 novel set in rural Natal.

It was from the west and the south that the Dutch had come, a few families venturing farther than any. Venturing like Scythians over rocky illimitable wastes, in those days unmeasured, they had come in mighty tented waggons that creaked and groaned, crude magnificent arks, on stupendous wheels, forced up and down the roadless uneven hills by straining teams of titanic oxen.

There were large gross men with flag-like beards, peasant-minds, and patriarchal names and manners; begetters of children. There were large gross women with wooden limbs and loud voices, bearers of children, their harsh heads hidden in prodigious flapping sun-bonnets of sheer black, as wickedly significant as the fell wings of unknown birds of ill-omen, in a landscape of clear dusty blue, and in an atmosphere as subtle as time and as vast as eternity.

Children came with them of all ages, babies and brats, quiet and mostly fascinated and bright-eyed (with black bright eyes like darting beetles, as all children have) and emulative (as all children are) of parents so wonderful as to be almost incredible. And young women with love insatiable, proud in their young womanliness; and young men were there, active, with young unshaven beards like bright wire in the sun.

Under the hoods of the waggons were secreted household goods – under every single hood a big black Bible, the holiest possession of each single family, massive, four-square, full of bitter biblical wisdom: and its pages turned oftenest by patriarchal thumbs in times of stress. 'Adversity,' as is written in each of those Bibles, 'teacheth a man to pray; prosperity never.'

The Boers, however, were not Britain's only problem. Back on the eastern frontier, in December 1850, the eighth 'kaffir war' had broken out, provoked by Sir Harry Smith's insultingly autocratic rule. If nothing else, it gave Thomas Baines (45), the artist and explorer, an opportunity he had been looking for. He had arrived in Cape Town as an immigrant in 1842, when he was 22, and taken a series of odd jobs.

I next obtained employment with a worthy but eccentric Scotch cabinet-maker who had relinquished his former calling for that of building wheeled carriages and, having then in cogitation a thousand and one schemes for the improvement of every department of mechanical science, required an assistant who could 'put his hand to a thing' and make himself generally useful. I soon became tolerably content with my situation; my wages, it is sure, were low and far from regularly paid, but my work was of a desultory character and nearly half my time was at my own disposal. The windows of the upper store commanded on one side the whole extent of the Bay, and on the other of the town and mountains, and the colours necessary to the decoration of a coach supplied me with the means of transferring to canvas much of the picturesque scenery I daily witnessed.

After about three years of poverty and hard though not incessant toil, a friend, the son of the late eminent musician Bernard Logier, enforcing his arguments by a commission for half a dozen pictures, persuaded me to profess myself an artist and trust entirely to my pencil for support; and, nothing loth though somewhat fearful for the result, I complied with his advice and soon found that I had no reason to repent the step that I had taken.

It was about this time [January 1847] that, during a severe gale from the north-north-west, two fine barques, the one a slaver and the other the ill-fated *Francis Spaight*, were driven on shore in Table Bay and twenty-seven of the crew of the latter and of those who volunteered to their assistance were drowned. For weeks afterward that fearful spectacle haunted my imagination. I could not close my eyes but the wild despairing countenances of the perishing seamen appeared before me 'plain and palpable to sense' as on the morning of the wreck, and it was long before I could reconcile myself to the idea of painting for profit a representation of that dreadful reality, of making money, as it were, of the sufferings of those whose grave was in the deep. At length I produced two pictures and disposed of them, and the subject soon became so general a favourite that I received commissions for it in every possible point of view; and this, with portraits of Indiamen and other vessels, and the never failing 'Cape Town with Table Bay and Mountain', kept me in full employment till the outbreak of the Kafir war induced me to turn my attention to landscape scenery and the delineation of the human figure. The departure of the various volunteer and burgher forces by sea and land formed my first subjects; and in the representation of the scenes of actual war-fare I received much valuable assistance from my friend and brother artist George Duff, whose beautifully pencilled native heads I have rarely seen equalled, and from many other officers and gentlemen who had visited the frontier. It was now impossible for me to execute all the commissions that poured in upon me; it was but seldom that I had opportunity to refresh my imagination and gather new ideas by a ramble among the mountains; and no sooner had I struck out something new than half a dozen persons, not a little to my annoyance, demanded 'an exact copy', which, if I undertook it, was sure to prove a failure.

It need not, however, be inferred that the roses which now appeared to strew my path concealed no difficulties or were entirely thornless. One great obstacle to my improvement was being obliged to bargain for the price of a picture before I commenced it; and perhaps a greater, was the rigorous exactitude to which, when painting to order, I was confined, and which many a time rendered what might otherwise have been an effective scene, tame and commonplace. Heaven forfend that there should be truth in Islam; for if, in the world beyond the grave, I be condemned to breathe a portion of my soul into every spiritless production of my pencil, Allah have mercy on the remainder, for little will be left to enter Paradise. Nevertheless, I rebelled sometimes against this thraldom, and refused now and then to spoil my pictures by the introduction of something glaringly in opposition to the rules of art, but my arguments were commonly met with 'What difference can it make to you if you get your money? If I pay for my picture have I not a right to have it painted as I please?' And among a host of absurdities of daily occurrence may be mentioned the remark of one gentleman who, dissatisfied with some apparent discrepancy in my charges, said he had understood the price of pictures to be 'a pound a foot' lengthwise.

Finding that the price at which I painted precluded the possibility of bestowing sufficient time upon my works to finish them very elaborately, I determined to attempt something of a rather superior character and not to fix its price till after its completion. I selected for my subject the defeat of the Kafirs by the 7th Dragoon Guards and Colonial forces at the Gwanga River, and, having collected all the sketches and information I could obtain, prevailed upon a young friend to stand in the various positions I required.

Among the groups was one of a burgher, a somewhat unusual circumstance, bayoneting an enemy, and, for this, two figures were necessary. My model Kafir, however, who refused to appear in other than full Parisian costume, was the most spiritless savage imaginable, and it was not until I took the weapon in my own hand and aimed a deadly thrust at his breast that he could be brought to see the propriety of appearing at all concerned in defending himself from the assault.

And so, in search of the real thing, Baines headed for the eastern frontier. By June 1851, pencil in hand, he was well to the east of the Great Fish River, where the eighth 'kaffir war' was in full swing.

My attention was now directed by a soldier to the advance of the 74th, who, having descended by a rugged path to the left of our position, were moving across the valley; and, perched upon a commanding mass of rock, I was busily engaged in sketching when a bullet sung through the air in close proximity to my head. 'That's he', said a Cape Corps man, pointing to a figure just visible in a small cloud of blue smoke about a hundred and fifty yards below. In another moment he disappeared behind the rock, and, just as I had resumed my pencil, treated me to another bullet, not quite so well directed as the first. Not relishing these interruptions and thinking myself entitled to a return shot, I was waiting his reappearance, when I was advised by an officer not to fire as there were Fingoes[3] in the bush; and almost immediately I saw them emerge from the cover beneath my feet, fire a volley at the rock, and gather round it, as if examining some object of unusual interest; though, whether that object were the body of the Kafir or not, the distance and the thickness of the foliage prevented my observing. The Seventy-fourth, meanwhile, were ascending a steep grassy ridge, so destitute of cover that every movement was plainly discernible, in the direction of a bold headland crowned by enormous rocks and backed, after a short interval of table land, by a dense forest communicating with, or, rather, forming part of, that in the basin of the Amatola Mountain, the Great Peak of which seemed almost to pierce the skies but a short distance on the left. On the right of the Regiment were the Port Elizabeth Fingoes, advancing with small regard to order and taking advantage as they moved of every object that could afford them cover; and on the left, tall columns of light-grey smoke, rising perpendicularly through the tranquil air and contrasting with the dark forest behind, marked the progress of those levied in Fort Beaufort.

Jet after jet of smoke now issued from the heights, while from the ranks of the Seventy-fourth, as they extended into line with as much steadiness as if upon parade, arose, in answer, a denser cloud, and in a few seconds the irregular rattle of the rebels' guns, followed by the heavy roll of Highland musketry, fell upon our ears. Under this galling fire from enemies who had been sitting at their ease in this almost impregnable position, while they had been toiling for at least three hours over mountain and valley, the gallant fellows advanced and, crowning the heights, followed the retreating enemy into the forest, from the depths of which rose pillars of smoke evidencing the conflagration of the huts, while the incessant rattle of small arms told of the conflict that was raging within [...]

In the afternoon we descended to the Amatola valley, the Seventy-fourth going round by the scene of their engagement to bury their dead, three in number, as we learned from the volleys fired over them as they were consigned to a soldier's grave. The bodies had already been stripped, and there is little reason to discredit the report that they were afterwards torn from their graves and exposed to the rapacity of creatures scarcely more savage than the enemy by whose hand they fell. Scarcely had the funereal volleys ceased, when the sharp rattle of musketry shewed that the regiment was again attacked, and as they descended the hill, another soldier received a wound which eventually proved fatal [...]

Most of the casualties occurred as the regiment was advancing up the exposed slope; men were wounded, the dress, the mess tins – worn on the blanket at the back of the neck – and even the musket-barrels of many others were perforated, and many of the officers, especially the Colonel, escaped narrowly. The Fingoes, on the contrary, disregarding military order and darting from cover to cover as they advanced, reached the heights without losing a man.

The British army's failure to adapt to fighting in the South African bush – so precisely observed by Baines – was to bedevil its later confrontations with the Zulus and the Boers.

The eighth 'kaffir war' – the most savage yet – finally ended in March 1853, 27 months after it had begun. More than 1 400 colonial troops were killed and 16 000 Xhosa. By then, Sir Harry Smith had been recalled in disgrace and Maqoma, the chief he humiliated on the beach at Port Elizabeth, sent to Robben Island. There then occurred one of those events so monstrous and tragic that it is never entirely forgotten. In the memory of the people, it is known as the Great Cattle Killing; the Europeans called it the national suicide of the Xhosa. CW de Kiewiet tells the story.

In 1857 the Eastern Frontier was stricken by a disaster which must be told for its tragedy and its meaning. The deep unrest of the Kafirs turned for help to magic instead of the assagai. Prophets amongst them proclaimed that they must kill their cattle and consume their corn even to their seed. Then a day would come when the spirits would write their power in the heavens, unleash the tempest to blow the white men into the sea, and make their land to be fat with corn and cattle. It is men who are in want that are most given to dream of plenty. The fat acres and lubberlands of joy of Ama-Xosa and Tembu superstition point to the intimate causes of their unrest. The proud white cattle that were to rise from the earth would take the place of the thin and diseased beasts that were really in their herds; the grain that would shoot to sudden ripeness would yield the abundance they did not have. Most desired miracle of all, the white man would be driven into the sea. The Kafirs appealed to their spirits to do what they had been unable to do in half a dozen wars. But the spirits of the tribe failed them too. How many cattle were killed, what tons of grain were destroyed cannot be told. It is enough to know that the tribes that took this fantastic gamble against fate were broken beyond repair. Besides the thousands, some say 25,000, that perished of hunger, many thousands more tramped into the colony begging for work that they might not die. Yet it was more than famine that drove them. It was the admission that they could no longer defend or maintain their own way of life. It was a movement of economic submission. Henceforth Kafirland was a reservoir of labour.

Contemporary estimates put the toll higher: at least 40 000 Xhosa dead of starvation; 400 000 cattle slaughtered. In the words of Noel Mostert, it was 'probably the greatest self-inflicted immolation of a people in all history'.

Underlining the life-or-death significance of cattle in rural South Africa is this account by Monica Hunter (46), the eminent social anthropologist, of their place in Pondo society. She carried out her study among the Xhosa's eastern neighbours in the early 1930s.

Before contact with Europeans, clothing was made of hide, supplemented by the skins of goats and wild animals, and cattle were the principal medium of exchange and the medium in which court fines were levied. Wealth was accumulated mainly in cattle. Further, cattle are the means of keeping on good terms with the ancestral spirits *(amathongo)*, and so of securing health and prosperity, because the maintenance of good relations with the ancestral spirits depends upon making the proper ritual killings of cattle at various stages in the life of the individual, and in sickness. In folk-tales the hero is often saved by a miraculous ox. Cattle are also the means of obtaining sexual satisfaction, since a legal marriage cannot take place without the passage of cattle; the right to limited sexual relations is legalized by the passage of a beast, and the fines for illegal relations are levied in cattle. The possession of cattle gives social importance, for they are the means of securing many wives and adherents, and of dispensing hospitality and showing generosity, on which virtues status largely depends. Also the possession of cattle in itself gives weight and dignity to the owner.

Considering the importance of cattle, therefore, in satisfying economic and sexual needs, and in keeping on good terms with the ancestral spirits, and as a ground of social standing, it is not surprising that the thought and interest of Pondo men should centre in them as it does. As boys they spend their days with cattle. The pride of a small urchin when he is promoted from goat to cattle herd is great, and always he is conscious that cattle are a most important concern of men. Each beast in the kraal has its name, usually given by the herd, and the boys maintain that the cattle know their names. As they grow older men take no part in herding, but they still take a great interest in the cattle and supervise the milking. I have seen middle-aged men walking several miles to watch their cattle being dipped, although sons and grandsons were in charge of them. Men sit a great deal in the shelter of the kraal fence where morning and evening the cattle are under their eye, and conversation constantly reverts to them. They talk of the pedigrees of the cattle, boast how many calves each cow has had, and tell what happened to each. Cattle are intimately known, and a man will describe accurately any beast in a neighbour's kraal. If a stray beast comes among the cattle of neighbours it will be noticed at once. This interest and knowledge is reflected in the language in which there are at least fifty-seven different terms describing cattle of different markings, as well as five terms describing the horns. That pasturage is of importance, as well as agriculture, is shown by the number of names of the month referring to the state of the pasture. Land is appraised by its pastural and agricultural value. Again and again I was asked about districts which I had visited, and which the inquirers had not seen: 'Is it good country for cattle? Have they many cattle there?' The most usual question about England was, 'What sort of cattle do they have there?'

This intense interest in cattle is among men and boys only. The women being dangerous to cattle, and having nothing to do with them talk little about them and are more interested in their gardens and crops than in cattle. Women usually do not know many of the terms referring to cattle. I found when learning them that I could get little help from girls, and it always aroused much mirth among men when I showed an interest in, and knowledge of, terms referring to cattle.

Cattle and people are the only things about which diviners are consulted, and serious illness and death in cattle is attributed to witches and sorcerers, as is sickness in human beings.

There is what may almost be termed an aesthetic appreciation of cattle. To the Pondo they are beautiful to look upon. 'Oh, but we love to fill our eyes with cattle,' pleaded a Native when a European was pointing out the dangers of overstocking, and the necessity of banking capital instead of buying cattle which the land could not support. The seriousness of the overstocking in South Africa is in itself proof that the economic aspect in the possession of cattle is not, to the Bantu, the most important.

In Zululand, Dingane had been overthrown in 1839 – soon after the Battle of Blood River – by his brother, Mpande, with the assistance of the Boers. He fled to Swaziland and was there duly murdered.

Rider Haggard (47), who arrived in Natal in 1875 at the age of 19 as an assistant to the colony's governor, became fascinated by the Zulus and later celebrated their history in a series of adventures featuring his hero, Allan Quatermain. Here, in a non-fiction work, he gives his version of the events leading up to the Zulu war and the defeat of the British at Isandlwana in January 1879.

Panda[4] was a man of different character to the remainder of his race, and seems to have been well content to reign in peace, only killing enough people to keep up his authority. Two of his sons, Umbelazi and Cetywayo,[5] of whom Umbelazi was the elder and Panda's favourite, began, as their father grew old, to quarrel about the succession to the crown. On the question being referred to Panda, he is reported to have remarked that when two young cocks quarrelled the best thing they could do was to fight it out. Acting on this hint, each prince collected his forces, Panda sending down one of his favourite regiments to help Umbelazi. The fight took place in 1856 on the banks of the Tugela. A friend of the writer, happening to be on the Natal side of the river the day before the battle, and knowing it was going to take place, swam his horse across in the darkness, taking his chance of the alligators, and hid in some bush on a hillock commanding the battlefield. It was a hazardous proceeding, but the sight repaid the risk, though he describes it as very awful, more especially when the regiment of veterans sent by Panda joined in the fray. It came up at the charge, between two and three thousand strong, and was met near his hiding-place by one of Cetywayo's young regiments. The noise of the clash of their shields was like the roar of the sea, but the old regiment, after a struggle in which men fell thick and fast, annihilated the other, and passed on with thinned ranks. Another of Cetywayo's regiments took the place of the one that had been destroyed, and this time the combat was fierce and long, till victory again declared for the veterans' spears. But they had brought it dear, and were in no position to continue their charge; so the leaders of that brave battalion formed its remnants into a ring, and, like the Scotch at Flodden –

'The stubborn spearmen still made good

The dark, impenetrable wood;

Each stepping where his comrade stood

The instant that he fell,' –

till there were none left to fall. The ground around them was piled with dead.

But this gallant charge availed Umbelazi but little, and by degrees Cetywayo's forces pressed his men back to the banks of the Tugela, and finally into it. Thousands fell upon the field and thousands perished in the river. When my friend swam back that night, he had nothing to fear from the alligators: they were too well fed. Umbelazi died on the battlefield of a broken heart, at least it is said that no wound could be found on his person [...]

A period of sixteen years elapsed before Cetywayo reaped the fruits of the battle of the Tugela by succeeding to the throne on the death of his father, Panda, the only Zulu monarch who has as yet come to his end by natural causes [...]

It must be remembered that for some years before Panda's death the

Zulus had not been engaged in any foreign war. When Cetywayo ascended the throne, it was the general hope and expectation of the army, and therefore of the nation, that this period of inaction would come to an end, and that the new king would inaugurate an active foreign policy. They did not greatly care in what direction the activity developed itself, provided it did develop. It must also be borne in mind that every able-bodied man in the Zulu country was a member of a regiment, even the lads being attached to regiments as carriers, and the women being similarly enrolled, though they did not fight. The Zulu military system was the universal-service system of Germany brought to an absolute perfection, obtained by subordinating all the ties and duties of civil life to military ends. Thus, for instance, marriage could not be contracted at will, but only by the permission of the king, which was generally delayed until a regiment was well advanced in years, when a number of girls were handed over to it to take to wife. This regulation came into force because it was found that men without home ties were more ferocious and made better soldiers, and the result of these harsh rules was that the Zulu warrior, living as he did under the shadow of a savage discipline, for any breach of which there was but one punishment, death, can hardly be said to have led a life of domestic comfort, such as men of all times and nations have thought their common right. But even a Zulu must have some object in life, some shrine at which to worship, some mistress of his affections. Home he had none, religion he had none, mistress he had none, but in their stead he had his career as a warrior, and his hope of honour and riches to be gained by the assegai. His home was on the war-track with his regiment, his religion the fierce denunciation of the isanusi (witch-doctors) and his affections were fixed on the sudden rush of battle, the red slaughter, and the spoils of the slain. Desirable as such a state of feeling may be in an army just leaving for the battlefield, it is obvious that for some fifty thousand men, comprising the whole manhood of the nation, to be continually on the boil with sanguinary animosity against the human race in general, is an awkward element to fit into the peaceable government of a state.

Yet this was doubtless the state of affairs with which Cetywayo had to contend during the latter years of his reign. He found himself surrounded by a great army, in a high state of efficiency and warlike preparation, proclaiming itself wearied with camp life, and clamouring to be led against an enemy, that it might justify its traditions and find employment for its spears. Often and often he must have been sorely puzzled to find excuses wherewithal to put it off. Indeed his position was both awkward and dangerous: on the one hand was Scylla in the shape of the English Government, and on the other the stormy and uncertain Charybdis of his clamouring regiments. Slowly the idea must have began to dawn upon him that unless he found employment for the army, which, besides being disgusted with his inactivity, was somewhat wearied with his cruelties, for domestic slaughter had ceased to divert and had begun to irritate: the army, or some enterprising members of it, might put it beyond his power ever to find employment for it at all, and bring one of his brothers to rule in his stead [...]

At this juncture Sir Bartle Frere[6] appeared upon the scene, and after a few preliminaries and the presentation of a strong ultimatum, which was quite impracticable so far as Cetywayo was concerned, since it demanded what it was almost impossible for him to concede – the disbandment of his army – invaded Zululand. The fact of the matter was, that Sir Bartle Frere was a statesman who had the courage of his convictions; he saw that a Zulu disturbance of one kind or another was inevitable, so he boldly took the initiative. If things had gone right with him, as he supposed they would, praise would have been lavished on him by the Home authorities, and he would have been made a peer, and perhaps Governor-General of India to boot; but he reckoned without his Lord Chelmsford,[7] and the element of success which was necessary to gild his policy in the eyes of the home public was conspicuous by its absence. As it was, no language was considered to be too bad to apply to this 'imperious proconsul' who had taken upon himself to declare a war.

That, at any rate, was how the colonists saw it. The truth is that Cetshwayo's 'cruelties' were greatly exaggerated and if his regiments were indeed 'clamouring', he had shown no intention of unleashing them. Contrary to Rider Haggard's view, the real villain was Sir Bartle Frere. Determined to subjugate the Zulus and regarding Cetshwayo as an 'ignorant and bloodthirsty despot', he decided – in direct contravention of his orders from the British government (shades of Sir Harry Smith) – to provoke a war.

So on 11 January 1879 the hapless Lord Chelmsford led his troops north across the Tugela River into Zululand, still then an independent country. There, on 22 January, Isandlwana and Rorke's Drift were written into the history books. At Isandlwana, a hill 30 miles north of the Tugela, 20 000 Zulus destroyed a poorly defended British camp, killing 900 white troops and 500 black. Armed only with assegais and cow-hide shields, some 2 000 Zulus died. Later that afternoon, 4 000 Zulus attacked a British outpost at Rorke's

Drift, which is nearby. They were beaten off. Eleven of the 140 defenders were awarded the Victoria Cross, Britain then being sorely in need of heroes.

According to Paul Kruger (48), four times president of the South African Republic, Sir Bartle Frere had only himself to blame for Isandlwana. The date is December 1878. Kruger is smarting at the British annexation of his republic a year earlier and wants it back. To make matters worse, 'Shepstone' – Sir Theophilus Shepstone – was the man who had done the annexing on the British government's behalf.

Sir Bartle Frere asked me, on my arrival at Durban, to assist the British Commander-in-chief, Lord Chelmsford, with information as to the best ways and means of waging war against the Zulus. I gave a ready and sincere compliance with this request. I advised the British commander to make every halting-place into a camp, by collecting the wagons together, as the Boers had been used to do, and always to be well provided with good spies and scouts, so as to keep thoroughly informed of the enemy's movements. Sir Bartle Frere asked me to accompany one of the Commander-in-chief's columns as adviser and leader. I at first refused. But, when he pressed me and declared that I might name my own reward for this service, I said: 'Very well, I accept. I will take 500 burghers and hand Zululand over to you, if you will give me the reward I want.' Sir Bartle Frere was a little of-fended when I offered to do with 500 men the work for which the English had placed so many soldiers in the field, and asked: 'Do you mean to say that your people are so much better than our soldiers?' 'Not that,' I replied, 'but our method of fighting is better than yours, and we know the country.' Sir Bartle now asked what reward I required. I said, 'The independence of my country and people,' whereupon the High Commissioner refused to discuss the subject further. Later, Shepstone also asked me, by letter, to come to the assistance of the English with a Boer commando. I replied that the annexation and the breach which this had caused between the people of the South African Republic and the British Government made a friendly co-operation of the two races impossible. I could not but refuse my assistance to those who paid no attention to the urgent entreaty of the people that their independence should be restored to them. With their usual arrogance, the English despised the Zulu impis, and the result was the bloody defeat of Isandhlwana (22 January, 1879), in which about 1,200 English soldiers were cut to pieces. This taught them wisdom; they went to work more cautiously and, in the Battle of Ulundi (July, 1879), Lord

Chelmsford succeeded in completely defeating the Zulus. Later, Cetewayo was taken prisoner and the war brought to an end.

Cetshwayo's imprisonment was brief. Three-and-a-half years after Isandlwana, the 'ignorant and bloodthirsty despot' was invited to London and an audience with Queen Victoria. Sir Bartle Frere was sacked

NOTES
1 i.e. missionary.
2 Induna: a councillor.
3 Properly, the Mfengu. They had been driven out of Natal by Shaka and fought with the British against the Xhosa.
4 i.e. Mpande; he reigned from 1839 to 1872.
5 i.e. Cetshwayo.
6 Appointed High Commissioner for southern Africa in 1877.
7 The commander of the British troops in Natal.

CHAPTER 8

DIAMONDS, GOLD AND CECIL RHODES

Aside from Xhosa, Zulu and Boer wars, 19th-century South Africa had had little to offer the world except Cape wine, merino wool and ostrich feathers. Then, in 1867, alluvial diamonds were found along the banks of the Vaal. Ten thousand prospectors flocked to the area. The pickings, however, were thin and by 1871 many had moved on to the north-eastern Transvaal, where gold had been discovered at Lydenburg and Pilgrim's Rest. Then, a few miles south of the Vaal, near a flat-topped hill called Colesberg Koppie, diamonds were found on the ground – and not just on the ground but beneath it, where they lay in a profusion beyond all imagining. There to take part in the rush and come tantalising close to making his fortune was WC Scully, whom we met in Chapter 5, describing the last great trek of the springbok. His family had emigrated from Dublin four years earlier, when he was 12, and were sheep farming on the eastern frontier. Talk of diamonds had drawn him north.

I will now relate how I very nearly became the discoverer of the world-famed Kimberley Mine. Being somewhat slightly built, I was not of much use at heavy work in the claim, so it was arranged that our Hottentot lad, David, should take my place, I taking his in the matter of herding the twelve oxen. This arrangement suited me exactly. Small game abounded, and I had the use of a gun.

My favourite pasturage area was the big shallow basin to the westward, within the perimeter of which was a low, oblong rise covered with long grass, and at the eastern end of which stood a grove of exceptionally large camelthorn trees. This rise afterwards came to be known as 'Colesberg

Koppie'; eventually it was named 'Kimberley', after Lord Kimberley, who was Secretary of State for the Colonies at the time of the annexation of the diamond fields. On it were usually to be found hares, Namaqua partridges, korhaan, and an occasional steenbok. Antbears and jackals had been at work at various places. One burrow was exceptionally deep, and the gravel thrown up from it looked exactly like that of the claim in which I had been working. I determined to do some prospecting on my own account at this spot.

Unfortunately I mentioned my intention at the camp. One of my peculiarities as a youngster was a morbid sensitiveness in respect of anything like chaff. This was so marked that the least attempt at teasing was enough to send me away in a state of misery. My mates knew this, and accordingly often made me the butt of their cheap witticisms. When I spoke of the burrow and the resemblance of the gravel at its mouth to the diamondiferous soil in which we were working, this was made a pretext for derision.

Day by day I was bantered about my supposed diamond mine; mockingly I would be asked how many carats my last find weighed, and so on. Consequently, I was afraid again to mention the subject. Had it been possible secretly to obtain the necessary appliances for prospecting, and to get them away without the knowledge of my mates, I would have done so. I often thought of asking some of my friends in the other camps to lend me tools, but the dread of my enterprise becoming known and being made the subject of more chaff deterred me, so I kept putting the thing off. However, I never abandoned the intention of one day carrying out the prospect. But I delayed too long; the clue dangled by Fortune within my reach was grasped by other hands.

One day when I drove my oxen to their usual pasturage I noticed that the camelthorn grove had been invaded. A tent had been pitched there, and the smoke of a fire arose from the camp. This annoyed me exceedingly; not because it in any way interfered with my intention of prospecting – I could still have done that freely, and the tent was nowhere near my burrow – but for the, to me, more important reason that the advent of a camp right in the middle of my preserve was bound to spoil my shooting. The camp turned out to be that of Mr. Ortlepp, of Colesberg, and his party. Mr. Ortlepp I afterwards got to know, but at that time we had not met. So for the future I avoided the area in which I had been accustomed to spend most of my days, and sought new and more lonely pastures. But game had now become so scarce that I usually left my gun at home.

Early one afternoon, when I was herding my cattle on that ridge which runs south-east from Kimberley in the direction of Du Toit's Pan, I noticed a stream of men flowing from De Beers towards the north-west, and at once correctly inferred what had happened. Diamonds had been discovered by the Ortlepp party, and a 'rush' was in progress.

Leaving the cattle to fend for themselves, I started at a run across the veld towards the objective of the rushers. My burrow! – on that my thoughts were centred; I longed to reach the spot before any one else had pegged it out.

Three or four times I paused to take breath, and each time I managed to pause in the vicinity of some patch of scrub, so that I could therefrom cut pegs wherewith to mark out my claim. When I reached the koppie – which, by the way, never was a koppie at all – men were swarming over it like ants over a heap of sugar. But I noticed with delight that my burrow and the area immediately surrounding it were still unappropriated. Accordingly I got in my pegs, enclosing a square with sides measuring approximately thirty-one feet six inches (or thirty Dutch feet), the burrow being exactly in the middle. Then I fell to the ground, panting from exhaustion.

I remained on my claim until darkness fell. One by one I watched the prospectors depart; I was not going to risk being dispossessed of my burrow, so stuck to my post as long as a human being was in sight. I had managed to get a message through to Brown, some time before sunset, asking him to send David out to look for the oxen. When I reached the camp I was roundly pitched into for my foolishness in abandoning the cattle and running after 'wild cat'. However, my blood was now up, so I told Brown that for the present I would do no more cattle-herding, as I meant to return next morning to my claim. Brown forbade my doing this, and ordered me to resume charge of the cattle, but I defied him.

The stars were still shining; there was, in fact, no hint of dawn in the sky when I arrived at my claim next morning. I was first in the field, having reached my destination some time even before the fire was lit in the Ortlepp camp. I brought with me a pick, a small circular sieve, a piece of plank about eighteen inches square for use as a sorting table, and a small iron scraper – an instrument used in the sorting of sifted gravel. Day soon began to break, so I filled my sieve and separated the sand from the gravel, placing the latter in a heap on the plank.

There was not enough light for sorting. I sat on a tussock and watched the east grow white. But the morning was chill, so I sprang up and went to work with the pick, uprooting the grass and bushes. Day waxed and a few men appeared.

When I thought the light strong enough, I crouched down and began sorting the gravel on the board. With the scraper I separated a small handful from the heap and spread it out so that every individual pebble became visible. These would be swept off the board and the former process repeated.

But before I got half-way through the heap my heart leaped and I almost swooned with ecstasy – there in the middle of the spread out gravel glittered a diamond. It was very small, not much more than half a carat in weight; still, it was most indubitably a diamond.

I searched in the pockets of my somewhat ragged coat for a scrap of paper in which to wrap my treasure. Then I put the diminutive parcel away – very carefully, as I thought. I finished sorting the heap of gravel and again filled the sieve. I sorted this and loosened more ground. I worked hard and feverishly, loosening the ground with the pick, filling the sieve with my bare hands, sifting out the sand, and sorting what remained.

However, no more diamonds could I find. I had brought in my pocket a lump of roosterkoek (unleavened dough, flattened out and roasted on a gridiron). This I munched as I worked. More and more people arrived. Soon the thudding of picks and the whish, whish of sieves sounded from every direction.

Someone shouted. I looked up and saw numbers of people running towards a certain spot. I leapt up and ran too. A diamond had been found. Around the lucky finder an excited and curious crowd soon collected. The stone, a clear yellow octahedron of about ten carats' weight, was passed from hand to hand to be admired and appraised. After an enthusiastic 'hip-hip-hurrah' the crowd dispersed, each one eager to test his claim.

I hugged my secret; no one should know of my good fortune until after my partners had arrived and I had confounded their scepticism. I rehearsed the prospective scene in imagination; what a lofty lecture I meant to read them on the unreasonableness of their incredulity.

Within a few minutes another shout rang out; another crowd collected. Once more a diamond had been found. This sort of thing went on, at more or less short intervals, ail day long.

It must have been nearly eleven o'clock before Brown and Beranger strolled up. I watched their approach.

'Well, have you made our fortune?' asked Brown.

'I have found a diamond,' I replied loftily.

'What!' he said, with a start. 'Where is it?'

I searched through all the pockets and interstices of my coat with trembling fingers. I turned every pocket inside out, but no diamond could I find. I vainly searched the surrounding surface of the sand. But all in vain; my treasure had disappeared.

Brown and Beranger smiled superciliously, and strolled back to De Beers. That was to me an hour of bitter humiliation.

However, as the day went on, more and more diamonds, some of considerable size, were found. Indubitable evidence of this having reached my partners, they came back post-haste in the hope of being able to mark out claims.

They even went so far as to peg one out. This was on the western edge of the koppie, clean outside the diamond bearing area. But this circumstance was not yet known, for here the red soil lay nearly ten feet deep over the bedrock. However, we exchanged this worthless site for a piece of ground in No. 9 Road – a half claim belonging to Alick McIntosh. The latter piece of ground turned out to be very valuable.

Whilst affecting still to disbelieve in my find, my partners now treated me with more respect. Towards them I assumed a patronising attitude. They no longer tried to force me to do cattle-herding. Day by day the finds grew richer and more important. So far as I remember, it was on the third day that Government sent officials to verify boundaries and make a general survey of the surface of the mine. Each individual had been, I think, permitted to mark out two claims. But the rush had been so swift that very few had been able to avail themselves of this privilege.

A certain amount of 'hustling' was attempted; 'roughs', who had come in late, occasionally tried to bully those who looked 'soft' out of their ground. Being quite a youngster, I was, naturally, the kind of game these gentry were seeking. However, I sought and obtained help among my Kaffrarian friends, so when two glib-tongued scoundrels endeavoured to claim my burrow on the score of prior occupation, they were soon hunted off.

Within a few weeks it was amply proved that the new mine was one of enormous richness. Day by day large and valuable stones were unearthed. On some sorting tables the finds ran up to as many as five and twenty diamonds per day. People flocked in by thousands from the surrounding camps. At Du Toit's Pan, Bultfontein, and De Beers claims were abandoned wholesale.

As though by magic the vast plains surrounding New Rush, as it now came to be called, became populous. A great city of tents and wagons sprang up like mushrooms in a night. There was at first no attempt at orderly arrangement; each pitched his camp wherever he listed. How, eventually, streets and a market square came to be laid out is more than I can explain. I would not like to guess at the number of people and tents surrounding the mine three months after the latter was rushed, but the tents alone must have figured to many thousands.

The ground at Du Toit's Pan, Bultfontein and De Beers turned out to be on the fringe of the volcanic vent in which the diamonds nestled. Anthony Trollope (49), hugely successful chronicler of English middle-class life and tireless traveller, reached Kimberley six years later, in 1877. He was 62 and had come by horse-drawn cart from Cape Town via the Eastern Cape – then on the brink of the ninth and last 'kaffir war' – to Natal, which was simmering with apprehension of the Zulus, and the recently-annexed Transvaal. At Kimberley, a sizeable mining town had sprung up around an enormous hole.

The Colesberg hill is in fact hardly a hill at all, – what little summit may once have entitled it to the name having been cut off. On reaching the spot by one of the streets from the square you see no hill but are called upon to rise over a mound, which is circular and looks to be no more than the debris of the mine though it is in fact the remainder of the slight natural ascent. It is but a few feet high and on getting to the top you look down into a huge hole. This is the Kimberley mine. You immediately feel that it is the largest and most complete hole ever made by human agency.

At Du Toit's Pan and Bultfontein the works are scattered. Here everything is so gathered together and collected that it is not at first easy to understand that the hole should contain the operations of a large number of separate speculators. It is so completely one that you are driven at first to think that it must be the property of one firm, – or at any rate be entrusted to the management of one director. It is very far from being so. In the pit beneath your feet, hard as it is at first to your imagination to separate it into various enterprises, the persons making or marring their fortunes have as little connection with each other as have the different banking firms in Lombard Street. There too the neighbourhood is very close, and common precautions have to be taken as to roadway, fires, and general convenience.

You are told that the pit has a surface area of 9 acres; – but for your purposes as you will care little for diamondiferous or non-diamondiferous soil, the aperture really occupies 12 acres. The slope of the reef around the diamond soil has forced itself back over an increased surface as the mine has become deeper. The diamond claims cover 9 acres.

You stand upon the marge and there, suddenly, beneath your feet lies the entirety of the Kimberley mine, so open, so manifest, and so uncovered that if your eyes were good enough you might examine the separate operations of each of the three or four thousand human beings who are at work there. It looks to be so steep down that there can be no way to the bottom other than the aerial contrivances which I will presently endeavour to explain. It is as though you were looking into a vast bowl, the sides of which are smooth as should be the sides of a bowl, while round the bottom are various marvellous incrustations among which ants are working with all the usual energy of the ant-tribe. And these incrustations are not simply at the bottom, but come up the curves and slopes of the bowl irregularly, – half-way up perhaps in one place, while on another side they are confined quite to the lower deep. The pit is 230 feet deep, nearly circular, though after awhile the eye becomes aware of the fact that it is oblong. At the top the diameter is about 300 yards of which 250 cover what is technically called 'blue', – meaning diamondiferous soil. Near the surface and for some way down, the sides are light brown, and as blue is the recognized diamond colour you will at first suppose that no diamonds were found near the surface; – but the light brown has been in all respects the same as the blue, the colour of the soil to a certain depth having been affected by a mixture of iron. Below this everything is blue, all the constructions in the pit having been made out of some blue matter which at first sight would seem to have been carried down for the purpose. But there are other colours on the wall which give a peculiar picturesqueness to the mines. The top edge as you look at it with your back to the setting sun is red with the gravel of the upper reef, while below, in places, the beating of rain and running of water has produced peculiar hues, all of which are a delight to the eye.

As you stand at the edge you will find large high-raised boxes at your right hand and at your left, and you will see all round the margin crowds of such erections, each box being as big as a little house and higher than most of the houses in Kimberley. These are the first recipients for the stuff that is brought up out of the mine. And behind these, so that you will often find that you have walked between them, are the whims by means of which the stuff is raised, each whim being worked by two horses. Originally the operation was done by hand-windlasses which were turned by Kafirs – and the practice is continued at some of the smaller enterprises; – but the horse whims are now so general that there is a world of them round the claim. The stuff is raised on aerial tramways, – and the method of an aerial tram-way is as follows. Wires are stretched taught from the wooden boxes slant-ing down to the claims at the bottom, – never less than four wires for each box, two for the ascending and two for the descending bucket. As one bucket runs down empty on one set of wires, another comes up full on the other set. The ascending bucket is of course full of 'blue'. The buckets were at first simply leathern bags. Now they have increased in size and importance of construction, – to half barrels and so upwards to large iron cylinders which sit easily upon wheels running in the wires as they ascend and descend and bring up their loads, half a cart load at each journey.

As this is going on round the entire circle it follows that there are wires starting everywhere from the rim and converging to a centre at the bottom, on which the buckets are always scudding through the air. They drop down and creep up not altogether noiselessly but with a gentle trembling sound which mixes itself pleasantly with the murmur from the voices below. And the wires seem to be the strings of some wonderful harp, – aerial or perhaps infernal, – from which the beholder expects that a louder twang will soon be heard. The wires are there always of course, but by some lights they are hardly visible. The mine is seen best in the afternoon and the visitor looking at it should stand with his back to the setting sun; – but as he so stands and so looks he will hardly be aware that there is a wire at all if his visit be made, say on a Saturday afternoon, when the works are stopped and the mine is mute.

When the world below is busy there are about 3,500 Kafirs at work; – some small proportion upon the reef which has to be got into order so that it shall neither tumble in, nor impede the work, nor overlay the diamondiferous soil as it still does in some places; but by far the greater number are employed in digging. Their task is to pick up the earth and shovel it into the buckets and iron receptacles. Much of it is loosened for them by blasting which is done after the Kafirs have left the mine at 6 o'clock. You look down and see the swarm of black ants busy at every hole and corner with their picks moving and shovelling the loose blue soil.

But the most peculiar phase of the mine, as you gaze into its one large pit, is the subdivision into claims and portions. Could a person see the sight without having heard any word of explanation it would be impossible, I think, to conceive the meaning of all those straight cut narrow dikes, of those mud walls all at right angles to each other, of those square separate pits, and again of those square upstanding blocks, looking like houses without doors or windows. You can see that nothing on earth was ever less level than the bottom of the bowl, – and that the black ants in traversing it, as they are always doing, go up and down almost at every step, jumping here on to a narrow wall and skipping there across a deep dividing channel as though some diabolically ingenious architect had contrived a house with 500 rooms, not one of which should be on the same floor, and to and from none of which should there be a pair of stairs or a door or a window. In addition to this it must be imagined that the architect had omitted the roof in order that the wires of the harp above described might be brought into every chamber. The house has then been furnished with picks, shovels, planks, and a few barrels, populated with its black legions; and there it is for you to look at ...

I must add also that a visitor to Kimberley should if possible take an opportunity of looking down upon the mine by moonlight. It is weird and wonderful sight, and may almost be called sublime in its peculiar strangeness.

But Trollope saw not only a hole. With remarkable prescience, he saw the economic future of South Africa, 'a land not of white but of black men'.

Having described the diamond mines in the Kimberley district I must say a word about the town of Kimberley to which the mines have given birth. The total population as given by a census taken in 1877 was 13,590, shewing the town to be the second largest in South Africa. By joining to this Du Toit's Pan and Bultfontein which are in fact suburbs of Kimberley we get a total urban population of about 18,000. Of these nearly 10,000 are coloured, and something over 8,000 are Europeans. At present both the one and the other are a shifting people; – but the Kafirs shift much the quickest. Each man remains generally six or eight months on the Fields and then returns home to his tribe. This mode of life, however, is already somewhat on the decrease, and as the love of making money grows, and as tribal reverence for the Chieftains dies out, the men will learn to remain more constantly at their work. Unless the diamonds come to an end all together, – which one cannot but always feel to be possible, – the place will become a large town with a settled Kafir population which will fall gradually into civilized ways of life. There is no other place in South Africa where this has been done, or for many years can be done to the same extent. I mention this here because it seems to be so essentially necessary to remember that South Africa is a land not of white but of black men, and that the progress to be most desired is that which will quickest induce the Kafir to put off his savagery and live after the manner of his white brothers.

Throughout the whole country which the English and the Dutch between them have occupied as their own, the Kafirs are the superiors in numbers in much greater proportion than that stated above in reference to the town of Kimberley; – but these numbers are to be found, not in towns, but out in their own hitherto untouched districts, where they live altogether after their old ways, where the Kafirs of today are as were the Kafirs of fifty years ago. And even with those who have come under our dominion and who live to some degree intermixed with us, the greater proportion still follow their old customs of which idleness and dependence on the work of women for what is absolutely necessary to existence, may be said to be the most prominent. The work of civilizing as it has been carried out by simple philanthropy or by religion is terribly slow. One is tempted sometimes to say that nothing is done by religion and very little by philanthropy. But love of money works very fast. In Griqualand West, especially in the Diamond Fields, and above all at Kimberley, it is not only out in the wilds, by the river sides, on the veld, and in their own kraals, that the black men outnumber the white; but in the streets of the city also and in the work shops of the mine. And here they are brought together not by the spasmodic energy of missionaries or by the unalluring attraction of schools but by the certainty of earning wages. The seeker after diamonds is determined to have them because the making of his fortune depends upon them; and the Kafir himself is determined to come to Kimberley because he has learned the loveliness of 10s. a week paid regularly into his hand every Saturday night.

Who can doubt but that work is the great civilizer of the world, – work and the growing desire for those good things which work will only bring? If there be one who does he should come here to see how those dusky troops of labourers, who ten years since were living in the wildest state of unalloyed savagery, whose only occupation was the slaughter of each other in tribal wars, each of whom was the slave of his Chief, who were subject to the dominion of most brutalizing and cruel superstitions, have already put themselves on the path towards civilization. They are thieves no doubt; – that is they steal diamonds though not often other things. They are not Christians. They do not yet care much about breeches. They do not go to school. But they are orderly. They come to work at six in the morning and go away at six in the evening. They have an hour in the middle of the day, and know that they have to work during the other hours. They take their meals regularly and, what is the best of all, they are learning to spend their money instead of carrying it back to their Chiefs.

Civilization can not come at once. The coming I fear under any circumstances must be slow. But this is the quickest way towards it that has yet been found. The simple teaching of religion has never brought large numbers of Natives to live in European habits; but I have no doubt that European habits will bring about religion. The black man when he lives with the white man and works under the white man's guidance will learn to believe really what the white man really believes himself. Surely we should not expect him to go faster. But the missionary has endeavoured to gratify his own soul by making here and there a model Christian before the pupil has been able to understand any of the purposes of Christianity. I have not myself seen the model Christian perfected; but when I have looked down into the Kimberley mine and seen three or four thousand of them at work, – although each of them would willingly have stolen a diamond if the occasion came, – I have felt that I was looking at three or four thousand growing Christians.

Because of this I regard Kimberley as one of the most interesting places on the face of the earth. I know no other spot on which the work of civilizing a Savage is being carried on with so signal a success. The Savages whom we have encountered in our great task of populating the world have for the most part eluded our grasp by perishing while we have been considering how we might best deal with them. Here, in South Africa, a healthy nation remains and assures us by its prolific tendency that when protected from self-destruction by our fostering care it will spread and increase beneath our hands. But what was to be done with these people? Having found that they do not mean to die, by what means might we instruct them how to live? Teach them to sing hymns, and all will be well. That is one receipt. Turn them into slaves, and make them work. That is another receipt. Divide the land with them, and let them live after their own fashions; – only subject to some little control from us. That was a third. The hymns have done nothing. The slavery was of course impossible. And that division of land has been, perhaps not equally futile, but insufficient for the growing needs of the people; – insufficient also for our own needs. Though we abuse the Kafir we want his service, and we want more than our share of his land. But that which no effort of intelligence could produce has been brought about by circumstances. The Diamond Fields have been discovered and now there are ten thousand of these people receiving regular wages and quite capable of rushing to a magistrate for protection if they be paid a shilling short on Saturday night.

This the diamonds have done, and it is the great thing which they have done. We have fair reason to believe that other similar industries will arise. There are already copper mines at work in Namaqualand, on the western coast of South Africa, in which the Natives are employed, and lead mines in the Transvaal. There are gold fields in the Transvaal at which little is now being done, because the difficulties of working them are at present overwhelming. But as years roll quickly on these, too, will become hives of coloured labour, and in this way Kimberleys will arise in various parts of the continent.

However, as De Kiewiet, the liberal historian, explains, the diamond mines did not just draw the black man into the white man's economy, thereby 'civilising the Savage'; it did so on the white man's terms, thereby laying the economic foundations of apartheid.

Labour in diamond mining was, therefore, divided into two classes. One was a large body of black labour earning low wages; the other was a much smaller group of white labour earning high wages. This division, so endlessly important in the subsequent social and industrial development of South Africa, must be clearly understood. It was not simply the result of the prejudice of colour. The natives who came to the fields had no skill to sell. Expertness and craftsmanship were the natural monopoly of the white workers. The natives came and went, for their homes and their hearts were in their kraals, whither they returned when their short contracts expired. By contrast the whites were a permanent population, bound by many ties to the place of their work. They had a compactness and self-consciousness which native labour, drawn from many tribes and speaking several tongues, could not have. The white workers stood out still more sharply because they were for the most part not of South African birth. Except for its wagon-builders South Africa simply had no skilled workers upon whom the mines could draw. Hence the special position of skilled labour was made still more emphatic because it was imported labour. Thus the apartness of white and black labour was the result of many circumstances. One other most important peculiarity in the pattern of labour in the diamond mines must be observed. Labour in most modern industry may be likened to a ladder with skilled workers at the top and unskilled workers at the bottom. Between them are the rungs of semi-skilled occupations by which men through their effort and the increase of their experience may mount upwards. In South Africa the emphatic separation of white and black in industry eliminated this intermediate region. It became a doctrine of South African labour economics that skill and high wages were a privilege of the white race, while the heavy labour and menial tasks were the province of the black race. The position of each group was guarded by the absence of competition, for into the area between them the one did not sink and the other did not rise. Such a disposition of labour conferred a great advantage upon the diamond mining industry. It was the advantage of being able to employ each year on an average of 10,000 native workers at rates of pay which were low and, because native labour was voiceless and constrained, did not vary from year to year. South Africa's new prosperity was not built up on diamonds alone nor upon the gold whose discovery was at hand. Of the resources which permitted South Africa at long last to take its place beside the Australian colonies, New Zealand, and Canada in the economy of the world, native labour was one of the most important. What an abundance of rain and grass was to New Zealand mutton, what a plenty of cheap grazing land was to Australian wool, what the fertile prairie acres were to Canadian wheat, cheap native labour was to South African mining and industrial enterprise.

As we shall see, securing a continuing supply of that cheap labour and ensuring South Africa's prosperity was to mean driving the blacks off the land and regulating every aspect of their lives.

The impact of gold on the economy was still to come because the deposits at Lydenburg and Pilgrim's Rest were soon exhausted. WC Scully, who had drifted there from Kimberley, describes the spell and frustration of prospecting.

Then, in the early part of 1875, after I had left the Reef, I worked for a short time near the head of the Creek. One day a friend named McCallum came and showed me a piece of gold he had picked up on a headland which jutted over the Blyde River near Peach-tree Creek. Next day was Sunday so we went together to the spot and took a prospect. The result was most encouraging; not alone was there a good yield for the amount of wash we had panned, but the quality of the gold suggested that it belonged to a genuine lead. Next morning we struck our tents and moved down to the scene of the discovery. As the area was not far enough from the nearest proclaimed diggings to entitle us to an extended miner's right, we just marked out a claim apiece and made no report of the matter. We pitched our tent in a little grove of peach trees below the bluff, close to the riverbank.

The thing was a 'surface' proposition; that is to say, the wash was only a few inches deep; it lay on a soft slate bottom. We fixed our sluice-box in a rapid of the river which was some two hundred yards from the claim and was reached by a footpath we scarped down the face of the bluff. We hired a couple of boys to carry down the wash. I did the pick-and-shovel work, which included the filling of the gunny-bags. McCallum washed out each instalment as it arrived. This was the easiest contract I ever took on; it meant about one minute's work, alternating with nearly ten minutes' rest, all day long. The first couple of days' work gave splendid results; from the gravel cleared off a space about eight feet square we got, so far as I can remember, about a pound weight of gold.

Naturally, we considered that at length our fortunes were made. Our claims measured together forty-five thousand square feet, the area we had cleared was but sixty-four. The latter number, when worked into the former, went nearly seven hundred times. And the surface appeared to be exactly the same over the whole area.

Assuming that any reliance could be placed on arithmetic, we were potential capitalists. We began to speculate as to what we would do with our money. £14,000 apiece was a large sum. I think McCallum decided to go to Scotland, there to recommence some lawsuit he had been obliged to drop for want of funds. My own firm intention was to organise an expedition to the Zambesi – not to go 'foot-slogging', as I had been doing in the Low Country, but with properly equipped waggons, the most modern armament, salted horses – and all the rest of it. Well, for one night, at all events, we enjoyed ourselves. I do not think we slept at all.

But we never found so much as another half ounce of gold in those claims; we had struck the one little 'patch' they contained. We hired more natives, we ran prospecting trenches in every direction, we worked late and early – often carrying the bags of wash down the scarped footpath ourselves, long after the natives had knocked off. But all was in vain. Our pound of gold melted like an icicle in the sun.

We were, in local parlance, bust.

One man who would never go bust – financially, anyway – was Cecil Rhodes. He made Kimberley and Kimberley in its turn made him a 19th-century master of the universe. The eighth child of an Anglican vicar, Rhodes arrived in South Africa in 1870, when he was 17. He had come partly for his health – he suffered from a weak heart – and joined an elder brother planting cotton in Natal. He reached Kimberley a year later – just after the new rush had begun – and started digging for diamonds; soon, he was buying up other men's claims. By 19 he was already tolerably wealthy. At 20, treating Kimberley as a kind of gap-year experience, he enrolled at Oxford. In his first term there, he came across the text of a lecture given three years earlier by John Ruskin, the writer, artist, social critic and visionary. 'Will you youths of England,' Ruskin had demanded of his undergraduate audience, 'make your country a royal throne of kings, a sceptred isle, for all the world a source of light, a centre of peace …? This is what England must do or perish. She must found colonies as fast and as far as she is able, formed of the most energetic and worthiest of men; seizing any piece of fruitful waste ground she can set her foot on, and there teaching her colonists that their chief virtue is to be fidelity to their country, and their first aim is to be to advance the power of England by land and sea.'

Rhodes was an instant convert. Suspending his studies, he hurried back to Kimberley and set about buying every claim he could. Convinced that 'the more of the world we – the English – inhabit, the better it is for the human race', he resolved to use his mining profits to fund the expansion of the Empire. Fifteen years later, the Big Hole was his. At the age of 35, he controlled 90 per cent of the world's diamonds. He had also become a Cape Colony MP – the Cape had been granted self-government in 1872 – and graduated from Oxford. It was time to turn his gaze northwards for, as the inscription on the plinth of his statue in Van Riebeeck's garden in Cape Town so forcefully reminds us, 'Your hinterland is there'. Rhodes had decided to 'give Africa to England'.

It could very well have been with him in mind that Joseph Conrad has Marlow say in *Heart of Darkness*, first published in 1902: 'The conquest of the earth, which mostly means the taking it away from those who have a different complexion or slightly flatter noses than ourselves, is not a pretty thing when you look into it too much. What redeems it is the idea only. An idea at the back of it; not a sentimental pretence but an idea; and an unselfish belief in the idea – something you can set up, and bow down before, and offer a sacrifice to ...'

But first there was the little matter of Kruger's gold and Kruger's republic. When diamonds were discovered, Britain had simply annexed the relevant part of the Orange Free State and renamed it Griqualand West – 'one of the most scandalous acts recorded in our history,' commented JA Froude, the English historian. However, when in 1886 gold was discovered at Witwatersrand 30 miles south of Pretoria – again, as it turned out, in unimaginable quantities – the sturdy Kruger was not to be annexed. So in 1895, Rhodes, who had by then become Prime Minister of the Cape Colony, secretly conspired with Joseph Chamberlain, Britain's Colonial Secretary, to engineer a coup in the Transvaal. The pretext was to be Kruger's refusal to give the vote to the thousands of foreigners – 'Uitlanders', as they were called – who had flooded into the republic to mine the gold; by 1895 they outnumbered the burghers by nearly four to one. The instrument was to be Dr Leander Starr Jameson, one of Rhodes's most trusted and devoted aides, who had already helped him seize, by a mixture of trickery and armed force, what was to become Rhodesia. The plan was that a group of co-conspirators in Johannesburg – among them Percy FitzPatrick, author of *Jock of the Bushveld* – would stage an uprising, at which point Jameson and an 800-strong private army would ride to their aid from Bechuanaland (now Botswana), the British protectorate on the republic's western border. The uprising failed to materialise but, on the night of 29 December 1895, Jameson and about 500 men crossed the border anyway. Three days later, they were rounded up by the Boers 25 miles short of Johannesburg. Sixty of the co-conspirators – including FitzPatrick – were charged with high treason; Jameson and three other leaders, including one of Rhodes's brothers, were sentenced to death, commuted by President Kruger to a heavy fine. The farce effectively ended Rhodes's political career. Jameson, oddly, was later to become Prime Minister of the Cape. Even more oddly, it was in tribute to Jameson that Rudyard Kipling (50), Rhodes's close friend and fellow Imperialist, wrote his most famous poem. It was first published in 1896.

If

If you can keep your head when all about you
Are losing theirs and blaming it on you,
If you can trust yourself when all men doubt you,
But make allowance for their doubting too;
If you can wait and not be tired by waiting,

Or being lied about, don't deal in lies,
Or being hated, don't give way to hating,
And yet don't look too good, nor talk too wise:

If you can dream – and not make dreams your master;
If you can think – and not make thoughts your aim;
If you can meet with Triumph and Disaster
And treat those two impostors just the same;
If you can bear to hear the truth you've spoken
Twisted by knaves to make a trap for fools,
Or watch the things you gave your life to, broken,
And stoop and build 'em up with worn-out tools:

If you can make one heap of all your winnings
And risk it on one turn of pitch-and-toss,
And lose, and start again at your beginnings
And never breathe a word about your loss;
If you can force your heart and nerve and sinew
To serve your turn long after they are gone,
And so hold on when there is nothing in you
Except the Will which says to them: 'Hold on!'

If you can talk with crowds and keep your virtue,
Or walk with Kings – nor lose the common touch,
If neither foes nor loving friends can hurt you,
If all men count with you, but none too much;
If you can fill the unforgiving minute
With sixty seconds' worth of distance run,
Yours is the Earth and everything that's in it,
And – which is more – you'll be a Man, my son!

If nothing else, it radiates the spirit of the times. Jameson, alas – never breathing a word about his loss – left no record of his role in the raid with which his name was for ever to be associated. Indeed, two years after it, he published his 'personal reminiscences' of Rhodes (51) without even mentioning it. Instead, he dilated on Rhodes's 'big schemes'.

The best part of twenty years has passed since I first met Mr. Rhodes. It was at Kimberley, in 1878. I had come out and settled there to practice as a doctor. From the day of my arrival at Kimberley, when I fell in with him, we drew closely together, and quickly became great friends.

Rhodes was then steadily working at his great scheme for the amalgamation of the diamond mines. He had been at work at it for years, and had still nearly ten years of persevering effort before him, for the amalgamation was not completed till 1888. We were young men together then, and naturally saw a great deal of each other. We shared a quiet little bachelor establishment together, walked and rode out together, shared our meals, exchanged our views on men and things, and discussed his big schemes, which even then filled me with admiration. I soon admitted to myself that for sheer natural power I had never met a man to come near Cecil Rhodes; and I still retain my early impressions of him, which have been fully justified by experience.

Even at that early period, Cecil Rhodes, then a man of twenty-six or twenty-seven, had mapped out, in his clear brain, his whole policy just as it has since been developed. He had obtained his opinions from no book, and no other man. He had thought out everything for himself independently; his success when he put thoughts into action increased his confidence in himself. He has good reason for his self-confidence. Where are you to find so large a man of ideas combined with so big a man of action? The rare amalgamation of these two kinds of men in Cecil Rhodes results in a statesman compared with whom a mere parliamentary leader in England, however consummate his skill, looks very small indeed.

I remember his first big speech at Cape Town. He was living with me at Kimberley, and was down with fever. He had not written a note, or a line of the speech. In fact, he had not put it into shape at all. He thought the subject out the night before he got up from his sick bed, and, though still very shaky, travelled down to Cape Town. This was in 1884. The speech was a big success. It was the first statement made in the Cape House as to his Northern Expansion policy, and shows the continuity of that policy. That policy consisted of the occupation of the hinterland of the Cape, by which he proposed to effect the ultimate federation of South Africa. He used to talk over all his plans and schemes with me, and, looking back at them now, it surprises me to note how little change there is in his policy. It is substantially the same to-day as it was then. He had, for instance, even at that early date (1878-9) formed the idea of doing a great work for the over-crowded British public at home, by opening up fresh markets for their manufactures. He was deeply impressed with a belief in the ultimate destiny of the Anglo-Saxon race. He dwelt repeatedly on the fact that their great want was new territory fit for the overflow population to settle in permanently, and thus provide markets for the wares of the old country – the workshop of the world.

This purpose of occupying the interior and ultimately federating South Africa was always before his eyes. The means to that end were the conciliation, the winning of the Cape Dutch support. They were the majority in the country, he used to say, and they must be worked with. 'I recognise the conditions and I shall make all the concessions necessary to win them. I mean to have the whole unmarked country north of the colony for England, and I know I can only get it and develop it through the Cape Colony – that is, at present, through the Dutch majority.' This idea of the occupation of unoccupied Africa, both South and Central, for England's benefit, was always in Cecil Rhodes's mind, from the time I knew him; and how long before I cannot, of course, say. I only know he talked about it just as freely and frankly when I first knew him, and his schemes seemed all in the air, in 1878, as when they grew ripe for fulfilment ten years later, in 1888.

1888 was the year that Rhodes, with Jameson's help, had set about grabbing the 'unoccupied Africa' north of the Limpopo that was to become Rhodesia. Having gained a foothold by bribing Lobengula, the chief of the Matabele, with the promise of a monthly salary, a thousand rifles and an armed steamboat on the Zambezi, he conquered the rest of the country behind the screen of a paramilitary chartered company while the British government studiously looked the other way.

In the memoirs he dictated in exile during the Boer War, President Kruger (48) told his version of the story.

Cecil Rhodes is the man who bore by far the most prominent part in the disaster that struck the country. In spite of the high eulogiums passed upon him by his friends, he was one of the most unscrupulous characters that have ever existed. The Jesuitical maxim that 'the end justifies the means' formed his only political creed. This man was the curse of South Africa [...]

As early as 1888, he induced Sir Hercules Robinson, the High Commissioner of that time, to enter into a treaty with Lobengula, the chief of the Matabele.

Later, he managed to turn this to his advantage when, through the payment of a large sum of money, supplemented by a quantity of fire-arms, he succeeded in obtaining a concession from Lobengula for himself. This concession merely gave him the right to search for gold or other metals in the country; but he used it to obtain a firm footing in Matabeleland, with the intention of preventing the extension of the South African Republic in this direction.

He soon saw that he would not be able to carry out his plans without protection from England. So he went to England to obtain a charter giving him the right to certain monopolies and independent action. He procured it without much difficulty, for he found bribery a useful ally when fine speeches were insufficient for his purpose, and he was not the man to spare money if some object was to be attained. It is certain that a number of influential persons in England received shares in his Chartered Company. He even tried to win over the Irish faction in Parliament, which was not at all in harmony with his plans, by a present of £10,000. Who knows how many more large sums he spent with the same object! This will never be revealed. Rhodes was capital incarnate. No matter how base, no matter how contemptible, be it lying, bribery or treachery, all and every means were welcome to him, if they led to the attainment of his objects. Rhodes obtained his charter, although one might well ask what rights England possessed over this district to enable her to grant a charter; and a company was formed with a capital of one million sterling.

Soon afterwards, in 1890, Rhodes fitted out an expedition to take possession of 'his' territory. The protest of the Matabele king was ignored. Rhodes took possession of Mashonaland, and built several forts: Fort Charter, Fort Salisbury and Fort Victoria. It soon became evident, however, that Mashonaland was of little value, either agriculturally or as a mining district. Under the impression that Matabeleland possessed valuable gold-fields, he set about to annex it. In order to do so, he must involve Lobengula in a war, and he succeeded but too well. It is affirmed in Africa that it was Rhodes, through his administrator, who informed Lobengula that the Mashonas had stolen cattle, and that it was his duty to punish the raiders. Lobengula at once dispatched a band of his people, as was the custom in such cases, to revenge the robbery. Rhodes used this fact as an excuse to demand Lobengula's punishment, on account of the massacre of the Mashonas. Whether there be truth in this statement or not, one thing is certain: Rhodes had his way and his war. A force under Dr. Jameson quickly dispersed the Matabele; the Maxim guns cut them down by hundreds.

It is said that Lobengula died near the Zambesi during his flight. What must have been the thoughts of the black potentate, during those last few hours of his life, when they dwelt on the arts of a so-called Christian nation? Such thoughts never influenced a man like Rhodes. He forthwith explored Matabeleland in all directions in search of gold, but with poor results. So he deliberately made up his mind to possess himself of the rich gold-fields of the South African Republic, the highroad to which was the possession of South Africa itself. History knows the successful issue of this base design!

The other aspect of Rhodes that most attracted the attention of admirers and detractors alike was his attitude to what came to be known in South Africa as the 'native question'. Here is another of Dr Jameson's reminiscences.

I was forgetting one of Mr. Rhodes's most prominent characteristics, which from the first impressed me greatly. This characteristic is his great liking for, and sympathy with the black men, the natives of the country. He likes to be with them, he is fond of them and trusts them, and they admire and trust him. He had thousands of natives under him in the De Beers mines. He carefully provided for their comfort, recreation and health. He was always looking after their interests. He liked to be with them, and his favourite recreation every Sunday afternoon was to go into the De Beers native compound, where he had built them a fine swimming bath, and throw in shillings for natives to dive for. He knew enough of their languages to talk to them freely, and they looked up to him – indeed, fairly worshipped the great white man.

It was just the same at a later date. He likes to have the natives round him, and be a sort of father to them. Need I say that Mr. Rhodes is absolutely free from contempt for the black man. He looks upon him and treats him as a fellow man, differing simply in his lower level of development.

He is really, by nature, strangely and deeply in sympathy with the natives. He regards them as children, with something of pity in his affection for them, and he treats them like children, affectionately but firmly. They like and trust him in return. I have never seen any one else who had the same sympathy with them. If there is a man in South Africa who deserves the title of the black man's friend, it is Cecil Rhodes.

What Jameson unaccountably fails to mention is that, to prevent the natives walking off with any diamonds they found, Rhodes had them locked up in his compound for the duration of their six-month contract – the gold mines were later to adopt the same system – and fed laxatives for the week before they left.

Central to Rhodes's approach to the 'native question' was his notion of 'civilisation'. His electioneering slogan became 'equal rights for every civilised man south of the Zambezi'. A civilised man he defined as one had 'sufficient education to write his name, has some property, or works – in fact is not a loafer'. All the rest were 'barbarians' and had to be treated as such; in particular, they were to be denied the vote. 'We are to be lords over them,' Rhodes explained. 'The native is to be treated as a child … We must adopt a system of despotism in our relations with the barbarians of South Africa.'

The result was the Glen Grey Act of 1894 – 'a Bill for Africa', Rhodes called it when he introduced it to the Cape Parliament – the foundation of all segregationist and apartheid legislation for the next 100 years. In essence, it set aside a block of land for Africans where they were to be allowed a limited degree of self-government, so foreshadowing the 'native reserves' and, ultimately, 'independent homelands'. Those who did not work on the land – it could be passed on only to the eldest son – were to be taxed and thus forced to work for the white man – or, as Rhodes preferred to put it, 'provided with a gentle stimulus to come forth and find the dignity of labour'. As always with despots, a glimpse of the private man behind the public face is especially illuminating. This one is provided by William Plomer (52), the South African novelist and poet, whose biography of Rhodes, published in 1933, is a little gem.

Here are three stories to illustrate Rhodes's approach to the 'native question' as it presents itself in its early stages, when the white man thrusts himself into the black man's country. In October 1890, after a champagne supper at Macloutsi,[1] he found, on leaving early in the morning, that his Cape-cart was not ready, and went into a 'terrible rage', saying that all natives were alike and ought to be severely flogged, and leaving orders for the offending driver to be arrested and kept without food. In August 1896, when he was on his way to England to attend the Commission of Enquiry into the Raid,[2] he arrived at Enkeldoorn[3] and found that the Dutch settlers there were troubled by the presence of a native chief whose kraal was a few miles off and who 'refused to surrender'. He immediately said, 'We'll go out and attack the kraal', and himself led the commando up a kopje at midnight. At early dawn the whites attacked the unsuspecting natives, who were shot like rats as they ran from their huts. Seventy of them were killed; one white man was wounded. When the column returned to the foot of the kopje, an argument arose as to the number of natives killed, and in order to settle it Rhodes returned alone to count the bodies again. There is something ghoulish in the picture of this heavy, Semitic-looking man, wearing slightly soiled white flannel trousers and carrying a riding-crop, picking his way all alone among the beautiful corpses on that African hillside, while the groans of the wounded rose up in the incomparable freshness of the early morning air.

A year later he was in the same neighbourhood and had a talk with a police officer who told him of a fight that had lately taken place between his own men and some natives. On Rhodes asking how many of the natives had been killed, the officer replied, 'Very few, as the natives threw down their arms, went on their knees, and begged for mercy.' 'Well,' said Rhodes, 'you should not spare them. You should kill all you can, as it serves as a lesson to them when they talk things over at their fires at night. They count up the killed, and say So-and-so is dead, and So-and-so is no longer here, and they begin to fear you.' This advice shows that Rhodes held the crude colonial belief that the welfare of a country can be permanently based on fear felt by the majority for a powerful ruling minority. It is a piece of evidence that Rhodes was more colonial than English by nature. Incidentally, 'Kill all you can' seems an odd motto for a man who considers himself civilised.

It was at about this time that a satirical magazine in Cape Town published a poem by an anonymous author 'with apologies to Pringle'. (For the original, see pages 114–116.)

A War (?) in the Desert

Afar in the desert I love to ride,
While the manacled Bush-boy to my stirrup is tied,
Away from the haunts of civilized men;
Away from the fear of the journalist's pen;
In places remote, where reporters are not,
And the captured Bechuana may safely be shot.
With my Burgher contingent I daily patrol,
And search every cranny, every bush, every hole;
And woe to the 'rebel' whose spoor we can trace,

For we'll treat and maltreat him and spit in his face;
Then his handcuffs are loosened, he's told to 'voetzak,'[4]
But he's almost immediately shot in the back.

Afar in the desert I love to ride,
With the captured Bush-boy no more by my side.
O'er the brown burnt veldt, where his pleading cry
Went up to his Maker so plaintively;
We were deaf to his cries, nor thought it a sin
To blow him to bits and his skull to smash in.
To see him lie there, a mere human mess,
Was to us first-class sport, no more, and no less.
Our thirst for the blood of the nigger is strong,
And a sharp look-out's kept as we canter along;
Lest by untoward chance we should fail to descry
The spot where a possible victim may lie.

NOTES
1 In present-day Botswana.
2 i.e. the Jameson Raid.
3 Now Chivu in present-day Zimbabwe.
4 In polite terms, push off.

CHAPTER 9

AN EMERGENT COUNTRY

By the end of the 19th century South Africa was producing nearly a third of the world's gold and hardly anyone could get married without buying a South African diamond. Writers were now drawn not by an uncharted land but an emergent country. As in the earlier days, however, it was the singularity of the Boers that caught their attention, starting, in Anthony Trollope's case, with how young Boers went courting.

We can hardly be entitled to expect more refinement today among the Boers of South Africa than among the English of the time of Queen Elizabeth. They are very great at making love, or 'freying' as they call it, and have their recognised forms for the operation. A most amusing and clever young lady whom I met on my way up to Pretoria was kind enough to describe to me at length the proper way to engage or to attempt to engage the affections of a Boer's daughter. The young Boer who thinks that he wants a wife and has made up his mind to look for one begins by riding round the country to find the article that will suit him. On this occasion he does not trouble himself with the hard work of courtship, but merely sees what there is within the circle to which he extends his inspection. He will have dressed himself with more than ordinary care so that any impression which he may make may be favourable, and it is probable that the young ladies in the district know what he is about. But when he has made his choice, then he puts on his very best, and cleans his saddle or borrows a new one, and sticks a feather in his cap, and goes forth determined to carry his purpose. He takes with him a bottle of sugar plums, – an article in great favour among the Boers and to be purchased at every store, – with which to soften the heart of the mother, and a candle. Everything depends upon the candle. It should be of wax, or of some wax-like composition; but tallow will suffice if the proposed bride be not of very high standing. Arrived at the door he enters, and his purpose is known at once. The clean trousers and the feather declare it, and the sugar plums which are immediately brought forth, – and always consumed, – leave not a shadow of doubt. Then the candle is at once offered to the young lady. If she refuses it, which my informant seemed to think was unusual, then the swain goes on without remonstrating and offers it to the next lady upon his list. If she take it, then the candle is lighted, and the mother retires, sticking a pin into the candle as an intimation that the young couple may remain to-gether, explaining their feelings to each other, till the flame shall have come down to the pin. A little salt, I was assured, is often employed to make the flame weak and so prolong the happy hour. But the mother, who has per-haps had occasion to use salt in her own time, may probably provide for this when arranging the distance for the pin. A day or two afterwards the cou-ple are married, – so that there is nothing of the 'nonsense' and occasional heartbreak of long engagements. It is thus that 'freying' is carried on among the Boers of the Transvaal.

What came next is described by Olive Schreiner (53) in her novel, *The Story of an African Farm*. First published in 1883, it is a gothic fantasy set against the everyday life of the Karoo.

It was eight o'clock when they neared the farm-house: a red-brick building, with kraals to the right and a small orchard to the left. Already there were signs of unusual life and bustle: one cart, a waggon, and a couple of saddles against the wall betokened the arrival of a few early guests, whose numbers would soon be largely increased. To a Dutch country wedding guests start up in numbers astonishing to one who has merely ridden through the plains of sparsely-inhabited karroo.

As the morning advances, riders on many shades of steeds appear from all directions, and add their saddles to the long rows against the walls, shake hands, drink coffee, and stand about outside in groups to watch the arriv-ing carts and ox-waggons, as they are unburdened of their heavy freight of massive Tantes and comely daughters, followed by swarms of children of all sizes, dressed in all manner of print and moleskin, who are taken care of by

Hottentot, Kaffir, and half-caste nurses, whose many-shaded complexions, ranging from light yellow up to ebony black, add variety to the animated scene. Everywhere is excitement and bustle, which gradually increases as the time for the return of the wedding party approaches. Preparations for the feast are actively advancing in the kitchen; coffee is liberally handed round, and amid a profound sensation, and the firing of guns, the horse-waggon draws up, and the wedding party alight. Bride and bridegroom, with their attendants, march solemnly to the marriage chamber, where bed and box are decked out in white, with ends of ribbon and artificial flowers, and where on a row of chairs the party solemnly seat themselves. After a time bridesmaid and best man rise, and conduct in with ceremony each individual guest, to wish success and to kiss bride and bridegroom. Then the feast is set on the table, and it is almost sunset before the dishes are cleared away, and the pleasure of the day begins. Everything is removed from the great front room, and the mud floor, well rubbed with bullock's blood, glistens like polished mahogany. The female portion of the assembly flock into the side-rooms to attire themselves for the evening; and reissue clad in white muslin, and gay with bright ribbons and brass jewellery. The dancing begins as the first tallow candles are stuck up about the walls, the music coming from a couple of fiddlers in a corner of the room. Bride and bridegroom open the ball, and the floor is soon covered with whirling couples, and everyone's spirits rise. The bridal pair mingle freely in the throng, and here and there a musical man sings vigorously as he drags his partner through the Blue Water or John Speriwig; boys shout and applaud, and the enjoyment and confusion are intense, till eleven o'clock comes. By this time the children who swarm in the side-rooms are not to be kept quiet longer, even by hunches of bread and cake; there is a general howl and wail, that rises yet higher than the scraping of fiddles, and mothers rush from their partners to knock small heads together, and cuff little nursemaids, and force the wailers down into unoccupied corners of beds, under tables, and behind boxes. In half an hour every variety of childish snore is heard on all sides, and it has become perilous to raise or set down a foot in any of the side-rooms lest a small head or hand should be crushed. Now, too, the busy feet have broken the solid coating of the floor, and a cloud of fine dust arises, that makes a yellow halo round the candles, and sets asthmatic people coughing, and grows denser, till to recognize any one on the opposite side of the room becomes impossible, and a partner's face is seen through a yellow mist.

At twelve o'clock the bride is led to the marriage-chamber and undressed; the lights are blown out, and the bridegroom is brought to the door by the best man, who gives him the key; then the door is shut and locked, and the revels rise higher than ever. There is no thought of sleep till morning, and no unoccupied spot where sleep may be found.

No one wrote more gently or apparently sympathetically about the Boers and their belief that they, like the Israelites, were God's chosen people than Pauline Smith (54). Born in 1882, a generation after Olive Schreiner, she grew up in the Little Karoo – a self-contained world south of Schreiner's Great Karoo – which she lovingly described in her 1927 novel, *The Beadle*. Henry Nind, a young Englishman, has arrived in the Aangenaam valley to stay with a Boer family preparing for 'Nagtmaal', the Dutch Reformed Church's quarterly communion service.

In the bright, clear spring days which followed his arrival, and in spite of the bustle of preparation for the coming Sacrament which occupied the entire household, the Englishman settled down quickly to the life at Harmonie. The young man was determined to prove to himself, to his relatives over the mountains, and to the world in general that happiness lay for him in complete freedom of action, and with his craving for sympathy there went now a desire to please that was not entirely unconscious. To gain his freedom, to prove his happiness, he submitted with grace to ways of life which were only less narrow because they were simpler, and only more tolerable because they were strange, than those from which, in the Princestown district, he had so recently escaped.

Of the slow-moving thoughts of the Dutch, and of all that made the coming Sacrament so great a social and religious event in the lives of the Aangenaam valley people, the young Englishman, with no feeling for, and no interest in, the history of any race but his own, understood but little. He accepted the hospitality of the men and women around him with the same careless grace with which he accepted every gift of heaven, but he never explored the sombre background of their minds. And in the Aangenaam valley, as in every other South African community, the Dutch retained their own direct Biblical interpretation of life. They were the descendants of a race formed by the mingling of the early Dutch settlers under the Dutch East India Company with those French Huguenots who, fleeing to the Netherlands after the Revocation of the Edict of Nantes, had been offered a refuge at the Cape of Good Hope under the rule of the Company. At the Cape, a few years after their arrival there, the French refugees had been forbidden the use of their own tongue, and only in the names of their descendants, and in the often beautiful names of their farms, do traces of it still linger. But though the Dutch Governors robbed the French Huguenots of their language, it was from the latter that, in the mingling of the two races, there came, through the memory of past sufferings and sacrifices, that intensity of religious feeling which still makes the Boers a race apart.

For these early settlers, as for many generations of their descendants, the literature of the world was limited to a single book, the Bible. In that strange new land of their adoption it was to the Bible that they turned for help, guidance and comfort in all the crises of a life which, in its simplicity and in the physical conditions of the country in which it was led, closely resembled that of the Patriarchs of the Old Testament. In their long treks through unexplored desert and veld, in search of water and green pasture for their flocks and herds; in the dangers which beset them from wild beasts and heathen savages; in the weeks, months, years perhaps, of isolation from any forms of civilization but those which they carried with them in their wagons, they were sustained by the intensity and simplicity of their faith. Through the wide open spaces of the Karoo Jan van der Merwe from Holland, Pierre de Villiers from France, moved as through eternity, conscious always of the presence of their God. They were not now Jan van der Merwe of Holland, Pierre de Villiers of France. Together they were, like Israel of old, a people chosen of God for the redeeming of this portion of the earth.

When the colony fell into the hands of the English it was to preserve this Heaven-granted sense of nationality that many Dutchmen, in succeeding generations, trekked still further north into unknown country with their wives and their families, their flocks and their herds, their Bibles and their guns. Nor among those who remained in what was now called 'the old colony' was this sense of nationality, this belief in themselves as a chosen people, ever lost. Throughout the colony, under English rule, the Dutchman felt himself to be, in the sight of the Lord, the rightful owner of a country which he, and not the Englishman, had taken from the heathen. For the heathen he had something of the bitter contempt of the writers of the Old Testament. The freeing of the slaves by the English was for him, and remains for many of his descendants, an incomprehensible act of injustice towards himself and of indifference to the warnings of the prophets. And with each succeeding act of injustice towards himself the Dutchman has been driven to a deeper, fiercer belief in his race as a persecuted but chosen people whose pilgrimage is not yet over.

To this people the Quarterly Sacrament of their church, drawing men and women together from their far-lying farms and lands, remains the great religious and social event of their life. To their church in the township of the district, men, women and children journey by ox-cart, ox-wagon, donkey-wagon and Cape-cart for the spring or the summer, the autumn or winter Sacrament. From the outlying farms in the Platkops district this journey to Sacrament in Platkops dorp might take two or three days, and for the poor who had no means of their own of conveyance it was a journey that, to be made at all, depended upon the kindness of others. To bring the Sacrament within easier reach to such as these in the Aangenaam valley Stephan van der Merwe had built the church at Harmonie where the pastor from Platkops dorp now came several times a year to minister to his people.

Stephan Cornelius van der Merwe, the wealthiest and most highly respected of all Aangenaam valley farmers, was a tall, loosely jointed man, slow in speech and in movement, just, generous, and patient. Both men and women stood a little in awe of him and he had a quiet nobility of carriage which made even little Jantje, whose joy in life it was to jump, step more gravely when he walked by Ou-pa's side. To his pupil, the Englishman, this tall, quiet man, who so seldom spoke yet spoke always with authority, seemed a somewhat lonely figure. But though he might live much of his life withdrawn from those around him Stephan van der Merwe was in fact never lonely. In his lands, in the veld, and on the mountain-side; in the cool, lofty rooms of the old gabled house where his wife, Alida de Villiers, still smiled upon his love; in the square white church where men and women gathered together for the Sacrament, he was conscious always of the presence of his God. His God was not, as He was for his wife Alida, a God of love drawing His people towards Him like little children. He was Jehovah – the God of Justice and of righteousness; the God to whom vengeance belongeth; the God who, showing mercy unto thousands of them that keep His commandments, would, in His own time, bring His chosen people into their full inheritance.

In *Cetywayo and his White Neighbours*, Rider Haggard, writing in the aftermath of the 1881 Anglo-Boer War, focused both on the Boers' singularity and their relations with their black neighbours.

The Boers are certainly a peculiar people, though they can hardly be said to be 'zealous of good works.' They are very religious, but their religion takes its colour from the darkest portions of the Old Testament; lessons of mercy and gentleness are not at all to their liking, and they seldom care to read the Gospels. What they delight in are the stories of wholesale butchery by the Israelites of old; and in their own position they find a reproduction of that of the first settlers in the Holy Land. Like them they think they are entrusted by the Almighty with the task of exterminating the heathen native tribes around them, and are always ready with a scriptural precedent for slaughter and robbery […]

Personally Boers are fine men, but as a rule ugly. Their women-folk are good-looking in early life, but get very stout as they grow older. They, in common with most of their sex, understand how to use their tongues; indeed, it is said that it was the women who caused the rising against the English Government. None of the refinements of civilisation enter into the life of an ordinary Transvaal Boer. He lives in a way that would shock an English labourer at twenty-five shillings the week, although he is very probably worth fifteen or twenty thousand pounds. His home is but too frequently squalid and filthy to an extraordinary degree. He himself has no education, and does not care that his children should receive any. He lives by himself in the middle of a great plot of land, his nearest neighbour being perhaps ten or twelve miles away, caring but little for the news of the out-side world and nothing for its opinions, doing very little work, but growing daily richer through the increase of his flocks and herds. His expenses are almost nothing, and as he gets older wealth increases upon him. The events in his life consist of an occasional trip on 'commando' against some native tribe, attending a few political meetings, and the journeys he makes with his family to the nearest town, some four times a year, in order to be present at 'Nachtmaal' or communion. Foreigners, especially Englishmen, he detests, but he is kindly and hospitable to his own people. Living isolated as he does, the lord of a little kingdom, he naturally comes to have a great idea of him-self, and a corresponding contempt for all the rest of mankind. Laws and taxes are things distasteful to him, and he looks upon it as an impertinence that any court should venture to call him to account for his doings. He is rich and prosperous, and the cares of poverty, and all the other troubles that fall to the lot of civilised men, do not affect him. He has no romance in him, nor any of the higher feelings and aspirations that are found in almost every other race; in short, unlike the Zulu he despises, there is little of the gentle-man in his composition, though he is at times capable of acts of kindness and even generosity. His happiness is to live alone in the great wilderness, with his children, his men-servants, and his maid-servants, his flocks and his herds, the monarch of all he surveys. If civilisation presses him too closely, his remedy is a simple one. He sells his farm, packs up his goods and cash in his waggon, and starts for regions more congenially wild. Such are some of the leading characteristics of that remarkable product of South Africa, the Transvaal Boer, who resembles no other white man in the world.

Perhaps, however, the most striking of all his oddities is his abhorrence of all government, more especially if that government be carried out according to English principles. The Boers have always been more or less in rebellion; they rebelled against the rule of the Company when the Cape belonged to Holland, they rebelled against the English Government in the Cape, they were always in a state of semi-rebellion against their own Government in the Transvaal, and now they have for the second time, with the most complete success, rebelled against the English Government. The fact of the matter is that the bulk of their number hate all Governments, because Governments enforce law and order, and they hate the English Government worst of all because it enforces law and order most of all. It is not liberty they long for, but license. The 'sturdy independence' of the Boer resolves itself into a determination not to have his affairs interfered with by any su-perior power whatsoever, and not to pay taxes if he can possibly avoid it. But he has also a specific cause of complaint against the English Government, which would alone cause him to do his utmost to get rid of it, and that is its mode of dealing with natives, which is radically opposite to his own. This is the secret of Boer patriotism. To understand it, it must be remembered that the Englishman and the Boer look at natives from a very different point of view. The Englishman, though he may not be very fond of him, at any rate regards the Kafir as a fellow human being with feelings like his own. The average Boer does not. He looks upon the 'black creature' as having been de-livered into his hand by the 'Lord' for his own purposes, that is, to shoot and enslave. He must not be blamed too harshly for this, for, besides being natu-rally of a somewhat hard disposition, hatred of the native is hereditary, and is partly induced by the history of many a bloody struggle. Also the native hates the Boer fully as much as the Boer hates the native, though with better reason. Now native labour is a necessity to the Boer, because he will not as a rule do hard manual labour himself, and there must be someone to plant and garner the crops and herd the cattle. On the other hand, the natives are not anxious to serve the Boers, which means little or no pay and plenty of thick stick, and sometimes worse. The result of this state of affairs is that the Boer often has to rely on forced labour to a very great extent. But this is a thing that an English Government will not tolerate, and the consequence is that under its rule he cannot get the labour that is necessary to him [...]

These remarks must not be taken to apply to the Cape Boers, who are a superior class of men, since they, living under a settled and civilised Government, have been steadily improving, whilst their cousins, living every man for his own hand, have been deteriorating.

JA Froude (55), the eminent English historian, who toured South Africa in 1874 and 1875, agreed with much of that but looked more kindly on the Boers' treatment of the natives.

The Transvaal Boer, when he settles on his land, intends it for the home of his family. His estate is from 6,000 to 20,000 acres, and his wealth is in his sheep and cattle. He comes on the ground in his waggon. He builds sheds or pens for his stock. He encloses three or four acres of garden, carrying a stream of water through it. He plants peaches, apricots, oranges, lemons, figs, apples, pears, olives, and almonds. In a few years they are all in full bearing. The garden being planted, he builds a modest house; a central hall, with a kitchen behind, and a couple of rooms opening out of it at each end. In his hall he places his old chairs and tables, which his father brought from the Colony; his sofa, strung with strips of antelope hide and spread with antelope skins. He has generally but one book – a large clasped Bible, with the births, deaths, and marriages of the family for half a dozen generations on the fly-leaf. He breaks up fifty acres of adjoining land for his corn and green crops. There he lives, and begets a huge family, huge in all senses, for he has often a dozen children, and his boys grow to the size of Patagonians. When a son or daughter marries, another house is built for them on the property; fresh land is brought under tillage; and the Transvaal is thus being gradually filled up in patriarchal fashion by a people who know nothing of the world, and care nothing for it; who never read a newspaper, whose one idea beyond their own concerns is hatred of the English, but who are civil and hospitable to English travellers and sportsmen. They are a proud stubborn race, free, and resolute to remain free, made of the same stuff as their ancestors who drove the Spaniards out of Holland.

I stayed with more than one of them. The beds (I may say this for them) were scrupulously clean, the food plain and abundant. Before and after meals there is a long grace. The day begins with a psalm, sung by the girls. They are strict Calvinists, ignorant, obstinate, and bigoted. But even Calvinism has its merits. They are, I suppose, not unlike what Scotch farmers were two hundred years ago. I enquired much about the slavery which was said to prevail there. I never saw a slave or anything like one. If they were not afraid of us, I daresay they would treat the natives as their countrymen do in Java, but otherwise they are not unkind to them. By far the most thriving native villages which I saw in South Africa were in the neighbourhood of the Dutch towns. The worst and most miserable was at Port Elizabeth – the great English commercial capital – where notwithstanding the coloured people have votes at the elections.

Mark Twain (56), renowned for his tales of the American South, arrived in 1896 at the end of a round-the-world lecture tour, when the Jameson Raid was still fresh in everyone's mind. 'This,' he proclaimed, having evidently done his homework, 'is the Boer …'

He is deeply religious, profoundly ignorant, dull, obstinate, bigoted, uncleanly in his habits, hospitable, honest in his dealings with the whites, a hard master to his black servant, lazy, a good shot, good horseman, addicted to the chase, a lover of political independence, a good husband and father, not fond of herding together in towns, but liking the seclusion and remoteness and solitude and empty vastness and silence of the veldt; a man of a mighty appetite, and not delicate about what he appeases it with – well-satisfied with pork and Indian corn and biltong, requiring only that the quantity shall not be stinted; willing to ride a long journey to take a hand in a rude all-night dance interspersed with vigorous feeding and boisterous jollity, but ready to ride twice as far for a prayer-meeting; proud of his Dutch and Huguenot origin and its religious and military history; proud of his race's achievements in South Africa, its bold plunges into hostile and uncharted deserts in search of free solitudes unvexed by the pestering and detested English, also its victories over the natives and the British; proudest of all, of the direct and effusive personal interest which the Deity has always taken in its affairs. He cannot read, he cannot write; he has one or two newspapers, but he is, apparently, not aware of it; until latterly he had no schools, and taught his children nothing; news is a term which has no meaning to him, and the thing itself he cares nothing about. He hates to be taxed and resents it. He has stood stock still in South Africa for two centuries and a half, and would like to stand still till the end of time, for he has no sympathy with Uitlander notions of progress. He is hungry to be rich, for he is human; but his preference has been for riches in cattle, not in fine clothes and fine houses and gold and diamonds. The gold and the diamonds have brought the godless stranger within his gates, also contamination and broken repose, and he wishes that they had never been discovered.

I think that the bulk of those details can be found in Olive Schreiner's books, and she would not be accused of sketching the Boer's portrait with an unfair hand.

Now what would you expect from that unpromising material? What ought you to expect from it? Laws inimical to religious liberty? Yes. Laws denying, representation and suffrage to the intruder? Yes. Laws unfriendly to educational institutions? Yes. Laws obstructive of gold production? Yes. Discouragement of railway expansion? Yes. Laws heavily taxing the intruder and overlooking the Boer? Yes.

For Mahatma Gandhi (57), there was nothing theoretical about what to expect from the 'unpromising material'. Arriving in Durban from India in 1893, the 24-year-old London-educated lawyer had barely stepped off the boat when he encountered the reality of how 'coloured' people were treated – not just in the Boer's South African Republic but in the proudly British colony of Natal too. He needed to get to Pretoria, where he had been engaged to represent a client. His account of racial humiliation is a classic of the genre.

On the seventh or eighth day after my arrival, I left Durban. A first class seat was booked for me. It was usual there to pay five shillings extra, if one needed a bedding. Abdulla Sheth insisted that I should book one bedding but, out of obstinacy and pride and with a view to saving five shillings, I declined. Abdulla Sheth warned me. 'Look, now,' said he, 'this is a different country from India. Thank God, we have enough and to spare. Please do not stint yourself in anything that you may need.'

I thanked him and asked him not to be anxious.

The train reached Maritzburg,[1] the capital of Natal, at about 9 p.m.

Beddings used to be provided at this station. A railway servant came and asked me if I wanted one. 'No,' said I, 'I have one with me.' He went away. But a passenger came next, and looked me up and down. He saw that I was a 'coloured' man. This disturbed him. Out he went and came in again with one or two officials. They all kept quiet, when another official came to me and said, 'Come along, you must go to the van compartment.'

'But I have a first class ticket,' said I.

'That doesn't matter,' rejoined the other. 'I tell you, you must go to the van compartment.'

'I tell you, I was permitted to travel in this compartment at Durban, and I insist on going on in it.'

'No, you won't,' said the official. 'You must leave this compartment, or else I shall have to call a police constable to push you out.'

'Yes, you may. I refuse to get out voluntarily.'

The constable came. He took me by the hand and pushed me out. My luggage was also taken out. I refused to go to the other compartment and the train steamed away. I went and sat in the waiting room, keeping my hand-bag with me, and leaving the other luggage where it was. The railway authorities had taken charge of it.

It was winter, and winter in the higher regions of South Africa is severely cold. Maritzburg being at a high altitude, the cold was extremely bitter. My overcoat was in my luggage, but I did not dare to ask for it lest I should be insulted again, so I sat and shivered. There was no light in the room. A passenger came in at about midnight and possibly wanted to talk to me. But I was in no mood to talk.

I began to think of my duty. Should I fight for my rights or go back to India, or should I go on to Pretoria without minding the insults, and return to India after finishing the case? It would be cowardice to run back to India without fulfilling my obligation. The hardship to which I was subjected was superficial – only a symptom of the deep disease of colour prejudice. I should try, if possible, to root out the disease and suffer hardships in the process. Redress for wrongs I should seek only to the extent that would be necessary for the removal of the colour prejudice.

So I decided to take the next available train to Pretoria.

The following morning I sent a long telegram to the General Manager of the Railway and also informed Abdulla Sheth, who immediately met the General Manager. The Manager justified the conduct of the railway authorities, but informed him that he had already instructed the Station Master to see that I reached my destination safely. Abdulla Sheth wired to the Indian merchants in Maritzburg and to friends in other places to meet me and look after me. The merchants came to see me at the station and tried to comfort me by narrating their own hardships and explaining that what had happened to me was nothing unusual. They also said that Indians travelling first or second class had to expect trouble from railway officials and white passengers. The day was thus spent in listening to these tales of woe. The evening train arrived. There was a reserved berth for me. I now purchased at Maritzburg the bedding ticket I had refused to book at Durban.

The train reached Charlestown in the morning. There was no railway, in those days, between Charlestown and Johannesburg, but only a stage-coach, which halted at Standerton for the night *en route*. I possessed a ticket for the coach, which was not cancelled by the break of the journey at Maritzburg for a day; besides, Abdulla Sheth had sent a wire to the coach agent at Charlestown.

But the agent only needed a pretext for putting me off, and so, when he discovered me to be a stranger, he said, 'Your ticket is cancelled.' I gave him the proper reply. The reason at the back of his mind was not want of accommodation, but quite another. Passengers had to be accommodated inside the coach, but as I was regarded as a 'coolie' and looked a stranger, it would be proper, thought the 'leader', as the white man in charge of the coach was called, not to seat me with the white passengers. There were seats on either side of the coachbox. The leader sat on one of these as a rule. Today he sat inside and gave me his seat. I knew it was sheer injustice and an insult, but I thought it better to pocket it, I could not have forced myself inside, and if I had raised a protest, the coach would have gone off without me. This would have meant the loss of another day, and Heaven only knows what would have happened the next day. So, much as I fretted within myself, I prudently sat next the coachman.

At about three o'clock the coach reached Pardekoph. Now the leader desired to sit where I was seated, as he wanted to smoke and possibly to have some fresh air. So he took a piece of dirty sack-cloth from the driver, spread it on the footboard and, addressing me said, '*Sami*, you sit on this, I want to sit near the driver.' The insult was more than I could bear. In fear and trembling I said to him, 'It was you who seated me here, though I should have been accommodated inside. I put up with the insult. Now that you want to sit outside and smoke, you would have me sit at your feet. I will not do so, but I am prepared to sit inside.'

As I was struggling through these sentences, the man came down upon me and began heavily to box my ears. He seized me by the arm and tried to drag me down. I clung to the brass rails of the coachbox and was determined to keep my hold even at the risk of breaking my wrist bones. The passengers were witnessing the scene – the man swearing at me, dragging and belabouring me, and I remaining still. He was strong and I was weak. Some of the passengers were moved to pity and exclaimed: 'Man, let him alone. Don't beat him. He is not to blame. He is right. If he can't stay there, let him come and sit with us.' 'No fear,' cried the man, but he seemed somewhat crestfallen and stopped beating me. He let go my arm, swore at me a little more, and asking the Hottentot servant who was sitting on the other side of the coachbox to sit on the footboard, took the seat so vacated.

The passengers took their seats and, the whistle given, the coach rattled away. My heart was beating fast within my breast, and I was wondering whether I should ever reach my destination alive. The man cast an angry look at me now and then and, pointing his finger at me, growled: 'Take care, let me once get to Standerton and I shall show you what I do.' I sat speechless and prayed to God to help me.

After dark we reached Standerton and I heaved a sigh of relief on seeing some Indian faces. As soon as I got down, these friends said: 'We are here to receive you and take you to Isa Sheth's shop. We have had a telegram from Dada Abdulla.' I was very glad, and we went to Sheth Isa Haji Sumar's shop. The Sheth and his clerks gathered round me. I told them all that I had gone through. They were very sorry to hear it and comforted me by relating to me their own bitter experiences.

I wanted to inform the agent of the Coach Company of the whole affair. So I wrote him a letter, narrating everything that had happened, and drawing his attention to the threat his man had held out. I also asked for an assurance that he would accommodate me with the other passengers inside the coach when we started the next morning. To which the agent replied to this effect: 'From Standerton we have a bigger coach with different men in charge. The man complained of will not be there tomorrow, and you will have a seat with the other passengers.' This somewhat relieved me. I had, of course, no intention of proceeding against the man who had assaulted me, and so the chapter of the assault closed there.

In the morning Isa Sheth's man took me to the coach, I got a good seat and reached Johannesburg quite safely that night.

Standerton is a small village and Johannesburg a big city. Abdulla Sheth had wired to Johannesburg also, and given me the name and address of Muhammad Kasam Kamruddin's firm there. Their man had come to receive me at the stage, but neither did I see him nor did he recognize me. So I decided to go to a hotel. I knew the names of several. Taking a cab I asked to be driven to the Grand National Hotel. I saw the Manager and asked for a room. He eyed me for a moment, and politely saying, 'I am very sorry, we are full up', bade me good-bye. So I asked the cabman to drive to Muhammad Kasam Kamruddin's shop. Here I found Abdul Gani Sheth expecting me, and he gave me a cordial greeting. He had a hearty laugh over the story of my experience at the hotel.

'How ever did you expect to be admitted to a hotel?' he said.

'Why not?' I asked.

'You will come to know after you have stayed here a few days,' said he. 'Only *we* can live in a land like this, because, for making money, we do not mind pocketing insults, and here we are.' With this he narrated to me the story of the hardships of Indians in South Africa.

Of Sheth Abdul Gani we shall know more as we proceed.

He said: 'This country is not for men like you. Look now, you have to go to Pretoria tomorrow. You will *have* to travel third class. Conditions in the Transvaal are worse than in Natal. First and second class tickets are never issued to Indians.'

'You cannot have made persistent efforts in this direction.'

'We have sent representations, but I confess our own men too do not want as a rule to travel first or second.

I sent for the railway regulations and read them. There was a loophole. The language of the old Transvaal enactments was not very exact or precise; that of the railway regulations was even less so.

I said to the Sheth: 'I wish to go first class, and if I cannot, I shall prefer to take a cab to Pretoria, a matter of only thirty-seven miles.'

Sheth Abdul Gani drew my attention to the extra time and money this would mean, but agreed to my proposal to travel first, and accordingly we sent a note to the station master. I mentioned in my note that I was a barrister and that I always travelled first. I also stated in the letter that I needed to reach Pretoria as early as possible, that as there was no time to await his reply I would receive it in person at the station, and that I should expect to get a first class ticket. There was of course a purpose behind asking for the reply in person. I thought that if the Station master gave a written reply, he would certainly say 'no', especially because he would have his own notion of a 'coolie' barrister. I would therefore appear before him in faultless English dress, talk to him and possibly persuade him to issue a first class ticket. So I went to the station in a frock-coat and necktie, placed a sovereign for my fare on the counter and asked for a first class ticket.

'You sent me that note?' he asked.

'That is so. I shall be much obliged if you will give me a ticket. I must reach Pretoria today.'

He smiled and, moved to pity, said: 'I am not a Transvaaler. I am a Hollander. I appreciate your feelings, and you have my sympathy. I do want to give you a ticket, – on one condition, however, that, if the guard should ask you to shift to the third class, you will not involve me in the affair, by which I mean that you should not proceed against the railway company. I wish you a safe journey. I can see you are a gentleman.'

With these words he booked the ticket. I thanked him and gave him the necessary assurance.

Sheth Abdul Gani had come to see me off at the station. The incident gave him an agreeable surprise, but he warned me saying: 'I shall be thankful if you reach Pretoria all right. I am afraid the guard will not leave you in peace in the first class and even if he does, the passengers will not.'

I took my seat in a first class compartment and the train started. At Germiston the guard came to examine the tickets. He was angry to find me there, and signalled to me with his finger to go to the third class. I showed him my first class ticket. 'That doesn't matter,' said he, 'remove to the third class.'

There was only one English passenger in the compartment. He took the guard to task. 'Don't you see he has a first class ticket? I do not mind in the least his travelling with me.' Addressing me, he said, 'You should make yourself comfortable where you are.'

The guard muttered: 'If you want to travel with a coolie, what do I care?' and went away. At about eight o'clock in the evening the train reached Pretoria.

I had expected someone on behalf of Dada Abdulla's attorney to meet me at Pretoria station. I knew that no Indian would be there to receive me, since I had particularly promised not to put up at an Indian house. But the attorney had sent no one. I understood later that, as I had arrived on a Sunday, he could not have sent anyone without inconvenience. I was perplexed, and wondered where to go, as I feared that no hotel would accept me.

Pretoria station in 1893 was quite different from what it was in 1914. The lights were burning dimly. The travellers were few. I let all the other passengers go and thought that, as soon as the ticket collector was fairly free, I would hand him my ticket and ask him if he could direct me to some small hotel or any other such place where I might go; otherwise I would spend the night at the station. I must confess I shrank from asking him even this, for I was afraid of being insulted.

The station became clear of all passengers. I gave my ticket to the ticket collector and began my inquiries. He replied to me courteously, but I saw that he could not be of any considerable help. But an American Negro who was standing near by broke into the conversation.

'I see,' said he, 'that you are an utter stranger here, without any friends. If you will come with me, I will take you to a small hotel, of which the proprietor is an American who is very well known to me. I think he will accept you.'

I had my own doubts about the offer, but I thanked him and accepted his suggestion. He took me to Johnston's Family Hotel. He drew Mr. Johnston aside to speak to him, and the latter agreed to accommodate me for the night, on condition that I should have my dinner served in my room.

'I assure you,' said he, 'that I have no colour prejudice. But I have only European custom, and, if I allowed you to eat in the dining-room, my guests might be offended and even go away.'

'Thank you,' said I, 'even for accommodating me for the night. I am now more or less acquainted with the conditions here, and I understand your difficulty. I do not mind your serving the dinner in my room. I hope to be able to make some other arrangement tomorrow.'

I was shown into a room, where I now sat waiting for the dinner and musing, as I was quite alone. There were not many guests in the hotel, and I had expected the waiter to come very shortly with the dinner. Instead Mr. Johnston appeared. He said: 'I was ashamed of having asked you to have your dinner here. So I spoke to the other guests about you, and asked them if they would mind your having your dinner in the dining-room. They said they had no objection, and that they did not mind your staying here as long as you liked. Please, therefore, come to the dining-room, if you will, and stay here as long as you wish.'

I thanked him again, went to the dining-room and had a hearty dinner.

Indians had first been brought to South Africa in 1860 to work as indentured labourers on Natal's sugar plantations, the Zulus preferring to sell their labour in the diamond fields where they were paid in guns. Of the 150 000 who signed up, the great majority chose to remain after their contracts had expired. Gandhi stayed for 21 years, fighting for their civil and political rights (but not, interestingly, for those of Africans) and perfecting the technique of 'satyagraha' – passive resistance – that he was later to use with such effect against the British Raj. A statue of him now stands outside Pietermaritzburg station.

What stirred the imagination of John Buchan (58) was a widespread fear among whites of a black uprising, intensified by the 1906 Bambata rebellion in Natal. Named after the Zulu chief who led it, the revolt was against British attempts to force blacks into the labour market by seizing their land and imposing a poll tax. More than 3 000 Zulus died. Buchan set his novel, *Prester John*, in the north-eastern Transvaal of the 1890s. (The legendary Prester John was believed to have ruled Ethiopia in the 13th century.)

Mr Wardlaw thought that we were underrating the capacity of the native. This opinion was natural enough in a schoolmaster, but not in the precise form Wardlaw put it. It was not his intelligence which he thought we underrated, but his dangerousness. His reasons, shortly, were these: There were five or six of them to every white man; they were all, roughly speaking, of the same stock, with the same tribal beliefs; they had only just ceased being a warrior race, with a powerful military discipline; and, most important, they lived round the rim of the high-veld plateau, and if they combined could cut off the white man from the sea. I pointed out to him that it would only be a matter of time before we opened the road again. 'Ay,' he said, 'but think of what would happen before then. Think of the lonely farms and the little dorps wiped out of the map. It would be a second and bloodier Indian mutiny.

'I'm not saying it's likely,' he went on, 'but I maintain it's possible. Supposing a second Chaka turned up, who could get the different tribes to work together. It wouldn't be so very hard to smuggle in arms. Think of the long, unwatched coast in Gazaland and Tongaland. If they got a leader with prestige enough to organize a crusade against the white man, I don't see what could prevent a rising.'

'We should get wind of it in time to crush it at the start,' I said.

'I'm not so sure. They are cunning fellows, and have arts that we know nothing about. You have heard of native telepathy. They can send news over a thousand miles as quick as the telegraph, and we have no means of tapping the wires. If they ever combined they could keep it as secret as the grave. My houseboy might be in the rising, and I would never suspect it till one fine morning he cut my throat.'

'But they would never find a leader. If there was some exiled prince of Chaka's blood, who came back like Prince Charlie to free his people, there might be danger; but their royalties are fat men with top hats and old frock-coats, who live in dirty locations.' Wardlaw admitted this, but said that there might be other kinds of leaders. He had been reading a lot about Ethiopianism, which educated American Negroes had been trying to preach in South Africa. He did not see why a kind of bastard Christianity should not be the motive of a rising. 'The Kaffir finds it an easy job to mix up Christian emotion and pagan practice. Look at Haiti and some of the performances in the Southern States.'

Then he shook the ashes out of his pipe and leaned forward with a solemn face. 'I'll admit the truth to you, Davie. I'm black afraid.'

An uprising does indeed materialise but, after much intrigue and many fearless deeds, our hero, Davie Crawfurd, with the help of his friend, Aitken, nips it in the bud. 'The Kaffirs' are disarmed and Laputa, their charismatic leader, arrested. Davie falls to reflecting on the burdens of Imperialism.

Yet it was an experience for which I shall ever be grateful, for it turned me from a rash boy into a serious man. I knew then the meaning of the white man's duty. He has to take all risks, recking nothing of his life or his fortunes, and well content to find his reward in the fulfilment of his task. That is the difference between white and black, the gift of responsibility, the power of being in a little way a king; and so long as we know this and practise it, we will rule not in Africa alone but wherever there are dark men who live only for the day and their own bellies. Moreover, the work made me pitiful and kindly. I learned much of the untold grievances of the natives, and saw something of their strange, twisted reasoning. Before we had got Laputa's army back to their kraals, with food enough to tide them over the spring sowing, Aitken and I had got sounder policy in our heads than you will find in the towns, where men sit in offices and see the world through a mist of papers.

Buchan, a benevolent Imperialist, ended *Prester John* with a vision of the future inspired by his work on the reconstruction of South Africa after the Boer War. In this extract, Aitken has made his fortune from diamonds.

But Aitken did more than mine diamonds, for he had not forgotten the lesson we had learned together in the work of resettlement. He laid down a big fund for the education and amelioration of the native races, and the first fruit of it was the establishment at Blaauwildebeestefontein itself of a great native training college. It was no factory for making missionaries and black teachers, but an institution for giving the Kaffirs the kind of training which fits them to be good citizens of the state. There you will find every kind of technical workshop, and the finest experimental farms, where the blacks are taught modern agriculture. They have proved themselves apt pupils, and today you will see in the glens of the Berg and in the plains Kaffir tillage which is as scientific as any in Africa. They have created a huge export trade in tobacco and fruit; the cotton promises well; and there is talk of a new fibre which will do wonders. Also along the river bottoms the india-rubber business is prospering.

There are playing-fields and baths and reading-rooms and libraries just as in a school at home. In front of the great hall of the college a statue stands, the figure of a black man shading his eyes with his hands and looking far over the plains to the Rooirand. On the pedestal it is lettered 'Prester John,' but the face is the face of Laputa. So the last of the kings of Africa does not lack his monument.

Of this institution Mr Wardlaw is the head. He writes to me weekly, for I am one of the governors, as well as an old friend, and from a recent letter I take this passage:

'I often cast my mind back to the afternoon when you and I sat on the stoep of the schoolhouse, and talked of the Kaffirs and our future. I had about a dozen pupils then, and now I have nearly three thousand; and in place of a tin-roofed shanty and a yard, I have a whole countryside. You laughed at me for my keenness, Davie, but I've seen it justified. I was never a man of war like you, and so I had to bide at home while you and your like were straightening out the troubles. But when it was all over my job began, for I could do what you couldn't do – I was the physician to heal wounds. You mind how nervous I was when I heard the drums beat. I hear them every evening now, for we have made a rule that all the Kaffir farms on the Berg sound a kind of curfew. It reminds me of old times, and tells me that though it is peace nowadays we mean to keep all the manhood in them that they used to exercise in war. It would do your eyes good to see the garden we have made out of the Klein Labongo glen. The place is one big orchard with every kind of tropical fruit in it, and the irrigation dam is as full of fish as it will hold. Out at Umvelos' there is a tobacco-factory, and all round Sikitola's we have square miles of mealie and cotton fields. The loch on the Rooirand is stocked with Lochleven trout, and we have made a bridle-path up to it in a gully east of the one you climbed. You ask about Machudi's. The last time I was there the place was white with sheep, for we have got the edge of the plateau grazed down, and sheep can get the short bite there. We have cleaned up all the kraals, and the chiefs are members of our county council, and are as fond of hearing their own voices as an Aberdeen bailie. It's a queer transformation we have wrought, and when I sit and smoke my pipe in the evening, and look over the plains and then at the big black statue you and Aitken set up, I thank the Providence that has guided me so far. I hope and trust that, in the Bible words, 'the wilderness and the solitary place are glad for us'. At any rate it will not be my fault if they don't 'blossom as the rose'. Come out and visit us soon, man, and see the work you had a hand in starting …'

I am thinking seriously of taking Wardlaw's advice.

There was, of course, no such transformation. Writing 20 years later, Sarah Gertrude Millin (59), the South African novelist and biographer, took a rather less optimistic view of 'the native question'.

Here, then, is an impasse. The white man has awakened the native, and, like a dream, the old savage life is ended. He has been called. He has arisen. He is on the road – travelling in the shadow of the white man, carrying his chattels.

The white man looks around at this being he has himself aroused, who is following him; who is serving him; who is dependent on him; for whom, on the journey, he must provide. And he thinks how useful it is that someone else's back shall be bowed under his burden, while he is free to exult in the air and sun of Africa.

The native follows patiently. Now it is time to take food. The white man throws the native a scrap. They go on again. The native is useful to the white man, but also he makes demands on the white man's resources. The master begins to wonder, a little resentfully, if he would not, on the whole, have been happier without his servant.

The journey is an arduous one. The white man opens up again his bundle of food, and thinks that, really, he cannot afford to give any more away, that he needs it all himself. He begins to be resentfully conscious of this creature who makes demands on him. If only he could shake him off, he mutters to himself. He begins to feel that he is being dogged. He begins to suspect that the native isn't keeping a decent distance. He begins to distrust him, to fear him. The native, he knows, is not getting enough to eat. What if he were suddenly to take it into his head to spring upon him, and rob him of his means of subsistence, and run away ahead of him, and leave him there to starve?

How can he get rid of the native? How can he get rid of him?

He begins to make suggestions to the native that he should retrace his steps, return home to his beginnings.

'Look here,' he says,' this journey of ours has been a mistake. You and I can't do it together.'

'It is hard for both of us,' admits the native.

'You'd better leave me,' says the white man. 'You'd better go back home.'

'Go back?' says the native. 'Home? … But the road has fallen in behind us. And my home is broken up. How can I go home now? '

'You are taking the bread out of my mouth,' protests the white man.

'But I am carrying your load.'

'I could have carried it myself. It would have been better.'

'Then why did you call me?'

They face one another, unable to move forward, unable to move back. And 'I wish to God I never had called you,' mutters the white man.

A few pages further on, Millin offers an even more sombre variation on the theme.

Here, then, is the black man, and South Africa, for better or worse, has been built on the foundation of his existence. Nowhere in the world is life for the European so easy as in South Africa. All the unpleasant work is done by natives. No white woman need scrub a floor. No white man need remove the garbage. The digger does not dig, and the farmer does not hoe, and the miner does not break the ground. The black man, with all the tradition of idleness behind him, toils for the white man, whose ancestors believed in the dignity of labour – he toils, if it is demanded, from sun-up to sun-down.

It is no wonder the South African feels he cannot live without the Kaffir. The housewife points to her sister in America or Australia – a domestic slave. The mine-owner points to the mines in America and Australia – their output diminished by half. The farmer explains how, since only three out of five seasons are beneficent, he cannot afford white labour.

Wherever he turns, the need of the moment glares in the eye of the beholder, and dazzles his sight so that he cannot see the future [...]

But what is the future? There are some who say that South Africa will be ruined if it does not exploit the black man, and there are some who say it will be ruined if it does. There are those who maintain that if he is not repressed, kept poor and ignorant and uncivilised, he will, one day, in his pride, rise up and challenge the white races; and there are others who prophesy: 'Take heed. Make not an enemy of him.'

Many believe that if the native is not rigorously dealt with at once, the opportunity will soon be gone for ever, and South Africa will become a black man's country; and a few think that the white man must do his duty, without regard to consequence, without regard to himself; for not by the colour of his skin, but by the colour of his conscience, does a man find salvation.

One white woman who had hoped never to have to scrub floors was Eliza Feilden (60). She was among 5 000 British, mostly middle-class, settlers brought to Natal in the 1850s under a scheme devised by Joseph Byrne, a money-making adventurer. Feilden's memoirs offer the first authentic glimpse of what white women in South Africa for at least the next 100 years would call 'the servant problem'.

Louisa is a nice creature, but wilful, and the difficulty of teaching her to understand in English first what she is to do, then how she is to do it, and lastly, seeing that she does it, is very fatiguing. She comes to me, 'What me do now?' Her mind is active, and her body strong. If we can only have patience with her she may turn out a fine creature and learn to be very useful, but you cannot reason with one of another language, who has no ideas upon daily duties. She reads pretty well in Zulu, and opens my English books with a sort of longing look. She opened my little sketch-book, I turned to where some figures were squatted. 'Oh, Caffres!' she cried, with a merry laugh. I pointed to herself under the tree, and Gudgeon, but she did not think it like her.

She came to me on Saturday, 'You know me want?'

'What do you want, Louisa?'

'Me want go church, all man love God; go church, not work Sunday.'

'Quite right, Louisa, you shall go to church. I cannot walk so far, so we have church here to worship God. You must come soon back at night.'

'No! me stay all night, me go church, me not work, God rest.' So I suppose we must help ourselves on a Sunday in future.

She was back before seven in the morning on Monday, having walked from the station, a distance of six or seven miles. She said the service was part in English and part in Caffre, and they taught her to read. She would like to learn everything, provided I go with her, and do as much as she. I asked if she would like to teach her people. She replied, 'Yes, but they not like to learn.' When she brings her 'Genesis' and seats herself on the floor at my feet I am reminded of the Eastern saying of the maid sitting at her mistress's feet. It sounds very pretty as a picture, a dark shining skin and eyes, a pink frock, and the Bible in her hand; but in reality she is a great, clumsy, walloping young woman in rags, though she can sew well. But there is something nice about her, and when she can understand us better, we may be able to reason with and teach her many things. She has taken a great fancy to my sketch-book, and is always turning over the leaves …

I have drawn a pretty picture of my dark maiden, Louisa, just such an one as the missionaries would seize upon for their reports, which take with the benevolent at home; but it is the sunny side. She is a fine, able-bodied creature, about five feet eight or ten in height, and very stout and thick-set. She looks magnificent as she appears coming up the steep hill out of the wood, with her bucket of water on her head and branches of green standing in it to keep the water steady, her form or bench (for she has been washing) under her arm, and walking erect. But, though active-minded, she is very idle, spares labour on everything, is never anxious to oblige, or to do a single thing she is not ordered to set about. She loves eating as all Caffres do, and stuffs till she is stupid, and then I have to do all, instead of three parts of the work. She talks of love to God, but does not strive to please her mistress, and, so far as I can judge, she does not know that she is a sinner, and yet I suppose

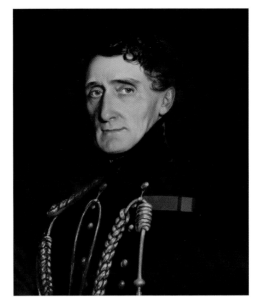

Left: Sir Harry Smith – prone to histrionics and driven by an insatiable lust for glory – became High Commissioner of South Africa in 1847. He called the Xhosa his children and made their chiefs kiss his foot. [MuseumAfrica]

Left: An ox wagon crossing the Drakensberg Mountains – one of the iconic symbols of the Boers' Great Trek from the Cape in the 1830s in search of freedom from British rule. [MuseumAfrica]

Below: A tapestry celebrating the Great Trek displayed in the Voortrekker Monument, Pretoria, a mausoleum commemorating the 'lives and endeavours of the Voortrekkers' in their search for the 'promised land'. [Voortrekker Monument, Pretoria.]

Left: A marble relief from the Voortrekker Monument showing women and children being slaughtered by Zulus. They were among a party of Voortrekkers led over the Drakensberg by Piet Retief, who thought Natal was their promised land.
[Photo by Don Boroughs / PictureNET Africa]

Below: A tapestry commemorating the Battle of Blood River, where, on 16 December 1838, a party of Boers avenged the massacre of Piet Retief and his followers by killing 3 000 Zulus. [Voortrekker Monument, Pretoria]

Bottom: A re-creation in bronze at the site of the Battle of Blood River of the 64 wagons drawn up in a laager (defensive circle) from within which the invading Boers repelled the Zulu attack, suffering only three wounded. [Gallo Images / Rapport]

Left: Robert Moffat, who ran the London Missionary Society's station at Kuruman in the Northern Cape for over 50 years and became David Livingstone's father-in-law. The painting, by William Wallis Scott, includes the two children adopted by Moffat and his wife, Mary. [WILLIAM WALLIS SCOTT. ROBERT MOFFAT, 1795–1883. MISSIONARY (WITH JOHN MOKOTERI AND SARAH). SCOTTISH NATIONAL PORTRAIT GALLERY]

Below: The Great Pit at Kimberley, where diamond mining began in 1871. The photograph, taken a few years later, captures the chaos that reigned until Cecil Rhodes succeeded in buying out scores of individually-mined claims, so making his fortune. [MUSEUMAFRICA]

Bottom: The Battle of Isandlwana in January 1879, a humiliating defeat for the British Army at the hands of Zulus armed only with assegais and cow-hide shields. Later the same day, British honour was restored by the heroic defence of Rorke's Drift, a military outpost nearby. [MUSEUMAFRICA]

A Boer family, the characteristic size of which was much remarked upon by late-Victorian writers such as Anthony Trollope, Henry Rider Haggard and Mark Twain. [MuseumAfrica]

Below left: Paul Kruger, the Boer leader, photographed in 1898 after being elected president of the South African Republic (Transvaal to the British) for the fourth time. The Boer War broke out a year later and he fled into exile in Europe, where he died. [MuseumAfrica]

Below right: Dr Leander Starr Jameson, Cecil Rhodes's right-hand man in the conquest of Southern Rhodesia and leader, in 1895, of an illegal and disastrous raid on Kruger's republic. He later became prime minister of the Cape. [MuseumAfrica]

she is as good a specimen of a convert to Christianity as most of those – the accounts of whom draw tears – in books or at meetings. She went to church as usual in the afternoon, but I told her she must be back before six in the morning to make breakfast. She arrived when I was washing the breakfast things and putting them away, and expressed no regret [...]

Louisa is a strange, untutored creature; she observed that I look out for my husband when I expect his return of an evening. She came to me one day saying he was visible. I went out to look, but he was hid from sight by bushes. I stood a moment looking. Louisa came behind (she is a sort of giantess), seized me round the ankles, and lifted me into the air, to look over the bushes! I was powerless as a struggling infant in her grasp. At last she set me down with a merry laugh at my discomfiture. She has got a new blue frock now, and did her best to wait at our Christmas party, as well as two Caffres in their best, i.e. they wore a bob of scarlet worsted the size of a pomegranate flower on their foreheads, and brass bracelets; beyond a few strips of rags the size of a philabeg hanging down before and behind, their shining dark skin of nature's bestowing was their only other covering. They drank our healths and seemed to enjoy the fun as much as any of us.

Louisa has gone off to visit her mother for a week. She has only been eight weeks with me, yet she must have as much holiday as she asks.

'Who will do your work, Louisa?' said I.

'I don't know, ma'am.'

'Am I to clean the pans, Louisa?'

'Oh no, ma'am!'

'Who then?' She shrugged her shoulders, and suggested 'Boy'.

'But Boy is busy in the garden; don't you think you could find me a good girl to do your work if I let you go?'

'No, ma'am, no Caffre girl, only one Caffre girl at Mr. B – 's.'

'But you could find one, I think?'

'No, ma'am, no girl, they all wife.'

So I must manage as I can until Louisa chooses to return. But with all her faults she is truthful and honest [...]

About this time (February, 1853) I observed a smartly-dressed Caffre man came occasionally to pay his respects to Louisa. I guessed what the result must be, so I spoke to her, and she frankly tells me she 'tink she like him. Him pray in me in church.' And soon she told me when I paid her wages, that she must go away, and live at the mission where her lover is; and so she set off, crying when I told her she ought not to leave me unprovided with another, it was ungrateful after all I had taught her. She shrugged her shoulders and was very sorry, but selfishness prevailed, and she set off there and then.

Louisa has interested me greatly. She has considerable reasoning powers, and was so desirous to learn to read English, and was beginning to speak and understand it so well, that I wonder she did not see her interest in remaining a little longer. She was very truthful; only once have I known her persist in an untruth. I have known her after a first denial and a little hesitation say, 'Yes, ma'am, I did.' She took a great fancy to my India-rubber galoshes, telling me they were too large for me, and when I found them split down the front I accused her of trying them on her own great foot. She denied, but I fear she had done it. Louisa is only sixteen years old, but full-grown, and her lover is twenty. Under a missionary she may become useful to her people, though her knowledge is scanty, and her mental education slow. She tells me she is a fugitive Zulu from Faku's country, where her father was killed. Her mother snatched her up on her back, and as she was running off, the child got struck on the back, where she always feels a pain during a cold. She would on no account go back to Faku's land. All in Natal are similar fugitives, and prefer being under English rule, as safer and less tyrannical.

In 1897, WC Scully, the sometime prospector for diamonds and gold, was the resident magistrate responsible for administering part of the Transkei, the Xhosa area on the Cape Colony's eastern frontier. Just 40 years after the Great Cattle Killing, it was struck by rinderpest, a lethal and highly contagious cattle disease that had been working its way south for the past five years. It killed 90 per cent of the cattle that were the main source of wealth for Boers and Africans alike. Scully takes up the story.

We knew it was coming and to a certain extent discounted its consequences. We read appalling accounts of its ravages: of how the wild buffaloes were found dead in heaps upon its track; of how enormous areas had been utterly denuded of horned stock throughout South-Eastern Africa. In the early part of the year the pest had reached Herschel and was withering up the herds of the Basuto. We knew that the smiting of the scourge was inevitable, but expected to have warning of its nearer approach. When the pestilence broke out, its advent was like a bolt from the blue. It suddenly appeared in the middle of the district and we were never able to trace the source of the infection.

Early in June a report reached us to the effect that cattle were dying suddenly from an unknown disease at the kraal of a man named Mtotyo, near a place called Xilinxa, about twelve miles from the Residency. I at once requisitioned the services of a veterinary surgeon, at the same time drawing a cordon around the infected spot. Within a few days the veterinary surgeon arrived. He happened to be Jotello Soga, son of my old friend Tiyo Soga. I accompanied him to Xilinxa and he at once pronounced the disease to be the dreaded rinderpest.

Immediately the infection began to spread, its first advance being along two lines almost at right angles to each other, each line being that of an alternately prevailing wind. The district was rich in cattle: it probably contained about eighty thousand head. The excitement among the people became acute. The Native loves his cattle as he loves nothing else, and a preposterous rumour gained ground to the effect that the Government had introduced the disease for the purpose of impoverishing the people and thus forcing them to go out and work at the mines. From various secret sources of information I learnt that the situation was growing distinctly dangerous, so I at once sent my wife and family over the border into the Colony and requisitioned a hundred Martini rifles and a large supply of ammunition. These I stored at the Residency.

Now arose the enormously important question: what was the best course to follow? Dr Koch's great discovery as to the preventive effect of inoculation with the bile of infected animals had hardly as yet been tested. Experiments with bile had been made in the district of Herschel, but the results were indeterminate. Soga had gained experience of the inoculation process at Herschel, but had left there before any convincing results had eventuated.

But neglect spelt certain ruin, so I proposed to Government that the inoculation method should be introduced at Nqamakwe. The step was sanctioned, but under most stringent conditions to the effect that the people were only to be 'advised' to adopt it and that no pressure whatever was to be exercised. These conditions were several times repeated in the most emphatic terms.

I called a mass meeting of the people and explained the situation to them. I told them of the experiences of other tribes. I explained that, if nothing were done, all their cattle would surely die; that, on the other hand, inoculation would most probably save at all events a few of them. Some of the people were sullen; some wildly excited; all were in the deepest distress. The terror and indignation induced by the suspicion which still haunted their minds seemed to render them incapable of reasonable thought.

After a long debate, from the close of which I was requested to retire, the great majority of the people remained opposed to taking my advice. However, one man of influence – his name was Henry Shosha, and it deserves to be placed on public record – stood up and said that he was prepared to consent to his cattle being inoculated. A few others followed suit.

So next morning I went out to the kraal of one Baleni, whose herd of beautiful cattle had been attacked, and bought some of his sick animals. These I caused to be shot at once and then I filled several large jars with bile from their immensely distended gall bladders. Post-haste I rode to Shosha's village, accompanied by Soga, and there superintended the inoculation of some hundreds of animals. Immediately several men from other parts of the district, influenced by Shosha's example, grudgingly consented to having their cattle inoculated as well. It was, in such cases, highly necessary to have the bile pumped in at once as the owners were apt to change their minds. This, as a matter of fact, happened in several instances.

The weather turned bitterly cold; snow fell in all the high-lying parts of the district. The cattle died like flies in early winter. It was a heart-breaking situation; the misery of the people was a terrible thing to contemplate. I spent all my time riding about the district. In season and out of season I preached the gospel of bile. At every principal kraal I emphasised my belief that inoculation or ruin were the alternatives. Like Satan in the Book of Job, I went to and fro in the earth and up and down in it. In fact, I almost lived in the saddle, never heeding where I slept or what I ate [...]

In the meantime the disease was spreading with appalling rapidity; fortunately, however, so far only along the two wind-courses leading from the original infection centre. But it soon became abundantly clear that the bile treatment was highly beneficial, for the murrain swept on like a veld fire, destroying the uninoculated herds, leaving the inoculated ones unscathed or, if touched at all, only very slightly. Then an immense reversal of feeling set in; about two-thirds of the cattle owners of the district hurried to the Residency, clamouring to have their herds treated. The rest remained recalcitrant and developed a very dangerous temper [...]

I should here say that as soon as I had satisfied myself that inoculation was of at least some use, I decided to disobey the order of Government: that is, I determined to use every available ounce of pressure towards making the people inoculate. I kept four horses under saddle and rode continually from one part of the district to another, preaching, advising, threatening and cajoling – doing everything, in fact, that might be calculated to bring over waverers. Just then I had but one object in life, namely, to save cattle. I felt that I was justified in acting as I did; that if Government had possessed my knowledge no attempt would have been made to tie my hands. It is a most true truism that orders are often more honoured in the breach than the observance. Risks must often be taken at a crisis by the man on the spot.

The psychology of the Natives under stress of their sharp trial afforded an interesting study. Fear, levity, desperation and suspicion passed like waves over the febrile general mind. But as experience in every direction showed indubitably that inoculation was proving an immense success, this dangerous mixture of explosive gases evaporated, leaving in its place a sense of deep gratitude for the efforts being made to avert disaster and a trust which was complete and full of pathos. In those dark, dangerous days I learnt to love and respect the Fingo people and they will always occupy a warm corner in my heart.

Only one who knows the intense affection a Native bears towards his cattle can realise how hard, how cruelly these people were hit. In some of the locations not a single bovine animal was left. This was more especially the case in the high, exposed regions. In some of the warmer river valleys about four per cent of the uninoculated animals survived. Most of these were cattle naturally immune, for there were hardly any recoveries. Had the visitation come in summer, when the grass was tender and succulent, the mortality would probably not have been quite so great [...]

It was not until October that the agony came to an end. By that time all uninoculated cattle, with the exception of perhaps sixty immunes which could not contract the disease, were dead. Over the surface of two-thirds of the district the carcasses lay thick: it was difficult to get out of sight of them or to avoid the pervading stench. It was but rarely one saw a vulture: the mortality was so general and so widespread that these loathsome but useful birds had flocked northward, to where the weather was warmer.

I was nearly dead too, for I broke down and became almost a wreck as soon as the strain slackened. I found it almost impossible to sleep. But we had saved over twenty thousand head of cattle.

In the surrounding districts the magistrates had obeyed the orders of Government (in abstaining from pressing inoculation upon the people), with the result that practically all the cattle died. We were nearly starving, except in the matter of meat, for a cordon had been drawn between the Colony and the Territories, and no waggon was allowed to cross from either side. This restriction was kept up quite unnecessarily long after the disease had leaped over the Kei River and spread southward and westward.

On the day the cordon was removed I had forty waggons with full spans of rinderpest-proof oxen waiting to cross the Kei and there was not a single ox-drawn vehicle from any other district present. The waggons pushed through to King William's Town and within a week or so returned laden with much needed supplies – not alone for Nqamakwe, but for the surrounding districts.

Next ploughing season, after my people had worked up their own fields, they went forth into the surrounding districts, hiring out their plough teams. By this means they made a great deal of money. My fame grew great in the land.

I remember once sending a message to Mxamli's Location, requiring the people to attend at the office in connection with some administrative matter. I received the following reply: 'We have no time to go and see you, for rain has fallen and we are busy cultivating. All you have to do is to let us know what the order is. We will obey it – even if it be that we are to send our ears in a basket.'

With South Africa now on the brink of the Boer War, Olive Schreiner (61) sums up the state of the nation. President Kruger, contemplating his troublesome Uitlanders, would have warmly agreed with her analysis.

South Africa is a young country, and taken as a whole it is an arid, barren country agriculturally. Our unrivalled climate, our sublime and rugged natural scenery, the Joy and Pride of the South African heart, is largely the result of this very aridity and rockiness. Parts are fruitful, but we have no vast corn-producing plains, which for generations may be cultivated almost without replenishing, as in Russia and America; we have few facilities for producing those vast supplies of flesh which are poured forth from Australia and New Zealand; already we import a large portion of the grain and flesh we consume. We may, with care, become a great fruit-producing country, and create some rich and heavy wines, but, on the whole, agriculturally, we are, and must remain, as compared with most other countries, a poor nation. Nor have we any great inland lakes, seas, and rivers, or arms of the sea, to enable us to become a great maritime or carrying people. One thing only we have which saves us from being the poorest country on the earth, and should make us one of the richest. We have our vast stores of mineral wealth, of gold and diamonds, and probably of other wealth yet unfound. This is all we have. Nature has given us nothing else; we are a poor people but for these.

Out of the veins running through rocks and hills, and the mud-beds, heavy with jewels, that lie in our arid plains, must be reared and created our great national institutions, our colleges and museums, our art galleries and universities; by means of these our system of education must be extended; and on the material side, out of these must the great future of South Africa be built up – or not at all. The discovery of our mineral wealth came somewhat suddenly upon us. We were not prepared for its appearance by wise legislative enactments, as in New Zealand or some other countries. Before the people of South Africa as a whole had had time to wake up to the truth and to learn the first great and terrible lesson our diamonds should have taught us, the gold mines of the Transvaal were discovered.

We South Africans, Dutch and English alike, are a curious folk, strong, brave, with a terrible intensity and perseverance, but we are not a sharp people well versed in the movements of the speculative world. In a few years the entire wealth of South Africa, its mines of gold and diamonds, its coalfields, and even its most intractable lands from the lovely Hex River Valley to Magaliesberg, had largely passed into the hands of a very small knot of speculators. In hardly any instances are they South Africans. That they were not South African born would in itself matter less than nothing, had they thrown in their lot with us, if in sympathies, hopes, and fears they were one with us. They are not.

It is not merely that the wealth which should have made us one of the richest peoples in the world has left us one of the poorest, and is exported to other countries, that it builds palaces in Park Lane, buys yachts in the Mediterranean, fills the bags of the croupiers at Monte Carlo, decks foreign women with jewels, while our citizens toil in poverty; this is a small matter. But those men are not of us! That South Africa we love whose great future is dearer to us than our own interests, in the thought of whose great and noble destiny lies the source of our patriotism and highest inspiration, for whose good in a far-distant future we, Dutch and English alike, would sacrifice all in the present this future is no more to them than the future of the Galapagos Islands. We are a hunting ground to them, a field for extracting wealth, for Building up Fame and Fortune; nothing more.

NOTES
1 i.e. Pietermaritzburg

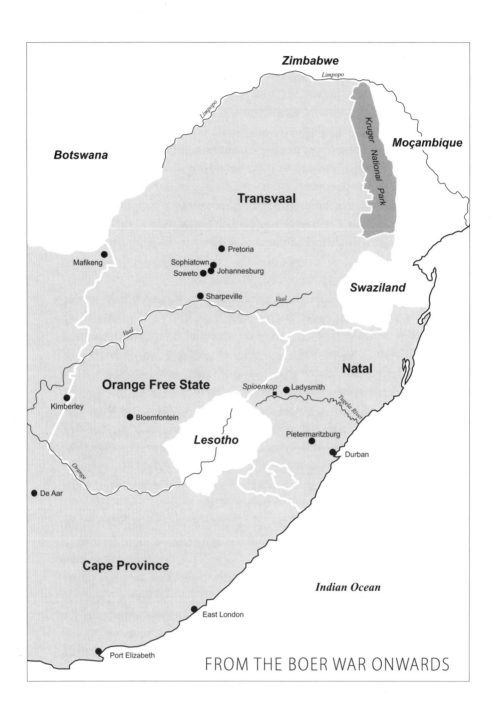

FROM THE BOER WAR ONWARDS

CHAPTER 10

THE BOER WAR

The Boer War became inevitable once Joseph Chamberlain, the British Colonial Secretary, who had been secretly complicit in the Jameson Raid, appointed Sir Alfred Milner High Commissioner for South Africa. Milner, an exceptionally able civil servant, shared Chamberlain's Imperialist creed; like him, he was determined to re-assert British sovereignty over the two Boer republics. First, though, he had to become acquainted with the realities of life in the Colony. In June 1897, a month after arriving in Cape Town, he addressed 6 000 school children assembled in the grounds of Government House to celebrate Queen Victoria's diamond jubilee. Being a bachelor, Milner was accompanied by the wife of his military secretary, John Hanbury-Williams, acting as hostess. Two of the children, both girls, one white, one Cape Coloured, presented her with bouquets. She kissed them both. In a letter to a friend back home (62), Milner reflected on the consequences.

As you say, the papers tell you mighty little, which is a good thing, for my first prayer, when I came out, was that S. Africa might cease to be the subject of continual, mostly mischievous, comment in the English Press. Whatever has to be put right here (and almost everything is at sixes and sevens) can best be put right 'on the quiet'. In one respect, however, I must vindicate my friends of the Press. You say that they have reported nothing except that Mrs. Hanbury-Williams kissed a black child as well as a white one. But that really is the most important thing that has happened since I came here – at least it has excited the greatest amount of general public interest and controversy. I think she was right. Most white people in S. Africa think she was wrong. There you have the great S. African problem posed at once. It is the Native Question. The Anglo-Dutch friction is bad enough. But it is child's play compared with the antagonism of White and Black. That the white man must rule is clear – but *How?* That is the point, where my views and those of most Englishmen differ radically from those of most Colonists. And this, and not the Dutch business, is the subject with respect to which I foresee the greatest difficulty.

A few weeks later, Milner elaborated on the 'difficulty' in a letter to his Oxford friend, Henry Asquith, later to become Liberal Prime Minister.

18/11/97 [CONFIDENTIAL]. I have just been reading with great interest the substance of a speech in which you dealt largely with our S. African difficulties. With your great two principles that (1) we should seek 'to restore the good relations between the Dutch and English' and (2) we should 'secure for the Natives, particularly in that part of Africa called Rhodesia, adequate and sufficient protection against oppression and wrong', I most cordially agree, with this reservation, that I don't quite see the ground for your 'particularly'. It seems to me, we are equally bound to secure the good treatment of the natives in the Transvaal, where we specially and most solemnly promised them protection when we gave back the country to the Boers, and inserted the provision in the Convention giving us the fullest right to intervene in their behalf. This, however, though an important point, is not the particular point, which I want to make in this letter. What I am so anxious that you and other English Statesmen, especially Liberal Statesmen, should understand is that object No. 2 is the principal obstacle to the attainment of object No. 1, is, and always has been. I should feel quite confident of being able to get over the Dutch-English difficulty if it were not so horribly complicated by the Native question. Rhodesia is a case in point. The blacks have been scandalously used. Even now, *though there is great amendment*, and though the position of the black man in Rhodesia is now probably more hopeful than in any part of South Africa not under direct imperial control, except Natal, I am not at all confident that many bad things will not happen. I am doing my best, in fact there is nothing out here which I consider so important or so difficult – but I have to walk with extreme caution, for nothing is more certain than that if the Imperial Government *were to be seen taking a strong line* against the Company[1] for the protection of the blacks, the whole of Dutch opinion in South Africa would swing round to the side of the Company and the bulk of – not the whole of – British Colonial opinion would go with it. You have, therefore, this singular situation, that you might indeed unite Dutch and English by protecting the black man, but you would unite them against yourself and your policy of protection. There is the whole crux of the S. African position. By far the worst is the Transvaal. Here the black has no rights whatever and there is neither kindliness nor wisdom to restrain the brutality of the ruling oligarchy [...]

I tell you all this, not to magnify my difficulties but to help you to understand them. I feel that, if I fail out here, it will be over the Native question. Nothing else is of the same seriousness.

Milner was absolutely right about the position of the blacks in the Transvaal. Both Boer republics had included a clause in their constitution that said: 'The people desire to permit no equality between coloured people and the white inhabitants either in Church or State' – and they meant it. But that was not why Britain was about to make war on the Boers. Indeed, Britain, as later events were to confirm, was not overly concerned about the position of the blacks. Instead, as in the run-up to the Jameson Raid in 1895, all attention was focused on the grievances of the Uitlanders, who – so Milner assured Chamberlain – were 'being kept in the position of helots', making the case for intervention 'overwhelming'. Once again, this was to be the pretence for seizing Kruger's golden republic. In 1899, with Milner's secret encouragement, Percy FitzPatrick, the author of *Jock of the Bushveld*, who had been implicated in the Jameson Raid, organised a petition to the Queen, which 21 000 Uitlanders signed.

The condition of Your Majesty's subjects in this State has indeed become wellnigh intolerable. The acknowledged and admitted grievances, of which Your Majesty's subjects complained, prior to 1895, not only are not redressed, but exist to-day in an aggravated form. They are still deprived of all political rights, they are denied any voice in the Government of the country, they are taxed far above the requirements of the country, the revenue of which is misapplied and devoted to objects which keep alive a continuous and well-founded feeling of irritation, without in any way advancing the general interest of the State. Maladministration and peculation of public moneys go hand in hand, without any vigorous measures being adopted to put a stop to the scandal. The education of the Uitlander children is made subject to impossible conditions. The police afford no adequate protection to the lives and properties of the inhabitants of Johannesburg; they are rather a source of danger to the peace and safety of the Uitlander population [...]

[We beseech] Your Most Gracious Majesty to extend Your Majesty's protection to Your Majesty's loyal subjects resident in this State, and to cause an inquiry to be made into grievances and complaints enumerated and set forth in this humble petition, and to direct Your Majesty's Government in South Africa to take measures which will secure the speedy reform of the abuses complained of, and to obtain substantial guarantees from the Government of this State for recognition of their rights as British subjects.

That, asserted President Kruger in his 1902 memoirs, was all nonsense. He had another explanation.

It is quite certain that, had no gold been found in the Transvaal, there would have been no war. No matter how great the influx of Englishmen, no matter how varied and manifold their complaints, the British Government would not have lifted a finger in their defence, had it not been tempted by the wealth of the country. The question of the franchise, which in reality caused no hardships to foreigners, was made use of by intriguers to further their plans. The words uttered by the late General Joubert, when a burgher came gleefully to tell him that a new gold-reef had been discovered, were prophetic: 'Instead of rejoicing,' he said, 'you would do better to weep; for this gold will cause our country to be soaked in blood.'

On the eve of the war, the Boers published a spirited account of their 'great struggle' for independence. Called 'A Century of Wrong', it was largely written by Jan Smuts (63), a brilliant, 29-year-old Cambridge law graduate whom Kruger had just appointed State Attorney. It is a lengthy document but these extracts capture its thrust.

Once more in the annals of our bloodstained history has the day dawned when we are forced to grasp our weapons in order to resume the struggle for liberty and existence, entrusting our national cause to that Providence which has guided our people throughout South Africa in such a miraculous way.

The struggle of now nearly a century, which began when a foreign rule was forced upon the people of the Cape of Good Hope, hastens to an end; we are approaching the last act in that great drama which is so momentous for all South Africa; we have reached a stage when it will be decided whether the sacrifices which both our fathers and we ourselves have made in the cause of freedom have been offered in vain, whether the blood of our race, with which every part of South Africa has been, as it were, consecrated, has been shed in vain; and whether by the grace of God the last stone will now be built into the edifice which our fathers began with so much toil and so much sorrow.

The hour has struck which will decide whether South Africa, in jealously guarding its liberty, will enter upon a new phase of its history, or whether our existence as a people will come to an end, whether we shall be exterminated in the deadly struggle for that liberty which we have prized above all earthly treasures, and whether South Africa will be dominated by capitalists without conscience, acting in the name and under the protection of an unjust and hated Government 7,000 miles away from here.

In this hour it behoves us to cast a glance back at the history of this great struggle. We do so not to justify ourselves, because liberty, for which we have sacrificed everything, has justified us and screened our faults and failings, but we do so in order that we may be, as it were, sanctified and prepared for the conflict which lies before us, bearing in mind what our people have done and suffered by the help of God [...]

During this century there have been three periods which have been characterised by different attitudes of the British Government towards us. The first began in 1806,² and lasted until the middle of the century. During this period the chief feature of British policy was one of utter contempt, and the general trend of British feeling in regard to our unfortunate people can be summarised by the phrase, 'The stupid and dirty Dutch.' But the hypocritical ingenuity of British policy was perfectly competent to express this contempt in accents which harmonised with the loftiest sentiments then prevailing. The wave of sentimental philanthropy then passing over the civilised world was utilised by the British Government in order to represent the Boers to the world as oppressors of poor peace-loving natives, who were also men and brethren eminently capable of receiving religion and civilisation.

It may seem inexplicable that the Power which stood up boldly at the Treaty of Utrecht³ as the shameless champion of negro slavery was the very one which was celebrated in South Africa for its morbid love of the natives; the explanation, however, is that it was not so much love for the native that underlay the apparent negrophilistic policy as hatred and contempt of the Boer. As a result of this hatred of the Boer, disguised under the veneer of philanthropy in regard to the aborigines, the natives were employed as police against us; they were provided with arms and ammunition to be used against us; they were incited to fight us, and, wherever it was possible, they murdered and plundered us. In fact, our people were forced to bid farewell to the Cape Colony and all that was near and dear to them, and seek a shelter in the unknown wilderness of the North.

As an ultimate result of this hatred, our people had to pursue their pilgrimage of martyrdom throughout South Africa, until every portion of that unhappy country has been painted red with the blood, not so much of men capable of resistance as with that of our murdered and defenceless women and children.

The second period lasted until the year 1881.[4] The fundamental principle then underlying British policy was no longer one of unqualified hatred. Results had already proved that hatred was powerless to subdue the Africander; it had, on the other hand, contributed largely to the consolidation of Africanderdom and to the fact that they spread over the whole of South Africa, thus forming the predominant nationality almost everywhere. In a moment of disinterestedness or absent-minded dejection England had concluded treaties with the Boers in 1852 and 1854,[5] by which they were guaranteed in the undisturbed possession of certain wild and apparently worthless tracts of territory.

The fundamental sentiment which governed the policy of the second period was a feeling of regret at having made this mistake, coupled with the firm determination to set aside its results. These wild and useless tracts, which had been guaranteed to the Boers, appeared to be very valuable after the Boers had rescued them from barbarism, and opened them up for civilisation [...]

The third period of our history is characterised by the amalgamation of the old and well-known policy of fraud and violence with the new forces of Capitalism, which had developed so powerfully owing to the mineral riches of the South African Republic. Our existence as a people and as a State is now threatened by an unparalleled combination of forces. Arrayed against us we find numerical strength, the public opinion of the United Kingdom thirsting and shouting for blood and revenge, the world-wide and cosmopolitan power of Capitalism, and all the forces which underlie the lust of robbery and the spirit of plunder. Our lot has of late become more and more perilous. The cordon of beasts of plunder and birds of prey has been narrowed and drawn closer and closer around this poor doomed people during the last ten years. As the wounded antelope awaits the coming of the lion, the jackal, and the vulture, so do our poor people all over South Africa contemplate the approach of the foe, encircled as they are by the forces of hatred and revenge, and by the stratagems and covetousness of their enemies. Every sea in the world is being furrowed by the ships which are conveying British troops from every corner of the globe in order to smash this little handful of people. Even Xerxes, with his millions against little Greece, does not afford a stranger spectacle to the wonder and astonishment of mankind than this gentle and kind-hearted Mother of Nations, as, wrapped in all the panoply of her might, riches, and exalted traditions, she approaches the little child grovelling in the dust with a sharpened knife in her hand. This is no War – it is an attempt at Infanticide.

And as the brain of the onlooker reels, and as his thoughts fade away into uneasy slumbers, there arises before him in a dream the distant prospect of Bantu children playing amongst the gardens and ruins of the sunny south around thousands of graves in which the descendants of the European heroes of Faith and Freedom lie sleeping.

For the marauding hordes of the Bantu are once more roving where European dwellings used to stand. And when the question is asked – why all this has happened? Why the heroic children of an heroic race, to which civilisation owes its most priceless blessings, should lie murdered there in that distant quarter of the globe? An invisible spirit of mockery answers, 'Civilisation is a failure; the Caucasian is played out!' and the dreamer awakens with the echo of the word 'Gold! gold! gold!' in his ears [...]

If it is ordained that we, insignificant as we are, should be the first among all peoples to begin the struggle against the new-world tyranny of Capitalism, then we are ready to do so, even if that tyranny is reinforced by the power of Jingoism.

May the hope which glowed in our hearts during 1880, and which buoyed us up during that struggle, burn on steadily! May it prove a beacon of light in our path, invincibly moving onwards through blood and through tears, until it leads us to a real Union of South Africa.

As in 1880, we now submit our cause with perfect confidence to the whole world. Whether the result be Victory or Death, Liberty will assuredly rise in South Africa like the sun from out the mists of the morning, just as Freedom dawned over the United States of America a little more than a century ago. Then from the Zambesi to Simon's Bay it will be

'AFRICA FOR THE AFRICANDER.'

As we shall see, 'a morbid love of the natives' was not a charge that could ever be laid against Smuts, later to be Prime Minister of South Africa for 14 years.
The Imperialist vision was summed up by John Buchan, the novelist, who after the war was to join Milner's 'kindergarten'. He later became Governor-General of Canada.

I dreamed of a world-wide brotherhood with the background of a common race and creed, consecrated to the service of peace; Britain enriching the rest out of her culture and traditions, and the spirit of the Dominions like a strong wind freshening the stuffiness of the old lands. I saw in the Empire a means of giving to the congested masses at home open country instead of a blind alley. I saw hope for a new afflatus in art and literature and thought. Our creed was not based on antagonism to any other people. It was humanitarian and international; we believed that we were laying the basis of a federation of the world. As for the native races under our rule, we had a high conscientiousness; Milner and Rhodes had a far-sighted native policy. The 'white man's burden' is now an almost meaningless phrase; then it involved a new philosophy of politics, and an ethical standard, serious and surely not ignoble.

On 11 October 1899, the two sides went to war: the Boers for their independence and the freedom it would give them to continue oppressing and exploiting the blacks; the British for the right to continue expanding the Empire and ensure that they retained control of the gold. Winston Churchill (64), just short of his 24th birthday and already a veteran of wars in Cuba, India and the Sudan, sailed for Cape Town on the same ship as

General Sir Redvers Buller VC, a veteran of both the ninth 'Kaffir War' and the 1879 Zulu war, who had been appointed Commander-in-Chief of the British forces.

Great quarrels, it has been said, often arise from small occasions but never from small causes. The immediate preliminaries of the South African War were followed throughout England, and indeed the whole world, with minute attention. The long story of the relations of Briton and Boer since Majuba Hill, and the still longer tale of misunderstandings which had preceded that ill-omened episode, were familiar to wide publics. Every step in the negotiations and dispute of 1899 was watched with unceasing vigilance and debated in the sharpest challenge by the Opposition in the House of Commons. As the months of the summer and autumn passed, the dividing line in British politics was drawn between those who felt that war with the Boer Republics was necessary and inevitable and those who were resolved by every effort of argument, patience and prevision to prevent it.

The summer months were sultry. The atmosphere gradually but steadily became tense, charged with electricity, laden with the presage of storm. Ever since the Jameson Raid three years before, the Transvaal had been arming heavily. A well-armed Police held the Outlanders in strict subjection, and German engineers were tracing the outlines of a fort overlooking Johannesburg to dominate the city with its artillery. Cannon, ammunition, rifles streamed in from Holland and Germany in quantities sufficient not only to equip the populations of the two Boer Republics, but to arm a still larger number of the Dutch race throughout the Cape Colony. Threatened by rebellion as well as war, the British Government slowly increased its garrisons in Natal and at the Cape. Meanwhile notes and dispatches of everdeepening gravity, between Downing Street and Pretoria, succeeded one another in a sombre chain.

Suddenly in the early days of October the bold, daring men who directed the policy of the Transvaal resolved to bring the issue to a head. An ultimatum requiring the withdrawal of the British forces from the neighbourhood of the Republican frontiers, and the arrest of further reinforcements, was telegraphed from Pretoria on the 8th. The notice allowed before its expiry was limited to three days. And from that moment war was certain.

The Boer ultimatum had not ticked out on the tape machines for an hour before Oliver Borthwick came to offer me an appointment as principal warcorrespondent of the *Morning Post*. £250 a month, all expenses paid, entire discretion as to movements and opinions, four months' minimum guarantee of employment – such were the terms; higher, I think, than any previously paid in British journalism to war-correspondents, and certainly attractive to a young man of twenty-four with no responsibilities but to earn his own living. The earliest steamer, the *Dunottar Castle,* sailed on the 11th, and I took my passage forthwith.

On the Boer side, Deneys Reitz (65), seven years younger than Churchill, had also been born to the purple. His father had been President of the Orange Free State and was now State Secretary of the South African Republic. Deneys would one day be Deputy Prime Minister of South Africa. He published his marvellously vivid memoir in 1929.

When we reached Pretoria, affairs were moving to a climax. Peremptory notes had been exchanged between the Transvaal and the British Governments, and excitement was rising as each cable and its reply was published. Already the Transvaal capital was an armed camp. Batteries of artillery paraded the streets, commandos from the country districts rode through the town almost daily, bound for the Natal border, and the crack of rifles echoed from the surrounding hills where hundreds of men were having target practice. Crowded trains left for the coast with refugees flying from the coming storm, and business was at a standstill.

Looking back, I think that war was inevitable. I have no doubt that the British Government had made up its mind to force the issue, and was the chief culprit, but the Transvaalers were also spoiling for a fight, and, from what I saw in Pretoria during the few weeks that preceded the ultimatum I feel sure that the Boers would in any case have insisted on a rupture.

I myself had no hatred of the British people; from my father's side I come of Dutch and French Huguenot blood, whilst my mother (dead for many years) was a pure-bred Norwegian from the North Cape, so one race was much like another to me. Yet, as a South African, one had to fight for one's country, and for the rest I did not concern myself overmuch with the merits or demerits of the quarrel. I looked on the prospect of war and adventure with the eyes of youth, seeing only the glamour, but knowing nothing of the horror and the misery.

I was seventeen years old and thus too young to be enrolled as a burgher. President Kruger himself solved this difficulty for me. One morning when I was at the Government buildings, I met him and my father in the corridor and I told the President that the Field-Cornet's office had refused to enrol me for active service. The old man looked me up and down for a moment and growled: 'Piet Joubert says the English are three to one – *'Sal jij mij drie rooi-nekke lever?'* (Will you stand me good for three of them?) I answered boldly: 'President, if I get close enough I'm good for three with one shot.' He gave a hoarse chuckle at my youthful conceit and, turning to my father, asked how old I was. When he heard my age he said: 'Well then, Mr State Secretary, the boy must go – I started fighting earlier than that', and he took me straight to the Commandant-General's room close by, where Piet Joubert in person handed me a new Mauser carbine, and a bandolier of ammunition, with which I returned home pleased and proud [...]

On the 10th of October a great parade was held in honour of President Kruger's birthday.[6] We mustered what was than probably the largest body of mounted men ever seen in South Africa. It was magnificent to see commando after commando file past the Commandant-General, each man brandishing hat or rifle according to his individual idea of a military salute. After the march-past we formed in mass, and galloped cheering up the slopes where Piet Joubert sat his horse beneath an embroidered banner. When we came to a halt he addressed us from the saddle. I was jammed among the horsemen, so could not get close enough to hear what he was saying, but soon word was passed that an ultimatum (written and signed by my father) had been sent to the British, giving them twenty-four hours in which to withdraw their troops from the borders of the Republic, failing which there was to be war.

The excitement that followed was immense. The great throng stood in its stirrups and shouted itself hoarse, and it was not until long after the Commandant-General and his retinue had fought their way through the crowd that the commandos began to disperse.

The jubilation continued far into the night, and as we sat around our fires discussing the coming struggle, we heard singing and shouting from the neighbouring camps until cock-crow.

Next day England accepted the challenge and the war began. Once more the excitement was unbounded. Fiery speeches were made, and General Joubert was received with tumultuous cheering as he rode through to address the men [...]

At dawn on the morning of the 12th, the assembled commandos moved off and we started on our first march.

As far as the eye could see the plain was alive with horsemen, guns, and cattle, all steadily going forward to the frontier. The scene was a stirring one, and I shall never forget riding to war with that great host.

Arthur Conan Doyle (66), the creator of Sherlock Holmes, who was to run a British military hospital in Bloemfontein, began his magnificent account of the Boer War with an estimate of the enemy the British were up against. His starting point is the long Protestant Dutch revolt against Catholic Spanish rule of the Netherlands, which began in 1568.

Take a community of Dutchmen of the type of those who defended themselves for fifty years against all the power of Spain at a time when Spain was the greatest power in the world. Intermix with them a strain of those inflexible French Huguenots who gave up home and fortune and left their country for ever at the time of the revocation of the Edict of Nantes. The product must obviously be one of the most rugged, virile, unconquerable races ever seen upon earth. Take this formidable people and train them for seven generations in constant warfare against savage men and ferocious beasts, in circumstances under which no weakling could survive, place them so that they acquire exceptional skill with weapons and in horsemanship, give them a country which is eminently suited to the tactics of the huntsman, the marksman, and the rider. Then, finally, put a finer temper upon their military qualities by a dour fatalistic Old Testament religion and an ardent and consuming patriotism. Combine all these qualities and all these impulses in one individual, and you have the modern Boer – the most formidable antagonist who ever crossed the path of Imperial Britain.

Kruger had decided that attack was the best form of defence and at first the war went well for the Boers' citizens' army. Within the first three days, they had invaded the Cape Colony and laid siege to Mafeking – just across the border from the Transvaal and commanded by Col Robert Baden-Powell, who was later to found the Boy Scouts – and Kimberley, four miles over the border from the Orange Free State and under the sternly proprietorial eye of Cecil Rhodes. In Natal, the Boers had to fight hard to reach Ladysmith, 100 miles inside enemy territory, but the prize was the greater. Three weeks after war had been declared, 12 000 British troops were besieged in the town, and General Buller's 45 000-strong army was still at sea. Later in November 1899, Winston Churchill was on an armoured train 20 miles south of Ladysmith when it was ambushed and derailed. A fierce fight ensued as the troops struggled to clear the tracks.

We then agreed that the engine should go slowly back along the line with all the wounded, who were now numerous, and that the Dublins and the Durban men should retreat on foot, sheltering themselves behind the engine which would go at a foot's pace. Upwards of forty persons, of whom the greater part were streaming with blood, were crowded on the engine and its tender, and we began to move slowly forward. I was in the cab of the engine directing the engine-driver. It was crammed so full of wounded men that one could scarcely move. The shells burst all around, some striking the engine, others dashing the gravel of the track upon it and its unhappy human freight. The pace increased, the infantry outside began to lag and then to be left behind. At last I forced the engine driver to stop altogether, but before I could get the engine stopped we were already 300 yards away from our infantry. Close at hand was the bridge across the Blue Krantz River, a considerable span. I told the engine-driver to cross the bridge and wait on the other side, and forcing my way out of the cab I got down on to the line and went back along it to find Captain Haldane, and to bring him and his Dublin Fusiliers along.

But while these events had been taking place everything else had been in movement. I had not retraced my steps 200 yards when, instead of Haldane and his company, two figures in plain clothes appeared upon the line. 'Platelayers!' I said to myself, and then with a surge of realization, 'Boers!' My mind retains its impression of these tall figures, full of energy, clad in dark, flapping clothes, with slouch, storm-driven hats, poising on their levelled rifles hardly a hundred yards away. I turned again and ran back towards the engine, the two Boers firing as I ran between the metals. Their bullets, sucking to right and left, seemed to miss only by inches. We were in a small cutting with banks about six feet high on either side. I flung myself against the bank of the cutting. It gave no cover. Another glance at the two figures; one was now kneeling to aim. Movement seemed the only chance. Again I darted forward: again two soft kisses sucked in the air; but nothing struck me. This could not endure. I must get out of the cutting – that damnable corridor! I jigged to the left, and scrambled up the bank. The earth sprang up beside me. I got through the wire fence unhurt. Outside the cutting was a tiny depression. I crouched in this, struggling to get my breath again.

Fifty yards away was a small platelayer's cabin of masonry; there was cover there. About 200 yards away was the rocky gorge of the Blue Krantz River; there was plenty of cover there. I determined to make a dash for the river. I rose to my feet. Suddenly on the other side of the railway, separated from me by the rails and two uncut wire fences, I saw a horseman gallop-ing furiously, a tall, dark figure, holding his rifle in his right hand. He pulled up his horse almost in its own length and shaking the rifle at me shouted a loud command. We were forty yards apart. That morning I had taken with me, Correspondent-status notwithstanding, my Mauser pistol. I thought I could kill this man, and after the treatment I had received I earnestly desired to do so. I put my hand to my belt, the pistol was not there. When engaged in clearing the line, getting in and out of the engine, etc., I had taken it off. It came safely home on the engine. I have it now! But at this moment I was quite unarmed. Meanwhile, I suppose in about the time this takes to tell, the Boer horseman, still seated on his horse, had covered me with his rifle. The animal stood stock still, so did he, and so did I. I looked towards the river, I looked towards the platelayer's hut. The Boer continued to look along his sights. I thought there was absolutely no chance of escape, if he fired he would surely hit me, so I held up my hands and surrendered myself a pris-oner of war.

'When one is alone and unarmed,' said the great Napoleon, in words which flowed into my mind in the poignant minutes that followed, 'a sur-render may be pardoned.' Still he might have missed; and the Blue Krantz ravine was very near and the two wire fences were still uncut. However, the deed was done. Thereupon my captor lowered his rifle and beckoned to me to come across to him. I obeyed. I walked through the wire fences and across the line and stood by his side. He sprang off his horse and began firing in the direction of the bridge upon the retreating engine and a few straggling British figures. Then when the last had disappeared he re-mounted and at his side I tramped back towards the spot where I had left Captain Haldane and his company. I saw none of them. They were already prisoners. I noticed that it was raining hard. As I plodded through the high grass by the side of my captor a disquieting and timely reflection came into my mind. I had two clips of Mauser ammunition, each holding ten rounds, in two little breast pockets one on each side of my khaki coat. These cartridges were the same as I had used at Omdurman, and were the only kind supplied for the Mauser pistol. They were what are called 'soft-nosed bullets'. I had never given them a thought until now; and it was borne in upon me that they might be a very dangerous possession. I dropped the right-hand clip on the ground without being seen. I had got the left-hand clip in my hand and was about to drop it, when my captor looked down sharply and said in English, 'What have you got there?'

'What is it?' I said, opening the palm of my hand, 'I picked it up.'

He took it, looked at it and threw it away. We continued to plod on until we reached the general gang of prisoners and found ourselves speedily in the midst of many hundreds of mounted Boers who streamed into view, in long columns of twos and threes, many holding umbrellas over their heads in the pouring rain.

Churchill was sent to Pretoria as a prisoner of war, quickly made a bold escape and hurried back to Natal.

It was not until three years later[7], when the Boer Generals visited England to ask for some loan or assistance on behalf of their devastated country, that I was introduced at a private luncheon to their leader, General Botha. We talked of the war and I briefly told the story of my capture. Botha listened in silence; then he said, 'Don't you recognize me? I was that man. It was I who took you prisoner. I, myself,' and his bright eyes twinkled with pleasure. Botha in white shirt and frock-coat looked very different in all save size and darkness of complexion from the wild war-time figure I had seen that rough day in Natal. But about the extraordinary fact there can be no doubt. He had entered upon the invasion of Natal as a burgher; his own disapproval of the war had excluded him from any high command at its outset. This was his first action. But as a simple private burgher serving in the ranks he had galloped on ahead and in front of the whole Boer forces in the ardour of pursuit. Thus we met.

Few men that I have known have interested me more than Louis Botha. An acquaintance formed in strange circumstances and upon an almost unbelievable introduction ripened into a friendship which I greatly valued. I saw in this grand, rugged figure, the Father of his country, the wise and profound statesman, the farmer-warrior, the crafty hunter of the wilderness, the deep, sure man of solitude.

In 1906 when, as newly-elected first Prime Minister of the Transvaal, he came to London to attend the Imperial Conference, a great banquet was given to the Dominion Prime Ministers in Westminster Hall. I was Under-Secretary of State for the Colonies, and as the Boer Leader, so recently our enemy, passed up the hall to his place, he paused to say to my mother, who stood by my side, 'He and I have been out in all weathers.' It was surely true.

By the end of November 1899, Buller's army had landed and 8 000 men under General Lord Methuen were on their way north from Cape Town to relieve Kimberley. Slogging across the veld from the rail junction at De Aar, they did not know that 3 000 Boers under General Piet Cronjé were waiting for them on the banks of the Modder River, 10 miles south of their destination. Conan Doyle, writing less than two years later, takes up the story.

Commandant Cronje was at the time of the war sixty-five years of age, a hard, swarthy man, quiet of manner, fierce of soul, with a reputation among a nation of resolute men for unsurpassed resolution. His dark face was bearded and virile, but sedate and gentle in expression. He spoke little, but what he said was to the point, and he had the gift of those fire-words which brace and strengthen weaker men. In hunting expeditions and in native wars he had first won the admiration of his countrymen by his courage and his fertility of resource. In the war of 1880 he had led the Boers who besieged Potchefstroom, and he had pushed the attack with a relentless vigour which was not hampered by the chivalrous usages of war. Eventually he compelled the surrender of the place by concealing from the garrison that a general armistice had been signed, an act which was afterwards disowned by his own government. In the succeeding years he lived as an autocrat and a patriarch amid his farms and his herds, respected by many and feared by all. For a time he was Native Commissioner and left a reputation for hard dealing behind him. Called into the field again by the Jameson raid, he grimly herded his enemies into an impossible position and desired, as it is stated, that the hardest measure should be dealt out to the captives. This was the man, capable, crafty, iron-hard, magnetic, who lay with a reinforced and formidable army across the path of Lord Methuen's tired soldiers. It was a fair match. On the one side the hardy men, the trained shots, a good artillery, and the defensive; on the other the historical British infantry, duty, discipline, and a fiery courage. With a high heart the dust-coloured column moved on over the dusty veld.

So entirely had hills and Boer fighting become associated in the minds of our leaders, that when it was known that Modder River wound over a plain, the idea of a resistance there appears to have passed away from their minds.

So great was the confidence or so lax the scouting that a force equalling their own in numbers had assembled with many guns within seven miles of them, and yet the advance appears to have been conducted without any expectation of impending battle. The supposition, obvious even to a civilian, that a river would be a likely place to meet with an obstinate resistance, seems to have been ignored ...

On the morning of Tuesday, November 28th, the British troops were told that they would march at once, and have their breakfast when they reached the Modder River – a grim joke to those who lived to appreciate it.

The army had been reinforced the night before by the welcome addition of the Argyll and Sutherland Highlanders, which made up for the losses of the week. It was a cloudless morning, and a dazzling sun rose in a deep blue sky. The men, though hungry, marched cheerily, the reek of their tobacco-pipes floating up from their ranks. It cheered them to see that the murderous kopjes had, for the time, been left behind, and that the great plain inclined slightly downwards to where a line of green showed the course of the river. On the further bank were a few scattered buildings, with one considerable hotel, used as a week-end resort by the businessmen of Kimberley. It lay now calm and innocent, with its open windows looking out upon a smiling garden; but death lurked at the windows and death in the garden, and the little dark man who stood by the door, peering through his glass at the approaching column, was the minister of death, the dangerous Cronje. In consultation with him was one who was to prove even more formidable, and for a longer time. Semitic in face, high-nosed, bushy-bearded, and eagle-eyed, with skin burned brown by a life of the veld – it was De la Rey, one of the trio of fighting chiefs whose name will always be associated with the gallant resistance of the Boers. He was there as adviser, but Cronje was in supreme command.

His dispositions had been both masterly and original. Contrary to the usual military practice in the defence of rivers, he had concealed his men upon both banks, placing, as it is stated, those in whose staunchness he had least confidence upon the British side of the river, so that they could only retreat under the rifles of their inexorable companions. The trenches had been so dug with such a regard for the slopes of the ground that in some places a triple line of fire was secured. His artillery, consisting of several heavy pieces and a number of machine guns (including one of the diabolical 'pom-poms'), was cleverly placed upon the further side of the stream, and was not only provided with shelter pits but had rows of reserve pits, so that the guns could be readily shifted when their range was found. Rows of trenches, a broadish river, fresh rows of trenches, fortified houses, and a good artillery well worked and well placed, it was a serious task which lay in front of the gallant little army. The whole position covered between four and five miles.

An obvious question must here occur to the mind of every non-military reader – 'Why should this position be attacked at all? Why should we not cross higher up where there were no such formidable obstacles?' The answer, so far as one can answer it, must be that so little was known of the dispositions of our enemy that we were hopelessly involved in the action before we knew of it, and that then it was more dangerous to extricate the army than to push the attack. A retirement over that open plain at a range of under a thousand yards would have been a dangerous and disastrous movement. Having once got there, it was wisest and best to see it through.

The dark Cronje still waited reflective in the hotel garden. Across the veld streamed the lines of infantry, the poor fellows eager, after seven miles of that upland air, for the breakfast which had been promised them. It was a quarter to seven when our patrols of Lancers were fired upon. There were Boers, then, between them and their meal! The artillery was ordered up, the Guards were sent forward on the right, the 9th Brigade under Pole-Carew on the left, including the newly arrived Argyll and Sutherland Highlanders. They swept onwards into the fatal fire zone – and then, and only then, there blazed out upon them four miles of rifles, cannon, and machine guns, and they realised, from general to private, that they had walked unwittingly into the fiercest battle yet fought in the war.

Before the position was understood the Guards were within seven hundred yards of the Boer trenches, and the other troops about nine hundred, on the side of a very gentle slope which made it most difficult to find any cover. In front of them lay a serene landscape, the river, the houses, the hotel, no movement of men, no smoke – everything peaceful and deserted save for an occasional quick flash and sparkle of flame. But the noise was horrible and appalling. Men whose nerves had been steeled to the crash of the big guns, or the monotonous roar of Maxims and the rattle of Mauser fire, found a new terror in the malignant 'ploop-plooping' of the automatic quick-firer. The Maxim of the Scots Guards was caught in the hell-blizzard from this thing – each shell no bigger than a large walnut, but flying in strings of a score – and men and gun were destroyed in an instant. As to the rifle bullets the air was humming and throbbing with them, and the sand was mottled like a pond in a shower. To advance was impossible, to retire was hateful. The men fell upon their faces and huddled close to the earth, too happy if some friendly ant-heap gave them a precarious shelter. And always, tier above tier, the lines of rifle fire rippled and palpitated in front of them. The infantry fired also, and fired, and fired – but what was there to fire at? An occasional eye and hand over the edge of a trench or behind a stone is no mark at seven hundred yards. It would be instructive to know how many British bullets found a billet that day.

The cavalry was useless, the infantry was powerless – there only remained the guns. When any army is helpless and harried it always casts an imploring eye upon the guns, and rarely indeed is it that the gallant guns do not respond. Now the 75th and 18th Field Batteries came rattling and dashing to the front, and unlimbered at one thousand yards. The naval guns were working at four thousand, but the two combined were insufficient to master the fire of the pieces of large calibre which were opposed to them. Lord Methuen must have prayed for guns as Wellington did for night, and never was a prayer answered more dramatically. A strange battery came lurching up from the British rear, unheralded, unknown, the weary gasping horses panting at the traces, the men, caked with sweat and dirt, urging them on into a last spasmodic trot. The bodies of horses which had died of pure fatigue marked their course, the sergeants' horses tugged in the gun-teams, and the sergeants staggered along by the limbers. It was the 62nd Field Battery, which had marched thirty-two miles in eight hours, and now, hearing the crash of battle in front of them, had with one last desperate effort thrown itself into the firing line […]

As the afternoon wore on, a curious condition of things was established. The guns could not advance, and, indeed, it was found necessary to withdraw them from a 1,200 to a 2,800-yard range, so heavy were the losses. At the time of the change the 75th Battery had lost three officers out of five, nineteen men, and twenty-two horses. The infantry could not advance and would not retire. The Guards on the right were prevented from opening out on the flank and getting round the enemy's line, by the presence of the Riet River, which joins the Modder almost at a right angle. All day they lay under a blistering sun, the sleet of bullets whizzing over their heads. 'It came in solid streaks like telegraph wires,' said a graphic correspondent. The men gossiped, smoked, and many of them slept. They lay on the barrels of their rifles to keep them cool enough for use. Now and again there came the dull thud of a bullet which had found its mark, and a man gasped, or drummed with his feet; but the casualties at this point were not numerous, for there was some little cover, and the piping bullets passed for the most part overhead.

But in the meantime there had been a development upon the left which was to turn the action into a British victory. At this side there was ample room to extend, and the 9th Brigade spread out, feeling its way down the enemy's line, until it came to a point where the fire was less murderous and the approach to the river more in favour of the attack. Here the Yorkshires, a party of whom under Lieutenant Fox had stormed a farmhouse, obtained the command of a drift, over which a mixed force of Highlanders and Fusiliers forced their way, led by their Brigadier in person. This body of infantry, which does not appear to have exceeded five hundred in number, were assailed both by the Boer riflemen and by the guns of both parties, our own gunners being unaware that the Modder had been successfully crossed. A small hamlet called Rosmead formed, however, a *point d'appui*, and to this the infantry clung tenaciously, while reinforcements dribbled across to them from the farther side. 'Now, boys, who's for otter hunting?' cried Major Coleridge, of the North Lancashires, as he sprang into the water. How gladly on that baking, scorching day did the men jump into the river and splash over, to climb the opposite bank with their wet khaki clinging to their figures! Some blundered into holes and were rescued by grasping the unwound putties of their comrades. And so between three and four o'clock a strong party of the British had established their position upon the right flank of the Boers, and were holding on like grim death with an intelligent appreciation that the fortunes of the day depended upon their retaining their grip.

'Hollo, here is a river!' cried Codrington when he led his forlorn hope to the right and found that the Riet had to be crossed. 'I was given to understand that the Modder was fordable everywhere,' says Lord Methuen in his official despatch. One cannot read the account of the operations without being struck by the casual, sketchy knowledge which cost us so dearly. The soldiers slogged their way through, as they have slogged it before; but the task might have been made much lighter for them had we but clearly known what it was that we were trying to do. On the other hand, it is but fair to Lord Methuen to say that his own personal gallantry and unflinching resolution set the most stimulating example to his troops. No General could have done more to put heart into his men.

And now, as the long weary scorching hungry day came to an end, the Boers began at last to flinch from their trenches. The shrapnel was finding them out and this force upon their flank filled them with vague alarm and with fears for their precious guns. And so as night fell they stole across the river, the cannon were withdrawn, the trenches evacuated, and next morning, when the weary British and their anxious General turned themselves to their grim task once more, they found a deserted village, a line of empty houses, and a litter of empty Mauser cartridge-cases to show where their tenacious enemy had stood.

For the British, it was a Pyrrhic victory: 460 dead and wounded against 80 Boer casualties. Unmistakable defeat followed two weeks later at Magersfontein, where the British toll was twice as heavy. Kimberley and Cecil Rhodes would have to wait another two months to be relieved.

Things were going badly, too, for Buller, now in Natal. Stubbornly barring his way to Ladysmith, the Boers, under General Botha, were dug in along the north bank of the Tugela. In London, an impatient War Office replaced Buller as Commander-in-Chief with Field-Marshal Lord Roberts, who had spent 40 years imposing the Imperial will on India. His Chief of Staff was to be Lord Kitchener of Khartoum, conqueror of the Sudan, and they were to sail immediately with another 45 000 troops. At the suggestion of the London *Daily Mail*, Rudyard Kipling, the Imperial bard, dashed off a piece of doggerel to raise pocket money for the men. Called 'The Absent-Minded Beggar' (67) and set to an excruciating tune by Sir Arthur Sullivan, it was widely performed in music halls and quickly yielded £250 000. The first verse – there were many more – was:

> When you've shouted 'Rule Britannia,' when you've sung 'God save
>   the Queen,'
> When you've finished killing Kruger with your mouth,
> Will you kindly drop a shilling in my little tambourine
> For a gentleman in khaki ordered South?
> He's an absent-minded beggar, and his weaknesses are great –
> But we and Paul must take him as we find him –
> He is out on active service, wiping something off a slate –
> And he's left a lot of little things behind him!
> Duke's son – cook's son – son of a hundred kings –

(Fifty thousand horse and foot going to Table Bay!)
Each of 'em doing his country's work
(and who's to look after their things?)
Pass the hat for your credit's sake,
and pay – pay – pay!

Then, in January 1900, Buller, still trying to force his way through to Ladysmith, sent his deputy, General Sir Charles Warren, to take a hill north of the Tugela called Spioenkop. Conan Doyle describes the tragedy that unfolded on what was to be called 'the acre of massacre'.

On the right front, commanding the Boer lines on either side, towered the stark eminence of Spion Kop, so called because from its summit the Boer Voortrekkers had first in 1835 gazed down upon the promised land of Natal. If that could only be seized and held! Buller and Warren swept its bald summit with their field-glasses. It was a venture. But all war is a venture; and the brave man is he who ventures most. One fiery rush and the master-key of all these locked doors might be in our keeping. That evening there came a telegram to London which left the whole Empire in a hush of anticipation. Spion Kop was to be attacked that night.

The troops which were selected for the task were eight companies of the 2nd Lancashire Fusiliers, six of the 2nd Royal Lancasters, two of the 1st South Lancashires, 180 of Thorneycroft's, and half a company of Sappers. It was to be a North of England job.

Under the friendly cover of a starless night the men, in Indian file, like a party of Iroquois braves upon the war trail, stole up the winding and ill-defined path which led to the summit. Woodgate, the Lancashire Brigadier, and Blomfield of the Fusiliers led the way. It was a severe climb of 2,000 feet, coming after arduous work over broken ground, but the affair was well-timed, and it was at that blackest hour which precedes the dawn that the last steep ascent was reached. The Fusiliers crouched down among the rocks to recover their breath, and saw far down in the plain beneath them the placid lights which showed where their comrades were resting. A fine rain was falling, and rolling clouds hung low over their heads. The men with unloaded rifles and fixed bayonets stole on once more, their bodies bent, their eyes peering through the mirk for the first sign of the enemy – that enemy whose first sign has usually been a shattering volley. Thorneycroft's men with their gallant leader had threaded their way up into the advance. Then the leading files found that they were walking on the level. The crest had been gained.

With slow steps and bated breath, the open line of skirmishers stole across it. Was it possible that it had been entirely abandoned? Suddenly a raucous shout of 'Wie da?' came out of the darkness, then a shot, then a splutter of musketry and a yell, as the Fusiliers sprang onwards with their bayonets. The Boer post of Vryheid burghers clattered and scrambled away into the darkness, and a cheer that roused both the sleeping armies told that the surprise had been complete and the position won.

In the grey light of the breaking day the men advanced along the narrow undulating ridge, the prominent end of which they had captured. Another trench faced them, but it was weakly held and abandoned. Then the men, uncertain what remained beyond, halted and waited for full light to see where they were, and what the work was which lay before them – a fatal halt, as the result proved, and yet one so natural that it is hard to blame the officer who ordered it.

Indeed, he might have seemed more culpable had he pushed blindly on, and so lost the advantage which had been already gained.

About eight o'clock, with the clearing of the mist, General Woodgate saw how matters stood. The ridge, one end of which he held, extended away, rising and falling for some miles. Had he the whole of the end plateau, and had he guns, he might hope to command the rest of the position. But he held only half the plateau, and at the further end of it the Boers were strongly entrenched. The Spion Kop mountain was really the salient or sharp angle of the Boer position, so that the British were exposed to a cross fire both from the left and right. Beyond were other eminences which sheltered strings of riflemen and several guns. The plateau which the British held was very much narrower than was usually represented in the press. In many places the possible front was not much more than a hundred yards wide, and the troops were compelled to bunch together, as there was not room for a single company to take an extended formation. The cover upon this plateau was scanty, far too scanty for the force upon it, and the shell fire – especially the fire of the pom-poms – soon became very murderous. To mass the troops under the cover of the edge of the plateau might naturally suggest itself, but with great tactical skill the Boer advanced line from Commandant Prinsloo's Heidelberg and Carolina commandos kept so aggressive an attitude that the British could not weaken the lines opposed to them. Their skirmishers were

273

creeping round too in such a way that the fire was really coming from three separate points, left, centre, and right, and every corner of the position was searched by their bullets. Early in the action the gallant Woodgate and many of his Lancashire men were shot down. The others spread out and held on, firing occasionally at the whisk of a rifle-barrel or the glimpse of a broad-brimmed hat.

From morning to midday, the shell, Maxim, and rifle fire swept across the kop in a continual driving shower. The British guns in the plain below failed to localise the position of the enemy's, and they were able to vent their concentrated spite upon the exposed infantry. No blame attaches to the gunners for this, as a hill intervened to screen the Boer artillery, which consisted of five big guns and two pom-poms.

Upon the fall of Woodgate, Thorneycroft, who bore the reputation of a determined fighter, was placed at the suggestion of Buller in charge of the defence of the hill, and he was reinforced after noon by Coke's brigade, the Middlesex, the Dorsets, and the Somersets, together with the Imperial Light Infantry. The addition of this force to the defenders of the plateau tended to increase the casualty returns rather than the strength of the defence. Three thousand more rifles could do nothing to check the fire of the invisible cannon, and it was this which was the main source of the losses, while on the other hand the plateau had become so cumbered with troops that a shell could hardly fail to do damage. There was no cover to shelter them and no room for them to extend. The pressure was most severe upon the shallow trenches in the front, which had been abandoned by the Boers and were held by the Lancashire Fusiliers. They were enfiladed by rifle and cannon, and the dead and wounded outnumbered the hale. So close were the skirmishers that on at least one occasion Boer and Briton found themselves on each side of the same rock. Once a handful of men, tormented beyond endurance, sprang up as a sign that they had had enough, but Thorneycroft, a man of huge physique, rushed forward to the advancing Boers. 'You may go to hell!' he yelled. 'I command here, and allow no surrender. Go on with your firing.' Nothing could exceed the gallantry of Louis Botha's men in pushing the attack. Again and again they made their way up to the British firing line, exposing themselves with a recklessness which, with the exception of the grand attack upon Ladysmith, was unique in our experience of them. About two o'clock they rushed one trench occupied by the Fusiliers and secured the survivors of two companies as prisoners, but were subsequently driven out again. A detached group of the South Lancashires was summoned to surrender. 'When I surrender,' cried Colour-Sergeant Nolan, 'it will be my dead body!' Hour after hour of the unintermitting crash of the shells among the rocks and of the groans and screams of men torn and burst by the most horrible of all wounds had shaken the troops badly. Spectators from below who saw the shells pitching at the rate of seven a minute on to the crowded plateau marvelled at the endurance which held the devoted men to their post. Men were wounded and wounded and wounded yet again, and still went on fighting. Never since Inkerman had we had so grim a soldier's battle. The company officers were superb. Captain Muriel of the Middlesex was shot through the check while giving a cigarette to a wounded man, continued to lead his company, and was shot again through the brain. Scott Moncrieff of the same regiment was only disabled by the fourth bullet which hit him. Grenfell of Thorneycroft's was shot, and exclaimed, 'That's all right. It's not much.' A second wound made him remark, 'I can get on all right.' The third killed him. Ross of the Lancasters, who had crawled from a sickbed, was found dead upon the furthest crest. Young Murray of the Scottish Rifles, dripping from five wounds, still staggered about among his men. And the men were worthy of such officers. 'No retreat! No retreat!' they yelled when some of the front line were driven in. In all regiments there are weaklings and hang-backs, and many a man was wandering down the reverse slopes when he should have been facing death upon the top, but as a body British troops have never stood firm through a more fiery ordeal than on that fatal hill.

The position was so bad that no efforts of officers or men could do anything to mend it. They were in a murderous dilemma. If they fell back for cover the Boer riflemen would rush the position. If they held their ground this horrible shell fire must continue, which they had no means of answering [...]

There remains the debated question whether the British guns could have been taken to the top. Mr. Winston Churchill, the soundness of whose judgment has been frequently demonstrated during the war, asserts that it might have been done. Without venturing to contradict one who was personally present,[8] I venture to think that there is strong evidence to show that it could not have been done without blasting and other measures, for which there was no possible time [...]

Throughout the day reinforcements had pushed up the hill, until two full brigades had been drawn into the fight. From the other side of the ridge Lyttelton sent up the Scottish Rifles, who reached the summit, and added their share to the shambles upon the top. As the shades of night closed in, and the glare of the bursting shells became more lurid, the men lay extended upon the rocky ground, parched and exhausted. They were hopelessly jumbled together, with the exception of the Dorsets, whose cohesion may have been due to superior discipline, less exposure, or to the fact that their khaki differed somewhat in colour from that of the others. Twelve hours of so terrible an experience had had a strange effect upon many of the men. Some were dazed and battle-struck, incapable of clear understanding. Some were as incoherent as drunkards. Some lay in an overpowering drowsiness. The most were doggedly patient and long-suffering, with a mighty longing for water obliterating every other emotion.

Before evening fell a most gallant and successful attempt had been made by the third battalion of the King's Royal Rifles from Lyttelton's Brigade to relieve the pressure upon their comrades on Spion Kop. In order to draw part of the Boer fire away they ascended from the northern side and carried the hills which formed a continuation of the same ridge. The movement was meant to be no more than a strong demonstration, but the riflemen pushed it until, breathless but victorious, they stood upon the very crest of the position, leaving nearly a hundred dead or dying to show the path which they had taken. Their advance being much further than was desired, they were recalled ...

And now, under the shadow of night, but with the shells bursting thickly over the plateau, the much-tried Thorneycroft had to make up his mind whether he should hold on for another such day as he had endured, or whether now, in the friendly darkness, he should remove his shattered force. Could he have seen the discouragement of the Boers and the preparations which they had made for retirement, he would have held his ground. But this was hidden from him, while the horror of his own losses was but too apparent. Forty per cent of his men were down. Thirteen hundred dead and dying are a grim sight upon a wide-spread battle-field, but when this number is heaped upon a confined space, where from a single high rock the whole litter of broken and shattered bodies can be seen, and the groans of the stricken rise in one long droning chorus to the ear, then it is an iron mind indeed which can resist such evidence of disaster. In a harder age Wellington was able to survey four thousand bodies piled in the narrow compass of the breach of Badajos, but his resolution was sustained by the knowledge that the military end for which they fell had been accomplished. Had his task been unfinished it is doubtful whether even his steadfast soul would not have flinched from its completion. Thorneycroft saw the frightful havoc of one day, and he shrank from the thought of such another. 'Better six battalions safely down the hill than a mop up in the morning,' said he, and he gave the word to retire. One who had met the troops as they staggered down has told me how far they were from being routed. In mixed array, but steadily and in order, the long thin line trudged through the darkness. Their parched lips would not articulate, but they whispered 'Water! Where is water?' as they toiled upon their way. At the bottom of the hill they formed into regiments once more, and marched back to the camp. In the morning the blood-spattered hill-top, with its piles of dead and of wounded, were in the hands of Botha and his men, whose valour and perseverance deserved the victory which they had won. There is no doubt now that at 3 A.M. of that morning Botha, knowing that the Rifles had carried Burger's position, regarded the affair as hopeless, and that no one was more astonished than he when he found, on the report of two scouts, that it was a victory and not a defeat which had come to him.

The death toll in this tragically futile battle was 350 British soldiers and 75 Boers; more than 1 000 were wounded. Among those who tended them was Mahatma Gandhi, who had volunteered as a stretcher bearer. Today, the 'acre of massacre' is a war memorial to both sides. The British mass graves, marked out by whitewashed stones, look like the trenches the men never had time to dig. William Plomer's laconic poem is called 'The Boer War'.

The Boer War

The whip-crack of a Union Jack
In a stiff breeze (the ship will roll),
Deft abracadabra drums
Enchant the patriotic soul –

A grandsire in St. James's Street
Sat at the window of his club,
His second son, shot through the throat,
Slid backwards down a slope of scrub,

Gargled his last breaths, one by one by one,
In too much blood, too good to spill,
Died difficultly, drop by drop by drop –
'By your son's courage, sir, we took the hill.'

They took the hill (Whose hill? What for?)
But what a climb they left to do!
Out of that bungled, unwise war
An alp of unforgiveness grew.

A month later, Buller finally made his break-through to Ladysmith at Pieters Hill, north of the Tugela. Deneys Reitz, who had earlier fought at Spioenkop, was here, too.

As we went along, a bombardment more violent than that of yesterday broke out ahead of us, and, when we came to the rear of Pieters Heights, we saw the ridge on which lay the Bethal men (and our own) going up in smoke and flame. It was an alarming sight. The English batteries were so concentrating on the crest that it was almost invisible under the clouds of flying earth and fumes, while the volume of sound was beyond anything that I have ever heard. At intervals the curtain lifted, letting us catch a glimpse of the trenches above, but we could see no sign of movement, nor could we hear whether the men up there were still firing, for the din of the guns drowned all lesser sounds.

We reined in about four hundred yards from the foot of the hill, at a loss what to do. To approach our men through that inferno was to court destruction, while not to try seemed like desertion. For a minute or two we debated and then, suddenly, the gun-fire ceased, and for a space we caught the fierce rattle of Mauser rifles followed by British infantry swamping over the skyline, their bayonets flashing in the sun. Shouts and cries reached us, and we could see men desperately thrusting and clubbing. Then a rout of burghers broke back from the hill, streaming towards us in disorderly flight. The soldiers fired into them, bringing many down as they made blindly past us, not looking to right or left. We went, too, for the troops, cheering loudly, came shooting and running down the slope.

Of our Pretoria men who had been on the ridge not one came back. They had been holding an advanced position to the right of the Bethal section, and had been overwhelmed there. They stood their ground until the enemy was on them, and they were bayoneted or taken to the last man. Thus our corporalship was wiped out, with its leader, Isaac Malherbe, the bravest of them all, and their going at this calamitous time was scarcely noticed. For this day marked the beginning of the end in Natal. The British had blasted a gap through which the victorious soldiery came pouring and, wherever we looked, Boer horsemen, wagons and guns went streaming to the rear in headlong retreat.

We followed the current, hemmed in by a great throng, all making for the various fords of the Klip River, and it was lucky indeed that the English sent no cavalry in pursuit, for the passages across the river were steep and narrow, and there was frightful confusion of men and wagons struggling to get past.

By nightfall my uncle and my brother and I had managed to cross, and as it started to rain we annexed a deserted tent behind Lombaardskop, picketed and fed our tired horses, and slept there till morning. We now resumed our journey as far as the head laager, where we spent a dismal hour or two watching the tide of defeat roll northward.

We knew that the siege of Ladysmith would have to be raised, and now came the news, while we were halted here, that Kimberley had also been relieved, and that General Cronje had been captured at Paardeberg with four thousand men, so that the whole universe seemed to be toppling about our ears.

From the way in which the commandos were hurrying past, it looked that morning as if the Boer cause was going to pieces before our eyes, and it would have taken a bold man to prophesy that the war had still more than two long years to run.

We hung about the dismantled head laager till midday, after which the three of us rode on gloomily to the Pretoria camp, arriving towards five in the afternoon. Word of the disaster to our men on the Tugela had already preceded us, as is the way with evil tidings, and, as it was not known that my brother and I had escaped, our unexpected appearance caused a sensation, men running up from all sides to hear the truth. My other brothers had returned and their welcome was a warm one.

It was by now clear enough that the siege could no longer be maintained and, indeed, orders had already been received that all commandos were to evacuate their positions around Ladysmith after dark. Our wagons were standing packed, but at the last moment it was found that someone had levanted with the transport mules, so everything had to be burned. It came on to rain heavily by nightfall. Peals of thunder growled across the sky, and, wet to the skin, we stood huddled against the storm in depressed groups, awaiting our final orders. At last, long after dark, Field-Cornet Zeederberg gave the word that we were to move off to Elandslaagte some twenty miles to the rear. It was an inky night, with rain in torrents, through which we had to feel our way, and thus we turned our backs on Ladysmith for good and all.

No march order was attempted; we were simply told to go, and it was left to each man to carry out his own retirement.

At the outset we travelled in company with many others, but, as I knew a short cut, threading the hills to the railway depot at Modderspruit, my brothers and I decided to go thither, for we saw no use in floundering about in mud and water, and the four of us, with my uncle and our native boy Charley, branched away by ourselves.

We reached the depot after two hours and found shelter until daybreak, after which we rode on.

The rain now stopped and the sun rose warm and bright, but it looked on a dismal scene. In all directions the plain was covered with a multitude of men, wagons, and guns ploughing across the sodden veld in the greatest disorder. Wherever a spruit or nullah barred the way there arose fierce quarrels between the frightened teamsters, each wanting to cross first, with the result that whole parks of vehicles got their wheels so interlocked that at times it seemed as if the bulk of the transport and artillery would have to be abandoned, for the mounted men pressed steadily on without concerning themselves with the convoys. Had the British fired a single gun at this surging mob everything on wheels would have fallen into their hands, but by great good luck there was no pursuit and towards afternoon the tangle gradually straightened itself out.

Our little family party remained behind with a number of others as a rearguard and we did not reach Elandslaagte until late that night. This place had been the chief supply centre for the Natal forces, and there were still huge quantities of stores that had been left to the enemy. These we burnt, lighting a conflagration that must have been visible for fifty miles around.

By now the bulk of the retreat had passed on, and next day we rode along leisurely, climbing up the Washbank valley to Glencoe near Dundee by the following evening. Here were stray remnants of almost every commando that had been in Natal, but things were in such confusion that most of the army had continued straight on, and there was scarcely a man who could tell us what had become of his officers, or what we were supposed to do next.

Mr Zeederberg, however, was at Glencoe when we got there, and during the next few days he succeeded in collecting about three hundred Pretoria men, while more drifted back later on, as did stragglers from the other commandos, until after a week or ten days there was quite a respectable body of men numbering well over five thousand.

During this time my brothers and I with our uncle subsisted on what we could loot from the supply trains at the station, for there were practically no commissariat arrangements, but by raiding the trucks at night we did not do badly.

After a while General Botha reorganized everything, and a new line of defence was established along the forward slopes of the Biggarsbergen, to which all available men were marched. We of the Pretoria commando were assigned a post on the shoulder of the mountain to the right of where the Washbank valley reaches the plain below, and here we lay amongst pleasant scenery, from which we looked regretfully over the wide sweep of country to the south from which we had been driven, but we enjoyed the spell of peace and quiet after the turmoil of the past weeks.

At about the same time Olive Schreiner, whose brother, William, was then Prime Minister of the Cape Colony, gave an interview to 'Banjo' Paterson (68), an Australian poet and journalist, who had written the lyrics of 'Waltzing Matilda'. Nearly 50 000 troops from Australia, New Zealand and Canada fought against the Boers on behalf of the Mother Country.

'Our friend the enemy'! For six weeks the New South Wales Lancers (with whom the present scribe is associated as war correspondent) had been in daily touch with the Boers. Six weeks of blazing hot days and freezing cold nights, spent in tents where the dust-storms coated everything with a dull-red powder, out on picket duty lying in the scorching sun among the rocks of a koppie, or on patrol trying how near we could get to the enemy without being shot dead; six weeks of hurried movements, of midnight marches and rapid shiftings of camp, of night-long watches out in the cold of the veld with the shivering horses standing alongside; and all with the object of killing, capturing or dispersing the unknown and practically unseen enemy that clung so tenaciously to his heaven-built fortress of rocky koppie, and who was so ready to shoot on the slightest provocation.

We had given up thinking what the Boers were like or of considering them as human beings at all. To us they were simply so much enemy – as impersonal as the Maxim guns and the rifles that they used. For six weeks we had seen no letters, no books and practically no newspapers. The world was narrowed down to ourselves and the enemy. All our time was fully occupied in fighting, and we gave no thought to the question of what the fighting was about. It was a great change, therefore, in visiting Cape Town to call on Olive Schreiner, a bitter opponent of the war, and to hear the Boer side of the question.

The authoress of The Story of an African Farm needs no introduction to Australians. While her brother (the Premier of the Cape Colony) has been very reserved in expressing opinions, Olive Schreiner has been most outspoken in denouncing the war and those who, in her opinion, are responsible for it.

She was at Newlands, a suburb of Cape Town, and no Australian city has such a suburb. On leaving the train one walks down an avenue overhung with splendid trees, and more like a private carriageway than a public road; it is hard to believe that one is not trespassing on somebody's private garden. There is no sidewalk – just the red-earth avenue between the trees. The flowers and trees grow most luxuriantly, sunflowers, box-hedges, roses and all manner of grasses flourishing everywhere, an inexpressible relief after the miles of sunburnt Karoo desert we have been staring over lately. The houses that front on the avenue all stand back in their own gardens, but instead of having a forbidding six-foot paling fence round each property there is usually a low iron-standard fence or a box-hedge as boundary, and the passer-by sees into these beautiful gardens as he goes along. If a few residences were erected in Sydney Botanic Gardens, that would be like Newlands. The trees are just as beautiful and luxuriant. In these surroundings lives the woman who made her name famous by The Story of an African Farm. She is married now, but still prefers to be known as Olive Schreiner. She is a little woman, small in stature, but of very strong physique, broad and powerful; her face olive-complexioned, with bright, restless eyes and a quick mobile mouth.

She talks fluently, and with tremendous energy, and one is not long in arriving at the conclusion that she is thoroughly in earnest – deadly earnest – over this question of the Boer War. It may be news to many Australians to hear that in the Cape Colony there are more people against the war than for it, not necessarily Boer sympathisers, but people who think that the war should never have been entered upon. When our troops landed from Australia we were astonished to find that the Cape Colony was so much against the war. The local papers that were for the war were all clamouring for the arrest or dismissal of W P Schreiner, the Premier, but when the House went to a division Schreiner had a majority behind him and Schreiner has always declared that England is not justified in this war. Olive Schreiner was not long in stating her views to the present writer. She talks rapidly and energetically, emphasising her remarks with uplifted finger.

'You Australians and New Zealanders and Canadians,' she said, 'I cannot understand it at all, why you come here light-heartedly to shoot down other colonists of whom you know nothing – it is terrible. Such fine men too – fine fellows. I went to Green Point and saw your men in camp; oh, they were fine men – (these were Colonel Williams' A. M. C. troops) – and to think that they are going out to kill and be killed, just to please the capitalists! There was one officer – oh, a fine man, so like a Boer, he might have been a Boer commandant. It is terrible – such men to come and fight against those fighting for their liberty and their country. The English Tommy Atkins goes where he is sent he fights because he is ordered; but you people – you are all volunteers! Why have you come?

'You say that England was at war, and you wished to show the world that when the mother country got into war the colonies were prepared to take their place beside her! Yes, but you ought to ask, you ought to make inquiries before you come over. You Australians do not understand. This is a capitalists' war! They want to get control of the Rand and the mines. You have nothing like it in your country. You have a working class that votes and that cannot be bought to vote against its own interests; but in the Transvaal there are just a handful of Boer farmers, a small but enormously wealthy mine-owning class and their dependants – professional men, shopkeepers and so on, and the rest are all Kaffirs.'

'Why didn't the Boers grant the franchise?'

'It was not really wanted. I was in Johannesburg a few months before the war broke out, and hundreds of men there said that they would not forego their British nationality for the sake of voting as a Boer. They are all nomads, wanderers, over there to make money, and if Oom Paul[9] had gone on his knees and asked them to accept the franchise they would not have accepted it. They would not relinquish being British subjects. But the capitalists insist on getting hold of the mines, and all the white people are so concerned with them, their interests so depend on the mine-owners, that they must go along with them, and now they want the franchise to take control of the mines from the Boers. It is a monstrous war, and England will regret it; it is just to take the country from the Boers for the benefit of the speculators. For years this war has been worked up – all sorts of stories have been printed of the Boers and their ignorance and their savagery. They are all lies. I was a governess among the Boers for years, and no kinder people exist. They are clever, too. Young Boers go to England and succeed at the universities; they become doctors, lawyers and politicians. It is much like Australia from what I have read. They are such hospitable people.

'Oh, this war is a terrible thing; it will be a war of extermination. What do you think will be the end of it? There will be no end. The Boers are fighting for life or death, and they have no idea of giving in. If they are beaten back into the Free State and the Transvaal that is just the time they will be most dangerous. When the English get to Pretoria with their army they will then be in a worse position than they are now. They will have hundreds and hundreds of miles of railway line to defend, and even if the Boers are scattered and beaten they will still fight. The Boer women now are heart and soul for the war. The Boer farmer is a curious man. He marries early, usually about eighteen or nineteen, and there is not one man in the army against you but has his wife and child somewhere. And those wives and children are reaping the crops and working the farms, so that their husbands can go to the war.

'After Elandslaagte, where the Boers were defeated, one Boer went home. His wife said, "What has happened: are you wounded?" "No." "Is the enemy fled?" "No." "Well, back you go to the laager and fight with the rest." Another old man of seventy-five, when he heard of the defeat, rose up and took his rifle. "I am going to the front," he said. "Why, you cannot see," said his grandchildren. "I cannot see at a thousand yards," he said, "but I can see at a hundred"; and off he went in a Cape cart as he was too old to ride.

'The small boys at school at the Cape Town schools have all been brought back to the farms to fight – boys of fourteen and fifteen are in the ranks. And all of these people have their relatives all through Cape Colony; and they are to be butchered, and the English soldiers are to be butchered, to suit a few capitalists. It will benefit no one else. The effect of this war on South Africa will be everlasting; we have such a large population here who feel that the war is unjust, and they will never forgive the English people for forcing it on. Perhaps the memory of Majuba Hill had a good deal to do with it? I cannot think so – the English are not so narrow as to treasure up memories of a small thing like that. But now it is a long, terrible war that is before us, and the Boers will be more dangerous after a few reverses. A few defeats will not crush them! When the English get to Pretoria then there will begin the trouble.'

Whatever may be the correctness of Olive Schreiner's views, there is no doubt of her sincerity. She says openly what most, or at any rate very many, South Africans think, and it is always well to hear both sides, so I have put down without comment exactly what her views were.

Talking on literary matters, Olive Schreiner said that though she was constantly writing she did not publish much. The cares of household life interfered much with work. When a governess in the Eastern Cape, after the day's work was done, she would sit in her room and work with a mind free from care. It was then that *The African Farm* was written. Nowadays she has too much to think about – household worries and so on. She was asked to act as war correspondent for a New York paper, but the authorities would not hear of her going – in which, by the way, they were quite right. The front is no place for a woman.

It seems a pity that this woman, who is no doubt a great literary genius, should be wasting her time and wearing out her energies over this Boer War question, instead of giving us another book as good as her first one; but after an interview with her one comes away with a much more lively and human interest in 'our friends the enemy'. If things are as she says, if the Boers are going to make it a war to the bitter end, then England has a sorry task before her. If the Boers scatter and break to the mountains they will be practically unreachable, and the English people are too humane to care about levying reprisals by destroying their homesteads and leaving their wives and children without shelter. The result will be that even after the war is over a large force will have to be kept in the country to maintain order, and with the Cape disaffected there will be serious trouble for politicians after the soldiers have got through with their work. One is more inclined to hope that after a defeat or two the Boer, sensible man that he is, will come in under English rule and rely on the forbearance of that Power rather than maintain a hopeless straggling fight which will only prolong the misery of the present war.

Schreiner was right, of course. Scattered and beaten though the Boers were to be in the coming months, they would still fight. Paterson, however, was wrong: the English would not shrink from levying reprisals.

By March 1900, Roberts had marched unopposed into Bloemfontein, the capital of the Orange Free State. He wrote to Queen Victoria assuring her the war would soon be over. In May, having annexed the Free State as the Orange River Colony, he swept on to Pretoria at the head of a 45 000-strong army. The Boers melted away into the veld. In October 1900, the first anniversary of the war, Roberts annexed the Transvaal. In December, he handed over command to Kitchener, sailed for home and was rewarded with an earldom. But few in Britain realised what a catastrophe he had set in train or could imagine the tragic heights it would attain under Kitchener's command. Six months earlier, the Boers – the 'bitter-enders', as they were now called – had turned to guerrilla warfare and Roberts, initially to punish them for attacking railways and telegraph lines, had started burning their farms. Pretty soon, however, any excuse would do, as the following remarkable account by Lisle March-Phillipps (69) confirms. He was a captain in Rimington's Guides, a detachment serving under Lord Methuen in the Orange River Colony. From there, March-Phillipps wrote a series of letters home. They were published in 1902.

Kronstadt, September 6, 1900.

The army seems to be adopting very severe measures to try and end the campaign out of hand, and the papers at home are loudly calling for such measures, I see, and justifying them. Nevertheless, it is childish to pretend that it is a crime in the Boers to continue fighting, or that they have done anything to disentitle them to the usages of civilised warfare. The various columns that are now marching about the country are carrying on the work of destruction pretty indiscriminately, and we have burnt and destroyed by now many scores of farms. Ruin, with great hardship and want, which may ultimately border on starvation, must be the result to many families. These measures are not likely, I am afraid, to conduce much to the united South Africa we talk so much of and thought we were fighting for.

I had to go myself the other day, at the General's bidding, to burn a farm near the line of march. We got to the place, and I gave the inmates, three women and some children, ten minutes to clear their clothes and things out of the house, and my men then fetched bundles of straw and we proceeded to burn it down. The old grandmother was very angry. She told me that, though I was making a fine blaze now, it was nothing compared to the flames that I myself should be consumed in hereafter. Most of them, however, were too miserable to curse. The women cried and the children stood by holding on to them and looking with large frightened eyes at the burning house. They won't forget that sight, I'll bet a sovereign, not even when they grow up. We rode away and left them, a forlorn little group, standing among their household goods – beds, furniture, and gimcracks strewn about the veldt; the crackling of the fire in their ears, and smoke and flame streaming overhead. The worst moment is when you first come to the house. The people thought we had called for refreshments, and one of the women went to get milk. Then we had to tell them that we had come to burn the place down. I simply didn't know which way to look. One of the women's husbands had been killed at Magersfontein. There were others, men and boys, away fighting; whether dead or alive they did not know.

I give you this as a sample of what is going on pretty generally. Our troops are everywhere at work burning and laying waste, and enormous reserves of famine and misery are being laid up for these countries in the future.

How far do you mean to go in this? Are you going to burn down every house, and turn the whole country into a desert? I don't think it can be done. You can't carry out the Cromwellian method in the nineteenth century. Too many people know what is going on, and consciences are too tender. On the other hand, nothing is so disastrous as that method half carried out. We can't exterminate the Dutch or seriously reduce their numbers. We can do enough to make hatred of England and thirst for revenge the first duty of every Dutchman, and we can't effectively reduce the numbers of the men who will carry that duty out. Of course it is not a question of the war only. It is a question of governing the country afterwards.

Frankfort, November 23, 1900.
Kronstadt, Lindley, Heilbron, Frankfort, has been our round so far. We now turn westward along the south of the Vaal. Farm burning goes merrily on, and our course through the country is marked as in prehistoric ages, by pillars of smoke by day and fire by night. We usually burn from six to a dozen farms a day; these being about all that in this sparsely-inhabited country we encounter. I do not gather that any special reason or cause is alleged or proved against the farms burnt. If Boers have used the farm; if the owner is on commando; if the line within a certain distance has been blown up; or even if there are Boers in the neighbourhood who persist in fighting – these are some of the reasons. Of course the people living in the farms have no

say in these matters, and are quite powerless to interfere with the plans of the fighting Boers. Anyway we find that one reason or other generally covers pretty nearly every farm we come to, and so to save trouble we burn the lot without inquiry; unless, indeed, which sometimes happens, some names are given in before marching in the morning of farms to be spared.

The men belonging to the farm are always away and only the women left. Of these there are often three or four generations; grandmother, mother, and family of girls. The boys over thirteen or fourteen are usually fighting with their papas. The people are disconcertingly like English, especially the girls and children – fair and big and healthy looking. These folk we invite out on to the veldt or into the little garden in front, where they huddle together in their cotton frocks and big cotton sun-bonnets, while our men set fire to the house. Sometimes they entreat that it may be spared, and once or twice in an agony of rage they have invoked curses on our heads. But this is quite the exception. As a rule they make no sign, and simply look on and say nothing. One young woman in a farm yesterday, which I think she had not started life long in, went into a fit of hysterics when she saw the flames breaking out, and finally fainted away.

I wish I had my camera. Unfortunately it got damaged, and I have not been able to take any photographs. These farms would make a good subject. They are dry and burn well. The fire bursts out of windows and doors with a loud roaring, and black volumes of smoke roll overhead. Standing round are a dozen or two of men holding horses. The women, in a little group, cling together, comforting each other or hiding their faces in each other's laps. In the background a number of Tommies are seen chasing poultry, flinging stones, and throwing themselves prostrate on maimed chickens and ducks, whose melancholy squawks fill the air. Further off still, herds and flocks and horses are being collected and driven off, while, on the top of the nearest high ground, a party of men, rifles in hand, guard against a surprise from the enemy, a few of whom can generally be seen in the distance watching the destruction of their homes.

Here, dating from the same period, is a victim's account (70) of her experience of Roberts's policy.

I had thought that the enemy would not come again but on the 14th November, 1900, they came again from Belfast[10] by the road over the farm

Schoonuitzicht, and reached Witpoort in the afternoon at 4 o'clock. After they had first fired a cannonade with Maxims over the house and trees, they came up to my house. A man said to me:

'Tante, I give you half an hour's time to take what you want out of your house for I am come to set it on fire.'

I asked him: 'Why will you burn the house? I am weak, suffering from fever. What will become of me under the naked sky?'

I spoke to the officer asking him to spare the house: he refused to do so. I said to him:

'With God in Heaven there is mercy, have you then no mercy for a poor woman? Because you cannot get the men into your hands will you fight the women?'

The man turned white, gave me no answer and rode away. The others remained sitting upon their horses. One of them said:

'Tante, this is an order and we must carry it out, but bring everything out of the house that you can.'

Then they dismounted and began to help me carry out the things, such as the furniture in the sitting and dining rooms, the beds and other goods. Also they brought out for me three sacks of corn and two sacks of meal. They also helped my daughter-in-law to carry out her things. From my storeroom I could save nothing for they refused to allow me to fetch anything from there except my veld-tent which a man carried out and gave me. It speaks for itself that I could do nothing, being but just out of a sick bed where I had lain for three months and my right arm was still powerless. I had spoken gently and had besought; but nothing availed – the house must be burnt. When I went to the pantry to fetch something I found a man there with two packets of fuel. He set fire to it. One packet he threw upon the ceiling of the sitting room the other in a bedroom. The flames rose up instantly in the gable of the house. I stood looking at it – no pen can write what was in my heart. Suddenly flashed into my mind: 'Vengeance is mine, I will repay, saith the Lord.' When I thought of this I felt steadfast – the dear Lord has more than this to give me – but it was terrible to see everything in flames. As the house stood in flames from gable to gable they took the three sacks of corn and put them in the passage of the house and threw the one sack of meal through the window of the sittingroom.

I asked them why they burnt my food: a man made answer: 'Your husband gives you food.'

I said then: 'The devil thanks you for this: my husband has given me food enough – but you have burnt it.'

A Kaffir in the service of the enemy who stood gazing at the house as it burnt said: 'It is awful.'

I remained silent.

He said for the second time: 'It is awful.' and added, 'it is sin.' Then spoke I and said: 'Yes, God will punish you for this.' Then they went back to their camp taking with them my two Kaffirs to carry the goods plundered from me to their camp.

Accounts of farm burning had begun appearing in British newspapers months before. In July 1900, for example, the *Manchester Guardian's* correspondent rode from Bloemfontein to Kimberley and reported: 'The way is a line of desolation; the farm-houses have not merely been sacked, they have been savagely destroyed.' Yet hardly anyone seemed to hear or, more importantly, want to listen. The outstanding exception was Emily Hobhouse, a redoubtable and well-connected philanthropist. In September 1900, she had heard enough about farm burning and the resulting destitution to help found the South African Women and Children's Distress Fund. Early in December – when Milner was claiming it would be 'preposterous to countenance the now fully exploded calumny about the ill-treatment of women and children' – she set sail for Cape Town determined to see for herself. By now, Kitchener as commander-in-chief was pursuing Roberts's scorched-earth policy with deadly vigour: the land was to be laid waste, its civilian inhabitants herded into concentration camps and his troops would sweep the veld as if they were conducting a pheasant drive. Deneys Reitz was with a Boer commando south of Pretoria when he heard the news.

At Olifantsfontein, General Botha came up with a small escort. He looked thinner than when I had last seen him in the Lydenburg Mountains four months ago, but he was full of energy and confidence. He told us that Lord Roberts had decided to bring the Boers to their knees by a series of drives, in which vast numbers of troops were to sweep across the country like a drag-net. To that end, all through this month of January (1901) they were assembling fifty thousand men along the Johannesburg-Natal railway line, ready to move over the high veld on a front of sixty or seventy miles, with the intention of clearing the Eastern Transvaal, after which the process was to be repeated elsewhere, until every one was dead or taken.

The Boers were as yet mercifully unaware that this new system was to include the burning of farms, the destruction of crops and herds, and the carrying into concentration camps of their wives and children, but they were soon enough to learn that the British had taken the dread decision of laying waste the two republics, regardless of the suffering of the non-combatant population, and ignorant of the fact that these methods, so far from subduing the Boers would merely serve to stiffen their resistance.

Two days after General Botha had ridden away, the storm broke upon us. As the sun rose, the skyline from west to east was dotted with English horsemen riding in a line that stretched as far as the eye could see, and behind this screen every road was black with columns, guns, and wagons slowly moving forward on the first great drive of the war.

General Beyers, when he grasped the situation, divided his force in two, and rode away with one half to find the left flank of the enemy, while the rest of us were told to do what we could in front of the advance.

Far away, to our left, parties of General Botha's men were visible from rise to rise, scattered specks before the great host.

All that day we fell back, delaying the enemy horsemen by rifle-fire as far as possible, and breaking away when the gun-fire grew too hot. This went on till sunset without heavy losses on our side, despite the many batteries brought into play from every knoll and kopje. Once I saw my brother disappear from sight as a shrapnel shell burst on him, but he rode out laughing, he and his horse uninjured.

During the course of the morning, pillars of smoke began to rise behind the English advance, and to our astonishment we saw that they were burning the farmhouses as they came. Towards noon word spread that, not only were they destroying all before them, but were actually capturing and sending away the women and children.

At first we could hardly credit this, but when one wild-eyed woman after another galloped by, it was borne in on us that a more terrible chapter of the war was opening.

The intention was to undermine the morale of the fighting men, but the effect was exactly the opposite, from what I saw. Instead of weakening, they became only the more resolved to hold out, and this policy instead of shortening the war, prolonged it by a year or more.

(The *Times History of the War* says: 'The policy of burning down farmhouses and destroying crops as a measure of intimidation had nothing to recommend it and no other measure aroused such deep and lasting resentment. The Dutch race is not one that can be easily beguiled by threats, and farm-burning as a policy of intimidation totally failed, as anyone acquainted with the Dutch race and the Dutch history could have foreseen. Applying this system against a white race defending their homes with a bravery and resource which has rightly won the admiration of the world was the least happy of Lord Roberts' inspirations and must plainly be set down as a serious error of judgment ...)

Towards dark the chase slowed down. It rained steadily all night, and we spent a miserable time lying in mud and water on the bare hillsides. At daybreak we were all on the move again, but, owing to the rain and the heavy going, the English could only crawl in our wake, and we had little difficulty in keeping our distance. By now, the news had spread that the English were clearing the country, with the result that the entire civil population from the farms was moving

The plain was alive with wagons, carts, and vehicles of all descriptions, laden with women and children, while great numbers of horses, cattle, and sheep were being hurried onward by native herd boys, homes and ricks going up in flames behind them.

General Botha directed all non-combatants, wagons, and live-stock to make for Swaziland, and he ordered us to give way before the troops, and let them expend their blow in thin air.

Owing to these measures the drive went to pieces during the next few days. The British could not maintain a continuous front over the increased distances, and the troops were left groping about after the elusive Boer forces, which easily evaded the lumbering columns plodding through the mud far in the rear.

The drive caused an immense amount of material damage to farmhouses and crops, and much live-stock was taken, but so far as its effect on the burghers went it was a complete failure, for it left them more determined than ever to continue fighting.

By January 1901, Emily Hobhouse was reporting back to London: 'I call this camp system a wholesale cruelty. It can never be wiped out of the memories of the people. It presses hardest on the children. They droop in the terrible heat, and with the insufficient, unsuitable food ... Thousands, physically unfit, are placed in conditions of life which they have not strength to endure.' But still no one was listening. Johanna Brandt (71) worked for the Boers' secret service and had been a volunteer nurse in one of the camps. She published her memoir in 1913.

A systematic devastation of the two Boer Republics then took place. Only the towns were spared; for the rest, the farms and homesteads and even small villages, throughout the length and breadth of the country, were laid waste. Trees were cut down, crops destroyed, homes, pillaged of valuables, burnt with everything they contained, and the women and children removed to camps in the districts to which they belonged [...]

Sickness broke out in the camps – scarlet fever, measles, whooping-cough, enteric, pneumonia, and a thousand ills brought by exposure, overcrowding, underfeeding, and untold hardships. Expectant mothers, tender babes, the aged and infirm, torn from their homes and herded together under conditions impossible to describe, exposed to the bitter inclemency of the South African winters and the scorching, germ-breeding heat of the summer, succumbed in their thousands, while daily, fresh people, ruddy, healthy, straight from their wholesome life on the farms, were brought into the infected camps and left to face sickness and the imminent risk of death.

By August 1901, the concentration camps held 94 000 whites and 25 000 blacks; by October, 110 000 whites and 40 000 blacks. In the white camps, the death rate was running at 4 000 a month and British public opinion was at last becoming outraged. By November, even Milner – now Lord Milner – was getting cold feet. 'If present death rate continues,' he telegraphed Chamberlain, 'some at least of camps may have to be abandoned.' A month later he told Chamberlain that the policy had been 'a mistake' – 'a fiasco', he called it in a confidential letter to a friend – and they would have to put the best face on it they could.

The black spot – the one very black spot – in the picture is the frightful mortality in the Concentration Camps. I entirely agree with you in thinking, that while a hundred explanations may be offered and a hundred excuses made, they do not really amount to an adequate defence. I should much prefer to say at once, as far as the Civil authorities are concerned, that we were suddenly confronted with a problem not of our making, with which it was beyond our power properly to grapple. And no doubt its vastness was not realized soon enough. It was not till six weeks or two months ago that it dawned on me personally (I cannot speak for others), that the enormous mortality was not merely incidental to the first formation of the camps and the sudden inrush of thousands of people already sick and starving, but was going to continue. The fact that it continues is no doubt a condemnation of the Camp system. The whole thing, I think now, has been a mistake. At the same time, a sudden reversal of policy would only make matters worse. At the present moment certainly, everything we know of is being done, both to improve the camps and to reduce the numbers in them. I believe we shall mitigate the evil, but we shall never get rid of it. While I say all this, I do not admit that the mortality would have been less if the people had been left in the veldt. I do not think it would. But our great error has been in taking a course which made us responsible, or partly responsible, for mischiefs which ought to have rested on the shoulders of the enemy. But it is easy to be wise after the event. The state of affairs which led to the formation of the camps was wholly novel and of unusual difficulty, and I believe no General in the world would not have felt compelled to deal with it in some drastic manner.

In the end, the death toll in the camps was put at 42 000: 28 000 whites, of whom 20 000 were children, and 14 000 blacks, most of them children, too. As Emily Hobhouse later pointed out, more adult Boers died in the camps than on the battlefield, and three times as many children. The biggest killers were measles, typhoid, jaundice, malaria and pneumonia, all of them exacerbated by the conditions in which the prisoners were held. Kitchener, a notably pitiless soldier, was never much interested, which is one reason why the camps, besides being poorly provisioned and equipped, were so badly run and criminally insanitary. Instead, he devoted his energies to trying to win the guerrilla war. In a mostly vain attempt to trap the Boer commandos, he built 8 000 blockhouses along the railway lines at intervals of one-and-a-half miles. Between them, he strung 3 700 miles of barbed wire guarded by 50 000 troops – by now he had 230 000 at his disposal – and 16 000 African scouts. In all, 30 000 farm buildings and more than half the Boers' livestock were destroyed. But the 'bitter-enders' slipped through the wire at night and crossed the borders into Natal and the Cape Colony. Between June and October 1901, for example, General Smuts led a marauding commando of about 300 men – including Deneys Reitz – more than 1 000 miles down the length of South Africa, from the north-west Transvaal to within sight of Table Mountain. It was all futile, of course. Rudyard Kipling (72), by now disenchanted, probably put it best.

Eventually the 'war' petered out on political lines. Brother Boer – and all ranks called him that – would do everything except die. Our men did not see why they should perish chasing stray commandoes, or festering in block-houses, and there followed a sort of demoralising 'handy-pandy' of alternate surrenders complicated by exchange of Army tobacco for Boer brandy which was bad for both sides.

At long last, we were left apologising to a deeply indignant people, whom we had been nursing and doctoring for a year or two; and who now expected, and received, all manner of free gifts and appliances for the farming they had never practised. We put them in a position to uphold and expand their primitive lust for racial domination, and thanked God we were 'rid of a knave'.

The war ended with the signing of the Peace of Vereeniging on 31 May 1902, when 20 000 Boers laid down their arms. Britain had achieved sovereignty over the whole of South Africa and, as everyone knew, would surrender it as soon as it conveniently could. Twenty-two thousand British soldiers had died – 13 000 of disease, mostly typhoid – and 7 000 Boers. The Boers, at least, knew what they were fighting for; Thomas Hardy (73), the Wessex poet, wondered whether the British troops did. His poem was published just six weeks after the war began.

Drummer Hodge

I
They throw in Drummer Hodge, to rest
Uncoffined – just as found:
His landmark is a kopje-crest
That breaks the veldt around;
And foreign constellations west
Each night above his mound.

II
Young Hodge the Drummer never knew –
Fresh from his Wessex home –
The meaning of the broad Karoo,
The Bush, the dusty loam,
And why uprose to nightly view
Strange stars amid the gloom.

III

Yet portion of that unknown plain
Will Hodge forever be;
His homely Northern breast and brain
Grow to some Southern tree,
And strange-eyed constellation reign
His stars eternally.

NOTES
1 The chartered company Rhodes had used as a cover for his conquest of Rhodesia and through which he now ran it.
2 The year Britain finally took the Cape from the Dutch.
3 In 1713, the treaty, which ended the War of the Spanish Succession, gave Britain a 30-year monopoly on supplying slaves to Spain's colonies.
4 The year the Boers, at the battle of Majuba Hill, reclaimed the South African Republic, which Britain had annexed in 1877 and renamed the Transvaal.
5 Granting independence to the South African Republic and the Orange Free State respectively.
6 He was 74.
7 1902, by when Churchill was a Conservative MP.
8 Churchill climbed Spioenkop that night after the fighting had stopped.
9 President Kruger.
10 In the eastern Transvaal.

CHAPTER 11

SEGREGATION AND MISCEGENATION

Seven years after losing the war, the Boers were handed everything they had fought for and more than they could have ever dreamed possible. Milner set the stage by inserting a clause into the Peace of Vereeniging that said: 'The question of granting the franchise to natives will not be decided until after the introduction of self-government.' That, as everyone knew, meant there would be no native franchise. Self-government for the Transvaal followed in December 1906 and for the Orange River Colony six months later. Finally, in 1909, Britain washed its hands of the whole affair by granting Dominion status to a unified South Africa under a segregationist constitution, an all-white Parliament and a franchise from which all non-whites, except for a small number of 'civilised' Africans and Coloureds in the Cape, were excluded. Underlining the cynicism was the new country's official motto: 'Unity is Strength'. Of its population of six million, just 21 per cent were white, just over half of whom were Afrikaners. They dominated the Union government from the start. Indeed, all three prime ministers between 1910 and 1948 had been Boer generals: Louis Botha, Jan Smuts and Barry Hertzog.

Even before the war ended, Milner, in a despatch to Chamberlain, the British Colonial Secretary, sketched out his plans for three of what were to become the most prominent features of apartheid: an inferior education for blacks, a pass system to control their movements and a prohibition on liquor because it reduced their productivity. His reasoning was to be rehearsed by apartheid's apologists for the next 90 years.

I think that much more should be done for the education of the natives than has ever yet been attempted in the Transvaal. I do not mean that they should be educated like Europeans, for their requirements and capacities are very different, but that they should be trained to develop their natural aptitudes for their own good and that of the community. Undoubtedly the greatest benefit that could be bestowed upon them or South Africa generally would be to teach them habits of regular and skilled labour [...]

The root idea of the old Pass Law was not a wrong one. If aboriginal natives are to come and go in large numbers in search of labour, and to reside for considerable periods in the midst of a white community, there must be some passport system, else the place will be a pandemonium. Alike for the protection of the natives and for the protection of the whites, it is absolutely essential to have some reasonable arrangements by which the incoming native can be identified, and his movements traced [...]

But undoubtedly the greatest benefit which it is in the power of the Government to confer, alike upon mine owner and native, is the suppression of the illicit drink traffic. But this more than anything else depends, not on the terms of the law, but on its administration. In the Proclamation dealing with this matter, which forms one of the series recently sent to you, we have taken over the principle of total prohibition embodied in the legislation of the late Government. Indeed, the new law on this point differs from the old in no important particular, except that the penalties for supplying natives with drink are rendered more severe, and especially that no option of a fine is allowed [...]

Generally speaking, I claim for the Native Code which we are trying to introduce, and of which these Proclamations are the first instalment, that it is conceived in the best interests of the natives, and that any restrictions imposed on their personal liberty do not go beyond what is necessary, not only for the protection of the white population, but for the good of the natives themselves. Moreover, the control which it is proposed to exercise over the natives, is so devised as to improve and not degrade them [...]

There is now a better appreciation at home of the difficulties confronting the colonists, and of the impracticability of governing natives, who, at best, are children, needing and appreciating a just paternal government, on the same principles as apply to the government of full-grown men. On the other hand, there is an increasing recognition on the part of the colonists of the heavy responsibility involved in the government of a vast native population, and of the duty and necessity of raising them in the scale of civilization. But this hopeful process of approximation would be utterly upset if the Imperial

Government were to approach this delicate question in the prejudiced and ill-informed spirit which seems to animate many well-meaning people at home, but which would be justly resented by the whole of white South Africa, including those men who are most active in the defence of native rights.

Addressing a municipal government conference in May 1903, Milner expounded on Cecil Rhodes's belief in the white man's duty to rule over 'uncivilised' blacks. White supremacy, he assured his audience, would probably last to eternity for the white man's level of civilisation was one that the great majority of blacks were never likely to attain.

There is a well-defined dislike of what are known as the opinions of Exeter Hall.[1] Speaking for myself, there is no man who more condemns what are popularly known as Exeter Hall opinions, by which I mean the sentimental and ignorant view of native questions, than I do. More than that, there is no man more prepared if need were – I do not say there is any cause, for I think Exeter Hall is a bugbear in these days – to fight that view of the native question than I. But I am not sure that, while we denounce the claptrap of Exeter Hall, we do not keep and cherish in this country an opposite sort of claptrap, which really advances the question as little as the extreme views of Exeter Hall. What is the good, for instance, of perpetually going on shouting that this is a white man's country? Does it mean that it is a country only inhabited by white men? That, of course, is an obvious absurdity, as the blacks outnumber us as five to one. Does it mean a country which ought only to be inhabited by white men? Well, as an ideal that would possibly be all very well, but as a practical statement it surely is perfectly useless. If it means anything, it means that we ought to try and expel the black population, thereby instantly ruining all the industries of the country. What it does mean, I suppose, if any sane meaning can be applied to it, is that the white man should rule. Well, if that is its meaning, there is nobody more absolutely agreed with it than I; but then let us say that plainly, and do not let us only say it, but let us justify it. There is only one ground on which we can justify it, and that is the ground of superior civilization.

The white man must rule, because he is elevated by many, many steps above the black man; steps which it will take the latter centuries to climb, and which it is quite possible that the vast bulk of the black population may never be able to climb at all. But then, if we justify, what I believe we all hold to, the necessity of the rule of the white man by his superior civilization, what does that involve? Does it involve an attempt to keep a black man always at the very low level of civilization at which he is to-day? I believe you will all reject such an idea. One of the strongest arguments why the white man must rule is because that is the only possible means of gradually raising the black man, not to our level of civilization – which it is doubtful whether he would ever attain – but up to a much higher level than that which he at present occupies.

But if you are going to defend white supremacy on this ground, and if at the same time you recognize, as I believe you do, the duty and wisdom of doing everything you can to raise the black man as far as he can be raised, what is the consequence? Is it not a consequence of taking your ground on the firm and inexpugnable ground of civilization as against the rotten and indefensible ground of colour, that if a black man, one in a thousand – perhaps it would be more correct to say one in a hundred thousand – raises himself to a white level of civilization – I will not speak now of the very highest level attained by white, because a black man getting to that level is at present entirely out of sight in South Africa, but to the average white level – should not his treatment be that which you accord to a white man, because you justify your especial treatment of white men by a civilization to which, *ex hypothesi*, he has attained?

I am not speaking of the question of political rights. Those of the black men, the natives, have been relegated, and I think wisely relegated, to the future for decision. It stands firm and is unquestionable, that that must be decided by a legislature elected by the white population of this country alone. But I am speaking of other privileges accorded to civilized men. Can you, if you base the supremacy of the white man upon his civilization, deny to other men who have attained his level in that respect, the rights which are granted to him? Now there are two practical ways in which that matter arises. One has already been decided. In the native legislation of this Colony, containing as it does very special regulation of natives, which their low state of civilization requires, we have made certain exceptions. They apply to very few people, but the natives who attain a high degree of education and culture are exempted from the restrictions placed on natives generally. The practical importance of the matter is very small, because this class is extremely limited, and will be so for a long time, but the principle is very important. Well, then the principle crops up again in connection with municipal rights.

Is it to be laid down that the native, who has even a high degree of education and civilization, and who is, I think, to be admired on that account, is, nevertheless, to be ignored in the management of those municipal questions and matters of health and sanitation, which, if he is a civilized man, must affect him as much as they affect the white? Is he to have no voice whatever in such matters? For all our sakes, it is of profound importance that the general standard of native civilization should be immensely raised. Even as a purely material question, it is one of the greatest importance, for if there is one thing that has come out in this discussion of this labour question, it is that the mere mechanical value of the native who has risen to some state of civilization is enormously greater than that of the man still on bed-rock. But if you are going to raise the mass of natives, and mind you, it will take years and years to raise them even so far as to the level of your waist, it stands to reason that a certain number of them will rise to the level of your shoulder. Are you going to put back the whole progress of civilization by banging them on the head the moment that they do so?

I feel even more strongly perhaps about the coloured class.[2] The vast majority of them are in a deplorably low state of civilization. There is a small section, a very small section, unfortunately, who have overcome the enormous disadvantages of their origin, and who have attained to a considerable degree of civilization. It is a further consideration, which I do not wish to lay too much stress upon, that throughout South Africa men of that class, for whom personally I feel the deepest sympathy, have stood most loyally in the great struggle for enfranchisement by the side of those who have been in favour of that wider extension of popular liberties, which is what the triumph of the British idea in this country means. They have been amongst its most ardent supporters; I should be sorry if one of the first fruits of our victory was to place an indelible stigma upon them. Speaking again my personal opinions, opinions, perhaps not shared by the majority of those here, perhaps not shared by any of them, I shall think it an unhappy day when any large British community in South Africa completely and finally repudiates the doctrine of one of the greatest of South African statesmen – 'equal rights for every civilized man.'

Rhodes was also much in the minds of Generals Botha and Smuts, the Prime Minister and Deputy Prime Minister respectively of the Union's first government. Taking up where Rhodes's Glen Grey Act of 1894 had left off, their 1913 Natives Land Act decreed that 93 per cent of the land of South Africa belonged to the whites and that Africans could live on it only as wage-earning labourers. At a stroke, tens of thousands of people, including those living as tenants and share-croppers on white farms, were deprived of their homes and their livelihoods. Sol Plaatje (74), one of South Africa's first black journalists, travelled round the country to record the Act's consequences. The natives, he concluded, had been deprived of their earthly home.

Awaking on Friday morning, June 20, 1913, the South African native found himself, not actually a slave, but a pariah in the land of his birth.

The 4,500,000 black South Africans are domiciled as follows: one and three-quarter million in locations and reserves, over half a million within municipalities or in urban areas, and nearly a million as squatters on farms owned by Europeans. The remainder are employed either on the public roads or railway lines, or as servants by European farmers, qualifying, that is, by hard work and saving to start farming on their own account.

A squatter in South Africa is a native who owns some livestock and, having no land of his own, hires a farm or grazing and ploughing rights from a landowner, to raise grain for his own use and feed his stock. Hence, these squatters are hit very hard by an Act which passed both Houses of Parliament during the session of 1913 [...]

But the great revolutionary change thus wrought by a single stroke of the pen, in the condition of the native, was not realized until about the end of June. As a rule many farm tenancies expire at the end of the half-year, so that in June 1913, not knowing that it was impracticable to make fresh contracts, some natives unwittingly went to search for new places of abode, which some farmers, ignorant of the law, quite as unwittingly accorded them. It was only when they went to register the new tenancies that the law officers of the Crown laid bare the cruel fact that to provide a landless native with accommodation was forbidden under a penalty of £100, or six months' imprisonment. Then only was the situation realized [...]

We are told to forgive our enemies and not to let the sun go down upon our wrath, so we breathe the prayer that peace may be to the white races, and that they, including our present persecutors of the Union Parliament, may never live to find themselves deprived of all occupation and property rights in their native country as is now the case with the Native. History does not tell us of any other continent where the Bantu lived besides Africa, and if this systematic ill-treatment of the Natives by the colonists is to be the guiding principle of Europe's scramble for Africa, slavery is our only alternative; for now it is only as serfs that the Natives are legally entitled to live here. Is it to be thought that God is using the South African Parliament to hound us out of our ancestral homes in order to quicken our pace heavenward? But go from where to heaven? In the beginning, we are told, God created heaven and earth, and peopled the earth, for people do not shoot up to heaven from nowhere. They must have had an earthly home. Enoch, Melchizedek, Elijah, and other saints, came to heaven from earth. God did not say to the Israelites in their bondage: 'Cheer up, boys; bear it all in good part for I have bright mansions on high awaiting you all.' But he said: 'I have surely seen the affliction of my people which are in Egypt, and have heard their cry by reason of their taskmasters; for I know their sorrows, and I am come down to bring them out of the hands of the Egyptians, and to bring them up out of that land unto a good land and a large, unto a land flowing with milk and honey.' And He used Moses to carry out the promise He made to their ancestor Abraham in Canaan, that 'unto thy seed will I give this land.' It is to be hoped that in the Boer churches, entrance to which is barred against coloured people during divine service, they also read the Pentateuch.

It was to be nearly 80 years before the Natives Land Act was repealed. In the interim, the proportion of the land designated for African ownership was raised to 14 per cent, when Africans were 68 per cent of the population. Thus the 'reserves' – or 'homelands', as they were later called – became the reservoirs of cheap, unskilled labour that Rhodes's Glen Grey Act had envisaged. In 1920, Smuts, who had become Prime Minister on Botha's death a year earlier, extended the Glen Grey Act's grant of limited self-government – in reality, a form of indirect rule through tribal chiefs – to all African reserves. He then completed his grand plan with the 1923 Natives (Urban Areas) Act, which barred blacks from living in urban areas unless they were serving the white man's needs. The Act also required municipalities to set up 'native locations', so establishing the characteristic, segregated pattern of all South African cities and towns.

None of this, however, was enough to prevent Smuts's South African Party being defeated in 1924 by the even more right-wing National Party. Its leader was Barry Hertzog, who was to remain Prime Minister until 1939, when, on the outbreak of the Second World War, his Nazi sympathies forced him to quit. Smuts, who had served as his deputy in a post-Depression coalition government since 1933, took his place. While out of power, Smuts had time to reflect on the perennial 'native question'. The result was the two extraordinary Rhodes Memorial lectures (75) he delivered at Oxford in 1929, edited here into a continuous text. His justification of racial segregation – in the interest, among other things, of 'racial purity' – did not go down well with his audience.

What is wanted in Africa today is a wise far-sighted native policy. If we could evolve and pursue a policy which will promote the cause of civilization in Africa without injustice to the African, without injury to what is typical and specific in the African, we shall render a great service to the cause of humanity. For there is much that is good in the African and which ought to be preserved and developed. The negro and the negroid Bantu form a distinct human type which the world would be poorer without.

Here in this vast continent, with its wide geographical variety and its great climatic differences, this unique human type has been fixing itself for thousands of years. It is even possible, so some anthropologists hold, that this was the original mother-type of the human race and that Africa holds the cradle of mankind. But whether this is so or not, at any rate here we have the vast result of time, which we should conserve and develop with the same high respect which we feel towards all great natural facts. This type has some wonderful characteristics. It has largely remained a child type, with a child psychology and outlook. A child-like human cannot be a bad human, for are we not in spiritual matters bidden to be like unto little children? Perhaps as a direct result of this temperament the African is the only happy human I have come across. No other race is so easily satisfied, so good-tempered, so care-free. If this had not been the case, it could scarcely have survived the intolerable evils which have weighed on it like a nightmare through the ages. A race, which could survive the immemorial practice of the witch doctor and the slave trader, and preserve its inherent simplicity and sweetness of disposition, must have some very fine moral qualities. The African easily forgets past troubles, and does not anticipate future troubles. This happy-go-lucky disposition is a great asset, but it has also its drawbacks.

There is no inward incentive to improvement, there is no persistent effort in construction, and there is complete absorption in the present, its joys and sorrows. Wine, women, and song in their African forms remain the great consolations of life. No indigenous religion has been evolved, no literature, no art since the magnificent promise of the cavemen and the South African petroglyphist, no architecture since Zimbabwe (if that is African). Enough for the Africans the simple joys of village life, the dance, the tom-tom, the continual excitement of forms of fighting which cause little bloodshed. They can stand any amount of physical hardship and suffering, but when deprived of these simple enjoyments, they droop, sicken, and die. Travellers tell how for weeks the slaves would move impassively in captive gangs; but when they passed a village and heard the pleasant noises of children, the song and the dance, they would suddenly collapse and die, as if of a broken heart. These children of nature have not the inner toughness and persistence of the European, nor those social and moral incentives to progress which have built up European civilization in a comparatively short period. But they have a temperament which suits mother Africa, and which brings out the simple joys of life and deadens its pain, such as no other race possesses.

It is clear that a race so unique, and so different in its mentality and its cultures from those of Europe, requires a policy very unlike that which would suit Europeans. Nothing could be worse for Africa than the application of a policy, the object or tendency of which would be to destroy the basis of this African type, to de-Africanize the African and turn him either into a beast of the field or into a pseudo-European. And yet in the past we have tried both alternatives in our dealings with the Africans. First we looked upon the African as essentially inferior or sub-human, as having no soul, and as being only fit to be a slave. As a slave he became an article of commerce, and the greatest article of export from this continent for centuries. But the horrors of this trade became such that the modern conscience finally revolted and stamped out African slavery peacefully in the British Empire, but in America with the convulsions of civil war and a million dead.

Then we changed to the opposite extreme. The African now became a man and a brother. Religion and politics combined to shape this new African policy. The principles of the French Revolution which had emancipated Europe were applied to Africa; liberty, equality, and fraternity could turn bad Africans into good Europeans. The political system of the natives was ruthlessly destroyed in order to incorporate them as equals into the white system. The African was good as a potential European; his social and political culture was bad, barbarous, and only deserving to be stamped out root and branch.

In some of the British possessions in Africa the native just emerging from barbarism was accepted as an equal citizen with full political rights along with the whites. But his native institutions were ruthlessly proscribed and destroyed. The principle of equal rights was applied in its crudest form, and while it gave the native a semblance of equality with whites, which was little good to him, it destroyed the basis of his African system which was his highest good. These are the two extreme native policies which have prevailed in the past, and the second has been only less harmful than the first. If Africa has to be redeemed, if Africa has to make her own contribution to the world, if Africa is to take her rightful place among the continents, we shall have to proceed on different lines and evolve a policy which will not force her institutions into an alien European mould, but which will preserve her unity with her own past, conserve what is precious in her past, and build her future progress and civilization on specifically African foundations. That should be the new policy, and such a policy would be in line with the traditions of the British Empire. The British Empire does not stand for assimilation of its peoples into a common type, it does not stand for standardization, but for the fullest freest development of its peoples along their own specific lines. This principle applies not only to its European, but also to its Asiatic and its African constituents.

It is a significant fact that this new orientation of African policy had its origin in South Africa, and that its author was Cecil Rhodes in his celebrated Glen Grey Act. Rhodes's African policy embodied two main ideas: white settlement to supply the steel framework and the stimulus for an enduring civilization, and indigenous native institutions to express the specifically African character of the natives in their future development and civilization [...] As a practical policy of native government it has worked most successfully. Gradually the system of native councils and native self-government through their own tribal chiefs and elected councils has been extended from one native area to another in the Cape Province, until today about two-thirds of the Cape natives, or roughly over a million, fall under this system and manage their own local affairs according to their own ideas under the supervision of the European magistrates [...]

A sense of pride in their institutions and their own administration is rapidly developing, and, along with valuable experience in administration and public affairs, they are also acquiring a due sense of responsibility; where mistakes are made they feel satisfied that they have only themselves to blame. After the new system had worked successfully and with ever increasing efficiency for twenty-five years, I thought the time ripe in 1920 to extend it to the whole of the Union, and in that year an Act was passed which gave increased powers to the councils and authorized the Government to introduce them over the whole Union, wherever the advance of the natives might justify the step. A Native Affairs Commission was at the same time appointed to advise the natives and the Government in regard to the establishment of new Councils, as well as in reference to all legislation affecting the natives. And it is confidently expected that before many years have passed the greater portion of the native population of South Africa will be in charge of their own local affairs, under general white supervision; and in this way they will get an outlet for their political and administrative energies and ambitions which will give them the necessary training for eventual participation in a wider sphere of public life [...]

Another important consequence will follow from this system of native institutions. Wherever Europeans and natives live in the same country, it will mean separate parallel institutions for the two. The old practice mixed up black with white in the same institutions; and nothing else was possible, after the native institutions and traditions had been carelessly or deliberately destroyed. But in the new plan there will be what is called in South Africa 'segregation' – separate institutions for the two elements of the population, living in their own separate areas. Separate institutions involve territorial segregation of the white and black. If they live mixed up together it is not practicable to sort them out under separate institutions of their own. Institutional segregation carries with it territorial segregation. The new policy therefore gives the native his own traditional institutions on land which is set aside for his exclusive occupation. For agricultural and pastoral natives, living their tribal life, large areas or reserves are set aside, adequate for their present and future needs.

In not setting aside sufficient such areas in South Africa in the past we committed a grievous mistake, which is at the root of most of our difficulties in native policy. For urbanized natives, on the other hand, who live, not under tribal conditions but as domestic servants or industrial workers in white areas, there are set aside native villages or locations, adjoining to the European towns. In both rural reserves and town locations the natives take a part in or run their own local self-government. Such is the practice now in vogue in South Africa and it is likely to develop still further, and to spread all over Africa where white and black live and work together in the same countries. For residential and local government purposes a clean cleavage is becoming ever more marked, the white portion of the population living under more advanced European institutions, while the natives next door maintain their simpler indigenous system. This separation is imperative, not only in the interests of a native culture, and to prevent native traditions and institutions from being swamped by the more powerful organization of the whites, but also for other important purposes, such as public health, racial purity, and public good order. The mixing up of two such alien elements as white and black leads to unhappy social results: racial miscegenation, moral deterioration of both, racial antipathy and clashes, and to many other forms of social evil.

In these great matters of race, colour, and culture, residential separation and parallel institutions alone can do justice to the ideals of both sections of the population. The system is accepted and welcomed by the vast majority of natives; but it is resented by a small educated minority who claim 'equal rights' with the whites. It is, however, evident that the proper place of the educated minority of the natives is with the rest of their people, of whom they are the natural leaders, and from whom they should not in any way be dissociated.

Far more difficult questions arise on the industrial plane. It is not practicable to separate black and white in industry, and their working together in the same industry and in the same works leads to a certain amount of competition and friction and antagonism, for which no solution has yet been found. Unhappy attempts have been made in South Africa to introduce a colour bar, and an Act of that nature is actually on the Statute book, but happily no attempt has yet been made to apply it in practice. It empowers the Government to set aside separate spheres of work for the native and the non-native, the object being to confine the native to the more or less unskilled occupations or grades of work. The inherent economic difficulties of such a distribution of industrial functions, the universal objection of the native workers, and the sense of fair-play among the whites will make its practical application virtually impossible. No statutory barrier of that kind should be placed on the native who wishes to raise himself in the scale of civilization, nor could it be maintained for long against the weight of modern public opinion. As a worker the white man should be able to hold his own in competition with the native. Industrial as distinguished from territorial segregation would be both impracticable and an offence against the modern conscience.

There remains the big question how far the parallelism of native and white institutions is to go? Is it to be confined to local government, or is it to go all the way, up to the level of full political or parliamentary government? Should black and white co-operate in the same parliamentary institutions of the country? If so, should they have separate representatives in the same parliamentary institutions? Few acquainted with the facts and the difficulties can profess to see clear daylight in the tangle of this problem. In the older practice, embodied in the constitution of the former Cape Colony and in many other colonial institutions, political equality between the different races on the basis of a complete mixture of political rights was recognized. Justice is colour-blind and recognizes no political differences on grounds of colour or race. Hence the formula of equal 'rights for all civilized men' with which the name of Rhodes is identified, and which represents the traditional British policy.

That policy, however, arose at a time when the doctrine of native parallelism had not yet emerged, when native institutions were proscribed as barbarous, and the only place for the civilized native was therefore in the white man's system and the white man's institutions. The question is whether the new principle makes, or should make, any difference to the old tradition of mixed and equal political rights in the same parliamentary institutions [...]

If we had to do only with the tribal native voters the question would not be so difficult, and the application of the general segregation principle to the particular case of political rights might be justified. Unfortunately very large numbers of detribalized natives are spread all over the Cape, and are no longer resident or registered in the native areas. These urbanized natives living among the whites constitute the real crux, and it is a difficulty which goes far beyond the political issue. They raise a problem for the whole principle of segregation, as they claim to be civilized and Europeanized, and do not wish to be thrust back into the seclusion of their former tribal associations, or to forgo their new place in the sun among the whites. With the application of strict education and civilization tests it would probably be the better course to allow them to exercise their political rights along with the whites. Were it not for this case of the urbanized or detribalized natives, the colour problem, not only in South Africa but elsewhere in Africa, would be shorn of most of its difficulties. And the situation in South Africa is therefore a lesson to all the younger British communities farther north to prevent as much as possible the detachment of the native from his tribal connexion, and to enforce from the very start the system of segregation with its conservation of separate native institutions.

In conclusion I wish to refer to an apparent discrepancy between this lecture and my previous one. In that lecture I stressed the importance of white settlement in Africa as a potent means of furthering native progress and civilization. I pointed out that enduring contact with the white man's civilization is the surest way to civilize the native. In this lecture I have emphasized the importance of preserving native institutions, of keeping intact as far as possible the native system of organization and social discipline. It may be thought that there is a clash between these two aims, and that civilization by white contact must inevitably lead to the undermining and ultimately to the destruction of the native culture and social system. This, however, is not so.

So long as there is territorial segregation, so long as the native family home is not with the white man but in his own area, so long the native organization will not be materially affected. While the native may come voluntarily out of his own area for a limited period every year to work with a white employer, he will leave his wife and children behind in their native home. The family life in the native home will continue on the traditional lines; the routine of the family and of the tribe will not be altered in any material respect. The male adults, father and sons, will no doubt imbibe new ideas in their white employment, but their social system will not suffer on that account.

It is only when segregation breaks down, when the whole family migrates from the tribal home and out of the tribal jurisdiction to the white man's farm or the white man's town, that the tribal bond is snapped, and the traditional system falls into decay. And it is this migration of the native family, of the females and children, to the farms and the towns which should be prevented. As soon as this migration is permitted the process commences which ends in the urbanized detribalized native and the disappearance of the native organization. It is not white employment of the native males that works the mischief, but the abandonment of the native tribal home by the women and children. This the law should vigorously prevent, and the system whether it is administered through passes or in any other way should only allow the residence of males for limited periods, and for purposes of employment among the whites. If this is done there will be no serious danger that the indigenous native system will be unduly affected.

At the same time I wish to point out that the prevention of this migration will be no easy task, even where ample tribal lands are guaranteed to the natives. The whites like to have the families of their native servants with them. It means more continuous and less broken periods of labour, and it means more satisfied labourers. It means, moreover, the use of the women and children for such work as they are fit for.

These are considerable advantages, and the white employers will not be very keen to carry out a law against them. On the other hand, the native also very often likes to get away from the jurisdiction of the chief and the discipline of the tribe, and prefers to have his women and his children around him in his daily life. For the native the pressure to break away from the old bonds and live with his white master is thus very great [...]

There is, however, no reason why segregation, although it has broken down in South Africa in the past, should not be a workable and enforceable system in the future. The power of Government and the reach of the law are today very different from what they were under the primitive nomadic conditions of the old Cape frontier. The system of native administration is today so ramified and pervasive, the policeman is so ubiquitous, that segregation can be tried under far more favourable conditions than existed in South Africa in the past. The young countries to the north can start with a clean slate. They can learn from the mistakes which we made in South Africa, and can *ab initio* reserve ample lands for the natives to live and work on. They can check the abuses of the chiefs, and can effectively supervise the working of the native system, both in its administrative and judicial aspects. Witchcraft can be fought, official injustice and corruption can be largely prevented, schools can be established, and the simplest amenities of civilized life can be introduced, in the native villages and tribal areas.

The position is really very different from what it was generations ago, and the inducements for native families to remain on their tribal lands are such, or can be made such, that a segregation law will become comparatively easy to carry out. The women and children will continue to carry on their native life at home, will continue to work in the homes and in the fields as they have done from the immemorial past. The men, instead of lying in the sun, or brawling over their beer, or indulging in the dangerous sport of tribal warfare, will go out to work, and supplement the family income and render tolerable a weight which under the new conditions is becoming more and more difficult for the women and children. They should never be away long, and the physical and moral life of the family and the tribe need not suffer because of the short periods of absence. Theorists may pick holes in such a system, but there is no practical reason why it should not work in practice. There is no break in the communal village life, but among the men the thin end of the industrial wedge is quietly introduced, and they rightly become the bread-winners which they have seldom or never been. Such a system has great redeeming features, and compares more than favourably with the old ways, which meant absolute stagnation for the men, and virtual slavery for the women. It represents a compromise between the native routine of the past and the white man's industrial system, which may work tolerably well in the future.

Without breaking down what is good in the native system, it will graft on to it a wholesome economic development, which will yet not disturb too deeply the traditional ways of mother Africa. The white man's civilization and the steadily progressing native culture will live side by side and react on each other, and the problems of their contact will provide a fruitful theme for the statesmen of the future.

To appreciate the depth of Smuts's hypocrisy, one has to recall that in 1919 he had helped found the League of Nations 'as a living expression of the moral and spiritual unity of the human race'. Outside South Africa, he was widely revered for his 'sublime and lofty idealism', repeatedly extolling the virtues of 'liberty, freedom from oppression and justice for all'. As his son, JC Smuts, put it in a hagiography of his father, 'He reintroduced the code of higher spiritual and ethical values into the council chambers of the world.' In relation to South Africa, however, Smuts was happy to characterise the abolitionists' creed of 'a man and a brother' as the 'opposite extreme' of slavery and willing to introduce a system of migratory labour that would force the majority of African families to spend most of their lives apart. Similarly, his condemnation of the colour bar in industry as 'an offence against conscience' is hard to square with the fact that in 1911 he was Deputy Prime Minister of the government that first imposed it. By the same token, in 1936 he was Deputy Prime Minister of the government that removed 'civilised' Africans in the Cape from the common voters' roll – where they had been since 1853 – so depriving them of their 'place in the sun'. For one of his admissions, though, we should be grateful: that enforcing segregation depended on 'ubiquitous policemen'. The subsequent history of apartheid fully demonstrated it.

All this was driven by the inability of a substantial proportion of the Afrikaner people to make their way in the world unprotected. At the end of the 19th century, the great majority of Afrikaners were ill-educated, unskilled subsistence farmers dependent for their livelihoods on land worked for them by blacks. In the move to cities and towns that followed the Boer War – 'the new Great Trek' – they found themselves squeezed between European immigrants better qualified for the skilled and semi-skilled jobs and blacks who would do the unskilled work at a fraction of the cost. All the Afrikaners had to offer were their white skins and the entitlement that gave them to vote – as Botha, Smuts and, particularly, Hertzog well understood.

Smuts's international bluff was finally called in 1946. Just a year after he had drafted the preamble to the United Nations Charter expressing the organisation's 'faith in fundamental human rights and the dignity and worth of the human person', the General Assembly voted to condemn South Africa, of which he was still Prime Minister, for denying those rights and that dignity to its Indian population. For the next 45 years, the United Nations was to continue condemning South Africa for the apartheid policies Smuts had done so much to put in place; in 1966, it branded apartheid as a crime against humanity.

One curiosity remains: Smuts's reference to 'racial miscegenation' and the 'moral deterioration' that accompanies it. Again, there was to be one message for his international audience and quite another back home – where, it is worth remembering, nearly 10 per cent of the population now owed its origins to 250 years of inter-racial sex. 'It has now become an accepted axiom in our dealing with the natives,' Smuts assured white South Africans, 'that it is dishonourable to mix white and black blood.' But in a 1934 lecture on his philosophy of 'holism' he told the Royal Institute of International Affairs in London: 'More and more we are recognising that, in spite of racial and political barriers, humanity is really a whole [...] The driving force in this human world of ours should be, not morbid fears or other sickly obsessions, but this inner urge towards wholesome integration and co-operation.'

Such fears and obsessions were, of course, widely shared at the time. The saintly Olive Schreiner, for example, regarded 'half-castes' as 'our own open, self-inflicted wound – the flotsam and jetsam thrown up on the shores of life as the result of contact between the lowest waves of conflicting races, loved by none, honoured by none'. In her posthumously published *Thoughts on South Africa*, the tone was even more doom laden.

Future ages may attain to a knowledge of the exact laws of inheritance, and may then know certainly what the result of such commingling of widely distinct human varieties will be; but for us, today, it is a racial leap in the dark which no man except under the most exceptional conditions has the right to make. What the Black man is we know, what the White man is we know: what the ultimate result of this commingling will be no man today knows.

Of all the anti-social actions which can take place in a country situated as South Africa is to-day, for cowardice and recklessness perhaps none equals the action of the man who in obedience to his own selfish passions originates such a cross of races: for cowardice, because the pain and evil resulting from his action can never under any circumstances recoil on himself, but must be borne by others; for recklessness, because the results of his action must go on for generations after he has passed away, acting in ever-widening circles, in ways which he cannot predict, and producing results which cannot be modified [...]

Each society, as each age, has its own peculiar decalogue, applicable to its own peculiar conditions. For South Africa there are certain commandments little heard of in Europe, because the conditions of life raise no occasion for them, but which loom large in the list of social duties in this land. The first of these would appear to be – *Keep your breeds pure!*

No one, however, was more fearful of miscegenation than the white South African writer, Sarah Gertrude Millin (76). Her 1924 novel, *God's Step-Children*, must be one of the nastiest ever written on the subject. In her preface to an edition published in 1951 – the topic held an enduring fascination for white South Africans – Millin recalled the genesis of her obsession with 'the tragedy of mixed blood'.

But I began to understand the feelings of coloured people only after some years at school in Kimberley.

I was twelve when there came to our school a girl, not dark enough to be forbidden the school, but too dark for the other girls to treat as an equal – even I who, on the River, was friends with people of all colours, offered her no friendliness, dared not do what was not done.

Then, one day, in a shopping street, I saw the girl lagging along the pavement. A dark woman further on beckoned to her; and the girl looked this way and that to see if anyone was noticing; she walked towards the woman as if she were not walking towards her; she stood near her as if she was not standing near anyone she knew; she listened to her as if it was a stranger addressing her.

I saw that the coloured woman was the girl's mother and that the girl was ashamed of her. I began to think very much then of the tragedy of mixed blood, and the people I blamed altogether were the white fathers – the creators of this endless tragedy. I hated them.

My first short story had to do with mixed blood (I was seventeen when it was published in a Johannesburg paper); also, some years later, my first novel, my third novel, *God's Step-Children*, and other novels.

When people in these days speak of South Africa's racial problems, they mean the great black races, those races who are Africans together with all the other hundred and fifty millions of Africans in Africa. But history is on their side. Nothing remains in Africa of the European and Asiatic civilizations that once were here; and the age is coming of the dark peoples. I sometimes pity the white peoples.

Those, however, who must always suffer, are the mixed breeds of South Africa: the offspring of the careless and casual; unwanted in their birth; unwanted in their lives; unwanted, scorned by black and white alike. The blacks had once a greatness of their own, and will have it again. In the mixed breeds lies not so much their blood as the blood of slaves and feeble, vanished races; of white fathers blending their blood with outcasts, and disowning their offspring.

Yet, again, white men go to these offspring, and, in time, there emerge coloured people almost white: so nearly white that they have the anguish of not being altogether white; so nearly white that they may 'try for white' and slip in among the white – whereupon they cast off their folk who cannot pass for white.

Now there are laws in South Africa which not only prohibit concubinage or marriage between white and not-white, but tear apart white and not-white who have long lived together …

God's Step-Children is the story of four generations of the descendants of the Rev Andrew Flood, a deeply unappealing and ineffectual English missionary. Inspired by a belief in 'the essential equality of all human beings' – contemptuously dismissed by Millin as Britain's 'creed of the moment' – he arrives in Cape Town in 1821 to 'spread the Word among the Hottentots'. They are described as 'little yellow, monkey-like people', generally 'dazed and stupid' from dagga smoking and with a habit of 'squatting down like baboons'. At a remote mission station beyond the Orange River, Flood marries a Hottentot girl – taken as proof that he is 'mentally sick' – and proceeds to 'sow the seeds of disaster' by fathering a 'half-caste' daughter, Deborah. At 17, Deborah is made pregnant by a wandering Boer and gives birth to Kleinhans, who, being one-quarter Hottentot, has 'yellowish skin, a broad nose and high cheek-bones'. Kleinhans, though, 'yearns to be white'; he grows up hating his mother's 'fuzzy hair and thick lips' and 'the blood of savages and sin' that runs in his veins. But all his attempts to pass himself off as white are rebuffed. After being assaulted by some passing Boers, he is rescued by Adam Lindsell, an effete English immigrant, who has a servant called Lena.

And within a year he was married to Lena Smith.

She was quite a different type of half-caste from Kleinhans himself. She was a light-coloured Cape girl. Her father had been a German – his name Schmidt anglicized into Smith – and her mother a coloured woman, with a little Malay blood in her and a little St. Helena blood, and the usual incursion of white blood.

Lena herself showed in her delicacy of feature and clear yellowish skin her ancestral superiority over Kleinhans. For all she had the straight, coarse, black hair and shadowed black eyes of the Cape girl, and Kleinhans' hair and eyes were light in colour, it was quite obvious that she was further removed from the aboriginal than he was. The Hottentot blood in him expressed itself in his heavy, triangular-shaped face and wide nose; but she had the thin little nose, the well-cut mouth and the oval cheek-line of her Malay grandmother, her German blood showed in her paler skin, and her voice, too, was light and gentle where that of Kleinhans was heavy with nearness to the African earth. It is doubtful whether she would have married Kleinhans had he not been, for her standards, an exceedingly prosperous man; but having done so, she made him a meek and amiable wife.

And Kleinhans, except in moments of sudden recurrent bitterness, learnt to forget, in his successful domesticity and happy husbandry, that he had once intended to marry a pure white girl, and that he had been beaten almost to death for merely speaking to one.

Their eldest child, a daughter, was born within the first year of their marriage – in the year 1872, and they called her after Lena's mother, Elmira.

She looked at birth like a typical European baby. Deborah, who had come over from Kokstad for the event, shook her head at her in proud amazement.

'Such a white child I have never seen before,' she said.

Elmira turns out to have 'olive skin, delicate features, large eyes and straight, golden brown hair'. As long as her parents keep out of sight, she passes for white and is sent to boarding school in Cape Town, 600 miles away. After a promising start, 'her brain soon tired and lagged behind' – racially-induced arrested development is one of Millin's recurring themes – and, at 16, she 'ceased to make any mental advance'. At 17, Elmira marries 63-year-old Adam Lindsell, who, violating 'the sanctities of race', makes her pregnant. Enter Barry, the fourth generation of Flood's unfortunate descendants. He 'looks unquestionably white' but, we are reminded, being three-sixteenths black, he too

GOLDEN GATE
HIGHLANDS NATIONAL PARK

Nestled in the foothills of the Maluti mountains of the north-eastern Free State lies the Golden Gate Highlands National Park. This is true highland habitat, home to a variety of mammals - black wildebeest eland, blesbok, oribi, springbok and Burchell's zebra - and birds, including the rare bearded vulture (lammergeier) and the equally rare bald ibis, which breed on the ledges in the sandstone cliffs.

Generaalskop, the third highest point in the Park, reveals a breathtaking tapestry of red, yellow and purple hues as it warm shades merge with the cool mountain shadows towards evening. The park derives its name from the brilliant shades of gold cast by the sun on the sandstone cliffs, especially the imposing Brandwag rock, keeping vigil over the main rest camp.

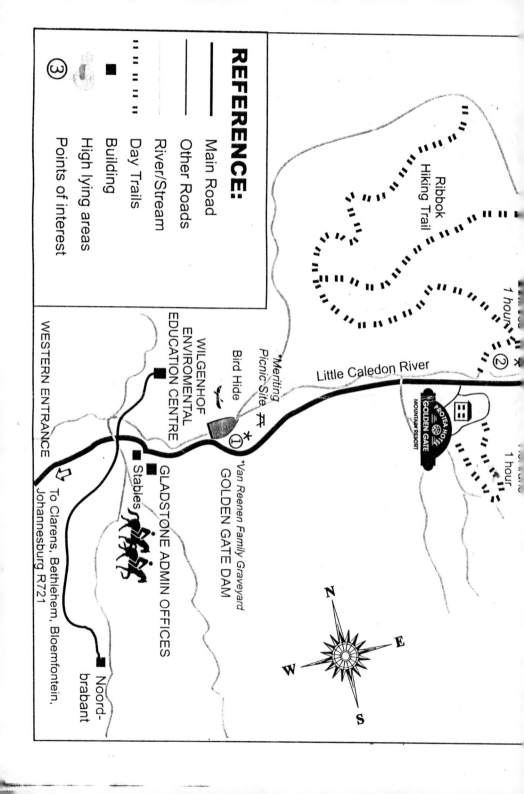

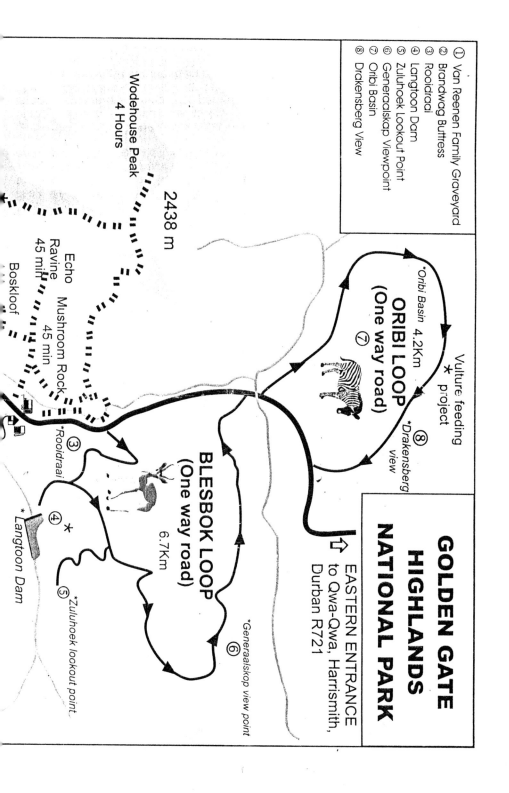

GOLDEN GATE HIGHLANDS NATIONAL PARK

⇨ EASTERN ENTRANCE
to Qwa-Qwa, Harrismith,
Durban R721

① Van Reenen Family Graveyard
② Brandwag Buttress
③ Rooidraai
④ Langtoon Dam
⑤ Zuluhoek Lookout Point
⑥ Generaalskop Viewpoint
⑦ Oribi Basin
⑧ Drakensberg View

Wodehouse Peak
4 Hours

2438 m

Echo   Mushroom Rock
Ravine   45 min
45 min

Boskloof

*Rooidraai ③

④ *

*Langtoon Dam

⑤ *Zuluhoek lookout point

BLESBOK LOOP
(One way road)
6.7Km

*Generaalskop view point ⑥

ORIBI LOOP
(One way road)
⑦

*Oribi Basin 4.2Km

Vulture feeding
* project

⑧
*Drakensberg
view

Rules:

The National Parks Act no. 57 of 1976, as amended and regulations made thereunder provide, inter, alia, that it shall be an offence to:

1. Alight from a motor vehicle elsewhere other than in a rest camp or at a picnic spot or any other authorized place (even if you are only partly out of your car.)

2. Drive elsewhere than on an authorized road.

3. Exceed the indicated speed limits.

4. Injure, feed or disturb any form of the wild.

5. Uproot, pick, cut or damage any plant or be in possession of any part of a plant indigenous to the Park.

6. Place any name, letter, figure, symbol, mark or picture on any object.

7. Discard a burning object in such manner or place as to cause fire.

8. Be in possession of any explosives or of an unsealed or loaded firearm.

9. Introduce into the Park any pets, whether domestic or otherwise.

10. Discard any article or any refuse otherwise than by placing it in a receptacle intended therefore.

11. Drive or park in such a manner that it is a nuisance or a disturbance or an inconvenience to any other person.

12. Make any noise after, 21:30 and before 6:00 which is likely to disturb any other person.

13. Advertise or offer any goods for sale.

14. Collect any money from the public or give public entertainment for reward.

15. Stay overnight in any rest camp without the knowledge of the supevisor.

16. Travel in the Park during times other than those as laid down by the regulations.

17. Stay overnight at any place other than in a rest camp or at a place other than designated by the Board.

18. Drive a vehicle in the Park without a valid Driver's licence.

19. Offences are liable to a fine not exceeding R800.00.

Notice:

It is an express condition of your visit to this Park that South African National Park's Board of Trustees shall not be responsible for any bodily injury whether fatal or otherwise, nor shall the Board of Trustees be responsible for any damage you may suffer arising from the loss or damage to your property brought into the park irrespective of whether such bodily injury, loss or damage arise as the result of fire, theft, floods or from the negligence or intentional act of any person whether or not in the employ of the Board, or cause by any animal in the Park. All visitors, whether or not they occupy accommodation within the rest camps are deemed to contract with the Board on this basis.

Printed by Hooglandpers

'has the blood of savages and slaves in his veins'. At the age of seven, his father having died and his mother run off with a commercial traveller, Barry moves to Cape Town to live with his all-white half-sister.

Barry was eaten up with a secret fear.

He feared his blood. The older he grew, the more was he obsessed with an instinctive sense of his own inferiority.

He was never comfortable with other children. He felt himself to be different. He had the contempt for black blood which is one of the nails in the cross that the black-blooded bear. No man so scornful of the native as the half-caste; no man so bitter against the half-caste as the native. 'Nigger!' the coloured man calls the black. 'Bastard!' the black man retaliates. No brotherhood in that blood so near the earth. Let the white man give his tolerance to whom he pleases, the degrees among the black blooded are viciously marked by themselves.

Never would Barry forget the horror of those brown people who had claimed him as their own – him, the Little Baas to all that was dark on Lindsell's Farm! Now there was not a day but he remembered the secret degradation under his skin.

Cape Town is as brown as it is white. Barry shuddered before the brown, and shivered before the white. One day, he was afraid, some Cape boy would come along and sense the hidden association between Barry and himself, claiming kinship. One day, he dreaded, some white person would feel that Barry was not as he was, and searching, would discover why. In his little childish arguments with other boys Barry always shrank back in anticipation that, sooner or later, the yell would break out that he was not white. When he saw boys or girls whispering or giggling together and he did not know any other cause for the whispering and giggling, he thought it must be that, at last, they had found out the truth about him. If, as the years passed, he ever got near enough to be friendly with a school fellow, he could not rest in peace for fear that the friendship would one day be disrupted by damaging discoveries. Sometimes he even wanted to say right out and have done with it: 'Look here, I must tell you. I am not really white.'

But then he never altogether dared do it. As soon as he had at last nerved himself to the confession, he would begin to think that, as long as he seemed white, he was white. For what was the whole affair, after all, but a question of skin? And, certainly, his skin was as white as anybody's. 'But it isn't only the skin,' some inner voice would whisper ... And 'It must be,' he would argue against that inner voice. 'See if there are light and dark children in the same coloured family, the light can go to white schools, but the dark cannot. Which proves that if you look white, that is all that matters.'

And, in the end, not only did he not confess, but he thrust his secret still deeper down, covering it with layers of shame and hate and invective. Of all the people he knew, no one spoke as passionately against black and brown and yellow as did Barry Lindsell.

It was the tradition among the school boys, as it was among their fathers, whose attitude they adopted, as it had been among the school mates of Elmira, that one preferred a real, straightforward black man to a half-caste. Whatever else the black man might be, he was, at least, pure. 'It stands to reason,' they would tell one another earnestly – for South African children are bound to discuss question of colour as soon as they discuss anything – 'that the white in them can't be good white.'

'And the black can't either. They say the decent natives don't like to be mixed up any more than we do.'

'So the coloured people must be worse than any one else.'

That was always the conclusion reached.

And with that conclusion Barry would eagerly agree.

More white than the whitest Barry tried to prove himself in his hostility to colour.

It was a fact that he could not find much to be proud of among the half-castes of Cape Town, the Cape people as they called themselves.

They had become, by the time the twentieth century had thrust away the nineteenth, not only an accident, or even an association, a group, a clan, a tribe – but actually a nation, a people. They had intermarried through generations and had established a type. There were among them many who were meritorious – what might shortly have been described as decent folk; but too often they were small and vicious, and craven and degenerate.

In the Cape Colony they had political and industrial, if not social, opportunities, but they barely availed themselves of them. They achieved nothing of any consequence. Now and then (very seldom) it might happen that a real black man, the son of some African chief, rich in land and cattle (not so many of these left, either), would struggle as far as an English or Scottish university, and, through it, to a profession; and would come back to South Africa to practise that profession. But he would never really succeed at it.

Putting aside all questions of prejudice, he could not hold his own against white competition. He had not the brain, the persistence, the temperament. Nor would his white colleagues greatly trouble their heads about him. They would hardly think him worth discussing. 'Not much good,' they would briefly say, and thus dismiss the subject.

And still this aboriginal would have done what practically no half-caste ever succeeded in doing.

As Barry grew into manhood and began jealously to look about him to see where the Cape people stood, he could find nowhere an obviously coloured man in a big commercial enterprise, in a learned profession or an artistic endeavour. They were many of them astonishingly capable with their hands, they made good masons, or carpenters, or mechanics; but there they ended. Either they had not the heart or they had not the head to strive for anything else. They often remained to the end of their days gamins by disposition, imitative and monkey like. And that was the far back Hottentot blood in them: as when, nearly a century ago, Barry's ancestor, the Rev. Andrew Flood, just come to Cape Town, had seen the little skin-clad, yellow folk, with their pepper-corn hair, and small mischievous eyes, capering behind their big white masters, over whom they held those tall umbrellas [...]

Something of that blood there still lived in Barry. And he could not see past it.

And yet there *was* something else to see.

For the brown people, the yellow people, might be as abandoned of hope as the inhabitants of Hell, but there were men and women all over South Africa, apparently white, but with an attenuated dark stain in them, and they were by no means hopeless. They were, on the contrary, not seldom among the best the land could show. However romantically South Africans might shudder at hidden drops of black blood; however Barry's school friends might traditionally assert that their flesh would crawl if they had to touch a person of colour, there were, nevertheless, people of whom literally dark things were said, and pure white folk were delighted to have the chance of shaking their hands. Nor did their flesh crawl, nor were they afraid to associate with them, or even marry them, forgetting the past and risking the future for the sake of the present. In spite of talk and talk and talk, if a man looked white, and had success enough, he was, in the fullest sense, accepted. That was the truth, and much of the shuddering and crawling was conventional hypocrisy.

Heaven knows through what generations of sorrow; through what daily bitterness of self-distrust; through what oceans of ostracism, the man with that fading, but never dying, darkness in him arrived at havens of social grace; but once arrived, his life was distinguished in no noticeable sense from the lives of those around him, and, as far as all outward appearances might indicate, the world held him to be as white as he looked.

But Barry, in his school-days, was far from being able to take a philosophic view of his position. Perhaps, indeed, however he might seem to be bold and unconscious, no man could really be at ease when there was something latent in his body which it was necessary for him and the world, in a kind of conspiracy, to ignore. It was really blackmail. As long as he paid the world in the coinage of success, the world would say nothing. But what if one day he ceased payment? No longer would his secret, which was no secret, be curiously whispered – it would be shouted in his face.

There is much, much more on the same lines: the 'unspeakable shame' of Barry's heritage; the 'flaw in his inferior black blood'; and the 'degeneracy' of people who are brown. The true villain, of course, is white prejudice but Millin, who apparently shared it, was incapable of seeing the absurdity – let alone the obscenity – of blaming the prejudice on its victims.

'Mixed blood' is treated rather more sympathetically in 'Cape Coloured Batman' (77) by Guy Butler, a fine poet and playwright, who for 35 years was professor of English at Rhodes University in Grahamstown. During the Second World War, he fought in North Africa and Italy.

Cape Coloured Batman

As the slanting sun drowsed lazily
On the terraced groves of Tuscany
At last I found him, back to a trunk:
Nelson, my batman, the bastard, drunk.

On the grass beneath an olive tree
His legs splayed in a khaki V
And all his body, relaxed, at ease,

Head thrown back, while over his knees
Strumming the banjo his yellow hands

Stirred all his sorrow from four steel strands.

His melancholy cries from Hollywood
'Where the coyotes cry' or 'Lady be Good'
In that declining light awoke

A tenderness for the stupid bloke,
So happy his sorrow, so at ease
Strumming the strings across his knees.

No doubt a pirate Javanese
From Malacca Straits or Sunda Seas
Shaped those almond eyes of his;

A Negress from the Cameroons –
Bought for brandy, sold for doubloons –
Gave him a voice that wails and croons;

An eagle Arab trading far
From Hadramaut to Zanzibar
Left him a nose like a scimitar;

A Bush-girl from the Namaqua sands
Bequeathed him bird-like, restless hands
Stirring his sorrow from four steel strands;

While English, Dutch and Portuguese
Sick of biscuits and sodden cheese
Put in at the Tavern of the Seas,

Northerners warm in the Southern night
Drank red Cape brandy, and got tight –
And left him a skin that's almost white.

This is the man the Empires made
From lesser breeds, the child of Trade
Left without hope in History's shade;

Shouldered aside into any old place,
Damned from birth by the great disgrace,
A touch of the tar-brush in his face.

Under pines, mimosas and mango trees
Strewn through the world lie men like these:
Drunk crooning voices, banjos on knees.

He fell asleep in a vinous mist,
Star in his mouth, bottle in fist,
The desperate, maudlin hedonist.

But the pathos of the human race
Sainted his drunken, relaxed face;
And a warm dusk wind through the olive trees
Touched mute strings across his knees
With sorrows from the Seven Seas.

What Butler calls 'a touch of the tar-brush' was as much of an obsession in segregationist South Africa as it was in the American South. Just as President Abraham Lincoln was said to exhibit signs of it, so too in South Africa were President Paul Kruger and Prime Minister Louis Botha.[3] One of the few South African writers capable of poking fun at the phenomenon was the whimsical Herman Charles Bosman (78), an Afrikaner who wrote in English. 'Marico Scandal', like all the short stories in *Mafeking Road*, is set in the north-west Transvaal, where Bosman was a school teacher in the 1920s, and is told by Oom (Uncle) Schalk Lourens, his alter ego.

When I passed young Gawie Erasmus by the wall of the new dam (Oom Schalk Lourens said) I could see clearly that he had had another disagreement with his employer, Koos Deventer. Because, as Gawie walked away from me, I saw, on the seat of his trousers, the still damp imprint of a muddy boot. The dried mud of another foot-print, higher up on his trousers, told of a similar disagreement that Gawie had had with his employer on the previous day. I thought that Gawie must be a high-spirited young man to disagree so frequently with his employer.

Nevertheless, I felt it my duty to speak to Koos Deventer about this matter when I sat with him in his voorkamer,[4] drinking coffee.

'I see that Gawie Erasmus still lays the stones unevenly on the wall of the new dam you are building,' I said to Koos Deventer.

'Indeed,' Koos answered, 'have you been looking at the front part of the wall?'

'No,' I said, 'I have been looking at Gawie's trousers. The back part of the trousers.'

'The trouble with Gawie Erasmus,' Koos said, 'is that he is not really a white man. It doesn't show in his hair or his finger-hails, of course. He is not as coloured as all that. But you can tell it easily in other ways. Yes, that is what's wrong with Gawie. His Hottentot forbears.'

*   *   *

At that moment Koos Deventer's eldest daughter, Francina, brought us in more coffee.

'It is not true father, what you said about Gawie Erasmus,' Francina said, 'Gawie is white. He is as white as I am.'

Francina was eighteen. She was tall and slender. She had a neat figure. And she looked very pretty in that voorkamer, with the yellow hair falling on to her cheeks from underneath a blue ribbon. Another thing I noticed about Francina, as she moved daintily towards me with the tray, was the scent that she bought in Zeerust at the last Nagmaal.[5] The perfume lay on her strangely, like the night.

Koos Deventer made no reply to Francina. And only after she had gone back into the kitchen, and the door was closed, did he return to the subject of Gawie Erasmus.

'He is so coloured,' Koos said, 'that he even sleeps with a blanket over his head, like a kafir does.'

It struck me that Koos Deventer's statements were rather peculiar. For, according to Koos, you couldn't tell that Gawie Erasmus was coloured, just by looking at his hair and finger-nails. You had to wait until Gawie lay underneath a blanket, so that you saw nothing of him at all.

But I remembered the way that Francina had walked out of the voorkamer with her head very high and her red lips closed. And it seemed to me, then, that Gawie's disagreements with his employer were not all due to the unevenness of the wall of the new dam. I did not see Gawie Erasmus again until the meeting of the Drogevlei Debating Society.

But in the meantime the story that Gawie was coloured gained much ground. Paulus Welman said that he knew a man once in Vryburg, who had known Gawie's grandfather. And this man said that Gawie's grandfather had a big belly and wore a copper ring through his nose. At other times, again, Paulus Welman said that Gawie's father did not wear the copper ring in his nose, but in his one ear. It was hard to know which story to believe. So most of the farmers in the Marico believed both.

*　*　*

The meeting of the Drogevlei Debating Society was held in the school-room. There was a good attendance. For the debate was to be on the Native Question. And that was always a popular subject in the Marico. You could say much about it without having to think hard.

I was standing under the thorn-trees talking to Paulus Welman and some others, when Koos Deventer arrived with his wife and Francina and Gawie. They got off the mule-cart, and the two women walked on towards the schoolroom. Koos and Gawie stayed behind, hitching the reins on to a tree. Several of the men with me shook their heads gravely, at what they saw. For Gawie, while stooping for a reim, had another hurried disagreement with his employer.

Francina, walking with her mother towards the school, sensed something was amiss. But when she turned round she was too late to see anything.

Francina and her mother greeted us as they passed. Paulus Welman said that Francina was a pretty girl, but rather stand-offish. He said her under-standing was a bit slow, too. He said that when he had told her that joke about the copper ring in the one ear of Gawie's father, Francina looked at him as though he had said there was a copper ring in his own ear. She didn't seem to be quite all there, Paulus Welman said.

But I didn't take much notice of Paulus.

I stood there, under the thorn-tree, where Francina had passed, and I breathed in stray breaths of that scent which Francina had bought in Zeerust. It was a sweet and strange fragrance. But it was sad, also, like youth that has gone.

I waited in the shadows. Gawie Erasmus came by. I scrutinised him carefully, but except that his hair was black and his skin rather dark, there seemed to be no justification for Koos Deventer to say that he was coloured.

It looked like some joke that Koos Deventer and Paulus Welman had got up between them. Gawie seemed to be just an ordinary and rather good-looking youth of about twenty.

★   ★   ★

By this time it was dark. Oupa van Tonder, an old farmer who was very keen on debates, lit an oil lamp that he had brought with him and put it on the table.

The Schoolmaster took the chair, as usual. He said that, as we all knew, the subject was that the Bantu should be allowed to develop along his own lines. He said he had got the idea for this debate from an article he had read in the Kerkbode.[6]

Oupa van Tonder then got up and said, the way the Schoolmaster put it, the subject was too hard to understand. He proposed, for the sake of the older debaters, who had not gone to school much, that they should just be allowed to talk about how the kafirs in the Marico were getting cheekier every day. The older debaters cheered Oupa van Tonder for putting the Schoolmaster in his place.

Oupa van Tonder was still talking when the Schoolmaster banged the table with a ruler and said that he was out of order. Oupa van Tonder got really annoyed then. He said he had lived in the Transvaal for eighty-eight years, and this was the first time in his life that he had been insulted. 'Anybody would think that I am the steam machine that threshes the mealies at Nietverdiend, that I can get out of order,' Oupa van Tonder said.

Some of the men started pulling Oupa van Tonder by his jacket to get him to sit down, but others shouted out that he was quite right, and that they should pull the Schoolmaster's jacket instead.

The Schoolmaster explained that if some people were talking on the Kerkbode subject, and others were talking on Oupa van Tonder's subject, it would mean that there were two different debates going on at the same time. Oupa van Tonder said that that was quite all right. It suited him, he said. And he told a long story about a kafir who had stolen his trek-chain. He also said that if the Schoolmaster kept on banging the table like that, while he was talking, he would go home and take his oil-lamp with him.

★   ★   ★

In the end the Schoolmaster said that we could talk about anything we liked. Only, he asked us not to use any of that coarse language that had spoilt the last three debates. 'Try to remember that there are ladies present,' he said in a weak sort of way.

The older debaters, who had not been to school much, spoke at great length.

Afterwards the Schoolmaster suggested that perhaps some of our younger members would like to debate a little, and he called on Gawie Erasmus to say a few words on behalf of the kafirs. The Schoolmaster spoke playfully.

Koos Deventer guffawed behind his hand. Some of the women tittered. On account of his unpopularity the Schoolmaster heard little of what went on in Marico. The only news he got was what he could glean from reading the compositions of the children in the higher classes. And we could see that the children had not yet mentioned, in their compositions, that Gawie Erasmus was supposed to be coloured.

You know how it is with a scandalous story. The last one to hear it is always the person that the scandal is about.

That crowd in the schoolroom realised quickly what the situation was. And there was much laughter all the time that Gawie spoke. I can still remember that half-perplexed look on his dark face, as though he had meant to make a funny speech, but had not expected quite that amount of appreciation. And I noticed that Francina's face was very red, and that her eyes were fixed steadily on the floor.

There was so much laughter, finally, that Gawie had to sit down, still looking slightly puzzled.

After that Paulus Welman got up and told funny stories about so-called white people whose grandfathers had big bellies and wore copper rings in their ears. I didn't know at what stage of the debate Gawie Erasmus found out at whom these funny remarks were being directed. Or when it was that he slipped out of the schoolroom, to leave Drogevlei and the Groot Marico for ever.

And some months later, when I again went to visit Koos Deventer, he did not once mention Gawie Erasmus to me. He seemed to have grown tired of Marico scandals. But when Francina brought in the coffee, it was as though she thought that Koos had again spoken about Gawie. For she looked at him in a disappointed sort of way and said: 'Gawie is white, father. He is as white as I am.'

I could not at first make out what the change was that had come over Francina. She was as good-looking as ever, but in a different sort of way. I began to think that perhaps it was because she no longer wore that strange perfume that she bought in Zeerust.

But at that moment she brought me my coffee.

And I saw then, when she came towards me, from behind the table, with the tray, why it was that Francina Deventer moved so heavily.

In his play, *The Blood Knot*, Athol Fugard (79), another Afrikaner who writes in English, approached the dual issues of inter-racial sex and passing for white from the other side of the colour line. His protagonists are two Cape Coloured brothers, dark-skinned Zachariah and light-skinned Morris. At Morris's urging, Zachariah acquires a pen-pal, Ethel Lange, '18 years old and well-developed'. She sends Zachariah a photograph of herself showing, to Morris's horror, that she is white and, to dark-skinned Zachariah's delight, that she assumes he is, too. Then she writes to say that she is planning a trip to Port Elizabeth, where the brothers live in a township shack. What follows is an extraordinarily powerful piece of South African theatre. It was first performed in 1961.

ZACHARIAH. Ethel …?

MORRIS. Is coming here.

ZACHARIAH. Coming here?

MORRIS [*puts down the letter and stands up*]. I warned you, didn't I? I said: I have a feeling about this business. I remember my words. And wise ones they turned out to be. I told you to leave it alone. Hands off! I said. Don't touch! Not for you! But oh no, Mr Z. Pietersen was clever. He knew how to handle it. Well, handle this, will you please?

ZACHARIAH [*dumbly*]. What else does she say?

MORRIS [*brutally*]. I'm not going to read it. You want to know why? Because it doesn't matter. The game's up, man. Nothing matters except: 'I'm coming down in June, so where can I meet you?' That is what Mr Z. Pietersen had better start thinking about … and quick, boy, quick!

ZACHARIAH. When's June?

MORRIS. Soon.

ZACHARIAH. How soon?

MORRIS [*ticking them off on his fingers*]. June, July, August, September, October, November, December, January, February, March, April, May, June. Satisfied?

ATHOL FUGARD

[*Another long pause.*]

ZACHARIAH. So?

MORRIS [*to the table, where he reads further into the letter*]. 'I'll be staying with my uncle at Kensington.' [*Little laugh.*] Kensington! Near enough for you, Zach? About five minutes walking from here, hey?

ZACHARIAH [*frightened*]. Morrie, I know. I'll tell her I can't see her.

MORRIS. She'll want to know why.

ZACHARIAH. Because I'm sick, with my heart.

MORRIS. And if she feels sorry and comes to comfort you?

ZACHARIAH [*growing desperation*]. No, but I'm going away.

MORRIS. When?

ZACHARIAH. Soon, soon. June. June! Morrie, June!

MORRIS. And what about where, and why and what, if she says she'll wait until you come back?

ZACHARIAH. Then I'll tell her …

[*Pause. He can think of nothing else to say.*]

MORRIS. What? You can't even tell her you're dead. You see, I happen to know. There is no white-washing away a man's facts. They'll speak for themselves at first sight, if you don't say it.

ZACHARIAH. Say what?

MORRIS. The truth. You know it.

ZACHARIAH. I don't. I know nothing.

MORRIS. Then listen, Zach, because I know it. 'Dear Ethel, forgive me, but I was born a dark sort of boy who wanted to play with whiteness …'

ZACHARIAH [*rebelling*]. No!

MORRIS. What else can you say? Come on. Let's hear it. What is there a man can say or pray that will change the colour of his skin or blind them to it?

ZACHARIAH. There must be something.

MORRIS. There's nothing … when it's a question of smiles and whispers and thoughts in strange eyes there is only the truth and … then … [*He pauses.*]

ZACHARIAH. And then what?

MORRIS. And then to make a run for it. They don't like these games with their whiteness, Zach. Ethel's got a policeman brother, remember, and an uncle and your address.

ZACHARIAH. What have I done, hey? I done nothing.

MORRIS. What have you thought, Zach! That's the crime. I seem to remem-

328

ber somebody saying: 'I like the thought of this little white girl.' And what about your dreams, Zach? They've kept me awake these past few nights. I've heard them mumbling and moaning away in the darkness. They'll hear them quick enough. When they get their hands on a dark-born boy playing with a white idea, you think they don't find out what he's been dreaming at night? They've got ways and means, Zach. Mean ways. Like confinement, in a cell, on bread and water, for days without end. They got time. All they need for evidence is a man's dreams. Not so much his hate. They say they can live with that. It's his dreams that they drag off to judgement. [*Pause: Goes back to the window. Turns to Zachariah.*] What are you going to do, Zach?

ZACHARIAH. I'm thinking about it, Morrie.

MORRIS. What are you thinking about it?

ZACHARIAH. What am I going to do?

MORRIS. You'd better be quick, man.

ZACHARIAH. Help me, Morrie.

MORRIS. Are you serious?

ZACHARIAH. I'm not smiling.

MORRIS. Okay, let's begin at the beginning, Zach. Give me the first fact.

ZACHARIAH [*severe and bitter*]. Ethel is white, and I am black.

MORRIS. That's a very good beginning, Zach.

ZACHARIAH. If she sees me …

MORRIS. Keep it up.

ZACHARIAH. … she'll be surprised.

MORRIS. Harder, Zach.

ZACHARIAH. She'll laugh.

MORRIS. Let it hurt, man!

ZACHARIAH. She'll scream!

MORRIS. Good! Now for yourself. She's surprised, remember?

ZACHARIAH. I'm not strange.

MORRIS. She swears?

ZACHARIAH. I'm no dog.

MORRIS. She screams!

ZACHARIAH. I just wanted to smell you, lady!

MORRIS. Good, Zach. Very good. You're seeing this clearly, man. But, re-member there is still the others.

ZACHARIAH. What others?

MORRIS. The uncles with fists and brothers in boots who come running

329

when a lady screams. What about them?

ZACHARIAH. What about them?

MORRIS. They've come to ransack you.

ZACHARIAH. I'll say it wasn't me.

MORRIS. They won't believe you.

ZACHARIAH. Leave me alone!

MORRIS. They'll hit you for that.

ZACHARIAH. I'll fight.

MORRIS. Too many for you.

ZACHARIAH. I'll call a policeman.

MORRIS. He's on their side.

ZACHARIAH. I'll run away!

MORRIS. That's better. Go back to the beginning. Give me that first fact, again. [*Pause.*] It started with Ethel, remember ... Ethel is

ZACHARIAH. ... is white.

MORRIS. That's it. And ...

ZACHARIAH. ... and I am black.

MORRIS. Let's hear it.

ZACHARIAH. Ethel is so ... so ... snow white.

MORRIS. And ... come on ...

ZACHARIAH. And I am too ... truly ... too black.

MORRIS. Now, this is the hard part, Zach. So let it hurt, man. It has to hurt a man to do him good. I know, just this one cry and then never again ... Come on, Zach ... let's hear it.

ZACHARIAH. I can never have her.

MORRIS. Never ever.

ZACHARIAH. She wouldn't want me anyway.

MORRIS. It's as simple as that.

ZACHARIAH. She's too white to want me anyway.

MORRIS. For better or for worse.

ZACHARIAH. So I won't want her anymore.

MORRIS. Not in this life, or that next one if death us do part, God help us! For ever and ever no more, thank you!

ZACHARIAH. The whole, rotten, stinking lot is all because I'm black! Black days, black ways, black things. They're me. I'm happy. Ha Ha Ha! Can you hear my black happiness? What is there is black as me?

MORRIS [*quietly, and with absolute sincerity*]. Oh, Zach! When I hear that certainty about whys and wherefores, about how to live and what not to love, I wish, believe me, man, I wish that old washerwoman[7] had bruised me too at birth. I wish I was as – [*The alarm goes off.*] Bedtime.

[*Morris looks up to find Zachariah staring strangely at him. Morris goes to the window to avoid Zachariah's eyes. He turns from the window to find Zachariah still staring at him. Morris goes to the table to turn off the lamp.*]

ZACHARIAH. Morris!

MORRIS. Zach?

ZACHARIAH. Keep on the light.

MORRIS. Why?

ZACHARIAH. I saw something.

MORRIS. What?

ZACHARIAH. Your skin. How can I put it? It's … [*Pause.*]

MORRIS [*easily*]. On the light side.

ZACHARIAH. *Ja.*

MORRIS [*very easily*]. One of those things. [*Another move to the lamp.*]

ZACHARIAH. No, wait, wait, Morrie! I want to have a good look at you, man.

MORRIS. It's a bit late in the day to be seeing your brother for the first time. I been here a whole year, now, you know.

ZACHARIAH. *Ja.* But after a whole life I only seen myself properly tonight. You helped me. I'm grateful.

MORRIS. It was nothing, Zach.

ZACHARIAH. No! I'm not a man that forgets a favour. I want to help you now.

MORRIS. I don't need any assistance, thank you, Zach.

ZACHARIAH. But you do. [*Morris sits.*] You're on the lighter side of life all right. You like that … all over? Your legs and things?

MORRIS. It's evenly spread.

ZACHARIAH. Not even a foot in the darker side, hey! I'd say you must be quite a bright boy with nothing on.

MORRIS. Please, Zach!

ZACHARIAH. You're shy! You always get undressed in the dark. Always well closed up. Like a woman. Like Ethel. I bet she shines. You know something? I bet if it was you she saw and not me she wouldn't say nothing.

[*Morris closes his eyes and gives a light, nervous laugh. Zachariah also laughs, but hollowly.*]

I'm sure she wouldn't be surprised, or laugh, or swear or scream. No one would come running. I bet all she would do is say: 'How do you do, Mr Pietersen?' [*Pause.*] There's a thought there, Morrie. You ever think of it?

MORRIS. No.

ZACHARIAH. Not even a little bit of it? Like there, where you say: 'Hello, Ethel –' and shake hands. Ah, yes, I see this now. You would manage all right, Morrie. One thing is for certain: you would look all right, with her, and that's the main thing.

MORRIS. You're dreaming again, Zach.

ZACHARIAH. This is not my sort of dream. My dream was different. [*He laughs.*] I didn't shake her hands, Morrie. You're the man for shaking hands, Morrie.

MORRIS. Are you finished now, Zach?

ZACHARIAH. No. We're still coming to the big thought. Why don't you meet her? [*Pause.*]

MORRIS. You want to know why?

ZACHARIAH. *Ja.*

MORRIS. You really want to know?

ZACHARIAH. *Ja.*

MORRIS. She's not my pen-pal.

[*Morris moves to get away. Zachariah stops him.*]

ZACHARIAH. Okay, okay. Let's try it this way. Would you like to meet her?

MORRIS. Listen, Zach. I've told you before. Ethel is your –

ZACHARIAH [*pained*]. Please, Morrie! Would – you – like – to – meet – her?

MORRIS. That's no sort of question.

ZACHARIAH. Why not?

MORRIS. Because all my life I've been interested in meeting people. Not just Ethel – anybody!

ZACHARIAH. Okay, let's try it another way. Would you like to see her, or hear her, or maybe touch her?

MORRIS. That still doesn't give the question any meaning! You know me, Zach. Don't I like to hear church bells? Don't I like to touch horses? And anyway, I've told you before, Zach, Ethel is your pen-pal.

ZACHARIAH. You can have her.

MORRIS. What's this now?

ZACHARIAH. I'm giving her to you.

MORRIS [*angry*]. This is no bloody game, Zach!

ZACHARIAH. But I mean it. Look. I can't use her. We seen that. She'll see it too. But why throw away a good pen-pal if somebody else can do it? You can. Morrie, I'm telling you now, as your brother, that when Ethel sees you all she will do is say: 'How do you do, Mr Pietersen?' She'll never know otherwise.

MORRIS. You think so?

ZACHARIAH. You could fool me, if I didn't know who you were, Morrie.

MORRIS. You mean that, Zach?

ZACHARIAH. Cross my heart and hope to die. And the way you can talk! She'd be impressed, man.

MORRIS. That's true. I like to talk.

ZACHARIAH. No harm in it, is there? A couple of words, a little walk, and a packet of monkey-nuts.

MORRIS. Monkey-nuts?

ZACHARIAH. *Ja.* Something to chew.

MORRIS. Good God, Zach! You take a lady friend to tea, man!

ZACHARIAH. To tea, hey!

MORRIS. *Ja*, with buns, if she's hungry. Hot-cross buns.

ZACHARIAH. Now, you see! I would have just bought monkey nuts. She's definitely not for me.

MORRIS. To tea. A pot of afternoon tea. When she wants to sit down, you pull out her chair ... like this. [*He demonstrates.*]

ZACHARIAH. Hey – I think I seen that.

MORRIS. The woman pours the tea but the man butters the bun.

ZACHARIAH. Well, well, well.

MORRIS. Only two spoons of sugar, and don't drink out of the saucer.

ZACHARIAH. That's very good.

MORRIS. If she wants to blow her nose, offer your hanky, which you keep in your breast pocket.

ZACHARIAH. Go on.

MORRIS [*waking up to reality*]. You're wasting my time, Zach. I'm going to bed.

ZACHARIAH. But what's the matter, man? You been telling me everything so damn nice. Come on. Tell me. [*Coaxing.*] Tell your brother what's the matter.

MORRIS. I haven't got a hanky.

ZACHARIAH. I think we can buy one.

MORRIS. And the breast pocket?

ZACHARIAH. What's the problem there? Let's also –

MORRIS. Don't be a bloody fool! You got to buy a whole suit to get a breast pocket. And that's still not all. What about socks, decent shoes, a spotty tie, and a clean white shirt? How do you think a man steps out to meet a waiting lady. On his bare feet, wearing rags, and stinking because he hasn't had a bath? She'd even laugh and scream at me if I went like this. So I'm giving Ethel back to you. There is nothing I can do with her, thank you very much.

[*Morris crosses to his bed. Zachariah thinks.*]

ZACHARIAH. Haven't we got that sort of money?

MORRIS. All I got left until you get paid tomorrow is twenty cents. What the hell am I talking about! You know what a right sort of for-a-meeting-with-the-lady type of suit costs? Rands and rands and rands. Shoes? Rands and rands. Shirt? Rands. Then there's still two socks and a tie.

ZACHARIAH [*patiently*]. We got that sort of money.

MORRIS. Here you are. Twenty cents. Go buy me a suit.

ZACHARIAH. Thank you, Morrie. Where's the tin?[8]

MORRIS. Tin?

ZACHARIAH. Square sort of tin.

MORRIS [*horror*]. You mean – our tin?

ZACHARIAH. There was sweets in it at Christmas.

MORRIS. Our future?

ZACHARIAH. That's the one. The future tin.

MORRIS. Our two-man farm?

ZACHARIAH. Yeah, where is it?

MORRIS. I won't tell you.

[*He runs and stands spread-eagled in front of the cupboard where the tin is hidden.*]

ZACHARIAH. Ah-ha!

MORRIS. No, Zach!

ZACHARIAH. Give it to me! Morrie!

MORRIS. No, Zach! – Zach, no …

[*Grabs the tin arid runs away. Zachariah lurches after him. Morris is quick and elusive.*]

Zach, please! Just stop! Please! Just stand still and listen to me. Everything

… everything we got, the most precious thing a man can have, a future, is in here. You've worked hard, I've done the saving.

ZACHARIAH. We'll start again.

MORRIS. It will take too long.

ZACHARIAH. I'll work overtime.

MORRIS. It won't be the same.

[*Zachariah lunges suddenly, but Morris escapes.*]

ZACHARIAH. Wait, Morrie! Wait! Fair is fair. Now this time you stand still … and listen.

MORRIS. I won't. I won't – no.

ZACHARIAH. Yes, you will, because Ethel is coming and you want to meet her. But like you say, not like any old *hotnot* in the street, but smartly. Now this is it. You're wearing a pretty-smart-for-a-meeting-with-the-lady type of suit.

[*Morris, clutching the tin to his chest, closes his eyes. Zachariah creeps closer.*]

Shiny shoes, white socks, a good shirt, and a spotty tie. And the people watch you go by and say: 'Hey! Who's you? There goes something!' And Ethel says: 'Who's this coming? Could it be my friend, Mr Pietersen?' And you say: 'Good day, Miss Ethel. Can I shake your white hands with my white hands?' 'Of course, Mr Pietersen.'

[*Zachariah has reached Morris. He takes the tin.*]

Thank you, Morrie.

[*Morris doesn't move. Zachariah opens the tin, takes out the money, and then callously throws the tin away. He takes the money to the table where he counts it.*]

MORRIS. Why are you doing this to me?

ZACHARIAH. Aren't we brothers? [*Pause.*] What sort of suit? And what about the shoes?

MORRIS. Go to a good shop. Ask for the outfit, for a gentleman.

SCENE FIVE

The next day.

Morris is lying on his bed, staring up at the ceiling. There is a knock at the door. Morris rises slowly on his bed.

MORRIS. Who's there? [*The knock is heard again.*] Speak up! I can't hear. [*Knocking.*] Who are you? [*Silence. Morris's fear is now apparent. He waits until the knock is heard a third time.*] Ethel … I mean, Madam … No! … I mean to say, Miss Ethel Lange, could that be you? [*In reply there is a raucous burst of laughter, unmistakably Zachariah's.*] What's this? [*Silence.*] What's the meaning of this? [*Morris rushes to his bed and looks at the alarm clock.*] It's still only the middle of the day.

ZACHARIAH. I know!

MORRIS. Go back to work! At once!

ZACHARIAH. I can't.

MORRIS. Why not?

ZACHARIAH. I took some leave, and left. Let me in, Morrie.

MORRIS. What's the matter with you? The door's not locked.

ZACHARIAH. My hands are full. [*Pause.*] I been shopping, Morrie.

[*Morris rushes to the door, but collects himself before opening it. Zachariah comes in, his arms piled with parcels. He smiles slyly at Morris, who has assumed a pose of indifference.*]

Oh no you don't. I heard you run. So you thought it was our little Miss Ethel. And a little bit poopy at that thought. Well, don't worry, Morrie, 'cause you know what this is? Your outfit! Number one, and what do we have? A wonderful hat … sir.

[*Takes it out and holds it up for approval. His manner is exaggerated, a caricature of the shopkeeper who sold him the clothing.*]

Which is guaranteed to protect the head on Sundays and rainy days. And next we have a good shirt and a grey tie, which is much better taste, because spots are too loud for a gentleman. Next we have – two grey socks, left and right, and a hanky to blow her nose. [*Next parcel.*] Aha! Now we've come to the suit. But before I show you the suit, my friend, I want to ask you, what does a man really look for in a good suit? A good cloth. Isn't that so?

MORRIS. What are you talking about?

ZACHARIAH. That's what he said. The fashion might be a season too old, but will you please feel the difference. It's lasted for years already. All what I can say is, take it or leave it. But only a fool would leave it at that price. So I took it. [*Next parcel.*] And next we have a real ostrich wallet.

MORRIS. What for?

ZACHARIAH, Your inside pocket. *Ja!* You forgot about the inside pocket. A gentleman always got a wallet for the inside pocket. [*Next parcel.*] And a cigarette case, and a cigarette lighter, for the outside pocket. Chramonium!

MORRIS. Since when do I smoke?

ZACHARIAH. I know, but Ethel might, he said.

MORRIS [*fear*]. You told him? Zach, are you out of your mind?

ZACHARIAH. Don't worry. I just said there was a lady who someone was going to meet. He winked at me and said it was a good thing, now and then, and reminded me that ladies like presents. [*Holds up a scarf.*] A pretty *doek* in case the wind blows her hair away. Ah-ha. And next we have an umbrella in case it's sopping wet. And over here … [*Last parcel.*] Guess what's in this box. I'll shake it. Listen.

MORRIS. Shoes.

ZACHARIAH [*triumphantly*]. No! It's boots! Ha, ha! *Ja.* [*Watching Morris's reaction.*] They frighten an *ou*, don't they? [*Happy.*] Satisfied, Morrie?

MORRIS [*looking at the pile of clothing*]. It seems all right.

ZACHARIAH. It wasn't easy. At the first shop, when I asked for the outfit for a gentleman, they said I was an agitator, *ja*, and was going to call the police. I had to get out, man … quick! Even this fellow … Mr Moses … 'You're drunk,' he said. But when I showed him our future he sobered up. You know what he said? He said, 'Are you the gentleman?' So I said, 'Do I look like a gentleman, Mr Moses?' He said: 'My friend, it takes all sorts of different sorts to make this world.' 'I'm the black sort,' I said. So he said: 'You don't say.' He also said to mention his name to any other gentlemen wanting reasonable outfits. Go ahead, Morrie. [*The clothing.*] Let's see the gentle sort of man.

MORRIS. Okay. Okay. Don't rush me.

[*Moves cautiously to the pile of clothing. Flicks an imaginary speck of dust off the hat. Zachariah is waiting.*]

ZACHARIAH. Well?

MORRIS. Give me time.

ZACHARIAH. What for? You got the clothes, man.

MORRIS. For God's sake, Zach! This is deep water. I'm not just going to jump right in. You must paddle around first.

ZACHARIAH. Paddle around?

MORRIS. Try it out!

ZACHARIAH [*offering him the hat*]. No, try it on.

MORRIS. The idea, man. I got to try it out. There's more to wearing a white skin than just putting on a hat. You've seen white men before without hats, but they're still white men, aren't they?

ZACHARIAH. *Ja.*

MORRIS. And without suits or socks, or shoes …

ZACHARIAH. No, Morrie. Never without socks and shoes. Never a barefoot white man.

MORRIS. Well, the suit then. Look, Zach, what I'm trying to say is this. The clothes will help, but only help. They don't maketh the white man. It's that white something inside you, that special meaning and manner of whiteness. I know what I'm talking about because ... I'll be honest with you now, Zach ... I've thought about it for a long time. And the first fruit of my thought, Zach, is that this whiteness of theirs is not just in the skin, otherwise ... well, I mean ... I'd be one of them, wouldn't I? Because, let me tell you, Zach, I seen them that's darker than me.

ZACHARIAH. *Ja?*

MORRIS. Yes. Really dark, man. Only they had that something I'm telling you about ... that's what I got to pin down in here.

ZACHARIAH. What?

MORRIS. White living, man! Like ... like ... like looking at things. Haven't you noticed it, Zach? They look at things differently. Haven't you seen their eyes when they look at you? It's even in their way of walking.

ZACHARIAH. Ah – so you must learn to walk properly then.

MORRIS. Yes.

ZACHARIAH. And to look right at things.

MORRIS. *Ja.*

ZACHARIAH. And to sound right.

MORRIS. Yes! There's that, as well. The sound of it.

ZACHARIAH. So go on. [*Again offering the hat.*] Try it. For size. Just for the sake of the size.

[*Morris takes the hat, plays with it for a few seconds, then impulsively puts it on.*]

MORRIS. Just for size, okay.

ZACHARIAH. Ha!

MORRIS. Yes?

ZACHARIAH. Aha!

MORRIS [*whipping off the hat in embarrassment*]. No.

ZACHARIAH. Yes.

MORRIS [*shaking his head*]. Uhuh!

ZACHARIAH. Come.

MORRIS. No, man.

ZACHARIAH. Man. I like the look of that on your head.

MORRIS. It looked right?

ZACHARIAH. I'm telling you.

MORRIS. It seemed to fit.

ZACHARIAH. It did, I know.

MORRIS [*using this as an excuse to get it back on his head*]. The brim was just right on the brow ... and with plenty of room for the brain! I'll try it again, shall I?

ZACHARIAH. Just for the sake of the size. A good fit.

MORRIS [*lifting the hat*]. Good morning!

ZACHARIAH. That's very good.

MORRIS [*again*]. Good morning ... Miss Ethel Lange!

[*Looks quickly to see Zachariah's reaction. He betrays nothing.*]

ZACHARIAH. Maybe a little higher.

MORRIS. Higher? [*Again.*]

ZACHARIAH. *Ja.*

MORRIS. Good morning ... [*A flourish.*] ... and how do you do today, Miss Ethel Lange! [*Laughing with delight.*]

ZACHARIAH. How about the jacket?

MORRIS. Okay.

[*Zachariah hands him the jacket. He puts it on.*]

[*Preening.*] Zach – how did you do it?

ZACHARIAH. I said: 'The gentleman is smaller than me, Mr Moses.'

MORRIS [*once again lifting his hat*]. Good morning, Miss Ethel Lange ... [*pleading, servile*]. I beg your pardon, but I do hope you wouldn't mind to take a little walk with ...

ZACHARIAH. Stop!

MORRIS. What's wrong?

ZACHARIAH. Your voice.

MORRIS. What's wrong with it?

ZACHARIAH. Too soft. They don't ever sound like that.

MORRIS. To a lady they do! I admit, if it wasn't Ethel I was addressing it would be different.

ZACHARIAH. Okay. Try me.

MORRIS. You?

ZACHARIAH. You're walking with Ethel. I'm selling monkey-nuts.

MORRIS. So?

ZACHARIAH. So you want some monkey-nuts. Something to chew.

MORRIS. Ah! ... [*His voice trails off.*]

ZACHARIAH. Go on. I'm selling monkey-nuts. Peanuts! Peanuts!

MORRIS [*after hesitation*]. I can't.

ZACHARIAH [*simulated shock*]. What!

MORRIS [*frightened*]. What I mean is … I don't want any monkey-nuts. I'm not hungry.

ZACHARIAH. Ethel wants some.

MORRIS. Ethel?

ZACHARIAH. *Ja*, and I'm selling them.

MORRIS. This is hard for me, Zach.

ZACHARIAH. You got to learn your lesson, Morrie. You want to pass, don't you? Peanuts! Peanuts!

MORRIS [*steeling himself*]. Excuse me!

ZACHARIAH, I'll never hear that. Peanuts!

MORRIS. Hey!

ZACHARIAH. Or that. Peanuts!

MORRIS. Boy!

ZACHARIAH. I'm ignoring you, man. I'm a cheeky one. Peanuts!

MORRIS. You're asking for it, Zach!

ZACHARIAH. I am.

MORRIS. I'm warning you. I will.

ZACHARIAH. Go on.

MORRIS [*with brutality and coarseness*]. Hey, *swartgat!*[9]

[*An immediate reaction from Zachariah. His head whips round. He stares at Morris in disbelief. Morris replies with a weak little laugh, which soon dies on his lips.*]

Just a joke! [*Softly.*] I didn't mean it, Zach. Don't look at me like that! [*A step to Zachariah, who backs away.*] Say something For God's sake, say anything! I'm your brother.

ZACHARIAH [*disbelief*]. My brother?

MORRIS. It's me, Zach, Morris!

ZACHARIAH. Morris?

MORRIS [*at last realizes what has happened. He tears off the jacket and hat in a frenzy.*] Now do you see?

ZACHARIAH. That's funny. I thought … I was looking at a different sort of man.

MORRIS. But don't you see, Zach? It was me! That different sort of man you saw was me. It's happened, man. And I swear I no longer wanted it. That's why I came back. Because … because … I'll tell you the whole truth now … because I did try it! It didn't seem a sin. If a man was born with a chance

at changing why not take it? I thought … thinking of worms lying warm in their silk, to come out one day with wings and things! Why not a man? If his dreams are soft and keep him warm at night, why not stand up the next morning? Different … Beautiful! So what was stopping me? You. There was always you. What sort of thing was that to do to your own flesh and blood brother? Anywhere, any place or road, there was always you, Zach. So I came back. I'm no Judas. Gentle Jesus, I'm no Judas.
[*Pause. The alarm rings. Neither responds.*]

In *The Blood Knot*, the fascination of inter-racial sex is just one theme in a complex and moving play. In *Too Late the Phalarope* by Alan Paton (80) it takes centre stage. His earlier novel, *Cry, the Beloved Country*, made him the first internationally recognised anti-apartheid novelist; later he became president of the non-racial South African Liberal Party. *Phalarope*, published in 1953, is presented as a classical tragedy: the hero brought down by a fatal flaw in his character. The hero is police lieutenant Pieter van Vlaanderen, an upright, rugby-playing, true-blue Afrikaner. His flaw is that, in violation of the mores of his community and Hertzog's 1927 Immorality Act, he cannot resist the temptation to have sex with Stephanie, a struggling, black single-mother. Before surrendering to the temptation, Van Vlaanderen muses about an incident from his university days.

As I sat there my mind went back suddenly, ten, no eleven years, to Stellenbosch. I could see the very room where we were sitting, five or six of us students, Moffie de Bruyn's room, with the old Vierkleur[10] on the wall and the picture of President Kruger. We were talking of South Africa, as we always talked when it was not football or psychology or religion. We were talking of colour and race, and whether such feelings were born in us or made; and Moffie told us the story of the accident in Cape Town, how the car crashed into the telephone box, and how he had gone rushing to help, and just when he got there the door of the car opened and a woman fell backwards into his arms. It nearly knocked him over, but he was able to hold her, and let her gently to the ground. And all the time the light was going off and on in the telephone box. And just when the light went on, he saw it was a Malay woman that he had in his arms, full of jewels and rings and blood. And he could not hold her any more; he let her go in horror, not even gently, he said, and even though a crowd was there. And without a word he pushed through the crowd and went on his way. For the touch of such a person was abhorrent to him, he said, and he did not think it was learned; he thought it was deep down in him, a part of his very nature. And many Afrikaners are the same.

Why Moffie's story should come back to me then I do not know, for I cannot remember that I had ever thought of it all these eleven years. But it came back to me now, and I thought of him, and of all those like him, with a deep envy, and a longing too, that I could have been like that myself.

How we laughed at Moffie's story, partly because of the way he told it, and partly, I suppose, because we were laughing at ourselves. I do not think we were laughing at the Malay woman, nor at the way he let her fall to the ground. And I suppose there was some shame in it too. But I would take the shame, and I would be like that myself, if I could; for to have such horror is to be safe. Therefore I envied him.

So far is Van Vlaanderen from having a horror of touching a non-white woman, he cannot keep his hands off Stephanie. In due course, his 'unspeakable offence' is discovered and a police captain arrives at his father's home to break the bad news. The narrator is Sophie, Van Vlaanderen's aunt, who had long suspected something was wrong.

Then my sister-in-law and I sat down, and my brother asked the captain to sit down also, but he said that he would stand.

– It is a very painful duty I have to perform, he said.

And my brother said in a low voice, perform it then.

– I was in Cape Town, said the captain, when Captain Jooste telephoned me, and asked me to return at once, on a most urgent matter.

– What is the urgent matter?

– The urgent matter, said the captain, is that a charge has been laid against your son, Lieutenant van Vlaanderen, that on Monday night of this week he committed an offence under the Immorality Act of 1927.

And my brother said unbelieving, the Immorality Act?

– Yes.

And my brother said nothing. He was sitting with his arms stretched out before him on the table, as he has them out when the Book is between them, only no book was between them now. He did not look at us nor at the captain but straight before him. And I did not look at my sister-in-law, but I could see her out of the corner of my eye, and she sat without moving. And I sat without moving also, thinking to myself, thinking to myself, but what does it matter what I thought to myself, except that I knew that the whole house was destroyed, because I had not hammered and hammered on the door, and cried out not ceasing. And the captain did not move either, but stood there gravely in front of us all.

Then my brother said, is the charge true?

– I fear it is true, said the captain.

Then my brother said, are you sure it is true?

Then the captain said, that is a matter for a court.

But my brother persisted, are you yourself sure?

And the captain said, he has confessed to me.

After that all was silence, except that my brother's breathing could be heard by us all, like the breathing of some creature in pain. But he did not look at us, he stared in front of him; and my sister-in-law looked down at her hands; and the captain stood like a soldier in front of us all.

Then the sound of my brother's breathing ceased, and he said to me, Sophie, the Book. So I brought him the Book, and put it between his arms, and wondered where he would read; but he did not read at all, he opened it at the beginning where are all the names of the van Vlaanderens, for more than a hundred and fifty years.

Then he said to me, Sophie, the pen and ink.

So he took the pen and ink, and he crossed out the name of Pieter van Vlaanderen from the Book, not once but many times, not with any anger or grief that could be seen, nor with any words.

Then he said to the captain, is there anything more?

Now whether the captain had anything more or not I could not say, but he had seen the crossing out of the name from the Book, and he went to my sister-in-law and took her hands, which she had in her lap not moving, and he said to her, you have my help in anything that you need.

And my brother said, no one will ask help from this house.

The captain looked at him, and then again at my sister-in-law, and he said to her, I'll stand by the boy. Then he looked again at my brother and said to him, I'll stand by the boy.

And my brother said, you will do what you wish, and then he looked at the captain, waiting for him to go. So the captain left us.

I followed the captain, and my brother said to me, lock the door and bolt it, and bring me the key.

I brought him the key, and he said to us, the door shall not be opened again.

Then he said to me, telephone to Buitenverwagting and tell Frans[11] to come at once, alone.

I went to the telephone, and left husband and wife together, and they sat there neither moving nor speaking. When I came back I said, he is coming at once.

– You will take the book, he said, and the pipe, and everything that the man ever gave me, and every likeness of him, and everything in this house that has anything to do with him, and you will burn and destroy them all. And bring me paper to write.

So while I collected together the pipe, and the book of birds, and every likeness of the man, and everything that had ever anything to do with him, he sat and wrote; he wrote to Dominee Stander, and to the Nationalist Party, and to the Farmers' Society, and to every other thing to which he belonged, and gave up all his offices and honours. And while I did the collecting and he did the writing, which took upwards of the hour, the mother of the man, of the child who had first opened the womb, sat with her hands in her lap, not moving, not speaking.

NOTES
1 The traditional London meeting place of missionary and humanitarian societies.
2 Cape Coloured – as distinct from (black) 'native'.
3 Ex-President FW de Klerk felt moved to record in his autobiography that one of his 17th-century ancestors had been the illegitimate daughter of an Indian slave.
4 Front room.
5 i.e. Nagtmaal, the quarterly communion service.
6 The official organ of the Dutch Reformed Church.
7 Their mother.
8 The tin in which they are saving from Zachariah's wages to buy a farm.
9 Afrikaans for black arse – in the context, an electrifying piece of invective.
10 The red, white, blue and green flag of Kruger's South African Republic.
11 The lieutenant's brother.

CHAPTER 12

GOLD AND NATIONALISM

Ever since it was discovered in 1886, gold has ruled South Africa's economy – the country produces half the world's output – influenced its politics, dominated its biggest city's skyline and fired its writers' imagination. One of the most enduring myths concerns 'Kruger's gold', supposedly a three-ton hoard that disappeared in October 1900, when, on the first anniversary of the Boer War, the ageing president fled into exile. Was the gold buried in the national park that today bears his name? Or did he take it with him to Switzerland? The theory that it was simply spirited away to prevent it falling into the hands of the British is the centrepiece of *The Long Silence of Mario Salviati*, a beguiling exercise in magical realism by the Afrikaans novelist, Etienne van Heerden (81), published in 2002. Most of the story is set at the end of the 20th century in Yearsonend, a 'dorp' (small town) in the Great Karoo, where nearly everyone's blood has been mixed by their Bushman, Hottentot, Xhosa, slave, Dutch, Huguenot, Indonesian and Italian ancestors. Looming symbolically over the town is Mount Improbable. (The significance of the children's hands will become clear.)

The black ox-wagon carrying part of the Kruger Millions and five children's hands reached Yearsonend on a quiet Saturday afternoon in 1901. It was the time of the South African war, fought from 1899 to 1902 when Great Britain challenged the two Boer republics in the southernmost region of Africa. The war was, of course, about gold.

The black ox-wagon moved through the country like the Ark of the Covenant: from Pretoria, over the endless plains of the Orange Free State, past Winburg, down towards the Cape Colony, skirting Ficksburg one cold winter when snow lay on the Maluti mountains, and further, over the green hills to East London, to Grahamstown, Port Elizabeth, Graaff-Reinet, Oudtshoorn, Prince Albert …

The wagon loaded with gold groaned forward, mostly at night, but on the open plains where there was no sign of life they'd push on in daylight, through the thirsty land. The small commando consisted of hand-picked scouts, appointed by President Paul Kruger himself the day before he left by train for Lourenco Marques *en route* to Switzerland, where he died on the shores of a lake. Their job until the war was over was to keep on the move and to preserve part of the treasury of the embattled republic as it staggered under the British invasion. Their instructions were never to rest; and to keep moving ahead of rumour, speculation and the enemy.

The ox-wagon was specially reinforced. Trunks were fastened to its base. An old State Bible, signed before his departure by the president himself, lay in the wagon-chest. The salted hands were packed in a sealed lead casket.

The oxen were tough and hardy, selected from the best northern herds, descendants of the stalwart beasts who'd trekked from the Cape Colony, through bloody skirmishes with the Zulus, braving spears, foot-and-mouth disease and marauding lions as they pushed on to the Transvaal, to the gold fields, and to the Highveld's beckoning grasslands where the Boers, hardened and craving independence in Africa, declared their own republic.

The Kruger gold was of the purest, cast into bars and coins stamped with President Paul Kruger's bearded head. The gold reserves were to be kept moving until the president returned from exile; they had to keep trekking from town to town, from friendly farm to loyal community. It didn't matter how far they detoured as long as they kept ahead of the enemy. And if they found a sympathetic ship, they were to use some of the gold to negotiate for the shipping of the children's hands.

They left a trail of rumour and myth behind them, and fabulous tales of the small commando of horsemen with their valuable cargo preceded them, even though everyone along the road who helped them had to swear, on pain of death, to keep silent about the black ox-wagon, which was guarded at night, hidden under bales of lucerne in isolated barns or under thorn-tree branches in lonely dry riverbeds.

Sometimes they had to buy secrecy, because the Cape Colony, in particular, was crawling with turncoats, and loyalists to the Queen. It was a journey of huge risks, along rough tracks, over mountain passes and across swollen rivers. When they arrived in Yearsonend that day in 1901, they were ragged and emaciated, nothing like the heroes they'd become in the legends.

They should have waited until nightfall in the ravines of Mount Improbable, but they'd come to the end of their tether, exhausted from keeping ahead of the British spies. They were sick of the outmanoeuvring, of hiding their tracks, of lies and threats and bribery; they were feverish with loneliness, hunger and longing; sickened by their own misdeeds. They were ready to murder one another; it was a journey marked by strife and dissent.

And they had to find women, desperately. The sole woman with them, astride an ox, had only brought trouble. And that was the one injunction the old president had given them before he heaved his heavy body on to the train: 'Stay away from women, my boys.'

For the first eight months of the journey, they had managed, until that night near Pedi in the Transkei. God have mercy on them, sons of the Republic: that night when the devil seized them.

That was a day that Field Cornet Pistorius, father of Lettie Pistorius, would remember for the rest of his life. The day before, when they had come across the small settlement, had been a disaster. The wagon stuck in a ditch. At dusk, as they battled to get out, one of the oxen broke its leg.

From then on the wagon would have to manage with fewer oxen. The extra ox, which had now lost its yoke fellow, was tied to the back of the wagon with a thong.

Pistorius and Fourie had to kill the crippled ox. They had to slit the beast's throat because a shot in the night would have attracted attention. First they tied him securely to a tree so that he couldn't jerk and then they tried to slash his artery while he bellowed and wrestled against the thongs. Eventually, sickened by the struggle, they hit the artery. As the beast's blood drained away, it sank, bellowing, to its knees, and then keeled over.

As it fell, the thong fastening it to the tree snapped and swiped Pistorius across his shoulders leaving a mark like a whiplash. That was the first task for the woman they called Siela Pedi, after they brought her to the wagon: to rub salve and herbs into that wound, as he lay groaning under her hands.

But before she joined them, while they were butchering the ox – the meat still steaming – one of the other men came up with the idea that before deciding which route they should now follow, they should go and see whether there was life down in the settlement they'd spied out that afternoon.

Perhaps they all knew exactly what lay behind this – for who had not seen the women hoeing in the maize field next to the small houses? The place was somewhere between a Xhosa kraal and a small settlement. The people were clearly not Xhosa – through the binoculars most looked coloured.

Pistorius gave the order that choice pieces of meat be wrapped in tarpaulin. He posted guards round the wagon and, with two gold pounds and two men, he set out for the settlement. They stumbled along, cursing, in the dark and in the distance they could hear a dog barking and people chattering – Afrikaans with snatches of Xhosa.

A heated debate was in progress, and as they approached, they realised that their arrival in the district had been noted and that the argument was about them, about the 'funeral wagon that had come past with Paul Kruger's body', and 'black riders' who were taking the president's body to the Queen of England to show her what the war was doing to the elderly and to beg for her mercy.

As the people chattered on round their fire Pistorius and his two men suddenly appeared. As long as he lived, Pistorius would never forget that scene. One moment it was all lively argument, with dogs lazing by the fire and children playing around the houses, and a group of youngsters romping and giggling a little way from the adults and their beer pots. The next moment there was no one: just fires, ash, empty seats, and a puff of dust in the air.

Only then did Pistorius realise how he and his men must have looked in their tattered black clothes. Their faces were drawn from hardship, from clinging to one grim command, and their clothes were caked with the blood that had spurted from the ox's artery, and with dust that clung to it from the walk.

Only later did he realise that the unsheathed slaughtering knife was still stuck in his belt, and that he'd smeared blood on his face when he'd wiped it after killing the ox. What was more, behind him stood two men carrying bloody chunks of meat on meat hooks. Who wouldn't be scared out of their wits at such a sight?

It took some time to entice the people outside again. Sweet talk and cajoling were necessary; the meat was laid down near the fire; explanations and yet more explanations. And eventually the two gold pounds were tossed with a flourish into the open space between the fire and the thatched huts.

Heads bobbed over windowsills and all eyes were on the coins that lay glittering in the firelight. A dog must have picked up the scent of ox blood, which had smeared from Pistorius' hands on to the coins, and came out of one of the doors to sniff at one. A stone flew from behind a house hitting it in the ribs, so that it ran off yelping.

'The blood on our bodies is from the ox we slaughtered for you,' called Pistorius. 'We aren't murderers, we are soldiers of the Zuid Afrikaansche Republic. And the president is not dead. He's on a ship *en route* to Europe. We come in peace. We are tired. God, can't you see what we look like?'

Siela peeped out first. Yes, it was the future Granny Siela Pedi who, at a tender age, first ventured out. She wasn't particularly beautiful, but radiated curiosity and a spirit of adventure – you could see it the moment she stuck her head round the door. And then she darted outside and scrambled on all fours in the dust to snatch up the coins as quickly as possible. The firelight played over her beautiful legs and strong body and around the mischievous smile she threw the haggard men, and then she was back indoors.

Silence fell. An old man appeared from the door through which Siela disappeared. He doesn't look in much better shape than us, thought Pistorius; a man cured by the sun and this rugged goat country, here on the border where the Xhosa, the Khoi, the San and the white pioneers had come to a stand-off.

'Why do you throw your money at us?' He held the two pounds in his hand.

'We are alone. We need salt. We're tired of eating unseasoned meat. We have travelled far. We're looking for news of the war.'

Pistorius kept quiet for a moment and thought: Is this my voice begging? His men drew up closer behind him. 'We haven't come to hurt you. We could have shot you all long ago if we wanted to. We are seven men with guns.'

There was murmuring in the houses. 'We could have crept up and murdered you tonight.'

Then, one after another, the people emerged. They picked up the meat and hung it on the hooks from a tree branch – before the dogs got at it. Someone began to cut slices and a grid was put over the coals. The old man came up to Pistorius: 'How long have you been on the road, Field Cornet?'

'Eight hard months.'

'And what is on the wagon?'

'This I cannot tell you.'

'We have heard it's the president's body, embalmed.'

'Rubbish.'

'The people also say you're carrying the severed right hands of children who died in the British concentration camps. You're taking the hands to the Queen as proof.'

'That is true,' answered Field Cornet Pistorius, his eyes resting on Siela's breasts as she straightened the grill. 'They are the salted hands of small children who died in the Winburg camp. The world won't believe us when we tell them women and children are dying like flies in Kitchener's concentration camps. We asked five of the mothers each to give up the right hand of her dead child before it was buried. We're taking them to England. The ship is waiting.'

'It's a wagon of doom,' mused the old man, studying Pistorius through narrowed eyes. 'And, with respect, you have the red beard of the devil.'

'We are exhausted,' answered Pistorius. Something in him had died during the trek over the endless plains to the mountain world in which they were now trapped; and still, the knowledge that these eight long months were just the beginning and much hardship lay ahead. At the same time he had no idea of the state of the war, where his men's women and children were, or whether their farms had been razed by the British troops.

The old man looked at him for a while, then offered him beer, and later on a piece of the ox, tenderly grilled. 'We have no salt, sorry,' he said. And then it happened, the thing that started it all. While Pistorius was eating, he saw one of his men reach for his gun. It was an innocent gesture, a soldier pulling his trusty weapon closer. But a woman saw it, read it as the beginning of a massacre, and began to scream. The fellow meant no harm, but as the woman screamed, one of the young men from the settlement produced a battered Mauser from behind a barrel. He was just getting to his feet when one of Pistorius' men shot him in the forehead – a neat red hole. His eyes rolled back and, with a look of surprise and a resigned sigh, he fell face down into the dust.

Pistorius had instinctively drawn and cocked his gun; he and his men had been handpicked because of their lightning-fast reflexes in a tight corner. He summed up the situation instantly: saw that no one was pointing a gun at him and fired a shot into the air.

'Murderers!' screeched the old man. Pistorius grabbed Siela by the arm and jerked her to one side. Carefully he and his men started to retreat, with the woman in front of them. The people, who'd fallen flat when Pistorius fired his shot, lay with their faces in the dust. This wasn't the first time something like this had happened to them, Pistorius realised. Blood dripped slowly into the dust from the meat on the hook.

For William Plomer, too, gold spelled trouble and regret.

Johannesburg

Along the Rand in eighty-five
Fortunes were founded overnight,
And mansions rose among the rocks
To blaze with girls and light;

In champagne baths men sluiced their skins
Grimy with auriferous dust,
Then oiled and scented, fought to enjoy
What young men must;

Took opportunities to cheat,
Or meet the most expensive whore,
And conjured up with cards and dice,
New orgies from new veins of ore;

Greybeards who now look back
To the old days
Find little in their past to blame
And much to praise –

Riding bareback under stars
As lordly anarchs of the veld,
Venison feasts and tribal wars
Free cruelty and a cartridge belt;

Pioneers, O pioneers,
Grey pillars of a Christian State,
Respectability has turned
Swashbuckler prim and scamp sedate;

Prospecting in the brain's recesses
Seek now the nuggets of your prime,
And sift the gold dust of your dreams
From drifted sands of time.

BW Vilakazi (82) was a Zulu poet. Born in rural Natal in 1906, he was the first African lecturer employed by the University of the Witwatersrand – the 'white water reef' where the gold was found. For him, gold represented the pillaging of the fatherland by foreign conquerors and the destruction of traditional Zulu society. It takes more than three tons of ore dug from a depth of as much as 12 000ft to produce a single ounce of gold.

From: **On the Gold Mines**

I've heard it said that down the pits
Are nations upon nations of the Blacks,
And men of these tribes raise the white dunes
That make the angry spirits wonder.
There's a story told about the mine machines
That when they shrieked a small black mouse
Peeped out stunned and in a daze;
It was trapped and turned into a mole,
Burrowed in the earth, and so was seen the gleam of gold.

Yes, these burrowers dug underground
And sent up the towering white dumps.
They rooted deep and the ground heaved higher,
Today outtopping the hill of Isandlwana;
I climb up sweeping the sweat out of my eyes,
And here at the crest I watch the dust-coils
Smoke-white that weave and shift
Below my feet, and under shaded eyes
I see how they blot out the world.

Rumble, machines of the gold mines,
Thunder on, clang louder, deeper,
Deafen with such uproar that we go unheard

Though we may groan forever and cry out
And our bodies' joints be gnawed by you.
Hoot your contempt, old machinery,
You have the laugh on us under our burden;
Unmeasured is your power and terrible,
Going your own way as you will, while we obey.

We yielded and came up from our thatched huts
And were herded here together like yoke-oxen;
We left our dark corn and curds and milk
To be fed instead an alien mess of porridge.
Our family pride is gone, we are children,
The world is clearly turned heels over head.
Wakened up at dawn, stood in a row!
Where have you known of a man once buried
Who sees with both eyes open and stands alive?

Thunder, machines of the gold mines
I am awake, not so sick and tottering
And today I am going underground
To drive a jumper drill into the rock.
You too at the pithead, unaware of me,
You'll see how well I work the jack-hammer
Of the white man down below, and watch
The frame trucks and the cocopans come up
Loaded with white rock and the blue ore.

My brother will plod along carrying a pick
A shovel slung over one shoulder,
And his feet cased in iron-shod boots;
He too will go below following me,
The ground takes us burrowers at a gulp.
If I should die down in the deep levels
What matter? Just who am I anyway?
Day after day, you poor sufferer,
The men drop dead, they keel over while I watch.

Such towers were not here to scale
That time I first went underground,
Still I recall the raw deal that I got.
I thought, I'll pack my goods and get home,
But there – ruins and bare fields struck me.
I scratched my head, went into a hut
And asked: Where is my wife, her parents?
They said: The whiteman called them up to work.
Then I was dumb, my mouth sewn up in silence.

Rumble on engines of the gold mines
Even though distant from the location
Your voice that beats sorely against the soul
How it nags and clatters on my ears
Like bronze bells sounding from far off,
It brings thoughts to me of tall chimneys,
Wealth and the wealthy whom I made rich,
Climbing to the rooms of plenty, while I stay
Squeezed of juice like flesh of a dead ox.

Not so loud there, you machines;
Though whitemen may be without pity
Must you too, made of iron, treat me thus?
Hold off your roaring now in those mines
And listen awhile to what we say to you
Just in case we may be unforgiving
On that fine day which is still to come
When we stand up and say: Things of iron
You are slaves to us, the children of the Blacks.

Be careful, though I go unarmed today
There was a time when from these worn-out arms
Long-bladed spears were flung far and wide
Whose whirling dimmed the whole earth;
They shook the empire of the She Elephant
Thinned out Paul's boers – then I was struck down.
Now I am forever dreaming, child of iron,

That this earth of my forefathers once again
Will be restored to the rightful Black hands.

But today there's no place to lay myself down
Under the shadow of man's affluence.
The soil of my fathers long has lain fallow
And unploughed, at which I sit and stare.
If ever I raised the hard cash to buy
And claim back the ground my forebears owned
This just right is still denied to me.
God above be witness, and you spirits gone,
Can you bring no end to evils such as these?

There in the region of the long-gone dead
Where the countless souls of our race were taken
They say you have an unconquerable power
When you raise up your voice to God
Who disregards the colour of men's skins.
The blood of my veins flows over the earth
Scorched by the sun, clotting and congealed
As I toil on and raise up my prayer to you,
But in reply hear not the smallest sound.

This your fatherland today and yesterday
Is pillaged by the foreign conquerors
Grown rich out of the spoil of nation on nation,
Yet I and this whole line of ours
Who are black are left with nothing of nothing.
We come to the surface and we see the grass
Green to the furthermost rim of sky,
We gaze all about us and call out loud
Wo! But again you do not reply.

Thunder on, engines of the gold mines,
My hands may tremble with the pain,
My feet swell in my boots and stab me,
I have no salve to soothe them for

The whitemen sell their drugs for cash.
Roar on, only stop jarring on my ears,
I have served the white employers well
And now my soul weighs heavily in me.
Run slow, let sleep come to me entranced,
Deep sleep that seals up my eyes
Thinking no longer of tomorrow and the dawn.
Come, release me sleep, to rise far off
Far in the ancient birthplace of my race:
Sleep and dreams from which there is no waking,
Clasped in my vanished people's arms
Under the green hills of the sky.

The destruction of Zulu society is also the theme of Alan Paton's *Cry, the Beloved Country* (83), which was published in 1948. Zululand, under the impact of the government's segregationist policies, has duly become a backward, impoverished, over-crowded reservoir of unskilled, cheap black labour. Stephen Kumalo, an elderly African priest, travels from the remote rural district of Ndotsheni to the booming, sinful city of Johannesburg in search of his son, who went there to look for work and has apparently fallen into bad company. Stephen appeals for help to his brother, John, who has fully adapted to city life and become a successful businessman with political aspirations.

– Is your wife Esther well, my brother? John Kumalo smiled his jolly knowing smile. My wife Esther has left me ten years, my brother.

– And have you married again?

– Well, well, not what the Church calls married, you know. But she is a good woman.

– You wrote nothing of this, brother.

– No, how could I write? You people in Ndotsheni do not understand the way life is in Johannesburg. I thought it better not to write.

– That is why you stopped writing?

– Well, well that could be why I stopped. Trouble, brother, unnecessary trouble.

– But I do not understand. How is life different in Johannesburg?

– Well, that is difficult. Do you mind if I speak in English? I can explain these things better in English.

– Speak in English, then, brother.

– You see I have had an experience here in Johannesburg. It is not like Ndotsheni. One must live here to understand it.

He looked at his brother. Something new is happening here, he said.

He did not sit down, but began to speak in a strange voice. He walked about, and looked through the window into the street, and up at the ceiling, and into the corners of the room as though something were there, and must be brought out.

– Down in Ndotsheni I am nobody, even as you are nobody, my brother. I am subject to the chief, who is an ignorant man. I must salute him and bow to him, but he is an uneducated man. Here in Johannesburg I am a man of some importance, of some influence. I have my own business, and when it is good, I can make ten, twelve pounds a week.

He began to sway to and fro, he was not speaking to them, he was speaking to people who were not there.

– I do not say we are free here. I do not say we are free as men should be. But at least I am free of the chief. At least I am free of an old and ignorant man, who is nothing but a white man's dog. He is a trick, a trick to hold together something that the white man desires to hold together.

He smiled his cunning and knowing smile, and for a moment addressed himself to his visitors.

– But it is not being held together, he said. It is breaking apart, your tribal society. It is here in Johannesburg that the new society is being built. Something is happening here, my brother.

He paused for a moment, then he said, I do not wish to offend you gentlemen, but the Church too is like the chief. You must do so and so and so. You are not free to have an experience. A man must be faithful and meek and obedient, and he must obey the laws, whatever the laws may be. It is true that the Church speaks with a fine voice, and that the Bishops speak against the laws. But this they have been doing for fifty years, and things get worse, not better.

His voice grew louder, and he was again addressing people who were not there. Here in Johannesburg it is the mines, he said, everything is the mines. These high buildings, this wonderful City Hall, this beautiful Parktown with its beautiful houses, all this is built with the gold from the mines. This wonderful hospital for Europeans, the biggest hospital south of the Equator, it is built with the gold from the mines.

There was a change in his voice, it became louder like the voice of a bull or a lion. Go to our hospital, he said, and see our people lying on the floors. They lie so close you cannot step over them. But it is they who dig the gold. For three shillings a day. We come from the Transkei, and from Basutoland, and from Bechuanaland, and from Swaziland, and from Zululand. And from Ndotsheni also. We live in the compounds, we must leave our wives and families behind. And when the new gold is found, it is not we who will get more for our labour. It is the white man's shares that will rise, you will read it in all the papers. They go mad when new gold is found. They bring more of us to live in the compounds, to dig under the ground for three shillings a day. They do not think, here is a chance to pay more for our labour. They think only, here is a chance to build a bigger house and buy a bigger car. It is important to find gold, they say, for all South Africa is built on the mines.

He growled, and his voice grew deep, it was like thunder that was rolling. But it is not built on the mines, he said, it is built on our backs, on our sweat, on our labour. Every factory, every theatre, every beautiful house, they are all built by us. And what does a chief know about that? But here in Johannesburg they know.

He stopped, and was silent. And his visitors were silent also, for there was something in this voice that compelled one to be silent. And Stephen Kumalo sat silent, for this was a new brother that he saw.

By the end of the novel, Kumalo's son has been hanged for murdering a young white man, who, unknown to him, was an anti-apartheid campaigner and the son of Ndotsheni's biggest landowner. The landowner, in tribute to his murdered son, sets about improving the rural Zulus' lot. Having built a dam and a cattle kraal (enclosure), he employs Napoleon Letsitsi, a young black agricultural demonstrator, to teach new ways of farming – and, as it turns out, new ways of thinking.

There was another Napoleon, said Kumalo, who was also a man who did many things. So many things did he do that many books were written about him.

The young demonstrator laughed, but he cast his eyes on the ground, and rubbed his one boot against the other.

– You can be proud, said Kumalo. For there is a new life in this valley. I have been here for many years, but I have never seen ploughing with such spirit.

– There is a new thing happening here, he said. It is not only these rains, though they too refresh the spirit. There is hope here, such as I have never seen before.

– You must not expect too much, said the young man anxiously. I do not expect much this year. The maize will be a little higher, and the harvest a little bigger, but the soil is poor indeed.

– But next year there will be the kraal.

– Yes, said the young man eagerly. We will save much dung in the kraal. They say to me, umfundisi,[1] that even if the winter is cold, they will not burn the dung.

– How long will it be before the trees are ready?

– Many years, said the demonstrator gloomily. Tell me, umfundisi, he said anxiously, do you think they will bear the winter for seven years?

– Have courage, young man. Both the chief and I are working for you.

– I am impatient for the dam, said the demonstrator. When the dam is made, there will be water for the pastures. I tell you, umfundisi, he said excitedly, there will be milk in this valley. It will not be necessary to take the white man's milk.

Kumalo looked at him. Where would we be without the white man's milk? he asked. Where would we be without all that this white man has done for us? Where would you be also? Would you be working for him here?

– It is true I am paid by him, said the young man stubbornly. I am not ungrateful.

– Then you should not speak so, said Kumalo coldly.

There fell a constraint between them, until the young demonstrator said quietly, Umfundisi, I work here with all my heart, is it not so?

– That is true indeed.

– I work so because I work for my country and my people. You must see that, umfundisi. I could not work so for any master.

– If you had no master, you would not be here at all.

– I understand you, said the young man. This man is a good man, and I respect him. But it is not the way it should be done, that is all.

– And what way should it be done?

Not this way, said the young man doggedly.

– What way then?

– Umfundisi, it was the white man who gave us so little land, it was the white man who took us away from the land to go to work. And we were ignorant also. It is all these things together that have made this valley desolate. Therefore, what this good white man does is only a repayment.

– I do not like this talk.

– I understand you, umfundisi, I understand you completely. But let me ask one thing of you.

– Ask it then.

– If this valley were restored, as you are always asking in your prayers, do you think it would hold all the people of this tribe if they all returned?

– I do not know indeed.

But I know, umfundisi. We can restore this valley for those who are here, but when the children grow up, there will again be too many. Some will have to go still.

And Kumalo was silent, having no answer. He sighed. You are too clever for me, he said.

– I am sorry, umfundisi.

– You need not be sorry. I see you have a love for truth.

– I was taught that, umfundisi. It was a white man who taught me. There is not even good farming, he said, without the truth.

– This man was wise.

– It was he also who taught me that we do not work for men, that we work for the land and the people. We do not even work for money, he said.

Kumalo was touched, and he said to the young man, Are there many who think as you do?

– I do not know, umfundisi. I do not know if there are many. But there are some.

He grew excited. We work for Africa, he said, not for this man or that man. Not for a white man or a black man, but for Africa.

– Why do you not say South Africa?

– We would if we could, said the young man soberly.

He reflected for a moment. We speak as we sing, he said, for we sing *Nkosi Sikelel' iAfrika*.[2]

– It is getting dark, said Kumalo, and it is time for us to wash.

– You must not misunderstand me, umfundisi, said the young man earnestly. I am not a man for politics. I am not a man to make trouble in your valley. I desire to restore it, that is all.

– May God give you your desire, said Kumalo with equal earnestness. My son, one word.

– Yes, umfundisi.

– I cannot stop you from thinking your thoughts. It is good that a young man has such deep thoughts. But hate no man, and desire power over no man. For I have a friend who taught me that power corrupts.

– I hate no man, umfundisi. I desire power over none.

– That is well. For there is enough hating in our land already.

The young man went into the house to wash, and Kumalo stood for a moment in the dark, where the stars were coming out over the valley that was to be restored. And that for him was enough, for his life was nearly finished. He was too old for new and disturbing thoughts and they hurt him also, for they struck at many things. Yes, they struck at the grave silent man at High Place, who after such deep hurt, had shown such deep compassion. He was too old for new and disturbing thoughts. A white man's dog, that is what they called him and his kind. Well, that was the way his life had been lived, that was the way he would die.

He turned and followed the young man into the house.

Advanced though it was for its time, Paton's sympathetic portrayal of African nationalism had already been superseded. In *Mine Boy* (84), published four years earlier, Peter Abrahams, a Cape Coloured writer, had looked to a future in which blacks not merely 'did things' for themselves but gave the white man orders. Here Xuma, a 'mine boy' recently arrived from the country, encounters Paddy, his red-haired Irish overseer, in a Johannesburg street.

He carried on up the street and turned down Eloff Street. This was the heart of the city and the crowd was thick. It was difficult to move among all these white people, one had to keep on stepping aside and to watch out for the motor cars that shot past.

Xuma smiled bitterly. The only place where he was completely free was underground in the mines. There he was a master and knew his way. There he did not even fear his white man, for his white man depended on him. He was the boss boy. He gave the orders to the other mine boys. They would do for him what they would not do for his white man or any other white man. He knew that, he had found it out. And underground his white man respected him and asked him for his opinion before they did anything. It was so and he was at home and at ease underground.

His white man had even tried to make friends with him because the other mine boys respected him so much. But a white man and a black man cannot be friends. They work together. That's all. He smiled. He did not want the things of the white man. He did not want to be friends with the white man. Work for him, yes, but that's all. And didn't the others respect him more than they respected Johannes.[3] It was because he did not say baas to the white man but knew how to deal with him.

Then he thought of Eliza again. And the pride vanished from his breast. He had tried to forget her but it was no good. Every day his longing for her grew more and more. But she wanted the things of the white man and for that reason he resented the white man.

'Look Di, there's Zuma!'[4]

Xuma turned. It was his white man. And with him was a woman. And there was laughter in his eyes and a smile on his lips. It was the first time Xuma had seen Paddy laughing.

'Hello, Zuma!'

Paddy held out his hand. Xuma hesitated then shook it. Xuma smiled. The Red One had been drinking. 'This is my girl, Zuma. How is my taste?' Paddy laughed.

Xuma looked at the woman. She smiled at him and gave him her hand. Passing white people stopped and turned. Xuma felt unhappy and wished the Red One would take his woman away. He took the woman's hand. It was small and soft.

'So this is Zuma,' the woman said.

'It begins with an X, dear,' Paddy said.

'The Red One talks about you a lot, Zuma,' she said.

'We are blocking traffic,' Paddy said and took Xuma's arm.

Paddy led him a little way down the street and turned off into a little alley.

'I live here,' Paddy told him.

'Bring him up, Red,' the woman said.

'Good idea!' Paddy exclaimed. 'Come, Zuma, you will eat with us?'

'No,' Xuma said.

'Come on!' Paddy insisted and half pushed him into the lift.

They got out and the woman led the way into the flat.

'This is my home,' Paddy said.

Xuma looked around. He had never seen a place like that before. There was no fire, but it was warm.

'Sit down, Zuma,' the woman said.

Xuma sat on the edge of the chair. The woman took off her coat and went into another room. Paddy stretched himself on a settee and smiled at Xuma.

The woman came in with three glasses.

'This will warm you,' she said, giving Xuma one.

Paddy raised his glass.

'To the best mine boy, Zuma!'

'To Zuma,' the woman said and smiled at him.

Paddy and Di emptied their glasses. Xuma sat holding his. He could still feel the woman's hand in his. It was so small and soft. And she was very good to look at but he didn't want to look at her.

'Drink yours, Zuma,' she said.

The wine warmed Xuma. She took the empty glass from him and turned on the radio.

'Everything is ready,' she said to Paddy. 'Put it on the trolley and bring it in.'

Paddy went out.

Xuma thought: now I understand what Eliza wants. But these things are only for white people. It is foolish to think we can get them.

He looked round the room. Yes, it was fine. Carpets on the floor, books, radio. Beautiful things everywhere. Fine, all fine, but all the white man's things. And all foolishness to want the white man's things. To drink wine and keep the bottle on the table without fear of the police, how could a black person do it. And how could Eliza be like this white woman of the Red One.

Di followed his gaze round the room.

'Do you like it?'

'Heh?' He looked startled.

'I mean the room,' she said.

'It is fine,' he said and looked at her.

Her eyes looked kindly at him and dimples appeared on her cheeks when she smiled. Just like Eliza's dimples. And it seemed that her eyes understood what he was thinking. He looked away from her.

'The Red One wants you to be his friend,' she said.

Again Xuma looked at her. And again it seemed that she understood everything that went on in his mind. And as he watched her a smile slowly broke over her face.

'He is white,' Xuma said.

The smile faded from her face and there was sadness in her eyes.

And suddenly Xuma felt sorry for her and was surprised at himself for feeling sorry for a white person. And there was no reason for it either.

'And so you cannot be friends,' she said, and in her eyes was the same look he had seen many times in the eyes of the Red One.

Paddy came in with the food. Xuma felt ill at ease. But Paddy and Di talked and did not notice him, and soon he forgot his discomfort and ate.

When they had finished eating they drank more wine. And Xuma and Paddy talked about the mines and the funny things that happened there and soon they were all laughing. And in spots Xuma forgot that they were white and even spoke to the woman. Then Paddy took the things away.

Xuma looked at the woman and suddenly wanted to tell her about Eliza. But he didn't know how to begin. She gave him a cigarette and smoked one herself. Eliza smoked too. Xuma looked at Di and smiled.

'What are you smiling at?'

'My girl smokes too.'

'What's wrong with that?'

Xuma was silent.

'What is she called?'

'Eliza.' He wanted to tell her then, but the words would not come.

'Tell me,' Di said.

'What?'

'What you want to tell me. The Red One will be back soon and I know you don't want him to hear.'

'You know everything.'

'No. But I know this. Tell me.'

Xuma stared at her. She met his stare and smiled.

'You are a good one,' he said.

'Thank you. I'm your friend. Tell me.'

'She's a teacher and she wants to be like white people. She wants a place like this place and clothes like yours and she wants to do the things you do. It is all foolishness for she is not white. But she cannot help herself and it makes her unhappy sometimes.'

'And you?'

'It makes me unhappy too, for she wants me and she does not want me. But it is foolishness.'

'It is not foolishness, Zuma.'

'She cannot have your things.'

'But is not the heart the same, Zuma?'

'No. I care only for my people.'

'No, Zuma.'

'But it is so and where is the good in wishing.'

'Listen, Zuma. I am white and your girl is black, but inside we are the same. She wants the things I want and I want the things she wants. Eliza and I are the same inside, truly, Zuma.'

'But it cannot be.'

'It is so, Zuma, we are the same inside. A black girl and a white girl, but the same inside.'

'The same?'

'The same.'

'But it is wrong.'

'It is right, Zuma, I know.'

'No!'

'Yes!'

'It cannot be. You are good, but it cannot be.'

'It is. You do not believe me but it is so …'

Paddy came in. Xuma looked at Di then got up.

'I must go,' he said.

'Not yet, Zuma,' Paddy said, 'it is early still.'

'All right, Zuma,' Di said.

Paddy looked at Di then at Xuma and smiled.

'Do you like my woman?'

Xuma smiled. 'She's a good one, and you are lucky, Red One.'

'I will take you down,' Paddy said.

Di took Xuma's hand and smiled into his eyes.

'I am right.'

'Maybe. But I don't think so.'

He followed Paddy to the lift.

★ ★ ★

Paddy returned and slowly shut the door behind him. Di watched him. He went to the settee and pulled her down beside him. He slipped his arm round her shoulder and they sat like that for a while.

'What do you think of him,' he asked finally.

'What is there to think? … He's just a mine boy.'

'He's a grand fellow.'

'Yes. Grand, but not a human being yet. Just a mine boy. His girl's human and he can't understand her. He can't understand her wanting the things I want and have. And another thing you're wrong about – he does not dislike you, you're just not of the same world, Red.'

'That's nonsense, Di.'

'Think it out for yourself.'

'That fellow's as human as I am.'

'No, Red, he accepts what you wouldn't. That's part of the reason why he's so popular among all the other whites. He's all right. You can't say the same about Chris's boy.'

'I think you are wrong, Di.'

She smiled bitterly and looked at him.

'Yes, I know, Red. A man's a man for a' that. A man's a man to the extent that he asserts himself. There's no assertion in your mine boy. There is confusion and bewilderment and acceptance. Nothing more. Oh, he's human all right; he talks, he eats, he feels, he thinks, he gets lonely; but that's all.'

'He has dignity and pride.'

'So has an animal, Red. You've got this all wrong. The man in your Zuma has not come out yet, so he looks beautiful and strong and perfect and has dignity, so you say that is your future native. That is not true.'

Paddy looked at her. His face clouded. They were silent for a very long time. Di got up and went into the kitchen.

'You make it very difficult, Di,' Paddy called out. 'You make it sound as though there's no hope anywhere.'

Di laughed and her voice was sweet.

'Never again will I take up with an Irishman,' she said. 'One moment you are at one extreme and the next you are at the other.'

'Be serious, Di.'

There was a pause from the kitchen. He waited. Then her voice came to him. It was slow and hesitant and yet very matter-of-fact.

'So many of the people who consider themselves progressive have their own weird notions about the native, but they all have one thing in common. They want to decide who the good native is and they want to do good things for him. You know what I mean. They want to lead him. To tell him what to do. They want to think for him and he must accept their thoughts. And they like him to depend on them. Your Zuma makes an excellent "good native" for progressive folk. That's why you like him.'

'That's not true, Di. And I think you're being unfair.'

'I'm sorry, Red, but I honestly believe that.'

'In any case your little theory holds no water with Zuma. He is unfriendly towards me.'

'Yes, that's the one snag, but it doesn't prove anything. And beside, he's not being unfriendly towards you; you two just belong to different worlds. But the whole point is that a native who wants the things the whites have is suspect if he does not apply to them for leadership.'

Di came back into the room and they sat facing each other.

'So?'

'So nothing.'

'That leaves a pretty hopeless position for your hypothetical progressives.'

'Yes, until they accept the fact that the natives can lead; not only themselves but the whites as well.'

But that was still nearly 50 years in the future. Meanwhile, 1948 was another watershed in South Africa's history. It was the year that Smuts, despite all his efforts to satisfy the demands of a racist white electorate, was again defeated by the right-wing National Party, just as he had been in 1924. This time, the party was led by the fanatical Afrikaner nationalist, Daniel Francois Malan. He spent the Boer War years studying divinity in Holland, became a minister of the Dutch Reformed Church and edited an Afrikaans newspaper. His government lost no time in passing a slew of laws that created what came to be known as Grand Apartheid. In essence, they merely reinforced the segregationist structure that Smuts and Hertzog had erected on the foundations laid by Rhodes and Milner 50 years earlier. The *Population Registration Act* divided people into four groups, European, African, Cape Coloured and Asiatic; the *Group Areas Act* decreed where each should – and should not – live; the *Urban Areas Act* defined where Africans needed written permission to be; various employment Acts reserved the best-paid jobs for whites; the *Bantu Education Act* ensured that Africans would for ever receive an inferior education appropriate to their divinely-assigned station in life[5]; the *Reservation of Separate Amenities Act* barred non-whites from white hotels, cinemas, theatres, lavatories, cemeteries and lifts and prevented 'Europeans' and 'Non-Europeans' from travelling, eating, drinking, playing sports, bathing, standing in queues or sitting in parks together; and the *Immorality* and *Prohibition of Mixed Marriages Acts* sought anew to keep them out of each other's beds. Although most of this, if not already legislated for, had become custom and practice under Hertzog and Smuts, the determination with which apartheid was now enforced meant it bore down more brutally on non-whites than ever before.

In *My Traitor's Heart* (85), published in 1990, by when apartheid was in its death throes, Rian Malan was moved to reflect on his forebears' contribution to South African history.

I'm burned out and starving to death, so I'm just going to lay this all upon you and trust that you're a visionary reader, because the grand design, such as it is, is going to be hard for you to see. I know you're interested in my ancestors, so I guess I should begin at the very beginning. I am a Malan, descendant of Jacques Malan, a Huguenot who fled the France of Louis XIV to escape being put to the sword for his Protestant faith. He sought refuge among the Dutch, only to be put aboard ship in 1688 and sent to the Dark Continent, to the rude Dutch colony at the Cape of Good Hope. Jacques the Huguenot was the first Malan in Africa. In the centuries since, a Malan has been present at all the great dramas and turning points in the history of the Afrikaner tribe.

Jacques tamed the Cape and planted vineyards. His sons built gracious gabled homesteads in the lee of Table Mountain. His grandson Dawid the Younger ran off to the wild frontier in 1788, where he fought the savage Xhosa and took part in Slagtersnek, the first Afrikaner rebellion against the British.

Hercules, son of Dawid the Younger, led the third wave of Voortrekkers into the heart of Africa. In February 1838 he sat in the kraal of the great king Dingaan, watching a huge Zulu army wheeling back and forth on the plain. The sun glinted off thousands of spears. Feet thundered in unison. Clouds of dust rose into the sky. And then Dingaan cried, 'Kill the wizards,' and Hercules and his seventy companions were murdered – stakes driven up their anuses, skulls smashed with stones, and their bodies left on a hill for the vultures.

Once the killing was done, King Dingaan pointed, and his army set off for the north at a run. They ran all day and most of the night, and it was still dark when they fell on the main Trekker party. The attack was unexpected. Men were disembowelled, women mutilated, and the brains of small children dashed out on wagon wheels. In all, 530 Trekkers died that dawn, in a place we still call Weenen – the Place of Weeping.

In the aftermath, the survivors drew their wagons into a circle on the bank of a nameless river and made ready for the final battle. On its eve, they laid hands on the Bible and swore a covenant with Jehovah: If he granted them victory over the heathen, they would hold true to his ways forever. A Malan was there – Jacob Jacobus Malan, brother of the fallen Hercules. As the sun rose on December 16, he saw something amazing: rank upon rank of Zulu warriors sitting silently on their haunches, waiting for the mist to rise. Two hours later, the river was red with black blood, and it was no longer nameless: It was Blood River. Mountains of Zulus lay dead on the battlefield, but not a single Boer was slain. It was surely a miracle, a sign that God's will was ours.

So we remember Jacob Jacobus Malan and still honour his solemn covenant. We also remember his sons Jacobus and Hercules, who survived the Zulu wars, dragged their covered wagons over the mountains, and smashed the black tribes on the high plain. There, on conquered land, they established Boer republics, where white men were free to rule blacks in accord with their stern Jehovistic covenant.

In 1881, Hercules Malan the second sat on an African hilltop watching another seminal event in the white tribe's bloody saga – the Battle of Majuba, turning point in our first war against the British. Kommandant Malan's soldiers were an undisciplined rabble of farm boys and greybeards, but they could drop a buck at a thousand yards, and every bullet counted. The redcoats were annihilated, and the British retired to lick their wounds. A few years later, however, gold was discovered on our land, and they came after us in earnest. In that next war – the Second War of Freedom – our forces were outnumbered nine to one. The largest army yet assembled on the planet rolled across our frontiers and occupied our towns. We fought on, though. A Malan was there, too: General Wynand Malan, the bravest of the brave, leader of a guerrilla band that ranged deep into enemy territory. To crush our resistance, the British scorched the earth and put Afrikaner women and children in concentration camps, but General Malan fought on to the bittersweet end, taking a bullet on the war's very last day.

In the aftermath, we became a backward peasantry, despised by our British bosses and betters. But we rose again, with yet another Malan at the fore – Daniel Francois Malan. His Afrikaner National Party came to power in 1948, vowing to throw off the imperial British yoke and devise a final solution for the 'native question'. This final solution was apartheid, a gridlock of more than a hundred laws designed to keep blacks and whites forever separate and to ensure, not at all coincidentally, that blacks remained in their God-ordained place, hewers of wood and drawers of water, forever and ever.

This fate was unacceptable to blacks, so they rose against us in earnest in 1976, in a rebellion that has never really ceased since. In this era, too, the destiny of the tribe is in the hands of a Malan – General Magnus Malan, minister of defence. There are those who say it is he who truly controls the country, through the awesome power of the white military establishment. In these troubled times, the name Malan is often heard on the lips of black comrades, in the chanted litany of those who will die when the day comes. I see them at the township rallies, thousands upon thousands of them, running to and fro in tight formation. Their feet thunder in unison. Their faces glisten with sweat and excitement. Dust rises. They cradle imaginary AK-47s in their arms, and chant, '*Voetsek*, Malan!' Fuck off, Malan! Fuck off! Fuck off! And then they wheel in formation and thunder away to the far side of some dusty township stadium, leaving me poised there on a cusp of history.

History, of course, is written by the conquerors. Bloke Modisane (86), a black journalist, recalled how he was taught it in the 1930s at school in Sophiatown, then an African suburb of Johannesburg.

South African history was amusing, we sat motionless, angelically attentive, whilst the history teacher recounted – as documented – the wars of the Boers against the 'savage and barbaric black hordes' for the dark interior of Africa; the ancestral heroes of our fathers, the great chiefs which our parents told stories about, were in class described as bloodthirsty animal brutes; Tshaka, the brilliant general who welded the Mnguni tribelets into a unified and powerful Zulu nation, the greatest war machine in South African history, was described as a psychopath. A group of us confronted our teacher.

'My lessons come from the history books,' he said, 'and if you want to pass exams you must reproduce the history lesson, straight from the book if you like.'

'What's the truth?' I said.

'That you must learn for yourself,' he said. 'This is only a historical phase, the situation may be reversed tomorrow and the history may have to be rewritten.'

'How did it happen?' I said. 'Why?'

'Your history lessons may answer that.'

Left: Lord (Alfred) Milner, ardent Imperialist and white supremacist, appointed I ligh Commissioner for South Africa in 1897. He helped to provoke the Boer War and lay the foundations of apartheid. [MUSEUMAFRICA]

Below left: Spion Kop, 24 January 1900 – 'the acre of massacre'. In the most tragically futile battle of the Boer War, British troops seized and then abandoned a hill barring the way to the relief of Ladysmith; 350 of them died and 75 Boers; more than 1 000 were wounded. [MUSEUMAFRICA]

Above: Winston Churchill, then a 24-year-old war correspondent, standing alone on the right with British soldiers captured by the Boers in the first month of the war. He soon escaped, returned to Natal and climbed Spion Kop on the night after the battle. [MUSEUMAFRICA]

Left: Mahatma Gandhi (circled), pacifist, civil rights lawyer and architect of Indian independence, arrived in Natal in 1893 aged 24 and stayed for 21 years. On the outbreak of the Boer War, he helped form an ambulance corps and was present at the Battle of Spion Kop. [MUSEUMAFRICA]

Top: One of 30 000 Boer farmhouses burned by British troops after the Boers, the capitals of their two republics having been captured, turned to guerrilla warfare in June 1900. [MuseumAfrica]

Above: One of more than 100 civilian concentration camps – all poorly provisioned and criminally insanitary – set up by Lord Kitchener, the British commander-in-chief and a notably pitiless soldier. Some 42 000 died, the great majority of them children. [MuseumAfrica]

Left: Emily Hobhouse, a determined, fearless and politically well-connected philanthropist, was the first to draw British public attention to the scandal of the concentration camps. She is still revered by Afrikaners. [Anglo-Boer War Museum, Bloemfontein]

Left: The death mask of Cecil Rhodes, whose reputed last words aged 48 were 'So little done, so much to do'. Charismatic and ruthless, he made a fortune from diamonds and gold, seized what became Zimbabwe and Zambia for the British Empire and dreamed of extending it from Cape to Cairo. [MuseumAfrica]

Right: 'Sophiatown 1956': a potent image of anti-apartheid resistance. The township, near Johannesburg, was one of the few where Africans could own their own homes – an 'anomaly' for the white Nationalist Government, which bulldozed it out of existence. [Jurgen Schadeberg]

Below: In January 1984 the ANC called for a 'people's war' to make South Africa ungovernable. Soon, a nationwide campaign of boycotts, strikes and violent resistance was under way. The Government's efforts to crush it – as, for example, at Katlehong, south of Johannesburg, in March 1985 – became increasingly desperate. In July 1985 a state of emergency was declared. It was to remain in force throughout apartheid's last years. [Drum Social Histories / Baileys African History Archive / Africa Media Online]

Above: 11 February 1990: Nelson Mandela – his then-wife, Winnie, by his side – walks free after 27 years as a prisoner of apartheid. Four years later, he became president of South Africa's first democratically elected government. [Gallo Images]

Below: Within sight of Table Mountain and one of the most affluent cities in Africa, Khayelitsha, an 'informal settlement' built mostly of corrugated iron, plastic sheeting and cardboard, is home to one-and-a-half million people. [Don Boroughs / PictureNET Africa]

The question has not been fully answered, but the history revealed that truth may have a double morality standard; the white man petitioned history to argue his cause and state his case, to represent the truth as he saw it; he invoked the aid and the blessing of God in subjugating the black man and dispossessing him of the land. It was impossible to understand history, it showed a truth I could not accept, so I learned my history of South Africa like a parrot, I reproduced the adjectives describing African chiefs, and for external examinations I added a few of my own adjectives to flatter the white examiners.

The Malans were bound together not only by a shared understanding of history but by their attachment to the Afrikaans language. By the end of the 18th century, the High Dutch of the early settlers had been so radically simplified by barely literate speakers that it had become a separate language, known as Cape Dutch or 'the Taal' or, more vulgarly, 'kitchen Dutch'. But although – or, perhaps, because – it was the *lingua franca* of the Boers and their servants, Afrikaans was looked down on by most educated Afrikaners. It had virtually no literature before 1900, it was not granted official status until 1925 and an Afrikaans translation of the Bible did not appear until 1933. It was in Dutch that the nationalism of the Boer republics expressed itself; Dutch was the language that Milner, the Imperialist High Commissioner, wanted to stamp out; and it was Dutch that, despite Milner's efforts, was given equal status with English in the 1910 Act of Union. Milner explained his prejudice in a letter to a colleague in November 1900.

There was a time when I leaned to greater equality of language, but when I see how Dutch is being worked in this Colony purely as a political engine, and how openly the rebel party declares its intention of playing the same game in the Republics, I feel that it is useless to give Dutch a position which will only be abused. What weighs with me greatly is the gross inequality, which I see daily illustrated at the Cape, of requiring all persons desiring to enter the public service to be able to speak and write both languages. To teach a Dutch child English is to teach him something of the greatest possible value to him, and which he would have to learn in any case if he wanted to get on in life in any other line except the most backward forms of agriculture. To teach an English child High Dutch is pure waste of time. It is a very difficult language, which is absolutely useless to him except for its artificial use in official business, into which it has been introduced with a political object – the promotion of Africanderdom. For ordinary life and intercourse with the common people it is no good at all, as the 'taal' is really almost a different language, and you might as well compel people to learn Chaucer in order to carry on business at the East End. High Dutch is simply kept up in opposition to English, and the only object of making Englishmen learn it is to make them pass under the Africander yoke. My policy would be to make English indispensable in the future, and to prepare the rising generation for that state of affairs by practically compelling them to learn it, but to admit Dutch until the Anglicizing process is consummated, in order to meet the necessities of the existing non-English speaking Boers, and to prevent them feeling themselves prejudiced by being unable to express their wants or assert their rights in the only language they know.

But the Anglicizing process was not to be completed and it was in Afrikaans that the Boers – the Afrikaners – were to express their wants and, increasingly, their rights. Soon, Afrikaans – in the mouths of white people, at least (it was always spoken by more Coloureds than whites) – became the language of apartheid, of brutality and oppression, wielded by its users 'like a club against their enemies'. The analogy is from *Boyhood* (87) by JM Coetzee, South Africa's greatest novelist, who won the Nobel Prize for Literature in 2003. In this memoir, published in 1997, of growing up in a mixed English-Afrikaans home, he writes of himself in the third person.

Because they speak English at home, because he always comes first in English at school, he thinks of himself as English. Though his surname is Afrikaans, though his father is more Afrikaans than English, though he himself speaks Afrikaans without any English accent, he could not pass for a moment as an Afrikaner. The range of Afrikaans he commands is thin and bodiless; there is a whole dense world of slang and allusion commanded by real Afrikaans boys – of which obscenity is only a part – to which he has no access.

There is a manner that Afrikaners have in common too – a surliness, an intransigence, and, not far behind it, a threat of physical force (he thinks of them as rhinoceroses, huge, lumbering, strong-sinewed, thudding against each other as they pass) – that he does not share and in fact shrinks from. They wield their language like a club against their enemies. On the streets it is best to avoid groups of them; even singly they have a truculent, menacing air. Sometimes when the classes line up in the quadrangle in the mornings he scans the ranks of Afrikaans boys looking for someone who is different, who has a touch of softness; but there is no one. It is unthinkable that he should ever be cast among them: they would crush him, kill the spirit in him.

Yet, to his surprise, he finds himself unwilling to yield up the Afrikaans language to them. He remembers his very first visit to Voelfontein, when he was four or five and could not speak Afrikaans at all. His brother was still a baby, kept indoors out of the sun; there was no one to play with but the Coloured children. With them he made boats out of seed-pods and floated them down the irrigation furrows. But he was like a mute creature: everything had to be mimed; at times he felt he was going to burst with the things he could not say. Then suddenly one day he opened his mouth and found he could speak, speak easily and fluently and without stopping to think. He still remembers how he burst in on his mother, shouting 'Listen! I can speak Afrikaans!'

When he speaks Afrikaans all the complications of life seem suddenly to fall away. Afrikaans is like a ghostly envelope that accompanies him everywhere, that he is free to slip into, becoming at once another person, simpler, gayer, lighter in his tread.

One thing about the English that disappoints him, that he will not imitate, is their contempt for Afrikaans. When they lift their eyebrows and superciliously mispronounce Afrikaans words, as if *veld* spoken with a *v* were the sign of a gentleman, he draws back from them: they are wrong, and, worse than wrong, comical. For his part, he makes no concessions, even among the English: he brings out the Afrikaans words as they ought to be brought out, with all their hard consonants and difficult vowels.

In his class there are several boys besides himself with Afrikaans surnames. In the Afrikaans classes, on the other hand, there are no boys with English surnames. In the senior school he knows of one Afrikaans Smith who might as well be a Smit; that is all. It is a pity, but understandable: what Englishman would want to marry an Afrikaans woman and have an Afrikaans family when Afrikaans women are either huge and fat, with puffed-out breasts and bullfrog necks, or bony and misshapen?

He thanks God that his mother speaks English. But he remains mistrustful of his father, despite Shakespeare and Wordsworth and the *Cape Times* crossword puzzle. He does not see why his father goes on making the effort to be English here in Worcester, where it would be so easy for him to slide back into being Afrikaans. The childhood in Prince Albert that he hears his father joking about with his brothers strikes him as no different from an Afrikaans life in Worcester. It centres just as much on being beaten and on nakedness, on body functions performed in front of other boys, on an animal indifference to privacy.

The thought of being turned into an Afrikaans boy, with shaven head and no shoes, makes him quail. It is like being sent to prison, to a life without privacy. He cannot live without privacy. If he were Afrikaans he would have to live every minute of every day and night in the company of others. It is a prospect he cannot bear.

NOTES

1 A term of respect.
2 God bless Africa – the anthem of the ANC.
3 A more experienced 'boss boy'.
4 Xuma is 'Zuma' when the white man pronounces it because the X represents a click sound.
5 'The Natives will be taught from childhood that equality with Europeans is not for them … There is no place for the Bantu child above the level of certain forms of labour' – Dr Hendrik Verwoerd, Minister of Education, 1953.

CHAPTER 13

FIGHTING FOR FREEDOM

Having been denied any say in the unification of South Africa, black activists responded in 1912 by setting up a national organisation of their own. Its aim was to unite Africans around a demand for 'equal rights and justice' and it became the African National Congress (ANC). For its first 30 years, it was a conservative, self-consciously 'respectable' and largely moribund body. Then in 1943, a small group of well-educated young men decided it was time to breathe life into it. Sharing a conviction that the answer to white supremacy was militant African nationalism, they formed a Youth League 'to give direction to the ANC', as they delicately put it, 'in its quest for political freedom'. Among them were Oliver Tambo and Nelson Mandela, both graduates of Fort Hare, the oldest black university in Southern Africa, and both then in their mid-twenties. The Afrikaner nationalists' victory in 1948 gave them the spur they needed, as Nelson Mandela (88) later recorded.

Africans could not vote, but that did not mean that we did not care who won elections. In the white general election of 1948, the ruling United Party, led by General Smuts, then at the height of his international regard, opposed the revived National Party. While Smuts had enlisted South Africa on the side of the Allies in the Second World War, the National Party refused to support Great Britain and publicly sympathized with Nazi Germany. The National Party's campaign centred on the *'swart gevaar'* (the 'black danger'), and they fought the election on the twin slogans of *'Die kaffer op sy plek'* ('the nigger in his place') and *'Die koelies uit die land'* ('the coolies out of the country') – coolies being the Afrikaner's derogatory term for Indians.

The Nationalists, led by Dr Daniel Malan, a former minister of the Dutch Reformed Church and a newspaper editor, were a party animated by bitterness – bitterness towards the English, who had treated them as inferiors for decades, and bitterness towards the African, who the Nationalists believed was threatening the prosperity and purity of Afrikaner culture. Africans had no loyalty to General Smuts, but we had even less for the National Party.

Malan's platform was known as apartheid. Apartheid was a new term but an old idea. It literally means 'apartness', and it represented the codification in one oppressive system of all the laws and regulations that had kept Africans in an inferior position to whites for centuries. What had been more or less *de facto* was to become relentlessly *de jure*. The often haphazard segregation of the past three hundred years was to be consolidated into a monolithic system that was diabolical in its detail, inescapable in its reach and overwhelming in its power. The premise of apartheid was that whites were superior to Africans, Coloureds and Indians, and the function of it was to entrench white supremacy for ever. As the Nationalists put it, *'Die wit man moet altyd baas wees'* ('The white man must always remain boss'). Their platform rested on the term: *baasskap*, literally 'boss-ship', a loaded word that stood for white supremacy in all its harshness. The policy was supported by the Dutch Reformed Church, which furnished apartheid with its religious underpinnings by suggesting that Afrikaners were God's chosen people and that blacks were a subservient species. In the Afrikaner's world view, apartheid and the church went hand in hand.

The Nationalists' victory was the beginning of the end of the domination of the Afrikaner by the Englishman. English would now take second place to Afrikaans as an official language. The Nationalists' slogan encapsulated their mission: *'Eie volk, eie taal, eie land'* – 'Our own people, our own language, our own land'. In the distorted cosmology of the Afrikaner, the Nationalist victory was like the Israelites' journey to the Promised Land. This was the fulfilment of God's promise, and the justification for their view that South Africa should be a white man's country for ever.

The victory was a shock. The United Party and General Smuts had beaten the Nazis, and surely they would defeat the National Party. On election day, I attended a meeting in Johannesburg with Oliver Tambo and several others. We barely discussed the question of a Nationalist government because we did not expect one. The meeting went on all night, and we emerged at dawn and found a newspaper stall selling the *Rand Daily Mail*: the Nationalists had triumphed. I was stunned and dismayed, but Oliver took a more considered line. 'I like this,' he said. 'I like this.' I could not imagine why. He explained, 'Now we will know exactly who our enemies are and where we stand.'

Bloke Modisane was one of a generation of gifted black journalists fostered by *Drum* magazine, which published their dramatic exposés of apartheid throughout the pre-censorship 1950s. For him, the new order was an assault on human dignity.

I am not suggesting there was no prejudice prior to the South Africa of 1948, but it was around then that the white man in South Africa decided to recognise the portentous presence of the black peril threatening his existence as a white man; it was that moment in history when he decided to rally round the flag of apartheid in defence of Christian principles, democratic ideals and Western civilization; the black peril was made to become synonymous with Communist infiltration.

Whilst the freedom-loving nations of the world, including the Government of South Africa, deliberated in New York to entrench the rights of man, to reaffirm for all time the dignity of man and to banish from the face of the earth the Hiroshima of wars, one single word was invading the imagination of South Africa; and whilst the free-world nations were smacking their lips over the eloquence of the Declaration of Human Rights, one word – with no specific dictionary meaning – changed the South African scene overnight, and won the general election for the Nationalist Party; one word, three-syllabled, charged with an emotional intensity which suited the general temper of white South Africa; a one-word ideology which inflated the political life of Dr Daniel Francois Malan and punctured that of General Jan Christian Smuts, and unleashed the race monster of our age.

Apartheid, the one-word onslaught on the human dignity which the men in New York were so lyrical over, became a parliamentary joke the opposition members of the United Party made undergraduate witticisms about, whilst it entrenched white supremacy and relegated the Native to his place; and as they did this the non-white races were dehumanised and defaced. The pigeon-hole philosophy of apartheid manifested itself when the segregation notices went up everywhere, particularly in Johannesburg: 'Europeans Only' and 'Non-European', but I noticed a peculiar – if not subtle – omission of the 'only' on the Non-European signs.

I was soon to find myself being forced – by the letter of the law – to use separate entrances into the post offices, banks, railway stations, public buildings; it became a criminal offence for me to use the amenities set aside for the whites, who were either indifferent or satisfied with this arrangement. There was no massive white indignation at this insult on the dignity of the black races. I found myself unable to use the Eloff Street entrance into Park Station, a habit I had cultivated over the years; I became resentful, it was a pleasing-to-the-eye entrance, there were flower-beds, a water fountain and other details I have not seen for so long that I have forgotten them; and, of course, the Non-European entrance, then still under construction, was dismal and bleak, and because I have been educated into an acceptance of the primacy of law and order I accommodated, rather than defied, this effrontery. Everywhere I turned there were these prohibitions taunting me, defying my manhood with their arrogance, their challenge was driving me out of my mind; but I am only a man, afraid and apprehensive, perhaps even a coward. I should have walked past the notices and registered, to myself, a protest against that which offended my manhood, but I was afraid to go to prison, rationalising that it would have been a futile gesture. Dear, dear God.

It got to a point where I became insensitive to the oppression around me; I accommodated the carrying of a Pass because it was the law; I sweated in the black igloo that was Sophiatown because it was the law; I walked through the 'Non-European' entrance, used the 'Natives and Goods' lifts, jogged from foot to foot at the 'Native Counter' in the banks and post offices, waited patiently for the green 'For Coloured Persons' buses; I permitted my labour to be exploited, accepted the discrimination against my colour, cowered under the will of the Immorality Act of 1957, which lays down that sexual acts between black and white are illegal, un-Christian and immoral, and was instead excited by the juvenile satisfaction of outsmarting the law by mating illegally, drinking behind locked doors. All these I did because I respected the law, because I was law-abiding. In the name of law and order I accommodated a variety of humiliations. I permitted sidewalk bullies to push me about, to poke their fingers into my nostrils, spitting insults into my eyes, and because I had arranged myself under the will of the law I permitted other men – armed by the letter of the law and under the protection of the law – to castrate me.

Of course, there was nothing new about humiliation and sidewalk bullies. In his autobiography, *Down Second Avenue* (89), Ezekiel Mphahlele, another *Drum* writer, recalled growing up in Pretoria in the 1930s.

I came to learn the hard way that one had to keep out of the white man's way. There was enough hardship in my home without deliberately waiting to absorb the cruder impacts from our surroundings. So if a group of whites walked, as they invariably did, abreast of one another on pavements, we gave way. In a sense we were happy enough that we could visit public places like the Museum, the Zoo, the Union Buildings and so on, on certain days only, when the whites would not be there as well. We Blacks were not even tolerated near the fence of a park. Such places were foreign to us, and so we loved to stand with our faces pressed against the wire fence, to admire and envy white children playing on swings and 'horses'. To us they were performing a feat, and we often shouted to congratulate them on their antics. When we were barked away by the white caretaker, I hated him, and hated the children and envied them.

But whites who liked to could enter public places on days set aside for Blacks: usually week-days and Sunday mornings, up to 12 noon. A couple were sitting near each other under a tree on a day the Foxes had decided to raid the Zoo. The couple spoke Afrikaans. Danie, Ratau and I stopped to watch a monkey on a tricycle. 'Ag, don't, Blikkies!' the white girl said, laughing hysterically. We cast furtive glances to see what was happening. It was evident that the man Blikkies was not very sober. He sat with his legs folded under him. The girl was on her knees, putting her hair in order. Her face was flushed up to the ears. Blikkies took her into his arms, laid her on her stomach on his lap, spanked her a few times, gently, and let her go. She laughed, and kept saying, 'Don't, don't, Blikkies. *Ag, Sies!*'[1] He drove his finger in between her buttocks, pushing in her dress as he did so. This seemed to propel her in a forward movement, and he followed behind, both of them on their knees. The man Blikkies kept his finger in the same area, while the girl, obviously tickled, laughed in shrill tones, crying, '*Eina*,[2] Blikkies, *Eina*, Blikkies, *Eina! Ag* don't, man *ag sies!*' And she laughed at intervals.

The three of us nudged one another and giggled. The couple got up and moved towards us, the man Blikkies staggering slightly.

'Kick me a Kaffir tonight, Blikkies,' the girl said, looking murderously civil. I remembered that during their little act our eyes met for a few seconds, hers and mine. 'Kick me a Kaffir tonight, *my lief*, won't you, my love? A nice kick on the arse of a nice black Kaffir monkey, eh?'

'Tonight, my little heart? Why not now?'

He came towards us. 'What are we looking for?' he said.

He swung his leg and missed Danie who was always agile. The man Blikkies' hoof struck the monkey's iron railings, and he fell, buckling from obvious pain. We bolted away. From behind the elephant we realized the monkey had stopped his tricycle antics, as if in deference to Blikkies, whom the girl was trying to help up.

Within a few moments all the Africans cleared that part of the gardens. 'Beware of the white man, he's very, very strong,' my mother often said. And all the years of my boyhood the words rang in my head.

December 16th was Dingaan's Day. A public holiday meant to commemorate the death of Piet Retief and his men at the hands of 'treacherous Dingaan', the Zulu king and Shaka's brother.

It was common for Afrikaners on Dingaan's Day to parade along Church Street in the centre of Pretoria on horseback. They wore Voortrekker clothing and large-brimmed hats and big broad bandoliers. It was quite a spectacle as these men, some of them Anglo-Boer War veterans, grimly filed down the street, obviously admired by the large crowds of whites on the sidewalks and roof tops.

I came from the suburbs that Dingaan's Day of 1934, when I saw these droves of horsemen go down the main street. Just then I spotted Rebone tentatively craning her neck on the fringe of the crowd of whites. When I joined her, she told me she had been to the station to see her aunt off to Johannesburg.

'Let's go deeper in,' she said in her usual animated fashion.

'I'm scared.'

'C'mon, Eseki, they won't bite us.'

'We never do it here.'

'But we're already here.' And she pulled me by the arm. It was no use now, we were already inside the crowd. We hadn't been standing long inside there when a huge bony Afrikaner prodded me in the ribs and said, 'Step out, Kaffir! This is no monkey show.'

'We're only looking,' Rebone said.

In a split second I felt a large hand take me by the scruff of the neck and push me out. Another hand from nowhere reached out for me. Another slapped me a few times on the cheek. My face ran into yet another object, so that I felt a sting on the bridge of my nose. I don't know how I was eventually thrust out of the crowd, but I stumbled down the curb. Only then did I feel that someone had kicked me in the back as well. Rebone joined me lower down the street.

We didn't speak for a while. Then, 'The stinking Boers!' she blurted.

'Boer or no Boer, it's your fault.'

'They'd have done it anyhow, wherever we might have been standing.'

'We could run.'

'They like to chase, these people. We'd be *lekker* sport for them.'

It hurt more because she was right. 'What did they do to you?' I asked.

'Just a few hard ones on my cheek.'

'Was Prospect Township like this?'

'They do it differently there. The Police do it for the rest of them.'

'We had no right to go in among that crowd, we shouldn't have gone in.' Tears were gathering in my eyes, and a lump of bitterness stopped in my throat, and I couldn't speak any more. But deep down in the cool depths of this well of bitterness, I felt a strong current of admiration for Rebone. And the cool freshness of it made itself felt deep down in the pit of my stomach.

For African men, one of the most pernicious humiliations was the requirement to carry a 'pass' at all times and produce it on demand to a policeman. First imposed on slaves in the 18th century and Hottentots in the early 19th century, it was a document that showed whether the bearer had the right to be where he was, that right being determined by whether his presence ministered to the white man's needs. During the 20th century, an estimated 17 million Africans were jailed under the pass laws, a process known officially as influx control. Bloke Modisane, who grew up in Sophiatown during the 1920s, never forgot the effect a pass raid had on his relationship with his father.

Then the walls of my world came tumbling down, everything collapsed around me, wrecking the relationship. My father shrunk into a midget. There was a Pass raid and two white police constables with their African 'police boys' were demanding to see the Passes of all adult African males.

'Pass jong, kaffir,' demanded the police constable from Uncle George, a distant relation of my father. 'Come on, we haven't all day.'

He would not dare to address my father in that tone, I bragged, my father is older than he.

'And you, why you sitting on your black arse?' the constable bawled at my father. 'Scratch out your Pass, and tax.'

I was diminished. My father was calm, the gentleness in his face was un-ruffled, only a hardness came in his eyes; he pulled out his wallet and showed his documents, an Exemption Pass certificate and a tax receipt for the cur-rent year. My hero image disintegrated, crumbling into an inch high heap of ashes; I could not face it, could not understand it, I hated the young consta-ble for destroying my father; questions flashed through my mind, I wanted to know why, and I think I resented my father, questioned his integrity as a man. I turned my face away and disappeared into the bedroom, searching for a parting in the earth that I could crawl into and huddle up into a ball of shame.

By the time he was a little older, however, Modisane had learnt the rules of the white man's game.

The shadow of apartheid spreads long over my life, I have to live with it, to come to terms with its reality and to arrange myself under the will of its authority. I have to be sane, calculating and ruthless in order to survive; I was sane that night as I walked from Lower Houghton to Sophiatown against curfew regulations in a restricted area for blacks. I realised my position and planned my strategy accordingly.

I had been confronted in the servant's quarters of a girl friend working as a domestic servant in Lower Houghton; she had smuggled me into her room, supposedly against the ruling of the white master. It was arranged for me to arrive during dinner, and whilst the white family was at the meal Esther came out through the kitchen door and signalled me through the back gate, past the refuse bins along a path lined with flower-beds.

'Take off your shoes,' Esther whispered, 'you'll trample the flowers of the missis.'

I removed my shoes, tippytoeing on, an impatient, panting open-eye of anticipation; I walked against an obstacle.

'Sh,' she said, ushering me into her room.

An hour later she brought me a bowl of soup, then a meat dish, steam pudding and coffee, all served in attractive china; it was the luxury we called 'dog's meat', from the stories told around the locations that kitchen girls served their boy friends dishes prepared from the rations for the dogs, which were fed more nutritiously than the children of the locations. And although some white employers pretended not to notice the traffic in the back-yards, they objected to their best china being used by Natives; I have worked for firms where separate cups were used by whites and by blacks, and I have seen a white typist break her own cup on the allegation that it had been used by a Native. A competent cook may be mollycoddled by being permitted to keep a 'husband' in the back-yard, but this is never extended to include the use of the china; Esther probably intended to impress me.

The radio was blaring throughout our conversation, and we were preparing to get into bed when there was a knock at the door. Esther motioned me behind the door as she slipped her nightie over her clothes.

'I'm sleeping, master,' she said, unlocking the door.

The door forced her back into the room; she gasped as a man walked in closing the door behind him. I felt stupid on being discovered behind the door.

'I'm sleeping, master,' he mimicked. 'I knew I would catch you one day.'

'This is my new boy friend,' she said, pointing at me. 'I told you I didn't want you any more.'

'Heit, bricade,'[3] he said, 'this is my cheerie; take a walk, friend, this cheerie is a rubberneck   a real Delilah.'

'Why, friend,' I said, bluffing a man I knew by reputation as the knife terror of Alexandra Township. 'She's also my cheerie.'

'Don't get hot running, friend,' he said, removing his jacket. 'Take a walk, bricade.'

'You better go, Willie,' she said, 'I don't want trouble.'

'That's right, bricade.'

I took my hat and went out; it was after midnight, I did not have a special Pass, Native public transport had stopped three hours ago. My pride had been hurt and I was too snobbish to lock myself in the servant's outdoor lavatory and spend the night there; I determined to brave the police and the tsotsis,[4] to walk the nine miles to Sophiatown. Two hours later, on the Jan Smuts Avenue, I was surprised by a police block.

'Nag Pass, kaffir,' the white constable said, shining a torch in my face. 'Night Special.'

I pulled my hat off and came to military attention; I squeezed a sob into my voice, shook my body with fear, trembling before the authority confronting me.

'My baas, my crown,' I said, in my textbook Afrikaans. 'I have a School Pass, my baas.'

'Skool kinders is almal aan die slaap,'[5] he said.

'Yes, my baasie,' I said. 'I was very stupid tonight, I was nearly led into the ways of the devil. This kaffir meid, my baas, was trying to trick me into sleeping in her room, but I know it is against the law, my baasie; so I said to her: the law says I must not sleep on the property of the white master. I know I didn't have a Special Pass, but I said to myself, this is wrong, you must go. This is the truth, my baasie.'

'Jy's 'n goei kaffir,' he said, becoming sickeningly paternal, 'a very good kaffir. Let me see your Pass – you must be careful, these kaffir women are bad, very bad. You must learn good at school and be a good Native; don't run after these bad women and don't mix with the trouble-makers.'

'Hier is dit, my baas,' I said, 'the Pass.'

'Ek sien,'[6] he said, looking at the Pass under the torch light. 'Now, tell the baas where you're going?'

'Sophiatown, my baas,' I said. 'I'm very sorry to be out so late, my baas; it's this kaffir meid, my baas, very bad; she delay me until it's too late for the buses, then she says I must sleep, but I say no, it's wrong; also I see, my baas, the clothes of a man, and I say to myself, trouble; but she try to stop me, say it belong to her brother, but I say she lie and I go home.'

'You must watch these meide,' the constable said, with fatherly concern. 'You watch out for them, they're the devil's work; now, listen here, weg is jy, gone with you.'

'Baie dankie, baasie,' I said, bowing my head several times, 'thank you very much, my baasie.'

'Don't let me catch you again,' he said, playfully kicking my bottom, but there was enough power behind it to make it playfully brutal.

'Thank you, my baasie.'

I was rubbing my hands over the spot where I was kicked, hopping forward and pretending a playful pain, all to the amusement of the white police constable and his African aides. Bloody swine, I mumbled through the laughing and the clowning. Two police blocks later, played with the same obsequiousness, I arrived home.

Dugmore Boetie (90) also grew up in Sophiatown. A barely-educated, habitual criminal with a wooden leg, he had an extraordinary gift for illuminating the darker absurdities of apartheid.

There was a big new building at 80 Albert Street. It was simply known as Influx Control. A beehive of black misery. They should have named it Liberty Control. This is where you had to report without the slightest delay after losing or resigning from a job. Failing which, you risked being charged under the Section 29 law, a law carrying a two-year jail sentence.

The trouble with this house of lawful humiliation is that here you are made to take any job they offer, whether it suits you or not. Here, black man must take work, not choose work. Remember, never talk back to your employer; you are not indispensable. You're in orbit around town. Don't accept employment twelve miles out of town, even if there's no work to be found where you live; you can lose, or forfeit, all right to live where you've always lived. Do not marry a girl who comes from a similar distance because she is regarded as a foreigner; they won't allow you to live together. If you want to visit relatives, see that your pass is properly stamped. Also, if you want to make some sort of celebration at your home, do not buy livestock to slaughter without getting a special permit from the superintendent. Most important of all, before going to bed at night, make sure that your passbook is either in the pocket of the trousers or the jacket you're going to wear the following morning.

Influx Control was my destination. I was going there with the hope of getting new employment. As I approached the place, I nearly turned back. Queues a half-mile long were snaking around the four-block building. The Africans were moving in pairs at a snail's pace. Misery was written on every face, as if they were walking the last mile. Maybe we were, who knew. Most of us were either going to be given twenty-four hours to leave the urban area of Johannesburg, or sold to potato farmers for failing to renew work-seeking permits in time.

In time? Look at that queue! By the time I reached the small gate so as to get the necessary rubber stamp in my passbook, it would be four-thirty, time for them to close, making me twelve hours behind schedule and liable for arrest by any street policeman who demanded to see my pass.

There's a tall tale about the trees of Canada. They say the trees are so high that if you look straight up, it will take you three weeks to see the top. Right here in Johannesburg is a queue like that. Every time you came to that gate, it would be four-thirty. Then they closed it in your face. If you tried to get back by five in the morning, you'd find that hundreds had had the same idea. If you spent the night there so as to be first in the morning, you risked arrest for Night Special.

Instead of joining the queue at the tail end, I made a beeline for the side entrance. Imagine having to stand in a queue the whole day with only one leg to support you. Clearly this was no place for cripples, respectable or otherwise. The side entrance was guarded by two municipal police, commonly known as Black Jacks because of their black uniforms. You were not allowed to stand on the pavements. The pavement was for Europeans only. Europeans who were looking for servants, or those who were trying to get their servants' passes in order.

'What do you want? Why don't you join the queue?' asked the Black Jack glaring at me.

'I'm not here to put my pass in order. I'm here to see the social workers.'

'What is social worker?' he asked aggressively.

'They are on the third floor. They are the people who help cripples.'

'You mean the doctor?'

'No! The social workers.' Not knowing what social workers were caused him to let me go through. I was seven years old when they called me a headache, I suppose I just had to go on being one.

Inside was a hall with a giant horseshoe-shaped counter. Behind the counter were divided cubicles. In each cubicle sat a white clerk. On the hall side, opposite each cubicle, were barroom stools where black interpreters sat. An iron grille divided the interpreters from the white clerks. Nowhere in this vast arena was there a place where the job-seekers could sit. This is where the queue ended.

The interpreter would hand your pass through the grille to the white clerk who would take his time studying it. If there was an irregularity, he'd give it back to the interpreter with instructions.

The interpreter would hang on to your pass which you didn't dare leave without. He'd then shout, 'Escort!' Two police would appear and escort you upstairs to the interrogation room.

If you fail to give satisfactory answers about why your work-seeking permits are not in order, they conclude that you don't want to work. You are then given twenty-four hours to get out of Johannesburg. Failing which, they charge you under Section 29. Two years' imprisonment. And after serving your sentence you still have to get out of Johannesburg.

If you tell them you were sick and couldn't come into town, they demand a doctor's certificate. Africans who have money go to private doctors and buy certificates. The best excuse is out. It doesn't work any more because too many Africans have used it. It was to tell the authorities that you were mad in the township and that you were treated by a witch doctor. Witch doctors don't issue certificates.

The procedure is to give you a first job. If you find you don't agree with your employer because of the wage, or because the work is too strenuous or because your baas is just plain mean, as is often the case, they'll give you a second and third job. If you don't accept them, they declare you a vagrant by refusing to give you a fourth work-seeking permit.

The best thing to do is to take any work they give you and stick to it no matter what the circumstances are, while you keep your eyes open for a better job. You are bound to get it. The black man is not indispensable. We are a rotating labour force. Here, there are no middle-class Africans. Whether you're educated or not, you are looked upon as an illiterate and treated as such. In this building the worse sufferer is the educated African. If you've been a teacher you'll be offered a job as a gravedigger, or coal-heaver, or a domestic servant. They hate the sight of an educated African.

The eponymous hero of *In the Name of Patrick Henry*, a 1967 short story by Jack Cope (91), is a skilled forger. Who better to unpick a society in which a man's identity is defined by a piece of paper?

These past years he had got along without any trouble under whatever name people chose to use for him; though in his own mind he clung to the conviction that he was Patrick Henry. Perhaps his mother had named him, or Ma-Sarina, or some bush-preacher. Children like him had never been registered, so it was useless, of course, to have a search made at the Registry. It was possible he had found the name for himself because he had been called all sorts of things as a child like Sa-Sa and Lam and Boetie and he had rolled them all up one day and thrown them off at a time when he knew they were babyish. From then he was to himself Patrick Henry just as a tree could not be anything else but a tree. Secretly he was proud and sometimes wrote the two names in his careful and practised script, turned the paper and examined it from all angles as if searching there for the very essence of himself.

He could put this skill of his with a pen to many uses and helped people with their identity papers, passes, tax receipts, work tickets and the different documents which allowed a man to exist. He copied handwriting and with blue or purple endorsing-ink and a soft pen he could make a perfect impression of any official rubber stamp. Patrick Henry's passes were the best on the market and he charged only a modest fee to cover his time and materials and enough, say, for a meal with a litre of beer and a four-ounce packet of Boxer tobacco.

He had not at any time made documents for himself and got through without them, or at least with only a second-hand registration book in reasonable condition and a bundle of papers in a greaseproof packet that he traded from a man who had no more use for them, having changed his identity. He had got through, until his misfortune. During a police raid for dynamite saboteurs or unlawful societies or something else that was equally no concern of his, Patrick Henry had been drawn into the net. He realised that his second-hand papers were not going to help with these people and he quickly lost them. But from that moment his real troubles began. He cleared himself, after four months, of any complicity in the revolutionary underground. But he lost his job meanwhile as a clerk in Beaumont & Ditchwell's law office. Endless complications followed for him. Twice he was sent to prison and for six months he worked as a convict labourer hired to an apple farmer far out in the country. In his red shirt and canvas shorts he soon was a trusted foreman, kept the records and was a weigh-clerk and dispatcher in control of the big export crop. The farmer called him Noah and wanted him back in a fulltime job. But this was not allowed by law and he was returned to prison, released and rearrested the same day.

Now he had to prove who he was, he had to prove he had been born in the city district, he had to show when and where and how he was born and what he was, what tribe and who was his Chief. After all the years of his life (he was not sure how many) he had to be given his place, his hole in the wall. If he was not born in the city he could not stay. He would be ordered home and not allowed back. But in that case he had to know where 'home' was, which reserve and Chief and headman. To all these questions he had one answer: he was Patrick Henry. Nobody believed him. For one moment he played with the idea of making a set of papers going back to his birth and inventing a father for himself and maybe a grandparent or two. So he would be the father of his own father. But he knew at this stage it was too late. They were watching closely; they checked numbers and dates and finger-prints and his papers were not likely to convince. He had appealed to his old employer, Mr Beaumont, and the lawyer had him released from the police cells. His money was finished, his clothes were worn out and his boots split. He had lost his room and blankets and tin box and also his woman whose name was Fidelity. Thinking of it as he drove along in the car behind the two silent men he reckoned up and found he had actually nothing left. Nothing, that is, except his name. The more he turned this over the stranger it became, and soon he startled the two with a surge of laughter. With one hand he quickly stifled the sound but his body went on shaking and his neck felt like bursting. The men did not condescend to turn, but after a minute the lawyer said severely: 'George, were you laughing or breaking wind?'

'My name is not George, sir. It is Patrick Henry, and I was laughing.'

'What at?'

'At that, at my name.'

'Well, don't splutter down my neck. Your name is no laughing matter, it's a handicap. I can't do anything for a boy with a handle like that. It's absurd, nobody can take it. Why don't you get rid of it and call yourself something plain like Tom Mabom?'

'No sir. I stick to my name. Honestly, I can't eat it or buy bread with it, and I can't smoke it in my pipe. But it is all I have got left. No sir, any other name but Patrick Henry is dishonest.'

'That's rich, coming from him,' the Inspector said. 'A fraud and a faker; I've seen some of his forgeries, I believe.'

'I did not forge my name, sir,' he said. 'I am not ashamed. I never stole six cents. I don't lie. I never swallow another man's bread. I never swallow another man's country.'

'Shut your mouth, Tom, you're talking out of turn,' Mr Beaumont warned.

They went on and Patrick Henry directed the lawyer until they left the tarmac and got on to a dirt road between ragged port-jackson wattles. A few trees were a grimy yellow with fading blossom. In a gap on one side they saw a stagnant swamp, then a straggle of tin shanties and a burnt-out brick church with a blackened cross still tilted on the gable. Children and chickens and dogs raced in front of the car.

'Should run a few over,' Mr Beaumont said.

The Inspector nodded a silent approval.

Another law with a long history that made criminals of Africans was liquor prohibition.

Bloke Modisane describes the consequences.

Ma-Willie and I had always pointed with pride to Dr Xuma, the African doctor who had studied in America, Glasgow and London; he had success, wealth, position and respect, and my mother was suddenly seized by the vision of a Dr Xuma in the family.

'You will be a doctor,' she said, determined.

She turned our home into a shebeen,[7] worked fourteen hours a day brewing and pressing home brews called skokiaan and barberton, and from the proceeds she educated me to high school level and the two girls to primary school level. They dropped out because they could not visualise the immediate benefit of education; but the value of it had been indelibly impressed into my mind.

Moralists and reformists, like Dr Xuma, whose existence did not depend on shebeens, spoke out publicly against the medical dangers of these concoctions, but prohibition anywhere places a premium upon the restricted commodity, and thus the churches, the welfare department, the cause-followers fastened on the campaign to stamp out the traffic, focusing on altruistic motives like: the health of the Native, the destitute family of the addict bread-winner; but the police departments, which put up half-hearted banner campaigns, were more realistic than the correctionists who overlooked the human factor; the Africans, like everybody else, wanted to, and would drink, whether it was or was not prohibited.

To the police departments shebeens were a source of unlimited funds, the tariffs for liquor offences were worked out with careful attention, reasonably steep but not calculated to discourage or inconvenience the budget of shebeen queens. The liquor squad was made up of 'reasonable men' always willing and prepared to listen to the pleas of the shebeen queens, to make accommodating adjustments. My mother always paid, and I often wondered why she had not taken out an insurance policy against this hazard.

Life in a shebeen exposed me to a rude introduction to the South African police, they made me realise the brutal, dominant presence of the white man in South Africa. I saw my mother insulted, sworn at and bundled into the kwela-kwela, the police wagon, so often it began to seem – and I perhaps accepted it – as a way of life, the life of being black. Listening to the young constables screaming obscenities at Ma-Willie emphasised the fact that we were black, and because my mother was black she was despised and humiliated, called 'kafir meid' and 'swart hell'. I was helpless in the coffin of my skin and began to resent the black of my skin, it offered no protection to my mother from the delinquency of the police constables who saw only the mask representative of a despised race; but Ma-Willie was not black, she was my mother, and if I had been white the whiteness of my skin would have protected her honour. I wished I was white.

Every night was Saturday night, house full, in the charge office of Newlands Police Station, new arrivals waiting to be charged were sardined in the yard immediately behind the office; a continual buzz flowing from the shebeen queens, the drunks, Pass offenders, thieves and all sorts, in a conspiracy of voices, making arrangements, sending out messages, to relations, to friends, about funds, fines.

Tell my wife.

Mother.

Friends.

Ten shillings.

It was always the same, the same voices, the same desperation, the same pleas, and throughout all this I waited outside the police station, waiting for my mother to be charged, fined and released, waiting to escort her home. The police clerks behind the desk were pedantically methodic in their job, and sitting out there with nothing to do I would find leisure in timing the changes of working relays. The offenders were shouted into the charge office.

'Stand against the wall,' the police clerk said. 'Shake up, this isn't a bed.'

'Silence, you devil,' the other shouted. 'You, you with the black face, shut your stink mouth.'

The offenders pushed against each other into a straight line against the wall. The clerk placed the pad in front of him, arranging two carbons between the pages, selected an indelible pencil, sharpened the lead and generally prepared himself for the session.

'Right,' he said. 'Name? God, these bloody names. Guilty or not guilty?'

'Guilty, my crown.'

'Two pounds.'

'My wife is bring it, my baas.'

'Lock him up.'

'Is coming, my baas,' he said, 'the money.'

'Silence. Next. Name? God. Guilty or not guilty? Eight pounds. Good, stand one side.'

And so it went on for two hours the clerk working like a robot, questions and instructions rattling away almost as if by reflex action, and at the end of that time the offenders would be ordered off into the yard.

'Hey, Ephraim, open a window,' the clerk shouted at the attendant African police boy. 'This place stinks.'

For the next half-hour the clerks would stretch, smoke and drink coffee and chat together; Ephraim would be fingering the roller and inking the pad.

'Ephraim, tell me,' the clerk said, 'what is it about you people that smells so bad?'

'Don't know, baas.'

'Like shit.'

'Yes, baas.'

'Bring those stink pots out.'

When all the offenders had been charged, there would be another break, then those with funds paid the admission-of-guilt fines and took their turn at being finger-printed by Ephraim; this done they wait against the wall whilst the receipts are being written out, then the names are called out against the receipts and the offenders start hurrying out through the door where the women find their escorts waiting. This would be around one-thirty and I would consider myself lucky if Ma-Willie was in this early batch.

My mother accepted her life, and, I suppose, so did the other shebeen queens; they chose this life and accommodated the hazards, my mother wanted a better life for her children, a kind of insurance against poverty by trying to give me a prestige profession, and if necessary would go to jail whilst doing it. And in our curious society going to jail carried very little social stigma, it was rather a social institution, something to be expected; it was Harry Bloom who wrote: more Africans go to prison than to school.

Such was the background to the Defiance of Unjust Laws campaign, which was launched on 26 June 1952 and marked the emergence of the rejuvenated ANC. The plan was that small groups of volunteers would do what apartheid outlawed. They entered proscribed areas without permits, stayed out on the streets after curfew and used facilities such as libraries, toilets, waiting rooms, railway compartments and post office entrances reserved for whites. Over the next six months, thousands were sent to jail for non-violent acts of civil disobedience, and the ANC's membership swelled. By now, its conservative leadership had been pushed aside. Chief Albert Luthuli, a man of courage and principle, who was later to be awarded the Nobel Peace Prize, became president; his deputy was Nelson Mandela, now truly embarked on the journey of a lifetime. In *Long Walk to Freedom*, his compulsively readable autobiography published in 1994, Mandela reflected on where he had come from.

The village of Qunu was situated in a narrow, grassy valley crisscrossed by clear streams, and overlooked by green hills. It consisted of no more than a few hundred people who lived in huts, which were beehive-shaped structures of mud walls, with a wooden pole in the centre holding up a peaked grass roof. The floor was made of crushed ant-heap, the hard dome of excavated earth above an ant colony, and was kept smooth by smearing it regularly with fresh cow dung. The smoke from the hearth escaped through the roof, and the only opening was a low doorway one had to stoop to walk through. The huts were generally grouped in a residential area that was some distance away from the maize fields. There were no roads, only paths through the grass worn away by barefooted boys and women. The women and children of the village wore blankets dyed in ochre; only the few Christians in the village wore Western-style clothing. Cattle, sheep, goats and horses grazed together in common pastures. The land around Qunu was mostly treeless except for a cluster of poplars on a hill overlooking the village. The land itself was owned by the state. With very few exceptions, Africans at that time did not enjoy private title to land in South Africa but were tenants paying rent annually to the government. In the area, there were two small primary schools, a general store, and a dipping tank to rid the cattle of ticks and diseases.

Maize (what we called mealies and people in the West call corn), sorghum, beans and pumpkins formed the largest portion of our diet, not because of any inherent preference for these foods, but because the people could not afford anything richer. The wealthier families in our village supplemented their diets with tea, coffee and sugar, but for most people in Qunu these were exotic luxuries far beyond their means. The water used for farming, cooking and washing had to be fetched in buckets from streams and springs. This was women's work and, indeed, Qunu was a village of women and children: most of the men spent the greater part of the year working on remote farms or in the mines along the Reef, the great ridge of gold-bearing rock and shale that forms the southern boundary of Johannesburg. They returned perhaps twice a year, mainly to plough their fields. The hoeing, weeding and harvesting were left to the women and children. Few if any of the people in the village knew how to read or write, and the concept of education was still a foreign one to many […]

From an early age, I spent most of my free time in the veld playing and fighting with the other boys of the village. A boy who remained at home tied to his mother's apron strings was regarded as a sissy. At night, I shared my food and blanket with these same boys. I was no more than five when I became a herd-boy looking after sheep and calves in the fields. I discovered the almost mystical attachment that the Xhosa have for cattle, not only as a source of food and wealth, but as a blessing from God and a source of happiness. It was in the fields that I learned how to knock birds out of the sky with a slingshot, to gather wild honey and fruits and edible roots, to drink warm, sweet milk straight from the udder of a cow, to swim in the clear, cold streams, and to catch fish with twine and sharpened bits of wire. I learned to stick-fight – essential knowledge to any rural African boy – and became adept at its various techniques, parrying blows, feinting in one direction and striking in another, breaking away from an opponent with quick footwork. From these days I date my love of the veld, of open spaces, the simple beauties of nature, the clean line of the horizon.

As was customary, Mandela was given an English name by his teacher on his first day at school. Why she chose Nelson, he never knew. Nor could he date when he became a rebel.

I cannot pinpoint a moment when I became politicized, when I knew that I would spend my life in the liberation struggle. To be an African in South Africa means that one is politicized from the moment of one's birth, whether one acknowledges it or not. An African child is born in an Africans Only hospital, taken home in an Africans Only bus, lives in an Africans Only area and attends Africans Only schools, if he attends school at all.

When he grows up, he can hold Africans Only jobs, rent a house in Africans Only townships, ride Africans Only trains and be stopped at any time of the day or night and be ordered to produce a pass, without which he can be arrested and thrown in jail. His life is circumscribed by racist laws and regulations that cripple his growth, dim his potential and stunt his life. This was the reality, and one could deal with it in a myriad of ways.

I had no epiphany, no singular revelation, no moment of truth, but a steady accumulation of a thousand slights, a thousand indignities and a thousand un-remembered moments produced in me an anger, a rebelliousness, a desire to fight the system that imprisoned my people. There was no particular day on which I said, Henceforth I will devote myself to the liberation of my people; instead, I simply found myself doing so, and could not do otherwise.

For the ANC, the next step on the road to liberation was to call a Congress of the People – 'irrespective of race or colour' – to draw up a Freedom Charter 'for the democratic South Africa of the future'. Held at Kliptown, a few miles outside Johannesburg, on 25 and 26 June 1955, the congress was attended by more than 3 000 delegates represent-ing a spread of anti-apartheid organisations. Towards the end of the second afternoon, it was broken up by the police, who took the names of everyone there. By then, each clause of the Freedom Charter had been passed with acclamation.

We, the People of South Africa, declare for all our country and the world to know:

that South Africa belongs to all who live in it, black and white, and that no government can justly claim authority unless it is based on the will of all the people;

that our people have been robbed of their birthright to land, liberty and peace by a form of government founded on injustice and inequality;

that our country will never be prosperous or free until all our people live in brotherhood, enjoying equal rights and opportunities;

that only a democratic state, based on the will of all the people, can secure to all their birthright without distinction of colour, race, sex or belief;

And therefore, we, the people of South Africa, black and white together equals, countrymen and brothers adopt this Freedom Charter;

And we pledge ourselves to strive together, sparing neither strength nor courage, until the democratic changes here set out have been won.

The People Shall Govern!

Every man and woman shall have the right to vote for and to stand as a can-didate for all bodies which make laws;

All people shall be entitled to take part in the administration of the country;

The rights of the people shall be the same, regardless of race, colour or sex;

All bodies of minority rule, advisory boards, councils and authorities shall be replaced by democratic organs of self-government.

All National Groups Shall have Equal Rights!

There shall be equal status in the bodies of state, in the courts and in the schools for all national groups and races;

All people shall have equal right to use their own languages, and to develop their own folk culture and customs;

All national groups shall be protected by law against insults to their race and national pride;

The preaching and practice of national, race or colour discrimination and contempt shall be a punishable crime;

All apartheid laws and practices shall be set aside.

The People Shall Share in the Country's Wealth!

The national wealth of our country, the heritage of South Africans, shall be restored to the people;

The mineral wealth beneath the soil, the Banks and monopoly industry shall be transferred to the ownership of the people as a whole;

All other industry and trade shall be controlled to assist the wellbeing of the people;

All people shall have equal rights to trade where they choose, to manufacture and to enter all trades, crafts and professions.

The Land Shall be Shared Among Those Who Work It!

Restrictions of land ownership on a racial basis shall be ended, and all the land re-divided amongst those who work it to banish famine and land hunger;

The state shall help the peasants with implements, seed, tractors and dams to save the soil and assist the tillers;

Freedom of movement shall be guaranteed to all who work on the land;

All shall have the right to occupy land wherever they choose;

People shall not be robbed of their cattle, and forced labour and farm prisons shall be abolished.

All Shall be Equal Before the Law!

No-one shall be imprisoned, deported or restricted without a fair trial;

No-one shall be condemned by the order of any Government official;

The courts shall be representative of all the people;

Imprisonment shall be only for serious crimes against the people, and shall aim at re-education, not vengeance;

The police force and army shall be open to all on an equal basis and shall be the helpers and protectors of the people;

All laws which discriminate on grounds of race, colour or belief shall be repealed.

All Shall Enjoy Equal Human Rights!

The law shall guarantee to all their right to speak, to organise, to meet together, to publish, to preach, to worship and to educate their children;

The privacy of the house from police raids shall be protected by law;

All shall be free to travel without restriction from countryside to town, from province to province, and from South Africa abroad;

Pass Laws, permits and all other laws restricting these freedoms shall be abolished.

There Shall be Work and Security!

All who work shall be free to form trade unions, to elect their officers and to make wage agreements with their employers;

The state shall recognise the right and duty of all to work, and to draw full unemployment benefits;

Men and women of all races shall receive equal pay for equal work;

There shall be a forty-hour working week, a national minimum wage, paid annual leave, and sick leave for all workers, and maternity leave on full pay for all working mothers;

Miners, domestic workers, farm workers and civil servants shall have the same rights as all others who work;

Child labour, compound labour, the tot system and contract labour shall be abolished.

The Doors of Learning and Culture Shall be Opened!

The government shall discover, develop and encourage national talent for the enhancement of our cultural life;

All the cultural treasures of mankind shall be open to all, by free exchange of books, ideas and contact with other lands;

The aim of education shall be to teach the youth to love their people and their culture, to honour human brotherhood, liberty and peace;

Education shall be free, compulsory, universal and equal for all children;

Higher education and technical training shall be opened to all by means of state allowances and scholarships awarded on the basis of merit;

Adult illiteracy shall be ended by a mass state education plan;

Teachers shall have all the rights of other citizens;

The colour bar in cultural life, in sport and in education shall be abolished.

There Shall be Houses, Security and Comfort!

All people shall have the right to live where they choose, be decently housed, and to bring up their families in comfort and security;

Unused housing space to be made available to the people;

Rent and prices shall be lowered, food plentiful and no-one shall go hungry;

A preventive health scheme shall be run by the state;

Free medical care and hospitalisation shall be provided for all, with special care for mothers and young children;

Slums shall be demolished, and new suburbs built where all have transport, roads, lighting, playing fields, crèches and social centres;

The aged, the orphans, the disabled and the sick shall be cared for by the state;

Rest, leisure and recreation shall be the right of all:

Fenced locations and ghettoes shall be abolished, and laws which break up families shall be repealed.

There Shall be Peace and Friendship!

South Africa shall be a fully independent state which respects the rights and sovereignty of all nations;

South Africa shall strive to maintain world peace and the settlement of all international disputes by negotiation – not war;

Peace and friendship amongst all our people shall be secured by upholding the equal rights, opportunities and status of all;

The people of the protectorates Basutoland, Bechuanaland and Swaziland shall be free to decide for themselves their own future;

The right of all peoples of Africa to independence and self-government shall
be recognised, and shall be the basis of close co-operation.

Let all people who love their people and their country now say, as we say
here:

**THESE FREEDOMS WE WILL FIGHT FOR, SIDE BY SIDE,
THROUGHOUT OUR LIVES, UNTIL WE HAVE WON OUR LIBERTY**

In his autobiography (92) published a few years later, Albert Luthuli captured something
of the feeling behind the charter.

Who owns South Africa?

With the exception of a small group of black nationalists who have
learned their politics from Dr. Verwoerd's and General Smuts's parties, *the
great majority of Africans* reply that the country now belongs to fourteen million people of different races – it is jointly owned by all its inhabitants, quite
regardless of their colour. This view, which I adhere to without qualification,
demands that people be regarded primarily as people. As far as culture and
habits of life are concerned, they may differ as radically as they wish. But
when it comes to participation in ownership and government, race must be
made wholly irrelevant.

With the exception of a small number of voices crying in the wilderness,
the overwhelming majority of whites reply that South Africa is exclusively
owned by three million whites. On this point General Smuts and his successors, and Dr. Malan and his successors, are in whole-hearted agreement. It
does not stop, either, with ownership of land and wealth, and participation
in government. In this view the whites, because they *are* 'white,' extend their
possession to ownership of the remaining eleven million people, who are
expected to regard themselves as fortunate to be allowed to live and breathe
– and work – in a 'white man's country.'

The whites who hold this view energetically repudiate the accusation that
those who do not belong to the 'master race' are owned as though they were
slaves. It is, of course, true that we are not bound in quite the same shackles
as in the days of conventional slavery. But the idiom of slavery changes with
the times. Nowadays, state ownership has replaced individual ownership to
some extent. The slave system has been nationalised. We are told where we
may work, and where we may not, where we may live and where we may

not; freehold rights are altogether taken from us and we are forbidden by law to strike or to protest against the edicts of an all-white parliament or against exploitation.

We have no safeguards whatever. There is nothing which our white owners cannot do to us simply by agreeing with each other to do it. And in law after law since the Act of Union in 1910, you will find this conception – whites own Africans, Indians, coloured people – expressing itself. In election after election you will see the 'native question' ('What shall we do with our movable property which our political opponents have not yet thought up?') used as a major successful means to sway an all-white electorate. We stand by and watch ourselves being used as the white man's football. This or that white group scores the points and wins the election, over what should be done with 'the natives.' Our lot is to feel the impact of the boot.

And the impact of the boot was exactly what came next. Returned with an increased majority in 1953, the Nationalist government was now led by JG Strijdom, a hard-line white supremacist determined to stamp out the growing opposition to apartheid. In December 1956, 156 of those who had been most active in promoting the Freedom Charter, including Luthuli and Mandela, were arrested in dawn raids, accused of 'acting with a common purpose to endanger the security of the state' and charged with high treason. By the time the Treason Trial ended with the acquittal of all the accused in March 1961, it had become an irrelevance. Almost exactly a year earlier, Sharpeville had branded itself on the world's consciousness; the government, now led by Hendrik Verwoerd, Grand Apartheid's ultimate messiah, had declared a state of emergency; and the ANC and its Pan-Africanist off-shoot, the PAC, led by Robert Sobukwe, had been outlawed. The background to Sharpeville, as Mandela explains, was an anti-pass campaign launched by the PAC on 21 March 1960.

Sharpeville was a small township about thirty-five miles south of Johannesburg in the grim industrial complex around Vereeniging. PAC activists had done an excellent job of organizing the area. In the early afternoon, a crowd of several thousand surrounded the police station. The demonstrators were controlled and unarmed. The police force of seventy-five was greatly outnumbered and panicky. No one heard warning shots or an order to shoot, but suddenly the police opened fire on the crowd and continued to shoot as the demonstrators turned and ran in fear. When the area had cleared, sixty-nine Africans lay dead, most of them shot in the back as they were fleeing. All told, more than seven hundred shots had been fired into the crowd, wounding more than four hundred people, including dozens of women and children. It was a massacre, and the next day press photos displayed the savagery on front pages around the world.

The shootings at Sharpeville provoked national turmoil and a government crisis. Outraged protests came in from across the globe, including one from the American State Department. For the first time, the UN Security Council intervened in South African affairs, blaming the government for the shootings and urging it to initiate measures to bring about racial equality. The Johannesburg stock exchange plunged, and capital started to flow out of the country. South African whites began making plans to emigrate. Liberals urged Verwoerd to offer concessions to Africans. The government insisted that Sharpeville was the result of a communist conspiracy.

The massacre at Sharpeville created a new situation in the country. In spite of the amateurishness and opportunism of their leaders, the PAC rank and file displayed great courage and fortitude in their demonstrations at Sharpeville and Langa. In just one day, they had moved to the front lines of the struggle, and Robert Sobukwe was being hailed inside and outside the country as the saviour of the liberation movement. We in the ANC had to make rapid adjustments to this new situation, and we did so.

A small group of us – Walter,[8] Duma Nokwe, Joe Slovo and I – held an all-night meeting in Johannesburg to plan a response. We knew we had to acknowledge the events in some way and give the people an outlet for their anger and grief. We conveyed our plans to Chief Luthuli, and he readily accepted them. On 26 March, in Pretoria, the chief publicly burned his pass, calling on others to do the same. He announced a nationwide stay-at-home for 28 March, a national Day of Mourning and protest for the atrocities at Sharpeville. In Orlando, Duma Nokwe and I then burned our passes before hundreds of people and dozens of press photographers.

Two days later, on the 28th, the country responded magnificently as several hundred thousand Africans observed the chief's call. Only a truly mass organization could coordinate such activities, and the ANC did so. In Cape Town a crowd of fifty thousand met in Langa township to protest against the shootings. Rioting broke out in many areas. The government declared a State of Emergency, suspending habeas corpus and assuming sweeping powers to act against all forms of subversion. South Africa was now under martial law.

With the ANC banned, Mandela went underground in March 1961 on the day the Treason trial ended.

Living underground requires a seismic psychological shift. One has to plan every action, however small and seemingly insignificant. Nothing is innocent. Everything is questioned. You cannot be yourself; you must fully inhabit whatever role you have assumed. In some ways, this was not much of an adaptation for a black man in South Africa. Under apartheid, a black man lived a shadowy life between legality and illegality, between openness and concealment. To be a black man in South Africa meant not to trust anything, which was not unlike living underground for one's entire life.

I became a creature of the night. I would keep to my hideout during the day, and emerge to do my work when it became dark. I operated mainly from Johannesburg, but I would travel as necessary. I stayed in empty flats, in people's houses, wherever I could be alone and inconspicuous. Although I am a gregarious person, I love solitude even more. I welcomed the opportunity to be by myself, to plan, to think, to plot. But one can have too much solitude. I was terribly lonesome for my wife and family.

The key to being underground is to be invisible. Just as there is a way to walk into a room in order to make yourself stand out, there is a way of walking and behaving that makes you inconspicuous. As a leader, one often seeks prominence; as an outlaw, the opposite is true. When underground I did not walk as tall or stand as straight. I spoke more softly, with less clarity and distinction. I was more passive, more unobtrusive; I did not ask for things but let people tell me what to do. I did not shave or cut my hair. My most frequent disguise was as a chauffeur, chef or a 'garden boy'. I would wear the blue overalls of the field-worker and often wore round, rimless glasses known as Mazzawatee tea-glasses. I had a car and I wore a chauffeur's cap with my overalls. The pose of chauffeur was convenient because I could travel under the pretext of driving my master's car.

During those early months, when there was a warrant for my arrest and I was being pursued by the police, my outlaw existence caught the imagination of the press. Articles claiming that I had been here and there were on the front pages. Roadblocks were instituted all over the country, but the police repeatedly came up empty-handed. I was dubbed the Black Pimpernel, a somewhat derogatory adaptation of Baroness Orczy's fictional character the Scarlet Pimpernel, who daringly evaded capture during the French Revolution.

I travelled secretly about the country: I was with Muslims in the Cape, with sugar-workers in Natal, with factory workers in Port Elizabeth. I moved through townships in different parts of the country attending secret meetings at night. I would even feed the mythology of the Black Pimpernel by taking a pocketful of 'tickeys' (threepenny bits) and phoning individual newspaper reporters from telephone boxes and relaying stories of what we were planning or of the ineptitude of the police. I would pop up here and there to the annoyance of the police and to the delight of the people.

There were many wild and inaccurate stories about my experiences underground. People love to embellish tales of daring. I did have a number of narrow escapes, however, which no one knew about. On one occasion, I was driving in town and stopped at a traffic light. I looked to my left and in an adjacent car saw Colonel Spengler, the chief of the Witwatersrand Security Branch. It would have been a great plum for him to catch the Black Pimpernel. I was wearing a workman's cap, my blue overalls, and my glasses. He never looked my way, but even so the seconds I spent waiting for the light to change seemed like hours.

One afternoon, when I was in Johannesburg posing as a chauffeur and wearing my long dust-coat and cap, I was waiting on a corner to be picked up and I saw an African policeman striding deliberately towards me. I looked around to see if I had a place to run, but before I did, he smiled at me and surreptitiously gave me the thumbs-up ANC salute and was gone. Incidents like this happened many times, and I was reassured when I saw that we had the loyalty of many African policemen. There was a black sergeant who used to tip off Winnie[9] as to what the police were doing. He would whisper to her, 'Make sure Madiba[10] is not in Alexandra on Wednesday night because there is going to be a raid.' Black policemen have often been severely criticized during the struggle, but many have played covert roles that have been extremely valuable.

When I was underground, I remained as unkempt as possible. My overalls looked as though they had been through a lifetime of hard toil. The police had one picture of me with a beard, which they widely distributed, and my colleagues urged me to shave it off. But I had become attached to my beard, and I resisted all their efforts.

Not only was I not recognized, I was sometimes snubbed. Once, I was planning to attend a meeting in a distant area of Johannesburg and a well-known priest arranged with friends of his to put me up for the night. I arrived at the door, and before I could announce who I was, the elderly lady who answered exclaimed, 'No, we don't want such a man as you here!' and shut the door.

By now Mandela had concluded that non-violence, which he had always regarded as a tactic rather than a principle, had run its course. By the end of 1961, he had persuaded the ANC to allow him to form an armed wing.

I who had never been a soldier, who had never fought in battle, who had never fired a gun at an enemy, had been given the task of starting an army. It would be a daunting task for a veteran general, much less a military novice. The name of this new organization was Umkhonto we Sizwe (The Spear of the Nation) – or MK for short. The symbol of the spear was chosen because with this simple weapon Africans had resisted the incursions of whites for centuries.

Although the Executive of the ANC did not allow white members, MK was not thus constrained. I immediately recruited Joe Slovo and along with Walter Sisulu we formed the High Command with myself as chairman. Through Joe, I enlisted the efforts of white Communist Party members who had resolved on a course of violence and had already executed acts of sabotage such as cutting government telephone and communication lines. We recruited Jack Hodgson, who had fought in the Second World War and was a member of the Springbok Legion, and Rusty Bernstein, both party members. Jack became our first demolition expert. Our mandate was to wage acts of violence against the state – precisely what form those acts would take was yet to be decided. Our intention was to begin with what was least violent to individuals but most damaging to the state.

I began in the only way I knew how, by reading and talking to experts. What I wanted to find out were the fundamental principles for starting a revolution. I discovered that there was a great deal of writing on this very subject, and I made my way through the available literature on armed warfare and in particular guerrilla warfare. I wanted to know what circumstances were appropriate for a guerrilla war; how one created, trained and maintained a guerrilla force; how it should be armed; where it gets its supplies – all basic and fundamental questions.

Any and every source was of interest to me. I read the report of Blas Roca, the general secretary of the Communist Party of Cuba, about their years as an illegal organization during the Batista regime. In *Commando* by Deneys Reitz, I read of the unconventional guerrilla tactics of the Boer generals during the Anglo-Boer War. I read works by and about Che Guevara, Mao Tsetung, Fidel Castro. In Edgar Snow's brilliant *Red Star Over China* I saw that it was Mao's determination and non-traditional thinking that had led him to victory. I read *The Revolt* by Menachem Begin and was encouraged by the fact that the Israeli leader had led a guerrilla force in a country with neither mountains nor forests, a situation similar to our own. I was eager to know more about the armed struggle of the people of Ethiopia against Mussolini, and of the guerrilla armies of Kenya, Algeria and the Cameroons.

I went into the South African past. I studied our history both before and after the white man. I probed the wars of African against African, of African against white, of white against white. I made a survey of the country's chief industrial areas, the nation's transportation system, its communication network. I accumulated detailed maps and systematically analysed the terrain of different regions of the country.

In August 1962, after Mandela had toured Africa, secretly visited England and received military training in Ethiopia, his luck ran out. He was captured by the police as he was being driven through Natal. It was to be nearly 28 years before he regained his freedom. At a trial in October 1962, he was charged with inciting Africans to strike and leaving the country without a passport. Dressed in a traditional Xhosa leopard-skin kaross (cloak), he began his defence by challenging the court's right to judge him.

Firstly, I challenge it because I fear that I will not be given a fair and proper trial. Secondly, I consider myself neither legally nor morally bound to obey laws made by a Parliament in which I have no representation. What sort of justice enables the aggrieved to sit in judgment over those against whom they have laid a charge?

The white man makes all the laws, he drags us before his courts and accuses us, and he sits in judgment over us. In this courtroom I face a white magistrate, I am confronted by a white prosecutor, and I am escorted into the dock by a white orderly. The atmosphere of white domination lurks all around in this courtroom. It reminds me that I am voteless because there is a Parliament in this country that is white-controlled. I am without land because the white minority has taken a lion's share of my country and forced my people to occupy poverty-stricken reserves, overpopulated and overstocked, in which we are ravaged by starvation and disease. These courts are not impartial tribunals dispensing justice but instruments used by the white man to punish those among us who clamour for deliverance from white rule.

I became a member of the African National Congress in 1944 and I have followed its aims for eighteen years. It sought the unity of all Africans, overriding tribal differences. It sought the acquisition of political power for Africans in the land of their birth. The African National Congress further believed that all people, irrespective of the national groups to which they may belong, and irrespective of the colour of their skins, all people whose home is South Africa and who believe in the principles of democracy and of the equality of men, should be treated as Africans; that all South Africans are entitled to live a free life on the basis of fullest equality of the rights and opportunities in every field, of full democratic rights, with a direct say in the affairs of the government.

Any thinking African in this country is driven continuously to a conflict between his conscience and the law. Throughout its fifty years of existence the African National Congress has done everything possible to bring its demands to the attention of successive South African governments. But this government has set the scene for violence by relying exclusively on violence with which to answer our people and their demands. We have been conditioned to our attitudes by history which is not of our making. We have been conditioned by the history of white governments in this country to accept the fact that Africans, when they make their demands powerfully enough to have some chance of success, are met with force and terror from the government.

Government violence can only breed counterviolence. Ultimately, if there is no dawning of sanity on the part of the government the dispute between the government and my people will be settled by force.

I hate all race discrimination, and in my hatred I am sustained by the fact that the overwhelming majority of people, here and abroad, hate it equally. I hate the systematic inculcation in children of colour prejudice and I am sustained in that hatred by the fact that the overwhelming majority of people, here and abroad, are with me in that. I hate the racial arrogance which decrees that the good things of life shall be retained as the exclusive right of a minority of the population, which reduces the majority of the population to a position of subservience and inferiority, and maintains them as voteless chattels to work where they are told and behave as they are told by the ruling minority. I am sustained in that hatred by the fact that the overwhelming majority of people both in this country and abroad are with me.

I have done my duty to my people and to South Africa. I have no doubt that posterity will pronounce that I was innocent and that the criminals who should have been brought before this court are the members of this government.

Mandela was sentenced to five years' imprisonment. Nine months later, in July 1963, he and nine others – the entire high command of Umkhonto we Sizwe – were accused of sabotage and conspiracy to overthrow the government, charges that carried the death penalty. Mandela opened the defence.

I am the First Accused. I hold a Bachelor's Degree in Arts and practised as an attorney in Johannesburg for a number of years in partnership with Oliver Tambo. I am a convicted prisoner serving five years for leaving the country without a permit and for inciting people to go on strike at the end of May 1961.

At the outset, I want to say that the suggestion made by the State in its opening that the struggle in South Africa is under the influence of foreigners or communists is wholly incorrect. I have done whatever I did, both as an individual and as a leader of my people, because of my experience in South Africa and my own African background, not because of what any outsider might have said. In my youth in the Transkei I listened to the elders of my tribe telling stories of the old days. Among the tales they related to me were those of wars fought by our ancestors in defence of the fatherland. I hoped then that life might offer me the opportunity to serve my people and make my own contribution to their freedom struggle. This is what has motivated me in all that I have done in relation to the charges made against me in this case.

Having said this, I must deal with the question of violence. Some of the things so far told to the court are true and some are untrue. I do not, however, deny that I planned sabotage. I did not plan it in a spirit of recklessness, nor because I have any love of violence. I planned it as a result of a calm and sober assessment of the political situation that had arisen after many years of tyranny, exploitation, and oppression of my people by the whites.

I admit immediately that I was one of the persons who helped to form

Umkhonto we Sizwe, and that I played a prominent role in its affairs until I was arrested in August 1962. I, and the others who started the organization, did so for two reasons. Firstly, we believed that as a result of government policy, violence by the African people had become inevitable, and that unless responsible leadership was given to channel and control the feelings of our people, there would be outbreaks of terrorism which would produce an intensity of bitterness and hostility between the various races of this country which is not produced even by war. Secondly, we felt that without violence there would be no way open to the African people to succeed in their struggle against the principle of white supremacy. All lawful methods of expressing opposition to this principle had been closed by legislation, and we were placed in a position in which we had either to accept a permanent state of inferiority, or to defy the government. We chose to defy the law. We first broke the law in a way which avoided any recourse to violence; when this form was legislated against, and the government resorted to a show of force to crush opposition to its policies, only then did we decide to answer violence with violence.

But the violence which we chose to adopt was not terrorism. We who formed Umkhonto were all members of the African National Congress, and had behind us the ANC tradition of non-violence and negotiation as a means of solving political disputes. We believed that South Africa belonged to all the people who lived in it, and not to one group, be it black or white. We did not want an inter-racial war, and tried to avoid it to the last. But the hard facts were that fifty years of non-violence had brought the African people nothing but more and more repressive legislation, and fewer and fewer rights. Four forms of violence were considered – sabotage, guerrilla warfare, terrorism, and open revolution. We chose to adopt the first method and to exhaust it before making any other decision.

The initial plan was based on a careful analysis of the political and economic situation of our country. We believed that South Africa depended to a large extent on foreign capital and foreign trade. We felt that planned destruction of power plants, and interference with rail and telephone communications, would tend to scare away capital from the country, make it more difficult for goods from the industrial areas to reach the seaports on schedule, and would in the long run be a heavy drain on the economic life of the country, thus compelling the voters of the country to reconsider their position.

Attacks on the economic lifelines of the country were to be linked with sabotage on government buildings and other symbols of apartheid. These attacks would serve as a source of inspiration to our people. In addition, they would provide an outlet for those people who were urging the adoption of violent methods and would enable us to give concrete proof to our followers that we had adopted a stronger line and were fighting back against government violence. In addition, if mass action was successfully organized, and mass reprisals taken, we felt that sympathy for our cause would be roused in other countries, and that greater pressure would be brought to bear on the South African government.

This then was the plan. Umkhonto was to perform sabotage, and strict instructions were given to its members that on no account were they to injure or kill people in planning or carrying out operations.

Experience convinced us that rebellion would offer the government limitless opportunities for the indiscriminate slaughter of our people, but it was precisely because the soil of South Africa was already drenched with the blood of innocent Africans that we felt it our duty to make preparations as a long-term undertaking to use force in order to defend ourselves against force. If war was inevitable, we wanted the fight to be conducted on terms most favourable to our people. The fight which held out prospects best for us and the least risk of life to both sides was guerrilla warfare. We decided, therefore, in our preparations for the future, to make provision for the possibility of guerrilla warfare. All whites undergo compulsory military training, but no such training was given to Africans. It was in our view essential to build up a nucleus of trained men who would be able to provide the leadership which would be required if guerrilla warfare started.

Another of the allegations made by the State is that the aims and objects of the ANC and the Communist party are the same. I wish to deal with this and with my own political position, because I must assume that the State may try to argue that I tried to introduce Marxism into the ANC. The allegation is false. The ideological creed of the ANC is, and always has been, the creed of African Nationalism. It is not the concept expressed in the cry, 'Drive the white man into the sea.' The African Nationalism for which the ANC stands is the concept of freedom and fulfilment for all as enshrined in our Freedom Charter, which is by no means a blueprint for a socialist state. It calls for redistribution, but not nationalization, of land; it provides for nationalization of mines, banks, and monopoly industry, because big monopolies are owned by one race only, and without such nationalization racial domination would be perpetuated despite the spread of political power.

As far as the Communist party is concerned, and if I understand its policy correctly, it stands for the establishment of a state based on the principles of Marxism. Although it is prepared to work for the Freedom Charter, as a short-term solution to the problems created by white supremacy, it regards the Freedom Charter as the beginning, and not the end, of its programme. The ANC's chief goal was for the African people to win unity and full political rights. The Communist party's main aim, on the other hand, was to remove the capitalists and to replace them with a working-class government. The Communist party sought to emphasize class distinctions while the ANC sought to harmonize them. This is a vital distinction [...]

Africans want a just share in the whole of South Africa, we want security and a stake in society. Above all, we want equal political rights, because without them our disabilities will be permanent. I know this sounds revolutionary to the whites in this country, because the majority of voters will be Africans. This makes the white man fear democracy. But his fear cannot be allowed to stand in the way of the only solution which will guarantee racial harmony and freedom for all. It is not true that the enfranchisement of all will result in racial domination. Political division based on colour is entirely artificial, and when it disappears so will the domination of one colour group by another. The ANC has spent half a century fighting against racism. When it triumphs it will not change that policy.

This then is what the ANC is fighting. Our struggle is a truly national one. It is a struggle of the African people, inspired by our own suffering and our own experience. It is a struggle for the right to live. During my lifetime I have dedicated myself to this struggle of the African people. I have fought against white domination, and I have fought against black domination. I have cherished the ideal of a democratic and free society in which all persons live together in harmony and with equal opportunities. It is an ideal which I hope to live for and to achieve. But if needs be, it is an ideal for which I am prepared to die.

At the end of what was known as the Rivonia Trial, Mandela and seven others were sentenced to life imprisonment. He arrived on Robben Island in June 1964.

Each cell had one window, about a foot square, covered with iron bars. The cell had two doors: a metal gate or grille with iron bars on the inside and a thick wooden door outside that. During the day, only the grille was locked; at night, the wooden door was locked as well.

The cells had been constructed hurriedly, and the walls were perpetually damp. When I mentioned this to the commanding officer, he told me our bodies would absorb the moisture. We were each issued with three blankets so flimsy and worn they were practically transparent. Our bedding consisted of a single sisal or straw mat. Later we were given a felt mat, and one placed the felt mat on top of the sisal one to provide some softness. At that time of year, the cells were so cold and the blankets provided so little warmth that we always slept fully dressed.

I was assigned a cell at the head of the corridor. It overlooked the courtyard and had a small eye-level window. I could walk the length of my cell in three paces. When I lay down, I could feel the wall with my feet and my head grazed the concrete at the other side. The width was about six feet, and the walls were at least two feet thick. Each cell had a white card posted outside it with our name and our prison service number. Mine read, 'N. Mandela 466/64', which meant I was the 466th prisoner admitted to the island in 1964. I was forty-six years old, a political prisoner with a life sentence, and that small cramped space was to be my home for I knew not how long.

NOTES
1 An expression of disgust.
2 Ouch.
3 Township argot.
4 Young hooligans.
5 School children are all asleep.
6 I see.
7 An illegal drinking den.
8 Walter Sisulu.
9 Mandela's wife at the time.
10 Mandela's honorific title.

CHAPTER 14

THE APOTHEOSIS OF APARTHEID

South Africa, renowned both far and wide
For politics and little else beside
Roy Campbell

Apartheid, composed almost equally of absurdity and brutality, presented writers with a challenge. One of the most successful at exploiting its comic potential was the English satirist, Tom Sharpe. He emigrated to Natal in 1951, when he was 23 and, being a natural subversive, was deported 10 years later. In his first novel, *Riotous Assembly* (93), published in 1971, he exacted his revenge.

Miss Hazelstone was telephoning to report that she had just shot her Zulu cook. Konstabel Els was perfectly capable of handling the matter. He had in his time as a police officer shot any number of Zulu cooks. Besides there was a regular procedure for dealing with such reports. Konstabel Els went into the routine.

'You wish to report the death of a kaffir,' he began.

'I have just murdered my Zulu cook,' snapped Miss Hazelstone.

Els was placatory. 'That's what I said. You wish to report the death of a coon.'

'I wish to do nothing of the sort. I told you I have just murdered Fivepence.'

Els tried again. 'The loss of a few coins doesn't count as murder.'

'Fivepence was my cook.'

'Killing a cook doesn't count as murder either.'

'What does it count as, then?' Miss Hazelstone's confidence in her own guilt was beginning to wilt under Konstabel Els' favourable diagnosis of the situation.

'Killing a white cook can be murder. It's unlikely but it can be. Killing a black cook can't. Not under any circumstances. Killing a black cook comes under self-defence, justifiable homicide or garbage disposal.' Els permitted himself a giggle. 'Have you tried the Health Department?' he inquired.

It was obvious to the Kommandant that Els had lost what little sense of social deference he had ever possessed. He pushed Els aside and took the call himself.

'Kommandant van Heerden here,' he said. 'I understand that there has been slight accident with your cook.'

Miss Hazelstone was adamant. 'I have just murdered my Zulu cook.'

Kommandant van Heerden ignored the self-accusation. 'The body is in the house?' he inquired.

'The body is on the lawn,' said Miss Hazelstone. The Kommandant sighed. It was always the same. Why couldn't people shoot blacks inside their houses where they were supposed to shoot them?

'I will be up at Jacaranda House in forty minutes,' he said, 'and when I arrive I will find the body in the house.'

'You won't,' Miss Hazelstone insisted, 'you'll find it on the back lawn.'

Kommandant van Heerden tried again.

'When I arrive the body will be in the house.' He said it very slowly this time.

Miss Hazelstone was not impressed. 'Are you suggesting that I move the body?' she asked angrily.

The Kommandant was appalled at the suggestion. 'Certainly not,' he said. 'I have no wish to put you to any inconvenience and besides there might be fingerprints. You can get the servants to move it for you.'

There was a pause while Miss Hazelstone considered the implications of this remark. 'It sounds to me as though you are suggesting that I should tamper with the evidence of a crime,' she said slowly and menacingly. 'It sounds to me as though you are trying to get me to interfere with the course of justice.'

'Madam,' interrupted the Kommandant, 'I am merely trying to help you to obey the law.' He paused, groping for words. 'The law says that it is a crime to shoot kaffirs outside your house. But the law also says it is perfectly permissible and proper to shoot them inside your house if they have entered illegally.'

'Fivepence was my cook and had every legal right to enter the house.'

'I'm afraid you're wrong there,' Kommandant van Heerden went on. 'Your house is a white area and no kaffir is entitled to enter a white area without permission. By shooting your cook you were refusing him permission to enter your house. I think it is safe to assume that.'

There was a silence at the other end of the line. Miss Hazelstone was evidently convinced.

'I'll be up in forty minutes,' continued van Heerden, adding hopefully, 'and I trust the body –'

'You'll be up here in five minutes and Fivepence will be on the lawn where I shot him,' snarled Miss Hazelstone and slammed down the phone.

Anthony Delius, a South African journalist and writer, published his epic poem, *The Last Division* (94), in 1959 just as Verwoerd was getting into his messianic stride. In a tight-lipped review, *Die Burger*, an Afrikaner nationalist newspaper once edited by Daniel Malan, observed: 'It is an unpleasant, bitter poem which will definitely be quoted to a considerable extent.' No part of it has been more quoted than the 'Ethnic Anthem', sung, Delius suggested, by all Nationalists 'at solemn feasts and junketings'.

> 'Ethnasia will last a thousand years,
> Our land is studded with its glories,
> Its monuments are separate bars
> And segregated lavatories.
>
> 'God has through us ordained it so
> Post Offices are split in two
> And separate pillar boxes fix
> That correspondence does not mix,
> No one has ever managed better
> To guard the spirit – and the letter.
>
> 'O ethnic trains and buses daily hurry
> Divided hues to earn divided bread,
> The races may not fornicate or marry,
> They even lie apart when they are dead.

'God may award his just damnation
For mixed or unmixed fornication,
Down here we warn the citizen
With whom it is a crime to sin,
And no man takes, with our cognisance,
A liberty without a licence.

'Yea, in our law men stand or fall
By rule of thumb or finger-nail,
So sensitive's our Roman-Dutch
It notes if lips protrude too much.

'We've split all difference so fine
No wider than a hair or skin,
To foil the trick of traits and needs
So shockingly the same in breeds –
For such success in our researches
We thank Thee, Lord, in separate churches.

'How wondrous is our work, our way,
And thine as well, Great Separator,
Who separating night from day
Left us to sort the rest out later.'

For that and a string of similarly inspired offences, Delius was forced to leave the country.

Adam Small (95), a Cape Coloured poet, showed that embracing his oppressors could be quite as effective as mocking them.

There's Somethin'

You can stop me
drinking a pepsi-cola
at the cafe in the Avenue
or goin' to an Alhambra revue,
you can stop me doin'

415

some silly thing like that
but o
there's somethin' you can
never never do;
you can stop me
boarding a carriage
on the Bellville run
white class
or sittin' in front
of the X-line
on the Hout Bay bus,
you can stop me doin'
some silly thing like that
but o
there's somethin' you can
never never do;
you can stop me goin' to
Groote Schuur
in the same ambulance
as you
or tryin' to go to Heaven
from a Groote Kerk pew
you can stop me doin'
some silly thing like that
but o
there's somethin' you can
never never do;
true's God
you can stop me doin'
all silly things of that sort
and to think of it
if it comes to that
you can even stop me hatin'
but o
there's somethin' you can
never never do –
you can't

ever
ever
ever stop me loving
even you!

Nadine Gordimer was the first South African to win the Nobel Prize for Literature, awarded to her in 1991. An anti-apartheid activist, she joined the ANC when it was an illegal organisation. Although the government banned many of her books, she was not a propagandist. Rather, her novels are intricate psychological studies of her characters' responses to apartheid. In *A World of Strangers* (96), one of the first, she explored the question of whether the victims of apartheid had a moral duty to enrol in the fight against it. The narrator is a young Englishman, the son of left-wing parents, recently arrived in 1950s Johannesburg; Steven Sitole is a black man-about-town; Anna, an anti-apartheid lawyer, regards him as a 'shebeen-lizard'.

In the kitchen she did everything unhurriedly but practisedly. When she lifted the lid of a pot, there was the comforting vegetable scent of a home-made soup, and there were two thick pats of fillet lying on a board, ready for grilling. I hung about, talking to her, getting in the way rather than helping, as you do in a kitchen when you don't know where things are kept. 'I'm glad to hear that you're not too down on Steven's romantic view of life – although I'm not sure, yet, that I agree about it being romantic.'

'It's romantic, all right,' said Anna, sending tomatoes seething into a hot pan, 'and I am down on it. I understand the need to be romantic in some way, but I'm down on this way. It's a waste of energy. You won't catch Steven working with Congress or any other African movement, for that matter. He never defied, either – I'm talking about the defiance campaign, the passive resistance movement of a year or two back. The only defiance he's interested in is not paying his bills, or buying drink. He's got this picture of himself as the embittered, devil-may-care African, and believe me, he's making a career of it. He doesn't care a damn about his people; he's only concerned with his own misfortune in being born one of them.' The sizzling of the tomatoes in butter spat angrily around her.

'Why should Steven *have* to be involved in these movements and congresses and what-not?' I said. 'I must admit, the whole idea would fill me with distaste. I'd run a mile at the thought.'

Over the tomatoes, she smiled the private smile of the old hand: the stoker when the ship's passenger marvels at the fact that anyone can work in such heat, the foundryman when someone says, 'How do you stand the noise?' 'Somebody's got to do it. Why should you expect somebody else to do it for you? Nobody really wants to.'

'Ah now, that's not so. I've always thought that there are two kinds of people, people with public lives, and people with private lives. The people with public lives are concerned with a collective fate, the private livers with an individual one. But – roughly, since the Kaiser's war, I suppose – the private livers have become hunted people. Hunted and defamed. You must join. You must be Communist or Anti-Communist, Nationalist or Kaffirboetie'[1] – she smiled at my pronunciation – 'you must protest, defy, non-co-operate. And all these things you must do; you can't leave it all in the infinitely more capable hands of the public livers.'

She turned from the stove with her answer all ready, but then paused a moment, filling in the pause by gesturing for me to pass her the soup bowls, and said, as if she had suddenly discarded her argument, 'Yes, there's less and less chance to live your own life. That's true. The pressure's too strong.'

'From outside, as well as within, that's my point,' I said, obstinately, not wishing to claim common ground where I did not think there was any. 'The public life people have always responded to pressure from within – their own conscience, sense of responsibility toward others, ambition, and so on; but the private livers, in whom these things are latent, weak, or differently directed, could go on simply going their own ways, unless the pressure from outside became too strong. Well, now it's just bloody irresistible. It isn't enough that a chap like Steven has all the bother of being a black man in this country, on top of it he's expected to give up to political action whatever small part of his life he can call his own.'

I followed Anna into the living-room, where she carried the soup. 'He wants the results of that political action, doesn't he?' she called, over her shoulder. 'He wants to be free of the pass laws and the colour bar and the whole caboodle? – Well, let him fight for it.' She laughed, indignant in spite of herself.

All the old, wild reluctant boredom with which I had borne with this sort of talk all my life was charged, this time, with something more personal; a nervous excitement, a touchiness. I felt the necessity to get the better of her; to punish her, almost. 'My dear Anna, you're so wrong, too. The private liver, the selfish man, the shirker, as you think him – he's a rebel. He's a rebel against rebellion. On the side, he's got a private revolution of his own; it's waged for himself, but quite a lot of other people may benefit. I think that about Steven. He won't troop along with your Congress, or get himself arrested in the public library, but, in spite of everything the white man does to knock the spirit out of him, he remains very much alive – getting drunk, getting in debt, running his insurance racket. Learning all the shady tricks, so that, in the end, he can beat dear old white civilization at its own games. He's muscling in; who's to say he won't get there first? While the Congress chaps are pounding fiercely on the front door, he's slipped in through a back window. But, most important of all, he's alive, isn't he? He's alive, in defiance of everything that would attempt to make him half-alive. I don't suppose he's been well fed, but he looks wiry, his schooling hasn't been anything much, but it seems to me he's got himself an education that works, all the same, well-paid jobs are closed to him, so he's invented one for himself. And when the Congress chaps get in at last, perhaps they'll find him there, waiting.' I laughed.

'Oh my God! What a horrible idea.' She pressed her napkin against her mouth and drew in her shoulders.

I was perversely triumphant. I added, with some arrogance 'Well, don't underestimate the Sitoles of this world, anyway. They're like history; their progress is inexorable. Let that be a consolation to you when your Congresses and protests don't seem to be getting very far.'

From the 1930s onwards, South African Jews made an enormous, disproportionate contribution to the anti-apartheid cause. Besides Nadine Gordimer, the most illustrious of them included Joe Slovo, chief of staff of the ANC's armed wing and later a minister in Mandela's first government, and Helen Suzman, for 36 years an opposition MP and one of apartheid's most persistent and effective critics. Many Jews were trade unionists, lawyers and journalists actively involved in the struggle. Of the 23 whites prosecuted in the Treason Trial, 15 were Jewish, as were all five whites in the Rivonia Trial. Reflecting on the cultural life of Johannesburg in the 1950s, Lewis Nkosi (97), a *Drum* journalist, paid tribute to them.

Johannesburg, unlike Durban, was also dense, rhythmic: it was swaggering and wasteful, totally without an inner life. People loved quickly, they lived fitfully; so profligate were they with emotion, so wasteful with their vitality, that it was very often difficult for them to pause and reflect on the passing scene. This I think partly explains why so many black South African writers have concentrated on the journalistic prose, more often on the short story but rarely on the long reflective novel. It is not so much the intense suffering (though this helped a great deal) which makes it impossible for black writers to produce long and complex works of literary genius as it is the very absorbing, violent and immediate nature of experience which impinges upon individual life. Unless literature is assumed to be important in itself, for its own sake, unless it is assumed to be its own justification, there was no reason whatever why anyone in our generation should have wanted to write. It seems to me that literature begins where life fails; in Johannesburg there was much too much of this direct experience to be had; there was no privacy in which to reflect, people called on you early in the morning, bringing bottles or asking you out to a shebeen, police raided you at night for permits and identity documents, parties were too numerous and sprang up too arbitrarily in the middle of some important work; and if one wasn't sure which jail one was going to be in on the morrow, or even whether one was going to be alive or cut down by a police bullet or perhaps by the knife of a thug, there was no reason not to grab at this life, at this gift, eagerly, without waiting even for the mediating intervention of art and literature. That did not mean, as it might be taken to mean, that we did not need literary heroes; those of us who could read wanted to test this vitality against someone else's vitality; what it merely meant was that we had not the time or the driving necessity to create a literature ourselves. Thus when we attacked white authors like Alan Paton for distorting African reality, when we repudiated the heroes they provided for us, we were rightly accused of having failed to provide South Africa with alternative heroes of our own. Where, it was scornfully asked, was the great African novel? Ultimately, it was the cacophonous, swaggering world of Elizabethan England which gave us the closest parallel to our own mode of existence; the cloak and dagger stories of Shakespeare; the marvellously gay and dangerous time of change in Great Britain, came closest to reflecting our own condition. Thus it was possible for an African musician returning home at night to inspire awe in a group of thugs surrounding him by declaiming in an impossibly archaic English: 'Unhand me, rogues!' Indeed, they did unhand him. The same thugs who were to be seen chewing on apples in the streets of Johannesburg after the manner of the gangsters they had seen in Richard Widmark's motion picture, *Street with No Name*, also delighted in the violent colour, the rolling rhetoric of Shakespearean theatre. Their favourite form of persecuting middle-class Africans was forcing them to stand at street corners, reciting some passage from Shakespeare, for which they would be showered with sincere applause.

However, Johannesburg had also the sense to have a large Jewish population, which, besides making money, also did a great deal to temper this crude urban landscape with what surely must be the innate Jewish gift for marshalling residual energy toward a life of contemplative culture. If Johannesburg is a cultural desert (indeed the whole of South Africa is) it would have been a worse desert without the mitigating Jewish presence. For instance, if one was foolhardy enough to have girl friends across the colour-line they were likely to be Jewish (as guilt-ridden as hell, naturally, and fixated on their fathers to boot); if one had white friends of any sort they were most likely Jewish; almost eighty per cent white South Africans who belonged to left wing and liberal organisations were Jewish; whatever cultural vitality Johannesburg enjoyed was contributed by this Jewish community, middle-class and moneyed; one community which can be counted on to produce a Helen Suzman. It is not very much, I admit, but in South Africa it staggers the imagination.

This was the city then conquered by big business and by Boer philistines, run by a gun-crazy police force and knife-happy African thugs, a city immune to all the graces of African tribal life and to the contemplative pleasures of European cultural life; finally it had to depend upon this Jewish community, upon its dogged sense of identity and the Jewish nostalgia for things of the heart and spirit.

The moment one understands the great South African poverty so far as tradition is concerned, the lack of any coherence in whatever intellectual life there is to be found there, the lack finally of any common assumptions or sense of shared nationhood, the sooner will the importance of this Jewish identity become apparent, however threadbare and shopsoiled – and it is threadbare and shopsoiled, for it buttressed the rather aimless, drifting existence of Johannesburg urban life. It was the Jews who tempered this harsh social order of apartheid with a tenuous liberalism and humane values for the liberals and the left wing were drawn mostly from this community; and it was they who provided whatever fusion there was between African native talent and European discipline and technique. They and the Africans made Johannesburg alive and absorbent in a way no other city of the Republic was.

Can Themba (98), another of the *Drum* kindergarten, was a close friend of Lewis Nkosi's. He personified what Nkosi called 'swaggering profligacy' and could almost have been a model for Gordimer's man-about-town.

There is a law that says (I'm afraid quite a bit of this will seem like *there is a law that says*), well, it says I cannot make love to a white woman. It is a law. But stronger still there is a custom – a tradition, it is called here – that shudders at the sheerest notion that any white man could contemplate, or any black man dare, a love affair across the colour line. They do: white men *do* meet and fall in love with black women; black men do explore 'ivory towers'. But all this is severely 'agin the law'.

There are also African nationalists who profess horror at the thought that any self-respecting black man could desire any white woman. They say that no African could ever debase himself as to love a white woman. This is highly cultivated and pious lying in the teeth of daily slavering in town and in cinema. African girls, who are torturing themselves all the time to gain a whiter complexion, straighter hair and corset-contained posteriors, surely know what their men secretly admire.

As for myself, I do not necessarily want to bed a white woman; I merely insist on my right to want her.

Once, I took a white girl to Sophiatown. She was a girl who liked to go with me and did not have the rumoured South African inhibitions. She did not even want the anthropological knowledge of 'how the other South Africans live'. She just wanted to be with me.

She had a car, an ancient Morris. On the way to Sophiatown of those days, you drove along Bree Street, past the Fordsburg Police Station in the Indian area, past Braamfontein railway station, under a bridge away past the cemetery, past Bridgetown Memorial Hospital (known, strangely, for bringing illegitimate non-European children into the world), up Hurst Hill, past Talitha Home (a place of detention for delinquent non-European girls), past aggressive Westdene (sore at the proximity of so many non-white townships around her), and into Sophiatown.

So that night a black man and a white woman went to Sophiatown. I first took Janet to my auntie's place in Victoria Road, just opposite the bus terminus. It was a sight to glad a cynic's heart to see my aunt shiver before Janet.

'Mama' – in my world all women equivalents of my mother are mother to me – 'Mama, this is my girl. Where is Tata?' This question, not because my uncle might or might not approve, but because I knew he was terribly fond of brandy, and I was just about to organise a little party; he would not forgive me for leaving him out. But he was not there. He had gone to some meeting of *amagosa* – church stewards, of whom he was the chief.

'Mama, how about a doek for Janet.'

The doek! God save our gracious doek. A doek is a colourful piece of cloth that the African woman wears as headgear. It is tied stylistically into various shapes from Accra to Cape Town. I do not know the history of this innocuous piece of cloth. In Afrikaans, the language of those of our white masters who are of Dutch and Huguenot descent, doek meant, variously, a tablecloth, a dirty rag, or a symbol of the slave. Perhaps it was later used by African women in contact with European ideas of beauty who realised that 'they had no hair' and subconsciously hid their heads under the doek. Whatever else, the doek had come to designate the African woman. So that evening when I said, 'Mama, how about a doek for Janet', I was proposing to transform her, despite her colour and her deep blue eyes, into an African girl for the while.

Ma dug into her chest and produced a multi-coloured chiffon doek. We stood before the wardrobe mirror while my sisters helped to tie Janet's doek in the current township style. To my sisters that night I was obviously a hell of a guy.

Then I took Janet to a shebeen in Gibson Street. I was well known in that particular shebeen, could get my liquor 'on tick' and could get VIP treatment even without the asset of Janet. With Janet, I was a sensation. Shebeens are noisy drinking places and as we approached that shebeen we could hear the blast of loud-mouthed conversation. But when we entered a haunted hush fell upon the house. The shebeen queen rushed two men off their chairs to make places for us, and: 'What would you have, Mr Themba?'

There are certain names that do not go with Mister, I don't have a clue why. But, for sure, you cannot imagine a Mr Charlie Chaplin or a Mr William Shakespeare or a Mr Jesus Christ. My name – Can Themba – operates in that sort of class. So you can see the kind of sensation we caused when the shebeen queen addressed me as Mr Themba.

I said, casually as you like, 'A half a jack for a start, and I suppose you'd like a beer, too, my dear?'

The other patrons of the shebeen were coming up for air, one by one, and I could see that they were wondering about Janet. Some thought that she was coloured, a South African mulatto. One said she was white, appending, 'These journalist boys get the best girls.' But it was clear that the doek flummoxed them. Even iron-coloureds, whose stubborn physical appearances veer strongly to the Negroid parent, are proud enough of whatever hair they have to expose it. But this girl wore a doek!

Then Janet spoke to me in that tinkling English voice of hers, and I spoke to her, easily, without inhibition, without madamising her. One chap, who could contain himself no longer, rose to shake my hand. He said, in the argot of the townships, 'Brer Can, you've eaten caustic soda. Look, man, get me fish-meat like this, and s'true's God, I'll buy you a *vung* (a car)!' That sort of thawed the house and everybody broke into raucous laughter.

Later, I collected a bottle of brandy and some ginger ale, and took Janet to my room in Gold Street. There were a few friends and their girls: Kaffertjie (Little Kaffer – he was quite defiantly proud of this name) and Hilda, Jazzboy and Pule, Jimmy, Rockefeller and a coloured girl we called Madame Defarge because day or night she always had clicking knitting needles with her. We drank, joked, conversed, sang and horse-played. It was a night of the Sophiatown of my time, before the government destroyed it.

Sophiatown, which looms so large in reminiscences of the period, was one of the few urban areas of South Africa where non-whites were allowed to own the freehold of their homes. To Afrikaner nationalists, it was an insulting anomaly. So in 1955, under the Group Areas Act, the government bulldozed Sophiatown out of existence, built a white suburb in its place and called it, with all the subtlety at its command, 'Triomf'. Similarly, District Six, a vibrantly multi-racial part of Cape Town ever since the abolition of slavery, was re-zoned as white in 1966 and finally bulldozed 18 years later after 60 000 people had been forced to move. In his fictionalised portrayal of the area where he was born, Richard Rive (99), a Cape Coloured writer, reflected on what District Six represented. It is New Year's Day and the Jungle Boys gang and their friends have gone to the beach – the 'wrong' beach, as it turns out.

After lunch the Jungle Boys went back to their unsuccessful fishing and everyone else relaxed on the sand or rocks. Pretty-Boy suggested to Moena Lelik that they could go for a stroll along the beaches to St James. As they walked he told her about Johannesburg, how he had learnt to swim and when he had first met Zoot. She in turn told him that she had never dared to tell how much she admired him. Her parents and brothers loved her as she loved them, but they were far too protective towards her. The two stood and held hands on the edge of the almost deserted tidal pool at Dalebrook, watching the few children cavorting in the water. Pretty-Boy held her tightly. Moena was blissfully happy.

A young white beach constable hurried towards them waving his arms.

'Come on, come on, get off this beach. You're not allowed here!'

'Why not?' Pretty-Boy asked, annoyed at the uncalled-for hostility.

'Can't you read the notices? This beach is for white people only.'

'We're not making any trouble. We're just looking,' Moena said.

'Well you've looked enough. Now clear off the beach.'

'You don't speak to any lady like that,' Pretty-Boy said angrily.

'Let's go,' Moena pleaded. 'We don't want any trouble.'

'There will be plenty of trouble if you don't move fast. Want me to fetch a railway policeman from the station?'

'You may do what you please. We'll move when we are ready,' Pretty-Boy said evenly. 'And we're not ready yet.'

'If that's the way you want it, then you can have it.' The beach constable hurried back through the subway.

'Let's go,' Moena said nervously.

'Don't worry about him,' Pretty-Boy reassured her. 'He's just bluffing. All whites bluff all the time. That's most probably the last we'll see of him.'

They started walking back towards Kalk Bay. The beach constable came running after them with a bored railway police sergeant in tow. Pretty-Boy did not quicken his pace although Moena nervously gripped his hand.

'Hey you, you there, stop where you are,' the beach constable shouted.

They went on walking at the same pace, ignoring the shouts.

'Can't you hear me? I said, stop there!'

Pretty-Boy and Moena waited until they came up.

'These are the two, sergeant.'

The railway policeman was obviously more annoyed with the beach constable than with them.

'You know you're on the wrong beach?' he said, going through the motions.

'I wasn't aware of it,' Pretty-Boy said.

'Well, you are now, and you are breaking the law. I can arrest you and that's not a pleasant way to start the new year, is it?'

'You must do what you mean to do,' Pretty-Boy answered flatly.

'I don't understand you people. You have your own beaches. Why must

425

you come here to swim? White people don't go to your part.'

'We were not going to swim. We were just walking across this section on our way to St James.'

'Please, sir,' Moena was now near to tears. 'We don't want any trouble. We are leaving now.'

'O.K. I'll let you off this time, but don't let me catch you here again. Stay on your own beach or, if you want to walk to St James, then take the Main Road.'

Pretty-Boy said nothing but there was a hostility in his blue eyes that was ugly and frightening.

'Come,' he said fiercely to Moena. They continued walking to Kalk Bay in silence.

Pretty-Boy would not speak about the incident but Moena burst into tears when she saw her mother, and blurted out the full story. The Jungle Boys were fetched and were all for sorting out the beach constable immediately. Their mother dissuaded them. There was no doubt that the spirit of the party was now dampened and that nothing would revive it. Then Zoot spoke, more to himself although the rest were listening.

'You know, it's a funny thing, but it's only in the District that I feel safe. District Six is like an island, if you follow me, an island in a sea of apartheid. The whole of District Six is one big apartheid, so we can't see it. We only see it when the white man comes and forces it on us, when he makes us see it – when the police come, and the council people and so on – or when we leave the District, when we leave our island and go into Cape Town or to Sea Point or come here to Kalk Bay. Then we again see apartheid. I know the District is dirty and poor and a slum, as the newspapers always remind us, but it's our own and we have never put up notices which say 'Slegs blankes' or 'Whites only'. *They* put up the notices. When the white man comes into the District with his notices he is a stranger, and when we come out of the District he makes us realise that we are strangers. It's funny but that's the way I see it.'

This was more than he had spoken for a long time, and the rest of the party did not interrupt or comment.

'Well, that's that. Now I suggest we have a last drink, pack up our things, and get the hell back to the District as soon as we can.'

They took an empty train back while crowded trains were still coming in.

426

Under Verwoerd, who became prime minister in 1958, apartheid reached its apotheosis. It was now known officially as 'separate development'. In *Brothers Under the Skin*, published in 2003, Christopher Hope (100), the South African-born novelist and poet, perfectly caught the lunatic spirit of it.

What made Hendrik Verwoerd a revolutionary was his appetite for theory and his will to power. He was prepared to face the question others had shirked. He had found the solution, and in this man who had once planned to become a religious minister, the missionary urge was strong; he was prepared to do what it took, he was going to improve the destiny of black people, whether they liked it or not. He had the answer that would be intellectually respectable, that would stand up to scrutiny, that was modern and, even, compassionate. He saw the winds of change were blowing in Africa in the direction of sovereignty, freedom and independence and he came up with a solution that embodied all these goals. He would set the Afrikaner free by setting everyone free. He would keep the Afrikaner separate and pure by keeping everyone separate and pure, within their 'homelands'.

What was to be done with 'others', your neighbours, excluded from this idea of South Africa – those who watched you strengthening your stockade, your laager, and growing rich and fat? His answer was – you declare them 'independent'. Everyone would be independent, in their own countries, under their own flags, and their own presidents. Parallel freedoms for all. Every 'race' under the sun would be penned in ethnic stockades and kept apart by law, barbed wire and bullets.

It was a doctrine built on complex ideas, and white South Africans were traditionally uneasy with ideas. They wanted superiority, they did not like theory. Yet they obeyed. They were in thrall to this blue-eyed mystic. Dr Verwoerd's theories may have seemed bizarre or bold or bunkum, but they fired in his followers passionate, violent loyalty. Distended, rampant power does not bring on mental collapse, rather it regularizes abnormality. Amongst those who bought into the dream, and most whites did so, it seemed perfectly normal.

Dr Verwoerd transformed the crude notion that whites were better than blacks into the mystical belief that the separation of races into parallel prisons was divinely sanctioned and intellectually respectable. In order to enforce his dream of 'homelands' for everyone, he was obliged to multiply the number of amenities that were to be equally available to each group:

schools, sex, buses, toilets, governments, flags, churches, graveyards. You might then separate children from mothers, wives from husbands, brothers from sisters, and remove whole towns and villages from their ancestral lands. It seemed astonishingly cruel, but really it was truly kind. Thousands of people administered the system and they believed it was the best solution in the best of worlds. No one understood its Byzantine complexities. It required an army of people who went around pushing pencils into children's hair to see if it was curly enough to hold the pencil for as long as it took for the child to be 'classified' as 'coloured' or 'Asian' or 'white' or 'black'. Teams of surveyors drew up maps of new, separate, race-based states, to be created in a separate but equal, Balkanized South Africa which was to be carved up into eight or ten or twelve or fourteen new 'homelands'. Model townships arose in the veld, vast projects which often advanced no further than a forest of concrete outhouses. Squads of police broke into the bedrooms of people suspected of having sex 'across the colour bar', and tested the bedclothes for signs of tell-tale warmth. Opponents went to jail, into exile, to the gallows.

Verwoerd believed in it and soon his people believed in it, and then even his English-speaking opponents amongst the white people believed in it, and voted for Verwoerd in increasing numbers throughout his reign. They feared him, they respected him, they were appalled by him – but they breathed in the perfume and in their heart of hearts they gave thanks because they needed a strong man, and here was a strong man. They needed answers and he had the answers. They needed to deal with their enemies, and he dealt with enemies without hesitation or remorse, not because he was bad, but because he knew he was right. Nothing more distinguished the tyranny of Hendrik Frensch Verwoerd than his unshakable ascetic mien, his sincere conviction that apartheid was not merely desirable it was morally right and divinely ordained. He brooked no argument. The crazier the ideas became, the more white people adopted them. The country was in the hands of a tribe that had literally lost its head.

Fulfilling Verwoerd's 'vision' was to lead to more than three million Africans being forcibly uprooted and transported to rural areas where there were no jobs and, as often as not, no homes, shops or schools. As apartheid bit deeper, the brutality with which it was enforced intensified. Verwoerd, assassinated in 1966 by an apparently crazed parliamentary messenger, was replaced by John Vorster, who had been interned during the Second World War for his Nazi sympathies. As Verwoerd's Minister of Justice, he had specialised in pulling the levers of repression. The most high-profile victim of his regime was Steve Biko, a charismatic leader, who in 1970 had helped found the Black Consciousness movement. Biko believed the first step to liberation was psychological emancipation from white tutelage. One of his most influential admirers was Donald Woods (101), editor of the liberal *Daily Dispatch*, which had a large African readership in the Eastern Cape. In his 1978 biography of 'the greatest man I ever had the privilege to know', Woods told the story of Biko's martyrdom.

On Tuesday, September 6, 1977, a close friend of mine named Bantu Stephen Biko was taken by South African political police to Room 619 of the Sanlam Building in Strand Street, Port Elizabeth, Cape Province, where he was hand-cuffed, put into leg irons, chained to a grille and subjected to twenty-two hours of interrogation in the course of which he was tortured and beaten, sustaining several blows to the head which damaged his brain fatally, causing him to lapse into a coma and die six days later.

The fatal blows were struck by one or more of the following members of the South African Security Police: Colonel P. Goosen; Major H. Snyman; Warrant Officers J. Beneke, R. Marx, B. Coetzee, J. Fouche; Captain D. Siebert; Lieutenant W. Wilken; Sergeant S. Nieuwoudt and Major T. Fischer. Most, if not all, of these men were members of two interrogation 'teams' – one operating by day and one by night. Detainees with personal experience of Security Police methods say the day interrogation teams specialize in coordinated questioning, psychological tactics and verbal abuse, but that the night teams are the assaulters, beating up detainees to 'soften them up' for the day teams. If this procedure was followed against Steve Biko, the fatal blows were struck by one or more of the 'night team' – Wilken, Coetzee and Fouche.

However, these men were simply agents. The man ultimately responsible for the death of Steve Biko was James Thomas Kruger, Minister of Police, because it was his indulgent attitude toward the homicidal tendencies of his Security Police that created the atmosphere within which the torturers were given scope to act. Kruger cannot validly claim to have known nothing of these matters, because two years previously I had warned him that there were criminal elements in his Security Police.

On the same occasion I told him of the importance of Steve Biko and later published a warning that if any harm came to him in detention, the consequences would be disastrous for the entire nation, and in particular for the Nationalist government. Mr. Kruger and his colleagues ignored this warning. Not only was Steve Biko detained several times, but he was increasingly persecuted, harrassed, put into solitary confinement and ultimately tortured and killed.

Kruger immediately implied that Steve had starved himself to death, but I knew this was nonsense. Steve and I had had a pact that if he should be detained, if he should die in detention, and if it should be claimed that he had taken his own life, I would know this to be untrue. Clearly, he had been killed by Security Police under the powers granted to them by the Nationalist government.

Therefore, in addition to being a personal testimony to Steve Biko, this book is an indictment of the Nationalist government and of the policy and the system it represents.

Steve Biko's death echoed around the world. He was only thirty years old when he died, and he had lived in obscurity, silenced from public utterance by banning orders and restricted to a small town remote from the metropolitan areas. He was forbidden to make speeches; forbidden to speak with more than one person at a time; forbidden to be quoted; forbidden to function fully as a political personality. Yet in his short life-time he influenced the lives and ideals of millions of his countrymen, and his death convulsed our nation and reverberated far beyond its boundaries.

True to South African judicial form, the inquest into Biko's death found that 'his head injuries were probably sustained in a scuffle in the security police office in Port Elizabeth … the death cannot be attributed to any act or omission amounting to a criminal offence on the part of any person.'[2] In a general election two months after Biko was murdered, Vorster's National Party was returned to power with a record number of seats. In *Burger's Daughter* (102), another of her banned novels (published in 1979), Nadine Gordimer identified – skewered would be more accurate – the sophistry of a new generation of government supporters.

Brandt Vermeulen is one of the 'New Afrikaners' from an old distinguished Afrikaner family. In each country families become distinguished for different reasons. Where there is no Almanach de Gotha, the building of railroads and sinking of oil wells becomes a pedigree, where no one can trace himself back to Argenteuil or the Crusades, colonial wars substitute for a college of heraldry. Brandt Vermeulen's great-great-grandfather was murdered by Dingaan with Piet Retief's party, his maternal grand-father was a Boer War general, there was a poet uncle whose seventieth birthday has been commemorated by the issue of a stamp, and another uncle interned during the Second World War, along with Mr Vorster, for pro-Nazi sympathies, there is even a cousin who was decorated posthumously for bravery in battle against Rommel at Alamein. Cornelius Vermeulen, a Moderator of the Dutch Reformed Church, was a Minister in the first National Party government after the triumph of the Afrikaner in 1948, when his son Brandt was eight years old, and held office in the successive Strydom, Verwoerd and Vorster governments before retiring to one of the family farms in the Bethal district of the Transvaal.

The sons of distinguished families also often move away from the traditional milieu and activities in discordance with whatever their particular level in frontier society has confined them to. Just as the successful Jewish or Indian country storekeeper's son becomes a doctor or lawyer in the city, or the son of the shift-boss on the gold-mine goes into business, Brandt Vermeulen left farm, church and party caucus and went to Leyden and Princeton to read politics, philosophy and economics, and to Paris and New York to see modern art. He did not come back, Europeanized, Americanized by foreign ideas of equality and liberty, to destroy what the great-great-grandfather died for at the hands of a kaffir and the Boer general fought the English for; he came back with a vocabulary and sophistry to transform the home-whittled destiny of white to rule over black in terms that the generation of late-twentieth-century orientated, Nationalist intellectuals would advance as the first true social evolution of the century, since nineteenth-century European liberalism showed itself spent in the failure of racial integration wherever this was tried, and Communism, accusing the Afrikaner of enslaving blacks under franchise of God's will, itself enslaved whites and yellows along with blacks in denial of God's existence. He and his kind were the first to be sophisticated enough to laugh at the sort of thing only denigrators of the Afrikaner volk were supposed to laugh at: the Dutch Reformed Churches' denouncement of the wickedness of Sunday sport or cinema performances, the censorship board's ruling that white breasts on a magazine cover were pornography while black ones were ethnic art. He did not shrink from open contact with blacks as his father's generation did, and he regarded the Immorality Act as the relic of an antiquated libidinous backyard guilt about sex that ought to be scrapped, since in the new society of separate nations each flying the flag of its own skin, the misplacement of the white man's semen in a black vagina would emerge, transformed out of all recognition of source, as the birth of yet another nation. He was a director of one of the first insurance companies that had broken into the Anglo-Saxon and Jewish domination of finance when he was a schoolboy, but his avocation was a small art publishing firm he indulged himself with at the sacrifice of losing in it his share of the profits of a wine farm inheritance from his mother's family. At symposia, where he was the invariable choice of white liberals to contribute views fascinatingly awful to them, he was animated on the platform in the company of black delegates, and widely quoted in press reports. *I don't see you through spectacles of fear and guilt ... my perceptions, like those of my fellow Afrikaner nationalists, are of positive and fruitful interaction between nation and nation, and not of racial rivalry. This will exclude political power-sharing within a single country. Frankly, Afrikaners will not accept that ... I foresee a future in which the different nations could reach a peaceful co-existence through hard bargaining ...*

An English-language newspaper exposé once named him a member of the Afrikaner political Mafia whose brethren rule the country from within parliament; and he was interviewed dealing with that, too, smilingly. *Why only the Broederbond? Why not the Ku-Klux-Klan or the League of Empire Loyalists?* So it was not revealed how high his influence in high places might go. He had close friendships in several ministries. An elegant photographic essay, very different from the usual sort of Come-to-sunny-South-Africa information publication, appeared under his imprint in all the country's embassies; there were people in the Department of Information who found 'dynamic' his ideas about improving the country's image without either deviating from principles or being so naive as to lie about them.

Another of Vorster's victims was Winnie Mandela (103), hounded throughout the years her husband was in prison. In May 1969, she was arrested, brutally interrogated and then detained in solitary confinement without charge or trial for 13 months.

Detention means that midnight knock when all about you is quiet. It means those blinding torches shone simultaneously through every window of your house before the door is kicked open. It means the exclusive right the Security Branch have to read each and every letter in the house, no matter how personal it might be. It means paging through each and every book on your shelves, lifting carpets, looking under beds, lifting sleeping children from mattresses and looking under the sheets. It means tasting your sugar, your mealie-meal and every spice you have on your kitchen shelf. Unpacking all your clothing on your shelves and in your suitcases, and going through each pocket. It means you no longer have a right to answer your telephone should a call come through, no right to speak to anyone who might come to find out if you need help. It means interrogating your employer to find out why you are employed, questioning fellow workers to find out what you discuss privately, planting informers at work, around your neighbourhood, amongst your friends, in church, in school, etc.

Ultimately it means your seizure at dawn, dragged away from little children screaming and clinging to your skirt, imploring the white man dragging mummy to leave her alone. It means leaving the comfort of your home with the bare essentials of life that hardly make life bearable in your cell. It means the haunting memories of those screams of the loved ones, the beginning of that horror story told many a time and that has become common knowledge, yet the actual experience remains petrifying.

To review but the minimum bare facts: it means, as it was for me, being held in a single cell with the light burning twenty-four hours so that I lost track of time and was unable to tell whether it was day or night. Every single moment of your life is strictly regulated and supervised. Complete isolation from the outside world, no privacy, no visitor, lawyer or minister. It means no-one to talk to each 24 hours, no knowledge of how long you will be imprisoned and why you are imprisoned, getting medical attention from the doctor only when you are seriously ill. It means a visit from one magistrate and a retinue of the prison officials against whom you may wish to lodge a complaint and at whose mercy you are held. The very manner in which you are asked for complaints in fact means 'How dare you complain'.

The frightful emptiness of those hours of solitude is unbearable. Your company is your solitude, your blanket, your mat, your sanitary bucket, your mug and yourself. You have no choice of what you are given to eat even though you have not been charged. You have only one hour exercise per day depending on whether there is enough staff to spare. To you, your very existence in prison seems to be a privilege. All this is in preparation for the inevitable HELL – interrogation. It is meant to crush your individuality completely, to change you into a docile being from whom no resistance can arise, to terrorise you, to intimidate you into silence. After you have suffered the first initial shock of imprisonment for those who are inexperienced, this initial shock followed by the detainee's adaptation to prison has an effect of changing the detainee's personality and outlook in life.

In some cases it means severe moods from fervent hope to deep despair. Each day of nothingness is a struggle to survive. What sustains you is the spontaneous defence mechanism, that granite desire to defend and protect at all cost [against] disintegration of personality. You ask yourself questions without answers day after day, week after week, month after month, and then you keep telling yourself – I am sane and I will remain sane.

You're subjected to countless stripping of all your clothes. You must be quite naked for the white prison wardress to search your body thoroughly, to run fingers through your hair, to look in your mouth and under your tongue. There have been alleged suicides in detention; you keep asking yourself whether you will leave the cell alive for you do not know what drove those who died to their deaths. Sometimes it is a serious effort to remember what happened, the mind becomes completely blank. Then suddenly when you have gone through all this you are whisked away from your cell to the interrogation room.

Here now you have to enter a debate within yourself. There are only two divisions, you decide whether you will emerge a collaborator with the system or continue your identification with whatever your cause is.

By the mid-1970s, South Africa's neighbours were in turmoil. Mozambique and Angola, having been handed their independence by Portugal, were immediately plunged into civil wars – wars in which South Africa directly intervened. The liberation struggles in South West Africa/Namibia and Rhodesia/Zimbabwe were also under way, again with South Africa's murderous involvement. In the country itself, the explosion came on 16 June 1976. Thousands of school children took to the streets of Soweto, the vast black township outside Johannesburg, to protest against the government's decision to force them to learn in Afrikaans, widely regarded as the language of the oppressor. The police opened fire; the rioting – in reality, against apartheid in all its forms – spread to other urban areas; by February 1977, nearly 600 people had been killed; and the genie was out of the bottle. Over the next 15 years, violence in South Africa became institutionalised. In *A Dry White Season* (104), published in 1979, André Brink, a novelist who writes in both English and Afrikaans, probed the anguished response of white liberals. His protagonist, Ben Du Toit, an Afrikaner school teacher, finds himself drawn into the aftermath of the Soweto riots when Gordon, a cleaner at the school, discovers that the police have murdered his teenage son. Gordon, in turn, is taken into police custody, where he meets a

Left: Bloke Modisane, Ezekiel Mphahlele (*below left*) and Can Themba (*below*) were all members of a group of gifted journalists who worked for *Drum* magazine in the 1950s. As well as exposing the cruelties of apartheid, they told in sparkling prose of its impact on their own lives. [DRUM STAFF / BAILEYS AFRICAN HISTORY ARCHIVE / AFRICA MEDIA ONLINE]

Above: In *My Traitor's Heart*, published in 1990, when apartheid was in its death throes, Rian Malan told how for 300 years his ancestors had been present 'at all the great dramas and turning points in the history of the Afrikaner tribe'. [JONATHAN KATZENELLENBOGEN / INDEPENDENT CONTRIBUTORS / AFRICA MEDIA ONLINE]

Right: JM Coetzee, probably the finest writer South Africa has produced, emigrated to Australia in 2002 and was awarded the Nobel Prize for Literature in 2003. [GALLO IMAGES / BEELD]

Above: Published in 1944, Peter Abrahams's *Mine Boy*, was one of the first novels to portray the lives of Africans under apartheid. Fifty years ahead of his time, he looked to a future in which blacks gave the orders and whites obeyed. [Drum Social Histories / Baileys African History Archive / Africa Media Online]

Above right: Adam Small, philosopher, poet and dramatist, was one of the early supporters of the Black Consciousness Movement. [Baileys African History Archive / Africa Media Online]

Right: Born in Sophiatown in 1944, Wally Serote, poet and novelist, is a veteran of the liberation struggle. Detained in solitary confinement for nine months in 1969, he became an ANC Member of Parliament after South Africa's first democratic election. [Cedric Nunn / Independent Contributors / Africa Media Online]

André Brink's long personal journey from a sternly Afrikaner, pro-apartheid background is reflected in many of his novels. However, post-apartheid South Africa has filled him with 'disillusionment, resentment, and rage tinged with despair'. [South Photographs / Africa Media Online]

In *Triomf*, her hilarious and scatalogical tale of a family of poor white Afrikaners, Marlene van Niekerk showed that apartheid, in the end, failed even those it was meant to benefit. [Lien Botha]

Left: Nadine Gordimer, a life-long opponent of apartheid, was the first South African to win the Nobel Prize for Literature. She joined the ANC when it was an illegal organisation and had her books banned by the apartheid régime. [GALLO IMAGES]

Above: Born on a farm in the Orange Free State in 1952, Antjie Krog, who writes in English and Afrikaans, is one of the most astute and sensitive observers of post-apartheid South Africa, as she demonstrated in *Country of My Skull*, her account of the Truth and Reconciliation Commission. [GALLO IMAGES / DIE BURGER]

Left: Zakes Mda's novels gently satirise the pretensions and ambitions of both whites and blacks in the new South Africa. [ERIC MILLER]

Below: In *A Country at War with Itself*, Antony Altbeker, a researcher and investigative journalist, argued that apartheid and the resistance to it followed by the 'disappointments of democracy' were at the root of the violent crime that plagues modern-day South Africa. (AUTHOR'S PRIVATE COLLECTION)

Above: In *A Portrait with Keys,* Ivan Vladislavić constructs a poetic, delicately observed kaleidoscope of the perils and attractions of life in post-apartheid Johannesburg. [MINKY SCHLESINGER]

Right: Jonny Steinberg, an outstanding investigative journalist and writer, has specialised in exploring the worms in the bud of the new South Africa, such as AIDS (the subject of *Three-letter Plague*), farm murders and prison gangs. (AUTHOR'S PRIVATE COLLECTION)

Below right: Ingrid de Kok is one of the finest poets writing in South Africa today. Her lyrical narrative verse captures moments of personal crisis against a political background. [KARINA TUROK]

Below: In *Trencherman* by Eben Venter, an Afrikaner novelist, post-apartheid means post-apocalypse – and the nightmare is just around the corner. [GALLO IMAGES / RAPPORT]

violent death. Ben, trying to uncover the truth of what happened, has just returned from visiting Stanley, a contact in Soweto, where he was stoned by a gang of black youths.

Back home I took a bath and changed my clothes. Swallowed a few tablets. Lay down. But I couldn't sleep. Every now and then I started shivering again, quite uncontrollably.

I had never been so close to death before.

For a long time, as I lay there trying to clear my mind, I couldn't think coherently at all, conscious only of a terrible, blind bitterness. Why had they singled me out? Didn't they understand? Had everything I'd gone through on their behalf been utterly in vain? Did it really count for nothing? What had happened to logic, meaning, sense?

But I feel much calmer now. It helps to discipline oneself like this writing it down to see it set out on paper, to try and weigh it and find some significance in it.

Prof Bruwer:[3] *There are only two kinds of madness one should guard against, Ben. One is the belief that we can do everything. The other is the belief that we can do nothing.*

I wanted to help. Right. I meant it very sincerely. But I wanted to do it on my terms. And I am white, they are black. I thought it was still possible to reach beyond our whiteness and blackness. I thought that to reach out and touch hands across the gulf would be sufficient in itself. But I grasped so little, really: as if good intentions from my side could solve it all. It was presumptuous of me. In an ordinary world, in a natural one, I might have succeeded. But not in this deranged, divided age. I can do all I can for Gordon or the scores of others who have come to me; I can imagine myself in their shoes, I can project myself into their suffering. But I cannot, ever, live their lives for them. So what else could come of it but failure?

Whether I like it or not, whether I feel like cursing my own condition or not — and that would only serve to confirm my impotence – I *am white.* This is the small, final, terrifying truth of my broken world. I am white. And because I'm white I am born into a state of privilege. Even if I fight the system that has reduced us to this I remain white, and favoured by the very circumstances I abhor. Even if I'm hated, and ostracised, and persecuted, and in the end destroyed, nothing can make me black. And so those who are cannot but remain suspicious of me. In their eyes my very efforts to identify myself with Gordon, with all the Gordons, would be obscene. Every gesture

I make, every act I commit in my efforts to help them makes it more difficult for them to define their real needs and discover for themselves their integrity and affirm their own dignity. How else could we hope to arrive beyond predator and prey, helper and helped, white and black, and find redemption?

On the other hand: what can I do but what I have done? I cannot choose not to intervene: that would be a denial and a mockery not only of everything I believe in, but of the hope that compassion may survive among men. By not acting as I did I would deny the very possibility of that gulf to be bridged.

If I act, I cannot but lose. But if I do not act, it is a different kind of defeat, equally decisive and maybe worse. Because then I will not even have a conscience left.

The end seems ineluctable: failure, defeat, loss. The only choice I have left is whether I am prepared to salvage a little honour, a little decency, a little humanity – or nothing. It seems as if a sacrifice is impossible to avoid, whatever way one looks at it. But at least one has the choice between a wholly futile sacrifice and one that might, in the long run, open up a possibility; however negligible or dubious, of something better, less sordid and more noble, for our children. My own, and Gordon's, and Stanley's.

They live on. We, the fathers, have lost.

Apartheid entered its final, manic phase in 1978, when Vorster, mired in a financial scandal, gave way to PW Botha, another wartime Nazi sympathiser. Although he claimed to be a 'pragmatist', Botha elaborated the segregationist fantasy by creating a 'tricameral' parliament with extra chambers for Cape Coloureds and Indians. Approved by an all-white referendum, it was speedily dubbed 'tri-partheid'. Africans, who by then constituted more than 70 per cent of the population, were expected to continue seeking their political salvation in the scattered rural areas known as 'independent homelands'. By 1985, violence in the townships had reached such a pitch that Botha was forced to declare a state of emergency. Appropriately, it remained in force throughout apartheid's last years.

Of all apartheid's chroniclers, Christopher Hope is one of the most savagely witty. Born in Johannesburg in 1944, he left the country in 1975. In 1987, he returned to report on the general election that was to be the last but one under apartheid. The following year, he recorded his experiences in *White Boy Running* (105).

In the bar of the Balfour Hotel[4] on this Saturday night patrons pack in as darkness falls. The serious drinkers on the stools around the wooden bar talk little, swallow their doubles, down their chasers, nod and leave, their silent sons padding behind them. The members of the rugby team, well into their third and fourth beers, are regaling each other with stories about women. Particularly enchanting to them is the joke about a Japanese named Sadie who, for various reasons, is having a baby. Only this phrase in the conversation is in English, everything else is in Afrikaans. But Sadie's baby is a catchword, a phrase so charged it bends them double with laughter. The serious drinkers look coldly upon this frivolity. Across the echoing cavern of a room the snooker players continue to weave around the table in their short-sleeved shirts, pushing beer bellies importantly before them; by now they are incapable of hitting a straight ball and spend a lot of time cursing, falling over or lying on the table, still pulling at their brandies and Cokes – and making a little Coke go a long way. The few dedicated drinkers remaining cup their glasses with protective hands and guard their conversation, which divides more or less equally into farm talk and politics; the subjects are not always distinguishable A man with a great half moon of a belly, wearing a little blue pork-pie hat, drinking a triple cane spirit and lemonade, is telling the man on the stool beside him about the trouble he has been having with a tractor driver. His friend, who has skin the colour of aged teak, nods sadly and swallows his beer very slowly:

'Yes, they're a lot of trouble.'

'That's what I say,' says the man in the pork-pie, 'they're a lot of trouble. Especially when you consider the trouble you have with them.'

'And the work you have, showing them how to do things.'

'Exactly,' says Pork-Pie. 'So in the end I had enough. I got up on the wheel and I knocked that uppity kaffir right out of the cab. Just like that!'

He mimics his assault and shows how the driver tumbled into the road by swaying dangerously on his bar stool.

'Nothing but bloody trouble,' his friend agrees.

'What could I do?' Pork-Pie demands plaintively. 'I told him nicely, but he didn't want to listen. He just didn't want to listen!'

This conversation is deeply instructive. There is a dimension to the relations between Black and White people in South Africa little known among foreign observers who imagine that the relationship is based on simple domination. Domination is, of course, its foundation, but to think that there is nothing more to it is to miss the metaphysics of South African race relations and the missionary zeal with which the religion is preached in bars, prisons, courtrooms and election battles. The underlying metaphysics of the relationships suggest that if God be pleased to see it so, Black and White will enjoy equality in the world to come. Or perhaps it is more sensible to talk of worlds to come, of separate but equal paradises with linking corridors or inter-leading doors by means of which the souls of the masters will mix freely with those of their former servants. But before the Chosen enter the world to come there is the struggle in the fallen world of here and now in which the White Afrikaner is divinely charged with the protection and moral uplift of his Black brother. Thus it is that, to most observers, the admission: 'I knocked that uppity kaffir right out of the cab,' will sound like an aggressive action, a brutal assault by the boss upon his employee. But this is a misconception and, in part, explains the resentment with which the South African Nationalist complains of interference by the 'outside world' in matters it does not understand. For although the Afrikaner's religion enjoins him to succour his Black brother, the moment he embarks upon this he finds it easier said than done; instead of co-operating in his salvation the Black man proves stubborn, subtle, perverse, recalcitrant and proud, and try as you may to help him, he finds ways of resisting. So it is finally, more in sorrow than in anger, that one is forced to, well ... *chastise* the simple soul in order to correct his thinking and improve his demeanour. It's always done reluctantly, as a last resort, after much pleading with the man to see the error of his ways, but it is in the end usually what things come down to – a fist, a boot, a bullet. It must be understood that what underlies the conversation of the man in the pork-pie hat and his nut-brown friend is genuine sorrow, wounded feelings and sad frustration at the unwillingness of the driver in the cab to be shown the light. If you watch the doleful expressions, sorrowful head-shakings and tongue-clickings as the story unfolds, if you hear the incidental music beneath the exchange, you know that these farmers truly expect the Black man to be the death of them one day ...

And of course, in ways perhaps unsuspected, they could be right.

Theodore Blanchaille, the protagonist of Hope's demonic novel, *Kruger's Alp* (106), is a renegade Catholic priest. His first posting had been to the transit camps where 'surplus' Africans were sent in the interests of 'separate development'. Assigned to a white parish, Blanchaille decides to tell his new congregation all about it.

After Pennyheaven, Blanchaille had been appointed to St Peter-in-the-Wild. The church was so new it still smelt of cement and the walls and ceiling were painted sky blue. The whole place was severely angular with pews of pale natural pine and a baptismal font at the back made of stainless steel, deeply shining, rather like the wash-basins found on trains. In a pulpit of steel and smoked glass with its directional microphone Blanchaille talked of Malanskop, his first camp. It had been, he said, a most terrible garden full of deadly melodies, a music of wonderful names: kwashiorkor and pellagra, enteritis, lekkerkrap and rickets. How they rolled off the tongue! How lovely they sounded! Children in particular found the music irresistible. They listened and died. Every day ended with perfunctory funerals. No less euphonious afflictions decimated the adults: tuberculosis, cystitis, scabies and salpingitis, cholera, typhoid ... The red burial mounds grew up overnight beyond the pit latrines as if an army of moles had passed that way. Later the little graves were piled with stones to keep the jackals off and finally came the clumsy wooden crosses tied with string, the names burnt into the wood in a charred scrawl, dates recording the months, weeks, days, hours, in the brief lives of 'Beauty' and 'Edgar', 'Sampson', 'Nicodemus' and 'Precious'.

The Church half emptied after this first sermon. Blanchaille began to feel rather better about his new appointment. At the second sermon he tried to encourage the congregation remaining to recite after him the names of the camps and perhaps to clap the beat: 'Kraaifontein, Witziesbek, Verneuk, Bittereind, Mooiplaats ...' The microphone gave a hard dry sound as he clapped his way through the litany. No one joined him. 'I want to suggest that in the foyer of the church we build models of these camps, of the shoe-box shantytowns, the tent villages, that we show their corrugated iron roofs, the towns built of paraffin tins, the three stand-pipes on which thousands of people relied for their water, the solitary borehole and of course the spreading graveyards. Everywhere the graveyards. We might use papier maché.'

At his third sermon the congregation had shrunk to those few who he later realised constituted the Consensus Committee: Makapan, the two Kretas, and Mary Muldoon. Mary wore a hat with bright red cherries. Her flower arrangements, he noticed, had not been changed since his first sermon. Before the altar the hyacinths were dying in their waterless brass vases.

'I wish to remember today, dear brethren, my third and final camp, Dolorosa, that tin and cardboard slum in the middle of nowhere which has since become so famous. In my day, the mortality rate for dysentery was a national record, the illness carried off three-quarters of the newborn in the first month after the camp was set up. People in their tin hovels with their sack doors died of despair, if they were lucky, before the more regular infections removed them. Dolorosa, as you know, is important because it caught the imagination of the country and the Church. It was called, in one of those detestable phrases, "a challenge to the conscience of the nation." Individuals arrived there in their private cars with loads of medicines and milk. Rotary Clubs collected blankets and bread. This charitable effort grew and teams of doctors and nurses, engineers and teachers made their way to Dolorosa. But more than anything else Dolorosa became the camp which the Church took up. It became, in the words of Bishop Blashford's episcopal letter, "the burning focal point of the charitable energies of the Catholic Church ..." A hospital was opened. Then a school. And a fine new church in the beehive style, this being judged as reflecting best the tribal architecture of the local people, was erected and dedicated. What was sought ... What *was* sought? Oh yes, I remember, what was sought was "a living, long-term commitment" – they actually said that! Farsighted superiors in distant seminaries saw the potential. Could not such a place, these wise men asked themselves, provide a training ground for their priestlings? Give their chaps a taste of real poverty, they said, by billeting them on me for short periods. The spiritual directors of these seminaries took to visiting me by bus and helicopter. They brought tales of increasing interest among their novices. Inspired by the new direction the Church had found, these young men wished to live, for short periods, a sympathetic mirror existence with their brother outcasts, to embrace Mother Africa. A small pilot scheme was begun and proved to be extremely popular. It was likened to young doctors doing a year of housemanship. Parcels of young priests arrived simply crackling with a desire to do good and discover for themselves the vision of the suffering Christ of the camps. Well, of course, the word got round and before long other sympathisers and wellwishers asked if they too could take part in this scheme in a more practical way. It was one thing to drive down every weekend with a load of powdered milk in the back of the Datsun – but that was no substitute for actually "living in" ... And if the priests were doing it, then why not the laity? The Church, keen to involve the faithful, agreed. Rather than to drive down to Dolorosa once a week with a fresh supply of saline drip, maybe people should get a taste of dysentery for themselves? A conference of bishops recognized the desire evident among the laity, and in their famous resolution called on them to "make living witness of their deep Christian concern for their dispossessed brethren by going among them, even as Our Lord did ..." Well, you can imagine what happened. The accommodation problem at Dolorosa, and I believe at other camps, became suddenly very acute. Sociologists, writers, journalists, health workers, students, nuns, priests, all began crowding in. I found I had to ration the shanties, the lean-to's and huts. I had to open a waiting list. Soon we were doubling up on our volunteer workers, five or six to a hovel, three or four to a tent, up to half-a-dozen in the mobile homes donated by the Society of St Vincent de Paul on the proceeds gathered from a number of sponsored walks. Even so it wasn't enough. It became increasingly difficult to separate the races as the laws of the Regime required that we do, and harder still to keep the sexes apart, as morality demanded. Who hasn't heard of the tragic case of the Redemptorist Brother accused of raping an African girl behind the soup kitchen run by the Sisters of Mercy? Of the nurse who died of dysentery? Of the Dominican novice taken to hospital suffering from malnutrition? Of the infestation of head lice among a party of visiting Canadian clergy? For a while it seemed as if the whole project of "embracing the poor" was in serious doubt since the faithful seemed unable to resist the very diseases they came to relieve. As a temporary measure all inhabitants, both victims and volunteers, had to be moved into tents miles away from the infected zone while the entire shantytown was fumigated by volunteers from the Knights of Columbus wearing breathing apparatus supplied free of charge by a local firm. At the time the problem seemed insurmountable but with that particular genius which has triumphed through the ages, the Church found a solution. The answer, as we now know, was the careful demarca-tion of areas of infection. This was achieved by driving sanitary corridors between the healthy volunteer forces on the outside and the infected slum people within; these were the so-called "fire breaks against infection", a kind of Hadrian's Wall of Defensive Medicine buttressed at strategic inter-vals by the SST's, camp jargon for the scour and shower ablutions, obliga-tory for all personnel passing between secure areas and infected zones. It was, according to the Bishop's Conference, a pioneering effort in disease control, a highly imaginative protective health measure sufficiently flexible to take into account the varying degrees of resistance (or lack of it) exist-ing among the ethnic plurality of groups which made up the rich diversity of Southern African peoples ...'

Blanchaille gripped the edge of the pulpit. His words no longer seemed to carry through the church. He tapped the microphone. Dead. The bastards had cut his mike. He peered at Mary Muldoon, the red cherries on her hat pulsed in the gloom. The rest of the parishioners stared back at him sullenly. 'It was at this time that I composed my letter to *The Cross*,' Blanchaille yelled. 'Perhaps you've heard of it? In it I said that if the people in the camps prayed for anything they should pray for the bulldozer. Enough of these smooth and resonant phrases, of plump churchmen talking of people living in a manner consonant with human dignity. Disease kills but so does charity, more slowly but just as surely. Flatten the camps, that is freedom! Release their inhabitants to a decent beggary, let them wander the countryside pleading for alms, calling on us to remember what we have done to them!'

It was his last sermon. After that the siege began.

Later, Blanchaille, whose journey echoes that of John Bunyan's Pilgrim, comes across a township where there has just been a Sharpeville-type massacre. Having helped clear up the bodies, he sits exhausted by the roadside.

And then I saw in my dream that a man driving a yellow Datsun estate stopped and offered him a lift. A short and balding man with a pleasant smile whose name was Derek Breslau. A commercial traveller for Lever Brothers dealing in ladies' shampoos. The inside of his car was so heavily perfumed it made Blanchaille swoon and he could barely find the words to thank him for his kindness.

'Don't mention it. Couldn't leave a guy sitting by the side of the road outside a bloody township. Normally I put my foot down and go like hell when I pass a township. You never know what's going on inside. Gee, you took a risk!' He examined Blanchaille's blood-stained, muddied clothes with interest.

'My bags are heavy and I can't go very far at a stretch.'

'Well, keep away from the townships.'

'It's a funny thing,' said Blanchaille, 'but I always believed that the townships were peaceful now.'

Breslau nodded. 'Well it depends on what you mean. If you mean the townships are peaceful except when there are riots, then I suppose that's correct. So I suppose you could say the townships are peaceful between riots.

And I must say they're pretty peaceful after riots. If we need to go to the townships that's usually when we go. They have a period of mourning then, you see, and you got time to get in, do the job and get out again.'

'I suppose then you could also say that townships are peaceful before riots,' said Blanchaille, trying to be helpful.

Breslau thought this over and nodded approvingly. 'Yes, I suppose that's right. I never thought of it that way. But leaving all this aside, the truth is you can never be sure when the townships are going to be peaceful. You can drive into a township, and I have no option since I do business there, and find yourself in the middle of a riot. You can find yourself humping dead bodies or driving wounded to hospital. You can find yourself dispensing aid and comfort.'

'Aid and comfort?'

'Sure! That comes after the riots, usually, when they've laid out the victims and the relatives come along to claim them. It's an emotional time, as you can imagine. What they usually do these days is to get the priest up from the church and he gives each relative a blessing. Well, one day I arrived just as the blessings had started. They didn't seem to be comforting people very much so the police officer in charge commandeered me and my vehicle and all my samples and he suggested that each relative should also get a sample of my shampoo, plus a blessing. Of course they weren't my samples to give, but on occasions like this you don't argue. Well, I stood next to the priest and he gave the blessing and I handed out the sample. Of course there was no question of matching hair types. I mean you can't stop the grieving relatives and ask them whether they suffer from dry, greasy or normal hair. I mean that's not exactly the time and place to start getting finicky. Can I drop you somewhere in town?'

Blanchaille mentioned the suburb where Bishop Blashford lived.

'Sure. Happy to help.'

'What disturbs the peace in the townships?'

Breslau shrugged. 'Everything – and nothing. Of course the trouble is not having what they want, and then getting what they want. Like I mean first of all they don't have any sewage so the cry goes up for piped sewage and they get it. Then there's no electricity, so a consortium of businessmen organised by Himmelfarber and his Consolidated Holdings put in a private scheme of electrification. Then a football pitch is asked for. And given. And after each of these improvements there's a riot. It's interesting, that.'

'It's almost as if the trouble with the townships is the townships,' Blanchaille suggested.

'You can't not have townships or you wouldn't have any of this,' the salesman gestured out of the window at the blank and featureless veld on either side of the road. 'Cities have townships the way people have shadows. It's in the nature of things.'

'But we haven't always had townships.'

'Of course we have. Look, a township is just a reservoir. A pool. A depot for labour. I mean you look back to how it was when the first white settlers came here. You look at Van Riebeeck who came in – when was it – in 1652? And he arrives at the Cape of Good Hope – what a name when you think how things turned out! A bloody long time ago, right? What does Van Riebeeck find when he arrives in this big open place? He finds he's got to build himself a fort. He finds the place occupied, there are all these damn Hottentots swanning around. Anyway he sees all these black guys wandering around and he thinks to himself – Jesus! This is Christmas! What I'm going to do is sit in my fort, grow lots of vegetables and sell them to passing ships. And all these black Hottentots I see wandering around here, they're going to work for me. If they don't work for me they get zapped. So he sits there at the Cape and the black guys work for him. Afterwards he gets to be so famous they put his face on all the money. It's been like that ever since.'

'But he didn't have a township.'

'What d'you mean, he didn't have a township? The whole damn country was his township.'

The bleak intensity of JM Coetzee's critique of authoritarianism puts him in a class of his own. The novel in which he confronts apartheid most directly is *Age of Iron* (107), published in 1990. It opens in 1986, when South Africa was reaping the whirlwind that the children of Soweto had sown 10 years earlier. Once again, 'witches' were being smelt out but this time car tyres were forced over their heads, filled with petrol and set alight. Known in the townships as necklacing, it killed hundreds. *Age of Iron* is written as a letter from Elizabeth Curren, who is dying of cancer, to her daughter in America. Vercueil, a drink-sodden vagrant, has moved into her woodshed. He has just been assaulted by two African boys, one of whom, 15-year-old Bheki, is the son of Mrs Curren's servant, Florence.

Like an old tom chased off by the rising males, Vercueil has gone into hiding to lick his wounds. I foresee myself searching the parks, calling softly, 'Mr Vercueil! Mr Vercueil!' An old woman in search of her cat.

Florence is openly proud of how Bheki got rid of the good-for-nothing, but predicts that he will be back as soon as it starts raining. As for me, I doubt we will see him as long as the boys are here. I said so to Florence. 'You are showing Bheki and his friends that they can raise their hands against their elders with impunity. That is a mistake. Yes, whatever you may think of him, Vercueil is their elder!

'The more you give in, Florence, the more outrageously the children will behave. You told me you admire your son's generation because they are afraid of nothing. Be careful: they may start by being careless of their own lives and end by being careless of everyone else's. What you admire in them is not necessarily what is best.

'I keep thinking of what you said the other day: that there are no more mothers and fathers. I can't believe you mean it. Children cannot grow up without mothers or fathers. The burnings and killings one hears of, the shocking callousness, even this matter of beating Mr Vercueil – whose fault is it in the end? Surely the blame must fall on parents who say, "Go, do as you wish, you are your own master now, I give up authority over you." What child in his heart truly wants to be told that? Surely he will turn away in con-fusion, thinking to himself, "I have no mother now, I have no father: then let my mother be death, let my father be death." You wash your hands of them and they turn into the children of death.'

Florence shook her head. 'No,' she said firmly.

'But do you remember what you told me last year, Florence, when those unspeakable things were happening in the townships? You said to me, "I saw a woman on fire, burning, and when she screamed for help, the children laughed and threw more petrol on her." You said, "I did not think I would live to see such a thing."'

'Yes, I did say that, and it is true. But who made them so cruel? It is the whites who made them so cruel! Yes!' She breathed deeply, passionately. We were in the kitchen. She was doing the ironing. The hand that held the iron pressed down hard. She glared at me. Lightly I touched her hand. She raised the iron. On the sheet was the beginning of a brown scorch-mark.

No mercy, I thought: a war without mercy, without limits. A good war to miss.

'And when they grow up one day,' I said softly, 'do you think the cruelty will leave them? What kind of parents will they become who were taught that the time of parents is over? Can parents be recreated once the idea of parents has been destroyed within us? They kick and beat a man because he drinks. They set people on fire and laugh while they burn to death. How will they treat their own children? What love will they be capable of? Their hearts are turning to stone before our eyes, and what do you say? You say, "This is not my child, this is the white man's child, this is the monster made by the white man." Is that all you can say? Are you going to blame them on the whites and turn your back?'

'No,' said Florence. 'That is not true. I do not turn my back on my children.' She folded the sheet crosswise and lengthwise, crosswise and lengthwise, the corners falling together neatly, decisively. 'These are good children, they are like iron, we are proud of them.' On the board she spread the first of the pillowslips. I waited for her to say more. But there was no more. She was not interested in debating with me.

Children of iron, I thought. Florence herself, too, not unlike iron. The age of iron. After which comes the age of bronze. How long, how long before the softer ages return in their cycle, the age of clay, the age of earth? A Spartan matron, iron-hearted, bearing warrior-sons for the nation. 'We are proud of them.' We. Come home either with your shield or on your shield.

And I? Where is my heart in all of this? My only child is thousands of miles away, safe; soon I will be smoke and ash; so what is it to me that a time has come when childhood is despised, when children school each other never to smile, never to cry, to raise fists in the air like hammers? Is it truly a time out of time, heaved up out of the earth, misbegotten, monstrous? What, after all, gave birth to the age of iron but the age of granite? Did we not have Voortrekkers, generation after generation of Voortrekkers, grim-faced, tight-lipped Afrikaner children, marching, singing their patriotic hymns, saluting their flag, vowing to die for their fatherland? *Ons sal lewe, ons sal sterwe.*[5] Are there not still white zealots preaching the old regime of discipline, work, obedience, self-sacrifice, a regime of death, to children some too young to tie their own shoelaces? What a nightmare from beginning to end! The spirit of Geneva triumphant in Africa. Calvin, black-robed, thin-blooded, forever cold, rubbing his hands in the after-world, smiling his wintry smile. Calvin victorious, reborn in the dogmatists and witch-hunters of both armies. How fortunate you are to have put all this behind you!

Marlene van Niekerk, who writes in Afrikaans, moves the story on to the eve of the 1994 general election, the first democratic vote in South Africa's history. In *Triomf* (108), her hilariously scatological tale, the Benades are a dysfunctional, incestuous family of poor whites – the descendants of generations of unemployable Boers – living in the eponymous suburb built by apartheid on the grave of Sophiatown. Lambert is epileptic and 'not right in his top storey'; Treppie, who speaks first, is officially his uncle but quite possibly his father; Pop is his official father.

'Come now, Lambert, we don't have all morning. What are the vital issues in this election?'

'Well,' Lambert says, 'it's the constitution, it's the people who're going to write the new constitution. We have to vote for them.'

'And?' Treppie's eyes are glittering.

'Well, um,' Lambert looks at Pop. Pop must help him now. 'We've always stuck with the NP.'[6]

'Oh yes?' Treppie says quickly. He waves at the flies. 'We've also stuck with Sunlight. That's how you keep the flies out, you wash yourself with Sunlight soap. Your arse and your head and your floor and your bed, the whole lot, whiter than snow.'

Lambert tries to straighten up. This is going too far now. If Treppie wants him, then he's going to get him. But his head's zinging. Pop signals: stop it now. He says please. Lambert shuts his eyes. Maybe that'll help his head a bit. Pop's voice is so soft, all Lambert hears is 'ease'. Then it's Treppie again. He's talking to Pop. Treppie sounds like a preacher.

'If you ask me, Pop, the National Party are a filthy lot. What's more, they're also confused and they're getting more confused by the day. One great fucken scrapyard, if you ask me. Now they say they're going to get their house in order, again. How, I ask you? How? Where will they begin? They must first get their fingers out of their backsides. That's what, and then wash them with Sunlight. That's all I can say, Pop. That's the hard reality. Old Lambert here, he knows very well what I'm talking about. He reads those pamphlets. And he's not stupid, not by a long shot.'

Lambert opens his eyes. The only thing you can do here is play along. 'At least they've stuck to one thing from beginning to end. It's like a golden thread,' he says.

'Oh yes?' Treppie says. 'Now that sounds better. What golden thread?'

Lambert leans forward so he can get his pamphlets. Pop helps him, pushing them closer.

'Wait, let me read it.' He looks through the pamphlets till he finds the right one. Then he looks up. Pop stares down at the floor. Treppie looks him straight in the face. He reads.

'"The National Party of today is no longer the National Party of yester-day, but"' – 'Fuck but!' Treppie says, shooting up like a jack-in-the-box and grabbing the pamphlet out of his hands. 'It's not even the same party you voted Yes for that last time. Remember, when you could still fit into your smart clothes, your black charcoal pants with the shiny leather belt, and those boots with no laces. What did it say again on the label of those pants? Smart pants, those!'

Treppie gets up and walks carefully over the broken glass to the steel cabinet against the wall. He tries to shake open the doors, but they're locked. 'Quickly, give me the keys so I can see what that label says.'

'Boom!' Treppie slams his hand against the steel door. Pop jumps.

'Man About Town! That's it. Now I remember. Man About Town! That's what it says on the label. I still remember. The coolie at the Plaza showed us the label, at the back, on the inside.'

'Can I carry on now?' Lambert asks. Talking politics is bad, but not as bad as talking about his pants. It's not his fault he got so fat. It's the pills.

'"But …"'Lambert reads, '"there's a golden thread that runs from the early years of the National Party right through until today."'

'Stuff and nonsense!' Treppie says. He sits on his crate again.

'"Our first priority remains our own, our own minority, our own language and culture, and our own Christian faith,"' he reads in stops and starts, the words swimming in front of his eyes.

'And our own postbox!' Treppie shouts.

Lambert raises his hand for silence. He reads: '"That's what we call the protection of minority rights. All minorities. So that there can be no domination by a black majority …"'

'So, do you buy that story, Lambert?' Treppie asks.

'Well, um, to an extent,' Lambert says.

'To an extent! You sound just like that pamphlet, old boy.'

'Well, if things don't work out then we've at least got a plan!' Lambert says. 'Remember what you said, then we take Molletjie[7] and we load the petrol into the front, and on the roof-rack, and in the dicky, and then we go, due north. All of us, even Gerty and Toby.[8] To Zimbabwe or Kenya. Where you can still live like a white man. With lots of kaffirboys and -girls to order around, just as we please! They're cheaper there!'

Treppie looks at him. He looks at Treppie. Why's Treppie looking at him like this now?

Treppie was after all the one who thought up the plan, one day when he, Lambert, was lying here at the back, when he couldn't pull himself together after a fit, and all he could do was pull his wire, but even that didn't want to work any more. When his mother was sick in the hospital. From asthma. At least that's what he thought. But then Treppie said it was a nervous break-down 'cause he had fits all the time, 'cause there was nothing for him to do and he was wearing his mother out. And then Treppie came and sat here on a crate and said he'd found just the thing to keep him busy: the Great North Plan for when the emergency came. Yes, they must start storing up petrol, Treppie said, 'cause you never knew. He, Lambert, must dig a cellar under his den to store up petrol, 'cause petrol couldn't be stored above ground, at least not here at the Benades'; there were too many sparks flying around when they started welding. Treppie said the silver bags inside wine boxes were the best for storing petrol. They took up the least space, and you could fold them up when you were finished, and then fill them up again later. He remembers thinking it was a real stroke of genius. Treppie's got a lot of plans. But that's not all he's got a lot of and he mustn't come and be a nuisance now. He, Lambert, didn't go scratching around rubbish dumps just for nothing. On Monday nights, when people put out their rubbish, he walked up and down the streets so he could check those rubbish bags for wine boxes. Then he'd pull out the silver bags and throw back the boxes. By the time he got home he was stinking of wine and old rubbish. Sometimes people heard the scratching at their gates, and a few times they even came out with their sjamboks and their catties,[9] 'cause they thought it was dogs eating their rubbish. Then they'd start shooting without even taking a good look to see who it was. One night a man with a pellet gun hit him a shot in the backside as he stood there scratching around. He hadn't even seen the man. And he didn't go looking for him, either, 'cause then he'd have to please explain what he was doing there in the rubbish. He couldn't very well go and tell other people about their plan, 'cause then they'd also start doing it, and then the petrol would run out too quickly. It's true what Treppie says, when there's trouble in the country it's always petrol that runs out first. Treppie said he, Lambert, could learn from the NP government – every time they got the country into trouble, they just stashed away more petrol. Treppie's like that when he talks politics. Actually when he talks anything. You never know if he means something's good or bad. And if you ask him, he says he's not interested in those two words, things are what they are and that's all there is to it.

NOTES

1 A contemptuous term for whites who are friendly to blacks.
2 Twenty-five years later, South Africa's Truth and Reconciliation Commission found that Biko sustained his fatal injuries when two security policemen held his arms and a third smashed his head against a wall.
3 A friend.
4 Balfour is a small town about 50 miles south-east of Johannesburg.
5 We shall live, we shall die (We for you, South Africa) – from 'Die Stem', the Afrikaners' national anthem.
6 National Party.
7 The family Volkswagen.
8 The dogs.
9 Catapults.

CHAPTER 15

A NEW BEGINNING

By 1989, State President PW Botha had lost his tenuous hold on reality and was shouldered aside by Frederik Willem (FW) de Klerk, a politician who fancied he felt the touch of history. In truth, he merely came face to face with the inevitable. Apartheid, of which he had been a life-long supporter, had finally become unsustainable: state repression was losing its grip; international pressure was mounting; disinvestment – the ultimate sanction – was gathering pace; and white prosperity, the point of it all, was in jeopardy. In Botha's phrase, as De Klerk recorded in his 1998 memoirs, *The Last Great Trek* (109), white South Africa faced a 'total onslaught' to which the only possible response was a 'total strategy'.

It has become fashionable to ridicule P. W. Botha's view that there was a total onslaught against South Africa. However, during the mid-1980s, fortnight after fortnight, the intelligence that we received in briefing after briefing in the State Security Council underlined the very grave situation that confronted us. We were faced not only with a concerted campaign to make South Africa ungovernable as the prelude to a general revolution, we also had to contend with extremely serious external threats. Seldom had such a comprehensive international campaign been mounted against a single country so relentlessly for so long a period, as the campaign that the international anti-apartheid alliance had mobilized against us. The sanctions net was beginning to tighten around South Africa in almost every sphere of its international relations. The Soviet Union and Cuban allies had established threatening positions in some of our neighbouring countries.

We were involved in a low intensity war in northern Namibia and southern Angola that had brought the South African Defence Force into direct conflict with Cuban and Russian-led forces. Guerrilla groups, based in neighbouring countries, had begun to launch attacks against South Africa.

In response to this, P. W. Botha and his security advisers developed the concept of a total strategy. The need for such a total strategy arose from military analyses of the fundamental changes that had taken place in the nature of warfare since the end of the Second World War. A new form of revolutionary warfare had evolved in which victory did not come from the clash of two armies on a field of battle. Instead, revolutionary forces sought to overthrow incumbent governments by mobilizing the masses; by making countries ungovernable; by fomenting strikes; by involving churches, trade unions and civil society in their campaigns; by using propaganda to destroy the image and undermine the confidence of governments; by eliminating opposition through the use of terrorism and intimidation; and by continuing to mount guerrilla attacks against its enemy.

What De Klerk calls 'eliminating opposition through the use of terrorism and intimidation' was precisely the policy that Botha, with De Klerk's support, then adopted. Official documents uncovered later show that from the mid-1980s onwards the State Security Council expected the police and the army to 'eliminate', 'take out' and 'destroy' apartheid's opponents. This they did by abducting, murdering and torturing thousands – something De Klerk has always insisted he knew nothing about. His strategy, once he took over, was to salvage what he could for Afrikaner nationalism, the way having been prepared by Botha, who, three years earlier had secretly instituted talks with Nelson Mandela. Here Mandela describes the drama of De Klerk's first move.

On 2 February 1990 F. W. de Klerk stood before Parliament to make the traditional opening speech and did something no other South African head of state had ever done: he truly began to dismantle the apartheid system and lay the groundwork for a democratic South Africa. In dramatic fashion, he announced the lifting of the bans on the ANC, the PAC, the South African Communist Party and thirty-one other illegal organizations; the freeing of political prisoners incarcerated for non-violent activities; the suspension of capital punishment; and the lifting of various restrictions imposed by the State of Emergency. 'The time for negotiation has arrived,' he said.

It was a breathtaking moment, for in one sweeping action he had virtually normalized the situation in South Africa. Our world had changed overnight. After forty years of persecution and banishment, the ANC was now a legal organization. I and all my comrades could no longer be arrested for being a member of the ANC, for carrying its green, yellow and black banner, for speaking its name. For the first time in almost thirty years, my picture and my words, and those of all my banned comrades, could appear in South African newspapers. The international community applauded de Klerk's bold actions. Amid all the good news, however, the ANC objected to the fact that Mr de Klerk had not completely lifted the State of Emergency or ordered the troops out of the townships.

On 9 February, seven days after Mr de Klerk's speech opening Parliament, I was informed that I was again going to Tuynhuys.[1] I arrived at six o'clock in the evening. I met a smiling Mr de Klerk in his office and, as we shook hands, he informed me that he was going to release me from prison the following day. Although the press in South Africa and around the world had been speculating for weeks that my release was imminent, the announcement nevertheless came as a surprise to me. I had not been told that the reason de Klerk wanted to see me was to tell me that he was making me a free man.

I felt a conflict between my blood and my brain. I deeply wanted to leave prison as soon as I could, but to do so on such short notice would not be wise. I thanked Mr de Klerk, and then said that at the risk of appearing ungrateful I would prefer to have a week's notice in order that my family and my organization could be prepared for my release. Simply to walk out tomorrow, I said, would cause chaos. I asked de Klerk to release me a week from that day. After waiting twenty-seven years, I could certainly wait another seven days.

De Klerk was taken aback by my response. Instead of replying, he continued to relate the plan for my release. He said that the government would fly me to Johannesburg and officially release me there. Before he went any further, I told him that I strongly objected to that. I wanted to walk out of the gates of Victor Verster[2] and be able to thank those who looked after me and greet the people of Cape Town. Though I was from Johannesburg, Cape Town had been my home for nearly three decades. I would make my way back to Johannesburg, but when I chose to, not when the government wanted me to. 'Once I am free,' I said, 'I will look after myself.'

De Klerk was again nonplussed. But this time my objections caused a reaction. He excused himself and left his office to consult with others. After ten minutes he returned with a rather long face and said, 'Mr Mandela, it is too late to change the plan now.' I replied that the plan was unacceptable and that I wanted to be released a week hence and at Victor Verster, not Johannesburg. It was a tense moment and, at the time, neither of us saw any irony in a prisoner asking not to be released and his jailer attempting to release him.

De Klerk again excused himself and left the room. After ten minutes he returned with a compromise: yes, I could be released at Victor Verster, but, no, the release could not be postponed. The government had already informed the foreign press that I was to be set free the next day and felt they could not renege on that statement. I felt I could not argue with that. In the end, we agreed on the compromise, and Mr de Klerk poured a tumbler of whisky for each of us to drink in celebration. I raised the glass in a toast, but only pretended to drink; such spirits are too strong for me.

Mandela spent his first night of freedom at Archbishop Desmond Tutu's official residence in the Cape Town suburb of Bishopscourt. Here, nearly 350 years before, Van Riebeeck had a farm. Now was the time for a new beginning.

In his memoirs, De Klerk gave his version of why the Afrikaners threw in the towel.

We urgently needed to gain access to foreign investment and to resume full economic relations with the rest of the world. Our economy had been stagnating for almost a decade and the lack of growth had already become a source of social unrest. We knew that it would be much easier for us to negotiate an acceptable constitutional solution if all the parties felt that their material circumstances were improving and would continue to improve. We needed to break free from the over-protection, restraints and distortions that decades of sanctions had created in our economy and to break into fiercely competitive global markets.

It was also essential for me to be able to show my own supporters, as soon as possible, that the course that we had adopted was producing dividends. Visible progress in eliminating the restrictions that had been imposed on South African citizens and companies would help in this regard. In particular, the removal of sanctions, a dramatic rise in our exports and our early return to international sporting competition would help to illustrate the benefits of rejoining the international community.

Finally, I wished to ensure that key international leaders would lend their

support to a balanced process of negotiations in which the reasonable concerns of all South Africans – its minorities as well as its majority – would
receive adequate attention. It was important to break down the stereotypes
that many people overseas had developed of white South Africans and the
National Party – and to persuade them that we were no longer the problem
but an indispensable part of the solution.

The next four years were among the most violent in South Africa's history. Nearly 15 000
died, mostly as the result of an internecine power struggle – in effect, a civil war – between the ANC and the Inkatha Freedom Party, the Zulu tribal machine controlled by
Chief Mangosuthu Buthelezi. It was secretly funded, armed and trained by the government, which encouraged it to attack ANC supporters. At first, De Klerk and the white
beneficiaries of apartheid looked smugly on. In March 1992, two years after Mandela's
release, white voters were asked in a referendum if they supported 'the continuation of
the reform process aimed at a new constitution through negotiations'. Thinking they
were being asked to approve a form of 'power sharing' that would leave them in effective control, 69 per cent said yes. Like De Klerk, they still fondly believed apartheid could
be reformed. Mandela, though, knew it could only be abolished – a disjunction that
seemed to escape the notice of those who decided they should share the 1993 Nobel
Peace Prize.

As Mandela tightened the negotiating screws, his relations with De Klerk – aggrieved
at being regarded as one of the architects of apartheid – deteriorated. Confronted at last
with the reality of democracy, De Klerk found himself powerless and out-manoeuvred.
On 27 April 1994, in South Africa's first democratic election, the ANC won 62.5 per cent
of the vote; Mandela, at the age of 76, became president. Nadine Gordimer (110) caught
the euphoria of it all.

Is there any South African for whom this day will be remembered by any
event, even the most personal, above its glowing significance as the day on
which we voted? Even for whites, all of whom have had the vote since they
were eighteen, this was the *first time*. This was my own overwhelming sense
of the day: the other elections, with their farcical show of a democratic procedure restricted to whites (and, later, to everyone *but* the black majority),
had no meaning for any of us *as South Africans*; only as a hegemony of the
skin.

Standing in the queue this morning, I was aware of a sense of silent bond-
ing. Businessmen in their jogging outfits, nurses in uniform (two, near me,

still wearing the plastic mob-caps that cover their hair in the cloistered asepsis of the operating theatre), women in their Zionist Church outfits, white women and black women who shared the mothering of white and black children winding about their legs, people who had brought folding stools to support their patient old bones, night-watchmen just off duty, girl students tossing long hair the way horses switch their tails – here we all were as we have never been. We have stood in line in banks and post offices together, yes, since the desegregation of public places; but until this day there was always the unseen difference between us, far more decisive than the different colours of our skins: some of us had the right that is the basis of all rights, the symbolic X, the sign of a touch on the controls of polity, the mark of citizenship, and others did not. But today we stood on new ground.

The abstract term 'equality' took on materiality as we moved towards the church hall polling station and the simple act, the drawing of an X, that ended over three centuries of privilege for some, deprivation of human dignity for others.

The first signature of the illiterate is the X. Before that there was only the thumb-print, the skin-impression of the powerless. I realised this with something like awe when, assigned by my local branch of the African National Congress to monitor procedures at a polling booth, I encountered black people who could not read or write. A member of the Independent Electoral Commission would guide them through what took on the solemnity of a ritual: tattered identity document presented, hands outstretched under the ultraviolet light, hands sprayed with invisible ink, and meticulously folded ballot paper – a missive ready to be despatched for the future – placed in those hands. Then an uncertain few steps towards a booth, accompanied by the IEC person and one of the party agents to make sure that when the voter said which party he or she wished to vote for the X would be placed in the appropriate square. Several times I was that party agent and witnessed a man or woman giving this signature to citizenship. A strange moment: the first time man scratched the mark of his identity, the conscious proof of his existence, on a stone must have been rather like this.

Of course nearby in city streets there were still destitute black children sniffing glue as the only substitute for nourishment and care; there were homeless families existing in rigged-up shelters in the crannies of the city. The law places the ground of equality underfoot; it did not feed the hungry or put up a roof over the head of the homeless, today, but it changed the base on which South African society was for so long built. The poor are still there, round the corner. But they are not The Outcast. They no longer can be decreed to be forcibly removed, deprived of land, and of the opportunity to change their lives. They count. The meaning of the counting of the vote, whoever wins the majority, is this, and not just the calculation of the contents of ballot boxes.

If to be alive on this day was not Wordsworth's 'very heaven' for those who have been crushed to the level of wretchedness by the decades of apartheid and the other structures of racism that preceded it, if they could not experience the euphoria I shared, standing in line, to be living at this hour has been extraordinary. The day has been captured for me by the men and women who couldn't read or write, but underwrote it, at last, with their kind of signature. May it be the seal on the end of illiteracy, of the pain of imposed ignorance, of the deprivation of the fullness of life.

At Mandela's presidential inauguration in front of the Union Buildings in Pretoria two weeks later, De Klerk, who has been thrown the sop of joint deputy president in what was to prove a short-lived 'government of national unity', emerged blinking furiously into the sunlight.

Also seated with me on the podium was Archbishop Desmond Tutu, resplendent in his purple robes. The diminutive priest had goaded us for years over the sins of apartheid – but he had also wept and threatened to leave South Africa if his comrades in the United Democratic Front[3] continued to necklace their enemies. He was referring to the particularly brutal form of execution by which the revolutionaries had burned their victims to death by fastening petrol-filled tyres around their necks and setting them alight. Somehow Winnie Mandela had also managed to make an appearance on the main platform, despite her estrangement from her famous husband. As always, she was a centre of attention. She had promised to free the people of South Africa with her matchboxes and necklaces. In the end they were liberated not by violence after a devastating racial war, but through peaceful negotiations and compromise. Also around us were the chiefs of South Africa's security forces, General Johan van der Merwe, the commissioner of the South African police; General Georg Meiring, the chief of the defence force accompanied by the chiefs of the army, navy and air force. Their uniforms, crisp and smart, bore rows of military decorations for campaigns waged primarily against the ANC and its allies. Until a week earlier Nelson Mandela and many of the key ANC leaders feared that they would mount a *coup d'état*, rather than surrender power to their erstwhile enemies.

The funeral of Dr Verwoerd – the architect of apartheid – had been held in this same amphitheatre. Now, twenty-eight years after his death, it was witnessing the final burial of his vision of an ethnically compartmentalized commonwealth of southern African states. It was filled with an assembly that would have been quite unthinkable during his lifetime. He had doggedly preferred international sporting isolation to the prospect of accepting Maori players in the rugby teams of our traditional arch-rivals, New Zealand. While he was in office visas were granted to black American diplomats only after weighty consideration by the cabinet. Now the amphitheatre was filled with South Africans and foreigners of all colours and races, mixing freely and happily together. Senior office bearers of the African National Congress mingled easily with National Party cabinet ministers whom they had come to know quite well during the tortuous negotiations that had preceded our first fully democratic elections on 27 April. Dr Mangosuthu Buthelezi, the leader of the Inkatha Freedom Party, found himself in the same audience as ANC leaders from Natal. For years members of his party had been locked in a murderous struggle with the ANC for the control of the province of KwaZulu-Natal.

The amphitheatre was also filled with numerous international guests for whom the idea of any public contact with South Africa would have been anathema during the long decades of our international isolation. Vice-President Al Gore and Hillary Clinton, Robert Mugabe and numerous heads of government and state were seated together in the sharp morning sunshine, shielding their eyes with their programmes as the ceremony proceeded. Among them was Fidel Castro and a senior representative of the Russian Federation. Less than seven years earlier our army had been locked in battle with Russian-and Cuban-led Angolan troops on the Lomba River, in southern Angola. It was probably one of the largest land battles in Africa since the Second World War. We had convincingly won that battle – but it had shown us how precariously isolated we had become.

The moment arrived when the chief justice called upon me to take the oath of office as one of the two executive deputy presidents in the Government of National Unity, which was about to take over the government of South

Africa. The other executive deputy president was Thabo Mbeki, widely regarded as the ANC leader who was most likely to succeed Nelson Mandela.

I was no longer president. I would be moving from the president's office behind the impressive colonnaded portico to my left to a mirror image office to my right. I had never had any illusions that this would be the outcome of the reform process that I began on 2 February 1990. I had equally few illusions about the difficulty of the task that lay ahead and about the problems and frustrations that would accompany the loss of power.

Judge Corbett administered the oath to me in my own language, Afrikaans. I made a point of swearing it in the name of *Drie-enige God* – the Afrikaans for the Holy Trinity. I did so because of the concern among Christians – and particularly the Afrikaans churches – about the ANC's approach to religious matters. I wished to illustrate my commitment to Christian values, within the framework of religious freedom.

I was deeply aware of my responsibility for assuring the best possible future for my own people – as well as for all the other peoples of our incredibly complex society. If I turned in my seat and looked out through the bullet-proof glass that had been erected around the ceremonial platform I could see the square mass of the Voortrekker Monument silhouetted against the southern sky. Out beyond the terraced gardens and sweeping lawns – now covered in festive marquees, huge public announcement systems and tens of thousands of eager South Africans – it was a stark reminder of my heritage. My people had erected the monument some fifty years earlier to the Afrikaner Voortrekkers – pioneers in Afrikaans – who had opened up the interior of South Africa with their flint-lock muskets and trains of lumbering ox wagons. The marble bas-reliefs that adorned its interior walls bore silent testimony to the tribulations that they had suffered in their quest to establish their own free republics in the interior of the sub-continent. The people depicted in the murals were the heroes of whose deeds I learned at my mother's knee. The dream that they had dreamt of being a free and separate people, with their own right to national self-determination in their own national state in southern Africa, had been the dream that had motivated the ancestors who stared sternly at me from our old family photographs. It had been the central goal of my own father, who had been cabinet minster during the 1950s and 60s. It was the ideal to which I myself had clung until I finally concluded, after a long process of deep introspection, that, if pursued, it would bring disaster to all the peoples of our country – including my own.

In his inaugural address, Mandela read a haunting poem by Ingrid Jonker (111), an Afrikaner poet. It was written in 1960 in the wake of the Sharpeville massacre and the nation-wide anti-pass demonstrations that followed. 'In the midst of despair,' Mandela said, 'she celebrated hope. Confronted with death, she asserted the beauty of life. To her and others like her, we owe a debt to life itself. To her and others like her, we owe a commitment to the poor, the oppressed, the wretched and the despised.' (Nyanga is a township outside Cape Town.)

The child who was shot dead by soldiers at Nyanga

The child is not dead
the child lifts his fists against his mother
who shouts Afrika! shouts the breath
of freedom and the veld
in the locations of the cordoned heart

The child lifts his fists against his father
in the march of the generations
who are shouting Afrika! shout the breath
of righteousness and blood
in the streets of his embattled pride

The child is not dead
not at Langa nor at Nyanga
nor at Orlando nor at Sharpeville
nor at the police post in Philippi
where he lies with a bullet through his brain

The child is the dark shadow of the soldiers
on guard with their rifles, saracens and batons
the child is present at all assemblies and law-givings
the child peers through the windows of houses and into the hearts of
    mothers
this child who wanted only to play in the sun at Nyanga is everywhere
the child grown to a man treks on through all Africa

the child grown into a giant journeys over the whole world
Without a pass

One of the most significant outcomes of the negotiations between Mandela and De Klerk was the decision to set up a Truth and Reconciliation Commission (TRC) to help lay the ghosts of the recent past. 'We can forgive,' said Mandela, 'but we can never forget.' Under the chairmanship of Archbishop Desmond Tutu, who had been awarded the Nobel Peace Prize in 1984 for his non-violent opposition to apartheid, the commission was assigned the daunting task of investigating all politically-inspired 'gross violations of human rights' – defined as 'killing, abduction, torture and severe ill-treatment' – since Sharpeville. This was to be no Nuremberg trial if only because the leaders of the apartheid regime had capitulated and not, as the Nazis had, been defeated. Instead, the victims would be given the opportunity to tell their stories and the perpetrators would be granted immunity in return for full disclosure. Never more than a one-sided deal – the word 'justice' was notably absent from the commission's title – it was thought to be the best that could be achieved in the fragile circumstances of a negotiated settlement in a deeply divided society. Among those who bitterly dissented was Steve Biko's widow, who went to court in an unsuccessful attempt to challenge the amnesty provision.

Over the two-and-a-half years of the commission's life, 21 000 victims recorded their appalling experiences – they included 10 000 allegations of killing – while 8 000 gross violators of human rights – many of them murderers in anyone's book – applied for amnesty and got off scot-free. Ingrid de Kok's poem (112) is called 'The Archbishop Chairs the First Session'.

The Archbishop Chairs the First Session

The Truth and Reconciliation Commission.
April 1996. East London, South Africa

On the first day
after a few hours of testimony
the Archbishop wept.
He put his grey head
on the long table
of papers and protocols
and he wept.

The national and international cameramen
filmed his weeping,
his misted glasses,

his sobbing shoulders,
the call for a recess.

It doesn't matter what you thought
of the Archbishop before or after,
of the settlement, the commission,
or what the anthropologists flying in
from less studied crimes and sorrows
said about the discourse,
or how many doctorates,
books, and installations followed,
or even if you think this poem
simplifies, lionises
romanticises, mystifies.

There was a long table, starched purple vestment
and after a few hours of testimony,
the Archbishop, chair of the commission,
laid down his head, and wept.

That's how it began.

Anjtie Krog, an Afrikaner poet and journalist, sat through the entire proceedings on behalf of the South African Broadcasting Corporation. *Country of My Skull* (113) is her sensitive, sometimes tortured, account of what she saw and heard.

It is ordinary people who appear before the Truth Commission. People you meet daily in the street, on the bus and train – people with the signs of poverty and hard work on their bodies and their clothes. In their faces you can read astonishment, bewilderment, sown by the callousness of the security police and the unfairness of the justice system. 'We were treated like garbage: worse even than dogs. Even ants were treated better than us.'

And everyone wants to know: Who? Why? Out of the sighing arises more than the need for facts or the longing to get closure on someone's life. The victims ask the hardest of all the questions: How is it possible that the person I loved so much lit no spark of humanity in you?

A mother stumbles on to the fact that her child is dead. She sends one child to go and buy fish. He hears on the street: 'They shot your little brother just now.'

The abnormality of South African society strikes Commissioner Mary Burton. 'In a normal society if your child is not at home on time, you think he might still be at his friends. But under Apartheid you go and look at the police station, then at the jails, then at the hospital and eventually at the morgue.'

What gradually becomes clear is that the Apartheid system worked like a finely woven net – starting with the Broederbond who appointed leaders. In turn these leaders appointed ministers, judges, generals. Security forces, courts, administrations were tangled in. Through Parliament legislation was launched that would keep the brutal enforcement of Apartheid out of sight.

It is striking that no politicians attend the hearings. Is it because they respect the independence of the Commission, or do they simply not want to know what price ordinary people paid for the end of Apartheid and the new dispensation? Many of those testifying are unemployed and live in squatter camps.

Now that people are able to tell their stories, the lid of the Pandora's box is lifted; for the first time these individual truths sound unhindered in the ears of all South Africans. The black people in the audience are seldom upset. They have known the truth for years. The whites are often disconcerted: they didn't realize the magnitude of the outrage, the 'depth of depravity' as Tutu calls it.

Where does the truth lie? What does it have to do with reconciliation and justice?

'For me, justice lies in the fact that everything is being laid out on the same table,' says my colleague Mondli. 'The truth that rules our fears, our deeds and our dreams is coming to light. From now on you don't only see a smiling black man in front of you, but you also know what I carry inside of me. I've always known it – now you also know.'

'And reconciliation?'

'Reconciliation will only be possible when the dignity of black people has been restored and when whites become compassionate. Reconciliation and amnesty I don't find important. That people are able to tell their stories – that's the important thing.'

'For me, it's a new beginning,' I say. 'It is not about skin colour, culture, language, but about people. The personal pain puts an end to all stereotypes. Where we connect now has nothing to do with group or colour, we connect with our humanity ...' I keep quiet. Drunk or embarrassed.

'Let us drink to the end of three centuries of fractured morality,' says Mondli and lifts his glass. 'Here people are finally breaking through to one another and you and I are experiencing it.'

'And maybe this is how we should measure our success – if we manage to formulate a morality based on our common humanity.'

Mondli laughs and says: 'We're all starting to talk like Tutu.'

De Klerk was one politician who did attend the hearings and give evidence, though neither side found it a rewarding experience.

I repeated, in more impassioned terms than ever before, my apology for apartheid.

I said that apartheid was wrong. On my own behalf and on behalf of the National Party I apologized to the millions of South Africans who had suffered the wrenching disruption of being arbitrarily deprived of their homes, businesses and land because of forced removals; who over the years, had suffered the shame of being arrested for pass law offences; who over the decades – and indeed, centuries – suffered the indignities and humiliation of racial discrimination; who were prevented from exercising their full democratic rights in the land of their birth; who were unable to achieve their full potential because of job reservation; and who received inadequate and unequal social, medical and educational services.

The second point that I made was that since the National Party's reform policies began – at first tentatively, and later with increasing boldness and vigour – we had been part of the solution, and not part of the problem. The new South Africa was just as much our creation as it was the creation of any other party. We refused to allow any party or any organ to deprive us of our rightful place in our new society.

I said that we, like the ANC and all the other parties of South Africa, were the product of a complex and tormented history. We did not regard ourselves as being morally superior – or inferior – to any other party. The glory of the past seven years had been that, together, we had been able to overcome the divisions and bitterness of our history and, together, we had been able to create the basis for a better and more peaceful future for all our people.

It was soon clear that the TRC had little interest in such sentiments. It had already determined its agenda – and its agenda was to discredit and humiliate me.

What particularly irritated the commission was De Klerk's insistence that, despite having been a cabinet minister since 1978 and State President since 1989, he had known nothing about the horrors perpetrated throughout those years in the interests of apartheid. He had also angrily rejected Tutu's plea to say he was sorry for his involvement. The commission's frustration was best expressed by Alex Boraine (114), its deputy chairman, who, having been an opposition MP from 1974 to 1986, knew where the bodies were buried.

De Klerk saw himself, to use his own words, as a 'co-liberator' of South Africa. When he came to see us, he described himself as a man of integrity, needed by the new South Africa to consolidate democracy and to establish stability. He clearly believed that he still had a critical leadership role to play and that we should be careful not to blur his image. He was deeply resentful that he had not received the same praise and acceptance that was afforded Mandela. It is quite astonishing that he should feel that way, bearing in mind what Mandela had stood for, fought for, and suffered for for so long, in strong contrast to what De Klerk had participated in. What he refused to accept was that the policies of the National Party had created a climate which made it possible for some of the worst offences and extra-legal practices to take place, particularly during the 1980s. I have no doubt that he could grasp this intellectually, but it seemed impossible for him to do so emotionally, perhaps because of his father's role as a senior member of the National Party, and because he had spent his own life defending the principles, and therefore the practice, of apartheid.

I also found it extraordinary that he should maintain over and over again that he hadn't been aware of what was happening. During my twelve years in Parliament I had been approached on many occasions by individuals, organisations, and groups, who shared with me and my party something of their personal suffering and sorrow. I went to many areas where forced removals were taking place. I went to morgues and saw the bodies of people who clearly had been shot in the back by police and spoke on these matters in Parliament time and time again. In this regard, the former Minister of Law and Order, Adriaan Vlok, made a telling statement when he appeared before the Commission. On his own initiative, he said that it was true that 'Commissioner Boraine did tell us about some of these things that were taking place but we didn't believe him and did not want to accept what he was saying because we saw him as being part of the enemy of South Africa.' Leon Wessels, a former deputy minister in De Klerk's Cabinet, said in his statement to the Commission, 'It was not that we didn't know, we didn't want to know. We didn't talk about it, we whispered it in the corridors of Parliament.' It may be that De Klerk was unable to hear what some of us were trying to say and couldn't understand the force of Tutu's plea to him. I am deeply saddened that he did not leave politics in 1994. I think he would then have gone out on the crest of a wave, as it were, as a major contributor to our new democracy. But it was not to be. I think he believed that he would continue to be a leader in South Africa on a par with Mandela, which of course was unthinkable.

'There are those', observed the ANC's 1994 election manifesto, 'who would like us to believe that the past doesn't exist: that decades of apartheid rule have suddenly disappeared. But the economic and social devastation of apartheid remains. Our country is in a mess.' Re-visiting the country of his birth on the eve of the election, Dan Jacobson (115), the novelist and academic, contemplated the mess and was filled with foreboding.

The disparities of wealth and poverty in South Africa can produce in resident and visitor alike a kind of vertigo, a disbelief in the evidence of their own eyes. The wealthier groups are not a thin layer of expatriates and a yet thinner, positively molecular, layer of middle-class locals, as they are in many Third World countries. They can be seen almost everywhere, in town and country alike, and so can their possessions – houses, cars, swimming-pools, furnishings, electronic goods. Yet the poor, a category which includes the overwhelming majority of unskilled or semi-skilled blacks lucky enough to be employed and housed after a fashion, are incomparably more numerous; while beside them, beyond them, beneath them, are the armies of the truly poor – hungry, houseless, uneducated, unemployed, half-clothed; at once disregarded, even 'transparent', and yet never forgotten.

Now, to such disparities add the following. The rich are usually, indeed almost invariably, of a different colour from the poor, though there is some degree of overlap. Rich and poor speak different languages from one another, and it is in the languages of the rich (in English, above all) that the important, skills-giving books are written. Rich and poor have different histories and national identities (or so most of them believe, and belief in these matters is more important than any question of 'fact'). Their cultural habits and expectations are different. The gulfs in education and training between them, above all in the technological, mathematical, and accounting disciplines which more and more determine who has power over whom – these gulfs may be somewhat narrower than they once were, but they remain huge nevertheless.

Add the angers engendered by an embedded conviction of racial superiority on the one side, and a centuries-old experience of displacement and contempt on the other. Add too the fears arising from a consciousness of the disasters (political, economic, social, medical) which have overtaken so many African countries to the north – fears felt not only by whites in South Africa but by many blacks too, and almost all Asians and Coloureds.

The strange thing is that in such circumstances, under such pressures, it is possible that some of the dispossessed may actually find it easier not to attack those of a different colour who own everything they lack, but to pursue instead ancient, internecine enmities among themselves. Or to turn only on the most vulnerable of the wealthier groups, the Indians especially, many of whom today feel themselves to be even more threatened than they were by the manias and humiliations of the apartheid era.

Nowhere are the disparities of wealth and poverty more vertiginous than in Cape Town, a lurid stage-set on which whites in their affluent homes cling to the slopes of Table Mountain while the tide of Africa laps around their feet. Here, in the foreground, sprawling across the Cape Flats, the sandy isthmus where in Van Riebeeck's time Hottentots grazed their multitudinous cattle and sheep, is Khayelitsha, part formal township, part squatter camp. First established in the mid-1980s as an apartheid dormitory for Cape Town's black workers, it now provides a home – of sorts – for an estimated one-and-a-half million Africans. Steven Otter (116), a white journalist, first went to live there in 2002 'to break down my inner prejudices and feel truly South African'; he gradually found himself accepted. Following an unhappy spell in Europe, where he 'pined after the feeling of belonging, of being part of a powerful spirit of kinship', he decided to return.

The Table Mountain sunset behind us was less than an hour away as we sped along the N2 highway past the turn-off to Cape Town International Airport. The rush hour traffic heading out of the city had thinned out slightly and

467

we were racing down the busy highway towards Khayelitsha at a terrifying speed. But there was more to the adrenalin being pumped into my veins than that: after two and a half years away from the rambling black township I was coming back to live there. Europe could not have felt more distant as I watched the crooked shacks hurtling past on the right-hand side of the road. One of those shacks would be my home and the thought filled me with a combination of excitement and anxiety. This was the real Khayelitsha, the massive informal settlements known for their ugly poverty and rampant crime. This was the nemesis of the rich, where disorganised groups of tsotsis daily made the decision, consciously or otherwise, to take on the beneficiaries of the system.

It had been a mistake taking the middle front seat of the taxi, I realised as the taxi driver screeched to a halt on the grass verge of the highway. No matter your age, intelligence, religion or race, in the middle seat up front you are required to count the taxi fares sent forward from the back, not an easy task if someone forgets to pay, makes a mistake, or takes a chance. To be fair, the driver had handled my news that the money was 'short' quite well. Repeatedly turning his head towards the passengers seated behind us, he'd asked over and over again for the culprit to pay up. His ire having peaked, with a lightning quick glance in the left-hand side mirror, he'd swerved from the fast to the slow lane and applied the brakes.

'We are not going any further until that fare is in,' he said in Xhosa, as we ground to a stop. After an angry conversation involving most of the passengers, the culprit, a shifty-eyed boy of around seventeen was eventually identified and paid up. He received a robust scolding from the mama sitting beside him, the driver started the engine and we were on our way again. The debate among the passengers had required a person by person explanation of their virtuousness.

'I gave you that ten rand note,' the woman sitting behind me had said, looking pleased with herself. 'Do you remember giving me change?' '

And so it went on, until it became obvious that the devious youth had no evidence of his innocence. Once the mama's scolding was over, all was forgiven and we drove on in a comfortable silence.

It wasn't long before we were on Mew Way moving over the bridge above the highway and heading towards TR Informal Settlement. As we neared the first four-way stop, a little hill sprinkled with shacks, some large, some small, some wide, some high, but all of them ragtag and decrepit, came into sight.

In the air above this beautiful scene, the evening fire was being taken on by darkness, with the dust from the shack lands and the smog from the city hanging wearily beneath the sky. The sun was already eroding the usually sharp contours of Table Mountain, its target the Atlantic Ocean flowing out before Camps Bay. Different worlds perhaps, but with the African sun they are linked forever.

Although there was not a tree in sight, I could feel by the ease with which the taxi crossed over the four-way stop that even the wind had paused for this sunset, its breath held in anticipation of reunion.

'Four-way please, my brother,' I said to the driver, who nodded that he'd heard.

Its momentum lost, the taxi moved over the little bridge leading to the four-way stop between TR and W Sections. The driver sluggishly dodged a few cars and brought us to a lazy halt.

'Sharp,' he answered my thanks.

And there he was, my old friend, on the other side of Mew Way. He was wearing beige baggy tsotsi-style pants with white braces. On his head, Fumanekile, aka Ta-fumsa, wore his lopsided revolutionary beret. Although this felt like a first meeting, this time, the gaps between his teeth, his rough skin, rugged looks and soft voice represented all that I liked most about this place in Khayelitsha's heart.

'Welcome back, my brother,' Fumanekile said just loudly enough for me to hear, as he crossed the road towards me.

I threw my heavy rucksack over my shoulder.

'Luvuyo,'[5] he said, dragging the word out slowly, as he came out from behind the taxi, 'welcome home!'

We shook hands, going through the multifaceted handshake over and over again.

'This is Banana,' Fumanekile said, his left hand on the shoulder of the tall, thin man in his early twenties who was standing to one side, 'and this is your homeboy[6] Gigs.'

I could see where Banana got his nickname. Exactly my height, he wore a pair of brown Bermudas which, with his sloping back, gave him the appearance of the longest KwaZulu-Natal banana ever. Gigs was a short man with a floppy white hat on his head. His lively eyes were set in a youthful face, untouched by cynicism or distrust.

'Are you from iLitha Park?' I asked.

'*Haai, mlungu*,[7] from Uitenhage,' he said, shaking my hand vigorously.

'That's amazing,' I told him. 'I don't meet people from Uitenhage very often. I also don't like to admit that I come from there, you know?'

'Why? Uitenhage's a lekker[8] place,' he replied. 'You know KwaNobuhle?'

I told him I did as we walked off, waiting on the island to cross the street, taxis hauling over the white lines in front of us. Fumanekile took my bag.

'Don't worry about it, Luvuyo,' he answered my protest.

'Yes, yes, hi, my brother,' Gigs said in a deep voice, the open smile on his face placing a lasting emphasis on his assertion that we were related. 'What clan are you from?'

'The Madiba[9] clan,' I said, to laughter from all three of them.

As we headed down a side street in the direction of Fumanekile's shack and into the centre of TR, the kwaito singer Zola's 'Bhambatha' blared out from a pair of speakers outside a roadside shebeen. Instead of making me feel homesick, as it had when I'd played it while braai-ing[10] on my own in Europe, his tough township gangster rap inspired me to take the cue from my three companions – without thinking about it too much, I added an extra drag and a spring to my step.

In the distance I could see the other end of the road, up which I had walked from the Site C train station to visit Fumanekile more than three years before. The tar on the road where a group of children were playing a game of cricket, with a beer crate as the wickets, was as thin as everywhere else, looking like leftovers from an upgrading of the nearby highway. Whacked hard by a boy the height of my waist, the tennis ball the children were playing with shot between Fumanekile and me, with three boys in hot pursuit.

The smiles of passers-by, acknowledging us with a grin or a wave, ran contrary to the hardship written like graffiti all over my new surroundings, where the cheapest metals and the throwaway things of the wealthy had been used with great care to create the best living conditions possible. This was a great camping ground away from the rural areas, set up in acknowledgement of the contradictory magnetism of the city. Gone were the valley forests and green rolling hilltops of the Xhosa ancestral lands in the Transkei; in their place was a mix of sea sand, soil and never-ending flatness. The round, cow dung huts, which are cool in summer and warm in winter, had been sacrificed for tin shacks that would, if not for the cardboard insulators on the inside, have made the rough Cape Town seasons still worse, while the ancient radios – their aerials struggling periscope-like to catch a signal above the giant Transkei hills – had been exchanged for taxi rank hi-fis. The old-fashioned dark suit pants and collared shirts and traditional ladies' dresses, meanwhile, had been laid on the altar of tsotsi culture, where youthful rebellion lasted into the thirties. There was poverty all sides here, yet the smiles of the people told a different story – a story of cultural survival against all odds. As Zola rapped on in the distance, the angry tone in his voice intensified for a moment, then faded into his chorus, filled with courage and strength. Then a new track killed Zola's voice in that squatter camp that holds tens of thousands of residents, most of whom, like me, had initially travelled from the impoverished Eastern Cape in search of work.

We walked down the stairs and into Fumanekile's sunken lounge.

'What's on your mind?' he asked me.

'I've been away for too long,' I replied, and we both smiled.

The Transkei, where colonists and Xhosa once fought nine 'kaffir wars', is the contemporary setting for Zakes Mda's delightful novel, *The Heart of Redness*[11] (117), published in 2000. The people of Qolorha-by-Sea, the village on the Wild Coast where Nongqawuse, the Xhosa prophetess, precipitated the Great Cattle Killing of 1856-57, are divided between Believers and Unbelievers. The Believers, led by Zim, are the fourth-generation descendants of those who, in obedience to Nongqawuse's instructions, killed their cattle and destroyed their crops in the hope that the dead would arise and drive the white man into the sea. The Unbelievers, led by Bhonco, are descended from those who thought Nongqawuse a foolish girl and a false prophet whose teachings, probably inspired by the British colonists, would lead to the destruction of the Xhosa nation. Now the *casus belli* is a developers' plan to turn the area around Qolorha into a 'tourist paradise', complete with casino. To Bhonco and the Unbelievers, the development represents progress and civilisation; to the Believers, who want the Wild Coast to stay wild, it is a threat to traditionalism and the environment. Into the controversy steps Camagu, son of Cesane, recently returned from 30 years' exile in the United States with a PhD in development economics. He has just scandalised the villagers by publicly declaring his love for Zim's daughter. They had thought the object of his fancy was Bhonco's daughter, Xoliswa Ximiya.

One day he gets a surprise visit from John Dalton.[12] He says they need to bury their differences because there are greater things at stake. The developers are coming to hold a public meeting with the villagers, to explain their plans to turn Qolorha-by-Sea into a tourist paradise. Dalton will not be able to attend this imbhizo[13] because he is going to Ficksburg in the Free State on an urgent family matter. He has come to ask Camagu to attend the meeting because it is important that someone should be there who will be able to articulate the view of those villagers who are opposed to the tourist paradise as envisaged by the developers.

'It is good that you want us to bury our differences,' says Camagu. 'I never had any differences with you in the first place. I merely expressed a different point of view about the water project … after you had solicited my opinion!'

'Okay, maybe it was childish of me to take it personally,' admits Dalton, 'but let's talk about this imbhizo. Will you be able to attend?'

'Who will listen to me after what I did at the concert?'

Dalton laughs.

'I don't know what came over you,' he says. 'But this meeting is important. The whole future of the village depends on it. We cannot let your personal problems –'

'Okay, okay, I will go.'

The developers, two bald white men and a young black man, come early on a Saturday morning and insist that the meeting be held at the lagoon so that they can demonstrate their grand plans for the village. The young black man is introduced as Lefa Leballo, the new chief executive officer of the black empowerment company that is going to develop the village into a tourist heaven. He looks very handsome in his navy-blue suit, blue shirt and colourful tie. The two elderly white men – both in black suits – are Mr Smith and Mr Jones. They were chief executive and chairman of the company before they sold the majority shares to black empowerment consortia. Now they act as consultants for the company.

Most of the villagers have gathered. When Camagu arrives they titter and point fingers at him. He walks defiantly to the front, and to his consternation he finds himself standing next to the teachers of Qolorha-by-Sea Secondary School. Xoliswa Ximiya just looks forward and pretends that he does not exist. The history teacher who was the chairman at the concert smiles at him. He smiles back.

His eyes search for Bhonco, the most vocal supporter of the holiday resort project. There he is, surrounded by his supporters. The hadeda ibises have given him some respite and are no longer mocking him with their laughter. The abayiyizeli, the ululants, have also taken a break from slashing Zim's eardrums with their razor-sharp ululation, and have assumed the role of ordinary citizens. Zim sits with his daughter and a few supporters. Both elders look tired and drained.

After the chief has introduced the visitors, Lefa Leballo makes a brief speech. He tells the villagers how lucky they are to be living in a new and democratic South Africa where the key word is transparency. In the bad old days such projects would be done without consulting them at all. So, in the same spirit in which the government has respected them by consulting them, they must also show respect to these important visitors, by not voicing the objections that he heard some of the villagers were having about a project of such national importance. He then gives the floor to Mr Smith.

Mr Smith talks of the wonders that will happen at Qolorha-by-Sea. There will be boats and water-skiing and jet-skiing. People from across the seas will ride the waves in a sport called surfing. This place will be particularly good for that because the sea is rough most of the time. Surfing will be a challenge. There will be merry-go-rounds for the children, and rides that go up to the sky. Rides that twist and turn while the riders scream in ecstatic fright.

'Right here,' says Mr Smith, 'we shall see the biggest and most daring rides of all roller-coasters in the world ... over the rough sea. This will be the place for roller-coaster enthusiasts who spend their lives travelling the world in search of the biggest and most daring rides.'

Bhonco and his supporters applaud. Except for people like Xoliswa Ximiya, none of them have seen a roller-coaster before. But it does not matter. If it is something that brings civilisation, then it is good for Qolorha.

'That is not all, my dear friends,' says Mr Smith excitedly. 'We are going to have cable cars too. Cable cars shall move across the water from one end of the lagoon to the other.'

'These are wonderful things,' says Bhonco. 'But I am suspicious of this matter of riding the waves. The new people that were prophesied by the false prophet, Nongqawuse, were supposed to come riding on the waves too.'

Lefa Leballo explains that this has nothing to do with old superstitions. This riding of the waves is a sport that civilised people do in advanced countries and even here in South Africa, in cities like Durban and Cape Town. But the waves here are more suited to the sport than the waves of other big cities in South Africa. The waves here are big and wild.

Lefa Leballo then interprets Bhonco's concerns to the consultants. They find this rather funny and laugh for a long time. The villagers join in the laughter too.

But Camagu is not impressed.

'You talk of all these rides and all these wonderful things,' he says, 'but for whose benefit are they? What will these villagers who are sitting here get from all these things? Will their children ride on those merry-go-rounds and roller-coasters? On those cable cars and boats? Of course not! They will not have any money to pay for these things. These things will be enjoyed only by rich people who will come here and pollute our rivers and our ocean.'

'Who are you to talk for the people of Qolorha?' asks Bhonco. 'You talk of our rivers and our ocean. Since when do you belong here? Or do you think just because you run after daughters of Believers, that gives you the right to think you belong here?'

'Hey you, Bhonco! If you know what is good for you, you will leave my child out of this!' shouts Zim. 'She did not invite that stupid man to follow her. Today this son of Cesane is talking a lot of sense. This son of Cesane is right. They will destroy our trees and the plants of our forefathers for nothing. We, the people of Qolorha, will not gain anything from this.'

'You will get jobs,' says Lefa Leballo desperately. Then he looks at Camagu pleadingly. 'Please don't talk these people against a project of such national importance.'

'It is of national importance only to your company and shareholders, not to these people!' yells Camagu. 'Jobs? Bah! They will lose more that they will gain from jobs. I tell you, people of Qolorha, these visitors are interested only in profits for their company. This sea will no longer belong to you. You will have to pay to use it.'

'He has been put up to this by that white man, Dalton,' says Bhonco. 'He is Dalton's stooge. Dalton is hiding himself and has sent this man here because he has a black face. Dalton wants us to remain in the darkness of our fathers so that he can grab our land as his fathers did before him.'

'You are a liar, Bhonco!' cries Zim. 'You lie even in the middle of the night. This young man is talking common sense from his own brain. It has nothing to do with Dalton.'

'You have nothing to offer these people,' says Mr Jones to Camagu. 'If you fight against these wonderful developments, what do you have to offer in their place?'

'The promotion of the kind of tourism that will benefit the people, that will not destroy indigenous forests, that will not bring hordes of people who will pollute the rivers and drive away the birds.'

'That is just a dream,' shouts Lefa Leballo. 'There is no such tourism.'

'We can work it out, people of Qolorha,' appeals Camagu. 'We can sit down and plan it. There are many people out there who enjoy communing with unspoilt nature.'

'We are going ahead with our plans,' says Lefa Leballo adamantly. 'How will you stop us? The government has already approved this project. I belong to the ruling party. Many important people in the ruling party are directors of this company. The chairman himself was a cabinet minister until he was deployed to the corporate world. We'll see to it that you don't foil our efforts.'

'Well, how will you stop progress and development?' asks Mr Smith, chuckling triumphantly.

'Yes! How will he stop civilisation?' asks Xoliswa Ximiya.

For a while Camagu does not know how to answer this. Then in an inspired moment he suddenly shouts, 'How will I stop you? I will tell you how I will stop you! I will have this village declared a national heritage site. Then no one will touch it. The wonders of Nongqawuse that led to the cattle-killing movement of the amaXhosa happened here. On that basis, this can be declared a national heritage site!'

'That damned Nongqawuse again!' spits Bhonco.

'That Nongqawuse of yours is already burning in the fires of hell,' says Xoliswa Ximiya.

'This son of Cesane is brilliant!' cries Zim. 'I knew that Nongqawuse would one day save this village!'

It is clear that the majority of the people have been swayed by Camagu's intervention. Bhonco bursts out in desperation, 'This son of Cesane, I ask you my people, is he circumcised? Are we going to listen to uncircumcised boys here?'

'How do you know he is not circumcised?' asks Zim.

'Why should that matter?' says Camagu. 'Facts are facts, whether they come from somebody who is circumcised or not.'

'Yes, it does matter,' says Zim. 'That is why this Unbeliever brings it up. He has been defeated by facts and reason. That is why he now talks about circumcision. Of course, if this son of Cesane is uncircumcised we shall not deal with him, though he has been useful in our cause.'

At first Camagu is stubborn. He says he does not see why the worth of a man should be judged on whether he has a foreskin or not.

'You said you respected our customs,' says Bhonco. 'So you respect them only when it suits you? Clearly you are uncircumcised!'

'I challenge to you, Tat'uBhonco, to come and inspect me here in public to see if I have a foreskin,' says Camagu confidently. He knows that no one will dare take up that challenge. And if at any time they did, they would not find any foreskin. He was circumcised, albeit in the most unrespectable manner, at the hospital.

Zim's supporters applaud.

Mr Jones adopts a more conciliatory stance. In measured tones he tries to convince them how beautiful the place will be, with all the amenities of the city. There will be a shopping mall, tennis courts and an Olympic-size swimming pool.

He is struck by a new idea, which by the look on his face is quite brilliant. 'We can even build new blocks of townhouses as holiday timeshare units,' he says.

'Timeshare units? We didn't talk about timeshare units,' says Mr Smith. 'We talked about a hotel and a casino.'

'Well, plans can always change, can't they?' says Mr Jones.

'If the plans change at all, I rather fancy a retirement village for millionaires,' says Mr Smith. 'This place is ideal for that. We can call it Willowbrook Grove.'

'Grove?' exclaims Mr Jones. 'How can we call it a grove when we're going to cut down all these trees to make way for the rides?'

'We'll plant other trees imported from England. We'll uproot a lot of these native shrubs and wild bushes and plant a beautiful English garden.'

The developers seem to have forgotten about the rest of the people as they argue about the profitability of creating a beautiful English countryside versus that of constructing a crime-free timeshare paradise. Even Lefa Leballo is left out as they bandy about the most appropriate names: names that end in Close, Dell and Downs. At first the villagers are amused. But soon they get bored and drift away to their homes, leaving the developers lost in their argument.

Two of the most sobering issues confronting post-apartheid South Africa are crime and AIDS. Crime, especially violent crime, both urban and rural, is as endemic now as violence was under apartheid. In *A Country at War with Itself* (118), published in 2007, Antony Altbeker, a researcher and journalist, summarises the textbook account of the link between the two.

Over the past 350 years or so, state power in this part of the world has been exercised exclusively in pursuit of the interests of a small minority. It has operated with the raw logic of the jungle: the strong dominated and everyone else had to bow down or be destroyed. The roots of this model of state power lie in the 17th century with the arrival of the first Europeans, but the process accelerated in the 19th century when colonists in the Cape extended their presence up the east coast and into the interior. In doing so, they used violence that was at once state-sanctioned and state-building to reshape the social, economic and political realities of the region. If anything, levels of institutionalised violence only worsened during the 20th century as the systems of migrant labour and apartheid were built and then consolidated. In the process, traditional society was ripped apart, turning whole generations of people into disenfranchised units of labour, disembodied hands and arms and backs and legs, with no more rights than a cart horse.

The gist of this account of the roots of crime is that the violence used in the shaping of modern South Africa has not dissipated; it lingers on as a kind of background radiation, deforming and dementing us even as the forms in which it is expressed have mutated. 'The past is never dead,' William Faulkner wrote. 'It isn't even past.'

But it is not just in the grand violence of conquest and submission – something common, surely, to all societies – that the origins of present-day violence are to be found, but in the details of the way that this power was exercised here, and the ways that this differed from other places and other times. In this, as the historian and criminologist Gary Kynoch has observed, what distinguishes apartheid and its predecessors from other colonial experiences was the nature of the institutional architecture on which it was premised: the mining hostels and the prisons. In these spaces, men, torn from the bosoms of their families, lived in a pressure-cooker world where the resort to violence to protect oneself and one's property was common, accepted and necessary. The emergence of gangs was inevitable, as was the legitimisation of violence and the transfer of its skills, processes that have shaped life in South Africa's urban townships ever since. In other colonial settings, by contrast, men worked where they lived, and the emergence of a violence-rich male subculture was much less pronounced.

Apart from the devaluation of human life implicit in the building of apartheid, apart also from the destruction of family and communal life it entailed, apartheid, because it denied the majority their freedom, was a system that could never renounce violence. Whether it was the policeman looking at passes or the urban planner plotting the removal of a 'blackspot', apartheid was premised on the sustained threat of coercive force. This was an essential by-product of the system, a greenhouse gas that was being pumped into the air and was changing the chemical composition of the atmosphere. Violence became part of the ambience of a society in which it was understood by everyone, even by those who denied it, that a small minority lived the good life only because it kept its boots firmly on the necks of everyone else.

Apartheid, then, produced violence in the same way that industrialisation produced and produces global warming – inevitably, insidiously and, now that we know better, cynically, too. It also taught anyone who was paying attention that one could do anything to secure one's material interests: any oppression could be inflicted if those with the power felt so inclined. Apartheid, it might be said, was a kind of raw Darwinism in which the only criterion by which a policy was to be judged was whether it advanced the needs of those with the power to institute it; moral rules were for everyone else.

Needless to say, this is not the kind of lesson law-makers should teach their subjects unless they are prepared to hold on to power forever.

If apartheid was premised on pervasive violence, both implicit and explicit, resistance to apartheid, by taking millions of children out of school and putting them on the frontline of the struggle, by legitimating the use of violence and teaching many its techniques, poisoned the same well. Noble as the cause might have been, honourable as most of its activists undoubtedly were, the violence of resistance was a crucial element of the country's ambience, its social atmosphere. Nor was it just the technology and techniques of violence that resistance contributed. More subtle contributions included the inevitable and justifiable building up of resentment that was both the origin of resistance to apartheid and its fuel. But resentment, in the absence of catharsis, is a volatile compound, one that corrodes everything it touches. It, too, is part of our heritage.

To the nature of apartheid and the resistance it engendered, accounts of present-day violence often add a third element: the disappointments of democracy.

Today, millions live on the margins of the formal economy, their hopes and expectations unmet and arguably unmeetable, even as the white community continues to dominate the economy along with an 'emerging' middle class. Everyone from the president down warns that those who have been left out will not be patient forever: owing nothing to a society that has given them nothing, some have already lost patience.

There have been other disappointments, too: urbanisation has left our cities struggling to cope with new demands; family structures have buckled and been swept away by a ghastly AIDS epidemic; the housing backlog has left millions of people living in quarters so cramped it is hard to see how they could develop an appreciation of their own rights to the integrity of their bodies, much less the rights of anyone else.

The fruits of liberation have not all been sweet.

These, then, are the basic building blocks of any reasonable account of the causes of crime. At root, the argument is that some kind of learnt savagery – the product of history and broken homes, sclerotic labour markets and broken souls – has driven a frustrated, angry fraction of South Africans into a life of crime. Indeed, by this reading, levels of violence are almost a metric of the injustices and cruelties of the past, and a gauge of the extent to which the process of social and economic transformation is still unfinished.

However, Altbeker questions whether this is a sufficient explanation for South Africa's place at the top of the world's league tables for violent crime. Here, about 60 people are murdered every day – a rate per head of population eight times higher than America's – and 120 are raped. Armed robbery is another record-setter, as is the hijacking of cars. Altbeker's thesis is that 'violence and criminality have themselves come to shape the context within which young men [overwhelmingly the perpetrators] make decisions about how to behave … As more and more people engage in criminality, its sheer prevalence drags in others, many of whom would not get involved if fewer people were not already doing it.' His solution, briefly, is a criminal justice system that 'comes down like a ton of bricks on people who commit violent crime' accompanied by other measures to instil respect for the rule of law. 'Ours,' he explains, 'is a half-made land … We have yet to learn the conventions and civilities, the social graces and the urbane niceties that are assumed in our constitution.'

Creating a 'culture of respect for the rule of law' was also one of the aims of the Truth and Reconciliation Commission. Whether pardoning apartheid's murderers and torturers promoted respect for the law is an interesting question.

For visitors and residents alike, perhaps the most striking feature of urban South Africa is the security apparatus that surrounds the homes of the well-off. High walls, electrified fences, impenetrable gates, burglar bars, razor wire, alarms, uniformed guards and aggressive warnings of a '24-hour armed response' are all seen as essential accessories. They inspired one of Nadine Gordimer's sharpest and most unforgettable short stories (119). It was published in 1989 before the demise of apartheid but not a lot has changed. She calls it 'a bedtime story'.

In a house, in a suburb, in a city, there were a man and his wife who loved each other very much and were living happily ever after. They had a little boy, and they loved him very much. They had a cat and a dog that the little boy loved very much. They had a car and a caravan trailer for holidays, and a swimming pool that was fenced so that the little boy and his playmates would not fall in and drown. They had a housemaid who was absolutely trustworthy and an itinerant gardener who was highly recommended by the neighbours. For when they began to live happily ever after they were warned, by that wise old witch, the husband's mother, not to take on anyone off the street. They were inscribed in a medical benefit society, their pet dog was licensed, they were insured against fire, flood damage and theft, and subscribed to the local Neighbourhood Watch, which supplied them with a plaque for their gates lettered YOU HAVE BEEN WARNED over the silhouette of a would-be intruder. He was masked; it could not be said if he was black or white, and therefore proved the property owner was no racist.

It was not possible to insure the house, the swimming pool or the car against riot damage. There were riots, but these were outside the city, where people of another colour were quartered. These people were not allowed into the suburb except as reliable housemaids and gardeners, so there was nothing to fear, the husband told the wife. Yet she was afraid that some day such people might come up the street and tear off the plaque YOU HAVE BEEN WARNED and open the gates and stream in … Nonsense, my dear, said the husband, there are police and soldiers and tear gas and guns to keep them away. But to please her – for he loved her very much and buses were being burned, cars stoned, and schoolchildren shot by the police in those quarters out of sight and hearing of the suburb – he had electronically-controlled gates fitted. Anyone who pulled off the sign YOU HAVE BEEN WARNED and tried to open the gates would have to announce his intentions by pressing a button and speaking into a receiver relayed to the house. The little boy was fascinated by the device and used it as a walkie-talkie in cops-and-robbers play with his small friends.

The riots were suppressed, but there were many burglaries in the suburb and somebody's trusted housemaid was tied up and shut in a cupboard by thieves while she was in charge of her employers' house. The trusted housemaid of the man and wife and little boy was so upset by this misfortune befalling a friend left, as she herself often was, with responsibility for the possessions of the man and his wife and the little boy that she implored her employers to have burglar bars attached to the doors and windows of the house, and an alarm system installed. The wife said, She is right, let us take heed of her advice. So from every window and door in the house where they were living happily ever after they now saw the trees and sky through bars, and when the little boy's pet cat tried to climb in by the fanlight to keep him company in his little bed at night, as it customarily had done, it set off the alarm keening through the house.

The alarm was often answered – it seemed – by other burglar alarms, in other houses, that had been triggered by pet cats or nibbling mice. The alarms called to one another across the gardens in shrills and bleats and wails that everyone soon became accustomed to, so that the din roused the inhabitants of the suburb no more than the croak of frogs and musical grating of cicadas' legs. Under cover of the electronic harpies' discourse intruders sawed the iron bars and broke into homes, taking away hi-fi equipment, television sets, cassette players, cameras and radios, jewellery and clothing, and sometimes were hungry enough to devour everything in the refrigerator or paused audaciously to drink the whisky in the cabinets or patio bars. Insurance companies paid no compensation for single malt, a loss made keener by the property owner's knowledge that the thieves wouldn't even have been able to appreciate what it was they were drinking.

Then the time came when many of the people who were not trusted housemaids and gardeners hung about the suburb because they were unemployed. Some importuned for a job: weeding or painting a roof; anything, baas, madam. But the man and his wife remembered the warning about taking on anyone off the street. Some drank liquor and fouled the street with discarded bottles. Some begged, waiting for the man or his wife to drive the car out of the electronically-operated gates. They sat about with their feet in the gutters, under the jacaranda trees that made a green tunnel of the street – for it was a beautiful suburb, spoilt only by their presence – and sometimes they fell asleep lying right before the gates in the midday sun. The wife could never see anyone go hungry. She sent the trusted housemaid out with bread and tea, but the trusted housemaid said these were loafers and tsotsis, who would come and tie her up and shut her in a cupboard. The husband said, She's right. Take heed of her advice. You only encourage them with your bread and tea. They are looking for their chance … And he brought the little boy's tricycle from the garden into the house every night, because if the house was surely secure, once locked and with the alarm set, someone might still be able to climb over the wall or the electronically-closed gates into the garden.

You are right, said the wife, then the wall should be higher. And the wise old witch, the husband's mother, paid for the extra bricks as her Christmas present to her son and his wife – the little boy got a Space Man outfit and a book of fairy tales.

But every week there were more reports of intrusion: in broad daylight and the dead of night, in the early hours of the morning, and even in the lovely summer twilight – a certain family was at dinner while the bedrooms were being ransacked upstairs. The man and his wife, talking of the latest armed robbery in the suburb, were distracted by the sight of the little boy's pet cat effortlessly arriving over the seven-foot wall, descending first with a rapid bracing of extended forepaws down on the sheer vertical surface, and then a graceful launch, landing with swishing tail within the property. The whitewashed wall was marked with the cat's comings and goings; and on the street side of the wall there were larger red-earth smudges that could have been made by the kind of broken running shoes, seen on the feet of unemployed loiterers, that had no innocent destination.

When the man and wife and little boy took the pet dog for its walk round the neighbourhood streets they no longer paused to admire this show of roses or that perfect lawn; these were hidden behind an array of different varieties of security fences, walls and devices. The man, wife, little boy and dog passed a remarkable choice: there was the low-cost option of pieces of broken glass embedded in cement along the top of walls, there were iron grilles ending in lance-points, there were attempts at reconciling the aesthetics of prison architecture with the Spanish Villa style (spikes painted pink) and with the plaster urns of neoclassical facades (twelve-inch pikes finned like zigzags of lightning and painted pure white). Some walls had a small board affixed, giving the name and telephone number of the firm responsible for the installation of the devices. While the little boy and the pet dog raced ahead, the husband and wife found themselves comparing the possible effectiveness of each style against its appearance; and after several weeks when they paused before this barricade or that without needing to speak, both came out with the conclusion that only one was worth considering. It was the ugliest but the most honest in its suggestion of the pure concentration-camp style, no frills, all evident efficacy. Placed the length of walls, it consisted of a continuous coil of stiff and shining metal serrated into jagged blades, so that there would be no way of climbing over it and no way through its tunnel without getting entangled in its fangs. There would be no way out, only a struggle getting bloodier and bloodier, a deeper and sharper hooking and tearing of flesh. The wife shuddered to look at it. You're right, said the husband, anyone would think twice … And they took heed of the advice on a small board fixed to the wall: Consult DRAGON'S TEETH The People For Total Security.

Next day a gang of workmen came and stretched the razor-bladed coils all round the walls of the house where the husband and wife and little boy and pet dog and cat were living happily ever after. The sunlight flashed and slashed off the serrations, the cornice of razor thorns encircled the home, shining. The husband said, Never mind. It will weather. The wife said, You're wrong. They guarantee it's rust-proof. And she waited until the little boy had run off to play before she said, I hope the cat will take heed … The husband said, Don't worry, my dear, cats always look before they leap. And it was true that from that day on the cat slept in the little boy's bed and kept to the garden, never risking a try at breaching security.

One evening, the mother read the little boy to sleep with a fairy story from the book the wise old witch had given him at Christmas. Next day he pretended to be the prince who braves the terrible thicket of thorns to enter the palace and kiss the Sleeping Beauty back to life: he dragged a ladder to the wall, the shining coiled tunnel was just wide enough for his little body to creep in, and with the first fixing of its razor-teeth in his knees and hands and head he screamed and struggled deeper into its tangle. The trusted housemaid and the itinerant gardener, whose 'day' it was, came running, the first to see and to scream with him, and the itinerant gardener tore his hands trying to get at the little boy. Then the man and his wife burst wildly into the garden and for some reason (the cat, probably) the alarm set up wailing against the screams while the bleeding mass of the little boy was hacked out of the security coil with saws, wire-cutters, choppers, and they carried it – the man, the wife, the hysterical trusted housemaid and the weeping gardener – into the house.

Ivan Vladislavić, who lives in Johannesburg, is another sharp observer of white South Africans' obsession with crime and security. In *Portrait with Keys* (120), published in 2006, he enumerates the 17 that hang from his interlocking rings, organised into 'separate working groups'. 'Coming and going through the front door: street-door deadlock, Yale, security gate (outside), front-door deadlock, Yale. Coming and going through the back: back-gate padlock, back-door deadlock, Yale, security gate (inside). Coming and going by car: garage door, car door, steering lock, immobilizer, ignition. Miscellaneous: window lock, cellar door, postbox.'

Having people to dinner adds a whole other dimension.

We have left the security arrangements for my birthday party until the last minute, resisting the imposition of it, hoping the problem will resolve itself. Once, your responsibilities as host extended no further than food and drink and a bit of mood music; now you must take steps to ensure the safety of your guests and their property.

'I think it's irresponsible of us to have a dinner party at all,' I say to Minky. 'There should be a municipal by-law that only people with long driveways and big dogs are allowed to entertain. We should call the whole thing off.'

'It'll be fine,' she says. 'Just stop obsessing.'

The last time we had people over, I had to keep going outside to check that their cars were still there. It spoilt my evening.

'We'll get a guard,' she says. She phones the armed response people. It is too late, all their guards are booked. But they recommend the Academy of Security, where trainees are registered for on-the-job experience. She phones the Academy. Yes, they do supply security guards for single functions. A dinner party? Sevenish? Can do. That will be the half-shift deal, unless you want him to stay past midnight, and pay the full-shift rate? Being inexperienced, the guard cannot be armed, of course, but he will be under constant supervision. They could arrange an armed guard from another company, probably – but at such short notice, it will be more expensive, you understand? We settle for inexperienced, unarmed, half-shift.

'The security costs more than the food,' I say, 'and he's still an appie.[14] We should have gone to a restaurant.'

The apprentice security guard is called Bongi. So far, he has only acquired the top half of a uniform, a navy-blue tunic that is too short in the sleeve. The checked pants and down-at-heel shoes are clearly his own. By way of equipment, he has a large silver torch and a panic button hanging around his neck. My theory is that he is earning the uniform item by item, as payment or incentive. After six months or so, he'll be fully qualified and fully clothed.

'I knew this was a bad idea,' I say to Minky. 'He's just a kid.'

Bongi is standing under a tree on the far side of the road. He looks vulnerable and lonely. It is starting to drizzle. Minky takes him an umbrella from the stand at the door, the grey and yellow one with the handle in the shape of a toucan, which once belonged to her dad. With this frivolous thing in his hand, Bongi looks even more poorly equipped to cope with the streets.

'This is unforgivable,' I say, 'this is a low point. I'd rather live in a flat than do this.'

'What difference would that make?' says Minky, who always sees through my rhetoric. 'People have still got to park their cars somewhere.'

'A complex, then, I'd rather live in a complex. Some place with secure parking.'

The guests begin to arrive. Bongi waves the torch around officiously, and then stands on the pavement under the toucan umbrella, embarrassed.

When dinner is served, Minky takes out a plate of food and a cup of coffee. 'Poor kid's starving,' she says when she comes back.

Excusing myself from the table, on the pretext of fetching more wine from the spare room, I sneak outside and gaze at him from the end of the stoep.[15] He's squatting on the kerb, with the plate between his feet on the tar, eating voraciously.

'He's a sitting duck,' I say to Minky in the kitchen, when we're dishing up seconds. 'What the hell is he expected to do if an armed gang tries to steal one of the cars, God forbid. Throw the panic button at them? This whole arrangement is immoral. Especially our part in it. Our friends are insured anyway, if someone steals Branko's car, he'll get another one. What if this kid gets hurt while we're sitting here feeding our faces and moaning about the crime rate? I think he'll have seconds too.'

With a plate of Thai chicken under his belt, and another in prospect, Bongi is looking better. We exchange a few words. He comes from a farm near Marikana, out near the Magaliesberg, and he's been in Joburg since June. His uncle found him this job, his uncle has been a 'full-time security' for five years. He looks quite pleased with himself. Perhaps he's thinking this is not such a bad job after all.

But we cannot see it that way. At ten thirty, Minky calls him inside to watch the cars from the stoep, over the wall. When the supervisor arrives an hour later, there's a hullabaloo. You've got to maintain standards, he says, especially when you're training these guys. You can't have them getting soft on the job.

That's it, we say to one another afterwards. No more parties. Never again.

Nowhere is the confrontation between the haves and the have-nots more intense or deeply rooted than in those parts of rural South Africa where large, white-owned commercial farms are surrounded by landless, black peasants struggling to scratch a living. And nowhere does the shadow of Zimbabwe's catastrophic 2007 response to the same problem loom more menacingly than in KwaZulu-Natal.

This is the setting for *Midlands* (121), a powerful anatomy of the land wars by Jonny Steinberg, an outstanding writer and journalist. His story, published in 2002, is built around the 1999 murder – assassination would be more accurate – of the 28-year-old son of a white farmer near Richmond, a small town 20 miles south of Pietermaritzburg. Here, the question of who really owns the land goes back to the 1820s and the upheavals caused by Shaka's empire-building. The answer to the question is muddied by the Voortrekkers' occupation of the land after Dingane's defeat at Blood River, and their subsequent abandonment of it after the British seized Natal in the 1840s. Then the land was bought by London-based speculators, who left it empty, which led those who lived on it to claim it as their own – a claim they did not surrender when it was eventually sold to white farmers. For most of the 20th century, their resentment, suppressed under apartheid, simmered. With the transition to democracy, accompanied as it was by promises of land redistribution and the intensification of the long-running civil war between Inkatha and the ANC, the resentment boiled over. Such is the turbulent background to Steinberg's investigation of the unsolved murder of the son of a man whose name he has changed to Arthur Mitchell. Mitchell had bought his farm two years earlier from an Afrikaner called Steyn. He evicted the squatters and made plain to his black tenants that he would tolerate no trespassing in future. (Elias is one of Steinberg's black informants.)

I am sitting with Elias in the downtown Pietermaritzburg pub. He has put down my pen and has spread out the serviette on which he doodled in front of him. He admires his artwork, rubs his fingers over it until the blue tornadoes smudge and traces of ink accumulate along his fingerprint lines. He drinks his beer leisurely, one modest sip at a time. I have just ordered my second; he is halfway through his first.

I watch him from the other side of the table, and I realise that despite the large, warm place he has occupied in my head for the last few months, we are to all intents and purposes strangers. On the two occasions we have met during the last year, I have treated him with the exaggerated deference one shows to an old man. There are things he has just said with which I want to take issue, and I am not sure that the boundaries of our relationship will allow for it.

'Elias,' I say, uttering his name so as to signal the heaviness of what I want to tell him. 'You talk as if Mitchell should have behaved like a new neighbour in the suburbs. Cracked open a few beers, laughed, told jokes. Do you really think that is possible on the border of Sarahdale and Izita?'

'Why not?' he replies, crumpling up his serviette and pushing it to the corner of the table.

'Because it is not simply a question of finding out about the families, where they collect firewood and draw water. The relationship between these people is antagonistic. He wanted to farm the land they had taken from Steyn. Drinking beer together is not going to make that go away.'

'Yes, their relationship is a delicate one.' He takes another sip of his beer and nods sagely. 'All the more reason for Mitchell to move with care.'

'Elias, there is a struggle for land out there. It has been going on for over a century. When people deliberately allow their cattle onto your field while it is resuscitating, just in order to disrupt your farming, you do not come to an agreement with them over a beer. When people out of sheer spite cut down the fences you have just built, you do not solve the matter by showing you are a nice guy.'

'So what do you do then?'

'I am not sure. I am not sure that there is any easy solution. But I want you to see that Mitchell's rules were not the rules of a maniac. They were about defending his business, every one of them. When your neighbours are deliberately sabotaging your farming operation, you need to control them. When your tomatoes are pinched every night, when your fields are being set alight, there is a limit to the logic of give and take. It's not as if there was a clear, easy space for compromise here. There was a war of attrition. He had to defend the boundaries of his farm.'

Elias looks at me closely. He did not expect me to defend Mitchell. The cautiousness of his body language, which had begun to ease during the course of the afternoon, returns quite suddenly.

'I see we are set for a battle this afternoon. So let me begin by conceding the first round. Yes, this is not a matter that can be resolved over a crate of beer. You're right. Every inch he gave they would have taken, and then some more. Mitchell's problem is that he approached the matter as if we are still living under apartheid. He pretended to himself that he could think up some rules, march onto the tenants' land, shout them out, go home and then everything would be all right.

'He was a fool to think that. He dug his son's grave.'

'Dug his son's grave? Are you saying that when tenants don't like their landlord's rules, they can be expected to kill his son?'

'They would not have killed him if this had happened in the 1980s,' Elias says. He smiles at me again, but curtly this time, humourlessly. 'Same families, same farmer, same rules. Nobody would have died. Do you know why that is, my friend? Do you know what was different then?'

'They were afraid then? They were afraid of the white state?'

'No.' Elias is getting into his stride now. He is less alienated by the strange surroundings. He motions to the bartender and points at his empty beer bottle. The bartender nods. 'In the 1980s there was hope. Change was around the corner. The ugly things would soon be leaving. Then democracy came. Mandela's government. Then another election. Mbeki's government. And the white farmers still run the countryside. Things are getting worse, in fact. The farmers are building these game reserves and taking over miles of land they have never used before. They don't trust the police any longer so they create their own private police forces. These men in their uniforms stand on the hilltops watching your every move with their binoculars and their night-vision glasses, defending the law of their land.

'There is nowhere to escape to. You can't go to the cities because there is no work there. You will starve to death. You are a prisoner in the white man's countryside, and now there is no prospect of anything different. It is you against him for the rest of time. So when he marches onto your land and tells you he is going to interview your future son-in-law and decide whether he can live in your house, you take matters into your own hands, because nobody else is going to.'

'You kill his son?'

'Yes. It has come to that.'

The most chilling response to post-apartheid crime is JM Coetzee's *Disgrace* (122), published in 1999. David Lurie, the novel's protagonist, has been dismissed from his university post after an affair with a student. He goes to live with his daughter, Lucy, who owns a remote smallholding in the Eastern Cape, where she kennels dogs and sells flowers. They are attacked by three blacks. David is knocked unconscious; Lucy is repeatedly raped. In the car some days later, she speaks about it for the first time.

He lays a protective hand on Lucy's shoulder. *My daughter*, he thinks; *my dearest daughter. Whom it has fallen to me to guide. Who one of these days will have to guide me.*

Can she smell his thoughts?

It is he who takes over the driving. Halfway home, Lucy, to his surprise, speaks. 'It was so personal,' she says. 'It was done with such personal hatred. That was what stunned me more than anything. The rest was … expected. But why did they hate me so? I had never set eyes on them.'

He waits for more, but there is no more, for the moment. 'It was history speaking through them,' he offers at last. 'A history of wrong. Think of it that way, if it helps. It may have seemed personal, but it wasn't. It came down from the ancestors.'

'That doesn't make it easier. The shock simply doesn't go away. The shock of being hated, I mean. In the act.'

In the act. Does she mean what he thinks she means?

'Are you still afraid?' he asks.

'Yes.'

'Afraid they are going to come back?'

'Yes.'

'Did you think, if you didn't lay a charge against them with the police, they wouldn't come back? Was that what you told yourself?'

'No.'

'Then what?' She is silent.

'Lucy, it could be so simple. Close down the kennels. Do it at once. Lock up the house, pay Petrus to guard it. Take a break for six months or a year, until things have improved in this country. Go overseas. Go to Holland. I'll pay. When you come back you can take stock, make a fresh start.'

'If I leave now, David, I won't come back. Thank you for the offer, but it won't work. There is nothing you can suggest that I haven't been through a hundred times myself.'

'Then what do you propose to do?'

'I don't know. But whatever I decide I want to decide by myself, without being pushed. There are things you just don't understand.'

'What don't I understand?'

'To begin with, you don't understand what happened to me that day. You are concerned for my sake, which I appreciate, you think you understand, but finally you don't. Because you can't.'

He slows down and pulls off the road. 'Don't,' says Lucy. 'Not here. This is a bad stretch, too risky to stop.'

He picks up speed. 'On the contrary, I understand all too well,' he says. 'I will pronounce the word we have avoided hitherto. You were raped. Multiply. By three men.'

'And?'

'You were in fear of your life. You were afraid that after you had been used you would be killed. Disposed of. Because you were nothing to them.'

'And?' Her voice is now a whisper.

'And I did nothing. I did not save you.'

That is his own confession.

She gives an impatient little flick of the hand. 'Don't blame yourself, David. You couldn't have been expected to rescue me. If they had come a week earlier, I would have been alone in the house. But you are right, I meant nothing to them, nothing. I could feel it.'

There is a pause. 'I think they have done it before,' she resumes, her voice steadier now. 'At least the two older ones have. I think they are rapists first and foremost. Stealing things is just incidental. A side-line. I think they *do* rape.'

'You think they will come back?'

'I think I am in their territory. They have marked me. They will come back for me.'

'Then you can't possibly stay.'

'Why not?'

'Because that would be an invitation to them to return.'

She broods a long while before she answers. 'But isn't there another way of looking at it, David? What if … what if that is the price one has to pay for staying on? Perhaps that is how they look at it; perhaps that is how I should look at it too. They see me as owing something. They see themselves as debt collectors, tax collectors. Why should I be allowed to live here without paying? Perhaps that is what they tell themselves.'

'I am sure they tell themselves many things. It is in their interest to make up stories that justify them. But trust your feelings. You said you felt only hatred from them.'

'Hatred … When it comes to men and sex, David, nothing surprises me any more. Maybe, for men, hating the woman makes sex more exciting. You are a man, you ought to know. When you have sex with someone strange – when you trap her, hold her down, get her under you, put all your weight on her – isn't it a bit like killing? Pushing the knife in; exiting afterwards, leaving the body behind covered in blood – doesn't it feel like murder, like getting away with murder?'

You are a man, you ought to know: does one speak to one's father like that? Are she and he on the same side?

'Perhaps,' he says. 'Sometimes. For some men.' And then rapidly, without forethought: 'Was it the same with both of them? Like fighting with death?'

'They spur each other on. That's probably why they do it together. Like dogs in a pack.'

'And the third one, the boy?'

'He was there to learn.'

They have passed the Cycads sign. Time is almost up.

'If they had been white you wouldn't talk about them in this way,' he says. 'If they had been white thugs from Despatch, for instance.'

'Wouldn't I?'

'No, you wouldn't. I am not blaming you, that is not the point. But it is something new you are talking about. Slavery. They want you for their slave.'

'Not slavery. Subjection. Subjugation.'

> He shakes his head. 'It's too much, Lucy. Sell up. Sell the farm
> to Petrus and come away.'
> 'No.'
> That is where the conversation ends.

So determined is Lucy to 'pay the price of staying on' that she decides to have the baby that results from the rapes and to hand over her land to Petrus, her sinister black farm manager, in return for his 'protection'. The past, Petrus tells David, is past – disturbingly, the same formulation Mandela used in his inaugural presidential address. Interestingly, Coetzee decided not to stay on and moved to Australia.

For Eben Venter (123), a much-lauded Afrikaans novelist, post-apartheid means post-apocalypse. *Trencherman*, published in 2006, is set in South Africa's not-too-distant future, when the country is in ruins. The Government is bankrupt, foreign investors have pulled out, corruption is rampant and most people are either dying of AIDS ('they've fucked themselves to death') or starving because they are too feckless to shift for themselves. Marlouw, the protagonist, returns after 20 years abroad to track down his nephew, Koert. (The tale is elaborately modelled on Marlow's search for Kurtz in Conrad's *Heart of Darkness*.) With heavy symbolism, Marlouw finds Koert bloated and dying of gangrene on the ancestral farm, which now belongs to the blacks who used to work on it. Here, Marlouw holds an imaginary conversation with Pappie, his dead father.

> There was a dream, Marlouw, a dream, I hear him murmur. My grandfather dreamt this dream, and my great-grandfather Daniel, and his grandfather before him, thirteen generations of us had this dream until it no longer felt like a dream. Let me tell you about it – that is if you don't yet know it yourself. Someone sneaks up in the night with a butcher's knife, the blade is shiny and smooth in the sliver of moonlight. The knife glints like body of a mermaid. He glides through the house filled with the breathing of the sleeping grown-ups and children. Without bumping into anything, he slinks right up to the side of bed where the man is sleeping. The knife takes on another form. Now it's the body of a crocodile, sharp and sleek. He's chosen the correct side of the bed, the side where the man sleeps …
> Where the father, the progenitor, sleeps – I take the words out of his mouth.
> You see, I knew you were familiar with the dream. As I was saying, he sleeps on his side, this patriarch with his hands strong like stone, his feet strong like stone. And suddenly he sits bolt upright. Then the knife-bearer

bends over the bed with his rancid breath and body, heavy like an ox car-
cass, black like ploughed soil, and in his claw: the white blade of the knife.
The patriarch screams until the whole house is awake. Everyone sits up,
bewildered. The primal call echoes and re-echoes in their ears. They lurch
towards the main bedroom, weepy, the little girls panicky. The patriarch sits
with his head in his hands and sweat drips from his forehead. One by one
the little boys step back, bump into the doorframe and return to their own
beds. They know what the dream was about. Quickly they pull the sheets
and blankets over their heads and weep sorrowfully at the terrible burden of
their inheritance.

Listen carefully: it's easy to misinterpret the dream. I'm not afraid of dying, or even that I'll be killed in some cruel way. Even if it's with a knife in
the night. My fear goes much further and deeper. I was afraid we Afrikaners
would be wiped out roots and all. That's the heart of my fear.

That is the heart of Pappie's dream. It's the source of the primal fear. I
understand, Pappie. The fear is rooted in your amygdala.

What would that be, my child?

It's a small almond-shaped segment deep inside the temporal lobe of the
brain.

I'm not so sure, Marlouw. That's your way of putting things.

We're talking about the same thing, Pappie. At the precise moment that
the man bends over his bed with the blade of his knife, the patriarch jumps
up. He's sensed the icy beat, the heart of fear. The primeval fear rises in
the patriarch's head, in the core of his grey matter, and throws him from
his bed like a chewed bone. He sits upright, wild-eyed; the inherited fear
has taken shape. He's ready to fight to the death for as long as he can protect his own. That's how it must be understood: the dream that we men
have all dreamt repeatedly is passed on from generation to generation in
our genes. It's the effect of the conditional stimulus on the amygdala, the almond deep in Pappie's brain, that makes the body react instinctively. Pappie
knows how fast your heart beats, how geared up your body is after you've
had that dream. It's the amygdala telling your body what to do. The next
thing Pappie does is fight or run away. The stimulus on the amygdala makes
you respond in the appropriate way – it's the basis of the survival of the species. Of our species.

It is as you say, Marlouw. I'm glad you understand me at last. I believe that
we've had this dream since our first forefather stepped onto these shores, to

warn us against life-threatening danger. It's exactly as you've put it. It's been handed to us so that we can get up, defend ourselves and survive.

But now the amygdala has fallen asleep. We didn't listen, we didn't read the signs accurately and that's why we didn't begin fighting in time, nor did we leave in time. We threw in the towel, we engineered our own demise.

By the end of the novel, Koert ('I am your destiny, your fear, your very heart of darkness') has also been butchered by the blacks, so marking 'the end of our people in this land'.

What *is* true about post-apartheid South Africa is that AIDS kills more than 900 people a day, eclipsing the death rate from violent crime. In 2003 – the year ex-President Thabo Mbeki appeared finally to abandon his lethal denial of the link with HIV – AIDS claimed its millionth victim. Five year later, the death toll had risen to over 2.5 million. An estimated 20 per cent of the adult population is HIV-positive and the epidemic is spreading. The only effective antidote – although not a cure – is antiretroviral (ARV) treatment, which requires people to submit to a blood test, acknowledge the virus if they have it and then take a pharmacopoeia of pills every 12 hours for the rest of their lives – a particularly challenging message to deliver in a poverty-stricken and superstitious rural society.

In 2005, Jonny Steinberg (124) embarked on a study of how Médecins Sans Frontières was rising to the challenge in Lusikisiki, a destitute and densely populated district of Pondoland, the remote area of the Eastern Cape where, 70 years earlier, Monica Hunter had researched *Reaction to Conquest*. Running through *Three-Letter Plague* are the apprehensions of Sizwe Magadla, Steinberg's 29-year-old Xhosa interpreter, who suspects he has been infected with HIV by a demon sent by his enemies. But he is too scared and ashamed to take the test.

Over the course of a three-month period in mid-2006, I sit in on several HIV support-group meetings at Lusikisiki clinics. Sometimes Sizwe accompanies me. Sometimes I go with activists from the Treatment Action Campaign and watch them work.

By mid-2006, the youngest of the clinic support groups is more than two years old. In theory, each of the twelve clinics has two support groups: one for HIV-positive people, another for those on, or about to initiate, ARV treatment. Some are chaired by Médecins Sans Frontières' adherence counsellors, others by Treatment Action Campaign activists, still others by long-standing support-group members. Each is held in the outdoors on clinic grounds, under a tree or against a clinic wall, the bum of every member on government-issue plastic chairs that were borrowed from the packed clinic waiting rooms. That they are conducted out in the open, in full view of passersby, is both their signature and an emblem of their most urgent aspiration: to take the virus and those it afflicts from their secret places of shame.

The most eccentric feature of the support groups is their cosmopolitanism. An odd observation, perhaps, in the context of a rural town in the depths of the old Transkei; but Lusikisiki is about as unequal and diverse a place as you will find in any countryside anywhere in the world. Around the town centre are tiny suburbs of four- or five-room houses with satellite dishes, a complete range of household appliances, and a good car or two in the driveway. Thirty kilometres away is MaMagadla, Sizwe's mother, who fetches water from the river and firewood from the forest, has never seen a working television or attended a day of school, or travelled any farther than the one-horse town of Kokstad.

The support groups assembled on their plastic chairs under the trees make for an unlikely sight: a cross-section of Lusikisiki, right through, from one side to the other. There are the adherence counsellors and the Treatment Action Campaign activists, young, clever, testing the limits of a new identity and a new confidence. Some wear jeans and TAC T-shirts, others crisply pressed, button-down shirts and chinos. Among them are women in baggy trousers, with cropped haircuts and cloth caps, who carry in their body language and their faces the universal signature of an out-of-the-closet dyke; the TAC has been the catalyst for the unlikely emergence of a lesbian subculture in Lusikisiki.

Alongside the dykes are middle-aged, buxom women from the villages in their starched skirts, their hair wrapped in brightly-coloured cloth, the accoutrements of their excursions to town in supermarket bags at their sides. Next to them, middle-aged gold miners returned to their home villages when they fell ill; young, unemployed men living on their grandparents' pensions; men and women cast out of their homes because of their illness and living in a tin shack settlement to the north of town.

From this motley jigsaw of Lusikisiki s people comes the most remarkable talk. Men and women who, under other circumstances, would have come no closer than to brush against one another on the town's main street, here exchange views on clitoral orgasms, and semen, and anal sex; proper conduct in matters of love, marriage, parenthood and nutrition; and, of course, drugs. There has surely been nothing remotely like this in Pondoland's history.

When a batch of people who have freshly tested positive join the support group, the discussion explodes into shards that disperse across every aspect of life.

A shy, middle-aged man in a red-and-black checked shirt clears his throat, tentatively tests his voice, and begins to speak: 'If I stay with my child,' he asks, 'is my baby safe? Can we still live in the same house?'

A hefty woman, her head wrapped in bright orange cloth, stands up and replies: 'That depends. Is this baby your girlfriend or your off-spring? Because some men refer to their girlfriends as their babies, and I need some clarity on exactly what you're talking about before I can give you useful information.'

'I'm talking about my son,' he says with indignation. 'He is fourteen months old.'

A TAC activist named Akona joins the discussion: 'The virus lives inside your body,' she says, 'mainly in your semen and in your blood. You cannot infect your child. You can cook for him and bathe him and do everything a parent does.'

'But when I cook for him, can I taste the food before I give it to him? And what happens, for instance, if I put his dummy in my mouth, and then he sucks it again straight afterward?'

'There is some of the virus in your spit,' Akona replies, 'but very, very little. The medical scientists say you need litres of spit to infect someone, much more spit than is in your mouth. You can taste your child's food. You can do everything normal. You will not infect him.'

Another man stands up to ask a question. At the beginning of the meeting, he had announced that he tested HIV-positive two months ago, that when his CD4-count results came back they measured 316.[16]

'My girlfriend doesn't know her status,' he says. 'I told her I was positive the day I got the results, but she refuses to test. And she says she would rather die than use condoms. But I have learned here that I must use condoms for my own health. I suspect she is HIV-positive, and that she has a plan. She wants to go to the police to tell them she got HIV from me. I do not understand her behaviour. I do not trust her.'

'You must not jump to conclusions,' a man responds. 'Denial is a very strong force. After I tested positive I went to the mother of my children and told her. She refused to believe me. It took three months before she went to test.'

'That's all very well,' the aggrieved man replies. 'But every time we have sex she could be infecting me with another strain.'

'You are right to worry about that,' Akona says. 'But you are probably wrong to suddenly treat your girlfriend as a stranger with criminal intentions. I do not know her, but I would be surprised if she is trying to harm you. Probably, she cannot come to terms with the fact that she might be positive. She is not ready to face that. You must try to help her.' […]

In April, I attend a support-group meeting at Village Clinic in the centre of Lusikisiki. It is the oldest, largest, and most cosmopolitan of all the support groups. Sizwe is with me. He places his chair against mine and translates the Xhosa proceedings in a quiet murmur. He is a natural: he listens and translates at the same time, his English unbroken and lively, his intonations performing each speaker's character.

It is clear from early on that there is going to be trouble. The meeting is chaired by a woman called Thembisa. I do not know whether she is from MSF or TAC, or just a long-standing member of the group, but she has about her the demeanour of an activist, of one who must guide the discussion without bulldozing it. There are two women in the group who have signalled from the start that they are going to challenge her authority. One has bright yellow cloth spun around her head. The other is strikingly obese. They whisper to each other while Thembisa is talking, and cluck their tongues loudly to show their displeasure.

Somebody has placed the question of condoms on the agenda. Thembisa leads the discussion.

'They are something that can make a hypocrite out of you,' she says. 'Today I tell people to condomise; tomorrow I come to you with a big, pregnant stomach.'

'It is hard,' a middle-aged woman in the group responds. 'For twenty-five years my husband and I have had sex without a condom. He is not used to it. He doesn't like it.'

'Your husband is one thing,' Thembisa says. 'He knows your status. But if you sleep with a man who doesn't … Yo! If he is negative, and you make him sick, he can take you to court and you can get ten years. You must disclose your status.'

The woman with the bright yellow headdress is shaking her head in disagreement. 'It is hard to tell someone you are positive,' she says sharply. 'If a man proposes love to me, I cannot tell him my status. Even at home it is difficult to disclose. How much more difficult with a stranger?'

Thembisa frowns irritably. 'You don't just jump into bed with someone. It goes slowly. When you are in bed with him, you ask him to use a condom. If he refuses, you suggest that you go and test together. If you walk out of here and sleep with someone flesh-to-flesh, I will blame you for killing him.'

The fat woman speaks for the first time. 'Maybe you see a man,' she says, 'and you really want to sleep with him.' She slams the back of her hand into the palm of the other. 'It is urgent. You want him. You must have him.'

A few people giggle shyly. Thembisa brushes off the challenge with a dismissive wave of the hand. 'There is no such situation,' she says.

'Yes there is. You can love a man immediately and propose love to him.'

'Please,' Thembisa says. 'If you love him and he loves you, you must know each other's status. Otherwise how can you even talk of love?'

A TAC activist has appeared from nowhere and joined the discussion. Her name is Nomasamaria.

'There is no debate here,' she says. 'Since you know your status, you must use condoms. It is simple.'

'I am not saying no condoms,' the fat woman says. 'I am saying you can meet someone today and sleep with him today if you love him. And in that situation, you cannot disclose your status.'

'In any case,' Thembisa says uncomfortably, suddenly changing the subject, 'people still need to be taught how to use a condom. It is no use using them if they are not going to work.'

She marches off in the direction of the clinic, leaving Nomasamaria to chair the meeting, and returns a moment later carrying a large wooden penis, a pair of surgical gloves, and a box of condoms. She stands on a chair in the middle of the meeting, tucks the penis under her arm, and puts on the surgical gloves. Some people giggle. Two very dour-looking women in long, starched shirts stare expressionlessly. Another takes out a scrap of paper and a pen and watches carefully, preparing to take notes.

A man who has been silent until now swaggers over to Thembisa and tries to grab the penis from her.

'You will embarrass yourself,' she says, lifting it high in the air, beyond his reach. 'You are *isishumane*.[17] You do not know how to do this. You have no experience.'

'Why the gloves?' he asks. 'Are you afraid to handle meat?'

'Go away. You are making a fool of yourself.' She stands on her toes and lifts the penis higher.

Thus, Sizwe and I look on as a mottled patchwork of Lusikisiki's citizenry gather around a young woman who stands on a chair and holds aloft a large wooden penis like a pagan idol.

I chuckle out loud. 'Is this what Moses saw when he came down the mountain with the Ten Commandments?' I ask Sizwe.

'I don't think Moses saw anything like this,' he says quietly.

A woman who has not spoken before puts up her hand.

'Is it true,' she asks, 'that if you put hot water in a condom, you will see fly larvae?'

'I have heard that, too,' another woman comments. 'I have heard that the slippery substance on the condom is HIV. Is that true?'

'It was true of the old condoms,' someone replies. 'The ones that used to come from America. Today they get the condoms from other poor countries, made by black people and Indian people. They are safe.'

'Indian people? Why should the ones made by the Indian people be safe?'

Thembisa is distracted by the gloves and the penis. Nomasamaria says nothing. The explanation goes unchallenged [...]

I am relishing talking to Sizwe now, for the meeting has delivered a veritable feast for discussion: the men largely silent, those who did speak curiously inarticulate or meek, the women boisterous and obstreperous and free with their mouths, the discussion proudly and unashamedly taken over by the question of female desire.

'Let's go,' he says, before I can say anything. 'This place has made me so anxious.'

I look at him properly for the first time in a while. All morning I have been listening to his voice without taking in his mood. He is grey and troubled. He fidgets with his hands.

'About what?'

'Everyone here today looked healthy. And yet everyone here was sick. I looked from one face to the next one and wondered whether it was possible that they were all sick. And if it is true, if they are all sick, it is possible that everyone in Ithanga[18] is sick. The whole village. Everyone. Me. My mother, my father, the people who drink in my shop. Everyone.'

That would be an unduly sombre note on which to end this anthology. A more optimistic, though sober enough, finale is offered by Wally Serote's hymn to Robben Island (125). It comes from his long poem, *History is the Home Address*, published in 2004. Harry the Hottentot, the island's first political prisoner, would have understood.

Robben Island: between you and the sea
I stand near the cannon pointing into the sea
I hear it go off in my imagination
and think of the smithereens which fly from its explosion
shattering
disintegrating men
women and children devastated
because there has been Robben Island
here
I walk close to the penguins for the first time
here
I sense a very cold wet hot weather
here
thorny bushes and dry plants
spread and sprawl the dry harsh earth
here
on Robben Island the earth is rocky
and rugged
here dust clings to the leaves and stones
it clings to the walls which
I wish could speak
for I wonder what they would say
and what we would hear
here where a degenerate mind ruled
but where also
hope primed the essence of the human race
and since then a wish and will for freedom
flew
took off into the blue sky ricocheting on the sea
in my country
thunder and storm reside in the belly of the elements
it groans and groans and groans
releasing hot air
at times it is not air but diarrhoea
Robben Island: at night I sleep

and toss and turn, toss and turn as the sea echoes and roars
seeking the spiritual hand of those who have been
those whose spirits were wrung by time
by cruelty
by loneliness
by bewilderment and wonder
when they asked –
why
why are the walls and the iron bars so wide
why are the doors and their keys so large
and the keys turn twice and thrice to lock
why
to keep the freedom of the breeze from itself
or
to stop the roar and rumble of the waves
who would
who can tell the ancestors what to do
who can break the particle of hope
who can bind the will to be free of a people?
I toss and turn

Robben Island: what have we learnt
what do we know now
when the cells and jails are empty
and echo ghosts only?

our address is
Robben Island
ask us we will tell you
Zizi[19]
Madiba and his comrades left the cells
and you and we know our addresses
and the roaring seas sing of them
as the breeze whistles and whistles and whistles
and the earth spins on its miracle pin
if you go away
remember your home address

As the historian Colin Bundy has noted, the negotiated settlement that freed South Africa from apartheid left the 'structures of production, property, wealth and poverty' virtually intact. So, as the Freedom Charter promised, the country does now belong to all who live in it but very unequally. In a 1998 speech Thabo Mbeki described South Africa as two nations: 'One is white and well-off; the second and larger is black and poor.' Quoting the Harlem poet, Langston Hughes, he asked: 'What happens to a dream deferred?' Since then, thanks to Mbeki's policy of Black Economic Empowerment allied to widespread corruption, the two nations have become three: one is white and well-off; the second is black and well-off; and the third and largest is black and poor. At the same time, South Africa has apparently overtaken Brazil as the world's most unequal society.

What, then, happens to a dream deferred? If South Africa's troubled history is a guide, it will eventually be fulfilled – but the way ahead, like the one behind, is likely to be a long and exceptionally difficult one.

NOTES

1 The State President's residence in Cape Town.
2 The prison 35 miles outside Cape Town where Mandela spent the last 14 months of his incarceration.
3 Founded in 1983, the United Democratic Front had been the public face of the banned ANC.
4 Clerics.
5 Steven Otter's Xhosa name; it means joy.
6 Someone who comes from the same area.
7 Mlungu: a white man.
8 Afrikaans for nice.
9 Mandela's honorific title.
10 Barbecuing.
11 Redness, derived from the ochre the Xhosa rubbed on themselves, is a symbol of traditionalism.
12 A white local trader.
13 A public meeting.
14 Apprentice.
15 Veranda.
16 A CD-4 count is a blood test measuring the strength of the body's immunity. ARV treatment begins when it falls from a normal count of over 1 000 to below 200.
17 A man who has few, if any, girlfriends.
18 Sizwe's village.
19 The late Walter Sisulu, one of Mandela's closest comrades.

ACKNOWLEDGEMENTS

John Clare and Jonathan Ball Publishers would like to express their sincere thanks to everyone who gave us permission to use the extracts from the sources listed below.

The page references, which appear in square brackets after each source, indicate the relevant page(s) in Captured in Time *on which the extracts from these sources appear.*

In the event of any authorised copyright holder having been omitted, please contact the author or publisher so that this can be remedied in the event of a reprint.

1 Luis de Camoes, *The Lusiads,* translated by Landeg White. Oxford University Press, 1997. [pp 3–11]

2 Jan van Riebeeck, *Journal of Jan van Riebeeck, 1651–1662.* AA Balkema, 1952. [pp 13–28, 98–99]

3 John Buchan, *Memory Hold-the-Door.* Hodder and Stoughton, 1940. [pp 30–32]

4 Olive Schreiner, *Thoughts on South Africa.* T Fisher Unwin, 1923. [pp 32–34, 313–314]

5 *Journals of the Expeditions of Olof Bergh and Isaq Schrijver, 1682–1689.* Van Riebeeck Society, 1931. [pp 34–36]

6 Anders Sparrman, *A Voyage to the Cape of Good Hope, 1772–1776.* Van Riebeeck Society, 1975–77. [pp 40–41, 42–44, 45–47, 60–62]

7 Carl Peter Thunberg, *Travels at the Cape of Good Hope, 1772–1775.* Van Riebeeck Society, 1986. [pp 41–42, 89–90, 99–101]

8 John Barrow, *Travels into the Interior of Southern Africa.* Cadell & Davies, 1806. [pp 44–45, 51–52, 80–81, 86–87]

9 Jonty Driver, from *So Far.* Snailpress, 2005. [pp 47–48]

10 George Thompson, *Travels and Adventures in Southern Africa.* Van Riebeeck Society, 1968. [pp 49–51]

11 Francois Le Vaillant, *Travels into the Interior of Africa via the Cape of Good Hope*. Van Riebeeck Society, 2007. [pp 52–54, 85, 88–89]

12 Mazisi Kunene, *Emperor Shaka the Great*. Heinemann, 1979. [pp 54–56]

13 John Campbell, *Travels Through South Africa 1812–14 & 1820–1822*. Religious Tract Society, 1834. [pp 57–58, 66–68]

14 William Burchell, *Travels in the Interior of South Africa, 1810–1815*. Longman, Hurst, Rees, Orme and Brown, 1822 & 1824. [pp 58–60, 118, 140–144]

15 Roualeyn Gordon Cumming, *Five Years' Adventures in the Far Interior of South Africa*. John Murray, 1904. [pp 62–64, 103–106, 110–113, 117–118]

16 Henry Lichtenstein, *Travels in Southern Africa, 1803–1806*. Henry Colburn, 1812 & 1815. [pp 65–66, 72-73, 82–84]

17 Lady Anne Barnard, *South Africa a Century Ago*. Smith, Elder, 1910. [pp 68–71, 90–93, 94–95, 138–139]

18 Col Robert Gordon, *Journal, 1777–1778*. Available online, translated by Patrick Cullinan, 1992. [pp 71–72]

19 Arthur Cowell Stark, *The Birds of South Africa*. EH Potkee, 1900. [p 73]

20 Mary Maytham Kidd, *Wild Flowers of the Cape Peninsula*. Oxford University Press, 1950. [pp 74–75]

21 William Cornwallis Harris, *Narrative of an Expedition in Southern Africa, 1836 & 1837*. American Mission Press, 1838. [pp 75–77, 101–103, 107–110]

22 CW de Kiewiet, *A History of South Africa*. Clarendon Press, 1941. [pp 78–80, 149–150, 187, 206–207]

23 Robert Semple, *Walks and Sketches at the Cape of Good Hope*. C and R Baldwin, 1803. [pp 87–88]

24 RM Ballantyne, *Six Months at the Cape*. J Nisbet, 1879. [pp 93–94, 131–134]

25 Roy Campbell, *The Flaming Terrapin*. Jonathan Cape, 1924. [pp 97–98]

26 WC Scully, *Unconventional Reminiscences*. © Cathy Knoetze, Penguin Books, 2006. [pp 106–107, 195–200, 207–209, 224–248]

27 Thomas Pringle, from *African Sketches*. Edward Moxon, 1834. [pp 114–116]

28 Percy FitzPatrick, *Jock of the Bushveld*. Longmans, Green, 1907. [pp 118–125]

29 James Stevenson-Hamilton, *South African Eden*. © James Stevenson-Hamilton, Cassell, 1937. [pp 125–127]

30 Thomas Pringle, *Narrative of a Residence in South Africa*. Edward Moxon, 1834. [pp 129–131, 134-137]

31 John Philip, *Researches on South Africa, illustrating the civil, moral and religious condition of the Native Tribes*. James Duncan, 1828. [p 140]

32 Robert Moffat, *Missionary Labours and Scenes in Southern Africa*. Robert Carter, 1850. [pp 144–146]

33 David Livingstone, *Missionary Travels and Researches in South Africa*. John Murray, 1857. [pp 146–148]

34 Harry Smith, *The Autobiography of Lt-Gen Sir Harry Smith*. John Murray, 1903. [pp 150–153, 158–162]

35 George McCall Theal, *Regarding the Kaffir*, from *Kaffir Folk-Lore*. Sonneschein, Le Bas & Lowrey, 1886. [pp 154–158]

36 Noel Mostert, *Frontiers*. Cape, 1992. [p 163]

37 William Plomer, *Collected Poems*. Cape, 1960. [pp 165, 277–278, 351–352]

38 Piet Retief, *Manifesto of the Emigrant Farmers*, from GW Eybers, *Select Constitutional Documents*. Routledge & Sons, 1918. [pp 166–168]

39 Nathaniel Isaacs, *Travels and Adventures in Eastern Africa*. Van Riebeeck Society, 1936. [pp 168–171]

40 Thomas Mofolo, *Chaka*. Heinemann, 1981. [pp 171–173]

41 Francis Owen, *The Diary of the Rev Francis Owen*. Van Riebeeck Society, 1926. [pp 173–179]

42 Jan Bantjes, *Journal of the Expedition of the Emigrant Farmers*, from Bird's *Annals of Natal*. Maskew Miller, 1885. [pp 179–180]

43 Francis Carey Slater, from *The Karroo*, Centenary Book of South African Verse. Longmans, Green, 1925. [pp 181–182]

44 William Plomer, *Turbott Wolfe: A Novel*. Hogarth Press, 1925. [p 182]

45 Thomas Baines, *Journal of Residence in Africa, 1842–1853*. Van Riebeeck Society, 1961. [pp 183–186]

46 Monica Hunter, *Reaction to Conquest*. OUP, 1936. [pp 187–189]

47 Rider Haggard, *Cetywayo and His White Neighbours*. K Paul, Trench, Trubner, 1906. [pp 189–192, 224–227]

48 Paul Kruger, *The Memoirs of Paul Kruger, Four Times President of the South African Republic*. Morang, 1902. [pp 193–194, 213–215, 254]

49 Anthony Trollope, *South Africa*. Chapman & Hall, 1878. [pp 200–206, 219–220]

50 Rudyard Kipling, from *Rewards and Fairies*. Macmillan, 1910. [pp 210–211]

51 LS Jameson, *Personal Reminiscences of Mr Rhodes*. Chapman & Hall, 1897. [pp 211–213, 215–216]

52 William Plomer, *Cecil Rhodes*. Thomas Nelson & Sons, 1933. [pp 216–217]

53 Olive Schreiner, *The Story of an African Farm*. T Fisher Unwin, 1924. [pp 220–222]

54 Pauline Smith, *The Beadle*. Vanguard Press, 1927. [pp 222–224]

55 JA Froude, *Two Lectures on South Africa*. Longmans, Green, 1880. [pp 227–228]

56 Mark Twain, *Following the Equator*. American Publishing Company, 1898. [pp 228–229]

57 Mahatma Gandhi, *The Story of My Experiments with Truth*. Phoenix, 1949. [pp 229–236]

58 John Buchan, *Prester John*. Thomas Nelson & Sons, 1910. [pp 236–239, 258]

59 Sarah Gertrude Millin, *The South Africans*. Constable, 1926. [pp 239–241]

60 Eliza Feilden, *My African Home, or, Bush Life in Natal*, TW Griggs, 1887, from

Women Writing Africa. Feminist Press, 2003. [pp 241–244]

61 Olive Schreiner, *Words in Season*. Hodder & Stoughton, 1899. [pp 248–249]

62 Alfred (Lord) Milner, *The Milner Papers*. Cassell & Co, 1931. [pp 251–254, 293–294, 297–301, 371–372]

63 Jan Smuts and others, 'A Century of Wrong'. 'Review of Reviews', 1900. [pp 254–258]

64 Winston Churchill, *My Early Life*. Thornton Butterworth, 1930. [pp 258–260, 262–266]

65 Deneys Reitz, *Commando*. Faber & Faber, 1929. [pp 260–262, 278–281, 290–292]

66 Arthur Conan Doyle, *The Great Boer War*. Smith Elder, 1901. [pp 262, 266–271, 272–277]

67 Rudyard Kipling, *The Absent-Minded Beggar*. Methuen, 1918. [pp 271–272]

68 'Banjo' Paterson, *An Interview with Olive Schreiner*, from *Words in Season*. Penguin Books, 2005. [pp 281–285]

69 Lisle March-Phillipps, *With Rimington*. Edward Arnold, 1901. [pp 286–288]

70 AM van den Berg, *Journal of the War*, from *Women Writing Africa*. Feminist Press, 2003. [pp 288–290]

71 Johanna Brandt, *The Petticoat Commando*. Mills & Boon, 1913. [pp 292–293]

72 Rudyard Kipling, *Something of Myself*. Macmillan, 1937. [pp 294–295]

73 Thomas Hardy, from *Collected Poems*. Macmillan, 1919. [pp 295–296]

74 Sol Plaatje, *Native Life in South Africa*. PS King and Son, 1916. [pp 302–303]

75 Jan Smuts, *Native Policy in Africa*, from *Toward a Better World*. World Book Company, 1944. [pp 303–312]

76 Sarah Gertrude Millin, *God's Step-Children*. Central News Agency, 1951. [pp 314–320]

77 Guy Butler, from *The Penguin Book of South African Verse*. Penguin Books, 1968. [pp 320–322]

78 Herman Charles Bosman, *Mafeking Road*. Central News Agency, 1947. [pp 322–327]

79 Athol Fugard, *The Blood Knot*. OUP, 1974. [pp 327–341]

80 Alan Paton, *Too Late the Phalarope*. Cape, 1953. [pp 341–344]

81 Etienne van Heerden, *The Long Silence of Mario Salviati*. Sceptre, 2002. [pp 345–351]

82 BW Vilakazi, from *The Penguin Book of South African Verse*. Penguin Books, 1968. [pp 352–356]

83 Alan Paton, *Cry, the Beloved Country*. Cape, 1948. [pp 356–361]

84 Peter Abrahams, *Mine Boy*. Faber and Faber, 1944. [pp 361–367]

85 Rian Malan, *My Traitor's Heart*. Vintage, 1990. [pp 368–370]

86 Bloke Modisane, *Blame Me on History*. Thames & Hudson, 1963. [pp 370–371, 377–378, 381–384, 390–392]

87 JM Coetzee, *Boyhood*. Secker & Warburg, 1997. [pp 372–374]

88 Nelson Mandela, *Long Walk to Freedom*. Little, Brown and Company, 1994. [pp 375–377, 393–395, 400–411, 452–454]

89 Ezekiel Mphahlele, *Down Second Avenue*. Seven Seas, 1959. [pp 379–381]

90 Dugmore Boetie, *Familiarity is the Kingdom of the Lost*. Barrie & Rockliff, 1969. [pp 384–387]

91 Jack Cope, *The Name of Patrick Henry*. Heinemann, 1967. [pp 387–389]

92 Albert Luthuli, *Let My People Go*. Collins, 1962. [pp 399–400]

93 Tom Sharpe, *Riotous Assembly*. Martin Secker & Warburg, 1971. [pp 412–414]

94 Anthony Delius, *The Last Division*. Human & Rousseau, 1959. [pp 414–415]

95 Adam Small, from *The Penguin Book of South African Verse*. Penguin Books, 1968. [pp 415–417]

96 Nadine Gordimer, *A World of Strangers*. Gollancz, 1958. [pp 417–419]

97 Lewis Nkosi, *Home and Exile*. Longmans, Green & Co, 1965. [pp 419–421]

98 Can Themba, *Crepuscule*, from *A Century of South African Short Stories*. AD Donker, 2007. [pp 422–424]

99 Richard Rive, *'Buckingham Palace', District Six*. David Philip, 1986. [pp 424–426]

100 Christopher Hope, *Brothers Under the Skin*. Macmillan, 2003. [pp 427–428]

101 Donald Woods, *Biko*. Paddington Press, 1978. [pp 429–430]

102 Nadine Gordimer, *Burger's Daughter*. Cape, 1979. [pp 430–432]

103 Winnie Mandela, 'Detention Alone is a Trial in Itself', from *Women Writing Africa*. Feminist Press, 2003. [pp 432–434]

104 André Brink, *A Dry White Season*. WH Allen, 1979. [pp 435–436]

105 Christopher Hope, *White Boy Running*. Martin Secker & Warburg, 1988. [pp 436–438]

106 Christopher Hope, *Kruger's Alp*. William Heinemann, 1984. [pp 438–444]

107 JM Coetzee, *Age of Iron*. Martin Secker & Warburg, 1990. [pp 444–446]

108 Marlene van Niekerk, *Triomf*. Little, Brown & Company 1999. [pp 447–450]

109 FW de Klerk, *The Last Trek – A New Beginning*. Macmillan, 1998. [pp 451–452, 454–455, 457–459, 464–465]

110 Nadine Gordimer, 'April 27: The First Time', from *Women Writing Africa*. Feminist Press, 2003. [pp 455–457]

111 Ingrid Jonker, from *Selected Poems*. Cape, 1968. [p 460]

112 Ingrid de Kok, from *Seasonal Fires*. Umuzi, 2006. [pp 461–462]

113 Antjie Krog, *Country of My Skull*. Vintage, 1999. [pp 462–464]

114 Alex Boraine, *A Country Unmasked*. Oxford University Press, 2000. [pp 465–466]

115 Dan Jacobson, *The Electronic Elephant*. Hamish Hamilton, 1994. [pp 466–467]

116 Steven Otter, *Khayelitsha, uMlungu in a Township*. Penguin, 2007. [pp 467–471]

117 Zakes Mda, *The Heart of Redness*. Oxford University Press, 2000. [pp 471–477]

118 Antony Altbeker, *A Country at War with Itself*. Jonathan Ball Publishers, 2007. [pp 477–479]

119 Nadine Gordimer, 'Once Upon a Time', from *Jump and Other Stories*. Bloomsbury, 1991. [pp 480–484]

120 Ivan Vladislavic, *Portrait with Keys*. Umuzi, 2006. [pp 484–486]

121 Jonny Steinberg, *Midlands*. Jonathan Ball Publishers, 2002. [pp 486–489]

122 JM Coetzee, *Disgrace*. Secker & Warburg, 1999. [pp 489–492]

123 Eben Venter, *Trencherman*. Tafelberg, 2006. [pp 492–494]

124 Jonny Steinberg, *Three-Letter Plague*. Jonathan Ball Publishers, 2008. [pp 494–501]

125 Wally Serote, from *History is the Home Address*. Kwela, 2004. [pp 499-501]

SELECT BIBLIOGRAPHY

Bunting, Brian, *The Rise of the South African Reich*. Penguin, 1964.

Davenport, TRH, *South Africa: A Modern History*. Macmillan, 1991.

David, Saul, *Zulu: The Heroism and Tragedy of the Zulu War of 1879*. Viking, 2004.

De Kiewiet, CW, *The Imperial Factor in South Africa*. Cambridge University Press, 1937.

Gevisser, Mark, *Thabo Mbeki: The Dream Deferred*. Jonathan Ball, 2007.

Giliomee, Hermann, *The Afrikaners: Biography of a People*. Hurst, 2003.

Hobhouse, Emily, *The Brunt of the War and Where it Fell*. Methuen, 1902.

Illustrated History of South Africa. Reader's Digest, 1988.

Johnson, RW, *South Africa: the First Man, the Last Nation*. Weidenfeld & Nicolson, 2004.

Johnson, RW, *South Africa's Brave New World: The Beloved Country Since the End of Apartheid*. Allen Lane, 2009.

Keegan, Timothy, *Colonial South Africa and the Origins of the Racial Order*. David Philip, 1996.

Macmillan, WM, *Bantu, Boer and Briton*. Oxford University Press, 1963.

Marais, JS, *The Cape Coloured People*. Witwatersrand University Press, 1962.

Meredith, Martin, *Diamonds, Gold and War: The Making of South Africa*. Simon & Schuster, 2007.

Morris, Donald R, *The Washing of the Spears*. Jonathan Cape, 1966.

Pakenham, Thomas, *The Boer War*. Weidenfeld & Nicolson, 1979.

Rotberg, Robert I, *The Founder: Cecil Rhodes and the Pursuit of Power*. Oxford University Press, 1988.

Roux, Edward, *Time Longer Than Rope*. University of Wisconsin Press, 1964.

Sampson, Anthony, *Mandela: The Authorised Biography*. HarperCollins, 1999.

Sparks, Allister, *Tomorrow is Another Country*. Heinemann, 1995.

Stow, George W, *The Native Races of South Africa*. Swan Sonnenschein, 1905.

Thompson, Leonard, *A History of South Africa*. Yale University Press, 2000.

Van der Post, Laurens, *The Lost World of the Kalahari*. Hogarth Press, 1961.

Van der Ross, RE, *Up from Slavery: Slaves at the Cape*. Ampersand Press, 2005.

Wilson, Francis & Ramphele, Mamphela, *Uprooting Poverty: The South African Challenge*. David Philip, 1989.